MYSTICAL PATHS

MYSTICAL PATHS

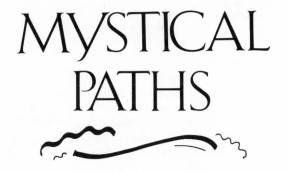

A NOVEL BY

Susan Howatch

ALFRED A. KNOPF

NEW YORK *1 9 9 2*

THIS IS A BORZOI BOOK
PUBLISHED BY ALFRED A. KNOPF, INC.

Library of Congress Cataloging-in-Publication Data
Howatch, Susan.
Mystical paths : a novel / by Susan Howatch.
p. cm.
ISBN 0-679-41205-0
I. Title.
PR6058.0912M97   1992
813'.54—dc20   91-58557
CIP

Manufactured in the United States of America
First Edition

Contents

PART ONE

THE JOURNEY
AROUND THE
CIRCLE

"Amidst the pressures and strains of life there is the longing of the self to realize itself by escaping from the dominance of the environment. There are many cults which offer such an escape, with an experience of a heightening of the faculties and a realization of the self in greater power of its own or of something beyond the self. But it is important to ask what is the reality which is experienced, and what is the effect not only upon the sensations but upon the life and character of the person who has had the experience. There is an old story of a man who was had up for being drunk. The magistrate asked, 'Why do you get drunk like this?' and the man replied, 'You see, your worship, it's the shortest way out of Manchester.' Alcohol, drugs, the mystical techniques of various religions, may be the shortest way out of Manchester . . . But it matters very much where you get to, and what you are like when you come back."

MICHAEL RAMSEY
Archbishop of Canterbury, 1961–1974
CANTERBURY PILGRIM

"God acts upon us inescapably through the people who touch and influence our lives."

CHRISTOPHER BRYANT
Member of the Society of St. John the Evangelist,
1935–1985
THE RIVER WITHIN

I

I

I HAD just returned from an exorcism and was flinging some shirts into the washing-machine when my colleague entered the kitchen. He was wearing his cassock and carrying a bottle of whisky. Beyond the window caked in city grime, sunlight blazed upon the battered dustbins in the backyard.

"How was the Gothic mansion haunted by the ravishing young ghost?"

"Non-existent. The trouble was in a council house where the previous occupant had overdosed on heroin in the lavatory."

"Ah well, that's 1988 for you . . . Drink?"

I declined but passed him a glass from the draining-board rack before I set the dials on the washing-machine. Meanwhile the electric kettle was coming to the boil. Absent-mindedly I reached for the teapot. "What's new?"

"Absolutely nothing. A drunk disrupted the lunch-time Eucharist, the Gay Christians demanded that we stock their literature on AIDS, and some neurotic female from the Movement for the Ordination of Women threatened to picket the church unless you sacked me—oh, and talking of neurotic women, someone called Venetia telephoned twice to say she had to talk to you. She sounded like a nymphomaniac." He drank deeply from his whisky before adding: "Now why should the name Venetia remind me of the 1960s?"

There was a silence broken only by the click of the kettle as it switched itself off. Then I said: "She was a friend of Christian Aysgarth's."

"Ah yes," said my colleague, suddenly motionless. "The Christian Aysgarth affair. 1968. Crisis, chaos and the Devil on the loose."

The phone rang. Moving to the extension, which hung on the wall by the dresser, I unhooked the receiver and said neutrally: "St. Benet's Rectory."

"Darling!" It was Venetia. "I thought I'd never get past that crusty old curate you keep!"

"He's not my curate. He's my colleague at the Healing Centre."

"Well, chain him up somewhere—I can't bear misogynists. Now darling, I know you were terribly sweet and madly keen that I should visit you for a little professional chat, but—"

"—you've got cold feet."

"Slightly shivery, yes. When I awoke this morning I began to wonder if a Healing Centre was really quite my scene, and—"

"Nobody's asking you to fall in love with it. Just think of it as a backdrop. *I'm* the scene."

"Oh yes, lovely, simply too thrilling—but I can't bear that word 'counselling'—quite ruined by the 1980s—all those wild-eyed social workers descending like vultures on disaster-victims—"

"I'm neither wild-eyed, nor a social worker, nor a vulture, and I'm not going to counsel. I'm going to listen."

"Oh, but I shall make a mess of talking—I make a mess of everything—I shall wind up totally speechless—"

"Fine. Then we can sit in silence and soak up the vibes."

"Soak up the vibes! Oh Nick, how that phrase takes me back! Do you know it's twenty years now—*twenty years*—since you came to see me about Christian? That mysterious quest of yours! You never did tell me the whole story, did you?"

" 'Whereof one cannot speak, thereof one must be silent.' "

"No, don't try and wriggle off the hook by quoting Wittgenstein! Look, let's forget my visit to the Healing Centre—come and dine with me instead and tell me exactly what happened in 1968. I always found that official version curiously unsatisfactory."

I realised it was time to take a firm line. "Sorry," I said, "but I don't dine out during the week and I've no intention of forgetting your promise to visit the Healing Centre. I'll see you on Thursday at eleven as we arranged yesterday in Starbridge."

"My dear, how masterful! Why is it I always find you so utterly impossible to resist?" said Venetia crossly, and hung up.

Turning my back on the phone I found that my colleague had made the tea for me. "That's the only woman I've ever met," I said, sitting down opposite him at the kitchen table, "who can instantly recognise a quotation from Wittgenstein."

"She sounds extremely dangerous. Do be careful, Nicholas."

I smiled at him. Then I drank my tea, stared into space and mentally turned back the clock to 1968, that demonic year when I had become so obsessed by Christian Aysgarth.

2

FOR most of 1968 I was twenty-five; my twenty-sixth birthday fell on Christmas Eve. Buried in that first quarter-century of my life were the time-bombs which exploded in 1968—or perhaps it would be more accurate, though less colourful, to write: weaving through those first twenty-five years were the paths which eventually converged to lead me into the Christian Aysgarth mystery. The first path followed my convoluted relationship with my father. The second path followed my disastrous career as a psychic. And the third path followed my friendship with Marina Markhampton. By 1968 all three paths were running side by side—in fact they had become a three-lane motorway where the words TO HELL came up on all the signboards—but in the beginning hell was a long way off and Path Number One led through the idyllic landscape of my childhood.

I was brought up in the country near the city of Starbridge where my father worked at the Theological College in the Cathedral Close. When I was still in the nursery he had been appointed Principal, but he had not been required to live on the premises and I can remember watching him ride off on his bicycle to the station where he would take the train to Starbridge, twelve miles away. If the weather was wet my mother insisted on giving him a lift in the Rolls, but he preferred to be independent. Born in the last century, he had never learnt to drive and he regarded travelling by Rolls-Royce as an inexcusable luxury for a priest. But then he became busier as the College Principal; soon the inexcusable luxury transformed itself into a time-saving necessity, and he stopped talking about the corrupting influence of the motor car.

I can just remember my mother's old chauffeur, who died in 1946. The Rolls, which I can remember clearly, died—or rather, was retired with honour—in 1947. Those were the days of the Labour Government when the rich had to tighten their belts, so my mother economised by replacing the Rolls with a Bentley and not replacing the chauffeur at all.

My mother worked. That was very unusual in those days for someone of her class. She ran the Home Farm which formed part of her estate at Starrington Magna, and every morning she would drive away to her office. I would stand on the doorstep of our manor house with Nanny and wave goodbye. Naturally I had no idea what a privileged childhood I was having, and naturally I took my doting parents and my beautiful home for granted. Nanny tried to bring me up sensibly but I soon mastered Nanny. By the time I was five I had evolved into a miniature tyrant.

This unpleasant phase of my development was brought to an end when I was nearly expelled from kindergarten for fighting over a boiled sweet. I remember it as the first time my father actively intervened in my life. Before that he had merely appeared at intervals and enfolded me in unqualified approval. But now the approval was withdrawn.

All he said was: "This won't do, Nicholas," and when he looked me straight in the eyes I suddenly realised that no, it wouldn't do at all because nothing was more important than that he should remain pleased with me. This insight in turn enabled me to articulate a truth which it seemed I had always known but had never been able to put into words. I said: "You're magic. You keep the bad things away," and as I spoke I knew that if he withdrew the protection of his magic anything might happen, anything, hobgoblins could haunt me, a witch could kidnap me, a monster could come down the nursery chimney and swallow me up. So I clutched the pectoral cross which my father always wore and I cried: "Save me from the Dark!"—a plea bizarre enough to alarm my mother, but my father merely wrapped his mind around mine to keep me safe, patted me on the head and said: "The word you want isn't 'magic.' It's 'psychic.'"

I liked this word but my mother didn't. She said sharply to my father: "Don't put ideas into his head!" but my father answered: "They're already there."

"Nonsense!" said my mother, and when she abruptly walked out of the room I realised that "psychic" could be a dangerous word, risky, not acceptable by some people, definitely not a word to be used with no thought for the consequences.

I tried the word out on Nanny and received the firm response: "That's not a nice word, dear, that's peculiar, and we don't have peculiar things in this nursery."

At kindergarten we were asked to write a sentence about our parents, and burning with curiosity to test my teacher I wrote: "Mummy is a farmer and Father is a sykick who saves me from the Dark." My teacher was appalled. In fact she was so disturbed that she even sent the composition to my mother, but my mother only commented briskly to me: "Silly woman! She might at least have taught you to spell 'psychic' correctly before she had hysterics." And to my father she said: "I refuse to let Nicholas go peculiar. What's all this rubbish about the Dark?"

"It's his way of referring to malign psychic forces."

"Well, I won't have it, it's bad for him, it'll give him nightmares."

"But my dear Anne, you can't alter the way he sees and senses the world!"

A flash of intuition lit up my juvenile brain. "I'm psychic too," I said triumphantly. "I'm just like Father!"

"Oh no, you're not!" said my mother, magnificently normal, superbly sane. "One Jon Darrow is all I can cope with. Two would finish me off altogether!" Then before we could get upset she kissed him, hugged me and declared: "You're Nicholas. You're not 'just like' anyone. You're you, your special self." And to my father she concluded sternly: *"No replicas."*

I asked what a replica was, and after he had given me the definition my father said: "But of course your mother's quite right and you must become not my replica but the special person God's designed you to be."

"Supposing God's designed me to be exactly like you?"

"Impossible!" said my mother robustly. "That would be very boring for God—much more fun for him to create someone different. And Nicholas, while we're talking of peculiar ideas, I think it would be very clever of you and much more grown up if you kept all psychic talk specially for your father, who understands such things. Other people don't understand, you see, with the result that they become uncomfortable, and a true gentleman must always do everything he can to lessen the discomfort of others."

I resolved to be a true gentleman.

And that was the beginning of my tortuous relationship with my father.

3

"BEWARE of those glamorous powers!" my father said to me years later before I went up to Cambridge. "Those psychic powers which come from God but which can so easily be purloined by the Devil!"

This warning I wrote off as an exaggeration, a typically Victorian piece of melodramatic tub-thumping. More fool me. Having noted the psychic affinity which formed the bedrock of my relationship with my father, I must now sketch my disastrous career as a psychic.

I followed in his footsteps by reading divinity up at Cambridge, but after my finals I decided not to proceed immediately to theological college to train for the priesthood. This decision arose out of a conversation I had with Christian and I shall describe it fully later, but at present it's sufficient to say that at twenty-one I was tired of living in all-male ghettos and hankered to experience what I called "The Real World." In consequence I wound up doing voluntary work in Africa, but within months I got in a mess with a witch-doctor and had to be flown home.

My father begged me to proceed without further delay to theological college, but I was determined to complete the two years I'd set aside for voluntary work; I felt the need to wipe out the failure by being a success. Accordingly I took a job at the Mission for Seamen, fifty miles from home on the South Coast, but again disaster struck: two sailors got in a fight over me and wrecked the canteen. In vain I protested to my supervisor that I wasn't a homosexual and had given neither sailor encouragement. I was judged a disruptive influence and asked to leave.

Despite my father's renewed pleadings I still refused to abandon my two-year plan, but my third job also ended chaotically. I started work as an orderly at the Starbridge Mental Hospital, but before long a schizophrenic girl fell in love with me and slashed her wrists when I explained to her (kindly) that I was unavailable for a grand passion. She survived the slashing, but I was very upset, particularly when I realised the doctors were looking at me askance. Worse was to follow. Plates began to be smashed mysteriously in the empty kitchens at night, and when the senior psychiatrist asked with interest if I had ever been involved in the phenomenon popularly known as poltergeist activity, I decided it would be smart to resign before I was sacked.

At that stage I realised I had to do something drastic before my father expired with worry, so I headed for Starwater Abbey where I had been a pupil at the famous public school. Standing in the Starbridge diocese not far from my home at Starrington Magna, the Abbey was run by Anglican-Benedictine monks from the Fordite Order of St. Benedict and St. Bernard. My father had been a Fordite monk once, and as the result of his special knowledge of the Order he had arranged for Starwater's resident expert on the paranormal to keep an eye on me during my schooldays. It was to this man that I now turned.

Father Peters recommended that I made a retreat at the Abbey while we tried to work out what was going wrong. As a tentative hypothesis he suggested I might be suffering from the cumulative stressful effect of my fiascos as a voluntary worker, with the result that an awkward situation had been generated. There was certainly no doubt about the awkwardness of the situation. Plates which soar off shelves and smash themselves to pieces apparently unaided by a human hand are really very awkward indeed.

At last I said: "Could I have done it while sleep-walking?"

"I doubt it, Nicholas—the noise would have been terrific. You'd have woken up."

"Then it must have been one of the inmates, someone who wasn't locked up. Surely I couldn't have triggered poltergeist activity now that I'm past adolescence!"

"It's unlikely, I agree, but not impossible. If you were to make a retreat we could try and solve the mystery by examining the entire situation in detail and reviewing your spiritual life—"

I switched off, knowing that the last thing I could face at that time was

Father Peters playing a spiritual Sherlock Holmes. Any discussion of how I was unconsciously expending my energy by generating psychic phenomena might lead to a discussion of how I was consciously expending my energy in messing around with girls, and I wanted no one to know I had an active sex-life. Admitting to sexual intercourse would only lead to spiritual questions which I didn't even like to think about.

Sex was a problem. As far as I could see it was now essential therapy, hiving off all the surplus energy so that I stopped smashing plates long-distance by mistake, but I knew any confessor would tell me there were other ways of calming an overstrained psyche, ways that didn't involve exploiting women and crashing around like an animal. The trouble was that it was such a relief to crash around like an animal when my attempts to be a decent human being, ministering without pay to the under-privileged and the sick, regularly ended in humiliation.

But of course I could confess none of this to Father Peters. All I could do was confess to God in private my exploits as a crasher and pray for the grace to become effortlessly ascetic once I was ordained.

"I'll think about a retreat," I said. "I really will." And away I went to muddle on.

"What happened?" said my father when I returned home, but I suspected he already knew.

"Oh, we had a good chat and I'm feeling much better."

"Nicholas—"

"No need for you to worry any more, I'm fine."

Sometimes when my father demonstrated his intuition I thought he knew about my sex-life, but most of the time I was sure he didn't. I was careful never to think about it in his presence, and every time I felt his mind prying into mine I mentally evicted him by thinking about cricket.

Back we come again to the relationship with my father, now clouded by my chaotic career as a psychic and muddied by his agonising anxiety.

Of course sex is a subject which children often find impossible to discuss with their parents, but in my case this wasn't my father's fault; certainly I don't mean to imply that just because he was a priest he was incapable of speaking frankly on the subject.

"Christianity has been much misunderstood on this matter," he had said to me at exactly the right moment in my adolescence, "but it has always claimed"—here centuries of clerical misogyny were swept aside—"that sex is good and right." With the slightest of smiles he conveyed the impression of surveying numerous pleasurable memories. "It's the *abuse* of sex, that gift from God, which Christianity condemns. That's a manifestation of the Devil, who hates God's generosity and longs to wreck it by converting a gift of joy into a trap of suffering."

This made sense to me. I liked it when my father talked in old-fashioned picture-language of the Devil in order to convey the strength of the Dark, that psychic reality which I had recognised at such an early age. But then my father stopped talking about the reality of the Dark and began talking of the unreality of the sexual rules. It turned out that almost anything was an abuse of sex. In fact in a world which was overflowing with sexual possibilities—and which was soon to explode into a sexual supermarket— he insisted that for the unmarried only deprivation was on offer. With a marriage certificate tucked under one's pillow one could have sex twenty-five hours a day and God would never bat an eyelid (provided that the sex was what my father called "wholesome"; I never failed to be amazed by his use of archaic language). But for the Christian it was either feast or famine where sex was concerned. No wonder the unchurched masses thought Christianity was peculiar on the subject.

"I expect you're thinking now that this is all idealism which has no relation to reality," said my father, reading my mind so accurately that I jumped, "but human beings must have ideals to look up to and examples to copy if they're not to sink to a most unedifying level." (More fascinating archaic language. Unedifying! Ye gods!) "In this world no one's perfect. But one can aim high and try to be good. To do so is a sign not only of maturity but of"—my father made a vast verbal leap forward into the twentieth century—"psychological integration. Religion is about integration, about successfully bringing the selfish ego into line with the centre of the personality where God exists, as a divine spark, in every human being. Religion is about helping man to live in harmony with his true self and to become the person God's designed him to be."

We seemed to have wandered away from the subject of sex, but the next moment my father was saying: "Casual sex is just the gratification of the ego. The ego sits in the driving-seat of the personality, but unless it's aligned with the true self it'll steer an erratic and possibly disastrous course."

"Hm," I said. I thought it was about time I said something.

"In addition, casual sex is the exploitation of another, and to exploit people is wrong . . ."

Later I felt he had exaggerated this. Later, when I was no longer so innocent, I thought: what exploitation? The girls loved it. I loved it. No one got hurt. Where was the harm? Of course there would always be people who made a mess of their pleasures, I realised that. But I wasn't one of those people.

After the disaster at the mental hospital I yielded to my father's pleas to bring my voluntary service to a premature end. By that time I had whiled away twenty months of the two years I had allotted myself, and I was due to begin my training at theological college that autumn, the autumn of 1966. The summer stretched before me, and telling my father that I was going to embark on some serious theological reading, I loafed around listening to my records and dipping into books on reincarnation.

It was then, quite without warning, that I got into a mess with a girl, but being me I didn't get into the usual mess young men get into with girls. It was a psychic mess. Typical.

Back we come again to my disastrous career as a psychic. "Beware of those glamorous powers!" my father had droned to me years earlier before I had gone up to Cambridge, and I had thought: yes, yes, quite so, of course I shall always be psychically well-behaved. But during my years as an undergraduate I had found it increasingly hard to resist a psychic flourish now and then. The girls loved it. I loved it. No one got hurt. Where was the harm?

In that summer of 1966 I found out. I was twenty-three years old and spending my Saturday nights with a little dolly-bird typist called Debbie who had a bed-sitting-room down in Langley Bottom, the working-class end of Starbridge. I'd met her in the Starbridge branch of Burgy's, which I had discovered was the ideal place for picking up girls whom I couldn't take home but couldn't do without. Being currently intrigued by the research into reincarnation, I hankered to reproduce the Bridey Murphy experiment, and with Debbie's eager consent I hypnotised her in order to find out if she could recall a past life. She could. Greatly excited I took notes as she described her life as a medieval nun. Then the disaster happened: I was unable to bring her out of the trance.

By that time she had stopped talking and evolved into a zombie, eyes open, responsive to my commands but unable to communicate. I panicked, terrified by the thought that I had produced permanent mental impairment. Having manoeuvred her into my car I headed for the emergency department of Starbridge General Hospital, but then I suffered a second bout of panic. Supposing they thought she was traumatised as the result of a sexual assault? Supposing a scandal aborted my career as a priest before it had even begun? Bathed in the coldest of cold sweats I drove past the hospital and fled home with the zombie to my father.

He asked me only one question. It was: "What's her name?" and when I told him he took her hand in his and said: "Debbie, in the name of JESUS CHRIST I command you to return to your body and reclaim it." The cure was instant. There was no permanent mental impairment. But I never went to bed with her again. She wanted me to; she cried, she pleaded, but I couldn't. I'd seen the Dark. I'd felt the Force. It had been shown to me very clearly how vulnerable my psychic powers made me to demonic infiltration and in my revulsion Debbie now seemed fatally contaminated.

"You used that child," said my father, hammering home the truth with a fury which failed to conceal his terror that I should be so vulnerable. "You exploited her in order to satisfy your curiosity about a psychological mystery which has been adopted by those who believe in the heretical doctrine of reincarnation. You've behaved absolutely disgracefully and I'm ashamed of you."

Strong words. I hated myself. Worse still, the temporary withdrawal of his love made me more aware of my vulnerability than ever. I saw that even though I was now a grown man of twenty-three I still had to have his powerful psyche enfolding mine in order to keep the Dark at bay.

"I shan't comment on the sexual relationship which you've obviously had with the girl," said my father. "You know exactly what I think of young men who are too selfish and immature to do anything with women but exploit them. Please don't attend mass until you've made a full confession to Aelred Peters."

This was the final horror. I couldn't bear the thought of Father Peters knowing how I'd behaved. *"You* hear my confession," I begged my father, but he refused.

"Confessing to Aelred would be a real penance," he said. "Confessing to me would be a soft option. Off you go to Starwater."

Away I sloped to the Abbey, but cowardice overwhelmed me as soon as I crossed the threshold, and although I told Father Peters about the psychic disaster I was unable to speak of the sexual relationship. Fortunately Father Peters was so fascinated by Debbie's story of life as a medieval nun that he quite forgot to ask me what I'd been doing in her bed-sitter, and after we had completed the travesty of my formal confession we settled down for a cosy psychic chat.

"How could she have invented such a detailed description of an utterly alien way of life?"

"Well, my theory is . . ." Father Peters expounded on his theory. He said that although we remembered everything that ever happened to us, only a small part of our memory was accessible to our conscious thoughts; Debbie had probably seen a film featuring a medieval nunnery and she could well have elided this memory with a theme from a novelette. So in fact it was not a former life which had been revealed, but the extraordinary depth of memory which lay buried deep in the subconscious mind.

This intriguing speculation certainly took my mind off my troubles, but as soon as I parted from Father Peters I realised that a cosy psychic chat was no substitute for a full confession. The chapel at Starwater had a section set aside for visitors. Scuttling in, I sank to my knees and served up the fullest possible confession, heavily garnished with expressions of remorse and repentance. What God thought of it all I have no idea, but afterwards I felt slightly less guilt-ridden. One of the best things about the Church of England is that it never says you must make a confession to a priest, only that you may. Anglo-Catholics may follow the Roman tradition of confession, but there's nothing to stop even an Anglo-Catholic taking the

Protestant path and confessing his sins to God without the aid of an intermediary.

"You made a full confession?" said my father when I arrived home.

"Yep," I said, mentally adding the words: "But not to Aelred."

There was a pause during which I became uncomfortably aware of his mind pussyfooting suspiciously around my own. Then just as I was daring to believe that my honest expression had convinced him all was well he announced: "Sometimes I think you tell me only what I want to hear," and gave me his most baleful stare.

God only knows how I kept my honest expression nailed in place. Sometimes I felt that having a psychic parent was an intolerable cross to bear.

4

I MUST now say something more about my father in order to flesh out this lethal relationship which was developing between us as my psychic career went from bad to worse. This particular path which led to the crisis of 1968 needs to be examined in more detail.

By the time of the Debbie débacle my father was very old. Born in 1880, he had been sixty-two when I had arrived in the world, and so every year of the 1960s was bringing him closer to his ninetieth birthday. By the time the Christian Aysgarth affair began in the spring of 1968, two years after the mess with Debbie, he was nearly eighty-eight.

Being over eighty was very difficult for my father because he finally had to face up to the fact that he was old. Previously, having excellent health and a strong will, he had avoided this truth by cantering around like a man twenty years his junior, but at eighty he was felled by a prostate operation and although the physical problem was successfully treated the psychological consequences lingered on. Old age now stared him in the face. My father was livid, then deeply depressed, then livid all over again. With his strong will unimpaired and his brain untouched by senility, he regarded his body's enfeeblement as nothing short of traitorous. Looking back I can see he was secretly frightened—not of death, which in his faith he could face with courage, but of dying without dignity. My father was a proud man. He always used to say that his pride was his biggest weakness. The thought of his body decaying in a humiliating fashion while his mind remained sharp enough to suffer every indignity to the full was intolerable to him.

I could sense all these secret fears and hidden rages, but I was too young then to understand the full dimensions of his psychological ordeal. All I could do was make renewed efforts to keep him happy. I had already realised that nothing should be allowed to worry him and impair his health;

in consequence, as he had wrapped his psyche around mine, keeping the Dark at bay, I had wrapped my psyche around his, keeping the Light alive, and gradually a sinister interlocking had taken place until we were like Siamese twins joined at the psyche. No wonder I now felt I would be unable to survive without him.

I suspected my mother had always feared my father and I might wind up in a muddle, and that this dread had stimulated her robust attitude to our psychic gifts. She was quite prepared to believe they existed, but she was determined that they should never be allowed to triumph over her resolute common sense. Early in their marriage my father had embarked on a short but disastrous ministry of healing, and I think this experience had made her nervous about any exercise of the "glamorous powers," those gifts from God which were so susceptible to corruption.

She had been my father's second wife, his first marriage having begun and ended before he had embarked on his career as a Fordite monk. This first marriage had been unsatisfactory, but my father's big love affair with the monastic life had lasted for seventeen years before he had been called back into the world at the age of sixty. My father had been at first ambivalent about this return, but since the call had been judged genuine by his superior there had been no alternative but to obey it. Two muddled years had followed during which he had married my mother. She had eventually sorted him out, and before he had embarked on a successful career in theological education they had produced a son, Gerald, who had died at birth. I had arrived on the scene seventeen months later.

I could never make up my mind whether little Gerald would have been a bigger bore alive than he was dead, but I had no doubt that I resented the effect his memory had on my parents. They were shockingly sentimental about him. There was a grave in the churchyard which had to be visited. His birthday was never forgotten. As a child I thought this behaviour was all quite idiotic and I was very rude about it to Nanny. I liked being an only child. It was bad enough having to share my father with the two children of his first marriage, both of whom were well over thirty years my senior and lived many miles away. To share him with a sibling close to me in age and on the spot would have been intolerable.

Fortunately my parents had no more children after I was born, and by 1945 my father was running the Starbridge Theological College. To cope with the huge influx of ex-servicemen who felt called to train for the priesthood once the war was over, he opened an extension of the College at our manor house in Starrington Magna. I can clearly remember the students—the ordinands, as I soon learnt to call them—pounding across the lawn on the way to our private chapel in the woods. I became their mascot. Some of them even gave me their sweet ration. No wonder I wound up spoilt rotten by the time I was five.

However, all good things come to an end, even life as a pampered mascot. In 1950 when I was seven—eight at Christmas—the last of the exceptionally large intakes of theological students achieved ordination, the College extension at our home was closed and my father, now seventy, retired from his position as Principal. My mother had looked forward to this day because she had cherished the belief that he would then sink into a quiet life and she would see more of him, but she soon discovered that he was becoming busier than ever. As a monk he had won a reputation as a spiritual director, and now that he had fulfilled his call from God to steer the College through the difficult post-war years, spiritual direction reclaimed him full-time. Hordes of people turned up for consultations. He led retreats, wrote copious letters, made himself constantly available to those seeking counsel. My mother and I became somewhat overlooked but we never doubted that he loved us. The problem was that there were only twenty-four hours in a day.

Then in 1957 when I was fourteen, my mother suddenly died. My father was almost killed by guilt. For a long time he could barely speak. His longest sentence was: "I didn't make enough time for her," and I knew, reading his mind, that in his grief and remorse he wanted to die too.

He promised me that he would never commit the sin of taking his own life but I remained terrified that his health had been fatally undermined. He became a recluse. He did eventually resume his spiritual counselling on a modest scale but he conducted the work almost entirely by letter. Meanwhile I had become what Matron at school called "strange" and my father had to drag himself out of seclusion to make special arrangements for my care. That was when Aelred Peters had been recruited to sort me out. Eventually plates stopped smashing themselves in the Abbey kitchens and inkpots stopped overturning themselves in unlikely places. Staggering home for the school holidays, I hoped for further help from my father but instead found myself obliged to grapple with his continuing bereavement.

I would sit with him for short periods of complete silence. Sometimes we stroked the cat together. My father always had a cat and the cat was always a tabby. After the death of my mother's cat William (annexed by my father after his marriage), he acquired Whitby the Second (died young of a kidney complaint), Whitby the Third (run over aged ten) and Whitby the Fourth. Whitby the First, a companion of my father's monastic years, had left a potent memory behind him and had been the hero of countless bedtime stories narrated to me by my father in the nursery.

When my father began to talk again it was the cat he spoke about. "Whitby's very fond of you," he said suddenly in the midst of one of our long silences. "That's because you're like me, good with cats." Then he paused before adding: "You're really very like me, Nicholas. Very like me indeed."

Unsure what to say I at first remained silent, but gradually it dawned on me that he was wrestling with some profound temptation. In an effort to be sympathetic and encouraging I then said: "Great. So what are you worried about?"

The invisible wrestling-match continued. My father pursed his lips and rubbed his nose and fondled the scruff of Whitby's neck before he at last managed to say: "There's something I'd like to tell you but Francis always said it would be better for you not to know." Francis Ingram, a Fordite monk, had been his confessor.

I never hesitated. "But Francis is dead," I said, "and everything's changed. You do exactly what you want, Father. You do whatever makes you happy."

And then he told me the most extraordinary story.

5

HE HAD seen me in a vision well over a year before I was born. He had seen me, aged three or four, in the garden of the Manor and had realised at once that I looked exactly as he had looked at the same age. Afterwards, during his struggle to interpret the vision, he had been tempted to believe God had given him the promise of a replica-son in order to cheer him up for the difficult times he had endured since leaving the Order, but Francis Ingram had later disputed this self-indulgent interpretation, and in fact my father had firmly believed that no parent should expect or desire his child to be a replica.

"But nevertheless . . ."

Nevertheless my father, longing for a son who shared his interests, had been unable to stop himself finding the vision irresistibly attractive.

"And then, Nicholas . . ."

Then, when I was three and a half, the vision had been enacted in reality and my father had fallen in love with it all over again.

"It was in 1946," he said. "Neville Aysgarth was visiting the Manor—Archdeacon Aysgarth, as he was in those days. As he crossed the lawn to join us, Nanny called your name from the terrace and you ran away to meet her—and I realised my vision had been replayed. I was so stunned that at first I could hardly hear a word Aysgarth said. I could only think: it's all come true. I have this son who's exactly like me and it's all according to God's plan. Although of course," said my father quickly, "I did realise you weren't a replica. Not exactly. Not quite. But nevertheless . . . It's extraordinary how like me you are! I've been telling myself I've nothing to look forward to now Anne's dead, but that's not true, is it? I've got *you* to look forward to, Nicholas. I shall so enjoy watching you live my life for me all over again—that's to say, I shall so enjoy watching you develop into the man that God obviously wants you to be. You won't be a replica, of course—never think that I want a replica, but—"

But he did want a replica. I could see he longed for a replica. And what was more, I could see the thought revived him, entranced him, gave him not only a new interest but the will to live which would ensure his survival.

"—but one can't deny the very exceptional likeness between us," he was saying, "and why shouldn't that be a comfort to me in my old age? Francis said I should never tell you about the vision because you might start believing you had to be a replica, but you wouldn't think that, would you, Nicholas? Francis was wrong. On this point I know best—I know you'll reverence my cherished vision as a gift from God, just as I do, and so therefore it can't possibly have a malign effect. I'm right, aren't I? I know I'm right. I know it."

Proud, arrogant, ancient, miserable and misguided, he glared at me in a pathetic plea for reassurance.

Taking his hand in mine I said: "Of course you're right, Father. You always are."

No doubt my mother would have made some very robust comment at that point.

But my mother was no longer there.

6

THE next holidays I returned from school to find that a cottage was being built for my father in the grounds by the chapel. He said it would make it easier for him to be secluded. Then he said I could visit him whenever I wished because I was quite different from everyone else and he didn't find my presence a strain. As an afterthought he added that he couldn't bear to go on living at the main house now that my mother was no longer there; he'd never liked living there much anyway; his middle-class upbringing as a schoolmaster's son had ensured he had never felt at ease in my mother's county setting.

I was stunned. My father, educated on scholarships at public school and university, had appeared to fit neatly into my mother's world. I had had no idea he had such a chip on his shoulder about class. I knew, of course, that his mother had been a parlourmaid, but my own mother had said how interesting that was and what a remarkable woman my unknown grand-mother must have been to succeed in marrying "above her station," so I had accepted my grandparents' mésalliance as merely an unusual piece of family history. Now for the first time I saw that my father also had married "above his station" and it occurred to me that my parents' marriage too had been, in a less obvious way, a mésalliance, which had caused problems.

I was still recovering from the shock that my father had never felt at ease in the home I loved, when he began to explain to me his plan for ensuring that my inheritance was properly looked after: he intended to let the Home Farm and found a small religious community which would run the house and tend the grounds.

I disliked this scheme—though I said nothing for fear of upsetting him—but as time passed I realised how clever the plan was. Not only did I never have to worry about the property but I never had to worry that my father was failing to take care of himself when I was away. The members of the Community tended the garden, looked after the house and worshipped my father whenever they weren't busy worshipping God. Their devotion was my passport to a normal life unburdened by abnormal anxieties.

I finished school, went up to Laud's, my father's old college at Cambridge, came down with my degree, dabbled disastrously with voluntary work and dabbled disastrously with Debbie. My father was still living as a recluse in his cottage, but now in 1966, nine years after my mother's death, he had come to terms with his loss and his biggest problem was the old age he hated so much. But I could see he was looking forward intensely to my life at the Starbridge Theological College. He said more than once how much vicarious pleasure he would receive from my career as an ordinand.

I went to the Theological College. It was awful. It seemed to have very little to do with religion—religion as I understood it from my personal experience. I was reprimanded for using terms like the Light and the Dark and told I was flirting with Gnosticism. "What about St. John?" I said. "He talks of the Light and the Dark," but I was told tartly that I was Nicholas Darrow, not St. John the Evangelist, and that it was the sin of pride to think I could flirt with the Gnostic heresy and get away with it. In vain I told my tutor that the Light and the Dark were code-names which I used to describe a reality which for me was as true as any reality acknowledged by a logical positivist. My tutor said I should beware of mysticism as mystics so often got into trouble with the Church.

The Church was exalted as a sort of idol. Enormous emphasis was put on teaching what was liturgically correct. Church history was taught in stupefying detail. A heavy-handed, outdated biblical theology still ruled the roost, the academic successor of the neo-orthodox thunderings of Karl Barth. Radical theology was ignored—and this was 1966, three years after John Robinson's Church-shattering blockbuster *Honest to God!* But the College refused to admit any shattering had taken place; the idol was not allowed to be chipped or cracked—or even renovated. Robinson was dismissed as "misguided" and "no theologian." There was certainly a case for propounding criticisms such as these, but I thought Robinson's ideas, misguided or not, should at least have been debated. And I didn't like this rampant ecclesiastical idolatry. What's the Church anyway? Just a man-made institution. It's God and Christ and the Holy Spirit that are important. I'm not saying we don't need a man-made institution to deal with worldly matters. Obviously we do. And I'm not saying (in defiance of Anglo-Catholic ideology) that the Church has no numinous value and that holy traditions are unimportant. Obviously it has and they are. All I'm saying is that setting the Church up on a pedestal and worshipping it is wrong.

I also took a dim view of the way the College staff played down mysticism as they converted theology into just another academic subject such as history or English literature. Theology ought to be alive, vivid, related to real life, not a system debated by intellectuals. Did the mystic Julian of Norwich have a theology degree? Of course she didn't. But she knew God. She had *gnosis,* special knowledge. She saw visions and she *knew.* But if she'd been unfortunate enough to attend that Theological College in the 1960s, the only vision she would have had would have been a vision of the bliss which marked the end of term.

Of course I couldn't tell my father what a travesty the College was. Having run the place so successfully in the forties, he would have been deeply upset to know how far it had gone downhill. I learnt to keep quiet at College too because I didn't want anyone thinking I was "unsuitable" and trying to boot me out. One ordinand did say: "I think we should have courses on pastoral work and discuss things like sex," but he didn't last long. Sex was the great unmentionable among the College staff because no one had the guts to discuss ethical issues realistically. As I mooched around, bored out of my mind, I wondered how the Church could survive the twentieth century when one of its most famous training-grounds had been so wholly smothered by the dead hand of an irrelevant past.

My boredom eventually produced the inevitable result: my interest in sex, damped down by the Debbie débacle, began to revive.

I may have given the impression that I was formidably promiscuous but in fact by the standards of the mid-sixties I was almost staid. My habit of going steady with one girl at a time—and usually only seeing her once a week—was my way of paying lip-service to my father's belief that men should try to be more than mindless animals, so before the affair with Debbie I had changed girlfriends no more than once a year. However now, goaded on by the mind-blowing boredom of College life, I traded them in every six months. Doreen was a waitress at The Copper Kettle, Angie was a salesgirl at Boots, and Tracy, like Debbie, was a little dolly-bird typist.

Naturally I went to great lengths to cover up this behaviour which was so very unacceptable for a would-be priest. Knowing my father would be wondering if I'd picked a successor to Debbie, I created a smoke screen by running a platonic romance in tandem with my sex exploits; this meant that I took a nice girl home and introduced her to my father so that he could see how virginal she was and deduce how well I was behaving. I need hardly add that I didn't take home girls called Doreen, Angie and Tracy. I took home girls called Celia, Lavinia and Rosalind, girls I met from time to time at the tedious upper-class parties that for some reason people expected me to enjoy.

At the beginning of 1968, the year of the Christian Aysgarth affair, the year I was due to be ordained, I was sleeping with Tracy and taking home Rosalind. "Sleeping with Tracy" meant a quick swill at the Adam and Eve in Starbridge's Chasuble Lane, a quick binge at Burgy's on the Market Place and a quick retreat to her bed-sit, which like Debbie's was down at Langley Bottom by the railway station. (It was actually quite difficult to find working-class girls with bed-sits; they tended to live at home with Mum unless there were family problems.)

On the other hand, "taking home Rosalind" meant a leisurely stroll through Starrington from her house to the Manor, a leisurely listen to my Beethoven records and a leisurely call on my father in his cottage by the chapel. Sometimes we would dine in Starbridge at The Quill Pen in Wheat Street and attend a performance at the Starbridge Playhouse. Hands were held. A good-night peck on the cheek became part of the routine. There was the occasional friendly letter. It was all light-years away from the world where I bucketed around the bed-sits of Langley Bottom.

This may sound to some people as if I had my private life in perfect order, but as an ordinand to whom religion was not just a dead letter but a vital part of life, I knew the apparent order masked a dangerous chaos. I found it spiritually exhausting to lead a double life, and this knowledge that I was becoming increasingly debilitated made me realise how far off-course I was. In other words, I knew that what I was doing was not only objectively wrong, violating a moral code which I planned to devote my life to upholding, but subjectively wrong in that it was preventing me from being integrated, dividing me from my true self. Why then, it may be asked by the moral stalwarts and the sexually pure, didn't I pull myself together and abandon this disgraceful behaviour which was so utterly unworthy of an ordinand?

Why indeed.

But I think at least two of the great saints of the Church would have sympathised with me. "For the good that I would I do not," St. Paul wrote, "but the evil which I would not, that I do." "Lord, give me chastity!" St.

Augustine had pleaded to God. "But not just yet." I bet those two knew all about how tempting it is to use sex to escape from one's problems, and of course they would have understood that ordinands aren't supermen, automatically sanctified by their calling. Ordinands are only human; I knew I wasn't the only student at that College who scooted around on the quiet in his spare time, and if the moral stalwarts and the sexually pure are now flinging up their hands in horror and gasping: "Surely not!" may I remind them that this was the 1960s, when the Church was being shaken to its foundations by the permissive society. If the Church had become the idol of the scared traditionalist die-hards who ran the Theological College, then sex without doubt had become the idol of the secular world which existed beyond the walls of the Cathedral Close. The Theological College staff thought they could avoid one form of idolatry by turning to embrace another, but they were wrong. You don't beat idolatry by holding fast to idols. You beat idolatry by holding fast to God, but that's easier said than done.

I lived my double life for over a year. Then in 1968 my nerve finally snapped and I asked Rosalind to marry me.

There were several reasons propelling me towards this proposal. The first, obviously, was that I could stand the strain of a double life no longer. The second was that I had begun to suspect my father had intuited what was going on, with the result that he was becoming ill with worry about me—and I just couldn't risk him getting sick; he was now at an age when any illness could kill him. The third reason was that my ordination was looming on the horizon and I knew that once I was a priest no more dabbling with Debbies and Doreens would be possible. And the fourth reason was that I had just had a bad fright when a condom had broken and Tracy had mused: "It might be kind of fun to be pregnant." This remark horrified me so much that I even felt it was a call from God to reform. I prayed feverishly for the grace to alter my life, and on the morning of the day when I was due for my next chaste date with Rosalind I opened my eyes, sat bolt upright in bed and thought: I'll do it.

So I did. I proposed and was accepted. Happy ending. Or was it?

The best thing about Rosalind was that I had known her all my life and found her familiarity relaxing. She was the grand-daughter of a certain Colonel Maitland, now dead, who had been a friend of my mother's and who had owned the largest house in Starrington Magna apart from the Manor. Rosalind still lived at this house with her parents. She was a churchgoer, musical, intelligent and good-looking in that slim, slightly equine way which is such a recurring feature among the English upper classes. She had a part-time job doing special flower arrangements for a Starbridge florist and was beginning to receive free-lance commissions to plan the floral side of weddings. Kind, friendly and a good organiser, she clearly had all the right attributes for a clerical wife, and I could now look forward to living happily ever after.

"There's one big favour I want to ask you," I said. "Could we keep the engagement unofficial at the moment? I'd like to announce it on the day of my ordination."

Now, why did I say that? I didn't like to think. But Rosalind, perfect Rosalind, said what a super idea, we'd then have a double reason to celebrate, what fun it would be tossing back all the champagne.

"Do we keep absolutely mum?" she added. "Or do we let the cat out of the bag to a favoured few?"

I was anxious to set my father's mind at rest. "Okay, a favoured few—but no notice in *The Times* yet."

Rosalind's parents were delighted. Rosalind's best friend was delighted. Rosalind's favourite godmother was delighted. My father professed himself delighted but went right on being crucified by an anxiety which was invisible to the eye but searing to the psyche.

A week later I wound up in bed with Tracy at Langley Bottom.

At that point, being twenty-five years old and no fool, I realised that unless I got help in double-quick time I was going to crash into the biggest mess of my life. I couldn't talk to my father. He might have died, finally tortured to death by his anxiety. I couldn't talk to Aelred Peters. Resourceful though Father Peters was in treating the problems caused by abnormal psychic activity, I felt that mopping up something so prosaic as a sex-mess would be beyond him. But there was still one man who I thought could help me.

I made an appointment to see the Bishop of Starbridge, Dr. Charles Ashworth.

7

BISHOP ASHWORTH was the main reason why the Theological College was a dead loss, but in my hour of need I didn't let that prejudice me against him. In his pre-episcopal days he had been a distinguished professor of divinity at Cambridge. That was the problem. It's dangerous to let divinity professors out of their ivory towers to roam unfettered through the Church of England; the temptation to convert theological colleges into minor outposts of major universities is apparently irresistible, but theological colleges are supposed to train priests for the priesthood, not intellectuals for the groves of academe.

To be fair to Uncle Charles I have to admit he was a good bishop, and I have to acknowledge that at least he had had the guts to come out of his ivory tower and shoulder a top executive position in the real world.

It wasn't his fault that he got his kicks out of an academic approach to religion. That was just the way he had been designed by God. The important thing was that this intellectual kink hadn't prevented him from being a devout Christian who had no hesitation in standing up for what he believed in. I wasn't sure I believed all he believed in—he was an ultra-conservative wedded to what he called the "absolute truths"—but I respected his courage and I admired him as a good man who had always been kind to me.

He was an old friend of my father's; my father had been his spiritual director since 1937. There were very few people my father saw any more, but the Bishop was one of them. Uncle Charles kept an eye on my father. He had also kept an eye on me since my mother's death, and he regularly invited me to the South Canonry, the bishop's official residence in the Cathedral Close.

During his Cambridge days the undergraduates had nicknamed him Anti-Sex Ashworth because of the hard line he always took against sexual transgression, but I had long since sensed, by that mysterious process so difficult for any psychic to describe, that he wasn't anti-sex at all but a man of the world who, somewhere along the line, had encountered a sexual catastrophe which had made him feel called to hammer out repeated warnings about how dangerous immorality could be. Seeking help from a conservative bishop tough on sexual sin—the bishop who would shortly be ordaining me—might seem as suicidal as putting my head in a lion's mouth, but I felt I needed someone morally tough to beat me into shape, just as I needed a priest who could tackle a sex-mess without flinching. I wasn't sure how much to tell him—obviously the minimum, but how minimal was the minimum?—and I wasn't even sure I'd be able to tell him anything, but all I knew was that I had to try.

I called him "Uncle Charles" because my father belonged to the generation who thought children should address their parents' close friends by courtesy titles. When I reached twenty-one the Bishop had invited me to drop the title, but this had proved impossible. He was so formidably elegant and distinguished, and his date of birth in 1900 was so very far removed from mine.

"Well, Nicholas!" he said, giving me his best smile as we settled ourselves in his study after the ritual exchange of small-talk. Uncle Charles' best smile always reminded me of a toothpaste advertisement. It flashed with great effect on television whenever he was hauled onto discussion programmes to oppose the permissive society.

"Well, Uncle Charles!" I responded warily, trying to beat back a burst of fright.

"How are things going?" enquired the Bishop, laying on the charm with a shovel in an effort to put me at ease.

"Great!" I said, feeling more nervous than ever.

"Splendid!" exclaimed the Bishop with enthusiasm.

We eyed each other in silence for some seconds while the Bishop kept his smile nailed in place and I struggled to master my panic, but at last I managed to say: "Uncle Charles, I wanted to see you because, well, I thought, that's to say, wondered if you might possibly, sort of, well, you know, help me."

"My dear Nicholas, of course!" said the Bishop, still oozing the charm which was such a famous feature of his public persona, but beyond this routine response I could sense his real self unfolding in a spontaneous surge of concern. The Bishop had an interesting psyche, where sensitivity and an idealistic nature were kept under ruthless control by his first-class intellect and his considerable sophistication. Yet this complex personality, which could have produced a divided man, was seamlessly integrated. The glittering public persona was the servant, not the master of his true self beyond; its job was not to impress people but to create a shield behind which his true self had the privacy to flourish.

I hadn't the experience in 1968 to put this judgement into words, but I did know by instinct that I had to ignore the toothpaste smile and the oozy charm in order to address myself to the genuinely sympathetic man beyond.

"I'm sort of bothered," I said, ploughing on in the incoherent way fashionable among the under-thirties, but then found myself unable to express what bothered me most. With renewed panic I grabbed the next most bothersome subject on my list. "I mean, the Theological College seems to be useless to me at the moment, and . . . well, the truth is I don't honestly think, to put the matter in a nutshell, it can help me in—" I hesitated but forced myself to add, "—in this muddle."

"My dear Nicholas!" said the Bishop again, professional charm still well to the fore but his genuine concern now so strong that he quite overlooked the signpost provided by my last three words. "But how can the College be useless? It's the most splendid place—I've entirely preserved it from the decadent spirit of the age!"

"Yes, Uncle Charles. Excuse me, sir, but I think that could be the problem: it's so well-preserved it's dead. Of course I'm not suggesting it should go all trendy and liberal like some of the other theological colleges—"

"I should think not indeed!"

"—but I do wish the staff were allowed to talk about relevant things sometimes, I mean things that are relevant to Real Life—like, in a manner of speaking, sex. It seems sort of, well, weird to go on and on about Church history and dogmatics yet never once mention—"

"Dear me, you young men of today with your passion for 'relevance'!

But tell me this: what makes you so sure that what you think is relevant isn't instead just a passing fashion? Who makes the judgement on what's relevant, and how is that judgement made? Subjective judgements made under the influence of passing fashion are dangerous, Nicholas. One must keep one's gaze fixed on absolute truths, not relative values."

"Sex looks like a pretty absolute truth from where I'm standing, Uncle Charles."

"Well, of course it does!" said the Bishop, shifting ground quickly in order to extricate us from the theological quicksands. "Don't think I've forgotten what it's like to be young!" Suddenly he got down to business. "Okay, I get the message," he said, very trendily for a conservative prelate. "Girl-trouble, isn't it?"

"Yep."

"You're strongly attracted to a girl and you want to go to bed with her."

"Um." The situation was now so delicate that I could only hold my breath and pray for courage.

"This is a very, very difficult problem," said the Bishop, finally casting aside the glittering public persona and speaking straight from the heart with profound sympathy. "Far be it from me to underestimate it. As you know, I wholly disapprove of fornication, but I'm also wholly aware how tempting it is to indulge in it. I shan't regale you with all the familiar arguments because you'll have encountered them numerous times before— you've read Austin Farrer on continence, I assume?"

"Yes, Uncle Charles."

"And Archbishop Ramsey on sex and society?"

"Yes, Uncle Charles."

"Then since Farrer and Ramsey are better priests than I am I can hardly hope to improve on what they say as they spell out the Christian point of view. So let me take a purely pragmatic—one might almost say worldly—approach. I've never been called to celibacy. At various times during my life this has created severe problems for me, but let me now attempt to share the fruits of my experience with you."

Clever old Uncle Charles, knowing perfectly well that the ruminations, no matter how truthful, of two saints like Farrer and Ramsey were of little practical use to someone battling away against maxi-erections. With bated breath I waited to sample the fruits of his experience.

"Fornication," said the Bishop with superb self-confidence and a total lack of embarrassment, "is like Russian roulette—by which I mean it can be tremendously exciting. It gives you all sorts of thrilling delusions about how dashing and masculine you are, but unfortunately the reality is that you may wind up destroyed. Now, that's not thrilling, that's not dashing, that's not even a boost to the masculine ego. It's just very silly and a tragic waste. Of course you may get away with your adventure; it's always possible to survive Russian roulette. But why be immature enough to take such a mindless risk once you're grown up? There's more to life than getting hooked on adrenaline—" The Bishop certainly knew how to turn on the trendy vocabulary; moving in the world of television had evidently taught him a thing or two. "—and smashing up your future for the sake of a night of pleasure just doesn't make sense, not if you've got anything that resembles a brain."

This was fine but he was only telling me what I already knew. What I really wanted him to tell me was how to muzzle the maxi-erection so that it only occurred with the right girl; or in other words, I wanted to know how I could stop being hooked on Tracy and start being hooked on Rosalind.

". . . and I need hardly point out to a young man of your intelligence," he was adding, "that fornication is worse than Russian roulette because a person other than yourself is also involved in this potentially suicidal gamble. Don't risk it, Nicholas. Wait for marriage. It may be the toughest exercise in self-restraint that you're ever called to make, but very often the most worthwhile things in life can only be achieved with considerable effort by people who have the strength and wisdom to act as mature human beings, not selfish children."

I nearly tied my tongue in a knot in my haste to say: "Right. Actually I'm getting married. In fact I'm unofficially engaged."

"You are? But that's wonderful—how very exciting!" said the Bishop, sagging with relief. "Who is she? Do I know her?"

"Rosalind Maitland."

"Oh, an excellent girl—what a splendid choice! And how pleased your father must be!"

"Um."

"Wait a minute—you're signalling there's a fly in the ointment—ah yes! Now I see what you were driving at: you're strongly tempted to try a spot of premarital sex."

"Well—"

"No, hang on, I'm on the wrong track again, aren't I? I'm talking too much—time for me to shut up and listen. Why don't you tell me exactly what's bothering you?"

This was the moment I had been dreading. "Well . . ." But disclosure was now impossible. After his resounding approval of Rosalind I could hardly admit I wasn't as enthusiastic as I should have been about marrying her. And I certainly couldn't admit that it was not Rosalind Maitland of Starrington Magna whom I found sexually irresistible but Tracy Dodds of Langley Bottom. A long and desperate silence ensued.

"I've got it!" said the Bishop suddenly. "You've sown a few wild oats and your conscience is troubling you. Well, of course young men do sow wild oats, even young men who want to be ordained; we're all liable to succumb to temptation, even the best of us. You'll remember St. Paul's words, of course. 'Let him who thinketh he standeth take heed lest he fall.' "

"Yes, Uncle Charles."

"What you have to do now, Nicholas, if you repent—and I'm sure you do or you wouldn't be here seeking my help—is to put the wild oats firmly behind you, set yourself a high standard of conduct for the future and ask God's grace to enable you to be a first-class husband to Rosalind. Getting married to an excellent girl who loves you is without doubt the best possible course you can take."

"Yes, Uncle Charles."

"Meanwhile I do see you still have the problem of abstaining from sex, even though chastity does become easier when there's a definite end to it in sight. Of course it would be easy for an old buffer like me to say to a young man like you: 'The solution is to take cold showers and work hard.' It would be easy—but it would be wrong. It would imply a view of man based on the Pelagian heresy, the view that man can improve himself by his own efforts without God's grace. But grace is all. And prayer is vital. I presume the Theological College has at least given you some useful teaching about prayer even if it hasn't been busy lecturing about sex?"

I seized the chance to race away from the subject of my sex-life. "Well, to be honest, Uncle Charles, I've found the College's teaching on prayer a dead loss. It doesn't connect with anything I do at all."

The Bishop, who had been so commendably open, now began to close up. He loved that College as a child loves a favourite toy. He had rescued it from the slough of sloth into which it had slumped during the years following my father's retirement. He had nurtured it, poured his precious time into it, attended every governors' meeting he could, redesigned its syllabus, basked in the glow of its rising reputation. To hear this cherished fiefdom repeatedly criticised by a mere ordinand was to experience the trial of his Christian patience to its limit. "And what, may I ask," he said dryly, "do you 'do' when you pray?"

"Flip a switch in my head and tune in."

There was a pause. Then Uncle Charles said: "Have you discussed this with your father?"

"Don't need to."

"Why not?"

"It's one of the subjects we don't have to talk about in words."

"I think most discussions are more profitable when conducted in words," said the Bishop, now speaking very dryly indeed, "and since your father's such a distinguished spiritual director—"

"He says he can't be my spiritual director because he's too emotionally involved."

"Ah well, yes, I'm sure that's right, but nonetheless I'd have thought that on such an important subject as prayer he . . . well, never mind. Remind me: who's your personal tutor at the College?"

"Dr. Hallet, but he's hopeless."

"Dr. Hallet is the most Christian man!"

"Yeah, but he's hopeless. Doesn't dig the mystics."

After another pause Dr. Ashworth said: "Do you still see Father Peters at Starwater?"

"Yes, but I wouldn't discuss prayer with him."

"Why not?"

"He's too tied up in Anglican-Benedictine convention, sort of old-fashioned, you know, square. I did try talking in my code-language once, but—"

"What code-language?"

"The symbols I use for ultimate reality—for you know, kind of, God. But Father Peters just said what Dr. Hallet said—warned me that I was talking like a Gnostic and ought to watch it. Well, so what if I do talk like a Gnostic if that's the best way I can put my experiences into words—experiences which can't actually be put into words anyway? Some of those Christian Gnostics in the old days were very good, holy men and I don't see why we should write them off just because they didn't quite conform to the Church's idea of orthodoxy."

"The Gnostic heresy," said the Bishop, who had written a book on the subject, "very nearly destroyed the Early Church."

I felt like saying: "Too bad it didn't succeed," but fortunately I resisted this temptation to take a swipe at that man-made idol THE CHURCH and made a mighty effort to rein myself in before Uncle Charles had apoplexy. I knew what had happened. After the conversation about sex, when I had been obliged to remain buttoned up, I was now lashing out in an unbuttoned frenzy at the Theological College and the Church in order to let off steam. Normally I would never have divulged my sympathy with the Gnostics to anyone who wore a clerical collar.

"Sorry, Uncle Charles, I know you must be thinking I'm a heretic, but—"

"No, no—just a trifle unusual," said the Bishop courteously as he prepared to play the champion of orthodoxy and bring me to heel. "Of course," he remarked, "it's an axiom of spiritual direction that each soul is different and that each soul must therefore pray in the method best suited to it, but I think you should always bear in mind, Nicholas"—here the full episcopal power was switched on—"that psychic gifts can be a danger to those following the spiritual way. For example, they tend to foster arrogance. Instead of writing off Dr. Hallet as hopeless and Father Peters as old-fashioned, you should approach them with more humility and consider the possibility that they might well have something important to teach you. You should also remember that undisciplined contemplative prayer can be dangerous and should never be undertaken without the guidance of a spiritual director."

"Yes, Uncle Charles." Abandoning the incoherent patois of the under-thirties, I adopted a crisp, formal tone.

Satisfied that his chilly reproof had had a sobering effect, the Bishop changed gears. The toothpaste smile flashed. Charm started to ooze again. No wonder he was such a success on television. "Well, so much for serious matters," he said lightly. "Now let's turn back to the very pleasant subject of your engagement—you must bring your fiancée to dinner soon! I'll ask my wife to get in touch with you about a date."

"Thanks—that would be very nice," I said, immaculately well-behaved, and parted from him in amity with all my problems quite unsolved.

The next day Marina Markhampton came to see me and the Christian Aysgarth affair began.

II

"Mysticism in the proper sense is an intense realisation of God within the self and the self embraced within God in vivid nearness. It is a phenomenon known in a number of religions, and in those religions very similar language is used in describing the experience . . . Now through the centuries Christian teaching has emphasised that the significant thing is not just the mystic experience but its place and its context within the whole life of a Christian."

MICHAEL RAMSEY
Archbishop of Canterbury, 1961–1974
CANTERBURY PILGRIM

I

I NOW come to the third path which led me to the crisis of 1968. Running parallel to my increasingly convoluted relationship with my father and my increasingly chaotic career as a psychic was my friendship with Marina Markhampton.

Since Marina was the fiancée of the Bishop's younger son, it was hardly surprising that I knew her; what was surprising was that I had become friends with her well before her engagement to Michael. She was a year my senior, one of those flashy debutantes who are forever having their photographs plastered all over the society magazines, and while still a teenager she had won herself the title of the biggest cock-tease in town. This was not the sort of woman who normally interested me and so there was no obvious reason why we should have continued to wander in and out of each other's lives, but ever since Marina had decided I should be a member of her famous Coterie I had never quite managed to disentangle myself from her.

Since my mother had come from an old county family I had been automatically granted access to the debutantes' social events in the diocese of Starbridge, but I had quickly fought my way out of this boring maelstrom and rejected all invitations to similar parties in London. This early antipathy of mine towards conventional socialising explains why I never met Marina until she turned up at my Cambridge College's May ball

in the summer of 1962, six years before my unprofitable interview with
Bishop Ashworth and the onset of the Christian Aysgarth affair.

The May ball was one of those rare events which I condescended to
attend; as everyone acquainted with Cambridge knows, the May balls are
a very big deal indeed and not even an oddball loner dares to miss them.
In 1962 I invited Rosalind to accompany me, but unfortunately she was
struck down by appendicitis so I wound up going on my own. The ball
marked the end of my first year up at Cambridge. I was nineteen. Apart
from Rosalind—who in those days was no more than my former childhood playmate—I had no girlfriend of any kind. Naturally, since I was
nineteen, I was obsessed with sex, but naturally, given my background, I
hadn't yet succeeded in working out what I could do about it. Alone and
innocent, I drifted along with mixed emotions (distaste ploughed under
by an overpowering sexual curiosity) to the event which all my contempo-
raries considered to be the last word in undergraduate chic.

By the time I met Marina the evening was far advanced. I had been
whiling away the hours by watching and listening and occasionally summoning the nerve to dance with girls who looked nice enough not to reject
a very plain teenager who felt like a goldfish marooned a long way from
his bowl. These girls all bored me very much. Eventually I confined myself
to observing the sultry sirens and wishing I had the guts to whip them away
from their preening partners. While all this was going on I drank much
more than usual out of sheer absent-mindedness; I was fantasising so hard
about the sirens that I forgot to notice what I was pouring down my throat.
Finally, unable to stand the frustration any longer, I staggered outside to
sample the moonlight, and as soon as I began to cross the lawn to the river
I saw Marina lying semi-naked in a punt.

The sight stopped me dead in my tracks. Then it dawned on me that
two would-be *gondolieri* were fighting on the jetty for the honour of
wielding the pole which would propel the punt downstream.

Drunk but by no means dead drunk, I said to myself: "He who dares
wins," and circumventing the brawling *gondolieri* I said politely to Marina:
"May I help you?"

"My dear," she said, "I thought you'd never ask," and stepping into the
punt I picked up the pole.

The *gondolieri* shouted: "I say, hang on!" and "What the hell do you
think you're doing?" but Marina and I were already gliding away from
the jetty. At that moment more opposition appeared: a small wiry figure
raced down to the bank and began to bounce up and down in an ecstasy
of disapproval. "Marina, nudity is *not* allowed—pull up your dress this
instant!" it thundered, and as I heard that familiar voice I realised this
curious creature was none other than the Bishop's son, not Michael but the
older one, Charley. He was at a theological college in Cambridge, but as

a graduate of Laud's he would have had no trouble obtaining a ticket for the May ball.

"Do you know this girl, Charley?" I called with interest, sinking the pole much too deep in the mud. My lack of interest in the debutante world and my lack of acquaintance with glossy society magazines had ensured my failure to recognise her.

"Of course I know her! She's the grand-daughter of Lady Markhampton who lives in the Close at Starbridge. Marina, for God's sake—"

"Take not the name of the Lord thy God in vain!" trilled Marina richly. "Remember your manners, Charley darling, and introduce me to this divine mystery-man!"

At that moment the divine mystery-man was trying to pull the pole out of the mud. For one agonising second I thought I was about to be dragged into the water, but the pole parted from the river-bed in the nick of time and I regained my balance. Meanwhile the *gondolieri* had stripped off their clothes and with cries of "Whoopee, Marina—we're coming!" they plunged into the river.

"This is disgraceful!" shouted Charley, outraged at the sight of more nudity. "Absolutely disgraceful!"

"Oh, buzz off before I order them to drown you!" exclaimed Marina crossly, and purred to the oncoming swimmers: "Darlings, you're terribly sweet but you've missed—quite literally—the boat. Punt on, mystery-man."

I shot the boat forward. Charley and the swimmers were left behind as I furiously propelled the punt towards the moonlit silhouette of Clare Bridge.

"Stop!" commanded Marina as we sped beneath the arch. "I want to feast my eyes on King's College Chapel."

I braked as dexterously as I could and tried to concentrate on drawing alongside the bank without a bump, but I was distracted by the sight of Marina's unsuccessful attempts to pull up her dress. Something had broken at the low neckline and her breasts kept falling out.

"I can't get my bosom to behave itself," she said, "but you don't mind, do you?"

"Not in the least."

"Introduce yourself. You fascinate me."

"Nick Darrow."

"What's your connection with that ghastly prig Charley Ashworth?"

"Our fathers are pals."

"Oh God, how awkward for you—I inevitably loathe all the offspring of my parents' friends. Where do you come from?"

"A village near Starbridge."

"Good heavens—in that case why haven't we met? I thought I knew absolutely everyone in the Starbridge area as the result of my visits to Granny in the Cathedral Close. Darrow, Darrow, Darrow . . . No, I don't know that name. How extraordinary."

"Your grandmother knew my mother. My mother's maiden name was Barton-Woods."

"Ah well, of course I've heard *that* name before—isn't there a rather heavenly manor house at Starrington Magna? And—gosh, wait a minute! Is your father the holy man who lives on communion wafers in a wood?"

"He's a priest who lives quietly in retirement."

"Exactly! Granny's told me all about him. Are you reading divinity in order to follow in his footsteps?"

"Yep."

"How sad—another good man lost to the Church!"

"Don't knock the Church too hard," I said, trying to work out where I could park the pole so that I could have both hands free to grab her breasts. "It could be in your future."

Instantly she was enthralled. "You sound as if you tell fortunes!"

"Of course I tell fortunes!" I said, and as I spoke a vision of how I could succeed with the sirens unfolded before my eyes. But still I couldn't work out where to park the pole.

Meanwhile Marina was stretching out her right hand and demanding: "Read my palm!" as her breasts appeared to float magically towards me in the moonlight.

"I don't go in for palmistry," I said. "I just tune into the vibrations." And still clutching the pole with one hand, I grasped her proffered fingers with the other. By this time my erection was so uncomfortable that I thought I might have to jump into the river to get my genitals under control.

"Go on—spill the beans!" said Marina impatiently. "How's the Church going to be in my future?"

I had no idea but I remembered the grandmother who lived in the Cathedral Close.

"I see you living in the shadow of a great cathedral," I invented, taking care to speak in portentous tones.

"Impossible! I never stay with Granny nowadays, there's no time, I simply drop in occasionally."

"Nevertheless I see that long shadow cast by the cathedral—and I see a man in your life there."

"There are always men in my life everywhere!" she said fractiously, and as she spoke I detected a touch of boredom with the male sex, perhaps even a trace of disappointment.

"This'll be a special man," I said, clued in by her tone of voice and deducing that the average panting male left her cold. Really, fortune-telling's so easy that I can't think why more people don't do it. All you have to do is put up a mental aerial to receive the unspoken signals and then wait for the subject to give herself away.

"The only special man I know," said Marina with a sigh, "is quite unobtainable." And as she disclosed this piece of information the alcoholic fog cleared in my psyche, my metaphorical aerial began to pick up strong signals and I understood that an unobtainable man was, in some mysterious way, exactly what she wanted. I was too young at the time to make the obvious deduction: that a desire for an unobtainable man coupled with a distaste for the men available hinted at a sexual hang-up. I just thought— and when I say "I thought" I mean I *knew,* it was the special knowledge I called *gnosis*—she doesn't do it. I'm wasting my time.

"The funny thing is," Marina was musing, "this man does actually have a connection with the Cathedral Close at Starbridge. But I don't see how I could ever wind up there living with him."

"I didn't say you would. I said you'd be living—or perhaps just temporarily staying—in the shadow of a great cathedral, and this man would at last be significantly present in your life."

"Will I get anywhere with him?"

"Yes, but not in the conventional sense," I said, inventing the answer I knew she wanted to hear, but then without warning I received the print-out that circumvents the ordinary processes of thought, the message that's hammered directly into the brain from some unknown source and appears instantly on the screen of the psyche. Without stopping to think— because thinking had been by-passed—I said: "You'll be very close to his wife. In fact she's already a friend of yours."

"Glory!" said Marina astounded. "You really are amazing! How could you possibly have known about my new friendship with Katie?"

And that was the moment when I elided the Cathedral Close connection with the wife called Katie and realised that the man we were talking about was Christian Aysgarth.

2

SINCE I had promised my father not to behave like a shady charlatan by performing psychic parlour-tricks, I felt guilty enough about the punt episode to try to avoid Marina afterwards, but she was like a child with a shrimping-net who had seen an exotic creature swimming in a rock-pool; she found herself compelled to kidnap me for her very own private aquarium.

I was netted, compulsorily enrolled in her Coterie and treated not as a fish but as a very expensive poodle. Marina called me the Coterie's soothsayer-in-residence. I hated all this rubbishy behaviour but of course I was flattered to have been singled out by the dazzling Marina Markhampton. Having been unsure how much sex-appeal I had (if any), I liked the way Marina made me feel like Errol Flynn and Elvis Presley rolled into one. No wonder I retained a soft spot in my heart for her afterwards and could never quite bear to sever myself completely from her boring old Coterie.

Ironically, sex was no longer a serious ingredient in our friendship once I'd sobered up. Marina's persistent pampering was based on the kind of attraction a smart woman feels towards a supremely original fashion accessory; it was covetousness, not lust, which lay at the root of her liking for me, and it was a flattered ego, not a libido in overdrive, which lay at the root of my liking for her. In fact once I was no longer drunk enough to feel like laying every woman in sight, I was surprised to discover how resistible I found her. The Venus de Milo type of torso has never been to my taste, and I happen to be one of those gentlemen who don't prefer blondes. I like steamy brunettes with large breasts, slim hips and legs that go on for ever. Marina was supposed to be a flawless example of feminine beauty, but I thought she looked like an intelligent sheep, all blazing light eyes and angular facial bones.

In the May of 1963, less than a year after our first meeting, she went to live temporarily in the Cathedral Close at Starbridge. (This reflects no credit on my fortune-telling skill, of course. My invented prophecy had merely given her an idea about how she could best further her friendship with Christian, and if I'd kept quiet in the punt it would never have occurred to her to offer to house-sit for her grandmother while Lady Markhampton was away in the south of France.)

Inevitably Marina threw a party and inevitably I was invited and inevitably I was afflicted by my usual ambivalence: I felt satisfaction that I should have been included, curiosity to see how the *jeunesse dorée* lived and annoyance that I was to be trotted out once more as Marina's psychic poodle. My friend Venetia seemed to think that the Starbridge party was the first occasion that Marina had displayed me as a fashion accessory, but there had been previous occasions in London when to my disgust I had been unable to resist being exhibited.

I now made a new resolution to waste no more time in this idiotic fashion, so I turned down the invitation to Lady Markhampton's house by saying I was too busy swotting for my second-year exams. Unfortunately Marina refused to take no for an answer. Discovering that I was planning to slip back to Starrington that weekend for my father's birthday, she bludgeoned me again with her invitation and almost before I could say "parlour-trick" I found myself mutinously turning up at the party—the "orgy" as Marina chose to call her parties in those days.

As a gesture of rebellion I arrived late and left early. In fact I behaved very badly, but then so did Marina, introducing me to her current gang as the Coterie's soothsayer-in-residence and fawning over me until I wanted to puke. There were about sixteen people present; Marina either gave small parties where couples continually formed and re-formed as everyone tried out everyone else, or she gave big bashes where couples tended to stick together in order to survive. On this select occasion it just so happened that I knew few of the guests, but there was nothing particularly surprising about this. Marina had a vast circle of acquaintances and liked to shuffle them around her guest-lists to keep everyone wondering whom they were going to meet next. The privileged inner circle, which she insisted on calling her Coterie, also varied, depending on who was in favour, and the only people I knew that night were her two closest girlfriends (Emma-Louise and Holly), my friend Venetia and Michael Ashworth, the younger son of the Bishop and the brother of Charley-the-Prig.

Anyway there I was, arriving hours late at Lady Markhampton's house in the Close, and there was Marina, not just introducing me as the Coterie's soothsayer-in-residence but even declaiming that I was the brother of Martin Darrow the actor (I'll get to that creep Martin later). If there was one thing I hated even more than being paraded as a psychic, it was being paraded as the brother of the famous Martin Darrow—who was only my half-brother anyway, the son of my father's first marriage, and so much older than I was that I felt he should be keeping little Gerald company in the hereafter.

It was before the drug era, so although everyone was stoned out of their minds the culprit was merely vintage Veuve Clicquot. I drank half a glass and asked for a Coke, just to be nasty. Marina gave a little tinkling laugh and said how original I was. Fortunately I discovered some excellent sausage rolls at the buffet. They kept me quiet for a bit. The nicest person in the room was my friend Venetia—Venetia Flaxton she was in those days. I'd met her a month earlier through Charley-the-Prig. It was curious how Charley Ashworth was present when I met both Marina and Venetia. The most unlikely people can turn up at crucial moments in one's life.

Venetia seemed a lot older than I was then because in 1963 she was twenty-six and I was only twenty, but I always liked her. I specially liked her at Marina's orgy that night. I could see she knew I hated being paraded as a soothsayer and the brother of Martin Darrow. "Give the poor child a chance to merge with the crowd!" I heard her mutter exasperated to Marina, and the next moment she had swooped to my rescue by leading me to the most striking couple in the room.

The woman was dark, not one of my steamy brunettes but a romantic heroine who looked as if she had stepped out of some Victorian novel where women were idealised as angels—or perhaps out of some Victorian painting where the female figure was supposed to represent Purity in its endless battles against Lust. She had delicate features, pale skin and fine-boned, well-bred hands. I remember thinking: I wouldn't want to go to bed with a woman like that because I'd be too afraid of breaking her.

The man who had apparently found this purity-on-a-pedestal fragility irresistible was lounging elegantly against the mantelshelf as if he owned not only the room but the house and the entire Cathedral Close. Tall, slim and dark, he coruscated with a glamour enhanced by an air of total self-confidence, the poise of a brilliant, sophisticated man who was well accustomed to the world grovelling at his feet. This aura of extreme worldly success fascinated me. I was also intrigued by the way the sensitivity of his face was marred by a thin, brutal mouth which had already, as if foreshadowing his middle age, begun to turn down slightly at the corners. I was surprised later when women sighed how handsome he was. That mouth ruined the film-star looks, but women, being women, obviously found it so sexy that they were incapable of seeing it as a blemish.

". . . and do you know the Aysgarths?" Venetia was saying to me. "This is Christian—and this is his wife Katie . . ."

I had heard much about this couple over the years, but I had never before managed to meet them. Christian's father was the Dean of Starbridge, the priest who ran the Cathedral. A self-made man, he had a considerable reputation as an administrator and no inhibitions about flaunting his powerful personality. My father disliked him but the Dean had many devoted friends and admirers not only in Starbridge itself but throughout the diocese. It was widely noted that the Bishop, like my father, was not among them.

In the early 1940s when my father had first met him, the Dean had been the Archdeacon of Starbridge, but in 1946 he had moved to London to become a canon of Westminster Abbey and an interval of eleven years had followed before he had returned to the diocese to take charge of the Cathedral. His eccentric second wife, Christian's stepmother, invited me to a few parties at the Deanery because I happened to be only eighteen months younger than Christian's brother Sandy, but when after one boring visit I consistently refused these invitations she at last gave up issuing them. I didn't care for Sandy, whose idea of fun consisted of reading Greek poetry—in Greek—and the Dean's other children were all either much older than I was or much younger.

Christian was fifteen years my senior, a fact which helps to explain why I had never met him before Marina's Starbridge orgy; by the time his father returned to the diocese in 1957, Christian was a don up at Oxford, and once I had rejected his stepmother's attempts to draw me into the Deanery's junior social set, there was no reason why he should ever have encountered me. I did go to the Cathedral Close regularly to see the Ashworths, but since the Bishop and the Dean were constantly at loggerheads, contact between the Deanery and the South Canonry was minimal. Certainly on my visits to the Bishop's house there was never an Aysgarth in sight.

Christian was the eldest child of the Dean's first marriage. The second son, Norman, was a barrister who lectured in law; he was also at Marina's orgy that night. There was a third son, James, whom at that time I had never met, a daughter, Primrose, whom I had glimpsed when Mrs. Aysgarth had initially succeeded in dragging me to the Deanery, and finally my contemporary, Sandy-the-Greek-Freak, whose real name was Alexander. Elizabeth and Pip, Dean Aysgarth's two offspring by his weird second wife, were still children at the time of Marina's Starbridge party, and I knew little about them except that Pip was a pupil at the Cathedral Choir School and Elizabeth had been nicknamed Lolita by various ordinands at the Theological College.

"Your father was the Principal of the Theological College back in the forties, wasn't he?" said Christian to me when we finally met that night. "I can remember him visiting us just before Father left Starbridge to take up the canonry at Westminster."

"Ah," I said, very young, very gauche.

"And I remember Sandy telling me about you," pursued Christian. " 'What's the point of reading Homer,' you said to him, 'when you could read Shakespeare instead?' Very shocking that was to Sandy! But I thought: there goes a man after my own xenophobic heart—a rampant chauvinist who goes to bed wrapped in the Union Jack every night!"

Everyone laughed as I tried to assemble a sentence which would prove I was no mental defective, but before I could speak, my friend Venetia exclaimed: "Stop teasing him, Christian! You don't have to be xenophobic to prefer Shakespeare to Homer!"

"No, but it helps." Suddenly he smiled at me and at once became the Oxford don who was well accustomed to socially inept undergraduates. "I seem to remember you're reading divinity at the Other Place," he said kindly. "How are you getting on?"

"Okay."

"I read theology up at Oxford, although my special subject is now medieval philosophy. Going to be ordained?"

"Yep."

"Good for you. You're a braver man than I ever was."

"Darling!" said his wife reproachfully. "You can't imply you're lacking in courage just because you weren't called to be a clergyman!"

"The Devil only knows what I was called to be," said Christian, turning his back on her, and at once I was aware of tension, of darkness, of a tingling on the spine.

Marina surged past me into the middle of the group. "Christian, did I ever tell you I met Nicky when I was lying semi-nude in a punt on the Cam?"

"I should think you met a lot of people, my love, if you lay around semi-nude in a punt on the Cam." He raised his voice to address a man who had begun to drift towards us from a group by the window. "Perry, come and meet the bravest man in this room—Marina's soothsayer's heading for a cassock and dog-collar!" And to me he added: "Nick, this is Peregrine Palmer, a very old friend of mine."

"Hullo, Nick," said Palmer. "Nice to meet someone under twenty-five who's committed to Jesus Christ instead of that crashing bore Elvis Presley."

"I'm mad about Elvis!" cried my friend Venetia hotly.

"I'm mad about you," said Palmer, "and how you could enjoy that kind of moronic music is quite beyond my power to imagine . . ."

An argument followed about whether rock 'n' roll had replaced religion as the opium of the masses. I wanted to talk to Christian but still I was unable to devise a remark worthy of his attention. Meanwhile Christian himself continued to lounge against the chimney-piece, his glass of champagne in one hand, a cigarette in the other, and his wife continued to gaze at him adoringly. So did Marina. That was when I realised that the secret hero-worship of last summer had blossomed into a passion which I had no doubt was platonic. Katie obviously had no doubt either. She was quite at ease, and when Marina offered her a cigarette she accepted it with a smile. By this time the debate had progressed from a disagreement about Marx's "opium of the masses" to a slanging match about Sartre's brand of existentialism, and I couldn't help admiring Venetia. Refusing to conform to the conventional pattern of feminine behaviour, she spoke up to both men, remained unintimidated when Palmer tried to undermine her argument, and finally won the debate by shouting out a quotation in Latin.

"Phew!" gasped Palmer pie-eyed.

I couldn't make up my mind whether he liked Venetia as much as he appeared to like her, or whether the friendly admiration was just an act, part of an adroit social manner which could be switched on and off without effort. There was something unreadable about Palmer. He had brown hair, neatly cut and parted, bland blue eyes and a square, unremarkable face which any poker-player would have envied; he economised constantly in his use of facial muscles. He was shorter than Christian. I remember noticing, as I glanced in the glass above the fireplace, that Christian and I were the same height: six feet exactly.

The party blazed on. Having reviewed my limited knowledge of Christian's special subject, I finally managed to compose a sentence suitable for opening a conversation with him ("Could the work of Joachim of Flora be considered a forerunner of the Marxian view of history?") but unfortunately I never managed to ask this mind-bending question because I was collared by Michael Ashworth. He wasn't engaged to Marina in those days and was busy being girl-mad, reacting against his father, the strait-laced bishop, and his brother, Charley-the-Prig. I had been watching him as I devised my question about Joachim of Flora. He had been sprawled on the sofa with two girls, his right arm squeezing the waist of the blonde (Emma-Louise) while his left hand squeezed the breast of the brunette. This unknown brunette interested me deeply. She was an ultra-steamy concoction of heaving cleavage, lissom legs and smouldering dark eyes.

"This is Dinkie," said Michael, having nobly abandoned his squeezing in order to look after me. Although nearly three years my senior, he always took a benevolent interest in my welfare.

"Hiya, gorgeous," said the steamy brunette in a show-stopping American drawl.

"Hi." Of course I could think of nothing else to say. What hell it is to be young.

"I just love to make passes," said this fabulous creature, "at guys who wear glasses."

This indeed was an education. I had lost my virginity a month after my encounter with Marina the previous summer, but I still knew very little about girls and I still thought my reflection in the mirror fell far short of the masculine ideal which would be demanded by any discerning steamy brunette. I was glad to be tall but I hated being so lanky and angular. I was glad not to be blind but I hated having to wear glasses. I was glad to be white, since life in England was such hell for blacks, but I hated the unusual pallor of my skin. I was glad not to be a hermaphrodite but I hated being so unremarkable below the waist. Since the loss of my virginity I had accepted that average-sized genitals were quite sufficient to see me through life, but nevertheless I remained discontented because I had hoped to be compensated for my plain looks by being supremely well endowed sexually. (What *hell* it is to be young.) No wonder I was so tempted to rely for sex-appeal not on my physique but on my psyche. It was all very well for my father to drone on about those "glamorous powers" which could be so easily purloined by the Devil, but at the insecure age of twenty it was hard to resist parading all the glamour at my disposal once a steamy brunette appeared on the horizon.

"A soothsayer, huh?" purred Dinkie Kauffman at Marina's party that night. "Tell my fortune, Wonder-Cat, and be sure you make it cool!"

But before I could begin to produce the usual intuitive rubbish, Christian clapped his hands to gain everyone's attention and I realised that the climax of the party had been reached. The lights were switched off, the curtains pulled back and as the floodlit Cathedral was revealed beyond the window, Christian proposed a toast to Starbridge. I had long since finished my Coke but I thought I might eat, rather than drink, the toast so I sidled to the buffet under cover of darkness and grabbed another of the sausage rolls. As I did so Dinkie suggested that we should all dance on the Cathedral roof and for some reason everyone seemed to think this was a brilliant idea. Funny the whims people get when they're drunk. But maybe the concept of polluting a numinous place by idiotic behaviour just has no meaning for non-psychics. For me it would have been like throwing paint at the Mona Lisa.

Deciding it was time to leave, I stuffed the last two sausage rolls into my pocket to keep me happy on the journey home, but unfortunately the lights were turned on again before I could complete this manoeuvre and my friend Venetia saw the second roll vanish. Immediately I felt embarrassed by my brazen greed, but almost before I had time to register her smile of sympathy my embarrassment was wiped out as the horror began.

The power was switched on in my psyche.

Knowledge began to be hammered directly into my brain, but this wasn't just a brief rattle of the computer keyboard followed by a quick flash on the blank screen. This was the long slam which seemed as if it would never end, this was the keyboard pounding so fast that the keys were no more than a blur to the psychic eye, this was the big print-out which cascaded all over my mind.

The shock was so profound that I almost lost consciousness. I could neither move nor speak. I could barely breathe.

The Dark began to pour into the room.

3

SOMETIMES foreknowledge is known as "second sight," but when I suffered such attacks they were never visual. In that respect I was less gifted than my father. As a psychic I experienced two kinds of special knowledge: one was the quick flash which could sometimes be written off as intuition; the other, much rarer, was the long slam which bore no more resemblance to intuition than an elephant bears to a mouse. Such episodes had a peculiarly vile, lucid quality which, unlike intuition, seemed to leave no room for ambiguity. This instant, uncontrollable destruction of all the shadows we depend on to shield us from searing truths was horrific. No wonder I nearly passed out with shock. It was as if I'd been sitting in an armchair by a cosy fireside and had been brutally blasted into Belsen.

Many people think it must be fun to be a psychic. Fun! When as a small child I first experienced the long slam I screamed non-stop until my father arrived to stitch up my shredded little psyche. Fortunately my mother was out at the estate office, but poor Nanny thought I'd gone mad. My father held me in his arms for a long time but eventually he slipped his pectoral cross into my hand and told me I was safe.

"No demon can withstand the power of Christ," he said, and when he spoke the name of the greatest exorcist who had ever lived, the image of the Light captured my brain and the Dark was conquered.

Much later in my life I read about autistic children. What interested me was that some doctors believed these children could be helped by being held tightly for long periods by a loving adult. I was never autistic; nor were all my profound psychic experiences equally terrifying. But they could be horrific enough to produce a reaction akin to mental illness, and never, by any stretch of the imagination, could they be described as "fun."

As soon as the Dark began to pour into the room that night at Marina's party, I was not only physically immobilised but mentally booted onto a plane not normally accessible to the conscious mind. I looked around the room and all the objects in it seemed to be hammering out messages to me, they were all speaking, although of course there were no words, no sounds, but I stood in that room, Lady Markhampton's drawing-room it was, the drawing-room of that house called the Chantry which stood in the Cathedral Close, and because all the objects there were vibrating with information, I experienced her essence quite clearly; the image was slapped on the computer screen of my psychic eye. That meant I could "see" her—but psychically, not visually—and at once I thought: nice old girl, sharp tongue, kind heart, well read, cleverer than her husband—and then I experienced the husband's essence too: old buffer, drank too much, liked cricket and Havana cigars, stupid old bore, forget him, and anyway the love of Lady Markhampton's life hadn't been her husband, it had been a slim, striking, middle-aged man with golden eyes—golden eyes just like Charley Ashworth's, how odd—and he was wearing a frock-coat and gaiters, a fact which was odder still, but no, he wasn't an actor in a costume melodrama, he was a twentieth-century bishop in full episcopal gear, interesting, fancy Lady Markhampton being in love with a bishop, but of course she'd kept her secret, and neither the bishop nor the silly old husband had ever guessed.

Then time suddenly went way out of alignment, and I knew that in that drawing-room, so civilised and elegant, a priest had been killed during the Civil War when the Roundheads had smashed up Royalist Starbridge. There was wall-to-wall blood, I couldn't see it, but it was there, I was wading in it, and all at once the Force—the psychic force—roared into top gear, like a gale it was, no, a hurricane, no, a nuclear wind, and it nearly deafened me, although of course there was no sound, just print-out, print-out, print-out, slam, slam, slam on the computer keyboard, and the word which kept flashing on the screen was DEATH, DEATH, DEATH, DEATH, DEATH.

Then I looked at my companions, that *jeunesse dorée,* those glamorous friends of Marina Markhampton all glittering in the Light, and I knew the Dark was closing in on them, I knew the Coterie was doomed. But Michael Ashworth was going to survive—odd how sure I was of that when popular opinion wrote him off as a rake who could only go from bad to worse, but no, Michael was going to live and someone else was going to live too, one of the girls—was it Marina, surviving with Michael?—but I couldn't quite read the name in the print-out—oh God, let it be my friend Venetia!—and meanwhile the keys were slamming on and the horrors were coming up brilliantly lit upon the screen.

I looked at Dinkie, the steamy brunette, and knew she'd become a walking corpse. I looked at Christian's brother Norman and knew his body would rot long before he died. I looked at Norman's wife Cynthia and heard her screaming in a locked room. I looked at Marina's friend Holly Carr and felt the pain as she slashed her wrists. I looked at Katie Aysgarth's brother Simon and knew the waters would close over his head. I looked at my friend Venetia and the word that roared through my brain was DANGER, DANGER, DANGER—and I thought: I've got to save her, got to act, got to speak—

But when I stepped forward Marina intercepted me. "Nicky—*Nicky!* You're not listening—what's the matter, have you gone deaf? I want you to tell all our fortunes once we get up to the Cathedral roof . . ."

I said something, don't know what, anything to brush her off, and then, thank God, Venetia saw me. She was on the other side of the room. I began to stagger towards her, and I think she realised I had a message to deliver because she came to meet me, but when we were face to face at last I was tongue-tied. I found I had no way of imparting my psychic knowledge; the *gnosis* wasn't transmissible to that part of the brain which controls speech, and when I finally opened my mouth the only words that came out were: "Don't go to the Cathedral."

Venetia's expression changed from curiosity to an amused indulgence. What a dear little psychic poodle, she was thinking, a nonsensical warning delivered with such an earnest expression, he really is rather adorable.

Overcome by an embarrassed fury, I bolted into the hall.

Someone—something—the cosmic equivalent of a hand—switched off the Force.

I just managed to reach the cloakroom basin before I threw up. Then I dashed cold water on my face and willed myself to stop shaking. I was wearing no cross but I tried to roll back the Dark by silently reciting the old Orthodox prayer which I used as a mantra. Lord Jesus Christ, Son of God, have mercy on me, a sinner, Lord Jesus Christ, Son of God, have mercy on me, a sinner, Lord Jesus Christ, Son of God—

Someone rattled the cloakroom door. "Yoo-hoo! Who's monopolising the lavatory? Hurry up!"

Struggling out, I found Marina giggling with her girlfriends Holly and Emma-Louise.

"Nicky, do change your mind about coming to the Cathedral!"

Incapable of speech, I merely shook my head, hurtled across the hall to the dining-room, which had been set aside for the guests' coats, and began to rummage around for my leather jacket.

"Ah, there you are!" said Christian, walking into the room a second later. "I was afraid you'd already gone. This hasn't been much fun for you, has it? Marina's very bold in bringing together widely differing age-groups, but it's a risky strategy for a hostess to adopt."

"I didn't mind." I pawed at a mink stole and finally found my jacket. "It was okay."

"Was it? You look a bit green."

"Too many sausage rolls—"

"—and not enough champagne!" he said laughing. To my surprise he added: "Look, I'm sorry I didn't have much chance to talk to you—I think you were probably the most original person in the room and I always admire originality. Come to Oxford to see me if ever you can tear yourself away from the Other Place!"

And then as he smiled straight into my eyes, the Force blasted back across my psyche and I thought: you'll die young.

III

"We sin because we are part of a sinful situation . . ."

MICHAEL RAMSEY
Archbishop of Canterbury, 1961–1974
CANTERBURY PILGRIM

I

HE DIED two years later in the summer of 1965. I met him only three times after that first encounter, but those meetings ensured I became involved in the mystery of 1968. They all took place within weeks of Marina's party.

I was anxious to respond to his invitation to Oxford, so as soon as my second-year exams were finished I wrote him a note which read: "Dear Dr. Aysgarth, If you have a moment to spare I'd like to ask you how far Joachim of Flora's philosophy predates Karl Marx's theory of history. I could come up to Oxford any time now. Yours sincerely, N. DARROW."

In reply he wrote back: "Dear Nick, How nice to hear from you! Now that term's ended and my undergraduates have finished having nervous breakdowns, I'm free as air. Come up for the weekend and we'll pull Joachim to pieces! Yours, CHRISTIAN."

I went up for the weekend. He had an unexpectedly large house in North Oxford, a fact which reminded me that Katie came from a wealthy family. There was a tousled garden with a bumpy tennis court in the middle of it. The house was comfortable, but its youngest inhabitants, two little Aysgarths aged five and two, ensured that it was not oppressively tidy. I knew little about children in those days, but these girls seemed unusually bright and well-behaved. An *au pair* female pitter-pattered in the background but Katie did most of the cooking herself. The food was Frenchified but plentiful. I ate voraciously and remembered to offer to help with the washing up. Katie said no, no, but was pleased I had volunteered. Christian said no, no, and bore me off to his study for mind-stretching conversations about Joachim of Flora, but since people kept dropping in and the phone kept ringing, our discussions tended to be fragmentary.

I was impressed by the Aysgarths' popularity and even more impressed by their ability to remain unflurried by the numerous interruptions. A successful partnership, I thought, a well-suited couple. I forgot that obscure moment of tension between them at Marina's party.

On the Sunday of my visit Christian showed me around his College and we attended Matins in Christ Church Cathedral. It was after this that I felt sufficiently self-assured in his company to say: "Since you're a churchgoer, I suppose your decision not to be ordained had nothing to do with a loss of faith."

"I don't usually go to church. But I happen to be fond of that Purcell anthem they sang this morning."

I was so startled by this confession that I was glad he gave me no chance to comment. "To tell the truth," he added, "I never intended to be ordained. I read theology just to please my father."

Automatically I heard myself say: "But how on earth did you break the news to him that you weren't going on to theological college?"

"I said something like: 'Brace yourself—tough news—I'm not going to be ordained.' And he said: 'Oh dear. Never mind, we can't all be Arch-bishop of Canterbury. Have a drink and tell me what you intend to do instead.' "

"What a fabulous father!" I exclaimed impressed, but Christian merely said: "I doubt if he was surprised. I think he'd already worked out that my decision to read theology was my way of discharging any filial obligation I had to follow in his footsteps."

"Even so," I said, "he took it very well. If I decided not to be ordained, I believe my father would sink into a depression and die."

"What about your mother?"

"She—"

"Oh God, no, I'm sorry, she's dead, isn't she?"

"Yes, she died when I was fourteen."

"I was fifteen when my mother died," said Christian. "It was absolute bloody hell. However, at least your father never remarried. Count your blessings." And when I heard the edge to his voice I knew he hated his stepmother.

I heard from her three weeks later. I was at home, trying to work out how I could trade in Lynda (my first girl, acquired in a frenzy the previous summer after my encounter with Marina in the punt) and take on some-thing with longer legs. I was just fantasising for the umpteenth time about Dinkie when Morgan, one of the Community, banged on the door of my private sitting-room and said: "The intercom's not working and that crazy wife of the Dean of Starbridge is on the phone screeching for you. Are you in or out?"

I opened the door. Morgan was an ex–pop singer who was now trying to write an opera about God in order to justify the free meals which he received as a member of the Community, but I didn't mind him. He was harmless. The members of the Community who drove me up the wall were Rowena and Agnes, the wives of the ex-monks Mark and Luke. I detest bossy old bitches who think priggishness is part of the Christian way of life.

"Okay, I'll take the call," I said, intrigued by Morgan's news, and moved to the bedroom, where I kept the phone.

"Nicholas my dear," said Mrs. Dean the instant I announced my presence, "this is Dido Aysgarth—as that peculiar man who answered the phone may or may not have told you, and really, I can't think why your father has to surround you with a bunch of cranks instead of engaging some motherly soul who would be a proper housekeeper, but then there's the problem of the garden, isn't there, and gardeners are almost impossible to obtain nowadays as I well know. Nevertheless it seems unwise to rely on religious maniacs, such a tragedy your mother died young, although she worked so hard running that estate that it's hardly surprising she had a massive stroke and personally I think women should stick to being wives and mothers and leave the masculine work in this world to men—and talking of men, my dear, Christian's coming down next weekend with his family and since he's taken a fancy to you he's insisting that I invite you over for Sunday lunch, and I thought *what* a good idea because it's years since you've seen Elizabeth and although she's only fourteen she's very mature—and in my opinion quite ravishing as well as utterly brilliant—but of course I'm prejudiced as I'm her mother, and talking of parents, I almost hesitate to ask for fear of hearing bad news, but how *is* that poor old father of yours?"

"Very well."

"So sad your mother's death unhinged him. All right, Nicholas, we'll look forward to your visit, Christian will be so—" And she hung up, cutting herself off. Probably she continued to talk even after the receiver had been replaced.

It says much for my desire to see Christian that I turned up at the Deanery despite the outrageous style of the invitation. Unfortunately I at first had no chance to talk to him. Mrs. Aysgarth was ruthless in clamping down on my efforts to escape from Nymphet-Elizabeth, Starbridge's very own version of Lolita, and when I did succeed in heading for the seclusion of the lavatory, Sandy-the-Greek-Freak waylaid me in the hall. I was just wishing I were a hundred miles away when Christian came to the rescue and bore me off for a stroll around the Close.

As we passed the South Canonry where the Ashworths lived he said: "Are you really psychic or is that just a fantasy of Marina's?"

"I get a bit of foreknowledge occasionally."

Hearing my guarded tone he realised I was nervous of ridicule and at once he sought to reassure me. "I ask purely out of friendly curiosity," he said, "not hostile scepticism."

"I'm not good at talking about it. In fact my father says I shouldn't talk about it, because in his opinion there are many futures and not all of them come true. You've got to allow for man's free will, you see, so when I do experience foreknowledge"—I repressed a shudder at the memory of Marina's party—"I always have to remind myself that the disclosed future may never happen."

"But presumably it does sometimes happen, and that's extraordinary in its implications, isn't it? It would seem to support Plato—to suggest that the world we know is only the shadow of another world, the real world where all time is eternally present. How can one see the future unless time, as it's popularly understood, is an illusion? What a kick in the teeth for modern philosophy, refusing to acknowledge any reality other than the one we perceive with our senses!"

"My father says modern philosophy is wholly unreal, just the spirit of the Enlightenment reaching its inevitable dead end. My father says the logical positivists prove only one thing: that it's possible to have a brilliant intellect and still wind up a spiritual ignoramus out of touch with ultimate reality."

"I'd like to talk to your father," said Christian, "but I hear he doesn't see anyone new nowadays."

"Oh, he'd see you, I'm sure," I said at once, "if I were to ask him."

"Would he? Then if you could mention my name I'd really be most grateful. Like the spirit of the Enlightenment, I seem to have reached a dead end."

I stared at him in astonishment, and when he saw my expression he said rapidly: "I've got everything a man could wish for, of course. But I feel I need a wise man like your father to give my life a new direction for the future."

This statement at least I could understand. Anyone could benefit from skilled spiritual direction, even those whose lives were successful and happy. My father had never confined himself merely to counselling the troubled in order to help them to pray; a considerable part of his ministry had consisted of advising those who were doing well in their journey along the spiritual way and wanted to sustain their progress. So I didn't automatically assume that Christian had severe personal problems. In fact I thought it far more likely that he had reached a point where his secession from the

Church bothered him and he was keen to re-examine whatever beliefs he still retained.

"I'll speak to my father as soon as I get home," I promised, pleased by the opportunity Christian had given me to repay his kindness, but to my dismay my father refused to see him.

"I'm not interested in Aysgarth's overeducated sons who are now finally realising that intellectual prowess is no substitute for spiritual growth."

"But Father—"

"I'm over eighty," said my father crossly, "I'm retired and nowadays I see only the people I want to see. However—" Realising that he was behaving like a very stubborn, tiresome old codger, he made a big effort. "—I'll write Christian a letter referring him to the Fordites at Grantchester. Since they're so close to Cambridge the monks there are well accustomed to helping clever men who have lost touch with their souls."

"I don't think he's lost touch with his soul. He just wants advice on shaping his future."

"When someone talks about reaching a dead end you can be certain his soul's well out of reach of his fingertips," said my father tartly, and pottered off to his little kitchen to prepare Whitby's evening fish.

I was so embarrassed by my failure to secure Christian an audience that I made no attempt to contact him, but in September, just as I was preparing to return to Cambridge for my final year, I received a phone call from his friend Perry Palmer in London.

"I'm throwing a party on the Saturday after next," he said pleasantly. "Any chance you'll be able to come? Marina and the gang will be there so you won't be entirely marooned among old fogeys in their mid-thirties like me."

I felt sure Christian had prompted the invitation. "Thanks, Perry," I said. "Great." As an afterthought I added warily: "Elizabeth Aysgarth won't be there, will she?" but Perry answered with a laugh: "No, I don't go in for nymphets!"

I then had to work out where I could stay the night. On previous visits to London I had stayed with the Fordite monks in the guest-wing of their headquarters near Marble Arch, but I knew from past experience that the guest-master became stroppy if I stayed out late. I decided I was tired of stroppy guest-masters, tired of my father behaving as if London were one big moral cesspit, tired of being treated as anything less than a fully-grown adult male.

"I'll stay with one of my friends," I said to my father.

"That's not acceptable to me, Nicholas. If you've got to go to London, you must stay with the monks."

"But that's such a pain in the neck!"

We eyed each other balefully. This was the danger zone where the generation gap yawned and my desire to be independent in the manner of the 1960s clashed with my father's antiquated ideas about what was proper for a young man of twenty.

"If you refuse to stay with the Fordites," said my father, "then you must stay with Martin. He'll look after you."

"I don't need looking after! Maybe I'll cadge a corner in Michael Ashworth's pad—surely you can't object if I stay with a bishop's son!"

"You may stay with Charley but not with Michael," said my father, who had somehow found out that Michael had been chucked out of medical school for laying every nurse in sight. "However, I must say that I don't approve of this modern habit of scrounging hospitality, and in my opinion you should always wait to be invited before you turn up on a friend's doorstep and put him to a certain amount of inconvenience. With members of one's family, of course, it's different. They have a duty to provide for you, but even so, a thoughtful, unselfish man will be scrupulous in trying not to impose himself on any household merely in order to make his life easier."

Hopeless old Victorian. "People are more casual nowadays, Father."

"Yes, I've noticed the decline in good manners over the last half-century. Now, Nicholas, why don't you approach Martin before you approach Charley? I'd really feel much happier if—"

"The last thing I'm going to do is stay with that old creep!"

Bad move, Nicholas. Bad, bad move. But the old man was driving me up the wall. Taking a deep breath I tried to grab some patience out of thin air. Mustn't upset the old boy. If he had a stroke and died—

"Father, I'm sorry, I didn't mean to sound so rude, the words just sort of slipped out, but you see, Martin and I . . . well, I mean . . . okay, I know we've got you in common and I know he's a good son, coming down here regularly and gushing all over you, and I'm sure you're right when you say he has many fine qualities, but . . . he's so old, you see, and not quite my sort of person, and—" I stopped before saying the words "I can't stand him" but my father heard them anyway as they flashed across my mind.

"I'm extremely disappointed by that speech," he said in the kind of voice priests use for funerals. "You've upset me very, very much."

I wanted to smash something. "Oh, I'm sorry, I'm sorry . . ." But I knew as I spoke that there was only one way of putting things right. Off I sloped to telephone my half-brother.

"Don't worry, Martin, I'm sure it's quite impossible—I know how busy you are—"

"Not too busy to help you out."

"I've refused to stay with the Fordites because they don't understand about late-night parties, and Father said I had to stay at your flat, but since I wouldn't dream of foisting myself on you—"

"Foist away."

"—there's no need for you to issue an invitation. I just have to tell Father, you see, that I've approached you but you can't help. Okay, Martin, sorry to have troubled you, 'bye."

I then phoned Charley-the-Prig Ashworth, who had been ordained that summer and was now working at St. Mary's church in Mayfair.

"I hate to make demands on your Christian charity, Charley," I said, "but can I sleep on your floor on Saturday week?"

"Of course you can! I admit it *is* a little tricky because we'll have four student Christians from Africa staying in the curates' flat then, but I'm sure we can find you a quiet corner somewhere—"

I didn't fancy student Christians from anywhere. "It's okay, Charley, I'll try Michael." I could always insist to my father that Michael had turned over a new leaf.

"I don't think you'd be terribly welcome there, old chap. He's got a new girlfriend who always seems to be around to answer the phone. Talks with an American accent and sounds as if she can't wait to be censored by the Lord Chamberlain."

"Gosh, not Dinkie!"

"You know her?" Charley was suddenly very cool.

"She's a friend of Marina Markhampton's."

"Honestly, Nick, I think you ought to watch it—that's a very fast crowd. Look, come and stay at the flat—you can have my bed. I'll kip down with the Africans in the living-room."

The thought of being "saved" by this evangelical crusader of unimpeachable virtue was enough to make me want to puke.

"No, don't worry, Charley, I'll go to the Fordites." I phoned Martin again. "Sorry to keep bothering you, but—"

"—but the old man's putting on his crucified look and you're at your wits' end."

"Don't you speak of my father like that!" I yelled, finally driven to the luxury of venting my rage.

"He's my father too, you know! Look, sonny, I don't know what your problem is, but—"

"Stop talking to me as if I was six!"

"Then stop behaving as if you were two! I'll see you on Saturday week—let me know what time you'll be arriving," said Martin, and hung up.

I decided I loathed everyone over thirty. Then I remembered Christian and amended thirty to forty. After that decision I found myself wondering how Michael had managed to convert Dinkie into his live-in telephone receptionist. Did his father know? And what could the Bishop have said once he had recovered from his apoplectic fit? Was it possible that Michael could pass Dinkie off as a "nice girl" and take her home to the South Canonry for visits? But no, Dinkie couldn't be passed off as anything but a siren, and Uncle Charles, being a man of the world, would recognise her type even at a distance of fifty paces. Surely Michael wouldn't dare tell his father! But how could he be sure Charley-the-Prig wouldn't split on him? And I thought *I* had problems, scrabbling around once a week with Lynda! It was consoling to know that some sons of priests lived even more dangerously than I did.

For a second I remembered my premonition that Dinkie would wind up as a walking corpse, but I blotted that memory right out by repeating my father's familiar words of comfort: "There are many futures and not all of them come true." I had long since decided that Christian wasn't going to die young. That particular premonition had been just a false blip on the screen, a stress reaction after the exceptionally gruesome psychic experience I had suffered minutes earlier.

I began to look forward to seeing him again at Perry's party.

2

MY FATHER said I had to take Martin a small present to signal my thanks for his hospitality so I bought some oranges from a barrow-boy at Water-loo station. Martin, a reformed alcoholic, regarded freshly-squeezed orange juice as a big treat. When I arrived at his flat in Chelsea he had just returned from a rehearsal at the theatre. A revival of Noel Coward's *Present Laughter* was due to open in the West End shortly, after a successful trial run in the provinces. My father and I had seen the production at the Starbridge Playhouse.

"Oranges!" exclaimed Martin as I mutely shoved the bag at him. "How clever of you!"

I tramped along behind him into the spare bedroom, where the wallpaper, curtains and bedspread all matched. The whole flat had this same manicured, expensive look, conjuring up images of a high-class tart. In the living-room middle-brow books sat on white shelves. Nasty examples of modern art leered from the walls. Signed photographs of show-business luminaries, all professing undying love, were positioned in various strategic points so that it was impossible to look anywhere without seeing a famous face who allegedly adored Martin. Below the middle-brow books were the middle-brow records where the noises of Frank Sinatra, Dean Martin and Peggy Lee were lavishly represented. The current copy of

Variety lay open on the coffee table. On the desk were scattered provincial press cuttings, all proclaiming how wonderful Martin was in *Present Laughter*. I wandered around feeling like a creature from another planet and tried to work out how I could stay in my bedroom till it was time to go to the party.

"Can I have a bath?" I said in a moment of inspiration.

I soaked and I soaked and I soaked. Eventually Martin called: "You haven't drowned, have you?" and I had to get out. When I finally reappeared, dressed in my best jeans and my favourite blue shirt, Martin said: "A casual party, is it? Whereabouts do you have to go?"

"Albany."

This impressed him. Martin, whose mother had been working-class, was a snob. "You mean *the* Albany? Off Piccadilly?"

"You don't say 'the' Albany. That's not done. You just say 'Albany,' " I said, very much the son of Anne Darrow, née Barton-Woods, of Starrington Manor.

"What's good enough for Oscar Wilde is good enough for me, you little snob—look up the reference in *The Importance of Being Earnest*! Who's your host?"

"A guy called Perry Palmer."

"Perry Palmer?" Martin's face, trained to express every conceivable emotion to every conceivable degree, now registered a profound astonishment. "What are you doing going to one of Perry's parties?"

I was equally astonished. "You know him?"

"Not well, no, but we've friends in common—friends in the theatre. How on earth did the two of you meet?"

"He's a friend of Christian Aysgarth's."

"Ah yes, the Starbridge connection—all is explained. But nevertheless, how extraordinary! If I were on stage I'd declare in my best sinister voice: 'It's a small world!' and a shiver would sweep through the audience!"

I experienced a moment of amnesia, as so often happens when one's confused. "Have you met any of the Aysgarths?"

"Almost the whole damned lot, yes—don't you remember me telling you? When *Present Laughter* played in Starbridge recently Dean Aysgarth and that fantastically bizarre wife of his gave a party for the cast."

"So they did, I remember now. And Christian was there, wasn't he—he came down specially from Oxford—"

"And Perry came down specially from London. Tell me, who else is going to this party of his tonight?"

"Oh, various people I know."

"Girls?"

"You bet."

"Thank God!" said Martin. "For one ghastly moment I thought I'd have to come to Albany to chaperone you, and all I want to do after that rehearsal is put my feet up and watch the box."

"Are you trying to tell me—"

"Perry moves in certain circles, yes. God, what a relief it is to live like a monk! I never thought I'd hear myself say it, but when one gets to the advanced age of fifty-eight, the thought of performing in bed as well as on the stage is simply too exhausting to contemplate, and now I find I'm hopelessly hooked on the delights of living alone." He laughed before adding: "Getting like Dad, aren't I? No wonder he's decided I'm a fit person to keep an eye on you when you come trundling up to London! I've even started to go to church. They do a first-class show at St. Mary's Bourne Street—brilliant stagecraft enhanced by the English lust for ceremonial! I'm wild about the whole gorgeous circus."

"Yeah," I said. "That type of Anglo-Catholic ritualism has always appealed to people like you." I stood up. "I've got to go."

"Well, watch yourself with Perry Palmer," said Martin smoothly as the conversation degenerated into a verbal punch-up. "Psychics are usually attractive to both sexes. I bet Dad's had plenty of men in love with him in his time."

"The most irritating thing about homosexuals," I said, heading for the door, "is that they believe everyone's secretly homosexual. A true triumph of hope over statistics."

"That's a great exit line!" cried Martin, genuinely amused, but I walked out without looking back.

3

I TOOK the tube to Green Park and wandered down Piccadilly to Albany, that fabulous ex-palace where the waiting-list is about twenty years long and no one gets a "set" of rooms unless they have a personal hotline to a bunch of nobs who appear to be less well-known than the Queen but more influential. How Perry had acquired this flat of his I had no idea. His grandmother was supposed to have been Edward VII's mistress, but a lot of women were supposed to have been Edward VII's mistress and presumably not all their grandsons had ended up in Albany. Anyway, there Perry lived in a ground-floor set that faced the Rope Walk, and there was I in the September of 1963 padding past the uniformed flunkey in the grand entrance hall.

Perry was a spy. Now that I had been informed that he was also a homosexual I thought: how typical! Apparently the Foreign Office had learnt nothing from the Burgess and Maclean affair. Then I remembered that it was only rumoured he was a spy; all that was known for certain was that he spoke fluent Russian and held some Foreign Office post which he refused to discuss. Possibly he just translated incoming mail from the Kremlin.

I had been bothered by Martin's revelations about Perry, but during my journey to Albany I became less bothered and more sceptical. Martin had denied knowing Perry well. It seemed obvious in retrospect that he'd rushed to judgement after seeing Perry carousing with a certain bunch of actors, but just because Perry dabbled in the social side of the acting profession in order to give himself a break from the tight-lipped job at the FO I didn't have to conclude he had a sex-life, lawful or unlawful. In fact Marina always said Perry was a eunuch. Perhaps he was just undersexed. Certainly I couldn't see Christian being close friends with an active homosexual. That didn't add up.

I rang the bell and seconds later Perry was flinging open the door. "Nick!" he exclaimed, very crisp in a grey suit, white shirt and old Wykehamist tie. "Welcome to my orgy!"

I smiled at him warily and prowled across the threshold.

4

THERE were far more people present than at Marina's Starbridge party in May. The large drawing-room was filled with cigarette-smoke and screeching voices and raucous laughter and overdressed bodies and (from the record-player) the muffled blaring of a big band, very forties, very square. Funny how the vast majority of the human race has to generate a repulsive amount of noise before it can convince itself it's having a good time.

Some sort of sea-green cocktail was circulating but I didn't like the look of it so I asked for a Coke. No luck. I settled for a glass of Rose's lime juice which Perry produced for me from his kitchen. The trouble with alcohol is that it tastes so disgusting, and if you start mixing lime juice with, for example, gin, the result always seems to me to be an affront to the taste-buds. Someone offered me a cigarette but I waved it away. I've never been able to see the point of smoking. It smells vile and all that ash makes such a mess. If you've got to do something with your mouth and hands between meals, why not sip Coke and chew gum? American civilisation could be pretty weird—all those obese cars—but some of the basic innovations, such as Coke and gum, were genuinely useful . . . Or so it seemed to me at the age of twenty.

Marina pounced on me within seconds. ("Nicky darling, heavenly to see you!") She was wearing a silvery cylinder squashed in the right places to show off her Venus de Milo figure. Her friends Emma-Louise and Holly also pounced ("Nicky—*super!*" one shrieked, and: "We've won our bet that you'd be wearing jeans—even to an orgy at Albany!" screamed the other.) But there was no sign of my friend Venetia. I was told she was too busy preparing for her wedding. I was just sighing with regret when Dinkie undulated by, entwined with Michael, and gave me a wink as she passed. This enthralled me. I spent some time wondering whether I should have winked back, but I wouldn't have wanted to offend Michael. Finally Perry ended my reverie by musing to me: "Christian and Katie are late— stuck in a traffic jam somewhere, I suppose," and I heard myself utter the *non sequitur:* "You never mentioned that you knew my brother Martin."

"Something told me," said Perry, "that you got very, very tired of people droning on about your brother," and suddenly I decided to like him.

I said: "Do you go to the theatre a lot?"

"All the time, yes, I'm an addict. Look, come and meet some of my thespian friends . . ."

I met his thespian friends of both sexes. Perry never mentioned my connection with Martin, but Katie's brother Simon, a pea-brained product of Eton, eventually let the cat out of the bag and then all the thespians started to gush over me, with the result that the party became tedious. I took refuge in the lavatory. Venturing out at last with reluctance, I found myself overpowered by the desire for more lime juice but before retiring to the kitchen to find the bottle I moseyed around, putting my nose in the dining-room where a buffet was laid out, casting an eye on Perry's bed-room where a single bed added weight to the theory that he was under-sexed, and taking a peek at the adjoining bathroom where I found a peculiar Picasso-style drawing of a mermaid.

Having noted the complete absence of any item which would have indicated homosexual leanings, I beetled down some stairs into the base-ment kitchen and came to a halt, mouth gaping and eyes wide, at the splendid sight which confronted me. The kitchen was a historical master-piece, untouched by the mid-twentieth-century mania for making kitchens look like poor relations of the morgue. I saw a large wooden table, very handsome, a gas stove which could only have been pre-war, and a distin-guished porcelain sink. The old range had been left in place for its orna-mental value, and beside it there was even a set of brass fire-irons: poker, tongs, shovel and soot-brush. Amazing! Anyone who lived in 1963 and kept fire-irons in his kitchen had to be exceptional, and I saw clearly then that Perry was no run-of-the-mill theatrical hanger-on with homosexual leanings but a highly original celibate who spoke Russian, lived in a palace, devoted his free time to civilised cultural pursuits—and kept Rose's lime juice in some corner I now had to find.

I opened the door of a gas—*gas!*—refrigerator that had to be at least thirty years old but no bottle of lime juice stood keeping cool on the shelves. Instead I found caviar from Fortnum's, a bottle of champagne, half a Melton Mowbray pie and a jar of olives. By this time I was beginning to think that all the kitchen lacked was one of the old-style butlers, complete with white hair, a stoop and corns.

I prowled on, pausing at an antique cupboard which housed some very grand china, and reached a door set in the wall near the back entrance—the tradesmen's entrance, as it would have been in the old days. Opening the door, I discovered a coal-cellar—a *coal-cellar!* Within spitting distance of Piccadilly!—and inside this astonishing relic of a vanished past was a *large load of coal.* Surreal. What kind of man kept a cellar full of coal in a designated smokeless zone? A man of infinite wit and style. I decided Perry was probably the one man in England who was worthy of being Christian's best friend.

But still no Rose's lime juice. Abandoning the coal-cellar, I opened yet another mysterious door and found a larder complete with a cooked pheasant sitting on a plate and a tub of Stilton exuding its famous pong. Nearby I spotted pâté de foie gras, Gentleman's Relish and—yes, Rose's lime juice. Grabbing the bottle I helped myself to a spare sliver of Stilton before moving to the table to replenish my glass.

Perry clattered down the stairs just as I was diluting the juice with water. He had an empty jug in his hands and Christian at his heels. ". . . playing with fire," he was saying as I tuned in to the conversation in mid-sentence. "Marina may be all talk and no action, but—" He saw me and broke off.

"Nick!" exclaimed Christian in delight.

"Hi!" I said pleased.

"Sorry, Nick—I've been neglecting you," said Perry, setting down the jug on the table and extracting some ice from the bag in the refrigerator. "Glad you found the lime juice. Would you like to see my coal-cellar?"

"It's a land-mark," said Christian, preparing to exhibit it to me. "The last full coal-cellar left in London. He shows it to everyone."

"Groovy," I said, feigning ignorance of the phenomenon and taking a peek. "But why all the coal?"

"I made a mistake with the coal-merchant just before the smokeless zone was declared. Pass that bottle of gin, would you, Christian?"

The doorbell rang in the distance.

"You answer that," said Christian to him. "I'll mix the jungle-juice."

"It's probably my neighbours complaining about the noise . . ." He clattered back upstairs.

"How are things going?" said Christian agreeably to me as he poured a huge slug of gin into the jug.

"Okay." Awkwardly I edged closer to him. "Sorry about my father,"

I said. "I really busted a gut trying to get him to see you. I hope you didn't feel I'd let you down."

"Of course I didn't!" He gave me his warmest smile. "He wrote a most helpful letter, so you needn't think you pleaded my cause in vain . . . All set for your final year at Cambridge?"

"Yep." I watched with amazement as he added liquid from three other bottles to the gin in the jug and then topped off the poison with Schweppes Bitter Lemon.

"I suppose you haven't been seduced since I last saw you by the current fashion among undergraduates for travelling around America once their finals are finished? I'm told that travel on a Greyhound bus is guaranteed to broaden the mind."

"Yeah?"

"Sounds a bit tame, if you ask me, but then I speak as someone who did two years' National Service in the army. Now, *there* was an experience that broadened the mind! I enjoyed that escape into a different world."

I had never before thought of National Service in a positive light. I had just assumed it would be boring and I had heaved a sigh of relief when it had been abolished, but the word "escape" in Christian's last sentence was now reverberating compellingly in my mind. I heard myself say: "I wouldn't mind getting away for a while. But my father would worry about me if I went off into the blue on my own, and *I'd* worry if I knew he was worrying."

"Obviously in that case the travel would need to be structured in some way which would win his approval and enable him to relax. How about doing voluntary work overseas for a Christian organisation? You'd be in the company of responsible people, and he'd recognise the work as useful experience for someone who planned to be a clergyman."

This struck me as such a brilliant suggestion that for a moment I was speechless with excitement. A vision of change blazed through my psyche. No more living with the Community and enduring their prim piety. No more feeling tethered to Starrington Manor. I could take two years off, just as if I were doing National Service, and work for a Christian organisa- tion in . . . The word "Africa" floated across my mind. Exotic, exciting Africa which I had longed to visit ever since I had seen Stewart Granger in *King Solomon's Mines. Distant* Africa, where no one would have heard of Jonathan Darrow, the famous spiritual director, and Martin Darrow, the famous actor. Africa, Africa, Africa . . . I could almost hear the drums beating to lure me on my way.

"That's cool," I said to Christian. "A great suggestion. Thanks."

He finished stirring the new batch of sea-green poison and smiled at me. Then he said idly: "Beware of getting too tied up with that father of yours. Are you sure you really want to be a clergyman?"

Instantly the Dark began to creep into the room. It appeared stealthily, eerily, billowing around Christian so that he became a shadowed figure, sinister and subversive, a skeleton cloaked in black, a nightmare from some medieval vision in which "the Dark" appeared not as a poisonous cloud but as a horned creature bent on destruction. I saw no horned creature but I felt that poisonous cloud, and as soon as I felt it I knew what it was, I just knew, I experienced *gnosis,* the knowledge that was special.

I stood facing Christian across the kitchen table while the party roared above us, and as the moment of *gnosis* hit me I knew there was something very wrong with him, I knew that his psyche was far out of alignment, utterly dislocated, and that the Dark was streaming into him through every fissure of his personality. Yet never had Christian seemed kinder to the man so many years his junior, and never had his words seemed more charming and benign.

The Dark was now a huge pressure on my psyche and I knew I had to blast myself free. "Yes, I do want to be a priest," I said. "I want to serve *Jesus Christ"*—instantly the pressure eased as I opened up the scene to the Light—"and nothing on this earth is going to stop me."

"Well done!" said Christian at once without a trace of condescension. Moving away from me with the jug of poison in his hands, he began to mount the stairs. "In that case I can only wish you the best of luck and every success in the Church."

In silence I followed him upstairs, the glass of lime juice still clutched in my sweating palm.

5

"I'M NOT at all sure you've got this right," said my father when I returned home and confided in him. Any manifestation of the Dark was always so horrifying, reeking as it did of death and disintegration, that my strongest instinct was still to seek sanctuary in his cottage, and as usual in such circumstances my father moved to reassure me by speaking very calmly. "I'm not at all sure you've got this right . . ." He often said that, but now I found the words not soothing but irritating. I didn't want my judgement queried. I *knew* what had happened. Having recognised that the Devil was infiltrating Christian, I wanted to know how to deal with this knowledge. How could I get Christian to an exorcist? How could I dare to face him in future? How could I be sure that the Devil wouldn't send a demon to infest me as the result of the scene in the kitchen when I'd defied him by declaiming the name—and thus invoking the power—of Christ? (I should perhaps apologise at this point for using old-fashioned picture-language, but some realities are almost impossible to express verbally without the

liberal use of symbols.) All these questions seemed to me to be very urgent, yet as far as I could see my father was far from brimming over with the desire to answer them.

"Father, it's no use you saying: 'I'm not at all sure you've got this right.' I *know* I've got it right, I know I have——"

"You 'know' no such thing! You've just jumped to a conclusion. Do please try not to be so arrogant, Nicholas!"

"I'm not being arrogant!"

The generation gap began to yawn between us again.

"Can we both make an effort to keep calm?" said my father. "If we start upsetting each other we'll get nowhere. Now let's review your story carefully. You say that the Devil was infiltrating Christian—or perhaps you would be using the traditional language more accurately if you said that Christian was being attacked by demons who were paving the way for their master to take possession of his soul. Very well. But this is a big claim to make and it would be wise to proceed with considerable caution before reaching such a diagnosis. Remember that the gift for recognising the presence of either God or the Devil—the charism of the discernment of spirits—is seldom granted to someone of limited spiritual experience."

Obstinate old fogey. I tried to be patient. "But I can pick up the vibes in my psyche and then I *know*, it's *gnosis.*"

My father began to get upset again. "That's a delusion. That's the Gnostic heresy in its most insidious form—the belief that you're one of an élite which has special access to God and special knowledge of spiritual mysteries. You're confusing psychic power with spiritual power, Nicholas, but it's quite possible to be psychically strong yet spiritually weak. Psychic powers must always be the servant of the personality, never the master, and all such powers should be offered with humility to God, not flaunted to boost one's self-esteem."

"I know all that, Father——"

"You're not behaving as if you know. You're being very proud and wilful, Nicholas."

Wilful! Another of those awful Victorian adjectives. I wanted to bang my head against the wall in exasperation. "Okay, okay, *okay!*" Mustn't upset the old boy. He might die. Taking a deep breath, I grasped my knees so tightly that my knuckles ached and said in my most soothing voice: "You tell me what really happened during that scene with Christian."

My father sulked for a moment but then said evenly enough: "First of all I would survey the background, and the first fact I notice is that he's taking an interest in you. Why? Possibly it's because as an Oxford don he deals with many young men of your age and he's intrigued because you're unusual. This is the most obvious explanation, although one could be more cynical and theorise that he wanted to see me and realised that cultivating you was the best way of getting what he wanted. Perhaps originally both explanations were true. Now, this second reason for his interest might be classified as self-centered, even ruthless, but I certainly wouldn't call it demonic, and since he's still willing to be friendly to you even though I've refused to see him, his interest at present would appear to be wholly benign."

"Yes, but—"

"Wait. Let's take this one step at a time. The next thing I notice is that he makes a most interesting suggestion: he proposes that you should do the Christian equivalent of National Service before you proceed to theological college. If you did want to do this, I must tell you that I certainly shouldn't oppose it. I firmly believe that the more experience young priests have of the world the better, and I often think, looking back, that I was ordained too young. Of course I should miss you dreadfully if you were away for a long time, but that's irrelevant. It would be very wrong indeed if I selfishly kept you hanging around here with the result that your growth to maturity was impeded. You've got your own life to live. You must live it.

"Very well—where have we got to? We seem to have concluded that Christian's behaviour towards you has been not only genuinely friendly but unexpectedly helpful. But then we come to his final question: 'Are you sure you really want to be a clergyman?' and immediately your psyche soars on to a very odd plane indeed. But why? This is a good question of Christian's and one which you should, in fact, be periodically asked."

"But Father—"

"Sometimes when a young man chooses to follow in his father's footsteps, it's a way of evading the difficult task of deciding what he's really called to do, and I for one don't want you falling into that particular trap. We're not all called to serve God as priests and I fully accept the possibility that He may wish you to serve Him in some other way."

"But if I've been designed by God to be specially like you—"

"He may still call you to serve Him in a different field. Of course it's very gratifying to me that you want to be ordained but you don't exist to ensure my selfish desire for gratification. You're here to serve God, not your father."

Nowadays my father regularly felt compelled to deny his desire for a replica, but since I had long since decided this denial was a mere formula to soothe his conscience, I never took the slightest notice. "So what you're really saying," I said after he had finished his new attempt to brainwash himself, "is that Christian was sanity personified and I reacted like a lunatic."

"Not like a lunatic—that seems a little harsh!—but I see no sign of the demonic in this conversation, and I'm wondering if you projected onto

Christian a particularly oppressive anxiety which you normally keep buried deep in your unconscious mind. Maybe you should interpret the scene not as a demonic manifestation—and certainly not as a sign that Christian was being infiltrated by the Devil—but as a hint from God that you should re-examine your call to be a priest."

"But that's all—" I bit back the word "balls." If there was one certainty in my life, it was my call to the priesthood. I had wanted to be a priest ever since I had learnt in my early childhood about Jesus the healer and the exorcist, the hero who always triumphed over the Dark.

Making a new effort to hold on to my patience, I said to my father: "Your explanation's so far from what I actually experienced. I *know* the Dark was there, billowing around Christian and seeping into him through all the cracks in his personality, so your whole interpretation of the scene falls as flat as a pancake."

My father then became very angry. "You understand nothing," he said. *"Nothing.* And what's worse, you don't want to understand, you refuse to be taught, your pride's convinced you that you know everything there is to know. But I tell you, Nicholas, that if Father Darcy were present in this room—"

I somehow managed to stifle a groan. It really was awful how old people repeated themselves. Cuthbert Darcy, who had once been the Abbot-General of the Fordite monks, was my father's hero. In fact I had been brought up on the extraordinary memories Father Darcy had left behind him. My father would reminisce about this peculiar old cove at the drop of a hat. Sometimes I felt I had heard each Darcy story at least twenty times.

"But Father Darcy isn't present in this room," I said. "Father Darcy's been dead for over twenty years."

"More's the pity—if only he could be here to train you as he trained me! Psychics have to be trained. When I think of the appalling messes I got into before I met him—and I didn't meet him until I became a monk at the age of forty-three—"

"I know, Father, I know, you've told me a million times—"

"Then you'll understand why I pray constantly that you'll meet your own version of Father Darcy very soon—and sometimes when I pray I feel he's quite close—or is it that he *will* be quite close? I'm not sure, but what I know for certain is that Aelred Peters is no longer right for you and you've got to have someone much tougher."

"But I like Father Peters! We get on."

"You mean you've reached the age when you can manipulate him. You need someone very strong, Nicholas, strong psychically and strong spiritually. Father Darcy . . ."

The reminiscences began. I stifled another groan.

". . . and he had the toughest psyche I ever encountered—strong as steel yet so extraordinarily flexible—like a magic rope his psyche was, I can see it quite distinctly in my mind's eye even now after all these years—forty years it is since I met him, imagine that! What a priest he was, so perfectly trained and disciplined, his psychic powers so striking yet so wholly under control, so entirely devoted to God's service—oh, I can see that first meeting of ours in 1923 as clearly as if it were yesterday . . ."

I picked up Whitby who had wandered over as if to sympathise with me. Lucky old cat, unable to understand my father's monologues.

". . . and there I was, six foot three, and there was he, no more than five foot nine, but within seconds I felt like a dwarf and he seemed seven foot tall. And all he did was look at me. He had very dark eyes, rather sunken, set in shadowed sockets . . ."

My father droned on but I switched off. The truth was that Cuthbert Darcy had been a monastic thug. Their first meeting had resulted in the thug beating him up. I never pretended to understand any of it. After that they had enjoyed a love-hate, father-son relationship for seventeen years even though they had never lived beneath the same roof. (My father denied any father-son relationship, of course, since this type of attachment was forbidden in the cloister, but it was obvious to me that Darcy had had all the spiritual glamour and psychic understanding which my Grandfather Darrow had lacked.) My father had spent some years at Ruydale, the Fordites' estate in Yorkshire, before he was appointed Abbot of the Grantchester house near Cambridge, and throughout this time Father Darcy had remained at the Fordite headquarters in London, the tarantula at the centre of the web. In consequence the two men had seldom seen each other. Initially they had met once a year, when the Abbot-General made his annual visitation. Later they had met twice a year, once during the visitation and once six months afterwards when my father was summoned to London for what was described as a "spiritual spring-cleaning." But despite the rarity of the meetings there had been copious correspondence. Apparently the strong psychic affinity between the two men had generated an interest powerful enough to overcome their temperamental incompatibility.

This exceedingly weird relationship should have served as a text-book example of how not to conduct an association arising from spiritual direction, but my father always said that Darcy had been the one spiritual director who had succeeded in keeping him on the rails. Indeed my father in old age was lyrical on the subject, and the saga of how the renegade psychic had been rescued, dusted down, shaken up, taught, trained and saved had now acquired the golden sheen of heroic legend. The darker side of this off-beat monastic *pas de deux*—all the bouts of un-Christian dislike, anger and truly scandalous violence—had long since faded away, obliterated by the rosy glow of my father's unflagging nostalgia.

". . . so Father Darcy said to Francis . . ." My father was still deep in his Fordite reminiscences. ". . . and then Cyril said to Aidan . . ."

I decided it was time to haul him back to 1963. "Can we return to Christian for a moment?"

My father recalled himself with an effort and said politely: "Of course."

"Are you saying I was completely deluded?"

"No. I'm not doubting for one moment that you experienced a dark force that frightened you. All I'm saying is that you may not only have misinterpreted this force but mislocated it as well. You're so young, you see, Nicholas, and you're not trained. If only we could find you your Father Darcy—"

Off he went again. Hopeless. I gave up, muttered some excuse and slipped away.

6

I CAME down from Cambridge in the summer of 1964. I hadn't seen Christian again. Eventually I came to accept my father's opinion that Christian's attitude to me had been wholly benign, but I couldn't forget my impression that something was far out of alignment in his psyche, and this dislocation, hinting at a personality being eroded by the Dark, made me unwilling to seek him out by attending Marina's parties. Declaring that I was wholly preoccupied with swotting for my finals, I refused every Coterie invitation that came my way.

However the Dark seemed to be waiting for me wherever I went in those days. It was certainly waiting for me when I blazed off to Africa to work for the Christian Trail Scheme which encouraged young people to bring the skills of the advanced countries to small rural villages in the Third World.

I was in such a bad state after I got in my mess with the witch-doctor that I had to be sent home. I thought I could handle the bastard by performing a simple exorcism, but I was far, far out of my depth. He put a curse on me. I began to feel ill. I knew the illness was psychosomatic and idiotic, but that made no difference. I wilted. Then I panicked. I flew home thinking the plane would crash. My father had been driven to Heathrow airport to meet me by Martin, who was in the midst of making a new series of his TV comedy *Down at the Surgery,* but I barely saw Martin. I just staggered into my father's arms and stuck there, once more transformed into the little boy, temporarily autistic, who had screamed in terror until his father had turned up to put things right.

As soon as I was alone with my father I said: "I'm never leaving you again, I can't live without you being nearby to save me," and I began to sob. Total regression. Pathetic. I'm almost too ashamed to admit it, but I was so frightened that I couldn't sleep at the house and had to camp at his cottage. Apart from the bathroom and the kitchen there was only one room, but I slept in a sleeping-bag on the hearth with the cat. Whitby the Fourth, all furry warmth, exuded comfort. Funny how well animals can relate to humans. I stroked and stroked that cat so often that it was a wonder all his fur didn't fall out. My father talked to me, prayed with me, helped me to be calm. Eventually the nightmares stopped and I no longer felt the Dark was trying to press through the huge cracks in my psyche. The cracks healed up, welded together by the Light which exuded steadily from my father.

"No demon can withstand the power of Christ," said my father, repeating the words he had used long ago, and what he meant was that no dissociated mind can withstand the integrating power of the Living God whose spark lies deep in the core of the unconscious mind and who can not only heal the shattered ego but unify the entire personality.

"Maybe you should forget about doing further voluntary work and go to the Theological College this autumn," said my father when I was better. I think he believed I'd meet my Father Darcy at Theological College, but at that point my pride staged a resurrection and I said no, that would mean the witch-doctor had won some sort of victory, and no one, least of all an old bugger of a witch-doctor, was going to deflect me from my chosen course.

But I didn't go far away again. The Mission for Seamen, scene of my next attempt at voluntary work, was fifty miles away in the port of Starmouth, but I had a car which enabled me to bolt for home on my days off. After that job too ended in chaos I moved even closer to my father, but I didn't start work at the Starbridge Mental Hospital until 1966. It was in the summer of 1965, when I was at the Mission for Seamen, that Christian drowned in the English Channel off the Isle of Wight.

He had been sailing with Perry Palmer. Perry kept a boat at Bosham, near Chichester, and they had formed the habit that summer of sailing every weekend. The catastrophe was caused by a freak wave which had flung Christian overboard; the theory was that he had hit his head and lost consciousness before he even entered the water, for he had apparently made no attempt to swim for survival. The incident was reported in the national press not because it was an unusual sailing accident but because any event touching the life of Marina Markhampton was judged to be fodder for the gossip columns.

The story ran its course. Eventually the tragedy was allowed to fade from the public consciousness and the newspapers stopped photographing Marina and Katie weeping into black handkerchiefs.

The body was never found.

7

LIFE lurched on. I staggered from mess to mess until I was so unnerved that I did take a premature retirement from voluntary work after all. Then I promptly fell into that other mess when I performed the Bridey Murphy experiment on Debbie and couldn't wake her from the trance. After that came the dead terms at Theological College culminating in the events of 1968 when I got engaged to Rosalind, found myself unable to stop bedding Tracy and sought help frantically but unsuccessfully from my formidable "Uncle" Charles Ashworth, the Bishop of Starbridge. And finally, in that same spring of 1968, nearly three years after Christian's death and five years after the Starbridge party where I had first met him, Marina arrived at Starrington Manor in a white Jaguar and asked to see me.

I was at home for the Easter vacation. That year Easter Sunday was not until the fourteenth of April, so even though March had finished there were still several days of Lent remaining. The Theological College at Starbridge aligned its terms with those of Oxford and Cambridge except in the summer; then the College slipped in a fourth term, but those who were due to be ordained on Trinity Sunday were allowed to skip this extra spell of labour and leave directly after ordination. I was heading for ordination and the third and final term of my second year.

On the morning of Marina's arrival I was trying to follow the Bishop's advice by praying for grace—the grace to be chaste while I waited for my trip to the altar—but praying in a conventional fashion (with words) didn't seem to be getting me very far. Praying in words hardly ever did. Finally I decided to pray my way, which meant I lit a candle, sat cross-legged on the floor, stared into the flame, flipped the switch in my head and tuned in.

Sometimes when I prayed I began by reciting the mantra but usually it wasn't necessary; other people might need a mantra in order to tune in, but I just flipped the switch. I tended to save the mantra for those times when I was overwrought and needed to calm myself down. Father Peters had originally taught me this technique after my mother died, and he favoured no one mantra but used various key phrases from the Bible. It was my father who always used the famous Orthodox prayer "Lord Jesus Christ, Son of God, have mercy on me, a sinner," and nowadays I followed his example. It's pathetic that so many people turn to the East for meditative techniques nowadays, and one of the greatest failures of the Church in this century lies in the fact that the strong tradition of meditation in Christianity is so little known.

I never thought of reciting the mantra as praying, although it is. For me the real prayer came afterwards when the mantra had done its work and the conscious mind was relaxed, beyond words, in touch with the centre, soaking luxuriously in the Light. Father Peters had told me that if I was in an overstrained state I should stop after the recitation of the mantra had been completed because otherwise I ran the risk that dark forces in my unconscious mind might elbow aside the benign effects of the mantra and rise to the surface with unpleasant results. I was quite prepared to follow this advice but I couldn't resist telling him that usually I didn't need the mantra and could achieve the same effect just by flipping the switch in my head.

That was when Father Peters had warned me against Gnosticism, which claimed, among other things, that only a spiritual élite with esoteric knowledge could attain salvation. He classed my act of flipping the switch as esoteric knowledge and said it was a psychic snare, fostered by the Devil, to make me think I was special. He said one must approach God through Christ; in this form of prayer saying a mantra which invoked Christ was the correct approach; with all my talk of the Light and the Dark I wasn't sufficiently Christ-concerned, but it was Christ in his humility who kept psychics like me on the rails, not Gnostic code-words, Gnostic elitism and that fatal Gnostic pride.

Well, of course as an Anglican-Benedictine monk he had to say that, no choice; he had to toe the orthodox line. But in my opinion I was quite sufficiently Christ-centred in my belief, and if God had given me a switch to flip in order to tune in to Him, why shouldn't I flip it? And what was wrong with using code-words? Father Peters used code-words himself when he resorted to old-fashioned picture-language and talked of the Devil. One used code-words and symbols all the time when dealing with spiritual reality; it was the equivalent of the way scientists used mathematics to express the truths of physics. Flipping the switch given by God to tune in to the Light—to switch on the current of Ultimate Reality—to merge with the Ground of One's Being—to touch the transcendent Creator who sustained the universe—whatever words one chose to describe the indescribable—was GOOD. And I knew that, I just knew; it was *gnosis*.

I did accept that when one was in a state of altered consciousness one had to be careful about warding off the dark forces in the unconscious mind, but I'd never found that a problem. Flipping the switch short-circuited them and the Light just blotted them out. I might suffer an attack by the Dark in other circumstances, but not when I was flipping the switch which Father Peters had so stuffily dismissed as a psychic snare.

"Oh, bugger Father Peters!" I said crossly to myself that morning as I lit the candle, stared into the flame and flipped the switch.

The candle went out.

I was so startled that I just stared open-mouthed at the smoking wick. Then I realised I'd left the window open and there was a draught. Closing the window I relit the candle, resumed my cross-legged position on the floor and switched on again, but now something had gone wrong with the switch. The Light was marred by a sort of cloud, or maybe it was mud—I mean, it was nothing I could see, but "cloud" and "mud" were the words which came closest to describing it. I felt as if I were driving a car with a dirty windscreen through thick fog.

Nasty. This psychic pollution meant I was overstrained and that in turn meant it was one of those occasions when I was unable to dispense with the mantra. I needed to have my conscious mind calmed by the constant repetition of words. Off I started. "Lord Jesus Christ, Son of God, have mercy on me, a sinner . . ." I kept that up with no problem for several minutes but then realised I was thinking of Tracy's breasts. I kept on reciting—that's very important with the mantra, one should never stop before the allotted time has finished—but I found myself wondering if I needed to do some special breathing exercises. In the end I broke off the mantra—bad practice but I was getting nowhere—and lay full length on the floor so that I could relax all my muscles in turn. My quest for a direct experience of God—a quest which should have resulted in the automatic elimination of all distracting images, even the sexual ones—looked now as if it might fail completely. I couldn't understand it. The switch in my head never let me down unless I was in a bad state, the sort of state I had been in as the result of the witch-doctor mess, but at that moment I was normal and well-balanced.

Or so I thought.

I was just taking my third deep breath and trying to kill the suspicion that what I really wanted to do was masturbate, when the intercom buzzed.

I sat up and grabbed the receiver. "Yep?"

"Marina Markhampton's here to see you, Nicholas," said Agnes, the bossiest member of the Community.

I can still remember the exact quality of my relief as I realised I was being diverted from my attempt to pray. "Okay, I'll come down."

When I saw Marina she called me Nick instead of Nicky. That made me realise how far we had travelled since that innocent night six years before in 1962 when I had commandeered her punt on the Cam. I was now twenty-five; she was twenty-six and had been engaged to Michael Ashworth since the previous autumn. When she called at the Manor that day to see me she was wearing a powder-blue mini-skirt, a clinging black sweater and a silver zodiac medallion. Her legs were encased in black stockings and her face was smothered in trendy make-up: white lipstick, black eyeliner and so much mascara that her eyelashes seemed to droop. Her natural blonde hair was very long and looked as if it had just been ironed.

We got on better now that we were older and could regard each other as people rather than accessories. When I started seeing her again after Christian's death it occurred to me that our friendship had endured because of a certain ineradicable compatibility, even though we had at first been too immature to do more than strike poses in each other's presence. I found her intelligent and pragmatic; beneath all the society gush there was something tough about Marina, the toughness of someone determined to survive no matter how adverse the circumstances. From a material point of view survival was hardly difficult for her. She was rich. But not all deprivation is financial.

I think she liked me because . . . well, why was it? Perhaps I represented reality amidst the phoniness of her society life. Or perhaps I represented safety in a world where most men were panting to bed her. Or perhaps I represented nothing at all but appeared to her as someone who (on his good days) could be just as intelligent and pragmatic as she was, one of those rare people in whose presence she could cast aside her affectations and be herself.

"Nick, I'm terribly worried about Katie," she said as we sat down with our mugs of coffee. "She's gone so peculiar."

Automatically I murmured: "The effects of a bad bereavement—" but Marina interrupted me.

"It'll be three years this summer since Christian died and she's not getting better, she's getting worse. She's started dabbling in spiritualism."

This did indeed sound tricky. "Dabbling?"

"Buying books about it. Seeking out people who go for it in a big way. Now don't get me wrong—I'm not particularly anti-spiritualism, there may well be something in it, I don't know. But what I do know is that it's a field stuffed with con-men who'd think nothing of exploiting a young widow who's slowly going crazy with grief."

"Obviously she needs professional help. Perhaps her doctor could recommend—"

"My dear, we're well past doctors, she's turned against anything orthodox, she's way out there on the nutty fringes. Now look, Nick. She's determined to try to contact Christian at a séance—and don't tell me I've got to stop her, because I know damn well I can't. That's why I've come to you for help."

My heart sank. "But Marina—"

"You've got to be the medium, Nick, got to be. You're the only psychic I trust."

I opened my mouth to say: "I don't mess around with my psychic powers any more, it's wrong, it's dangerous, it's asking for trouble," but the words which came out were: "Okay, where and when?"

I needed to be shaken till my teeth rattled.

The Christian Aysgarth affair had begun.

IV

"[Man's] failing has been the pride and egoism with which he aggrandizes himself, using his powers with aggressive or complacent self-assertion instead of using them in humble dependence."

MICHAEL RAMSEY
Archbishop of Canterbury, 1961–1974
CANTERBURY PILGRIM

I

I SHOULD never have involved myself in Marina's plan, but I felt so sure that for once I could use my powers with benign effect. After all, I was no longer an undergraduate messing around with Ouija boards—or even an innocent abroad locking horns with a witch-doctor. At twenty-five I thought I could give myself credit for some degree of maturity, but what I could never acknowledge was that in psychic matters I was no better than a precocious child who could recite the alphabet but who had never been taught to read and write.

There are basically two problems with séances. First, most dead people can be assumed to be at peace with God, in which case efforts to contact them are futile, and second, if the dead people aren't at peace with God, the most sensible thing one can do is to leave them well alone because lingering shreds of discarnate spirits, as my father had often told me, are either trivial or demonic. I had no doubt that Christian was now at peace with God. It was true he had died "unhousel'd" and "unanel'd," cut off from life by a violent death when he was possibly not in a state of grace, but during his life he had been a good man—or as good as most men can hope to be—and I had no doubt that since his death various people had prayed that he might rest in peace. Why shouldn't God have responded by exercising a loving forgiveness, healing those deep fissures which I had been so sure existed in Christian's personality, and finally enfolding his soul? It seemed a reasonable assumption to make in the circumstances.

From that reasonable assumption it followed that the chances of making contact with Christian were nil. What was much more likely to happen in the séance was that Katie's acute emotional distress would be projected from her psyche and cause havoc. That was why I planned not a séance but a pseudo-séance, a rite which might appear designed to contact Christian but which was in fact merely designed to help Katie. I thought that provided I kept my mind closed against any discarnate shreds of former personalities that happened to be floating around, I would be dealing not with the dead but with the living because what was really required of me in this situation was to be not a medium but a healer.

This attracted me, and was almost certainly why I had agreed against my better judgement to take part in Marina's plan. Even now, when my head was stuffed so full of theology that I could have written a thesis about the transformation of the historical Jesus into the Eternal Christ of the Church, I felt irresistibly compelled to look straight past that multi-symbol image to the charismatic Galilean wonder-worker who had healed the sick and raised the dead.

"I want to be a healer-priest when I grow up," I had announced at the age of eight after an enthralling game in which I had resurrected my tin soldiers, but my father had replied firmly that if I wanted to heal the sick I should train to be a doctor.

"It's true all priests are involved in the healing of souls," he had said, "but a ministry which centres on healing the physically and mentally sick is so extremely difficult and so fraught with danger that only priests with the strongest possible call to heal should attempt it."

It was not until later that I found out about his brief, unsuccessful attempt to be a healer. Naturally he had assumed, since I was so like him, that if I tried to be a healer I would fail too.

But the fascination with healing had persisted, and now, years later, I found myself seduced by the challenge of restoring Katie Aysgarth to full mental health. The result was that I planned the pseudo-séance in a haze of euphoria.

Disgusting. No wonder my father prayed daily for another religious thug like Cuthbert Darcy to knock the hell out of me. I was like one of those typhoid carriers who bounce through kitchen after kitchen and leave a trail of disaster in their wake.

God knows how anyone I met ever survived.

2

THE GIRLS came down from Oxford the next morning. It was a showery April day, cool and fresh. Marina was wearing a white coat which matched the Jaguar, and a scarlet mini-dress. Katie, seven years her senior, was dressed more conventionally in a mustard-coloured suit. She looked pale, drawn, fragile.

Starrington Manor was a large house, but since I shared it with the Community I had been obliged to take measures to ensure my privacy: I had designated certain areas for my use only and I had devised stringent rules to restrict intrusion to a minimum. The library, a long room lined with unreadable books and cases of stuffed fish, was part of my territory, although Rowena and Agnes were allowed in to clean it. Here I received visitors. I liked the library better than the drawing-room, which always reminded me too painfully of my mother.

The entire area upstairs in the main section of the house was also my domain. I slept in the room which had once been my father's study—his "cell" he had called it in memory of his monastic years—and I spent my leisure hours nearby in the room which had once been my parents' bed-room. Curiously, this area didn't remind me of my mother; my father had imprinted his personality too strongly there. Rowena and Agnes were never allowed to clean in this upstairs domain. Once a week I changed the sheets on my bed and showed the Hoover to the carpet. I seldom dusted, but the bathroom fittings received my regular attention. I rather liked muscling around with the Vim. That was a masculine art. Dusting's just for women.

Meanwhile, as I kept my domain utterly private and tolerably clean, the Community milled around on the ground floor (excluding the library) and slept in the wing which had been converted for the Theological College ordinands after the war. My father sometimes came up to the house for meals but usually he stayed in his cottage. In the chapel the Community said Matins and Evensong each day and my father celebrated mass. I always went to mass when I was at home, but except on Sundays I tended to avoid Matins and Evensong. I found that a little of the Community went a very long way.

When Marina and Katie arrived that morning I showed them into the library and brought them coffee to revive them after their journey. I could have held the pseudo-séance there, but I thought Rowena and Agnes might be tempted to listen at the door, so as soon as the coffee had disappeared I took the visitors to my sitting-room. None of the Community would have dared trespass on my upstairs domain without a valid reason. My father, who supported my quest for privacy, would have been too angry.

"I feel it ought to be night-time," said Marina as she sat down at the round table which I had pulled to the centre of the room. "Doesn't one get better results in the dark?"

"One gets better fakes. People can be more gullible and the mediums more fraudulent." I moved around the room at a measured pace in order to exude the right air of authority; in any ritual it's important to create a calm, dignified atmosphere which will not only impress the participants but put them at ease. I felt vaguely priest-like, pleasingly powerful. Having flicked an imaginary speck of dust from the table, I placed a heavy dictionary on top of the stack of *Private Eye* magazines by the bookcase, put away a couple of stray pencils in the top drawer of my desk and readjusted the engraving of Starbridge Cathedral which hung over the mantelshelf. Everything had to be securely in place. Although I was avoiding a traditional séance there was still the danger that Katie's psyche could create a disturbance, and I didn't want the magazines whooshing across the floor or the picture plunging off its hook. Such manifestations of kinetic energy can provoke hysteria.

Finally I drew the curtains. There was still plenty of light in the room afterwards and we could see one another clearly, but the fractional dimming was another device aimed at helping the girls relax.

"Okay," I said, sitting down with them at the table, "let me explain what I intend to do. Forget all the junk you may have read in books. I'm not going to grunt and groan and speak in a strange voice and say I'm the spirit of Tutankhamen, specially sent with a message from the astral plane. Nor am I going to conjure up mysterious tappings which spell out the letters of the alphabet. We're going to keep this very straight, very orthodox—no frills, no fancy touches, no Mumbo-Jumbo."

I paused. They were enrapt. So far so good.

"First of all," I resumed, "we'll all hold hands while I say a prayer. After that we'll keep holding hands as we remember Christian in silence; we'll picture him as clearly as possible and pray that we may share with him the peace which he now experiences as a departed soul enfolded by the love of God. We'll be silent for approximately five minutes. That'll probably seem a long time to you, but keep picturing and keep praying. Then I'll end the silence with another spoken prayer which will reinforce our silent prayers by asking for God's love to flow into us so that we may be at one with Christian's spirit. You'll know then," I said directly to Katie as I put the full force of my personality into my eyes, "that you're with Christian and he's with you because you'll feel this great peace and love . . . peace and love . . . peace and love."

I saw her eyes film over as her will knuckled under to mine. Easy. Emotional, romantic, very feminine women are never a problem to hypnotise. They like to be dominated by men. I glanced at Marina. Her blue eyes were round as saucers. I wondered whether to put her under too but decided against it. No need. Katie was the one who required healing. Marina, a far tougher personality, had survived her bereavement with her psyche scarred but unsplit.

"Are we ready?" I said. We were. I took Katie's right hand in my left and Marina's left hand in my right while the girls' spare hands touched and clasped. Then I said in my best priestly voice: "Almighty and Most Merciful Father, have pity, we beseech Thee, on Thy servant Katherine in her grief. Grant that she may accept her severance from her husband in this life so that she may now experience through Thy Grace the peace and love in which Thou enfoldest him. Help her to understand that this peace and love is eternal and that when we share in it, no matter how briefly, we are united with those who have gone before us into that world beyond time, beyond space, beyond the scope of our minds to conceive. Almighty Father, we make these requests in the name of Thy Only Son, Our Saviour Jesus Christ, who healed the sick and gave peace to those in torment. Lord, have mercy upon us and hear our prayer. Amen." I paused before saying with great care and clarity: "And now let us remember Christian in silence and pray again that we may share with him the peace he experiences as a departed soul enfolded by the love of God."

When I stopped speaking they started picturing Christian and exuding the silent yearnings which approximately reflected my suggestions to them, but I embarked on a mental recitation of the Lord's Prayer. I did this to keep at bay any discarnate shreds of former personalities who might have been attracted to the psychic activity and tempted to participate in it. I didn't want any uninvited guests muscling in on the action—or, to put the problem in modern terms instead of old-fashioned picture-language, I didn't want any irrelevant clutter stirring in the inaccessible realms of our unconscious minds and rising to the surface with bathetic results. This invasion from an unknown world would have corresponded to the point in a traditional séance where King Tutankhamen can drop in to say he's frightfully worried about the papyrus which fell in the Nile and he'd simply adore a spot of tea to soothe his fractured nerves.

"Our Father," I recited silently, "Which art in heaven, hallowed be Thy name; Thy kingdom come; Thy will be done on earth as it is in heaven; give us this day our daily bread, and forgive us our trespasses, as we forgive them that trespass against us; lead us not into temptation, but deliver us from—"

Katie moaned just as the word "evil" was projected from my brain, and at once my concentration snapped. It was an odd moan, not right, by which I mean off-key, not the kind of moan you would expect from a contralto like Katie. It was high-pitched, soul-less, abnormal.

"Lead us not into temptation," I repeated aloud, automatically trying to will her back on course, "but deliver us from evil—"

Above the mantelshelf the engraving of Starbridge Cathedral fell with a crash to the floor.

As Marina screamed I thought: bloody hell! Not the best of expletives for an ordinand, but I was very rattled. However, I knew what was happening. It wasn't King Tut muscling in on the action. It wasn't even an anonymous discarnate shred. It was Katie's disturbed psyche generating a level of energy that I hadn't anticipated. I'd been prepared for the odd breeze or two, but only a hurricane could have driven that carefully adjusted picture clean off the wall. Obviously she was too far under and I had to yank her upwards in order to put her back in control of her mind.

"It's okay," I said swiftly to Marina, "nothing to worry about, just a bit of energy on the loose." And to Katie I said: "Up—you're coming up—you're waking up—up—up—" I paused but nothing happened. She merely moaned again and her eyes remained closed. Instantly I thought of Debbie sunk in that trance I had been unable to break. But that had been in my younger days. Flexing my will, I steeled my psyche and tried again, doing my best to ignore the fright that was now crawling around the pit of my stomach.

"Katie, open your eyes. Wake up. Katie, I say to you in the name of Jesus Christ, open your eyes and—" She opened them. Thank God. "Katie, you're all right, you're fine, you just got diverted. Now think hard of Christian again—"

"Christian," she whispered. "Christian." Her lips were almost bloodless and her skin had a greyish tinge.

"Yes, that's it, think of Christian and I'll say the next prayer," I said, curtailing the allotted five minutes of contemplative silence, but then I found myself distracted by the wall where the fallen engraving had been hanging. The picture-nail, though still attached to the wall, was pointing downwards. Maybe the incident had had nothing to do with an explosion of kinetic energy but had been caused instead by the collapse of the nail, an event which would have happened anyway, no matter what was going on in the room. Glancing at the engraving on the floor I was astounded to see that the glass in the frame was intact, and at once this survival seemed far more freakish than the fall of the picture.

"Let us pray," I said, recalling my attention with an effort, but then Katie started to weep and immediately I broke off the prayer because I knew I had to put her under again. If I didn't she'd never experience peace and then the whole healing session would have been a failure.

"It's all right, Katie," I said. "You're all right now, Christian's at peace, you're at peace, you're both at peace, both of you . . ." She was under. Instantly I wrapped my psyche around hers to stop it sinking too far through her subconscious mind, but this was a mistake. I should have been concentrating on the prayer to God, not taking time out to play the hypnotist, and the result was we had now reached a stage where no one was praying; I was channelling my power in another direction, Katie was too unbalanced to focus and Marina was too worried about Katie to remember what she was supposed to be doing. Then the inevitable happened. I suddenly became aware of a discarnate shred elbowing its way into our circle, and it certainly wasn't King Tut turning up for tea. I experienced the shred as a strong, sinister pressure on the psyche.

Automatically I said: "Lord Jesus Christ, Son of God, have mercy on me, a sinner."

The pressure eased, but I had relaxed my psychic grip on Katie and she was giving that eerie moan again. *Hell.* Had to control Katie, had to control the shred, had to control Marina who was now on the brink of panic, had to control, control, control—

The table started to rock.

Marina screamed again.

Bloody hell, what was happening—Lord Jesus Christ, Son of God—"It's okay, Marina!"—have mercy on me, a—yes, that was better, I'd got the table back on its four legs and now all I had to do was calm down. Katie had been shooting off a gale-force blast of energy again, that was all, it was just an inconvenience, no reason for panic, but why couldn't I imprint the words PEACE and LOVE on her mind, why could I now make no contact with her whatsoever? It was as if during that moment of chaos someone had bolted and barred her psyche against mine—as if the sinister discarnate shred, repelled from my mind by the Jesus prayer, had slid sideways into hers and—

I suddenly realised the shred was closing in on me for another attack.

I could feel the pressure mounting, I could feel the power behind the pressure, and the next moment I knew that beyond the power, blasting it forward, was—

I leapt to my feet, my chair flew backwards and simultaneously the glass shattered to pieces in the frame of the fallen engraving. I had a fleeting glimpse of Marina's terrified face, and then as I slammed my psyche shut against the Dark by a colossal act of will I heard myself shout out: "IN THE NAME OF JESUS CHRIST, SATAN, BE GONE FROM THIS ROOM!"

The curtains billowed violently by the open window and Katie slumped forward across the table in a dead faint.

3

"*MARINA,* get some water—bathroom across the passage—tooth-mug by the basin—"

She obeyed me instantly. No idiotic questions. Admirable. Gathering Katie in my arms I tried to revive her by patting her cheeks and calling her name, but I was so frightened I might have driven her over the edge of the abyss into insanity that I hardly knew what I was doing.

Marina rushed back with the mug of water. I pressed it to Katie's lips but she was still unconscious. "Throw it over her," said Marina tersely. That too was admirable. Nothing's more helpful than a strong dose of common sense when one's scared out of one's wits. I threw the water. Katie moaned and her eyelashes fluttered. Thank God.

"Wake up, Katie," I repeated, trying to wipe out both the hypnosis and the mental disturbance. "You're all right now. Wake up."

She murmured our names.

"Yes, I'm here, darling," said Marina, grabbing her hand. "It's all right—it's over."

"What happened?" Her voice was louder, clearer, almost normal. I felt sick with relief.

"We made contact with a hostile force," I said glibly, "but that had nothing to do with Christian. He's at peace with God, Katie, I promise you, and now that you know he's at peace you're at peace too."

"I don't feel at peace," she whispered.

That disturbed me very much. She was supposed to wind up calm, serene and strengthened, not shattered, shocked and more tormented than ever. My attempt at healing by hypnosis coupled with prayer seemed to have been a complete failure, but the hypnosis should at least have had a temporary calming effect even if the prayer had failed to produce a permanent improvement. "Marina, fetch some more water," I said, trying not to sound as baffled as I felt, "and bring a towel from the bathroom so that she can mop herself up. Katie, you must lie down on my bed in the next room. No, don't try and get up—I'll carry you."

She was as light as a famine-victim, and when I became aware of the weight-loss which the cut of her suit had concealed I realised her mental disturbance had affected her physical health. I knew then I should never have meddled with her. She needed a doctor, not an ordinand playing the wonder-worker, and as this stark truth ploughed through my mind I felt overpowered by my guilt and my shame.

"Couldn't find a towel," said Marina, reappearing with the refilled tooth-mug. "There was nothing on the rail."

Laundry day. I'd forgotten. I'd turned in my towel after breakfast. "I'll get one from the airing cupboard—hang on, Katie—this way, Marina," I muttered, grabbing her wrist and drawing her out of the room. In the corridor I said rapidly: "Listen, I've got to talk to you, got to explain what happened so that you can understand what's got to be done. All those disturbances were caused by *her*. When a psyche's under extreme stress it can generate the paranormal happenings we witnessed just now when objects appear to move by themselves. The phenomenon's sometimes called poltergeist activity—it comes out of the unconscious, out of something we don't understand and don't normally have access to. When I said just now that we'd made contact with a hostile force, that was just old-fashioned picture-language—like talking about poltergeists. What we actually encountered was a violent emanation of psychic energy from Katie's unconscious mind."

"Then why did you yell out that command to Satan?"

"Oh, forget that, it was just a safety precaution. What I was really doing was gaining control over the emanations."

"But—"

"Look, just concentrate on the facts: Katie's disturbed. It's not the kind of disturbance that can be put right by prayer and meditation. She's got to see a psychiatrist."

Marina was shocked but remained well in control of herself. My admiration for her deepened. "Okay," she said, "I'll wheel on the big guns of Harley Street, but meanwhile how on earth do I get her home?"

"I'll fix her up, no need to worry, just give me an hour. Go for a drive."

"But what are you going to do?"

"Talk to her, make her some tea, try anything that'll get her back on her feet, but it's better if you're out of the way. Then I can focus on her without distraction."

"Okay, I understand."

"And as soon as you get her home call a doctor."

"Right." She glanced at her watch and walked briskly off down the corridor towards the main staircase.

I waited till I heard the front door close far away in the hall. Then I took a clean towel from the airing cupboard and returned to Katie.

4

SHE was crying. She lay face-down on the bed like a discarded doll and her body shook with sobs. As I came in she raised her head from the pillow and turned over to lie on her back. Her eyes were swollen, her skin looked like parchment, her hair was matted. I barely recognised her.

"I feel so guilty," she whispered.

I made what I prayed was the right response: wordless sympathy. Sitting down on the bed beside her I took her hand comfortingly in mine.

"I failed him somehow," she said. "I loved him so much but it wasn't enough."

She was putting us both in the confessional—which meant I was being given the chance to behave like a priest instead of a psychic maverick. Desperate to redeem my catastrophic error I said earnestly: "I know you loved him," and I clasped her other hand so that a symbolic double-lifeline was established. Then I tried to concentrate on supporting her damaged psyche. The image of the discarded doll was helpful; I pictured an imaginary china doll, very beautiful but chipped and cracked; then I visualised myself sealing up the cracks, painting over the chips and attending to each detail with immense care.

"In books love conquers everything," she said, "but it's not like that in reality. My love didn't conquer everything. My love ended in failure."

I had to be very cautious here. Some kind of reply was required but I was afraid of uttering a sentence which might be either a banality or simply untrue. I raised a metaphorical aerial to improve my reception of her thoughts but sensed nothing I could readily interpret. It was her guilt that interested me. I knew a surviving spouse could feel overpoweringly guilty—my father had been a classic example of that syndrome—but why Katie should be so full of guilt when she had done her best to be a model wife was not easy to perceive.

"I know he was disappointed when Grace and Helen were born," she said, sparing me the need to reply as she spoke of her daughters, "but I did put everything right in 1965 when John arrived and Christian had the son he'd always wanted. I was so happy. But then it began all over again."

"What began all over again, Katie?"

"It. I don't know what it was. But something had happened to Christian. Something had gone terribly wrong."

After a pause I said: "When did this begin?"

"Oh, ages ago, but it didn't become chronic until about six months before he died. I think it started in 1961 when Helen was born. 'You name it,' he said as if he couldn't have cared less. Oh, how I cried! But then he recovered and was nice again . . . for a while. By 1963 I was in despair—but then the miracle happened and Marina joined us." She withdrew one of her hands from mine in order to wipe her eyes, but the tears had stopped and I knew that by listening I was helping her.

I made a small noise indicating intense sympathy and deep interest. Then I reclasped her hand.

"I love Marina," she said. "She's such a wonderful friend. Christian loved her too because she was so bright and amusing and she never bored him. 'If Katie were as bright and amusing as you are,' he said to her in 1963, 'she wouldn't be driving me up the wall.' 'You absolute pig!' said Marina. 'How dare you be so beastly about darling Katie!' I was terrified when she said that, but do you know what happened? He laughed. He actually laughed—and then he apologised to me and said sorry, he knew he'd been a bastard but he was going to reform. Of course that was when I realized we had to have Marina in our marriage."

"Ah," I said, trying to sound as if she had made an unremarkable observation. On an impulse I added: "How very perceptive of you."

"Well, she had such a wonderfully benign effect on him, you see, and she was so devoted to both of us. We'd known her for a long time—that grandmother of hers living almost next door to my in-laws—but because she was so much younger than we were we didn't start to meet her at social occasions until about 1962. And then in the May of 1963 she gave that wonderful party at Lady Markhampton's house in the Close . . . you were there, weren't you? I can remember you dressed in jeans and eating a sausage roll—"

"—and I can remember Christian being on edge with you."

"Yes, he was—and that was when Marina made her stunning intervention and I realized we had to have her in our marriage . . . Of course sex didn't come into it at all."

"Ah."

"No, Marina finds the idea repulsive, but Christian quite accepted that sex wasn't on offer—in fact he liked that, found it original. Women were always throwing themselves at him, just as men were always throwing themselves at Marina."

"Sounds as if they were made for each other."

"Oh, we were all made for each other! It was quite perfect . . . for a while. But in the end, in 1965, not even Marina could stop him going off every weekend with Perry to that bloody boat at Bosham."

"How did you feel about Perry Palmer?"

"Jealous. Funny, wasn't it? You'd think I'd have been jealous of the woman and tolerant of the man, but it was quite the other way round."

"Was Christian as close to Perry as he was to Marina?"

"Oh, closer, because of their long shared past. But the relationship was certainly similar. Of course sex never came into it at all."

"Ah."

"No, Perry's no more interested in sex than Marina is, and anyway Christian was never drawn sexually to other men. My brother Simon used to say that Christian was very middle-class about sex," Katie added, unintentionally revealing her upbringing in an aristocratic world where sexual permutations failed to raise eyebrows, "but that was just because Christian found smutty jokes boring and immorality an unintelligent waste of time and energy. Christian was actually a very moral man. It was the clerical background."

As I knew so well, a clerical background was no guarantee of moral behaviour, but I understood what she was trying to say: a clerical upbringing at least makes one acutely aware of morality even if one fails to wind up as a replica of Sir Galahad.

"What's Perry's background?" I said, more to keep the therapeutic conversation going than to satisfy my curiosity.

"His father was some military VIP in India. Wealthy family but new money," said Katie, again offering a glimpse of a background where respectable fortunes had to be at least three hundred years old. "His grandfather manufactured something in Lancashire, a sort of hip-bath it was. Perry has a picture of the original drawing in his lavatory at Albany."

"I think I remember it. When exactly did Perry meet Christian?"

"On their first day at Winchester when they were both thirteen. I didn't meet Christian till much later, and we didn't marry till he was nearly thirty. Sometimes I feel I never caught up with Perry . . . oh, how baffling it all seems in retrospect! The truth is that at the end it was Perry he turned to, but why the marriage was disintegrating I don't know. I just feel increasingly sure that it was all my fault, and I've reached the stage where I don't know how to bear either my guilt or my ignorance."

"I understand," I said at once. But did I? One could say that she was being haunted to an abnormal degree by her unhappy memories, but beyond this dramatic symbolic language it seemed to me that a very commonplace situation was being described: a man had fallen out of love with a woman, got bored and hadn't quite been able to figure out how to extricate himself from the relationship. Love affairs disintegrated in that way every day, and so did marriages—although of course the disintegration of a marriage would usually be a more complex matter. It would be rarer too because in marriage friendship was supposed to take over when the sexual excitement had expired, but supposing one woke up one morning and realised that not only was desire dead but even the possibility of friendship had fizzled? Inevitably one would toy with the idea of divorce, but divorce might be undesirable for a number of social, professional and financial reasons. In such a jam what could be more natural than to escape from home as often as possible in order to relax with one's best friend? That all made sense. But it also made sense to note that none of this marital distress was necessarily the wife's fault. She could have been a model wife and still have induced boredom. The real difficulty almost certainly lay in the fact that the marriage had been based on illusions which time had mercilessly exposed.

I said with care: "It certainly seems that Christian had a problem which was putting a strain on the marriage, but that problem needn't have been connected with you."

"If he had a problem," she said at once, "I should have been told about it. The fact that he couldn't confide in me just underlines how deeply I failed him." And she added in a rush: "You do see now, don't you, why I wanted to contact him at the séance? I wanted to tell him I was sorry for whatever it was I did wrong and I wanted to hear him say: 'I forgive you.' "

The words "repentance," "forgiveness," "absolution" and "salvation" flashed across my mind in an automatic clerical reaction to the pastoral challenge which now confronted me. I had been about to draw the conversation around to the subject of seeking help—I had already phrased my opening remark on the prolonged physical stress which could result from the mental torment of guilt—but now I suddenly thought: maybe I can still fix this. And I felt driven to wipe out not just the fiasco of the séance but my guilt that I had only exacerbated her grief.

"Katie," I said, looking straight into her eyes and putting considerable emotion into my voice, "you did your best to be a good wife and we can never do more than our best. Set aside these bad feelings about yourself. If you did do something wrong, it's obvious you repent with all your heart and that means you're forgiven."

"But—"

I piled on the emotional pressure by leaning forward and tightening my grip on her hands. "Okay," I said, "I'm not Christian. I can't be him saying: 'I forgive you.' But I can be me saying: 'You're forgivable.' That's because you loved him and love generates forgiveness, it's automatic, it's assured, it's built into the system."

"But I feel my love was such a failure—I feel *I'm* such a failure—"

"Absolutely not. You loved him devotedly, with your whole heart— and that makes you a success, a great success, the greatest success you could possibly be."

"Oh Nick, you're being so kind, so—"

"A beautiful woman capable of a deep, unselfish love—of course Christian would forgive you if he were with us now! Any man would forgive you. *I* forgive you."

The next thing I knew I was kissing her and her arms were sliding around my neck. This was hardly what I had intended to happen, but I knew how important it was to restore her self-esteem. Christian had destroyed her sense of her own worth, I could see that now, but if I could give her back her faith in herself and in the power of love . . . I was dimly aware of my feet leaving the floor as my body arranged itself on the bed beside her.

She said in a low voice: "You're standing in for Christian, aren't you? Maybe the séance worked after all and he's speaking to me through you."

I couldn't answer. I just thought: a couple more kisses, then I stop, no harm done, total cure.

"Tell me again you forgive me."

"I forgive you, Katie," I said, saying Christian's lines for him. "I promise."

Immediately she clung to me with great passion.

Funny how difficult it was not to be passionate in return. No, it wasn't funny at all. And it wasn't just difficult either. It was quite impossible not to return that passion, especially when her fingers encountered the zip of my jeans. Her fingers? My fingers? The terrible part is I don't remember. No, they were her fingers, must have been. Mine were already unbuttoning her blouse.

Her last words before we copulated were: "I feel forgiven now."

Pathetic.

I can hardly bring myself to admit this, but I still honestly believed I was healing her.

Game, set and match to the Devil.

What a catastrophe.

5

IN MY rational moments, as I've already noted, I wasn't attracted to underweight women who looked fragile enough to break during intercourse. But this was not one of my rational moments. The obsession to achieve a healing had unplugged my brain.

She didn't break during intercourse. It was afterwards that she went to pieces.

As soon as she could speak she said in a shaking voice: "You're not standing in for Christian at all. You couldn't. You're quite different."

"It's okay, Katie, it's okay—"

But of course it wasn't.

"I never realised how different it could be—I thought all men made love in the same way."

"Look, don't be upset, I—"

"I've betrayed him. And *you've* betrayed *me!*"

"No, no—honestly—just think of it as a kind of therapy—"

"Therapy? My God, how utterly revolting!"

"But Katie, I didn't mean—"

"You've deliberately taken advantage of my grief—you've cold-bloodedly exploited me—"

"But all I wanted to do was help you!"

"You think *that* could help? You deceived me into thinking you could stand in for Christian and then raped me when I was in no fit state to fight you off!"

"It couldn't have been rape. Raped women don't have orgasms."

She hit me. I gasped. "Katie, for God's sake—" She hit me again. "Get away from me!" she said revolted. "Never come near me again! I hate you, *I hate you,* I HATE YOU—"

I grabbed my clothes and fled.

In my sitting-room I found I couldn't recite the Jesus prayer to calm me down, couldn't even remember it. I buttoned my shirt wrong, nearly fell over as I pulled on my jeans, and all the while I was becoming aware that the room was a shambles, the fallen chairs and smashed glass creating the impression of a violated space. The chilly air had a peculiarly desolate quality, and as I shuddered I at last remembered the mantra.

"Lord Jesus Christ, Son of God, have mercy on me, a sinner . . ."

Never had the prayer seemed more appropriate.

In the bedroom Katie began to scream for Marina.

I shuddered again and knew I was in hell.

6

MARINA returned ten minutes later. As soon as I saw the car I went to the bathroom, where Katie had barricaded herself, and told her the good news. She ran downstairs sobbing. Outside the two women embraced before Marina guided Katie into the car and drove away.

Leaving the landing window I stumbled downstairs. Sounds in the dining-room indicated that the members of the Community were having lunch. No conversation was permitted at meal-times but Dorothy the ex-missionary was reading aloud from *Pilgrim's Progress.* Silently I slunk into the kitchen and swiped the brandy bottle, which was kept in the house for medicinal purposes. It lived under the sink next to the spare bottles of lavatory-cleaner, a home reflecting the contempt with which the Community regarded alcohol. I had a swig straight from the bottle. My taste-buds felt as if they'd been mugged but within a minute I felt steadier. Burying the bottle in the cupboard again, I rinsed out my mouth with water and set off rapidly through the back garden to my father's cottage in the woods.

7

I KNEW I could tell my father only a highly censored version of what had happened, but nonetheless I knew I had to see him. Whenever I was in pieces there was only one person who could weld me together again.

"Ah, there you are," said my father as I entered his cottage. "Thank goodness. I had the feeling you were troubled in some way, perhaps even a little frightened."

"Oh, for heaven's sake, can't you switch off sometimes? I'm sick and tired of you invading my privacy with your ESP!" Of course I was terrified how much he had intuited.

My father's grey eyes filled with tears. He was very, very old now, almost eighty-eight, and he moved slowly. His great height had been reduced by a stoop. He was still *compos mentis* but his body was wearing out. Eight years after his successful prostate operation he was suffering from bladder problems again, and although tests had revealed there was no cancer the pain and difficulty continued. His digestion, which had always been excellent, had begun to cause trouble. He vomited, suffered headaches. The doctor continued to prove there was no cancer and in despair prescribed some tranquillisers which my father, much insulted, flushed down the lavatory. Now something had gone wrong with his hands and he refused to see the doctor at all. He made his own diagnosis, eczema, and rejecting all offers of help from Rowena, Agnes and Dorothy, he somehow managed to bandage the hands himself. Mark and Luke, the ex-monks, and Bob, the ex–naval chaplain, spent hours arguing about the dermatitis entry in the medical dictionary but came to no conclusion. Morgan, the ex–pop star, had left the Community long ago after abandoning his attempt to write an opera about God, and Theo, the ex-ordinand who thought he was being persecuted by Buddha, was now in a mental home. The Community had been reduced to six.

"Oh Father, I'm sorry, I'm sorry—I didn't mean to yell at you like that . . ." I couldn't stand it when his eyes filled with tears. This tendency to weepiness was new, another result of extreme old age. He couldn't control his emotions as well as he used to, and his psychic powers, once so formidably disciplined, were now more erratic. I was sure he hadn't deliberately tried to tune in to my activities; the tuning in would have been a mere reflex, triggered by his anxiety.

Hating myself for losing patience with him I said: "As a matter of fact you were right in sensing that I've been having an awkward time." Picking up Whitby, who was skulking around my ankles, I dumped him in my father's lap. I did this not just to give myself a chance to review the censored story I had prepared but because I thought it was once more time Whitby earned his keep by having a tranquillising effect on those nearest and dearest to him.

I stroked the striped fur. So did my father. Whitby tried to knead my father's knees but collapsed in ecstasy seconds later. The sonorous rise and fall of his purring thrummed around the room.

Having reviewed my story, I took a deep breath and said: "I've just had a very disturbing visit from Marina and Katie. They wanted me to hold a séance but of course I told them that was out of the question. However, when I realised Katie wanted to make contact with Christian in order to obtain his forgiveness, it occurred to me that this was a pastoral situation where I could be of use. I thought that if we all prayed together . . . the grace of God . . . love and peace . . . well, I might have been able to alleviate this mysterious burden of guilt, mightn't I? It really did seem as if I could be of use."

"Nicholas, you're not yet a priest. And you're certainly not a doctor.

If Mrs. Aysgarth was in such a troubled state, you should have advised her to seek professional help."

"Yes, of course. However—"

"Very well, tell me the worst. What happened?"

I prepared to skate on thin ice. "We sat down at the table in my sitting-room and I led them in prayer. I wanted to convey that Christian was at peace with God, so I prayed that we might be allowed to experience that peace. I didn't pray for his soul—I thought non-churchgoing Protestants might have balked at prayers for the dead—but I thought that if we simply remembered him before God . . . well, there's nothing wrong with that, is there?"

"No, but what exactly was your motive here, Nicholas? Did you act solely out of a desire to help Mrs. Aysgarth or were you perhaps attracted by the chance to adopt a powerful role in the presence of two beautiful and charming young women?"

"I most strongly deny—"

"Yes, of course you do. But Nicholas, even if your motive was as pure as driven snow, this apparently harmless attempt at prayer could still have been dangerous. If someone's emotionally disturbed—and in particular if they're haunted by guilt—any psychic activity, even prayer, can trigger an unpleasant reaction."

"But this was worse than just an unpleasant reaction from Katie! There was an interruption by a discarnate shred."

"Are you quite sure you weren't conducting a séance?"

"Oh no, Father! That was why I was so surprised when—"

"I too find it surprising. An emotional disturbance from Mrs. Aysgarth is easy to explain: the psychic activity of prayer might have caused her to break down as she sensed the opportunity to express her grief and guilt— she could easily have had hysterics or possibly even a psychotic episode if the channel of prayer wasn't wide enough to contain her emotions. But I wouldn't have expected an infiltration of the scene by a discarnate shred unless you were actively trying to align yourself with the dead."

"Father, it wasn't a séance. Honestly. It was just a pseudo-séance. I—"

"You appal me."

"But Father, listen—"

"Did you all hold hands and deliberately try to align yourselves with the spirit of a dead man?"

"Yes, but since Christian's at peace with God, surely an alignment could only be beneficial?"

"How do you know he's at peace with God?"

"Well, I—" I stared at him. Then as my scalp prickled I stammered: "I assumed—I felt sure—I mean, I just knew, it was *gnosis*—"

"Don't you dare use that word to me!"

"I'm not using it as a Gnostic—I'm using it as a Christian who needs a code-word for psychic certainties—"

"There *are* no psychic certainties."

"But Father—"

"Be quiet. Now listen to me. *Never* try to communicate with the dead, even those likely to be at peace with God, because even a seemingly harmless attempt to align yourself with a departed soul can have a profoundly disturbing effect on the living."

"Yes, but I still don't understand why what happened did happen. The discarnate shred was malign—I mean, it was *very* malign, it was driven by the most tremendous power, and in the end I realised that this power could only have been generated by—"

"I should think it most unlikely that the Devil could have been bothered to drop in on your shoddy little séance. It's much more probable that you lost your nerve and began to fantasise once the energy disturbances spiralled out of control. I assume that there were, in fact, energy disturbances?"

"Yes, and Katie was in a sort of coma, moaning and groaning as if she were possessed—"

"Rubbish, of course she wasn't possessed! She was merely manifesting her deep psychological troubles. Did you hypnotise her?"

"No, Father, certainly not."

"It would explain the appearance of coma. How on earth did you regain control of the scene?"

"I shouted to the Devil: 'In the name of Jesus Christ, Satan, be gone from this room!' and all the glass in the picture frame shattered as he went out of the window."

"Nothing went out of the window, Nicholas, except the vibrations of your guilt and your panic."

"But Father, that force I experienced—okay, maybe it wasn't the Devil himself, maybe it was just a malign shred acting alone—well, whatever it was, it came from without. It wasn't welling up from within."

"How did you experience it?"

"As a mounting pressure on the psyche."

"Exactly. It was a pressure exerted by your unconscious mind—which in your panic would have seemed quite external to your ego."

"But Father—"

"All right, Nicholas, calm down. I think our disagreement is an illusion created by the fact that we're mixing up two different languages, the religious language employing symbols such as 'the Devil,' and the scientific language which employs concepts such as 'the unconscious mind.' Why don't we try to produce a version of your story in each language so that we can see we're talking about a single truth? Then perhaps we won't get so cross with each other."

I was hooked, just as I always was when religion and psychology were seen not as mortal enemies—the grand illusion of so many people—but as complementary approaches to a multi-sided truth. I gave Whitby another long, lingering stroke. Then I said to my father: "Okay, go on."

8

"*WHICHEVER* language we adopt," said my father, "it's safe to say that some very unpleasant forces were on the loose in that room. It's also safe to say that Mrs. Aysgarth was in a highly disturbed state and that you too became disturbed when you found the scene was moving beyond your control.

"Very well, let's express ourselves in religious language first. We can say that something was infesting Mrs. Aysgarth; we can describe it by a symbol and call it the demon of guilt. When you finally saw how horrific that demon was, your psyche was opened up by your understanding, with the result that the demon was tempted to move from Mrs. Aysgarth to you. You experienced this demon as a strong pressure on the psyche. However, you then repelled this demonic invasion by calling on the greatest exorcist who ever lived and who we believe is living still; by invoking his name you aligned yourself with his power and succeeded in expelling the demon from the room.

"So much for the religious language. By the liberal use of important symbols we've created a true description of what happened, but there's another way of expressing the truth and it doesn't diminish the religious description—it merely complements and confirms it. Let's now turn to the verbal symbols of psychology.

"Something was infesting Mrs. Aysgarth, we said. We can express that in the other language by saying that she was suffering from a neurosis—obsessed by a sense of guilt. This neurotic guilt is rooted in her unconscious but has recently begun to break into her conscious mind and lead to an impairment of her health. When you interfered, conducting this séance and subjecting her to psychic manipulation, the control normally exercised by her conscious mind was removed, with the result that the darkest and most chaotic emotions began to rise out of the unconscious and manifest themselves in a variety of frightening ways.

"Mrs. Aysgarth may not, medically speaking, have been experiencing a psychotic episode, but I suspect her behaviour had the same effect on you as if you'd been witnessing the behaviour of a violent schizophrenic: you were terrified of what was going to happen next and your terror combined with your guilt that you'd induced such an appalling state of affairs. This made you unusually receptive to the guilt now spewing out of Mrs. Aysgarth's unconscious mind, and when her guilt merged with yours the merger appeared to you as a highly dangerous invasive force. In an instinctive gesture to repel the invasion you invoked the name of Our Lord—which is the point where the two languages meet. The invocation gave you the confidence to regain control; or in other words, the invocation resulted in an outpouring of grace which enabled you to triumph over the evil."

My father paused for a moment before concluding: "So the disaster can be accurately described in both languages and there would appear to be no mystery at all about what happened, but I confess there's one feature which still puzzles me: Mrs. Aysgarth's guilt. It must have been very extreme to create such a disturbance. Indeed it hints at something grossly abnormal."

I said cautiously: "Afterwards she revealed to me that even though she'd tried her hardest to be a good wife the marriage had been in bad shape."

"That would explain the existence of some degree of guilt on her part, certainly, but I'd suspect there was more she wasn't revealing to you— much more. Tell me, was she difficult to hypnotise?"

"No, she—" I stopped. He'd caught me. Clever, cunning old—

"So you did use hypnosis. I'm outraged, Nicholas, absolutely outraged. I've told you time and time again—"

"I know, I know, I'm sorry—"

"And how dare you lie to me about it earlier! Did you seriously think you'd take me in? As Father Darcy used to say—"

Here we went again. I knew what was coming. Father Darcy had said to anyone who he judged was making an unsatisfactory confession—

"—'You're saying the words you want me to hear but I hear the words you can't bring yourself to say,'" quoted my father, and added: "You've behaved absolutely disgracefully, and when I think that in a few weeks' time you'll be ordained I feel quite ill with despair."

"I'll drive over to Starwater straight away—see Father Peters—make my confession—"

"Yes, do all those things—and in future stay away from poor Mrs. Aysgarth, who quite obviously needs medical help as soon as possible. Which reminds me, how did you deal with her once you'd brought her out of the hypnotic state?"

"Oh, I just talked to her, held her hand for a bit, calmed her down—" By this time I was on my feet and hurtling from the room.

"If Father Darcy were here," said my father, intuitive powers now working full blast, "I think he'd demand a somewhat fuller explanation. In fact if Father Darcy were here—"

But he wasn't.

I flung open the door and fled.

9

I STAGGERED across to the chapel, which stood near my father's cottage on the floor of the dell. A hundred yards away I could see the wall which surrounded the grounds of the Manor, and I could also see the door there which the members of the Community used when they brought provisions to my father. It was easier to park the car beyond the wall and walk the few yards up the track to the cottage than to carry the shopping-bags for ten minutes along the meandering path from the main house, and in those days, before crime became a problem even in rural areas, my father kept the door in the wall unlocked during the daylight hours.

I was in such a state that I nearly bolted straight down the track to the road and hared to the village pub for another shot of brandy, but the chapel exerted its familiar magnetism and I headed across the floor of the dell instead. The chapel was young, about a hundred and twenty years old, and had been built in the style of Inigo Jones with such panache that it never seemed like a pastiche of his Palladian designs. It was small but perfectly proportioned, austere when viewed from the outside but fussier when viewed from within. This fussiness arose from the fact that my father had been unable to resist decorating the interior with various sumptuous Anglo-Catholic aids to worship. They formed a bizarre contrast with the plain, stark beauty of the altar's oak cross, made by my father before he had left the Order.

There were candles everywhere—my father was mad on candles—candles on the altar, candles to the side of the altar, prickets for the burning of votive candles at the back behind the pews. There was a holy-water stoup by the door. Another candle (no electricity; that would have been cheating) burned before the Blessed Sacrament, which was reserved (of course) in a pyx. The whole place reeked of incense but I didn't mind that; I'd grown up with it, and a strong whiff of the Fordite Special always made me feel relaxed and at home. What I minded were the pictures, florid representations of biblical scenes which in turn represented my father's uncertain taste in art. This uncertainty found its most embarrassing expression in a sentimental plaster statue of the Virgin and Child, vulgarly coloured and placed to the right of the altar on a fake-jewelled plinth. This had been installed after my mother's death. My mother, a Protestant who had loved my father not because of his Anglo-Catholicism but in spite of it, would have booted that statue out of her ancestors' chapel in no time flat.

It interested me that my father, who was extremely ascetic in so many of his habits, should choose to worship in this particular way. Ritualism does tend to be attractive to mystics because it's designed to express those mysteries which are beyond the power of words to describe, and indeed I believed my father when he said a rich liturgy infallibly created for him a deep sense of the numinous and a consciousness of the presence of Christ in the mass. Yet now that I was older I thought there was also a psychological reason for his attraction to this lavish, extravagant classical ritualism which had been such a daring liturgical fashion in his youth. He had had a sedate upbringing in a little Victorian villa where money had been far from plentiful, and this had given him not only austere tastes but an inverted snobbery about the luxuries money could buy; he always had to pretend he hated luxury, but I think deep down he found it attractive and the only way he could give vent to this attraction was in his religious life. That somehow sanctified the illicit passion which could never be consciously acknowledged, and becoming an Anglo-Catholic had been his way of escaping from the emotional constipation and straitened circumstances of that Victorian middle-class upbringing.

But I hadn't had that kind of upbringing, and now that I was old enough to think for myself, I felt increasingly confused about Anglo-Catholicism. It was well over a century since the Oxford Movement had relaunched the Catholic tradition within the Church of England, and the ageing of a once dynamic movement was becoming all too apparent. Undermined by Vatican II, which (so the traditionalists said) had Protestantised the Church of Rome, the Anglo-Catholics had been left high and dry with a bunch of rituals which were going out of fashion not only among the Romans but among the Anglicans. The new trend towards a weekly parish Eucharist, that watered-down version of the mass, now made the Anglo-Catholic services look archaic and—that most damning word of the 1960s—irrelevant. And the majority of English churchgoers—the Protestant majority—hated ritualism anyway.

Yet I had been brought up an Anglo-Catholic. It was my wing of my Church. I belonged there, and as a mystic I too was drawn to the numinous qualities of the services. Yet although I knew I couldn't abandon Anglo-Catholicism I was deeply dissatisfied with it. I felt strongly that it should be modernised but the traditionalists who ruled the roost were holding fast to the old ways as they developed a siege mentality. No hope of change there and meanwhile that fatal old-fashioned look was becoming tinged with decadence. Often it seemed to me that the idol of the die-hards was now a god called LITURGY—and there were other, even more unsavory hints of decadence than idolatry, hints that were beginning to surface in the sexual hothouse of the late 1960s. Anglo-Catholicism had always attracted a homosexual element, but in Victorian times the homosexual priests had committed themselves to the celibate ideal and followed the fashion for intense friendships which were never consummated. Now celibacy was on the wane and society worshipped the idol called SEX. No wonder Anglo-Catholicism was in trouble. Sometimes I thought even heterosexual Anglo-Catholics were only interested in providing a camp stage show of all the fashions imported from pre–Vatican II Rome.

I said nothing of my dissatisfaction to my father. A relic of another age, the age when Anglo-Catholicism had been a dynamic movement sweeping all before it, he would have been deeply upset by my critical thoughts. He might even have thought I was a closet-Protestant but I wasn't. I just hated seeing Anglo-Catholicism go down the drain, and during my terms at Theological College I had found it a relief to retreat into the churchmanship of the Middle Way which I found not only in the College chapel but in the Cathedral. There was an Anglo-Catholic church in Starbridge—St. Paul's at Langley Bottom—but I never went near it. The Principal of the College said it had fallen into the hands of cranks. ("Cranks" was his shorthand for homosexuals and/or nut-cases.) Even my father, who thanks to his small circle of distinguished visitors was well-primed with diocesan gossip, said once that he did hope I wouldn't go there, and I was relieved to find I had no difficulty in giving him the necessary reassurance. I had no interest whatsoever in a square, dated ritualism oozing eccentric decadence. It would have been far too painful to watch, particularly since I attended my father's services and knew how with the right priest even a dated ritualism could be made fresh, exciting and above all spiritually alive.

The big irony of this decline in Anglo-Catholicism was that a great many Anglo-Catholics were still able to kid themselves that everything was fine. This was because the Archbishop of Canterbury himself stood in the Church's Catholic tradition, but if one stopped being sentimentally proud of the Archbishop, the uneasiness soon began. Although Ramsey might look old-fashioned he certainly wasn't decadent and he certainly wasn't out of touch with the harsh ecclesiastical realities of the 1960s, but I was now convinced he wasn't typical of the High Church wing. That wing needed to be revamped, given a hormone shot, dragged kicking and screaming into the midst of the Now Generation . . . or so I found myself thinking for the umpteenth time as I sat down amidst the florid, old-fashioned Catholic trappings in our family chapel that afternoon, but then who was I to criticise my elders and betters? I was just a twenty-five-year-old ordinand who had gone clean off the spiritual rails.

As I tried to crawl back on the rails again I knelt in the front pew, gave thanks to God for my deliverance from the demonic power unleashed at the séance and prayed that Katie might be restored to full health. Then I set about making a comprehensive confession. I had become accustomed to making a private confession to God after every sexual lapse—a meaningless exercise, as I well knew, since I had had no intention of giving up fornication, but at least I'd found it helpful to go through the formal motions of repentance, and at least I had been able to tell myself that if I prayed regularly for the grace to be chaste there was always the chance that God might respond to my request. However, the catastrophe with Katie was in a very different league from my regular bouts of fornication and required not merely the acting out of a repentance-ritual but a full-blooded, utterly honest confession combined with an unqualified promise to God that I would never behave in such a disgusting way again. This time my prayer for the grace to reform would be unmarked by insincerity. As I begged on my knees for forgiveness, every word would come straight from the heart.

Off I started. One by one I dragged my sins out of my memory and laid them carefully before God like a cat laying all manner of mangled little corpses before his owner. Pride, arrogance, lust, selfishness, vanity, disobedience, deceit (these last two related to the interview with my father)—and worst of all, the sexual abuse of a damaged human being. This was cruelty, a sin which always seemed to me to be much worse than mere lust. Nobody got much worked up about lust nowadays except my Uncle Charles "Anti-Sex" Ashworth, but cruelty . . . Yet I hadn't meant to be cruel. I'd meant to be—no, God only knew what I'd meant to be.

Thinking of God recalled me to my confession. I went on kneeling, mentally pawing over all the sins, but eventually I recited the Jesus prayer. This had a calming effect. Afterwards I scooped up all the sins, offered them to God and said without words: sorry, sorry, sorry, I want to reform, I want to turn around and lead a better life, please forgive me, please help me, please rescue me from this awful mess my life's become. I prayed very hard, wordlessly, along these lines for some time. I did indeed feel deeply ashamed.

Finally I topped off the confession with the Lord's Prayer and flipped the switch in my head to tune in to the Light. To my great relief a calmness instantly enveloped me, and I knew I'd been forgiven, I just knew, it was—

But my father hated that word *gnosis* which recalled the Gnostic heresy.

Some people said Jung had been a Gnostic. My father had introduced me to Jung's writings on religion with the caveat that I should beware of anything he wrote about Christianity. Jung was sympathetic to religion but often got in a muddle about Christianity and misrepresented the orthodox view.

"Nevertheless he's a profoundly religious man," my father had said, "and his writings are of immense interest as we all, priests and laymen alike, struggle to understand the human spirit." My father had long since grasped that the languages of Christianity and psychology could form two ways of expressing one truth, but I longed for a detailed synthesis which would make Christianity blaze across the minds of the unchurched mid-twentieth-century masses and render its message meaningful. It's no good performing the classic academic exercise of expressing Christianity in terms of the latest fashionable philosophy. That appeals to no one outside the universities. For the mid-twentieth century you've got to express Christianity psychologically because even the average moron at a cocktail party has heard of the Oedipus complex. Or in other words, psychology's the grass-roots intellectual language of our time, and if you can translate Christianity into *that,* everyone will finally understand what the preachers are whittering on about in the pulpit—and then with understanding will come spiritual enlightenment . . .

I went on planning the conversion of England, but of course I was just an ordinand who had gone clean off the spiritual rails and was busy kidding himself he had crawled back onto them again.

At last, convinced that after such a successful confession I was now free to embark on the moral life which would signify my repentance, I set aside all thought of sin and realised I had missed lunch. To my surprise I found I was hungry. Back at the house I raided the larder, consumed two large roast-beef sandwiches, retired to my bedroom and slept.

Of course I never went to Starwater Abbey to see Father Peters.

I 0

MY FATHER had calmed me by his brisk dismissal of the Devil during his bilingual analysis; I was now able to believe that although I had encountered a demon, its master had been absent from the scene. Or, in the other language: I was now able to believe I had encountered neurosis but not the insanity which destroys the personality and prompts the murder and maiming of others. Nevertheless the memory of the paranormal phenomena continued to trouble me, and that evening in my sitting-room I began to reflect on the condition known in religious language as "possession." If Christian was occupying Katie's psyche in such a way that he was driving her to breakdown, could this perhaps represent the traditional "demonic possession" in an updated form? My father had brushed aside the possibility that Katie was, in a traditional sense, "possessed," but it seemed to me that the reality behind all the language did reflect a form of psychological possession.

I juggled with the two languages for a moment. One could say that Christian's memory was at the root of Katie's guilt, and that this guilt was making her neurotic. But could one say that Christian, not at peace with God as I had blithely supposed, was roaming around as a malign discarnate shred and infesting her? Perhaps, if one acknowledged the heavy use of symbolism, one could—but how confusing language was, how distracting! No wonder philosophers had become so bogged down in the problems it created for clear thinking.

The intercom buzzed on the side-table.

"Call for you, Nicholas," said Agnes as I responded with a grunt. "Marina Markhampton."

"Okay, I'll talk to her." I kept the bell of my telephone extension switched off because I liked the Community to screen my incoming calls; this was useful when I was meditating or studying or just feeling unsociable. Picking up the receiver I said: "Hang on, Marina," and waited for the click as Agnes hung up. It was always vital to wait for the click. Then I said: "Hi—how is she?"

"Look, we've got to talk."

The hairs rose on the nape of my neck. "What's happened?"

"When she got home she tried to cut her wrists."

I opened my mouth. No words emerged. I clutched the phone and started to sweat.

"It's all right," said Marina rapidly. "She didn't get far—the knife she chose was blunt. I got hold of the doctor and we managed to get her into that funny-farm near Banbury, the one where everyone goes to be dried out and detoxified. Emma-Louise went there after her first husband ran off with another man, Holly spent a month there after her first suicide attempt and Venetia's sister Arabella practically lives there, so it's all madly respectable."

I managed to say: "Katie needs a hospital, not a chic rest-home! She needs a psychiatrist!"

"My dear, there are oodles of psychiatrists there, they're wall-to-wall. Anyway, I got Katie settled in and now I'm back in Oxford waiting for Katie's mother to collect the children—that *au pair*'s good but I don't think it's right to give her total responsibility for three children in a crisis which could last some time. I plan to stay the night here, go back to the funny-farm tomorrow morning for a visit and then head for London. If you could come to my flat—"

"What time?"

"About three? Oh, and don't forget I've moved from Cadogan Place— you do have my new address, don't you?"

I flicked stiff-fingered through my address-book and eventually read aloud some words which included "Eaton Terrace."

"That's it. Thanks, Nick." She hung up.

That night I walked in my sleep, and when I awoke the next morning

I was lying on the library couch. That shocked me so much that I almost decided to visit Father Peters after all. Eleven years earlier, after my mother's death, he had cured me of somnambulism just as he had simultaneously cured me of triggering the poltergeist activity; he had taught me to stroke my psyche at regular intervals by prayer and meditation, and to channel the abnormal psychic energy out of my body by means of strenuous physical activity.

Remembering these vital lessons, I devoted myself to reciting the mantra for half an hour. Then after attending mass I meticulously expended a lavish amount of energy on washing and waxing my car until it looked like a four-wheeled fantasy in an advertisement. But all the effort was worthwhile. By this time I was feeling well in control of myself, and as soon as I had finished an early lunch I drove off in my jet-black Mini-Cooper towards the road which led to London.

I I

MARINA now lived in a large maisonette, the bottom two floors of one of those houses which cost a fortune a stone's throw from Eaton Square. There was a sixty-foot garden, all paved, with a fountain flanked by stone cherubs at the far end. Marina told me she planned to hold "happenings" there provided that the summer weather was benign and the neighbours were tame.

"Nice," I said as she indicated the garden from the drawing-room window, but in fact I thought the place was unpleasantly sterile. I don't like stone gardens where a cat can't even scrape an essential hole with his paw.

"Drink?" said Marina.

"Coke. Thanks." I prowled around the room, which was expensively furnished in exquisite taste. The atmosphere indoors was sterile too, but maybe this particular air of sterility arose from the fact that Marina had only recently moved in and hadn't had time to impress her personality on her surroundings. Or possibly the sterility reflected some off-key aspect of Marina herself: the beauty that was a little too perfect, the charm that was a little too artificial, the brain that she had long since consigned to mothballs. She had stopped pretending to work when she had become engaged to Michael Ashworth, but she had never attempted to be more than an ornamental secretary. I often wondered if her background had deformed her in some way. Her father was a typical upper-class oaf whose preoccupation in life was gambling at the races. Her mother, a far more intriguing character, was a minor painter of some repute but seemed to float through life without caring much about what went on outside her studio. Marina's brother Douglas ran a starchy antiques business in St. James's. There were two much older married sisters about whom I knew almost nothing. Marina was the afterthought, *sui generis,* emotionally detached from the other members of her family who seemed to bear so little resemblance to her. Perhaps it was because of this detachment that she devoted herself so intensely to friendships with people of both sexes. Uninterested in her family, uninterested in consummated love affairs, she chose this way to relate to the world.

"Michael's looking forward to living here after we're married," she said, returning to the room with my glass of Coke. "He's never been able to afford Belgravia before because the BBC are so mean about money."

Michael, a television producer, had been living for some years in a large, light, tousled flat in an excitingly seamy area of Maida Vale. I felt sorry for him having to leave it. "Skip Michael for the moment," I said, sitting down on a Georgian chair. "Tell me about Katie."

"I didn't see her when I called back at the funny-farm this morning—she'd been sedated." Marina paused to sip her drink, which I assumed was not just any old champagne but the Coterie's favourite: Veuve Clicquot. Her vanity ensured she didn't make a habit of drinking at odd hours but she was quite capable of hitting the bottle in mid-afternoon if life became unusually fraught.

"I can't tell you how awful it was yesterday," she added with a shudder as she set down her glass.

"Try."

"Well, after I'd got the knife away from her I was terrified she'd try again in some other way—stuff herself with pills perhaps when my back was turned—so I did something really idiotic. I was just so unnerved by that time—I kept remembering Holly when she finally succeeded in committing suicide—the bath-water bright red from her slashed wrists—"

"What did you do?"

"I gave Katie a shot of heroin."

"You gave—"

"It's okay, she's not a regular user! And neither am I. We only took it on a regular basis for a while after Christian died—we found it was the only thing that numbed the pain, and—"

"—and now she still likes to have the stuff around! Of course she's a regular user—you had the will-power to stop, but she kept on! No wonder she's as thin as a famine victim!"

"No, honestly, Nick, you've got it wrong! She doesn't use much—hell, I'm her supplier and I'd know if she was taking more than an occasional dose—"

"It's insane even to flirt with a drug like that. She might have spent three years not being addicted but she could go over the top into addiction at any time, particularly now that she's in a bad mental state. Who the hell do you get the stuff from?"

"Dinkie."

"Dinkie! What's happened to her? No," I said rapidly, fighting down the nausea which always accompanied my memory of the black blast of foreknowledge in 1963, and blotting out the horror of the futures which had consistently come true, "don't answer that, don't let's get side-tracked. You dosed Katie with heroin, you said—"

"—and she calmed down, well, passed out, and that was when I called the doctor. I hadn't had the chance before. But as soon as I put down the phone I realised I had to tell him what I'd done because otherwise he might give her a shot of something else which would react with the heroin and kill her. Oh God, what hell it was! The doctor was furious, said he'd have to call the police—"

"I bet. But of course you batted your eyelashes at him and he wound up saying he'd have done the same thing himself if he'd been in your shoes."

"Well, actually . . . yes. More or less. But Nick, although I know I was idiotic to give her the heroin, what else could I have done? She was as mad as a hatter, completely freaked out—"

"I know. A nightmare. All my fault. Dreadful." I guzzled my Coke and felt desperate.

"No, it wasn't all your fault, darling, honestly—she was heading that way before I brought her to you. If only she didn't feel so massively guilty—"

"That massive guilt," I said, "is what I just don't understand. It's almost as if she feels personally responsible for the drowning."

Marina stared at me. "But that's exactly what she does feel! Didn't she tell you?"

I stared back. "But how could Katie believe she was responsible for Christian being swept overboard by a freak wave?"

"Katie doesn't believe in the freak wave," said Marina. "She thinks he committed suicide."

V

I

"WE DECIDED not to mention the suicide possibility to you," said Marina rapidly, "because we wanted you to go into the séance uninfluenced by what we thought. But did Katie really never mention suicide afterwards when you were alone together?"

"She must have been too disturbed. But Marina, are you saying you seriously believe—"

"No. I'm sure the death was an accident. Katie's the one who's convinced it was suicide."

"But why would Christian have killed himself?"

"Well, you can make out some sort of case for it. He seemed to be fed up with everyone and everything by the summer of '65, so you could argue that he dived overboard in a fit of depression—and if his life had really become so meaningless that he preferred to die, then it's hardly surprising that Katie's now guilt-fixated. She'd see herself as part of the life he found so futile, part of the reason why he killed himself."

"But why did life become so meaningless?"

"My dear," said Marina after another gulp of champagne, "he was simply too successful. Wasn't it Alexander the Great who wept because he had no new worlds to conquer? Christian had achieved all his ambitions except getting the chair in medieval philosophy—and even that would have dropped into his lap in the end."

"If he did commit suicide there must have been much more going on than just a severe attack of *ennui.*"

"Exactly. That's why I'm sure it wasn't suicide. There was nothing else going on—and I'll tell you another reason too, Nick, why I'm sure the death was accidental. I shared a flat with Holly right up to the time she killed herself, and with the wisdom of hindsight I can now look back and spot the early signs which indicated which way she was going. I believe that if Christian had been working up to suicide, I could now look back and identify similar signs. But I can't because they don't exist."

"Maybe you simply missed them. After all, how often did you see Christian during the final months of his life?"

"Not so much as usual—all right, I'll admit that. He'd developed a craze for sailing and he used to go off to Bosham every weekend with Perry. But I did still see him and he did still confide in me—"

"But how far did he confide in you?"

"Oh, I'm sure he told me everything, he always did. He never talked to Katie of his problems because he hated it when she got upset and wept all over the place."

"Nevertheless," I said at once, "she was the one who was actually living with him and she strikes me as being an intuitive type. If she's now so convinced he committed suicide maybe she picked up some vibe you missed."

"Then why hasn't she told me about it?"

"It may be no more than an impression which she's buried deep in her subconscious mind. Tell me, did he ever think of leaving her?"

"Oh no! Christian was essentially good and kind and decent, and you don't walk out on an adoring wife, two beautiful children and a newborn baby unless you're a monster. Besides, it would have been bad for his career. The ruling élite's so old-fashioned up at Oxford. Immorality has to be discreet and private because immorality which is messy and public is an offence to all the great intellects. They think it's evidence not only of bad taste but of downright stupidity."

"Then maybe he was in the grip of an intolerable emotional conflict: he wanted to leave Katie but couldn't see how to do it without destroying her and wrecking his career. So death came to seem the only way out."

"No, that doesn't add up at all," said Marina without hesitation. "You're being much too melodramatic. The truth is he was content to jog along with Katie—okay, he'd reached the stage where he periodically found the marriage boring, but he did have me to pep it up, and if he'd wanted an orthodox mistress—which he didn't—he could have had his pick from any number of swooning women."

I decided not to comment; if I was going to hear the truth about Christian's sex-life it seemed unlikely that I would hear it from Marina, viewing the world through her platonic-sex spectacles. "Just supposing," I said instead, "that Christian did commit suicide. Why would Perry have concealed it from the police?"

"Oh, that's obvious: he'd have lied in order to protect Katie from unpleasantness."

She was making sense again. I thought her opinions were probably reliable so long as sex wasn't under discussion.

"Have you ever talked to Perry about the possibility of suicide?" I said.

"Of course—I went to see him as soon as Katie had trotted out her theory, but he insisted the freak wave was no fantasy."

"Did he actually see Christian go overboard? I seem to remember from the newspaper reports—"

"No, he was in a different part of the boat when the wave struck. It's true that Christian could have deliberately dived overboard—or he could have decided not to bother to swim after he'd been catapulted into the water—but Perry's as sure as I am that Christian wasn't suicidal."

I immediately wondered how far Perry would level with her if he wanted to protect Katie from unpleasantness. Adopting a different tack I said: "What do the rest of Christian's family think? Is Katie the only one who suspects suicide?"

"As far as I know Katie's out there on her own, but those Aysgarths can be very buttoned up when it suits them."

"I'd like to know what goes on under the buttons. If someone commits suicide the causes can usually be traced a long way back—and the further back you go, the closer you come to the suicide's family."

"Honestly, Nick, I'm sure it wasn't suicide!"

"Yes, but can't you see," I said, "we've got to prove it? The only way to cure Katie now is to prove that Christian's death really was accidental and that she herself was in no way to blame."

"If we could discover that he had a powerful motive for staying alive—"

"I'll work on it."

"Darling, you're a saint!"

But I wasn't. I was a sinner, driven to make amends in the only way now available to a woman he had almost destroyed. It was then that I realised my confession in the chapel had been a nullity. The slate of my conscience hadn't been wiped clean by the desire to repent; the graffiti of guilt remained unerased; so much for my delusion that I was free to set the catastrophic séance aside and make a fresh start.

"I'll see Perry first," my voice was saying, "and then I'll move on to the family. What about Christian's Oxford friends? Would they be any use to me?"

"I doubt it. He kept up a front for Oxford and only let his hair down with my Coterie—and since most members of my early-sixties Coterie are now either mad or dead, they're not much use to you either."

"There's your fiancé. What does Michael think about all this?"

"My dear, don't, I implore you, go stirring up Michael. He's madly jealous of my relationship with Christian because he can never quite believe it was all utterly platonic. But you might try Venetia. She knew Christian well."

"How well?"

"Oh, not *that* well! But they liked each other. They were good platonic friends."

"Uh-huh. This mystery's crawling with platonic friendships, isn't it? What happened to everyone's genitals?"

"What a typically masculine remark!"

"Come off it, Marina, just peep down from your platonic cloud-cuckoo-land for a moment! How sure are you that Christian wasn't sleeping with someone on the quiet?"

"One hundred percent sure. I know Christian and Katie were going through a rough patch but she never refused him—she told me so. He was free to have sex with her morning, noon and night."

"No wonder he got bored."

Marina decided to throw a tantrum on behalf of her sex. "God, what pigs men are sometimes! I'd like to hit you over the head with the champagne bottle!"

"All I meant was—"

"I know exactly what you meant! You can only see women as objects—you grab a girl, plunge up and down, get bored, toss her aside, pick up someone new and begin the whole shoddy charade all over again! I must say, I'm amazed—*amazed*—that you want to make a great big grown-up commitment like getting married, and if I were Rosalind Maitland—"

"How did you know about Rosalind?"

"Her sister Phyllida told someone who told someone else who told my sister Vivien. Well, Rosalind's a brave woman, that's all I can say, and I hope you don't get tired of plunging up and down with her before you even reach the altar!"

I said tersely: "I'm not sleeping with Rosalind. I'm about to become a priest."

"All the more reason to make hay while the sun shines!"

"Ordinands don't make hay."

"So you're currently as pure as driven snow, are you?"

"If you want to put it that way, yes. Certainly."

"My dear Nick," said Marina, becoming amicable again as she trium-phantly outmanoeuvred me, "do you really think I don't know you're lying to the back teeth?" And she smiled at me as I slumped winded with horror on my hard smart Georgian chair.

2

ALL I could say was: "So she told you."

"Of course. Katie tells me everything—but it's okay," she added kindly, abandoning all her hostility, "don't worry, I understand. You did it to make her feel better. It was a gesture of loving friendship."

I finished my Coke, slammed down my glass and said: "Don't be ridiculous. I did it to make myself feel better. I did it in the hope that I could still boost my pride by pulling off a cure." I hesitated, but only for a second. "It was a sin."

"Oh God! Well, I suppose you're honour-bound to take that dreary view, but frankly I can't think why the Church gets so hung up on sex when most of the time sex is no more important than a handshake between two people who like each other."

This time I never hesitated. I said: "That's the most pathetic remark you've ever made to me."

She was shocked. The glamorous, famous, sophisticated, socially success-ful, worldly-wise Marina Markhampton was never pathetic. She couldn't be. It was inconceivable.

"Pathetic?" she said incredulously.

"Yeah—*pathetic!* Why spend your life trying to be a run-of-the-mill animal when you've got the chance to be the greatest thing on earth—a fully integrated human being?" I stood up. "I've got to go."

"Nicholas."

I halted in my progress to the door. Never before had she called me by my full name.

"Don't go," she said. "Please."

I stayed. That was a big mistake. I knew instinctively what a big mistake it was, but I made it anyway. I suppose I thought I could handle the consequences.

"I can't tell you what a relief it is," she said, speaking rapidly, "to hear someone come out against casual sex. I mean, one just has to believe casual sex is right and normal these days, doesn't one, it's a sort of religion, and I've pretended to believe in it because I don't want anyone thinking I'm peculiar, but I don't believe in it, I *can't* believe in it, not when I look around and see the damage it causes not just to the guilty but to the innocent. A friend of mine's mother—" She broke off. Then she said: "No, forget the friend. *My* mother . . . My mother had a casual affair once. Well, I'm sure she's had lots of casual affairs, but this particular one . . . No, never mind, I don't care, not any more, it doesn't matter," said Marina as her eyes filled with tears, and then she exclaimed passionately: "Immorality *hurts,* and it's the innocent who suffer!"

She began to weep. Being Marina she wept beautifully, elegantly, pausing only to sip more champagne in an attempt to regain her composure. Her mascara had thickened but was holding up well. Her enormous blue eyes had assumed a dewy, vulnerable look. She was ravishing. "I feel so confused," she whispered. "Although deep down I don't believe in the casual-sex religion, it still seems to me that the only way to survive in life is to regard sex as no more important than a handshake, because so long as you stay uninvolved you protect yourself from the pain of rejection— from the pain of loving someone who doesn't care. I can't bear rejection," said Marina, "can't *bear* it. Being rejected by someone who ought to care is my idea of hell. So sex has to be neutralised somehow, and if one can't abstain altogether the next best thing is to make it meaningless. Only then can one feel safe."

She sank down slowly, gracefully, invitingly on the sofa and I sank down rapidly, clumsily, automatically beside her. Her left hand drifted towards my right. Our fingers touched, then intertwined. After a pause she murmured: "You do understand, don't you?"

"I'm working on it. Keep talking."

"Well, to cut a long story short, I'm currently in the most ghastly jam. When I get married, I don't expect to enjoy sex—well, I wouldn't dare enjoy it, if I enjoyed it I'd be too vulnerable to the pain of rejection—but I've got to appear to enjoy it, otherwise darling Michael will be so disappointed. So although I've got to be inwardly neutral I've got to be outwardly rampant, a sex-goddess de luxe. Yet how can I be a sex-goddess if I've had no previous experience?"

"You mean—"

"Yes. I've never done it. Not with Michael. Not with anyone. I almost did it several times when I was very young, but there were so many men to choose from and somehow it seemed more fun to keep them on tenterhooks. And then when I was twenty—" She stopped before forcing herself to add: "There was a man and I wanted him to love me but he turned his back on me and walked away."

"Bastard."

"Yes, but forget him, he doesn't matter any more, he can rot in hell for all I care. The one who matters now is Michael—which means I've simply got to have a five-star sex-lesson in order to get rid of the virginity and ensure I'm a sex-goddess de luxe on my wedding night. You do see, don't you, that bearing all the extremely tricky circumstances in mind, this is the only course I can possibly take?"

I opened my mouth to say: "You're nuts," but no words emerged. In the end I merely grabbed her glass and gulped down some champagne. Perhaps I thought it would give me instant oblivion.

"Katie said you were fantastic. In fact that was what upset her most: you being fantastic and giving her an orgasm. She'd never had one before."

I nearly dropped the glass. *"Never had one?"*

"No. Obviously Christian wasn't much good in bed. Funny, isn't it? He was so brilliant at everything else."

I poured out some more champagne and drank it straight off.

"Anyway," said Marina, topping up the glass, "although Katie was shattered I immediately thought: *there's* the man I need, the man who can rescue me from this ghastly fix, the man who can—"

"No," I said.

"But Nick, you'd be my saviour!"

"How can you say that after seeing how I wrecked Katie?"

"Katie was wrecked anyway, and besides, this situation's quite different. I'm asking you, as a dear friend of many years' standing—"

"It's not different. You're asking me to be a healer, but I can't heal you, not in that way."

"Are you worried about Michael? But I'd never tell him! I never tell Michael anything."

I took a deep breath. "Marina, are you really sure you want to marry Michael?"

"Yes. He's handsome and clever and charming and he adores me and I'm mad about him."

"I think the one you really love is Katie."

"Yes, but that's got nothing to do with real life. Real life is getting married and having a baby."

"No. Real life is being true to yourself, not trying to be something you're not."

"I really will hit you over the head with the champagne bottle in a minute! Look, Nick, I know what I want: I want to marry Michael and for his sake I want to be absolutely sensational in bed."

"Wonderful. But there's just one problem. That man in your past will lay a dead hand on your psyche and wreck all your efforts to be a sex-goddess unless you face his memory squarely, come to terms with the wrong he did you and forgive him."

"This *is* my way of coming to terms. If I become a sex-goddess and enslave darling Michael I shall triumph for ever over the past."

"And if you don't?"

"With you to teach me how to be rampant, I don't see how I can fail. Are you going to swill the rest of the champagne or am I?"

I swilled it. Then I said: "I'm sorry, but I've no choice but to turn you down."

"But you can't reject me like that!" said Marina. "Not now you know how brutally I was rejected in the past! It would be cruel."

This seemed, vaguely, to make sense. Then I realised, clearly, that I would be failing in my duty as her friend if I refused to help her. The whole success of her marriage was in the balance, and perhaps too I could somehow make amends for that unknown man whose cruelty had maimed her psyche. If I could bring a little healing—just a little—into Marina's life, then it would help atone for the wreck I'd made of Katie. Extraordinary about Katie, never having had an orgasm before. Maybe I'd achieved some sort of healing there after all. Maybe I hadn't been so misguided as I'd thought. Maybe I really was a sexual colossus despite the average-sized genitals and my failure to resemble Mr. Universe. Maybe—

"More champagne?" said Marina.

"Yeah, let's take a bath in it."

"Divine!" said Marina. "I think there are still eight bottles left in the case."

We raided the kitchen and adjourned upstairs.

3

WHEN I left, Marina, dead drunk, was lying unconscious on the massive double-bed which she would soon be sharing with Michael. So reminiscent was her marble-white body of the Venus de Milo that I was almost surprised by the sight of her arms.

I managed to get out of the house. Then I vomited into the gutter of Eaton Place.

A passer-by walking her poodle looked at me as if I were drunk, but I wasn't. I'd stopped drinking in order to play the sexual colossus. Marina was the one who'd gone on, muddled, maimed Marina who had breathed that everything was truly, honestly fabulous—and had then put herself beyond pain by passing out. No wonder I'd just thrown up. The triumph of the sexual colossus had been to put her through hell and reinforce her revulsion towards the sexual act. God only knew what Michael would make of her, but at least he would have the brains to get her to a psychiatrist and keep her away from any psychic healer on an ego-trip. Yet I could hardly call myself a healer, not after that travesty. All I was fit for was the naked-ape cage at the zoo.

Recoiling with a shudder from all these harsh truths I tried to focus my mind on Christian, and at once I remembered Marina's deduction that he had been no good in bed. I wondered how true that was—and if indeed it was true at all. Katie might normally be so frigid that even Casanova would have met his match. She hadn't been normal when I'd done my copulating catastrophe act, of course. I'd pulled her out of the earlier hypnosis, but in the sexual act her will had soon buckled beneath mine because she had been too damaged to resist further psychic pressure. The truth was that I'd made love to a zombie and obtained a zombie's mindless response. The orgasm had been a physical reflex signifying nothing. An impotent hypnotist could have produced the same effect without even touching her. So much for my ludicrous delusion that I was a sexual colossus.

Reaching my Mini-Cooper I slumped into the driver's seat, slammed the door and tried to refocus on Christian. Katie's frigidity certainly seemed to reveal a marriage with sexual problems . . . or did it? She could have been passionate and adoring in bed even though for some reason the orgasm had never quite happened. After all, prostitutes made their living out of being first-class in bed, but in the vast majority of cases, so I'd read somewhere, they were much too bored and detached to achieve any orgasmic reaction. So it was quite possible that Katie had satisfied Christian in bed—and even though the apex of the physical response had been missing it was quite possible that she had been emotionally satisfied in return. What you never have you never miss. And women were different from men anyway.

Having concluded that I should guard against making facile deductions about the Aysgarths' sex-life—and indeed that I should guard against making facile deductions about any aspect of the mystery which I now knew I'd been called to solve—I told myself I should stop thinking about sex and put myself in something that resembled working order. I said the Jesus prayer aloud, very slowly, until I stopped wanting to vomit in an orgy of self-hatred. Then I switched on the engine and drove south down Eaton Terrace in search of a phone-box.

4

I FOUND a kiosk on the Pimlico Road and glanced at my watch. Six o'clock. I dialled Perry Palmer. No reply. Returning to the car I realised that there was a void in my stomach which required filling, but all the day-time sandwich bars nearby were closed while the restaurants were too grand to offer a quick snack. I wished I was in America where there was a twenty-four-hour diner on every street-corner (or so it seemed in films).

Eventually I headed for Victoria, left the car in Carlisle Place and ate a simulated plastic sandwich in the station. Three cups of bad coffee later I felt less blitzed and more bullish. I decided it was no good continuing to agonise about the Marina mess. That was negative. What I had to do now was to devote myself to my mission. That was positive.

I called Perry again and this time he was at home.

"It's Nick Darrow," I said. "I'd really like to see you tonight—is it possible for me to drop in for about twenty minutes? I promise I won't stay longer than half an hour."

"Why the rush?" said Perry amused. "Stay and have some cold chicken and salad! Where are you phoning from?"

"Victoria."

"Fine. I'll have time to do the salad before you arrive," said Perry good-naturedly, and hung up before I could thank him.

I then wondered if I should telephone my fiancée, but I couldn't find the right coins and it seemed ungentlemanly to reverse the charges, almost as ungentlemanly as betraying her with other women twice in forty-eight hours. So revolted did I feel by this particular summary of my activities that I nearly vomited in the nearest gutter again, but instead I bought a postcard of Buckingham Palace at a souvenir shop which was still open by the station and wrote: "Darling—Sorry I've temporarily dropped out of sight. On a mission in London but will resurface soon. All love, N."

There was no need for me to send a postcard to Tracy. I had already decided I was in no mood to see her that weekend, and before my journey to London I had posted her a note cancelling our Burgy-binge on Saturday night. The note had read: "NO CAN DO SAT BUT STAY COOL COZ I LOVE-YA." Tracy was under strict instructions never to phone me at home but I thought she might get restive if I failed to turn up at her bed-sit as arranged.

I dropped Rosalind's card in the nearest pillar-box. Then I retrieved my car from Carlisle Place and drove to Albany.

5

WHEN PERRY opened the front door he immediately put a finger to his lips and whispered: "Sorry. Trying to get rid of him. Hang on." Then he exclaimed in a normal voice: "Nick—how nice to see you again! Come in."

Warily I crossed the threshold.

"Norman's just dropped in for a drink," said Perry cheerfully. "He's a grass widower at the moment and feeling a bit low."

In the drawing-room I found Norman Aysgarth, the second of Dean Aysgarth's four sons by his first marriage, slumped on the sofa. He was dead drunk but not, unfortunately, unconscious. Although he was formally dressed, his grey suit was creased, his shirt was crumpled and his tie was stained. The strong physical resemblance to Christian was unnerving. Norman was a fraction shorter, a fraction narrower and a fraction plainer, but at a quick glance one received the eerie impression of a *doppelgänger.*

"Christ!" said Norman before I could open my mouth. "It's Marina's pet charlatan! Or do I mean Venetia's pet talisman? Why does Venetia call you her talisman, you bloody psychotic—I mean psychic—hell, I can't get my words out, give me another drink, Perry, you bastard, I've got to have another drink before I can face this creep—or do I mean crook? What do I mean, for Christ's sake, what do I mean?"

"Don't let it bother you, old chap," said Perry, deftly filling the empty glass with soda-water. "And don't wallop Nick too hard—we may need him to help you into a taxi."

"What do you mean, a bloody taxi? Are you trying to boot me out? You wouldn't have booted out bloody Christian!"

"Christian wouldn't have been so bloody drunk. Rose's lime juice, Nick?"

"Great. Thanks, Perry."

"That's a bloody pansy thing to drink," said Norman, "and Perry, why have you only given me fucking soda-water? Where's the fucking whisky, for God's sake?"

"Okay, I give up. Here you are, here's the decanter. Now drink up and shut up and let's hope you pass out pretty damn quick."

"Why, you—" He tried to get up but crashed back on the sofa.

"How's Cynthia, Norman?" I said, hoping to create a diversion by asking after his wife.

"Wrong question," breathed Perry, passing me a glass of Rose's lime juice on ice.

"Cynthia's in the bloody loony-bin," said Norman.

"Oh yes? Which one?"

"What the hell's that got to do with you?"

This sort of conversation endured for five minutes during which I gathered that his wife had suffered a nervous breakdown after the committal of their elder child, an autistic boy, to an institution. "He's destroyed our marriage," said Norman, "bloody destroyed our marriage. My God, when I think of all we've been through, and it all started out so well, I was so pleased to get her because I was going one better than Christian—he only married an earl's grand-daughter but Cynthia's the daughter of a duke—and then I found out she'd wanted Christian all the time but Katie had pipped her at the post—which meant Cynthia had taken me as second-best—always bloody second-best—second-bloody-best I always come to that *shit* Christian—"

"I'm afraid this looks like going on for some time," said Perry to me, "but do please stick around if you can stand it."

"—and then I thought: aha! I've got a son and he's only got a daughter—I'm one up on him at last! But damn it, damn it, damn it, we find the little bugger isn't right in the head—"

"This sounds really rough," I said, sitting down cautiously beside him on the sofa. "I did know about Billy's illness, but I never realised—"

"Shut up, you creepy freak, you freaky creep, what do you know about marriage and fatherhood, nothing, absolutely bloody nothing—well, how could you know anything, you're going to be a clergyman and what do clergymen know—bloody nothing, and what's more they don't *want* to know anything, it's too uncomfortable, they just want life to be a Bible story rewritten for children—my God! When I think of all I went through with my father, all the times I put up a front and pretended nothing was wrong just so that his personal fairy-tale shouldn't be spoilt—Cynthia and I even pretended Billy was okay, Father was the last to know he had a mad grandchild, but of course Dido told him in the end, *that bloody Dido,* all stepmothers should be burnt at the stake—my poor mother, dying young like that, but why do I grieve for my mother, why bother, she only cared about Christian—"

"How old were you when she died, Norman?" I said, making another attempt to put out a sympathetic feeler. "My mother died when I was fourteen."

"I was twelve. 1942, that was, and then Father starts chasing that arch-bitch Dido and eventually marries her—Christ, what a mess! That bloody woman—do you know, she even made a pass at Christian? She didn't make a pass at me, of course. I didn't count, I was just second-best as usual, second-bloody-best to—"

"You mean she made a pass at Christian after she'd married your father?"

"You bet she did, but it was long ago, Christian was only twenty-one—which takes us back to 1948 when Dido was still in her early thirties. Yes, she fell in love with him, all women did, he was compulsive, addictive, worse than heroin—"

"How did your father react?"

"Oh, he never knew, we kept it from him, we all have to be perfect for Father, we all have to keep up a front, clerical families always have to be happy, happy, happy, all clean and bright and shining—why are you shaking your head like that, Perry? You visited us so often, you saw how it was!"

"I know all about being a member of a clerical family," I said. "I know how tough the pressures can be."

"Pressures! Don't talk to me about pressures! Christ, I can't tell you what life's been like—years and years of godawful torment with that child!

'You'd better put Billy in an institution,' says Christian. 'Can't you see it's driving Cynthia crazy? She's sleeping with every man in sight just to escape from the hell of it all.' My God, that *shit* Christian—"

"Count your blessings," said Perry crisply. "Christian's dead. You're still alive."

"Yes, but everyone looks at me and thinks: 'Why couldn't he have died instead of Christian?' *You* look at me and think: 'Why couldn't he have died instead of Christian?' But you've all got it wrong because *I'm* the one who's dead and *he's* the one who's alive, smashing me to pieces, driving me to drink—"

"Talking of drink," said Perry, "have another Scotch while Nick and I get something to eat."

"He hates me being here," said Norman to me. "He hates me for not being Christian—oh God, I can't get away from Christian, I can't shake him off, he's clinging to me—*clinging* to me, I tell you—I can even feel his fingernails—"

"Wait a moment, Norman," I said. "Couldn't that be an illusion caused by your present unhappiness? Maybe you're the one who's doing the clinging—raiding your memories of him to fuel your anger that life's currently so rough for you. But if you could stop the memory-raiding and focus on yourself—not the second-rate Christian but the first-rate Norman, the man God's designed you to be—"

"Sod God," said Norman, and passed out.

" 'For this relief,' " quoted Perry neatly, " 'much thanks.' " Norman's body started to slide to the floor but we heaved him back on the sofa.

"Does this happen often?" I said to Perry as we straightened our backs.

"This is the first time he's actually passed out, but of course he's worse today because of Cynthia's breakdown. I don't know why he's suddenly started calling on me. This is the fourth visit in six weeks."

"How do you stand it?"

Perry sighed before answering: "I've known Norman since he was a child. I can't just wash my hands of him because he's going through a bad patch, and besides . . . being kind to Norman is something I can do for Christian. They were fond of each other. They got on."

"*Got on?* But how do you explain—"

"Oh, Norman's crazy now—absolutely gone to pieces. In fact that whole family's gone to pieces since Christian died. It's as if he's haunting the lot of them." He moved towards the door. "Come on, let's have some dinner. I'm damned hungry."

Mesmerised by this new evidence of Christian as a malign discarnate shred, I followed Perry downstairs to the kitchen.

THE KITCHEN was still a unique monument to a past age, but the ancient gas refrigerator had expired. In its place stood a humming white slab. As I drifted past the ornamental range, still flanked by its classic fire-irons, Perry opened the door of the slab and pulled out the salad ingredients which he had had no time to mix before Norman's arrival.

"Did Mrs. Aysgarth—Dido—really make a pass at Christian back in the forties?" I said. "Or was that just something Norman dreamed up when he was stoned?"

"No, that bit was true. It was everything else which was out of focus, a typical alcoholic distortion . . . I say, would you mind carving the chicken? Then I can devote myself to the salad."

"Sure." I took the cooked bird he passed me before I added: "You're saying Norman's an alcoholic?"

"Oh, they're all alcoholics in that family—no, I'm sorry, let's be charitable and call them heavy drinkers. God knows I put away quite a bit myself occasionally."

"So what was the reality behind Norman's drunken distortions?"

"You mean what was the real relationship between Christian and Norman?" Perry thrust a lettuce under the tap and ruffled the leaves. Then he said: "They really did like each other, but that family has always had one very big problem."

"Which is?"

"They go in for suppressing emotion on a scale exceptional even for the British middle classes. Of course there was a degree of friction and jealousy between those two oldest boys, and in a normal family this discord would have been worked off in a few healthy fights, but fighting just wasn't the done thing in the Aysgarth family so inevitably a volcanic situation started to develop."

"All calm on the surface but explosive forces building up underneath?"

"Exactly. The affection on the surface was actually genuine, but the trouble was they could find no way of defusing the explosive forces except by resorting to alcohol. The result was that when they were drunk they always sounded as if they loathed each other, but they didn't. They were just letting off steam."

"You mean Christian could be as unpleasant as Norman?"

"Yes, but Christian had much better control over his drinking because he had an alternative method of letting off steam: he used to sound off to me, and our friendship was such that he didn't have to get drunk in order to sound off."

"You must be some kind of saint, Perry, patiently soaking up all these Aysgarth ravings!"

Perry laughed and said: "As a matter of fact, Christian used to call me his blotting-paper. I became rather adept at mopping up bad feelings—in fact that was what I was trying to do with Norman tonight, but I made a hash of it when I lost my temper at the end."

"You probably lost it because I was there and you felt you were being put in an awkward position. But Perry, if Norman and Christian had an acceptable fraternal relationship, how do you explain Christian crashing around in Norman's marriage and telling him Cynthia was sleeping with everyone in sight?"

"Well, of course he didn't and she wasn't. You've cited a prime example of Norman's alcoholic distortions."

"I thought that story didn't ring true! Cynthia was always so possessive with Norman—it's hard to imagine her looking seriously at anyone else."

"She did look at someone else, but she certainly didn't sleep with everyone in sight. And she only looked at someone else because Norman had got temporarily mixed up with Dinkie."

The carving knife slipped in my hand. I nearly cut off the top of my thumb.

"Nothing very startling about that, of course," mused Perry, too busy shredding the lettuce to notice my reaction. "Almost everyone I know has been temporarily mixed up with Dinkie."

"When did you say all this happened?"

"I didn't, but it was in the early spring of '64, just over a year before Christian died. Anyway, when Cynthia found out about Dinkie she decided to indulge in a spot of adultery to pay Norman back."

"Who—no, don't tell me, I can guess—"

"Yes, she did try Christian, but he was loyal to Norman and fobbed her off. Then she made the big mistake of tangling with Katie's brother Simon—"

"Bad news."

"—who by that time was in his terminal drug phase. It wasn't long afterwards that he drowned in that swimming-pool after drugging himself to the eyeballs. How he consummated the affair with Cynthia I've no idea, since pot's death to an active sex-life, but—"

"Cynthia's very sexy."

"She'd need to be, to get a rise out of poor Simon at that stage. However, no sooner had he made it with her than he was unable to resist boasting about his conquest to Katie—who told Christian—who decided action was called for. 'Leave *well* alone,' I said, but he couldn't. He was too involved with his brother and he felt Norman ought to know the truth so that he could take the right steps to save his marriage."

"Good intentions paving the road to hell?"

"I'm afraid so, yes. 'Cynthia's messing around with Simon,' Christian said to Norman in my presence. 'For God's sake lay off Dinkie before Cynthia sleeps with everyone in sight.' Norman, who'd known nothing about the affair with Simon, was very shocked. Then he said that if the marriage was on the rocks it was all Cynthia's fault because she'd neglected him—little Billy had been taking up all her time and energy. That was when Christian told him to institutionalise the child in order to save the marriage."

"What do you reckon the prognosis is?"

"For the child? Zero."

"No, for the parents."

"God knows. It all depends if Norman can get off the booze. Cynthia will probably crawl back eventually from the breakdown. She's at that rather chic place near Banbury."

"So's Katie."

Perry froze, his knife poised above the last tomato. *"Katie?"*

It was time I took the initiative in the conversation. Having carved the final slice of chicken, I sat down at the kitchen table and gave him a heavily censored résumé of my meeting with Katie and Marina.

7

"*... AND* I realised," I said, "when Katie fainted at the prayer-session, that she was in a very bad way, but it wasn't until I saw Marina this afternoon that I understood exactly what the trouble is: Katie's crucified by guilt because she thinks Christian committed suicide."

"Oh, my God!" said Perry. "I thought I'd laid that idiotic theory to rest! I told Marina—"

"I know. And she still agrees with you that the death was an accident. But Perry, this is a real *idée fixe* of Katie's and she needs help overcoming it—help that I'm very anxious to provide. I hate the thought that my prayer-session failed, and I feel I'm being . . . well, called, to put things right. Hope that doesn't sound too priggish."

"Not in the least. Very appropriate behaviour for an embryo-clergy-man. But I think you've set yourself a hard task."

"Have I? But surely if I can prove conclusively that Christian didn't commit suicide—"

"My dear Nick, that's not just a hard task; it's an impossible one because conclusive proof doesn't exist. I'm useless as a witness because I didn't see Christian go overboard and I was concussed for several minutes after the wave hit us."

"I realise that, but—"

"All I can offer you is my firm belief that he wasn't suicidal." Abandoning his food, Perry rose from his chair and retrieved an opened bottle of wine from the refrigerator. "Sorry," he said, "I didn't offer you wine because I thought you'd refuse, but you're not a teetotaller, are you?"

"No, but I'll stick to lime juice now, thanks. So Christian was in good spirits, was he, on the morning he died?"

"Yes, but that doesn't mean much; suicides often put up a front to their friends. When I said he wasn't suicidal I meant there was nothing going on in his life which would have driven him to drown himself on the spur of the moment during a freak accident at sea." He was pouring out the wine as he spoke. I noticed that he filled his glass almost to the brim.

"Okay," I said, "let's stand the question on its head. You and Marina both say he had no powerful motive for killing himself. But did he have some powerful motive for staying alive?"

"Of course. His wife, his children, his career."

"But Katie obviously thinks they don't count. I was wondering if he had some secret motive—a motive which only you, as his best friend, would know about."

"Such as?"

"Well . . . was he having an affair?"

"No, he needed all his energy to cope with Katie and Marina." Perry was still making no effort to eat but he was paying considerable attention to the wine.

"But supposing—just for the sake of argument—he'd reached the point where he was bored stiff with both of them. Mightn't he have wanted to take on someone new?"

"When Christian got bored with women his solution was to retreat into masculine company which didn't make demands on him."

"Uh-huh. Would it be fair to say he had some kind of a problem with women?"

"Most men have some kind of a problem with women."

"Yes, but—"

"I wouldn't call it a problem. A slight irritation perhaps. He always found no woman ever measured up to his mother, so he wound up being consistently disappointed."

"Did you know the first Mrs. Aysgarth?"

"Yes, Christian and I had been friends for two years when she died in 1942."

"What was she like?"

"Very special, very feminine, very . . . but it's difficult to find the right adjectives. 'Sweet' sounds common and 'gay' sounds banal. Perhaps nouns are more effective: she had intelligence and charm and sympathy; she was the heartbeat of the family, the source of their happiness. Her husband and children all adored her." He poured himself a second glass of wine.

"If all women failed to live up to this exceptional mother of his," I said, "doesn't that imply there was a continuous turnover of women in his life as he tried to find someone who could equal her?"

"The turnover wasn't sexual. I told you: Katie and Marina took all his time and energy. Katie in particular was like a leech," said Perry, betraying his first hint of animosity, and I knew at once he was annoyed by the indiscretion. I saw his fingers tighten for a second around the stem of his glass.

"So you're convinced," I persisted, "that this isn't a case of *cherchez la femme?*"

"It's not a 'case' of anything. The death was an accident, one of those random horrors which make one wonder how people can believe in a loving God."

"Jung says there's a dark side to God," I said, "just as there's a shadow side to humans."

"I didn't think Jung was a Christian."

"Jung played his cards close to his chest."

"My God, don't we all . . . What are you really after here, Nick?"

"The facts. Was Christian a homosexual?"

"No. Homosexuals were often attracted to him, but he found their advances a big bore." He paused, and in the silence that followed I could hear only the hum of the new refrigerator. Then he said: "That's why Christian liked me. Sheets of blotting-paper don't make sexual demands. He knew he could always relax in my company."

"Sure. But what turned you into a sheet of blotting-paper, Perry?"

He gave me a blank look before exclaiming: "How odd! No one's ever asked me that question before."

"Are you going to answer it?"

"I don't think so. More chicken?"

"No, thanks. Are you not answering because there's no answer?"

"Sorry, I don't follow."

"I could be asking the wrong question."

"I still don't follow."

"Maybe you're not really a sheet of blotting-paper after all. Maybe that's just a mask."

"Now you're getting spooky! Is this where you switch on the ESP?"

The telephone rang upstairs in the hall.

8

"*HELL!*" said Perry. "Excuse me for a moment." And he hurried off, taking the stairs two at a time. I finished my last slice of chicken and sat listening, but when I heard Perry say: "Oh hullo, James . . ." I allowed my thoughts to wander. Around me the kitchen jogged my memory. I could see Christian standing by the sink, wandering past the range, gesturing towards the door of Perry's fabled coal-cellar. But those were mere memories and psychically I "saw" nothing. Meanwhile my brain was continuing to digest the mounting evidence that Christian, who should have been at peace with God, was instead haunting those closest to him; it seemed clear to me now that I was witnessing the ghost of the dead in the torment of the living.

Suicide was the obvious explanation of the phenomenon, of course. So much guilt and anguish would be milling around in the conscious and unconscious minds of the living (as the language of psychology might put it) that one could easily say (in the religious metaphor) that Christian's disturbed spirit, alienated from God and unable to rest, was constantly manifesting itself to those most deeply involved with him. Again the two languages pointed to a single truth, and I thought how ironic it was that suicides so often killed themselves in the belief that they were being kind to those they loved. In truth the destructive act crippled the survivors by causing psychic damage on a massive scale.

Perry ran back downstairs. "That was James Aysgarth trying to find his brother," he said. "It seems Norman had arranged to dine with him at the 'In and Out' Club. Anyway I told James the corpse was here and he said he'd come round and remove it . . . Coffee?"

"Thanks. What's James doing nowadays?"

"He's got a desk-job at the Ministry of Defence and a house in one of those plush areas of Surrey where everyone's still living in the 1950s."

"What paradise!"

"You think so? What's wrong with the present day? Everyone knows this 'Swinging Sixties' rubbish is mostly a fabrication of the media."

"It seems true enough to me," I said. "Everyone sleeping with everyone else, getting stoned and going down the drain."

"Oh, people have always done that," said Perry comfortably. "The only difference now is that more people have more money to do it when they're young—and to the accompaniment of really frightful music. Are you a fan of today's noises?"

"Not particularly, although I listen now and then on the car radio. I get my kicks out of silence."

"You reassure me! I was afraid you'd think I was square."

"No, just sophisticated. Perry, why did Christian, who was every bit as sophisticated as you are, find Marina's Coterie amusing? After all, Marina's fifteen years your junior. Didn't she and her friends sometimes seem very juvenile?"

"But her friends were usually older than she was, and Marina herself was so sophisticated, even at twenty-one, that her parties always had great style."

"So you really did enjoy them?"

"Certainly—and so did Christian. He used to say they compensated him for his hard-working youth when he passed up so much fun in order to slave for his first in Mods and Greats and Theology. In some ways he felt he'd wasted his twenties . . . Milk and sugar?"

"No, thanks. Does regret for wasted years mean he suffered from depression?"

"He got a little blue now and then. But most people do, don't they? That's normal."

"There was never any abnormal depression—clinical depression?"

"Don't tell me you're still flirting with that idiotic suicide theory!"

"No, just trying to build up an in-depth picture. Remember, I didn't know Christian well."

"Well, I assure you he wasn't a depressive."

"But Perry, there was something dislocated about him, wasn't there? Something not quite right?"

Perry, who had been pouring out the coffee, swung to face me. "What do you mean?"

"I just sensed he was out of alignment somehow. As if his life and his self weren't properly related to each other."

Perry remained motionless, staring at me. At last he said: "He was all right. There were tensions in his life, but he was coping with them. In fact by the time he died he was coping well."

"That's not the impression I got from Katie. You're implying an up-swing—that things were getting better. But Katie implied a downswing—that in the final six months of his life things were getting worse."

"I hate to say this because it sounds so bizarre," said Perry, returning his attention to the coffee, "but I think I understood Christian rather better than she did."

"That may well be true, but the fact remains that she was the one who was living with him and I think she's an intuitive woman. So if she feels he was on a downswing—"

"Well, obviously she was talking about the marriage, which I agree was going through a rugged phase. But I'm talking about his whole life, and I think he was successfully getting his problems under control." He added an expletive as he accidentally slopped coffee into one of the saucers.

"Sorry, Perry," I said at once. "I'm upsetting you, aren't I, resurrecting a lot of tough memories. I'll stop."

"No, no, I'm all right." He carefully wiped the saucer with a cloth. "Maybe it's a good thing," he said, "for me to talk about my memories—and I'm sure it's a good thing that you're trying to help Katie, but Nick, let me present you with one very indiscreet comment before we close the conversation: Katie's a deeply neurotic woman, has been for years. It's not good to live entirely for someone else as she lived for Christian, and I wasn't exaggerating earlier when I called her a leech. She battened on him. She drained him of vitality. She was a disaster."

"You never liked her?"

"No, never. But let's change the subject. How's your brother Martin?"

We took our coffee upstairs to the drawing-room, but Norman was such an unattractive sight as he lay inert on the sofa that we quickly adjourned to the dining-room. Having spent some time discussing Martin's decision to play Sir Anthony Absolute in the current production of *The Rivals,* we had just agreed that the role was a welcome break from his mindless TV comedy series, when the doorbell rang.

"Enter James with stiff upper lip," muttered Perry, and headed for the hall to admit his latest guest.

I moved back through the communicating door into the drawing-room.

James Aysgarth was thirty-five, six years younger than Perry, three years younger than Norman, and had reached the rank of Lieutenant-Colonel in the army. An accident during a military exercise in Germany two years earlier had resulted in the amputation of a leg, the termination of his active service as a soldier and marriage to a nurse he had met in hospital. He had never been a member of the Coterie because Marina had judged him too dim to be amusing, but his career cast doubt on her estimate of his intelligence. His aggressively non-intellectual manner was probably his way of rebelling against the fate which had handed him two exceptionally clever older brothers. Tall, blue-eyed, square-jawed, thin-lipped and broad-shouldered, he wore his suit like a uniform. The bluff, jolly manner was deceptive. It was a tough, forceful face. I guessed he had been a terror on the parade ground in his younger days.

"My God, this is a bad show!" he said when he saw his prostrate brother. "Perry old boy, I really am damned sorry. Letting the side down and all that. Not the done thing at all."

It was amazing to learn that even in 1968 people still talked in this pre-war, public-school Pidgin-English. But James would hardly be interested in modern trends. No mid-Atlantic twang would ever soften his consonants or blur his vowels. The permissive society would have passed him by. One glance at his immaculately cut suit, gold watch-chain and snow-white shirt told me I was in the presence of a traditionalist who wanted to revive the death penalty, reintroduce flogging and jail every flower-laden drop-out in sight.

"Jolly tricky!" said James, having tried to rouse Norman without success. "I don't fancy carting him past that flunkey in the main hall. Is there a back entrance to this place?"

"Yes, at the other end of the Rope Walk. But perhaps he'd better spend the night here, James—I didn't realise he was incapable of even a mild revival."

"My dear chap, I couldn't *conceivably* let Norman inconvenience you in that fashion! Family honour and all that, my duty to remove the corpse. Now let's work out a master-plan . . ." James began to plot with military precision. We all had to synchronise our watches. He then asked the exact location of the back entrance, and having been told it faced up Savile Row, he proposed that he moved his car there. Perry advised him that he might have to double-park; smart restaurants nearby ensured that curb-space was limited in the evenings.

"All right, this is the plan," said James busily. "I'll now drive the car to the bottom of Savile Row. Perry, in five minutes' time you must leave here and meet me outside the back entrance in order to sit in my car. (Can't leave the old bus unattended if I have to ditch it in the middle of the street.) When you arrive to relieve me at my post I'll return here to remove the corpse with Nick's help. (Marvellous that you're here, Nick—jolly decent of you to help out.) Then we load the corpse in the back seat and the mission will be accomplished. Any questions?"

We shook our heads and somehow managed to restrain our laughter until he had departed.

"If you saw him on the stage," said Perry, "you'd say he was overacting."

"What goes on under the act?"

"Nothing, it's no act. That's just the way he is. James is the straightforward Aysgarth, the one with no problems."

"Losing a leg must have been a problem."

"He coped well with that. And he's got a good job now at the MOD. I warn you, don't be tempted to write him off as a fool."

"What's his wife like?"

"A thoroughly nice middle-class girl, quite different from the neurotic aristocrats Christian and Norman picked up. Let me repeat: he's no fool."

We waited. Perry eventually left to guard the car, and soon afterwards James returned to the flat.

"Now we come to the dodgy part," he said. "I couldn't ask Perry to help cart out the corpse, but my gammy leg makes things awkward. Question of balance."

"James, I'm sure Perry would be very willing to—"

"No, Norman's violated his hospitality and I can't ask more of Perry now than to keep an eye on the car. But can I ask you, as a clergyman-to-be, to exercise your Christian charity and take Norman's heaviest end?"

Off we staggered down the Rope Walk with Norman's corpse sagging between us. The long courtyard was eerily quiet. I felt like an ant scuttling along the bottom of an empty coffin.

Breathing hard we reached the back entrance and manoeuvred Norman into the waiting black Rover. James wiped the sweat from his brow, and suddenly I realised that the exertion had been not only difficult for him but painful.

"Many apologies again, Perry," he said. "I expect your neighbours are now phoning the police to report a murder, but at least they won't connect the corpse with you."

"I'm sure Norman's made their day. But don't start saying goodbye, James, because I'm coming with you—you'll need help at the other end."

"No, if Nick's willing to come I can manage," said James firmly. "No need for you to do any more, thank you. No need at all."

Perry turned to me for confirmation. "Nick?"

"Go back home and put your feet up," I said. "You need to recover from your guests."

He laughed. "It was good to see you again!"

"Thanks for the meal."

"Come back and have a better one soon."

"In you get, Nick," said James, still issuing orders.

I planted myself smartly in the car. In the back seat Norman began to snore. Tight-lipped and silent, James slid behind the wheel, slammed the door and drove swiftly away.

9

"POOR old Norman," said James, edging the car through the streets of Mayfair. "Having a tough time at the moment. Not quite himself. Sorry you should have seen him at his worst."

"That's okay, James. Priests often see people at their worst. All part of the job."

"Funny how Norman's got so chummy with Perry," said James, sufficiently reassured by my phlegmatic manner to become confidential. "Almost as if he were trying to take Christian's place . . . What do you make of Perry Palmer?"

"I'm not sure. What's your opinion?"

"Always seems a decent sort. One of Those, of course, but obviously doesn't practise. Couldn't hold down that job at the FO if he did."

"True."

"I hear you've just got engaged to Rosalind Maitland," said James, signalling to me that he knew I was officer material, even though he'd caught me hobnobbing with "One of Those." "I took out her older sister a few times. Nice girls. Nice family. Well done."

I was learning fast that there's really no such thing as an "unofficial engagement." "How did you hear the news?"

"My stepmother told me. She rang us last night to deliver her weekly monologue and after five minutes she happened to mention—"

"But how did she know?"

"Oh, Dido knows everything—she may be living in Surrey now, but she's still plugged in to the Starbridge grapevine. After her phone call last night I was trying to explain to my wife who you were—in relation to the Aysgarths, I mean—and I remembered Dido saying once to someone: 'Nicholas Darrow's father was the Bishop's *bête blanche* and the Dean's *bête noire.*' But that's not quite accurate, is it? I know our fathers were daggers drawn back in the 1940s when Father was still the Archdeacon, but by the time Father retired from the Deanery in 1965 he spoke very highly of Mr. Darrow. Father Darrow, I should say. He's one of those Anglo-Catholics, isn't he?"

"That's right."

"Never understood the point of Anglo-Catholicism. Why not just go over to Rome and be done with it?"

"Because Anglo-Catholics aren't Roman Catholics. They're loyal members of the Church of England, they admit no allegiance to the Pope—"

"I should think not! No Popery, no Romish Mumbo-Jumbo and thank God for the Reformation is what I say, but of course I'm just talking as a patriotic Englishman. I'm not a religious man."

"No? But since your father's such an eminent clergyman"—I didn't dare use the word "priest" after this display of Protestant bigotry so superbly awful that it was almost endearing—"doesn't that make life awkward sometimes?"

"Oh, he doesn't know I'm not religious. I always go to church if ever I visit him on a Sunday. Can't have the old boy upset."

"Ah."

"As a matter of fact I do believe in God sometimes but I never let it bother me."

I felt it was safer not to comment on this remarkable philosophy. "Norman seems to have wound up an atheist," I remarked instead.

"Yes, copying Christian as usual. Talking of Christian, I must say it was strange to go to Perry's tonight. Hadn't been there for ages. Perry's drifted apart from my family since Christian died—which is why I was so surprised when Norman told me earlier that he'd formed the habit of dropping in at Albany for a drink . . . Incidentally," said James, unable to muzzle his curiosity any longer, "how did you yourself wind up there tonight?"

"I wanted to find out more about Christian."

"How extraordinary! Why?" He swung the car at last into Knightsbridge.

"I'm trying to help Katie sort herself out. She's just been admitted to that place near Banbury where Cynthia is."

"Well, that's no surprise, I suppose—she was obviously heading that way, but I can't understand this current vogue for having nervous breakdowns. Grit your teeth, shut up and get on with it is my motto. Life's hard, life's tough. Amazing how many people think it ought to be all sunshine and roses."

"Has your life been so tough, James?"

"Well, it certainly hasn't been paradise. Paradise ended for me at nine when my mother died, and after that it was a case of 'God helps those who help themselves'—if God existed, which began to seem increasingly unlikely . . . Ah, we're almost there. Start flexing your muscles for the next round of weight-lifting."

Norman and Cynthia lived in a mews south of the Fulham Road, but the house was double-fronted, much larger than the chic boxes one usually finds in a former stableyard. Nevertheless perhaps Cynthia, the duke's daughter, felt that even a hulk in a smart mews was a come-down. The top storey, obviously a modern addition, had destroyed any symmetry the house had once possessed. The whole place had a bleak look. All the flowers were dying in the window-boxes.

"Norman and Cynthia have two children, don't they?" I said suddenly as it dawned on me that the house was deserted. "What's happened to the younger one?"

"Jill and I took him over along with the French *au pair* when Cynthia was carted off to Banbury. Billy's nurse had already left and the little Frog was making a fuss about being left alone with Norman."

Bearing in mind Norman's behaviour when he was drunk, I found my sympathy lay entirely with the French girl.

The moment James opened the front door with Norman's key, a decaying smell assaulted our nostrils. The living-room resembled a refuse dump: layers of dirt garnished with old newspapers, empty bottles and soiled coffee-cups. In the kitchen the sink was stacked high with unwashed dishes. A peculiarly foul smell was emanating from the saucepan on the stove.

"Disgusting!" said James as we both flinched.

Having reconnoitred the territory, we embarked on the ordeal of importing the corpse and James issued his last order of the evening. It was:

"Into the drawing-room, Nick—no sense in giving ourselves hernias by lugging him upstairs." Norman was dumped on the sofa. The next task was obviously to terminate the stink so I retired to the kitchen, opened the window and made liberal use of a bottle of disinfectant which I found in one of the cupboards. It finally dawned on me that the mess in the saucepan had once been Lancashire hotpot.

"This is damned good of you, Nick," said James, having concluded his quest to find pillows and blankets for his brother. "Trust a padre to turn up trumps in a crisis! Whisky?"

"Thanks." By this time I felt that I would have welcomed even a tot of methylated spirits to fight the nausea generated by the hotpot.

James poured us both double-whiskies. "Soda?"

"No, I'll take water." Moving to the sink I managed to pour off half the whisky and fill the tumbler to the brim.

Meanwhile James had sat down at the kitchen counter and was drinking his whisky neat. "What I can't understand," he was saying, "is what's got into Norman. Why's he going to pieces in this really spectacular fashion?"

"I suppose little Billy—"

"Oh, all that's been going on for years. Do you think that Cynthia could have gone round the bend as the result of a final marital bust-up? God, it would kill the old man if one of us got divorced!"

"It would?"

"Of course! He's got to believe we're all living happily ever after, but to be honest I wouldn't be exactly dumbfounded if Norman wound up in the divorce court. Big mistake, marrying out of one's class as he and Christian did. Christian developed social aspirations up at Oxford, that was the trouble, and then Norman felt he had to keep up with him. Very silly. Personally I've always ploughed my own furrow, charted my own course."

"Sounds a bit lonely."

"Oh, but I flourished best when I was on my own, away from my brothers! Thank God I never made it to Oxford! Well, I never even made it to Winchester. I went to St. John's, Leatherhead, the school for the sons of clergymen."

"Any good?"

"Absolutely splendid, a marvellous place. I was happy as a lark as soon as I crossed the threshold and realised no one there had ever heard of Christian, Norman and Sandy, the Aysgarth trio of geniuses. Sandy never bothered me, actually, as he was so much younger, but my God, how tired I used to get of Christian and Norman!"

"I can imagine."

"Couldn't say so, of course. Didn't want to upset Father. In Father's eyes we're all perfect—which means no fights, no rows, and everyone dedicated to getting on and travelling far. Quite right too. What's the point of life unless you make a success of it? I certainly slaved to be a success in the army . . . More whisky?"

"No, thanks."

"Mind if I do?"

"Not at all."

James poured himself another double-whisky. "I admit it was tough losing a leg," he said, "but I gritted my teeth and battled on and now I've carved myself just the right niche in the MOD. Father admired me for that. 'I'm very proud of you, James,' he said. First real compliment he ever paid me! Never mind, it was worth waiting for."

"Who was his favourite?"

"My sister Primrose. Oh, of the boys, you mean? Well, I think he always had a soft spot for me because I'm the only one who's normal and not a bloody genius, but Christian was the one he was really bound up with . . . Seems odd in retrospect."

"Why?"

"They didn't get on. Pretended they did, but . . . Maybe the trouble was they were too like each other. It doesn't always do, you know, for a father and son to be too alike."

"Is your father easy to get on with?"

"Very. A wonderful father he is, never a cross word. Of course, being a clergyman, he comes over as soft and woolly on some issues—my God, how he embarrassed me when he supported the publication of *Lady Chatterley's Lover!*—but I'll say this for him: he's never let God stand in his way when his career's been at stake."

"Remarkable."

"I mean, look how he got to be Dean of Starbridge despite my stepmother! No one ever knew how he managed to pull that one off. That bloody Dido . . . What did he ever see in her? Flat-chested, never stops talking and always winds up offending everyone in sight! I find it hard to believe a woman like that could ever give a man an erection."

"Since Elizabeth and Pip exist it would seem safe to assume your father had an erection at least twice."

"And there were three dead babies! That means five times he got it up with her—*five times!* Incredible . . . By Jove, this whisky tastes good! I feel a new man. Nothing like a couple of mild Scotches to perk one up after a hard day."

"How did Christian and Dido get on?"

"Loathed each other. Wait a minute, I've finally remembered you're trying to find out more about Christian in order to help Katie. But why should Katie be helped by you becoming a walking encyclopedia on her husband?"

"Well—"

"And why go to Perry? I wouldn't have thought Perry the Poof was too reliable on the subject of Christian, but don't worry, I can certainly tell you a thing or two . . . Cigarette?"

"No, thanks. Okay, go ahead—what can you tell me?"

"He turned into a certifiable lunatic," said James.

VI

I

"WHEN people are too bloody clever they often wind up going mad," said James after lighting his cigarette. "Look at Nietzsche. My sister Primrose told me about Nietzsche once. Wound up falling in love with a horse. Nietzsche, I mean, not Primrose."

"Weird. About Christian—"

"Ah yes. Mad as a hatter in the end. I saw that for myself shortly before he died—and it was unusual for Christian and me to get together, I might add, because we lived in such different worlds. Anyway, there I was in 1965, still out in Germany with the regiment, and lo and behold, Christian phones me out of the blue. He's bucketing around Europe on holiday with Perry—which was a bloody odd thing to do since Katie was eight months pregnant—and it turns out he's only a couple of miles from my base. 'Come on, you old sod!' shouts Christian down the phone—pissed as a newt he was—'Let's go out and have ourselves a ball!' Funny how he used Americanisms to try to sound young and trendy. Rather pathetic, I thought . . .

"Well, I wasn't too keen to accept the invitation because I had to be up early the next day, but I thought dash it all, he *is* my brother. So off I toddled to meet him. But my God—the next thing I knew we were in one of those bloody awful German dives where you're not sure what anyone's sex is."

"Transvestite bar?"

"More like a bloody freak-show. 'What the hell are we doing here?' I demanded, but Christian just laughed so hard he nearly passed out. 'Isn't it wonderful?' he said. 'Doesn't it make you long to put your finger on the nuclear button and blow up the world?' 'What's so wonderful about feeling homicidal?' I said, beginning to ask myself if he was more than just drunk. (Only a madman ever jokes about nuclear war.) 'It's so wonderful to feel anything at all!' shouted Christian. 'Welcome, revulsion! Welcome, sexual perversion! Now I know I'm alive!' Well, at that point Perry the Poof said nervously: 'You'll be lynched if you're not careful—for God's sake keep quiet about sexual perversion!' But Christian wasn't listening to him. 'I want you to get me a gun!' he bawled at me. 'I want you to get me a Luger, like the one James Bond had! Then I want to walk into a supermarket and *shoot everyone in sight!*' 'Ha-ha,' I said, 'funny joke,' but at once he denied he was joking. 'I want to shoot everyone in sight and then kill myself!' he screamed. 'Get me a gun, you stiff-necked bastard, or I'll tell your CO that you were here buggering bloody Krauts!'

"I said good-humouredly: 'You need a padded cell, not a gun!' But I tell you, Nick, I was rattled. It was because I felt that beneath all the drunken claptrap there was something serious going on. 'That's enough, Christian,' said Perry the Poof. 'We don't want to shock James into a heart-attack, do we? Time for the rag to end.' And he turned to me and said: 'Sorry, old chap, it was damn silly, I know, but Christian couldn't resist bringing you here to see your eyes pop out of your head. He seems to find it amusing to tease you.' Well, I never hesitated. I just said: 'I hope he laughs all the way to the lunatic asylum,' and then I walked out."

After a moment's silence I said: "That's the most extraordinary story. Did either of them comment to you on the incident afterwards when they were sober?"

"No, I didn't see them again during that trip, and in fact that was the last time I ever saw Christian. But as soon as I could wangle some compassionate leave after he died I flew to London, went straight to Albany and said to Perry: 'Did he succeed in getting that gun and shooting himself? And are you covering up the suicide by pretending he drowned in an accident?' "

"What did Perry say?"

"Oh, swore blind he'd told nothing but the truth. Urged me to forget the incident in Germany—repeated that it was all a rag, Christian had been drunk out of his mind, hadn't meant a word he said—et cetera, et cetera . . . Funny about Christian and Perry. Lovers at school, of course, but then Christian called a halt to that later . . . Have another whisky."

"No, thanks."

"Mind if I do?"

"Not at all. Do you know for a fact that they were lovers at school?"

"No, but I'd guess that was the way it was. Christian wasn't homosexual once he grew up but he still kept Perry around for sentimental reasons."

"Does that really add up, James? Wouldn't Christian have been more likely to wash his hands of Perry once he'd outgrown him?"

"Nothing about Christian adds up. I can't really believe he wanted to kill himself. He was so successful—had everything a man could want—"

"How many people have you told about this incident?"

"I've never told anyone. Didn't want the story getting back to Katie or, God forbid, to Father. And I didn't trust Norman not to tell Cynthia."

"What about Sandy or Primrose? Or your wife?"

"I'm not close to Sandy; it's that big age-gap. And Primrose and Jill are women. I couldn't have talked to a woman about that transvestite bar. God only knows why I'm telling you, a mere acquaintance, but perhaps it's because you've been such a brick about Norman tonight—and because one can always trust a padre to keep his mouth shut. Rather a relief to tell someone, actually. It's been bothering me for some time."

"I bet. Do you in fact believe Perry's denial?"

"Sometimes I do," said James, "but sometimes I don't—and that's what bothers me most: not knowing for sure what really happened. I'm a simple, straightforward type. I like to know where I stand."

"In that case I hesitate to add to your uncertainty, but I feel I must tell you that the suicide theory isn't new to me. You're not the only one who wonders if the death was accidental."

"Bloody hell, I hope to God this never reaches the old man! But Nick, why would Christian have committed suicide? I mean, it's just not good enough to say he went mad, as if he'd been attacked by an evil spirit. We don't believe in evil spirits any more, do we?"

"Yes, we do," I said, "but they're called by different names now."

"Sorry, I don't follow, but never mind, don't bother to explain, I must toddle off home. I think it's all right to leave Norman. I've wedged him on his side so that he doesn't suffocate if he vomits."

"Would you like me to stay with him?"

"My dear chap, I couldn't possibly ask—"

"You're not asking, I'm volunteering. To tell the truth, James, I'm being an opportunist. I need a bed for the night."

"Oh well, in that case make yourself at home . . . Damned decent of you, though. Three cheers for the Church. There's life in the old girl yet," said James obscurely, and tottered in a remarkably straight line outside to his car.

I wondered how much he had had to drink at his club while he was waiting for Norman to appear. Then as the Rover's rear lights disappeared beyond the archway at the far end of the mews, I stepped back into the hall and closed the door.

IN THE drawing-room I found that Norman had succeeded in rolling over onto his back but I wedged him on his side again by rearranging the pillows, two of which reeked of scent. This was the smelliest house I had ever encountered but at least the reek of putrefied lamb had died. Upstairs in the main bedroom I found a telephone extension and rang the Manor. "I'm staying the night with Norman Aysgarth," I said when Agnes answered. I gave her the number before adding: "How's Father?"

"Oh, very poorly! The eczema on his hands is getting worse—Rowena said she even saw blood on the bandages this afternoon."

I was silent.

"When are you coming home, Nicholas?"

"I don't know."

"But your father does so worry about you when you're away! In my opinion—"

I hung up and returned downstairs to inspect the contents of the kitchen refrigerator. Immediately I was assaulted by the stench of sour milk. I threw it out. I was beginning to find the house deeply revolting. It had a bad aura too, heavy and unhappy. To distract myself I switched on the television. Junk spewed forth. Norman moaned in his coma. I flicked off the switch and inspected the bookcases. Legal tomes reflected Norman's profession; legal literature, such as Henry Cecil's humorous novels and Cyril Hare's detective stories, disclosed his taste in light reading, but I saw no book that obviously belonged to Cynthia.

I decided to water the dying pot-plants. That took some time. Then I sat down and tried to think, but the aura was so oppressive that I was glad when I remembered my car, parked off Piccadilly and requiring to be rescued before it fell foul of the parking regulations at eight-thirty on the following morning. With relief I recalled the signboard saying the mews was a private road. That meant the car could sit outside Norman's front door indefinitely.

It took only a short time to perform the rescue because I got a taxi at once in the Fulham Road, and when I returned I was still in no mood for bed. I tried the television again. More junk. I switched on the radio instead and picked up the indignant squeaks of some old piece of deadwood who said society was going to pieces and the Church was responsible. He could have been right but he just made me want to wear a garland of flowers and smoke pot. Changing wavelengths I got the Rolling Stones shouting the same tired old drivel. Boring, boring, boring, almost worst than the piece of deadwood. I switched off the radio but for once I found the silence hard to take. It was the aura.

Returning to the kitchen, now the cleanest-smelling room on the ground floor, I tried to recite the mantra but got lost after five minutes. That was bad news. Unable to rest my mind in this way, I concentrated instead on framing a series of short spoken prayers in an effort to divert my attention from myself to others. I prayed briefly, shuddering, for Katie and Marina. Then I prayed at length, smoothly, for Cynthia, for the autistic child and for Norman. I even prayed for the *au pair* girl, severed from her French home and thrust among horrors.

After that I felt better. I decided I could finally face going to bed, but Norman and Cynthia's unkempt room stank of stale cigarette smoke, the stench of cheap scent in the French girl's room repulsed me, and I was too big for the cot in the nursery. I inspected the top floor, built beneath the dormer roof. Here the autistic child had been kept. I found barred windows and a smell of urine, but next door was the room which had belonged to the nurse. Since it proved to be neat and clean I decided I could at least try to sleep there.

Having found some string in the kitchen, I tied my ankle to the bed in order to abort any bout of somnambulism, and wished I could have said the Office properly but there was neither a Prayer Book nor a Bible in the house. Having muttered the General Confession (more shudders), I recited from memory the Twenty-third Psalm, the Magnificat, the Nunc Dimittis and the daily Evensong Collects before I concluded this formal attempt to communicate with God by begging Him to let my father live to be a hundred. Then I shouted to my father in my head: "STOP TORTURING ME—GET WELL," and fell asleep.

Appalling dreams, which I forgot the instant I woke up, hounded me constantly. The third time I awoke I sat bolt upright with a gasp as if I were in acute danger, and realised I had heard sounds downstairs. Norman must have surfaced. Untying the string around my ankle, I left my bedroom to see what was going on.

"Norman, it's Nick!" I called as I reached the hall.

He was being sick in the downstairs cloakroom.

"I'll make you some tea," I said as I passed the open door on my way to the kitchen.

He staggered out just as the kettle boiled. "What the hell are you doing here?"

"James and I thought it might be a good idea if one of us stayed."

"Christ, that's all I need. A bloody clergyman." He reeled back into the drawing-room and collapsed on the sofa. He looked about seventy.

"No milk," I said as I brought him a steaming mug, "but tea tastes good naked."

"Go to hell." He turned his back on me. I sat down and waited. After a while he started to snore but I knew he was shamming. He just wanted to get rid of me so that he could cure his hangover by hitting the bottle again.

"Okay," he said, finally realising that play-acting was getting him nowhere. "Give me the tea."

I handed over the mug. He drank, making a face. "Right," he said. "You can go now. Thanks for playing the nursemaid. Sorry I was a bit abusive."

"I'd prefer to stay in the house for a while, if you don't mind. It's three o'clock in the morning."

"No wonder I feel like a tramp's armpit! Okay, you can stay, but go back to bed, please."

"I don't think that would be helpful at the moment, Norman. Have some more tea."

"Now look here, you sod—"

"Talking of sods," I said, "were Christian and Perry lovers at Winchester?"

Norman boggled, miraculously diverted from all thought of alcohol. "No, of course not! I don't know what went on at your school, but—"

"Absolutely nothing, as far as I could see. The monks at Starwater Abbey had a talent for nipping 'particular friendships' in the bud."

"Well, there you are! The story that public schools are rife with homosexuality is a slander put out by the working classes . . . God, my head feels as if it's about to drop off. Get me some Alka-Seltzer, there's a good chap—top shelf, bathroom cupboard."

I sped upstairs and sped back but I still wasn't quick enough. By the time I returned with a foaming tooth-mug, he had found the bottle of Scotch.

"My God!" he said appalled. "Who's been knocking this back?"

"James. Don't worry, Norman, I'll look after the whisky. You focus on the Alka-Seltzer."

"Oh, go and be a clergyman somewhere else!"

"No, thanks, I'm getting interested in your case. Are you sure Christian never had any homosexual escapades at school?"

"Of course I'm sure! Neither of us did. If Father had ever heard we'd messed around like that it would have killed him."

"Your father means a lot to you all, doesn't he?"

"Of course. That's because he's always been a first-class father—except when he married Dido. God, what a catastrophe that was! Carved up the whole family. Christian never forgave him."

"How old was Christian when your father remarried?"

"Eighteen."

"That's old enough to stage a big rebellion. Did he run around getting drunk, driving too fast and screwing every girl in sight?"

"You're joking—this was 1945, not 1968! We weren't living in the permissive society then, teenagers didn't even exist. But Christian did rebel. In his own way."

"By not going into the Church?"

"Exactly. And I followed suit, even though back in the forties I still believed in God. But Christian never believed in God after Mother died."

"What did he believe in?"

"Nothing."

"People usually believe in something. Nature abhors a vacuum."

"He believed in himself. Getting on, going far, winning every prize in sight . . . God, this Alka-Seltzer tastes foul! Pass me the whisky so that I can give it a decent flavour."

"Are you busy today, Norman? I mean, do you have to be conscious for any reason?"

"What day's today?"

"Saturday."

"Oh my God, I'm supposed to be going down to Surrey to have lunch with the old boy himself! Okay, hide the whisky and make me some more tea."

The crisis was averted. I hid the whisky, made more tea and provided him with an ice-pack. Norman groaned and swore beneath his breath but fought tooth and nail to attain sobriety.

"Lucky you asked that question," he said at last. "I've got to pull myself together for Father. You won't tell anyone, will you, that I passed out at Perry's? If Father ever found out that I occasionally drink a little more than I should—"

"Relax. I'm about to become a priest, not a gossip columnist."

"Thank God." Norman sagged back among the pillows on the sofa. "Sorry I've been so bloody to you," he said. "You're not a bad chap, I know that, but you're just so damned odd. Why are you asking all these questions about Christian?"

"I'm trying to find out if he committed suicide."

Norman's dark eyes widened. Then without a word he clawed his way to his feet and bolted to the cloakroom for a second round of vomiting.

3

I FOUND a jug in the kitchen, and by the time Norman staggered back to the drawing-room I had a substantial supply of cold water waiting for him.

"Thanks," he said. He was becoming steadily nicer as the effects of the alcohol waned. I could now look at him and remember the Norman I had met at Marina's Starbridge party in 1963, the smartly dressed, sociable young barrister who was thriving in the field of academic law. "Why should you think," he said a glass and a half later, "that Christian committed suicide?"

"There's a rumour going around."

Norman began to shudder. In alarm I wondered if I was witnessing the onset of delirium tremens but it was merely an attack of revulsion. A moment later he had controlled himself sufficiently to say: "I know nothing about any rumour, but I've always wondered about the possibility of suicide, and that scared me shitless because if Christian committed suicide it would make a nonsense not only of his life but of mine as well . . . Sorry, I know that's far from lucid, but my brain feels like a wet sponge."

I said cautiously: "I think I see what you mean. You and Christian were ploughing similar furrows. If his life ended in nightmare, then a shadow falls not just across your furrow but across your decision to devote your life to ploughing."

"That's it." He groped for a cigarette but his hand was shaking so badly that he had trouble manipulating the lighter. "But maybe I was just projecting my own unhappiness onto him," he said. "Maybe my suspicion of suicide tells you more about me than about Christian."

"If the two of you were ploughing similar furrows, then your unhappiness could well be a mirror-image of his. Norman, what drove you and Christian to set out with your ploughs in this particular field?"

"Nothing. It just seemed the right and obvious thing to do." He wiped the sweat from his forehead before adding: "We were all brought up to succeed. Work hard, get on, travel far—that was my father's motto, the motto of the self-made man, and there's nothing wrong with that *per se*. It's what the Yanks call the Protestant Work Ethic. But as an idol it can have its problems for worshippers."

"So you're saying that because of the example your father set you when you were growing up—"

"Don't misunderstand. My father did weave the gospel of worldly success with the Gospel of Christ—somehow—but it was really only the former that came over loud and clear. I don't mean he gave us lectures. The message just seemed to ooze out of him as he travelled up the ecclesiastical ladder towards a top job. Yet I'm not saying he was corrupt and I'm certainly not saying he wasn't religious. Father's dedicated to Christianity, one hundred percent sincere. It's just that he has the brains and the toughness and the ambition to succeed in any big corporate structure . . . Do you follow what I'm trying to say?"

"All too clearly."

"Well, when I realised I couldn't go into the Church I cast around for another career which offered status and glamour at the top, and I picked the law. Fine. Father was very pleased, said the law offered wonderful opportunities to get on and travel far, so off I headed into the golden sunset."

"What went wrong?"

"Well, sometimes when I'm drunk I say that Cynthia ruined my career by refusing to leave London—she thinks Oxford and Cambridge are too provincial—but in fact my present lectureship at King's is a good job which could lead me right up the academic ladder. But it won't. Because deep down—*deep* down—I don't want to be a lawyer at all, and now I'm in my late thirties I'm running out of energy trying to hold down a job that no longer interests me."

"What do you want to do instead?"

"Write poetry—and if you laugh I'll hit you."

"I'm not laughing."

"I always wanted to be a poet. I started writing poetry in adolescence but unlike so many other teenage scribblers I kept on into my twenties. Published a few poems in various literary magazines when I was up at Oxford. Father said it was a nice little hobby. Of course I never dared tell him that what I wanted to do was to eke out a living in journalism and create as much spare time as possible for writing poetry. I knew a girl at the time who said I should, but I couldn't. Oh God, I can't forget that girl, I keep thinking about her, she's even started to turn up in my dreams—"

"Were you in love with her?"

"Yes, but she was the wrong class so nothing could come of it. I forgot all about her when I started to chase Cynthia. A duke's daughter! And keen on *me*—the grandson of a Yorkshire draper! What a catch, I thought, how well I'm doing, getting on, travelling far . . . oh, how *bloody* stupid it all seems in retrospect—and occasionally it even seemed stupid at the time, but whenever I had doubts I could always reassure myself by looking across at Christian, ploughing his parallel furrow and luxuriating amidst his wonderful career, wonderful wife, wonderful family. And I thought: if he can achieve happiness that way, I can too."

"So if he did commit suicide—if this happiness was just a sham—"

"It proves to me beyond all doubt that I've wasted my entire life chasing a grand illusion."

"Not your entire life, Norman. Go back to writing poetry."

"Oh, I can't write poetry any more—I can't even bear to read it, can't bear to have any books of poetry in the house. Christ, what a mess!" And he buried his face in his hands.

I realised that now was not the time to push the poetry and remind him of his lost opportunities, so in the hope of diverting him from the subject I bent the conversation back to his brother. "You were fond of Christian, weren't you, Norman?"

"Of course I was. Best brother a man ever had." He somehow kept his

upper lip stiff. Odd how often people talk in clichés when they're profoundly upset. It's as if the clichés become symbols pointing to a reality
which lies beyond verbal expression. "Look," he said when he finally
trusted himself to speak, "I don't know what I said earlier about Christian
at Perry's, but I've got a feeling I wasn't very complimentary. I never am
when I'm drunk. It's because I start to remember then what I make myself
forget when I'm sober: that our friendship went down the drain and it was
all my fault."

"There was a row?" I said, feigning ignorance as I realised his memory
of the tirade at Perry's was minimal.

"Yes, I thought he was meddling in my private life, giving me unsolic-
ited advice about Cynthia and Billy, but in fact the real reason why I got
so angry was because he was underlining that my life was in a mess while
he was still luxuriating happily in his perfect furrow. The underlining
wasn't intentional, but I just couldn't take it. I suppose you could say
jealousy finally won."

"You weren't jealous of him before?"

"Thanks to my mother, no. She brought us up to love and respect each
other—with the result that we became friends with plenty in common. But
in the end—"

"In the end the Dark blotted out the Light."

"Good God, what an extraordinary thing to say! You really are the
oddest chap I've ever—"

"I meant that your inauthentic existence prompted psychological disturbances which manifested themselves in inappropriate emotions. Like jealousy."

"Exactly. Well, as I was saying—"

"You were implying that you were estranged from Christian when he
died."

"That's right. We had the row in '64 and he died a year later. I spent
those last months trying to blot him out of my memory so that I didn't
have to think of him luxuriating in his furrow while I ploughed my way
into the abyss—but I found I couldn't blot him out, I was too deeply
connected to him, and I just couldn't get him out of my mind."

"Was it easier once he was dead?"

"No, harder. I began to feel as if his memory had become a corpse which
was strapped to my back, and that was such an irony because when he died
my first reaction was relief."

"No more being tormented by the demon of jealousy who had converted Christian into a destructive force?"

"*Demon?* Oh, come off it, Nick! This is the twentieth century!"

"Right. You mean that you thought his death would enable you to
make a satisfactory psychological adjustment to the malign aspects of his

memory and neutralise the phobic reaction which was making you un-happy."

"Yes, but I was wrong. Nothing was neutralised and gradually I've become not just unhappy but bloody frightened. I now feel it's exactly as if Christian can't rest until he's driven me too to suicide—oh my God, listen to me, I'm more or less saying I'm being haunted by his ghost, unable to exorcise the demon that's infesting me—"

"Oh no, no, no," I said, very soothing. "What you're really saying—of course—is that you're very troubled about that broken relationship which was unhealed when he died, and that your unassuaged guilt is now so massive that it's inducing all kinds of repulsive and terrifying thoughts."

"Well, I suppose that does make me sound slightly less certifiable, but—"

"You're not certifiable, Norman. You're just a normal man who's going through a traumatic time, but you do need help. You need—"

"If you say 'a psychiatrist' I'll knock you down, and if you say 'a clergyman' I'll knock you out. There's absolutely nothing wrong with me that can't be cured by will-power and a stiff upper lip! All I've got to do is say to myself firmly: 'Christian committed suicide, but I—' "

"No, wait a moment, Norman, hang on. We don't know for a fact that he did commit suicide, and so far I've turned up no convincing reason why he should have killed himself. Does one really commit suicide out of boredom and a spot of marriage trouble?"

"My God, it was a bit more than that, wasn't it?"

"What do you mean?"

"Well, Christian had this utterly surreal private life with three people who were all crazy about him. Surely you realised that!"

"But he had his eternal quadrangle so well organised! No sex with Marina or Perry, everyone knowing their place, no one overstepping the mark—"

"Balls. The truth was that he was in love with Marina but he didn't want to destroy Katie by leaving her. God knows what they all got up to, but you can bet your bottom dollar it wasn't that nice cosy little triangle they all pretended it was!"

"I'm sure he didn't have sex with Marina," said the man who had just relieved her of her virginity.

"God knows what he had with her, but if all three of them failed to end up in one bed I'd be very much surprised. Meanwhile, of course, Christian was taking time out from the two women to sleep with Perry."

I nearly fell off my chair. "But you said just now—"

"I said they never carried on at school, and I'm sure that's correct. But you can't convince me there was nothing between Christian and Perry at the end. My God, he even went on holiday with Perry when Katie was eight months pregnant! What kind of a husband does that?"

"But Norman—"

"This is how I see it: he was bored with Katie. I'd guess she wasn't too interested in sex. He wanted sex with Marina but had the brains to see that a full-scale love affair with her could trigger an explosion which would cripple his career. When these two women had driven him to the end of his tether he turned to Perry out of sheer desperation, but eventually he suffered a reaction from all these huge emotional dramas and decided he hated everyone, including himself. Result: suicide while the balance of the mind was disturbed. Or in other words: his outstanding worldly success ultimately counted for nothing and he ended his life when he realised how meaningless it was."

"But Norman, do you really think Christian would have dabbled in homosexual behaviour once he was grown up? I mean, I can just about accept that he might have messed around with Perry at school, but surely—"

"Where sex is concerned everyone's capable of anything."

"I don't think that's true," I said frankly. "For instance, I know very well I'll never copulate with a sheep."

"Just as well, since you're going to be a clergyman."

"Right. But what I'm trying to say is that the sex-myth you've just trotted out has only arisen because people are capable of experimenting widely. Once you get past the one-off experiments, it seems to me that most people prefer to express themselves sexually in a certain way. For example, I'm drawn only to women and within that gender I prefer brunettes. No matter how many experiments I tried I'm sure I'd always revert eventually to my special preference—and even my experiments would be limited by my personal taste. That's why copulating with a sheep wouldn't just be undesirable; it would be impossible. I'd never even get an erection."

"You sound most formidably normal, but obviously you haven't yet realized that not everyone's quite so normal as you are . . . God, my head feels as if it's about to drop off again—get some more Alka-Seltzer, would you? I threw the last lot up."

I mixed him another potion.

"You're a saint, Nick. Thanks." He drank the Alka-Seltzer, grimaced and slumped back on the pillows. "In my saner moments," he said, "I can convince myself that Christian died by accident, but unfortunately my saner moments are becoming less frequent and now I suspect that what's really slaying me is not knowing for sure how he died. That's why I've been cultivating Perry recently. It occurred to me that if I could get chummy with him he'd eventually open up and reveal what he was hiding—if anything—but I've begun to think I'm wasting my time."

"Why?"

"Two reasons. One: if Perry's telling the truth, he didn't see Christian die and therefore he's just as much in the dark as we are. And two: if Perry's lying, we'll never know because not all the chumminess in the world could coax him to open up. That one's like a steel clam. In the absence of the KGB and the Spanish Inquisition, we haven't a hope of hearing how his best friend committed suicide under his nose."

"If he ever did. Norman, is Perry really a spy?"

"Oh, I think so, but it's just a desk-job. He doesn't go waltzing off to Berlin with a Luger."

After a pause I said: "But presumably he could get a Luger if he wanted one."

"I'd imagine so, yes. In a hush-hush job like that he'd have access to all kinds of esoteric departments . . . God, I feel terrible! How the hell am I going to get to the station? Probably have to crawl to Victoria on all fours."

"No car?"

"Lost my licence for six months. Got nabbed when I was plastered on New Year's Eve."

"I'll drive you down to your father's," I said. "I've no plans for today."

"You'll grow a halo if you're not careful! Many thanks—I suppose I should cry: 'No, no!' but if you really want to be a Christian masochist, what right have I to stop you? And now I think I'm about to pass out again. Can you wake me at ten if I'm still alive?"

I promised to wake him. Then I waited in the kitchen until I heard him snoring and knew it was safe to search the house. This trawl for alcohol produced several bottles hidden in imaginative places; I also uncovered a cache in the dining-room sideboard and retrieved the bottle of whisky I had kidnapped earlier. Working methodically I removed all the bottles to the top-floor landing and hid them in the crawl-space under the roof next to the water-tank. Norman would soon find this hiding-place but at least if he woke before I did and came upstairs to search for sustenance there was a good chance that I'd hear him. I hardly fancied going downstairs for breakfast and finding him dead drunk in the kitchen.

I shut the small door which opened into the crawl-space. Then I returned to the nurse's room, tethered my ankle again and sank at once into unconsciousness.

4

I AWOKE at nine-thirty to find Norman creeping into the crawl-space. I could see him through the open door of my room. "Hey!" I said as soon as my brain had registered what was happening, and scrambled out of bed. Having forgotten my tethered ankle, I nearly fell flat on my face.

Meanwhile Norman, having heard my voice, was edging backwards out of the crawl-space. "You crafty bastard, what have you done with my drink?" I heard him yell in panic as I tore apart the knotted string around my ankle.

"It's behind the water-tank. Norman—"

"Don't worry, I only want the smallest possible nip of vodka. Got to keep myself sober for Father." He began to plough forward again towards the tank.

"Let me retrieve the bottle," I said, "because I know exactly where it is. You go and make us some coffee."

"If you think you can adulterate the bottle with water as soon as I'm out of the way—"

"No, I won't do that, I promise." Since it was obvious that I couldn't stop him drinking, one shot of undiluted vodka seemed a reasonable compromise.

Norman withdrew from the crawl-space and said: "I can't see a bloody thing in there, and I don't think the bottles are behind the tank at all. Christ, if you've poured everything down the drain, I'll—"

"I haven't. I'll retrieve the vodka," I said, acting on the principle that if one repeats something often enough people eventually hear it. "You make the coffee."

Norman hurtled downstairs in a cloud of four-letter words.

Having retrieved the bottle, I found yet another tooth-mug in the main bathroom and poured out a shot that was moderate but not stingy. Then I returned the vodka to the collection behind the water-tank. Downstairs I was astonished to discover that Norman had started to brew the coffee. Having assumed he'd be incapable of performing any task without first refreshing himself with alcohol, I'd given the order about coffee solely to get him out of the way while I dished up the drink.

"Sorry I sounded a trifle irritated," he said after knocking back the shot like a Cossack. "No offence meant."

"None taken." I made some delicious buttered toast out of some stale sliced bread. No marmalade, no milk, no eggs, no cornflakes in the house, but at least I'd caught the bread before it turned mouldy. Norman had also succeeded in making excellent coffee. I began to feel better.

"Can I borrow your razor?" I said to him when the toast had disappeared, but this decision to shave was a mistake. By the time I emerged from the bathroom Norman was reciting bright-eyed from *Henry V:* " 'Once more unto the breach, dear friends, once more . . .' " And I realised the bottle of vodka had been retrieved from the crawl-space.

"Norman, let's talk about how you can get back to writing poetry."

" 'I see you stand like greyhounds in the slips . . .' What's the point of writing poetry? I'll never be Shakespeare."

"No, but you could be Norman Aysgarth," I said, but that made no impression and I knew that once again I had failed to heal someone in distress. Suddenly my impotence seemed intolerable to me. "What you need, Norman," I said, unable to stop myself jettisoning the cool, calm, utterly controlled concern which had won his confidence at three in the morning, "is regeneration. You need to escape from this dead desert you're living in and save yourself by—"

"If you say 'by turning to Jesus' I'll smash your teeth in."

"No, I shan't say that! That's just a coded phrase that no longer has any meaning for you, but I'm going to break that code, I'm going to say instead: 'Salvation equals integration and self-realisation!' Integrate yourself by overcoming this false ego which is strangling you, and line yourself up with your *true* self, the man God created you to be—"

"Oh, belt up, for Christ's sake—"

"No, listen, Norman, *listen!*" I urged, now as fiery as the worst kind of evangelist, the kind guaranteed to make Norman recoil. "You're cut off from God. That's code-language for: you're living an inauthentic existence, you're living at odds with the man you've got the potential to become—"

"Piss off!"

The sad part was that everything I said was true but I was going about the healing in entirely the wrong way. As I was to be taught later, you can't heal the sick by force-feeding them with ideas they're not ready to accept; you can't cure people by the simple imposition of your will. It's the power of the Holy Spirit that heals, not the power of a would-be wonder-worker trying to play God.

"But don't you see?" I cried in exasperation. "You've got to live an authentic existence by being true to your real self! That's the point about Christ—he was uniquely integrated, he wasn't at the mercy of a false ego, he was wholly at one with God's design for him, and that's why we have to 'follow Jesus'—'following Jesus' is code-language signalling that because he's the finest example there's ever been of what it means to be fully human, we have to tread in his footsteps if we want to reach our maximum potential and—"

"Get out of my house!"

Having no choice then but to admit my failure, I withdrew reluctantly to my car.

At eleven o'clock Norman joined me. He was clean-shaven and dressed in fresh clothes, but I knew at once by his careful walk that he had polished off the remaining vodka in the bottle.

"Sorry I yelled at you," he said, "but I just can't stand all that Christ-talk. It always makes me feel so guilty that I disappointed Father by not going into the Church."

"You don't have to go into the Church, Norman. You have to write poetry."

"Oh, shut up, there's a good chap! It's all too late."

"It's never too late."

"It is for me."

Silence.

I drove out of London.

5

IT WAS a clear day, unseasonably warm, with small fleecy clouds bowling along in a bright sky, and as the car plunged down the hill past Putney Vale Cemetery the horizon looked as if it had been scored with a knife. Traffic was heavy. A fine spring Saturday always brings the city-dwellers roaring out of the woodwork. After the traffic jams by Putney Bridge it was a relief to hit the Kingston by-pass and pick up speed in the fast lane.

"By the way," said Norman, breaking a long silence, "for God's sake don't mention Christian while you're under my father's roof. We don't talk about him. Father thinks it's better that way."

I immediately wanted to burst into Dean Aysgarth's house and bawl out Christian's name at the top of my voice. "I see," I said politely.

"It nearly killed the old boy when Christian died. Lost all interest in his work. Took that premature retirement. Tragic. It was lucky he had your father to give him a helping hand."

"Did he?"

"You didn't know?"

"My father doesn't talk about his cases."

"Oh, Father wouldn't like to hear himself described as a 'case'! He just used to drop in on Father Darrow for tea and sympathy."

But since my father had begun to live as a recluse few people were allowed to call on him for either tea or sympathy or anything else. Martin visited, of course, and I was permitted to present friends, but otherwise my father saw no one who lived beyond the walls of the Manor except for a small circle of very old acquaintances, such as Bishop Ashworth, and the occasional desperate case. Dean Aysgarth had never belonged to the circle of very old acquaintances. Therefore he had to be one of the desperate cases. But naturally I said nothing of this to Norman.

"My father had two crises before he retired," Norman was reflecting. "The first one took place in 1963 when he got in a muddle over commissioning that pornographic sculpture for the Cathedral churchyard and the Bishop nearly sent him to the stake. Father was very depressed by that row for some reason—the depression was quite out of proportion to the rather ludicrous fiasco—but your father cheered him up, got him back on an even keel. I think Father had probably just been working too hard. Then the second crisis arose at the time of Christian's death."

"How's he doing at the moment?"

"Amazingly well—he's now a big fund-raiser for Guildford Cathedral and he's muscled his way into the British Council of Churches—he's got some part-time job working out how the Church of England can take over the Methodists. Oh, and he runs the local church, of course, keeps the vicar up to the mark and charms all the flower-ladies. He got himself appointed churchwarden in double-quick time."

"Does he miss Starbridge?"

"Yes, but he's adjusted. In fact he's absolutely fine nowadays so long as no one mentions Christian."

I made no comment. I was too busy wondering how Dean Aysgarth had managed to become one of my father's desperate cases in 1963, but I supposed my father had taken him on in order to do the Bishop a favour. Uncle Charles had probably been at his wits' end after the long-running feud with his dean had culminated in the pornographic sculpture scandal.

"I suppose your father's two crises weren't related?" I said suddenly to Norman. "He didn't take that early retirement in 1965 because he and the Bishop had a final bust-up?"

"Oh, good God, no! The premature retirement was all connected with Christian's death—Father felt he couldn't go on as he was, had to have a complete change. I believe a severe bereavement often takes people that way."

Another silence ensued but as I swung the car off the by-pass towards Leatherhead I said: "If we can go back to Christian for a moment—"

"Watch it—this is becoming an obsession!"

"Well, if I can't talk about him later I might as well talk about him now. Norman, could there have been a third woman in Christian's life?"

"You're thinking of Venetia, aren't you, but that was purely platonic."

"So outside his eternal quadrangle he didn't screw around at all?"

"Why can't you say 'fuck' and be done with it? Why do you have to use a bloody Americanism like 'screw'? I can't stand this tendency among the young to lapse into a mid-Atlantic patois—"

"Come on, Granddad, you're not that old!"

"—and I think you're looking back at the past through the sex-mad lens of 1968. I know everyone runs around nowadays with their flies permanently open, but—"

"No, they don't. They just say they do."

"—but the point to note about Christian was that he wasn't interested in being promiscuous. I'm not saying he was puritanical and I'm not saying he was undersexed; I think he probably did give promiscuity a whirl when he was young—" I noticed that Norman was speculating. Evidently where sex was concerned Christian had never confided in him. "—but once he found out he could have any woman he wanted, promiscuity would soon have seemed unutterably boring. Christian got his kicks out of challenges, not easy victories."

"But supposing that in the last year of his life he had met a big challenge?"

"All right, I concede he would have been capable of pursuing a big challenge to a promiscuous conclusion, but I don't believe he was behaving in that way before he died."

I reminded myself that the brothers had been estranged at the end of Christian's life. Clearly I was seeking information from the wrong person. "Okay, Norman," I said. "Point taken. I accept that outside his quadrangle Christian was as pure as driven snow."

Of course I accepted no such thing.

We drove on towards the Surrey Hills.

6

THE AYSGARTHS —the Dean, Dido and their two children, Elizabeth and Pip—now lived less than thirty miles from London in one of those Surrey villages which have the plastic, picture-book look of an old-fashioned film-set. Beyond the green I saw a fairy-tale church of idyllic proportions, a row of impossibly quaint old-world cottages and a pub called The Rose and Crown, a name which at once conjured up images of an idealised "Merrie Englande"—or perhaps memories of *Our Island Story,* that classic children's history book which sought to prove beyond dispute that England was the greatest country on God's earth and that any child born on such hallowed soil was incomparably blessed.

Into this intoxicatingly nostalgic cloud-cuckoo-land I drove with my alcoholic charge in my Mini-Cooper, a coarse reminder that the date was

1968. I had never before visited this village but I recognised that special Surrey quality of wealth married to a beautiful setting, of a meticulously preserved rural past which in fact resembled no rural past that had ever happened. I admit that wealth is often married to a beautiful setting in the Starbridge diocese; I don't mean to slam Surrey too hard, but my county has the good fortune to be farther from London, with the result that the villages avoid looking like set-pieces preserved by the National Trust as playgrounds for upper-class commuters.

"Here we are," said Norman, having directed me to his father's home which had once been a farmhouse. "Nice, isn't it?"

I grunted an assent, but I knew as soon as I saw the roses around the front door that the place was going to be one big country cliché. No expense would have been spared to achieve this city-dweller's dream; I was about to witness a sumptuous pastiche of The Simple Life.

The door opened and an Old English sheepdog bounded out. That was inevitable. There had to be a shaggy dog. It was as indispensable as the roses growing around the door.

Beyond the dog I saw Norman's half-sister Elizabeth, now no longer a nymphet but a full-blown nymphomaniac of nineteen, and alongside her was a youth whom I belatedly recognised as her brother Pip. He had grown since I had last seen him, and at fourteen was suffering from spots. I automatically thanked God I was no longer an adolescent.

"Wow!" said Nympho-Elizabeth. "It's Nick Darrow!"

"Hi," I said, emerging from the driving-seat and fending off the shaggy dog with my most baleful look.

The shaggy dog fell back and raced around the car to assault Norman.

"Here, Ringo, here!" exclaimed Pip, darting to the rescue as Norman let fly a stream of anti-canine abuse.

"That dog always wants to copulate with visitors," said Elizabeth, swinging her long dark hair over her shoulders and reminding me that she was now a fully-fledged steamy brunette. "Isn't that interesting?"

Before I could reply, the well-remembered phenomenon burst from the house. It looked like a cross between the Duchess of Windsor and Edith Sitwell and it talked in a high-pitched gabble which suggested a record being played at the wrong speed.

"Good God!" said Dido Aysgarth, boggling at me. "It's Nicholas Darrow—and still wearing jeans and a blue shirt, but I suppose you're making hay while the sun shines, my dear, because soon it'll be all black suits and clerical collars, won't it, and you'll have to start being grown up, which will be such a relief for your father, no doubt, poor old man, I hear he's dreadfully ill and has to be nursed night and day but at ninety-five what can one expect and really I daresay it would be a mercy if he was painlessly put out of his misery, though I don't approve of euthanasia myself and all killing of any kind should be regarded with suspicion which is why I do sympathise with vegetarians, although I've got roast beef for lunch today—and of course you *will* stay to lunch, won't you, *what* an act of Christian charity, driving poor Norman all the way down here, the least we can do is shower you with roast beef—do say you'll stay!"

"Thank you, Mrs. Aysgarth," I said politely in a voice of iron, and then as I looked past her I saw that the Dean himself was watching me from the threshold.

7

THE AYSGARTHS had been indefatigably hospitable when they had occupied the Deanery at Starbridge, and I soon realised that their gregarious inclinations remained unchanged. The pseudo-farmhouse was stuffed with an eclectic array of guests, all waiting to guzzle the roast beef, and I had no trouble losing myself in the crowd.

James and his wife Jill were present with their young daughter, Norman's younger son appeared with the French *au pair,* who looked as terrified as if the British were staging a rerun of Waterloo, and Sandy-the-Greek-Freak was circulating with his long-time best friend Boodle, whose real name I never succeeded in discovering. Half a dozen neighbours, all over sixty, were gulping hefty gin-and-tonics and talking in loud voices about how the country was going to the dogs. Mrs. Aysgarth's secretary-companion, Miss Carp, ran around wild-eyed, and from the kitchen came the faint shriek of voices as various minions sweated over the stove. Amidst this heaving racket Norman latched onto a lake of gin-and-French while I found myself clutching a glass of the Pimm's which had been provided for the younger generation. I didn't like Pimm's but I was so dazed by my plunge into this Surrey inferno that I forgot to ask for a Coke. I wondered whether I could tip my drink into the nearest vase of flowers but realised this would be futile as Pip, buzzing around with the Pimm's jug, would ensure my glass was immediately refilled.

"Are weekends in Surrey always like this?" I said when he next passed by.

"Yes, I'm afraid it's not so glamorous as Starbridge, but Mum works awfully hard to make the best of things. That paunchy number over there is a judge, and the lady in purple is—"

"I'm more interested in you, Pip. What's new?"

Social chit-chat followed. Pip was at Winchester but rather wishing he wasn't; life wasn't such fun now that his voice was breaking and his career as a choirboy was over; he wished he could spend more time studying music, but there seemed no point because everyone said music could never be more than a nice little hobby for anyone who wanted to get on and travel far—

"Study music," I said. "Study it morning, noon and night until quavers and dotted minims are coming out of your ears." I noticed that Norman was now on his second lake of gin-and-French but James was having a word with him and I decided to let James cope. When Pip left me I approached the *au pair* girl and found she spoke good English. Norman's younger son tried to crawl up my left leg. James's daughter was busy destroying something. I didn't connect with children at that time: too young. The shaggy dog was everywhere. Couldn't connect with him either. I was introduced to the paunchy judge, who said: "A clergyman, eh? Nice to know one of the younger generation isn't drugged to the eyeballs and wearing flowers." But he gave my jeans a very cool look indeed. Mrs. Judge asked where I had been at school and when I said: "Starwater Abbey," she remarked: "Oh, that's the Anglo-Catholic place, isn't it?" as if it were a zoo. The lady in purple said it had a good scholastic record and had I ever been tempted to go over to Rome, but before I could answer, Nympho-Elizabeth entwined her arm with mine and said Rome was heaven, she'd been there recently on holiday and would I like to see her photos of St. Peter's.

Fortunately at that point Sandy-the-Greek-Freak accosted me and said he was very keen to know what I thought of Vatican II and what a pity it was that the RCs had dropped Latin from the mass. Then Boodle, who I suddenly realised might be playing the same role in Sandy's life that Perry had played in Christian's, began to insist that the RCs should drop the mass altogether. Everyone was getting stoned out of their minds.

"Is there something wrong with that Pimm's?" enquired Pip worried as he arrived back at my side and saw my full glass.

"Have a gin-and-tonic," said Elizabeth, arm still entwined in mine, and managed to make the suggestion sound like an invitation to take my clothes off.

"My God!" I heard Dido breathe to Sandy. "Norman's tight as a tick!"

" '*Quousque tandem abutere,* Norman, *patientia nostra?*' " said Sandy, taking a holiday from Greek as he knocked back the Pimm's.

"Sandy darling, that's not terribly helpful, is it?"

James suddenly appeared at my elbow. "Nick, how much did Norman drink before he got here?"

"Too much."

"Why the hell didn't you stop him?"

"I'd temporarily forgotten my karate lessons."

". . . and of course it would all be quite different under a Conservative government," the lady in purple was declaring.

". . . can't think what the younger generation's coming to . . ."

". . . country's falling apart . . ."

". . . lack of moral fibre . . . failure of the Church . . ."

". . . in my young day . . ."

"My dear Nicholas," said Christian's father, unexpectedly confronting me as I inched around the room towards the door, "I'm so anxious to hear how you're getting on—come to my study after lunch and tell me all your news!"

I thought: he should be saying that to Norman. But Dr. Aysgarth had his back to Norman, now on his third gin-and-French; as far as Norman was concerned, I saw clearly, Dr. Aysgarth just didn't want to know.

"Thank you, sir," I said politely. "That's very kind of you."

8

THE former Dean of Starbridge had been awarded his doctorate in Divinity not by a university but by the Archbishop of Canterbury; it was a "Lambeth" doctorate, an honour conferred on distinguished servants of the Church. Dr. Aysgarth had won this ecclesiastical prize for his work after the war in promoting Anglo-German church fellowship, a cause in which his gift for fund-raising, his managerial skills and his ability to speak fluent German had all been lavishly displayed.

He was a short man, fat and plain, with a ruddy complexion, bright blue eyes and a thin, tough mouth which was periodically transformed into a wide, winning smile. He had interesting hands, square with short fingers, inelegant, incongruous and powerful. They suggested a farmer accustomed to wringing chickens' necks, not a priest who had collected a first in Greats up at Oxford and an honorary doctorate from Lambeth Palace. At first glance there seemed little to connect him with Christian, physically so different from his father, yet I knew from our previous meetings that the resemblance would become marked as the conversation progressed. The similarity lay in the mouth, the smile, the vocal inflections—and most strikingly of all, in the impression of intellectual force behind an effortlessly self-confident social manner.

"Sit down," he said, showing me into his study, which I realised was the one room that his wife had been forbidden to ruin with her extravagant taste. Books lined the walls from floor to ceiling; the desk, worn and chipped, was obviously a friend of many years' standing; the easy-chair nearby needed reupholstering; the faded patterned carpet was interestingly threadbare. "How good of you to bring Norman down from London," he said. "I'm afraid he's taking a pounding at the moment from 'the slings and arrows of outrageous fortune,' but he'll be fine once Cynthia returns from her little rest at Banbury."

"Yes, sir," I said, trying not to boggle at this conversion of extreme marital distress into a slightly off-colour romance with a guaranteed happy ending. I was being meticulous in addressing him as "sir" because as a dyed-in-the-wool Protestant whose biggest difficulty in ecclesiastical life consisted in being nice to Catholics, he might have passed out if I had addressed him as "Father." I suppose I could have addressed him as "Mr. Dean" in memory of his old job, but I agreed with my father, who thought that all Church dignitaries should drop their grand titles on retirement as a gesture of humility. It was true I often referred to Aysgarth by his old title, but that was just a convenient way of distinguishing him from his sons.

"I hear Katie's a bit under the weather too," Dr. Aysgarth was musing as he settled himself behind his desk and I sat down opposite him in the easy-chair. " 'When sorrows come, they come not single spies, but in battalions,' as the Bard says, but I'm sure everything will come right in the end. And talking of charming young women, I hear you've just got engaged to Rosalind Maitland. Congratulations! I knew her grandfather, Colonel Maitland, when he was a churchwarden at Starrington Magna and I was the Archdeacon of Starbridge back in the 1940s. How pleased your father must be by your engagement!"

"Yes, he is. Sir, please could you explain to your wife that he's eighty-seven, not ninety-five, and that he doesn't need nursing at all?"

Dr. Aysgarth laughed and said: "I'm afraid Dido favours an Aramaic style of speech—the exaggeration is supposed to underline what she believes to be the truth, and since she'd heard that your father's been a little unwell lately—"

"He's okay. Still living on his own and fending for himself."

"I'm delighted to hear it. And what a comfort you must be to him in his old age! My sons are a comfort to me too," said Dr. Aysgarth serenely, giving me his most charming smile. "They're all doing wonderfully well and so are my daughters. I confess I was fractionally worried when Elizabeth insisted on going up to Oxford, but now I know that was the right decision. You could never call Elizabeth a blue-stocking, could you?"

"Never, sir."

"Says she wants to be a novelist, which is fine because that's the kind of thing women can do in their spare time after they're married. Some women, of course, are cut out for a career and I wouldn't want to deprive them of it—indeed with my liberal principles, I'd demand that they should be employed on equal terms with men—but Elizabeth's obviously destined for marriage and motherhood."

I thought Elizabeth was obviously destined for a number of things, none of which had any connection with marriage and motherhood, but of course

I kept my mouth shut. I was becoming mesmerised by the conversation's increasing lack of anything that resembled reality.

"You must have a talk with her before you go," Dr. Aysgarth was saying. "You'll find her very entertaining—oh, and do have a word with Pip! I've suggested to him that he should go into the Church and aim at becoming the precentor of a great cathedral. That would seem the most satisfactory way for him to combine his interest in music with a first-class career."

Instantly I was overwhelmed by the urge to wave a bomb over cloud-cuckoo-land. "Maybe he should drop out and form a rock group," I said in my most deadpan voice. "There's plenty of scope nowadays in the music business for a young guy who wants to get on and travel far."

Dr. Aysgarth looked startled but made a quick recovery. "Oh, I'm all for being trendy!" he exclaimed. "But I'd still prefer Pip to go into the Church."

By this time I was quite unable to rein myself in. "What about God?" I said flatly.

"God?" said Dr. Aysgarth.

"Yeah, God," I said, very cool, very hip, very much the anarchic ordinand of the Swinging Sixties. "What do you think He'd prefer?"

"My dear Nicholas!"

"Don't you think God would prefer Pip to become the man God's designed him to be instead of the man you want him to become? Because isn't it true that until we become the people God's designed us to be, each one of us doing our own thing, we can't begin to serve Him as we should?"

There was a slight pause before Dr. Aysgarth said in his smoothest voice: "Quite. And naturally my dearest wish is for Pip to do whatever God calls him to do. But I think when you talk so blithely of 'doing our own thing' you should take care to distinguish between a God-given call and mere self-centred behaviour."

"Right. And we're all required to put our self-centred behaviour aside, aren't we? Even you."

Dr. Aysgarth's bright blue eyes widened. His eyebrows shot up. "Tell me," he said, "do you make a habit of being so very excessively rude?"

"No, and I apologise. But I've concluded that being rude is the only way to get through to you, Dr. Aysgarth, the only way to grab your attention."

"And why, may I ask, are you going to such outrageous lengths to grab my attention?"

"I want to talk about Christian," I said, finally detonating the H-bomb.

SILENCE.

The old man opposite me was expressionless. Not a muscle moved around his thin mouth. His brutal hands lay clenched upon the blotter.

"He's haunting Katie," I said. "He's haunting Norman. In fact I've begun to suspect he's haunting everyone who was close to him, and I believe I'm being called in to perform the necessary exorcism."

I'd gone too far. I'd not only reached Dr. Aysgarth but offered him the opportunity to embark on a verbal disembowelment. A cool, hip young ordinand should steer clear of old-fashioned picture-language which makes him sound like an actor in an occult B-movie.

"Oh, so you fancy yourself as an exorcist!" said Dr. Aysgarth, who as a liberal churchman had probably long ago decided that the Devil was the figment of a fevered mystical imagination. "You think you have some special power, no doubt, which enables you to play the wonder-worker, some special knowledge which humbler people don't possess, some mystical gift which makes you one of a spiritual élite. My dear Nicholas, you're wasting your time in the Christian Church where all men are equal in the sight of God! You should emigrate to California and found a cult based on the Gnostic heresy!"

"Sir, I was only speaking metaphorically—"

"You were speaking arrogantly—as arrogantly as your father used to speak when he erupted from his monastery in 1940 and created havoc in my archdeaconry with a scandalous ministry of healing!"

This was difficult ground. Even my father himself conceded that his attempt at a ministry of healing had been an embarrassing failure. I decided I had to be very meek. "I'm extremely sorry, sir; I didn't mean to give such offence."

"Oh yes, you did! You admitted a moment ago that you were being deliberately offensive in order to gain my attention!"

Too late I realised I was dealing with a formidable fighter who excelled in the punch-up, slash-down school of debate. "I know I must have appeared a trifle too frank, sir, but—"

"You were damned rude—why are you now hiding like a coward behind the word 'frank'? Do you think wearing jeans and being under thirty miraculously excludes you from a charge of lily-livered hypocrisy? Now listen to me, young man, and I'll show you how to call a spade a spade! You leave my family alone with their grief. I'll not stand for any half-baked interference, and if I hear you've been bounding around and upsetting everyone in sight, I'm going straight to your bishop to complain. Do I make myself entirely clear?"

"Yes, sir."

We sat in silence while he glared at me. The rage and pain streaming from him lacerated my psyche, and I knew then that he was haunted too.

Finally in an attempt to make peace with him I said: "I only want to be a good Christian, serving God in the Church."

"Then may I suggest you learn how to behave? You won't get far in the Church, you know, if you talk like a lout and act like a charlatan!"

Now it was he who had gone too far. Once again I was quite unable to rein myself in and once again I found myself reaching for an H-bomb. "This may amaze you, Dr. Aysgarth," I said, "but not all ordinands want to bust a gut pursuing worldly success in the Church, and maybe if Jesus had been born in 1942 as I was he wouldn't even have wanted to bust a gut to be an ordinand. Why are you reacting so violently when all I did was mention Christian's name and express a wish to help the people who are still suffering as the result of his death?"

"How dare you persist in repeatedly flinging Christian's name in my face!" he shouted. "I won't talk about him, do you hear? I absolutely and utterly refuse!"

"Why? What exactly are you afraid of here, Dr. Aysgarth?"

"AFRAID?" By this time he was scarlet with rage. "I'm not afraid of anything!"

"Then you should be. Your family's falling apart as the result of Christian's death."

He rose in his chair and for one moment I thought he was going to lunge across the desk and hit me. But he restrained himself. All he said in a shaking voice was: "Leave this room at once."

"Did it ever cross your mind that Christian might have committed suicide?"

My second H-bomb exploded. Dr. Aysgarth hurtled round his desk, flung wide the door so violently that it slammed against the wall, and yelled at the top of his voice: "OUT!"

Poor old bastard. The pain emanating from him was so acute that I could no longer sustain my dislike. Instead I found I wanted to help him—but once again, I didn't know how.

Deeply concerned, I withdrew from the room.

SANDY-THE-GREEK-FREAK waylaid me in the hall. "Come and play croquet."

"No, thanks. How's Norman?"

"Dire. Out cold on Pip's bed. Why do you always try to brush me off, Nick?"

"Do I?"

"Yes, you do. Look, come up to my room for a moment—there's something I want to ask you."

"Has it got anything to do with Latin or Greek?"

"No, nothing, I promise."

"Okay, let's go. Where's Boodle?"

"Walking off lunch with Pip and the dog."

We retired to the room which Sandy inhabited on his visits home. It was neat and impersonal. I guessed all his most cherished possessions were up at Oxford, where he taught Greek and worked on his doctoral thesis.

Sandy was short, like his father, and had thick brown hair, curly at the back. Unlike his father, he was thin and wiry. Dr. Aysgarth's remarkable blue eyes looked out of place in Sandy's unremarkable face.

"It's about girls," he said as I dumped myself on the window-seat.

This was certainly unexpected. "Oh?"

"Yes, I hear you're successful with them, one of Marina Markhampton's set and so on. And Elizabeth says you've got sex-appeal."

"Elizabeth would think anything in trousers had sex-appeal."

"No, she doesn't think I've got any, and she's right—I haven't. It's all rather awkward. I do try to get a girlfriend but I can't seem to keep them interested and I'm getting to the stage where I'm really worried."

I found myself compelled to ask: "You can't talk to your father about this?"

"Oh no, no, no!" Sandy looked horrified. "He's always saying how pleased he is that I'm doing so well with no problems whatsoever. But I'm sure you're the ideal person to consult, not just because you can give me some useful tips but because you're almost a clergyman and I can rely on you to keep this conversation confidential."

"Sure. But are your brothers no use to you here either, Sandy?"

"Oh, I never talk to them, I'm so much younger—and anyway, men don't normally talk about this sort of problem to one another, do they? It seems to be the unspoken rule that either you don't discuss women at all or else you give the impression that they all fall down like ninepins as soon as you cross their path. It's not the done thing to be anything but successful, is it?"

"Screw the done thing. Ever tried picking up a girl at Burgy's?"

Sandy looked at me as if I were talking Swahili. "Burgy's?"

"Burgy-Bliss, the hamburger chain. Find a working-class girl there who'll automatically think you're rich and fascinating as soon as she hears your accent."

"But what do I say?"

"You say: 'Is this seat taken?' and when she says no, you sit down at her table."

"But what do I say next?"

"Anything so long as it's not intellectual."

"My God, how difficult life is! But I've got to get a girlfriend somehow or people will think I'm not normal, and if Father thought I wasn't normal it would kill him."

"Screw normality. What gets me," I said, "is that all you Aysgarths behave as if your father's a fragile little flower who would wilt at the first whisper of unwelcome news, yet he's quite obviously as tough as a tank."

"He can give the impression of being tough, I agree, but underneath he's so sensitive, so kind, so good, so idealistic, so—"

"Yes, it's a lethal mixture, isn't it? You love him for all those good qualities, but once he's tough he's terrifying. So you're caught in this emotional bind, slaving away to keep him exuding sweetness and light."

"Oh no, you've got that quite wrong! How could we be afraid of him when he's never laid a finger on any of us?"

"That makes things worse. At least if he bashed you about a bit you could hate him occasionally, vent your true feelings, open the emotional sluice-gates—"

"But how could we ever hate him? He's so good, so kind, so sensitive, so—"

"Oh yeah? But he carved up his entire family when he married Dido, didn't he? In fact I heard someone say Christian never forgave him."

"Oh, I expect he did in the end."

"You don't know for sure?"

"Why should I? I hardly knew him, he was nearly fourteen years my senior, we were strangers. I only ever received one letter from him. After I got my first in Greats he wrote: 'Dear Sandy, How gratifying to know that one day, perhaps, you may be as clever as CHRISTIAN.' That was weird, wasn't it? I thought he was joking but I wasn't sure—one could never be sure what Christian was really thinking. He talked to Norman a bit, I believe, but not to James—James isn't very bright. And not to Primrose— she was just a girl. And I was just 'the baby,' even when I was grown up.

When I was in my teens I tried to make friends with him by chatting away in Greek, and he liked that but it didn't actually get me very far. For some reason I'm not good at communicating with people. Strange, isn't it?"

"No, inevitable. No one in your family really communicates at all." I stood up, casting around in my mind for a way to end the conversation kindly. "I think it was great you had those chats in Greek with Christian, Sandy," I said. "It suggests you've got the potential to be a first-class communicator, original and imaginative."

"You think so?" Sandy brightened.

"Sure, all you need is practice," I said, but in fact I couldn't see him getting anywhere at Burgy's. Perhaps I should have advised him to chat up blue-stockings in Oxford. Or perhaps . . . "Sandy, be honest," I said. "Are you seriously interested in girls? I mean, do you lie awake fantasising about them? Do you have an erection every time you pass a skimpy mini-skirt in the street? Do you ever masturbate and wonder if you're turning into a sex-maniac?"

"Oh yes!" he said, meaning: oh no.

"Maybe you're not meant to be married," I said. "Maybe you're called to celibacy, called to dedicate your life to scholarship without the distraction of female companionship."

"But how can I be called to celibacy?" said Sandy baffled. "This is 1968!"

"God doesn't care about time, Sandy. He's outside it. As far as He's concerned a call to celibacy is a call to celibacy whether it's 1968, 968 or 19,068."

"But how could I explain that to Father?"

I gave up. "It's a real problem," I said, exuding sympathy, and finally managed to escape.

II

AS I padded downstairs I became aware that the house was quiet. The Surrey antiques had lurched away to their tarted-up Georgian gems to dream of a Conservative Government; the sheepdog was still out being walked; the minions were apparently speechless with exhaustion in the kitchen—or perhaps the silence in that section of the house meant that they too had lurched away; as I paused in the hall I pictured them watching the Saturday afternoon sport on television in their Merrie-Englande-style council houses.

My one dread at that moment was that I would be collared by Nympho-Elizabeth. My weakness for steamy brunettes coupled with my current feebleness in controlling my sex-life meant that I could all too easily visualise her shedding her knickers in the shrubbery while I busted the zip on my jeans. But such a lapse would inevitably produce a catastrophe.

Elizabeth would never keep her mouth shut; she was the kind of girl born to create stormy scenes, and once Dr. Aysgarth discovered I'd messed around with his daughter he'd tip off Uncle Charles, who would refuse to ordain me.

I was still shuddering as I envisaged this nightmare, when I heard Elizabeth calling my name. Instantly I opened the nearest door and hid in the room beyond. It happened to be Dr. Aysgarth's study, but fortunately by this time Dr. Aysgarth himself was somewhere else. The room was empty. Nervously I prowled up and down. Again Elizabeth called my name, but when her footsteps crossed the hall without pausing I realised that the study was probably the one room which guests never entered without an invitation.

Heaving a sigh of relief I began to examine the books which lined the walls. Reams of Church history. The usual classic biographies, such as George Bell on Randall Davidson and F. A. Iremonger on William Temple. Hensley Henson's letters. The peculiarly boring memoirs of that most unboring bishop of Starbridge in the 1930s, Dr. Adam Alexander Jardine. The fragment of autobiography written by Charles Raven, the famous Regius Professor of Divinity at Cambridge. And a load of other books by Raven. Raven, Raven, Raven . . . And F. R. Barry. We were deep, deep in the country occupied by the old-fashioned Liberal Protestants, all glowing ideals and boundless optimism in a world from which evil and suffering had been mysteriously eliminated. And wait for it— yes, here we went, I might have guessed—Bishop John Robinson's *Honest to God,* very dog-eared, plus Dennis Nineham's *Saint Mark* and a whole slew of supremely clever but starkly unimaginative offerings from radical theologians. The trouble with the radicals, I always thought, was that they were so painfully restricted by their brilliant intellects. What could it be like to be born not only with no imagination but with no capacity for psychic insight? Worse than being a horse in blinkers. Tragic. I felt sorry for them.

It was strange to see this evidence that the formidable Dr. Aysgarth with his chicken-killer's hands was addicted to theology which was either sentimental, like that of the Liberal Protestants, or unconnected with any transcendent reality, like that of the Radicals. Or was it so strange? Sentimental and unconnected with reality. That exactly summed up the tenor of his conversation before I had started dropping my verbal H-bombs. But yes, it was still strange because he looked too tough to be sentimental and too down-to-earth to be adrift from reality. It was as if he were two men in one—which meant three people: person A, person B and person AB which produced the Dr. Aysgarth personality, the personality which had tied his children up in such convoluted emotional knots.

I was still pondering with deep interest on my host's complex psyche when the door of the room opened and Dido zipped in.

"Ah, there you are, Nicholas, I knew you must be hiding in the one place where nobody would dream of looking for you"—she closed the door with a bang—"and so naturally I came straight here because I've just spoken to Stephen and it's quite obvious that you need someone to talk to you candidly—and since I've always prided myself on my candour, I've elected myself to do the talking. Now—"

Stephen was Dr. Aysgarth. His real name was Neville but she had renamed him. She was that kind of woman, autocratic and anarchic, and suddenly I found myself wondering why that very masculine man, who had such set ideas about women, should have wound up with an eccentric who was obviously far beyond playing a conventional feminine role. Then in a moment of revelation I saw that this marriage was no mere intriguing little mystery but a profound enigma which had proved a malign force in Christian's life. How had it happened? What mysterious psychological drives had possessed Dr. Aysgarth and produced this extraordinary result? Why had he rebounded from the memory of his perfect first wife, grabbed this severely imperfect replacement and, as Norman had put it, carved up his whole family? I had no answers to these questions, of course. I could only think what a mystery life was, how little we can understand anyone, and how only God can know the whole truth of any given situation. All we have are partial glimpses of the truth, little fragments of a vast, multi-sided reality.

"—are you listening to me, Nicholas? You're looking very dreamy! You don't take drugs, do you?"

"Certainly not!" That was clever of her. She had stung me into paying attention, and I realised then that this woman communicated—even if it was only by putting people's backs up. "What is it you want to say, Mrs. Aysgarth?"

"What's all this about Christian committing suicide?"

"I'd heard a rumour—"

"Well, it's absolute balderdash and you should never have repeated it, least of all to my husband. Christian's death devastated Stephen, utterly devastated him, he adored that boy, worshipped him, he was so proud of Christian's brilliant academic success and his dazzling marriage—and personally I've always liked Katie better than Cynthia who struck me right from the start as dreadfully vain, and I'm not surprised she had a dotty child because everyone knows there's insanity in that family, that's the hazard of marrying into the aristocracy, you simply never know what congenital horror's going to surface next. And talking of dottiness—"

"I thought no one knew what causes autism."

"My dear, that's not autism, that's congenital syphilis. And as I was saying, talking of dottiness, what's all this about Katie and Norman being haunted and you being called in to exorcise them?"

"Well—"

"I've never heard such rubbish in my life! Katie's nerves are bad and Norman drinks like a fish, but they don't need an ordinand waltzing around mouthing nonsense, they need professional medical help!"

This impressed me. Here at last, apparently, was someone with a good grasp of reality.

"I agree with you," I said, "and I'm only trying to find out more about Christian's death because I want to help them in a conventional clerical way. When I used the word 'exorcism' to your husband, I didn't mean to imply—"

"Well, Christian didn't commit suicide. You don't kill yourself when you're being worshipped by everyone in sight. You get restless enough to look for new thrills, perhaps, but death isn't a thrill, it's a bore."

"Where did he look for new thrills?"

"Oh, in the last months of his life he was always running away to sea with Perry Palmer. Sometimes I think Englishmen never grow up. 'Let him go, my dear!' I said to Katie. 'If you want to keep him, don't cling—let him come and go as he pleases!' Men prefer women who don't put them under emotional pressure—which is why Christian liked Marina. Being a lesbian, she didn't wear him out with emotional demands, and I must say that if I were Charles Ashworth, which thank God I'm not, I'd be very worried about my son marrying Marina Markhampton, although God knows Michael's such a rake his father can probably only heave a sigh of relief that he's trying to be respectable at last."

"What makes you think Marina's a lesbian, Mrs. Aysgarth?"

"Oh my dear! The real action in that triangle was always between Marina and Katie. Everything else was just a fairy-tale. No wonder Christian wanted to go off with Perry all the time! No action there, of course. Perry's a eunuch."

"Oh yes? How do you know?"

"My dear, he's never been sexually interested in anything, that's why Christian found him so restful. Oh, I understood all about Christian and Perry! Christian was born normal but unfortunately he fell deeply in love with his mother—so clever of Freud to realise that this always has a disastrous effect on young men!—so he turned out to be rather peculiar with women and only comfortable with eunuchs. All that's been patently obvious to me for years, but I could never say so because poor Grace's name is never mentioned in this family, too upsetting for everyone, so sad her dying like that, although actually she was the most unsuitable wife for an ambitious clergyman, she came from Manchester and had no clothes. Well, as I was saying—"

"Mrs. Aysgarth, if you had to sum up Christian in one sentence, what would you say?"

"He was a pain in the neck," said his stepmother.

VII

"There is, as a result of the loss of touch with God, a deep frustration and fear, often subconscious and always divisive in its effects upon man's soul."

MICHAEL RAMSEY
Archbishop of Canterbury, 1961–1974
CANTERBURY ESSAYS AND ADDRESSES

I

"IT WAS an open secret," said Dido, "that Christian and I didn't get on, but of course we always kept up appearances so as not to upset my husband. Darling Stephen, being the most romantic idealist who ever lived, always wants to believe everything in the garden's lovely, and since he worshipped Christian and adored me he naturally longed for us to be devoted to each other. I'm sure he knew we weren't; he's no fool, but the point is he never saw any unpleasantness which would have upset him. Being a hard-bitten realist and famed for my candour, I'm always ironing out any little difficulty which Stephen would find upsetting, but I must say I was at my wits' end to keep Christian well-ironed because—poor boy!—he was so dreadfully neurotic."

"He was?"

"My dear, what else can one expect when a man's fallen irrevocably in love with his mother? The truth was he simply couldn't bear being touched by any woman but her—at least, not in his younger days, the days before he gritted his teeth, dragged himself to the altar and married Katie in order to disguise how deeply peculiar he was."

"When you say 'touched,' do you mean—"

"Embraced with genuine but asexual affection by a member of the opposite sex. I first found out about this phobia of his—no, let's be quite frank and say his really *kinky* maladjustment—in 1948 when he was twenty-one. I'd been trying for ages to have another baby—my first son was stillborn in 1946—and suddenly in 1948 I succeeded in getting pregnant, thank God, so when I whirled home from my doctor in Harley Street with the marvellous news that Elizabeth was on the way I was feeling utterly euphoric and bursting with *joie de vivre*. 'Christian darling!' I screamed when I opened the front door and saw him in the hall—he was down from Oxford for the Long Vacation—'Isn't life simply too divine? I'm having another baby!' And I threw my arms around him and gave him an ecstatic hug—and my dear! He looked like a woman who'd been sexually assaulted—dead white he was, dead white and sweating, and he was shaking from head to toe. 'You bloody bitch, keep your filthy hands off me!' he snarled and bolted up to his room. Obviously he thought I'd made the most obscene pass at him."

I was able to say with genuine sympathy: "How very unpleasant for you."

"It was worse than that, Nicholas, it was extremely hurtful, but at least I knew then he was so deeply neurotic that all I could do was pray for him every Sunday in church. 'Dear God,' I used to pray, 'please make Christian normal because darling Stephen will be so upset if he's not.' That's why I was so relieved when Christian finally nerved himself to marry Katie—a replica of his mother she was, of course, even though she came from Hampshire and had plenty of clothes—and I was even more relieved that the marriage produced three children, but if you ask me he was absolutely ruined by that doting mother of his, absolutely spoilt rotten, and darling Stephen couldn't redress the balance because he's soft as butter with all his children, he can't help himself, it's his noble nature, but if anyone needed a walloping it was Christian. He was arrogant, snooty, snobbish, vain and self-centred—and no doubt you're shocked that I should speak ill of the dead, but I pride myself on my candour and I've never had any time for that dreary old cliché *nil nisi bonum* thingummyjig. Well, there you are, my dear, that's Christian for you, and don't bother to listen to what anyone else says because it'll all be a fantasy. Will you stay to tea?"

"Well, I—"

"Do stay! Elizabeth's longing to show you her photos of Rome!"

That was what I was afraid of. "Well, actually—"

The door opened without warning and Dr. Aysgarth returned to his study.

2

"*STEPHEN* darling!" exclaimed Dido. "I've just explained Christian to Nicholas and he quite understands everything now, so you don't have to give his silly remarks a second thought—oh, and he's staying to tea because he wants to see Elizabeth's photos of St. Peter's, always so interesting for Anglo-Catholics, although I don't blame them in the least for preferring the Archbishop of Canterbury to the Pope, particularly since the Romans have now admitted we were right to hold services in the vernacular. Come along, Nicholas, we'll go and find Elizabeth. I"—the doorbell rang—"oh bother, that'll be the Browne-Bentleys arriving—excuse me for a moment—" And she flew away into the hall.

As the door banged shut Dr. Aysgarth and I eyed each other. I had just opened my mouth to attempt yet another apology when he said abruptly: "Sit down," and returned to the chair behind his desk.

Closing my mouth again I instantly did as I was told.

"I owe it to your father," he said, "to treat you with a little more patience than I displayed earlier. Back in the 1940s when I was trying to survive your father's invasion of my archdeaconry I lost count of the number of times I wanted to punch him on the nose, but I'll say this for him: in the 1960s no one could have been kinder during a couple of occasions when life became temporarily a little awkward for me. He's mentioned to you, I daresay, that I've been accustomed in the recent past to drop in on him for a little tea and sympathy now and then?"

"No, sir."

"No? Ah well, on second thoughts, why should he? There's nothing remarkable about an old acquaintance calling to pay his respects—an old acquaintance who can now say with truth that he has the greatest possible respect for your father as a clergyman. So bearing all that in mind"—he heaved a sigh as if this confession had been an exhausting exercise—"why don't we try to replay that previous scene in a way that does justice to us both? I'm sure you're fundamentally a good boy and I've no doubt you mean well."

Then I saw beyond the successful corporate manager to the priest who had the humility to say, no matter how obliquely, that he had been in the wrong and was sorry. Obviously I had been too quick to write him off with contempt as a worldly ecclesiastical careerist. I should have been more willing to remember Norman's insistence that his father was devout.

"It's very kind of you to give me a second chance, sir," I said. "I'm extremely sorry I upset you so much earlier, and naturally I shan't attempt to press you further about the subject of our previous conversation."

He smiled at me. "Congratulations!" he said. "That was admirably put—how well we're both behaving! Perhaps we should now pause to pat each other on the back!"

I laughed. It came as a relief to discover he had a sense of humour. I could see now he wasn't such a bad old boy after all.

"However," he said—and as soon as he spoke that qualifying word I sensed I was being not innocently befriended but subtly manipulated, "much as I would like to accept your offer to drop the subject of Christian, I now find I'm quite unable to do so. That's because my wife, by her own admission, has been giving you the benefit of her candour. Dido's candour," said Dr. Aysgarth, "is a most remarkable quality, but unfortunately her Aramaic style of speech can be a trifle misleading; all the nuances and subtleties tend to be buried beneath a tidal wave of hyperbole, and I really do feel that I can't let you leave this house until I've clarified her candour by giving you the whole truth, pure and simple. Of course Oscar Wilde said the truth was never pure and rarely simple," said Dr. Aysgarth wittily, now sparkling away like a well-cut diamond, "but let me at least strive to achieve a modest accuracy devoid of exaggeration."

"That's very good of you, sir," I said, and thought: if he's staging this type of high-quality performance he must be damned worried about what she said to me.

"Well, before I offer myself as a candidate for sainthood," said Dr. Aysgarth, still coruscating busily, "I wonder if I might ask you a few questions. First of all, why did you suddenly feel called to alleviate the misery resulting from Christian's death?"

"I had an encounter with Katie recently and I was appalled enough to try to figure out what I could do to help."

"Was it she who thought Christian had committed suicide?"

"I'm sorry, sir, but the conversations I've had with various people on this subject have all been confidential."

"Naturally I don't expect you to betray a confidence. And anyway, regardless of where the rumour came from I'm sure you wanted to help Katie by scotching it."

"Yes, sir. I decided to make a few enquiries in an attempt to establish he had a good reason for staying alive."

"And had he?"

"All I can say is that so far I've turned up no convincing motive for suicide. I've merely come across stories about him behaving oddly in the months before he died."

"I suppose you're referring to his decision to go on holiday with Perry when Katie was eight months pregnant—and his increasing obsession with sailing. I think there's no doubt he wasn't quite himself in those last months, but I must absolutely insist that he was in no way odd in the sense of neurotic. Dido, I'm afraid, will have declared that he was a bundle of the most extraordinary neuroses—how I wish garbled Freudian theory hadn't become so popular on the cocktail circuit!—but the reason she insists on believing he was neurotic is because she hates the idea that anyone could dislike her quite so much as he did. It's easier, as I'm sure you understand, for her simply to write him off as crazy."

Dr. Aysgarth paused, and suddenly I became aware of his psyche, blunt and dark but streaked with sharp bands of light, two contrasting strands of essence integrated miraculously but uneasily in that highly complex personality. I then had a strong impression of the light flaring up on all the bands, and at once it seemed to me that against all the odds he genuinely wanted to be truthful. The stylish manner, the subtle manipulative technique, the shady hallmarks of the sophisticated worldly fixer—all were set aside by a brief, tough act of will, and with surprise I found myself in the presence of a devout priest, emotionally buttoned up but passionately sincere, who was determined to live up to his ideals by being honest. At that point I realised that all three Aysgarths had been paraded before me that afternoon: Aysgarth Model A, the cosy idealist who preferred to look away from reality, had been succeeded by Aysgarth Model B, the worldly thug, who had in turn been contained and conquered by Aysgarth Model AB, who had somehow learnt how to hold the light and the dark side of his personality in a creative tension which produced a devout Christian. I thought how fascinated my father must have been by the spiritual challenges thrown up by this peculiar psyche. I could see now that the Bishop would hardly have needed to ask my father to take on Aysgarth as a desperate case in 1963; my father would have been only too willing to leap into the spiritual boxing-ring and rescue Aysgarth as he lay out for the count on the floor.

"Very well," the resurrected Aysgarth was saying firmly in 1968, "let's set Dido's biased opinion aside and have a go at delivering this truth that ought to be so pure and simple. Christian—" But he found he could no longer remain seated. Standing up he began to pace around the room.

"Christian," said Dr. Aysgarth, "was as sane and well-balanced as any normal person, but he wasn't an unimaginative type impervious to mental anguish. He was sensitive, romantic, an idealist. If he had been less sensitive, less romantic and less of an idealist, he would have recovered from the death of his mother, but he couldn't cope with that first brush with a harsh reality. I should have been able to talk to him, but I couldn't—I couldn't talk about the tragedy," said Dr. Aysgarth, speaking much more rapidly, "I couldn't talk about it, it was impossible for me. My failure, of course. My mistake. You're not a parent yourself yet, but let me tell you that even the most loving parents make hellish mistakes. One of the worst things for me about Christian's death is that I have no chance now to say to him: 'I'm sorry. I know I was at fault. Forgive me.' "

Pausing by the window, he stared out into the garden and I could no longer see his face.

"I don't believe he committed suicide," he said after another pause. "Of course I've faced the possibility that I don't dare believe it—I've faced the fact that I could be shying away from all the agony such a tragedy would involve. But once I try to consider the facts dispassionately I always wind up thinking: he wasn't the suicidal type. Something was wrong, perhaps even very wrong, but he was so like me, you see, and although I've gone through some horrifically difficult times in my life I've never once considered killing myself to escape from them."

"I accept that this is your considered, rational verdict, sir," I said, "but what was your initial, instinctive reaction when you heard the news?" I hardly dared to interrupt but I felt compelled to take every advantage of his desire to be truthful.

"Ah, now this is very odd," said Dr. Aysgarth, not in the least put out by the question and even becoming more confidential. "This'll surprise you. When I heard the news I thought: what a merciful release!"

"As if he'd been terminally ill?"

"Exactly. And I was so troubled by that reaction that I knew I had to talk it over with your father. How clearly I remember that day when I drove over to Starrington to see him . . . Dear old Jon, there he was, pottering around with that cat. Odd for a heterosexual male to keep a cat, I've always thought, and of course if he'd lived a few centuries ago they'd have called the cat his familiar and burnt the two of them at the stake. Strange how Jon's turned into the archetypal figure of the wise old man living in solitude! When I remember how he crashed around in 1940 . . . but no, I'm digressing. I think I must be playing for time while I nerve myself to deliver the truth—which, of course, is quite definitely neither pure nor simple.

"When I told your father I'd reacted to the death as if Christian had been terminally ill, he said: 'Perhaps subconsciously you'd felt for some time that he was very sick.' And then I saw it all.

"This is the truth, Nicholas; this is the truth your father and I worked out together: Christian *was* sick. It was a spiritual sickness. It arose because he'd turned away from God after his mother died and he'd never filled the vacuum satisfactorily. Of course there are many admirable people in this world who don't believe in God and yet lead moral, meaningful lives, but they've succeeded in filling the spiritual vacuum with sound humanist principles. For a long time I assumed Christian had done that, but in the end I began to wonder and then I started to worry, because if there's nothing substantial filling the vacuum . . . Well, as a good Liberal Protestant Modernist—dear me, how old-fashioned that sounds nowadays!—I've never believed in the Devil, but I do recognise that there are dark forces at work in the human mind, and I know they're only too adept at colonising a spiritual void.

"I said to your father that this void, this vacuum in Christian's soul, was all my fault because I'd failed to help him when his mother died—with the result that he'd turned his back on God. I also told your father that the real tragedy was not just that a believer had wound up an atheist; it was that Christian had rejected God's call to him to be a clergyman. I feel sure that if his mother had lived, Christian would have gone into the

Church. He was so like me, you see, and . . . no, it's not just wishful thinking. He was called to be a clergyman, I know he was, but he set his face against the call."

Dr. Aysgarth returned to the window again to study the view of the garden. Then he said: "Your father was so kind to me, so compassionate. He declared: 'I entirely disapprove of the Freudian theory that blames all a child's troubles on his hapless parents. You may have made mistakes with Christian, but that doesn't mean you were a bad father; it means you were human. And ultimately, regardless of your mistakes, his life was his own responsibility, not yours. Lay all your grief and pain before God,' your father said to me, 'and then let them go. Don't allow yourself to be haunted by these demons. Forgive yourself and forgive him so that you can both be at peace.'

"Well," said Dr. Aysgarth, moving away from the window to straighten the row of photographs on the mantelshelf, "that was without doubt the correct advice and I've tried to follow it, but it hasn't been easy—and it becomes very hard indeed when a brash young ordinand bulldozes his way into my study and blurts out abrasive remarks about Christian's death. However, let's forget that now and sum up the facts. One: Christian, I truly believe, died accidentally. Two: before he died he was troubled. And three: I don't know exactly what his troubles were, but that doesn't matter. What matters is that there was a widening split between the life he should have lived and the life he was actually living. This crucial problem, which is far from uncommon and which is essentially spiritual, was triggered in this case by his atheism—for which I was responsible because of my parental shortcomings during his adolescence."

Moving abruptly back to his desk, he planted himself beside his swivel-chair and looked me straight in the eyes. "Now, Nicholas, I've been exceedingly frank with you, not merely because I'm indebted to your father for all his kindness but because I want you to see as clearly as I do that it's both irresponsible and insensitive to run around asking questions about Christian and stirring up everyone's pain. It's good of you to be so concerned about poor Katie. But your enquiry into Christian's death is misconceived and you should now let the matter rest."

"Yes, sir. And thank you, sir, for taking me so deeply into your confidence. I respect that very much," I said, good as gold, but I wondered if Aysgarth Model B, the worldly thug, had secretly been in control of the scene all the time. It was not that I thought Aysgarth Model AB, the devout priest, had just told me a web of lies; I was sure he had told me what he believed to be the truth. (Whether it really was the truth was another matter altogether.) However I had the uncomfortable suspicion he had told me the truth not primarily because he had wanted to be truthful but because he had seen it as the best way of shutting me up; he had realised that nothing less than the truth was going to stop me asking questions, and he had felt compelled to stop me asking questions because he had been so afraid that he might eventually hear other people's answers—afraid, in other words, that there could be facts he didn't know and couldn't bear to know.

Poor old bastard.

But when all was said and done he was still manipulating me merely by proffering the truth as he saw it, the truth which by focusing on a lost vocation neatly excluded all such messy topics as sex, drink and binges in transvestite bars. I was very conscious that Christian had emerged from the conversation tragic, doomed yet sanitised.

". . . and now," Dr. Aysgarth was saying, slipping back into Aysgarth Model A, the genial idealist whose garden was perpetually lovely, "before we join the others for tea, do bring me up to date on the friends you shared with Christian! How's the beautiful Marina? And that splendidly curvaceous young American lady called after the toy motor cars—how's Dinkie? And let me see, who else is there . . . ah yes! How's Venetia?"

"I haven't seen any of them recently, sir, except Marina."

"Is she really going to marry that young rake Michael Ashworth?"

"Apparently."

"Poor Charles!" sighed Dr. Aysgarth, unable to resist taking a swipe at his old enemy—or was he merely driven to convince himself that his garden was still far lovelier than the Bishop's? "He's had such problems with his sons! I did feel so sorry for him when Charley ran away from home and Michael was thrown out of medical school."

I never hesitated. I was fond of my Uncle Charles, and this tough, convoluted little gardener, so manically weeding all the horrors from his messy herbaceous border, was a stranger to me. I knew where my loyalties lay. "But those disasters are all past history, aren't they?" I said. "Michael's doing so well in the BBC now and Charley's all set to be a big success in the Church."

Silence.

I'd detonated my last H-bomb.

"If you'll excuse me, sir," I mumbled, scuttling to the door, "I won't stay to tea. But many thanks for the lunch."

He just looked at me.

I fled.

3

I DROVE my Mini-Cooper to Dorking, the nearest town to the Aysgarths' film-set village, and after buying a Coke I sat drinking it in the car park which faced Box Hill. I found myself reflecting how magnificent Surrey must have been in the old days before it was tarted up by rich London commuters. Then it occurred to me that I was behaving like one of those antiques who had boomed earlier that the country was going to the dogs. Obviously I needed to escape from this seductive corner of England before I started reciting chunks of *Our Island Story* in Dorking High Street. The only problem was that I was unable to decide where to go next.

I wanted to see my friend Venetia, but I thought she would inevitably be out on a Saturday evening, and I was also wary of returning to London in case I succumbed to the impulse to loaf around one of the branches of Burgy's. I thought of going home, but I couldn't face my father, who would at once intuit that I had ignored his advice to leave Christian's mystery alone.

I had another think. I did have a wide circle of acquaintances, but I felt I needed to be somewhere very moral, very safe, and I couldn't at that moment recall a safe, moral acquaintance who would welcome an uninvited guest cadging a night's lodging. I wondered whether I should descend on the headquarters of the Fordite monks, but they were too moral, too safe, and I feared they could only depress me. There was Martin—a real last resort—but he would be at the theatre playing Sir Anthony Absolute and I might wind up at Burgy's while I waited for him to come home. I flirted with the idea of a hotel but God only knew what I would get up to there; the mere thought of a raven-haired chambermaid in black stockings made me want to tear off my jeans.

Finally I had a brain-wave. Charley-the-Prig Ashworth now had a parish at Fairlight Green on the Surrey-Hampshire border. I knew I could always dump myself on Charley, and no one could be safer, more moral and (unlike the Fordites) more easily managed by a sex-crazed ordinand on the loose. It did occur to me that the person I really couldn't manage was myself, but I decided I'd sort out that problem once I had solved the mystery surrounding Christian.

I studied my road-map. Then I headed west out of fake-farmhouse country to the Hampshire border.

4

FAIRLIGHT GREEN was a sprawling place situated on some bleak heathland. I drove past a couple of new office-blocks, rising like tombstones on the edge of the town, entered a Georgian high street and wound up on a council estate without having found the church. Backtracking to the centre of the town I finally spotted a Victorian hulk standing near a run-down cinema on the road parallel to the high street. Not exactly a picture-book parish. But better than a slum. I wondered how Charley was getting on.

Out of curiosity I took a look in the church porch and found it peppered with notices of parish activities. Clubs abounded. Flower rotas flourished. Lectures were threatened throughout Lent. Bible classes were trumpeted. Overseas missions were supported. An impressive list of services was flaunted. Could Charley conceivably be coping unaided with all these activities? I stared at the titles of the Lent Lectures and noted in particular the defiant: "Liberal-Radical Fallacies: An Evangelical Response." Here was someone who was obviously determined to fight the *zeitgeist* till he dropped. But when did he ever get time to pray or meditate or merely stare at the nearest wall? I could see he deserved a prize for effort, but I began to feel worried about him.

Next to the church was a large house, also Victorian, and beside the freshly painted front door was a highly polished brass plate inscribed THE VICARAGE. I noted the tiny front garden complete with trim lawn and weeded flowerbeds. Did he even get time for gardening? It hardly seemed possible, but how else could one explain the lack of weeds and mown grass? Feeling as if I were about to encounter a superhuman being from another planet, I warily pressed the front doorbell.

The door flew open. "Come in, come in!" sang Charley before his jaw sagged in surprise. Evidently he had been expecting a caller. (When *did* he get time to pray?) "Jumping Jehoshaphat—Nick Darrow!" he exclaimed. "What a splendid surprise! I thought you were my parish magazine delivery team—which would have been awkward as this month there are so many enclosures that the magazines have to go out in envelopes to make sure nothing gets lost, and I haven't yet finished envelope-stuffing. Come on in and give me a hand!"

An envelope certainly seemed a proper object to stuff. Feeling mentally flattened by all this dynamism, I drifted round-eyed over the threshold and was swept into a reception room where quantities of paper were strewn in stacks across a long table.

"I'll just put the kettle on," said Charley. "You'd like tea, wouldn't you? And I've got a smashing cake which one of the Mothers gave me yesterday before the MU outing. Tell you what: you start stuffing, and I'll whip up the feast."

I started stuffing. At intervals I tried to picture myself being such a sizzling parish priest, but my imagination failed me. After a minute I felt inadequate. After two minutes I felt depressed. After three minutes I wanted to bolt to the nearest branch of Burgy's.

"Here we are!" cried Charley, setting down a tray on the table. "Milk and sugar? Or have you given up sugar for Lent?"

"No, newspapers. I wouldn't miss sugar. Charley, can those really be cucumber sandwiches?"

"Yes, I just tossed them off as an afterthought as I was waiting for the kettle to boil."

"You're amazing!" I felt so weak I had to sit down.

"Everyone's amazing!" He beamed at me. "Wonderful to see you! How are you? All set for the big day?"

"What big day?"

"Ordination, fat-head!"

"Oh, that. Yes. Charley, is it possible for me to stay the night?" I really had to curb the urge to bolt for the nearest Burgy's.

"Of course you can—what fun! Now, I've got a prayer-group meeting at six and a Bible class at eight—"

"On a Saturday evening? Isn't everyone out enjoying themselves?"

"Of course! We have a wonderful time here, plenty of coffee, lots of laughs, stimulating conversation, fascinating things to talk about, challenging things to do—I think during Lent one should always offer an exciting spiritual alternative to the cinema or the pub, so—"

"Great. Well, don't worry about me, Charley, I won't get in your way, I'll just meditate in your spare-room."

"Oh, but I can't have you feeling shy and left out! And you'd really enjoy our prayer-group. Last week we accidentally got into the most interesting discussion of the Asians from Kenya and the Race Relations Bill—oh, and talking of race, wasn't it terrible about Martin Luther King?"

"What happened to him?"

"He was assassinated! Good Heavens, Nick, have you given up TV and radio along with the newspapers?"

"Well, I've been sort of preoccupied lately . . ." Having allowed my voice to trail away, I absent-mindedly disposed of a cucumber sandwich while Charley chattered on, eating cake and stuffing envelopes with remarkable manual dexterity. He was small but he had a neat, slim, well-proportioned figure. His dark hair was cut unfashionably short, his wide mouth reminded me of Donald Duck and his extraordinary eyes, almost golden in colour, seemed to be perpetually blazing with enthusiasm. He was thirty years old now and still unmarried but girls had never been high on his list of priorities. Poor old Charley. Rather a loser in that respect, but that was obviously God's will, forcing him to sublimate his sex-drive and pour all his energy into the task of being an outstanding parish priest.

The doorbell rang, heralding the arrival of the delivery gang—all young, eager and female, all regarding Charley with shining eyes. I blinked, wondering whether my imagination was running riot, but no, Charley was a success with these girls, they thought he was the hottest item in Fairlight Green. Extraordinary. It really was amazing what a bit of black cloth and a clerical collar could do.

One of the girls wore tall white leather boots and a mini-skirt which only just covered her bottom. I couldn't think how Charley controlled himself. I couldn't think how I controlled myself. I couldn't think how I was ever going to control myself.

Locking myself in the downstairs lavatory, I gave way to a bout of despair.

5

WELL, I got over that. Had to get over it. No time to do anything else. I stuffed some more envelopes, washed up the tea-things while Charley made some essential phone calls, attended the prayer-group session (interesting, but not to my taste), ate supper (delicious mixed grill whipped up by Charley in double-quick time) and joined the Bible class. This was astounding. The subject was the famous "hinge" of St. Mark's Gospel when Jesus began to talk of future suffering, and Charley brought to life each verse of that crucial passage by providing an exegesis which was both erudite and mesmerising. The class—all ages, all social groups, all enrapt—even clapped at the end.

I wondered if he would remember me when he was Archbishop of Canterbury, but I was sure he would. I could picture him heaving open the door of Lambeth Palace and exclaiming: "Nick! What a splendid surprise! I'm just off to consecrate a bishop, have tea with the Queen and make a speech at the House of Lords, but come in and make yourself at home . . ." God only knew what would have happened to me by then, but if skirts weren't lowered by at least six inches soon, my only hope of serving God properly would be to join the Fordite monks. What a prospect! As a loner I disliked community life, and how my father had endured a monastic existence from the age of forty-three to the age of sixty remained a mystery to me. And how had he coped with chastity from the time his first wife died until the time he entered the Order—an interval of eleven years? That was an even bigger mystery. Perhaps he had had little lapses occasionally, but no, that was inconceivable. My father was so dedicated, so gifted, and his call to be a priest was so strong that God would have automatically granted him the power to be chaste . . . I felt like banging my head against the wall in despair.

"Phew!" said Charley, having wrung the last hand, accepted the last compliment and closed the front door after the last parishioner. "So much for that! Now let's have some tea and biscuits before I toss off my sermon for Evensong tomorrow. I don't usually leave it so late in the day, but what with two funerals this week and the MU outing and the insurance man turning up out of the blue to inspect the lightning conductor on the church roof—and then of course I've had all the Easter services to plan—"

"If I were in your shoes I'd be unconscious. Charley, can I use your phone?"

I called the Manor. Rowena said my father was very depressed and had bandaged his hands more heavily than ever to conceal the eczema. He had eaten no lunch and hardly any dinner. When was I coming home?

"Tell him I'll write," I said. "And tell him I'm safe with Charley Ashworth at Fairlight Green." I gave her the number of the vicarage, beat back a twinge of nausea and returned to the kitchen where my host soon diverted me from frightening thoughts about my father's health. "Let's hear all your news!" Charley urged, offering me a packet of Lincoln Cream biscuits as I sat down opposite him at the table. "Dad mentioned to me on the phone last night . . ." Uncle Charles had revealed the existence of my engagement, which now seemed to be as official as if it had been printed in the Court Circular of *The Times*.

"Many congratulations!" sighed Charley. "There's nothing I'd like more than to get married, and I've only left it so long because I've been terrified of marrying the wrong girl. I've got this neurotic fear of winding up with some gorgeous creature who can only talk about the weather. Bishop Jardine did that and it was a disaster."

"Poor old Jardine. Wasn't he your godfather or something, Charley?"

"No, he just took an interest in me because Mum had been his wife's companion for years." Charley paused to munch his biscuit before announcing: "I do want a gorgeous creature, but she must be a gorgeous creature with a brain. I dream of a girl who's well-educated, glamorous, warm, dynamic—someone with the capacity to be a good Christian, a sex-symbol, a loyal partner, a devoted mother and a *cordon bleu* cook who can discuss the symbolism of William Blake while whipping up a Grand Marnier soufflé with one hand tied behind her back."

"Lead me to her."

"Ah, but you've got Rosalind!"

"Yeah. Charley," I said, finally unable to resist retreating into the one subject which kept my despair at bay, "what did you think of Christian Aysgarth?"

6

"*WHAT* an extraordinary question to ask out of the blue!" exclaimed Charley astonished. "What prompted it?"

"I had lunch with the Aysgarths today at their opulent fake-farmhouse near Dorking. They all seemed to be either drunk or nuts."

"Well, that's nothing new. Have another biscuit."

"Thanks." I took a second Lincoln Cream. "The subject of Christian kept coming up," I said, "and since I'm old enough now to realise how complex he was, I got intrigued."

"I don't see anything particularly complex about him. He was just a smart-aleck Wykehamist who failed to fulfil his potential and drowned his sorrows in a rather juvenile social life—oh sorry! I'm being tactless, aren't I? You yourself mingle on and off with Marina's gang."

"Mostly off. And anyway I *was* juvenile back in 1963 when I first met Christian at one of Marina's parties."

"Well, Christian certainly wasn't. In 1963 he would have been . . . let me see. I was born in 1938 and he was eleven years my senior—"

"He was thirty-six when I met him. Charley, why do you say he didn't fulfil his potential? It's well known he had a brilliant academic career."

"Oh, that was just Aysgarth propaganda churned out from the Deanery."

"You mean—"

"I strongly suspect his career had ground to a halt. Did you read his last book? It was terrible—just a rehash of other people's opinions. Dad read it and said: 'If that's the best he can do he'll never get the Chair.' "

"What had gone wrong?"

"No idea."

"Charley, this may sound ludicrous to you, but do you think there's any possibility that he committed suicide?"

"That's exactly the question Dad and I always asked ourselves," said Charley.

7

"AT THE time Michael said suicide was inconceivable," said Charley, pouring us both some more tea, "and since he was one of Marina's gang he knew Christian better than I did, but Michael was still very immature in those days and his judgements weren't too reliable. Dad and I were always much more sceptical about Christian. 'I wonder what goes on behind *that* glittering image!' Dad used to say with gloomy relish."

"Why should anything have been going on at all? Some people just naturally glitter."

"But a glamorous public facade so often masks a catastrophic private mess. Dad said Christian could have been trapped—even tormented— behind that glittering image of his."

"Uncle Charles saw Christian as tormented?"

"Potentially tormented. We've no proof he actually was."

"You didn't hear any inside gossip from the Deanery?"

"You're joking! Informal communications between the Deanery and the South Canonry were non-existent that summer."

"I knew, of course, that Uncle Charles and Dr. Aysgarth always had trouble getting on—"

"Trouble! They had the biggest ecclesiastical feud since Liddon rowed with Gore over *Lux Mundi*—which explains why Christian and I were almost strangers to each other and why Michael only came to know Christian as the result of his friendship with Marina . . . Incidentally, talking of Charles Gore and *Lux Mundi,* I came across a most interesting volume of sermons by Henry Scott Holland the other day—"

"Forget the *Lux Mundi* crowd for a moment. Charley, if you were so distanced from the Aysgarths, how did you and Uncle Charles collect enough facts to form a suicide theory? Surely you're not basing your case solely on the fact that Christian wrote a bad book!"

"Dad's theory ran like this: the bad book's critical reception made Christian realise he might not get the Chair, and the whole episode brought him face to face with failure for the first time in his life. The shock of this was so great that when he relapsed into the inevitable depression, his career crisis combined with the stress generated by his eternal triangle and fatally destabilised him."

"Trust Uncle Charles not to miss out on the sex-angle!"

"But don't you think Christian's relationship with Marina was extraordinarily odd? Of course Michael swears there was nothing sexual going on, and since he's now her fiancé one would certainly hope he knew what he was talking about, but—"

"I'm quite sure Marina and Christian didn't go to bed together. But maybe there was a third woman in Christian's life, a woman nobody knew about—"

"According to Michael there were hordes of women in Christian's life but he never had sex with any of them—and if Michael's right, that suggests a very obvious explanation of what was going on behind Christian's glittering image."

"And that is—"

"I'm convinced he was homosexual," said Charley.

8

"*AND* once you accept the theory of homosexuality," Charley added, "an even more plausible motive for suicide takes shape."

"Being blackmailed?"

"Not necessarily. My own theory is that Christian committed suicide as the result of the grinding strain of leading a double life. The career crisis created a strain, the emotional pressures of the two women created a strain, but it was the double life that finally finished him off." Charley paused to drink some tea before adding: "That curious social life he adopted suggests he'd formed the habit of dividing his personality in two: on the one hand he was moving among the stuffy, conventional society of an Oxford College, yet on the other hand he was rocketing around with Marina's groovy, much younger Coterie. It was as if Marina's parties gave him the chance to let off steam . . . Do you know if he took drugs?"

Automatically I answered: "I'm sure he didn't."

"A lot of that gang did—and do."

"Yes, but Christian—"

"I admit it *is* difficult to picture him as a drug-user," Charley conceded willingly enough. *"Pas si bête,* as the French say; not such a fool. Even Michael in his immature days used to do no more than smoke pot occasionally—or so he says, but I'm sure he's telling the truth because he was shocked when his ex-girlfriend Dinkie took to heroin."

There was a silence while I remembered Marina's shining Starbridge party in 1963. I could see Norman and Cynthia embracing, Michael squeezing Dinkie, Venetia gaily waving a bottle of Veuve Clicquot, Holly Carr full of life, Marina and Katie radiant, Christian raising his glass as if to drink to the brilliant future which seemed to stretch so inevitably before him—

I covered my face with my hands.

"Nick! Are you all right?"

"Yep." I shut out 1963, uncovered my face and grabbed another biscuit.

"I mean, are you really all right, turning up out of the blue like this? Did you perhaps come because there was something you wanted to talk over with an old friend who could be trusted to keep his mouth shut—something about Rosalind, for instance?"

That certainly made me snap out of my maudlin dive into the past. "No, I'm fine. Charley, are you casting Perry Palmer for the role of homosexual lover?"

"No," said Charley, instantly diverted. "If Perry's work at the Foreign Office involves handling classified information, he wouldn't be an active homosexual."

"Then who was the man?"

"I've no idea."

My psyche twitched. I suddenly realised he would hardly have expounded his theory so confidently if he hadn't had specific evidence to support it. Before I could stop myself I said: "You're lying."

Charley was so taken aback that he made no further effort to dissimulate. "My dear Nick, you really are quite uncanny sometimes—"

"But *why* are you lying? That's the interesting question! Does it involve confidential information, something that was told to you in the confessional?"

"I don't hear confessions. No, it's not confidential. It's just—" He stopped as if he were embarrassed, and as soon as I identified his emotion as embarrassment I knew what he was so reluctant to tell me.

"My God!" I exclaimed. "It's Martin, isn't it? It's my brother Martin . . ."

9

THE incident happened in 1964," said Charley. "Late November it was, several months before Christian died. I was still a curate at St. Mary's Mayfair, and I remember the Advent sermons were about to start. You were away in Africa, which is why you weren't at this party. I'm sure you'd have been invited otherwise.

"The party was given by Venetia, but it was completely conventional because her husband was the joint-host. It was he who invited me; when he'd worked in Starbridge he'd got on well with Dad, and he'd kept in touch with me after we both wound up in London.

"I was in two minds about whether to accept the invitation because I knew Marina and her gang would be there and I'd always taken care to look down my nose at them. (Those were my priggish days, when I was a lot less secure in my faith than I am now.) However in the end I just couldn't resist the chance to see Venetia again. I'd always secretly fancied her, but the trouble was I'd lacked the sophistication to do anything about it. Then she got married. What a lost opportunity! How I gnashed my teeth! I don't suppose she ever whipped up a Grand Marnier soufflé with one hand tied behind her back, but I bet she could recite Blake's 'Tyger, Tyger' backwards while opening a bottle of champagne with a flick of her wrist.

"Well, there I was, crammed into this smoke-filled room while everyone screamed at everyone else, and suddenly I recognised your brother. Apparently he'd met Venetia the year before when *Present Laughter* had arrived at the Starbridge Playhouse in a pre–West End run, and he'd met Christian then too. When I eventually spoke to Christian he said he was trying to persuade Martin to give up that ghastly TV comedy series, and I got the impression he knew Martin well—in fact I said to him: 'Is Martin a good friend of yours?' but Christian just answered casually: 'I see him now and then at Perry Palmer's.' Of course Martin was years older than Christian—how old is Martin exactly? He never looks more than fifty, but I suppose—"

"At the end of 1964 he would still have been in his fifties. Just."

"Well, he certainly looked younger that night. He was in great form, oozing charm—you know what actors are like—"

"Only too well."

"—lots of genuine feeling but all highly stylised. Well, I was just thinking it was time I left, when I caught sight of Martin and Christian talking in a corner. Martin was lighting Christian's cigarette, and suddenly . . . well, it's hard to describe, but in that one small gesture an entire hidden world seemed to be revealed. My instant reaction was: so that's the way the land lies. And for the first time I found I could believe Christian's relationship with Marina was platonic. I don't actually believe that a platonic friendship can exist between a man and a woman unless one of them's homosexual."

I refrained from arguing that a sexual hang-up could also ensure a friendship remained platonic. Deciding to focus on the scene which I was convinced Charley had misinterpreted, I said: "Are you sure you didn't just see Martin making a pass? I mean, did you actually see Christian responding in any off-key way?"

"Well, no, but—"

"I've heard evidence that he was attractive to both sexes, but if one excludes the possibility of an affair with Perry, there's nothing to suggest he ever responded to homosexuals."

"Evidence? Hang on, Nick! What's this—a criminal investigation?"

Damn. I tried to cover my tracks. "Well, to be honest—and this is confidential—I'm making a few enquiries for Marina. She's got obsessed by the past and she wants to find out the truth so that she can set Christian's memory completely aside before she marries Michael."

"Good heavens, does Michael know?"

"No idea, not my business to ask. Charley, can I use your phone again? I'll pay for these calls, of course . . ."

Having retrieved my address book from my leather jacket which was hanging in the hall, I checked my memory of Marina's new number and retired once more to Charley's study.

"It's Nick," I said to Marina when she answered the call. "How are you?"

"Radiant! I've been to a simply heavenly film called—"

"Is Michael there? Is that why you can't talk?"

"Darling, I'm absolutely alone and utterly yours!"

"I've been feeling very anxious about you—"

"How wonderfully chivalrous but *don't worry*. We'll just blot out yesterday, so you needn't give it a second thought."

"I'm doing nothing but give it second thoughts."

"Well, if I don't, you certainly shouldn't."

"If you don't now, you will later."

"Oh darling, *do* give your little crystal ball a rest, there's a pet!"

"Okay, how's Katie?"

"I've no news, but I'm going back to Banbury tomorrow to see her."

"Cynthia's there too."

"*God.* I'd heard she'd flipped out but I didn't know where she was . . . How's the Christian investigation?"

"Psychedelic. A jumble of weird patterns, all conflicting with one another. Marina, was Christian bisexual?"

"Was Christian *what?*"

"I was wondering if he'd ever had a homosexual affair."

"Darling, you've blown your mind! *Christian?*"

"Okay, forget it. Look, I want to see Venetia. Do you know if she's in town this weekend?"

"Yes, I've just been to the cinema with her. We saw this stunning film called—"

"Did she mention if she had any plans for tomorrow morning?"

"As far as I know, her only date's with the Sunday papers. Oh, by the way, she gave me a message for you. 'Undying love to my Talisman!' she said. 'And ask him when our orbits are due to intersect again!' She made it sound madly suggestive."

"Great. Okay, Marina, glad you're all right. I'll be in touch," I said, and hung up. I was just about to leave the study when I remembered my earlier promise to Rowena that I would write to my father. Sitting down at Charley's desk I found some headed paper, borrowed a pen and scribbled: "Dear Father: I'm okay. *Don't worry.* I'm staying with Charley (and here's the writing-paper to prove it). He's fantastic, a super-priest. I like him better now he's older. Tonight I joined his prayer-group and Bible class. The class even clapped. Amazing. Accidentally met a drunken atheist (Norman Aysgarth) yesterday and played the Good Samaritan. What a bad trip! It was a relief to get to Charley, so well, so integrated, so happy. Now that you know I'm all right, please make a big effort and put your body back in order. I'll be home soon and if I find your hands are still bandaged I shall be *very cross.* Love, NICHOLAS."

I reread the letter. Had to mention Norman because the Community would have told my father that I had spent the previous night in Norman's house. But there was no need to mention my exploits in fake-farmhouse country as I pursued my investigation of Christian. Better to keep quiet about those particular manoeuvres.

With the sealed letter in my hand I returned to the kitchen, where Charley was rapidly composing his Evensong sermon. On the table I saw *Peake's Commentary on the Bible,* books by Alan Richardson and John Stott, and an article from *The Church Gazette* on Donald Coggan, the evangelical Archbishop of York. No radicals for Charley; no John Robinson, no Maurice Wiles, no Dennis Nineham, not even that great 1960s liberal Ian Ramsey, who was the spiritual heir of Archbishop William Temple.

"What do you think of Ramsey, Charley?"

"Dunelm or Cantuar?" said Charley in ecclesiastical code-language, asking me whether I meant the Bishop of Durham or the Archbishop of Canterbury, both of whom, by a tiresome coincidence, had the same surname.

"Ramsey of Durham."

"I like his Lancashire accent. Good to see a great prince of the Church with Kipling's 'common touch.' "

"Is that all you can say about him?" I admired not only Ramsey's unflagging efforts to bring the Church into the heart of secular society but his deep interest in medicine and healing.

"Oh, of course he's a good man, but whenever I hear people say he's a churchman for our times, my blood runs cold. This mindless passion to reflect the spirit of the age is a disaster."

"You're bucking the trend, Charley!"

"So did Christ. He didn't embrace the spirit of his age; he consistently questioned it, and when you live in an age like this one, where all the old certainties are pouring down the drain, it's Christ you need to follow, not the latest liberal who does nothing but swim with the tide."

"Aren't you being rather unfair to Ramsey? Don't you admire him for engaging with the world in the way he does? Think what guts it must take to have philosophical dialogues with logical positivists!"

"Oh yes, yes, yes, very brave, very commendable, but what use are his philosophical dialogues to me as a parish priest? He's almost as bad as the Radicals—they're no use to me either."

This bothered me. I felt Charley was wrong to hook up only to the conservative line but I felt the Radicals were equally wrong to promulgate a theology which had no numinous value at the grass-roots level.

"Better Ramsey than the Radicals," I said, but in fact my admiration for Ramsey was limited. He was no mystic. He was a brilliant philosopher, but for me it was psychology, not philosophy, which opened up Christianity. "To be honest I can't really connect with him," I confessed to Charley. "Sometimes I feel I can't connect with anyone."

"What about the other Ramsey—Michael of Canterbury?"

"Oh, he's head and shoulders above the lot of them and he understands mysticism, but he's so old, isn't he, and that Father Christmas look makes him seem unreal to the under-thirties. He needs to be trendier."

"Rubbish! He's wonderful just as he is—holy and timeless! Beware of the quest for trendiness, Nick—it only leads to a liberalism gone berserk!"

"But liberalism has things to say about updating the Christian message, Charley—it's trying to talk to conservatives like you, the well-educated, dynamic priests who could transform the whole Evangelical wing of the Church. If the Evangelicals can get their act together as the result of the Keele conference—"

"The Evangelicals already have their act together! They're determined to stand by the absolute truths, and if you ask me, the Liberals' ceaseless quest for relative truth at the expense of absolute truth does nothing but open up cracks for the Devil to infiltrate—and I don't apologise for using the word Devil. It's a pity more people don't use it—why can't they call a spade a spade? This is the Devil's decade and most people can't even see him, let alone recognise him! It's pathetic. Imagine going down the drain and having no idea who's flushing you into the sewer!"

"I feel I'm going down the drain sometimes."

"My dear Nick!" Charley was horrified.

"It's okay, I'm not serious," I said, but I knew I was and suddenly before I could stop myself I was saying: "I think Christian went down the drain. I think the Devil grabbed him by the hair, tossed him into the lavatory with all the shit and flushed him screaming into the sewer."

"Nick, if I were you I'd stop this Christian Aysgarth investigation—I can see he's getting to you in some peculiar way, and that's not healthy. Look, why don't you stay here for a few days? You can assist me at Communion tomorrow, and—"

"I'd really like that, Charley, but my father will be disappointed if I don't turn up for mass in the chapel."

"Okay, but do talk to your father about this! You don't want to get overstrained just before your ordination."

"Right." I retired to the spare-room he had allocated me and spent some time sitting motionless on the edge of the bed. At least I'd managed to escape from his Communion service without making him suspicious. No choice but to get out of it; I knew how very far I was from being in a state of grace. No more self-deception. And no more pseudo-confessions which were worse than useless. I needed help—a lot of help—and as soon as I had solved the mystery surrounding Christian I'd go straight to Father Peters to be rehabilitated.

But meanwhile . . .

I began to plan a secular Sunday.

I O

ONE of my foibles is that I have to wear clean clothes; the fashion for being dirty, even smelly, passed me by. I had now been wearing the same clothes for two days and I knew that unless I went home I had either to raid Marks & Spencer for a new supply or to sit stark naked in a launderette while my clothes were being washed. As Marks & Spencer was closed on Sundays and since I had no wish to be arrested for indecent exposure, I was compelled to return to my wardrobe.

I timed my arrival for eight o'clock, when my father and the Community would be at mass. Having changed my clothes, I packed my shaving equipment and teeth-gear into a bag alongside some extra underwear and shirts, but when I looked for an additional pair of jeans I realised nothing clean was available so I was reduced to taking away a pair of ordinary trousers. I chose black ones to remind me that I would soon be a priest. I also grabbed my Prayer Book to convince myself that I hadn't yet gone down the drain.

Then I headed back to London.

I I

I WENT to Matins in Westminster Abbey and sat amidst a congregation of boggling tourists sternly stuffed into the transept seats by sidesmen skilled in crowd management. I felt I really couldn't let Sunday pass without attending church, particularly since Easter was now so close.

The service was straight, decent and well-oiled, no High Church frills, no Low Church fulminations, just the soothing, tasteful, uncontroversial splendour of the Church of England's famous "Middle Way," the broad valley between the opposing mountain peaks. Thinking of those ecclesiastical factions reminded me of Charley, embedded in Middle Way churchmanship but thundering like a Low Church tub-thumper as he hammered home his conservative views. Earlier in the twentieth century the Evangelical wing of the Church had faded through lack of effective leadership and the Anglo-Catholic wing had grabbed the reins of power, but now, with liberalism acting as a plague to the Anglo-Catholics and a spur to the Evangelicals, I thought Charley could be a portent of changing times. I saw him as one of a new breed, an Evangelical who was embarrassed by the anti-intellectual aura of old-fashioned fundamentalism, an Evangelical well-educated enough to read the Bible with sophisticated eyes, an Evangelical with a brain. The Anglo-Catholics needed to watch out. Unless they stopped living off their past glories they'd wake up one day to find that the Evangelicals had grabbed the reins of power at last, and then—

And then the great Catholic tradition of the Church of England would fragment beneath the wheels of a militant Protestantism. Was that what I wanted? No. But maybe that was what God wanted. Fewer elaborately beautiful, liturgically meaningful rituals and more roaring tub-thumpers to win back the decade from the Devil. Fewer limp-wristed performers in fancy dress and more fire-breathing, high-testosterone zealots. What a picture! Sex shouldn't come into the situation at all, of course; we were all equal in the sight of God—men, women and hermaphrodites—so why did sex keep muscling in on religion along with the faction-fighting, the power-grabbing and the money-grubbing? If I were God I'd despair. I was Nicholas Darrow and *I* despaired. Better to blot out that man-made Church, so painfully unsatisfactory, and tune in to the great truths beyond.

I looked at the rose window in the north transept and flicked the switch in my head to receive the Light.

Strange that it should be the *north* rose window, the one that never saw the sun. And how strange that the red glass should be so opaque, reminding me not of roses but of clotted blood. In fact I could see now it was a very dark window, heavy and threatening, and there was no light there, none, only a great blackness surging through the glass and streaming down on me in a huge, silent tide—

I switched off, sweating. One of the canons was preaching in the pulpit but I couldn't hear him, couldn't register what he said. I managed to recite the mantra soundlessly: Lord Jesus Christ, Son of God, have mercy on me, a sinner; Lord Jesus Christ, Son of God, have mercy on me, a sinner; Lord Jesus Christ . . . I began to relax but almost at once realised that this had nothing to do with the mantra. I was relaxing because another force was now invading my psyche, a benign force this time but painful and anguished. It was the Light emanating from my father as he came psychically to my rescue and enfolded me in a love that was distorted by his anxiety. I wanted to push him away, I wanted to be independent, but I didn't dare. I had to let my psyche interlock with his so that he could keep me safe. Twenty-five years old I was, and still I hadn't worked out how I could survive the onslaughts of the Dark without my father constantly propping me up and protecting me. Pathetic. And terrifying. If he were to die . . .

The Dean of Westminster pronounced the blessing that concluded the service.

Staggering out into the diesel fumes of Parliament Square I leant against the railings by St. Margaret's church. Big Ben was chiming. After a while I realised I was by the tube station but I had no memory of getting there. Nearby was a shop defying the Sunday trading laws by selling tourist junk. Hardly knowing what I was doing I bought an ice-cream, but as soon as I sank my teeth into the flavourless white mess the chill jolted me back to normality. It was as if I had finally got the stopper back on a bottle of sewage after I had opened it in the belief that it contained perfume.

I finished the ice-cream as I stood on Westminster Bridge and stared downstream. Then I returned to the tube station, found a phone-box and called my friend Venetia.

IT WAS curious how I always thought of her as "my friend Venetia," because the truth was we were mere acquaintances who occasionally bumped into each other, but as soon as we had been introduced in 1963 I had known she was to be special to me, just as I was to be special to her. This sense of unusual relatedness had nothing whatsoever to do with sex. The fact is that we're all interconnected with one another, but some people are more interconnected than others.

This vision of linked lives made me continually interested in her. When I suffered the annihilating shaft of foreknowledge in which I experienced the Coterie's ruin, I knew Venetia stood in great danger but I had no idea what that danger was or how I could save her from it. Could any would-be knight-errant have been more useless? I thought not, but later realised that God had no wish for me to play the knight-errant with Venetia; that glamorous role would only have gratified my ego. My role was to be powerless, but in my powerlessness I would eventually prove stronger than any knight-errant on a white horse.

It was with shock that I recognised this situation, but perhaps it's always a shock when a religious principle, accepted in faith, becomes a concrete, experienced reality. I had apparently been chosen to act out the great Christian paradox of strength achieved through weakness, the weakness which ultimately outstrips and triumphs over all the forces of evil. I had never pretended to understand how this mystery worked. All I knew was that in the end it would be proved true.

Over the years I regularly remembered her in my prayers, and often, not understanding the mystery, I wondered why I bothered, particularly when her life went from bad to worse. But I did bother. I went on praying and after a while it dawned on me that she hadn't overdosed on heroin, she hadn't died of cirrhosis, she hadn't slashed her wrists. The ranks of her friends had been decimated, but she was still alive. I read somewhere recently that the love of God is like a reservoir and when you pray you turn on the tap which releases the water. I turned on the tap for Venetia, and perhaps it was this small but constant flow of water which prevented her from dying of dehydration as she drifted farther and farther into her private desert.

She was now thirty-one, the same age as Christian's sister Primrose, who had once been her closest friend; Venetia's father, Lord Flaxton, was a landowner in the Starbridge diocese and an old crony of Dean Aysgarth's. However, the friendship with Primrose had withered, Primrose taking up the Church and Venetia taking up anything in trousers or a bottle. It was

well-known in the Coterie that her marriage was a disaster. I had heard
of spaced-out happenings at her country house in Norfolk. Her husband
seldom went there.

Something had gone very wrong with Venetia's life even before she
married, but I didn't know what it was. I could only be there periodically
in her darkness and offer her a profound but unspoken sympathy. She liked
me but found me juvenile. However, she took my psychic powers seriously
enough; she had believed me at our first meeting when I had told her I
would recur in her life, and she used to say that after any encounter with
me something extraordinary happened, not necessarily pleasant. Sometimes
she called me her Halley's Comet, that recurring phenomenon blamed for
unwelcome events, but usually she referred to me more flatteringly as her
Talisman, a mysterious object which produced unusual effects.

"And how's my Talisman?" she enquired, opening the front door of her
large cream-coloured house off Queensgate. "Still treading your mystical
paths?"

Venetia was tall, about five foot seven even when she was wearing
low-heeled shoes, and at first glance she appeared unattractive, having
broad shoulders, a flat chest and no hips. This shortage of curves gave her
an androgynous look, and her face, with its heavy dark eyebrows and
prominent jawline, conveyed an air of sullen aggression in repose. So much
for the casual observer's first glance. A second glance saw someone much
more intriguing, a woman who had extraordinary hair—long, thick, dark,
wavy and usually all over everywhere—and magnificent eyes, jungle-
green and fringed with long black eyelashes which spectacularly enhanced
her eccentric glamour. An exotic taste in clothes completed this impression
of a five-star Hollywood vamp who rose from her couch only to kick
convention in the teeth. On that morning she was wearing a scarlet robe
which was neither a dressing-gown nor a kimono nor an evening dress;
it had a zip up the front, suggesting it was designed for casual occasions,
but the low neckline and trailing sleeves suggested formality. The scarlet
silk was lavishly embroidered with green dragons. She also wore high-
heeled black slippers, open at the ends, and carried a very long cigarette-
holder. Her toenails were painted to match the dragons.

"Have a drink," she said, leading the way into the drawing-room and
waving the inevitable bottle of Veuve Clicquot in my direction. She spoke
in a husky contralto, very sexy.

"A bit early for me, thanks."

"Oh, don't be so square!" She poured me a glass of champagne and set
the bottle down on the coffee-table amidst the *Observer* and the *Sunday
Times*. "We'll drink a toast to your engagement," she said agreeably,
"although I must say I was surprised when Marina told me the news. I
wouldn't have thought Rosalind Maitland was quite your style."

"I wouldn't have thought your husband was quite yours."

That pulled her up short. Raising an eyebrow she gave me her best debonair smile, the one which was supposed to signal how worldly she was and how amusing she found life, but her pain lacerated my psyche so strongly that I flinched.

"Sorry," I said. "Oh Venetia, I'm sorry, sorry, sorry—"

"I can't imagine why! I was being catty about your fiancée and you quite rightly gave me a verbal biff on the nose. But darling, don't let's be *sombre,* it's so boring—electrify me by spilling the beans about your new mystical path! According to Marina, you're padding along with your crucifix in one hand and your crystal ball in the other while you pursue THE TRUTH about Christian's death so that you can help Katie, but frankly, my dear, I don't think anything can help Katie at this stage except either a religious conversion or a roaring love affair, preferably with another woman. (No man, of course, could ever measure up to Christian.) How far have you got with your investigation?"

"I'm beginning to feel I'm lost in a maze."

"Can I take you by the hand and lead you down the path to the centre?"

"I wish you would. Venetia, what on earth was going on during the last few months of Christian's life? Was he about to leave Katie? Had he finally fallen uncontrollably in love with Marina? What really went on with Perry Palmer? And regardless of whatever was going on with Perry, was Christian having a homosexual affair with someone else? Was he always bisexual? Or did he—"

"STOP!" thundered Venetia, holding up her hand, and as I obediently fell silent she exclaimed laughing: "My dear, what a pornographic farrago! Are we talking about Christian Aysgarth? Or are we talking about some demonic anti-hero conjured up by your baroque Anglo-Catholic imagination?"

I took a deep breath. "Okay, let's start from square one: how did you yourself see Christian?"

"He was my friend," said Venetia.

VIII

"Today there is in our society . . . a dwelling upon sex: the sex problem, the adjustments of sex, instruction for sex, adventures of sex, stories of sex, what to do with sex, brighter and better sex . . . But just as the uprush of sexuality in the decaying Graeco-Roman world was not due to sex impulses in themselves but to frustrations which caused men and women to turn to sex as an escape, so does it seem to be today."

MICHAEL RAMSEY
Archbishop of Canterbury, 1961–1974
CANTERBURY ESSAYS AND ADDRESSES

I

I SUDDENLY realised that her eyes were shining with tears. But the next moment she had blinked them back, reached for her glass and taken another dose of champagne.

My voice said: "You loved him."

"No. I loved someone else. But Christian . . . oh, I can't explain, but he reminded me of this other man . . . Never mind, it doesn't matter." She reached for the bottle to top up her glass. "Nothing matters any more."

"*You* matter, Venetia."

"Oh, I matter least of all—I'm just another decadent fool wasting all my opportunities, but don't let's talk about me; let me tell you about Christian. He was a good person, and when I say that, I don't mean he was churchy or priggish. He was kind, sensitive and . . . decent. Does 'decent' have any real meaning in 1968, or is it merely a pejorative adjective to be applied with a sneer? He loved Katie. He used to say that when he married he was happy for the first time since his mother died. He loved his children too, but he wasn't demonstrative about it—Christian wasn't demonstrative at all, but he did care for people and I believe that deep down he was very emotional, very idealistic. The glamorous manner was just part of a *persona*, a mask, which he used to keep people at a distance. He didn't like people coming too close. He was afraid of emotional involvement. He said that after his mother died he never wanted to be so close to anyone again because he could never run the risk of a second bereavement on that scale. That's why it took him so long to marry Katie. He'd known her for years but he had to dredge up all his courage to take the risk.

"I think he did love Marina, but not in a way which endangered his marriage. If Katie had objected he'd have given Marina up, but Katie realised it was all quite safe. Poor, hurt, muddled little Marina! She was such a 'little girl lost' behind *her* glamorous facade, and she wouldn't be planning to marry Michael now if Christian hadn't been so kind and decent, proving to her beyond dispute that not all men are bastards.

"Marina suited him too, of course, because she didn't threaten him by trying to come too close. It was the same with Perry. I think he loved Perry and I'm sure Perry loved him, but if Perry had ever tried to take the friendship too far Christian would have ended it instantly. The only reason he let Perry get so close was because he trusted him never to overstep the mark. I'll be quite frank and say I have no idea what goes on in Perry's life. All I know is what didn't go on between him and Christian.

"Now, if all this absence of consummated love seems odd to you it's because you're looking at it with a mind rooted in 1968. The Victorians would have thought the friendships normal, even commonplace, particularly the one between the two men. Strange how each generation is so utterly brainwashed by the times in which it lives . . . but Christian's psychology ensured that he behaved like someone from another age.

"By this time you'll have grasped the nature of the relationship I had with Christian after I joined Marina's Coterie back in 1963. Once I'd summed up the situation I was careful to offer him merely a warm, asexual friendship—and he took it, with gratitude. He got so tired of women slobbering all over him. In fact when they did overstep the mark he could be brutal in pushing them back—which meant he acted out of character, because brutality wasn't part of his real nature at all. Looking back I can see he must have been even more damaged than I realised by that bereavement in his teens. In many ways he made a good recovery, but there were some scars which never completely healed and in the end . . . in the end they broke open and began to suppurate."

Venetia paused. I was sitting motionless opposite her, my full glass of champagne clasped tightly in both hands as I leant forward with my elbows on my knees. At last I said: "What happened?" And she answered without hesitation: "The Great Pollutant came. I call it the Great Pollutant because . . . well, we don't talk of the Devil, do we, not nowadays, people just laugh."

"The word's a symbol that's lost its power," I said, "but the force the symbol represents is still going strong."

"Stronger than ever. It slammed into the whole Coterie in the end. I suppose it's a timeless phenomenon, isn't it? One moment the world's bright and clean and shining, and life's gay and carefree; then suddenly a crack opens up, and through that crack . . . In the end everything's dark and soiled and sordid and Death keeps turning up to leave his card. What happened to Christian, I'm convinced, is that a crack opened up in his life and the Great Pollutant began to spew its filth all over him."

She finished her champagne and stubbed out her cigarette. "It started about six months before he died," she said. "For some time I was dimly aware of it happening but I chose not to notice because it was so sinister. Then finally he did something so vile that I couldn't turn a blind eye any longer."

Again I said: "What happened?"

"He had the most brutal row with Katie, told her she was a boring old cow and went off with Perry for a continental holiday. Katie was eight months pregnant and God only knows how she managed to avoid going straight into labour. I heard all this from Marina, of course, who was shocked to the core and needed to consult someone in confidence."

"What happened when he came back?"

"Then Katie did go into labour and the longed-for boy arrived. Happy ending, I thought, Christian will be thrilled. But within days he was having a blazing row with Marina. She made the mistake of telling him exactly what she thought of his jaunt to the Continent, and he told her she was becoming as big a bitch as Dido—which was the nastiest thing he could have said because no one hated Dido more than Christian did. Anyway, at that point I realised I couldn't stand on the sidelines any longer. I had to get involved."

"Did he wind up quarrelling with you too?"

"No, because I was very careful not to criticise him; by that time I felt the most important thing was to discover *why* he was behaving so grossly out of character. I invited him here for some lethal champagne cocktails— guaranteed to destroy any emotional reserve on contact—and after he'd tossed off two of them he confessed he was worried about his work. After he'd tossed off a third he admitted he wanted to change his life radically. 'If I had the freedom to choose,' he said, 'I'd like to get right away from all women and sever myself from everyone I know.' And when I said: 'Thanks a lot!' he answered with a laugh: 'I'll make an exception where you're concerned—you can visit me once a year with a flask of champagne cocktails!' At that point I took my courage in both hands and said: 'What's gone wrong?' but he only said: 'Nothing that champagne cocktails can't cure.' It was not until I was standing up to produce a fourth round that he dropped the bombshell: he asked if I knew where to get heroin.

"I said: 'You're joking, of course,' and he said: 'Of course, but have you ever tried it?'

" 'Frankly,' I said, 'I've never fancied having to wear long-sleeved dresses in summer, and besides, it's so terribly bad for the complexion.' That amused him. He said: 'I'm sure that's the only sane line to take, but nevertheless I wouldn't mind trying it to see what all the fuss is about.'

"Then I knew he'd slipped far, far out of his true self again, just as he had with Katie and Marina—it was as if he kept dislocating his personality. All I could think was that the Christian I knew had always held himself aloof from the extremes of fashion and despised people who took hard drugs. It was at this point that I did a very stupid thing—not just because I was stoned on champagne cocktails but because I was so unnerved by the dislocation. I made a confession. I said: 'As a matter of fact I did try heroin once, just to see what all the fuss was about, but I decided afterwards to stick to dear old alcohol, so much safer, and one never winds up dead in a lavatory alongside a hypodermic needle.' At once he demanded: 'Who was your supplier?' and I answered: 'Dinkie.'

"Well, the weirdest part about this story is that Christian didn't— repeat: *didn't*—get hooked on heroin. In fact he told me later he'd never even bothered to try it."

"So what happened?"

"He got hooked on Dinkie," said Venetia.

2

"*I WAS* appalled," she added flatly, retrieving the cigarette-box from a distant table and returning not to her armchair but to the sofa where I was sitting. "I never liked Dinkie," she said, sinking down beside me and fitting a new cigarette into her holder. "Who was she anyway? Just an American carpet-bagger who happened to be working with Marina at that art gallery back in 1963. I wish to God Marina had never brought her into the Coterie."

"Did Marina—"

"No, she never knew about Dinkie and Christian, and neither did Katie. I never said a word. It would have killed them. Stunning, shining Christian, heaving away with that bosomy tart—ugh! Even now the thought makes me want to vomit."

"How did you find out?"

"I caught them *in flagrante* at my house in Norfolk. It was the spring of 1965 and the cherry-trees were flowering, I can see them now. Christian had been on holiday with Perry, had his row with Marina and confessed to me his urge to try heroin—in fact it was at our champagne-cocktail session that I invited him down to Norfolk. About two weeks elapsed between those London cocktails and that country weekend, time enough for him to look up Dinkie and for her to latch on to him. He admitted after I'd caught them in the act that it wasn't the first time they'd got together.

"Dinkie had broken up with Michael by that time and had latched on to Robert Welbeck, whom I'd always rather liked. Dinkie the latcher, latching on to anything capable of an erection . . . Did she ever latch on to you?"

"No, you're forgetting that I dropped out of the Coterie when I was doing my voluntary work, and by the time I resurfaced—"

"—she'd run off to the Bahamas with that millionaire who eventually ditched her. Yes, I remember now."

"Tell me about this weekend in Norfolk."

"I had a house-party of about a dozen people. I invited Katie to come with the baby, but he was very newborn still and although she accepted the invitation she later changed her mind and stayed at home. But Christian came; Katie insisted on it, martyred herself to keep him happy. Marina was there. And so was Dinkie—had to invite Dinkie because I wanted Robert to come. Everyone roared down on Friday night and we had a late dinner, the usual form. On Saturday morning we all flopped around recovering. A buffet lunch. Not quite warm enough for it to be *al fresco* but the weather was sunny. In the afternoon some of the guests played tennis and some went boating on the lake. I played clock-golf with Robert, but since I was the hostess I was continually keeping an eye on everyone and I noticed early on during the round that Dinkie had disappeared.

"That bothered me. I was worried in case she was either shooting up in the lavatory or screwing my new gardener in the potting-shed—being Dinkie she was *capable de tout,* and I didn't want any boring scenes. Then Marina appeared. She'd been boating with Christian but he'd gone indoors to phone Katie—or so he told her, and it never occurred to me that he might have been lying. Meanwhile I was still worrying about Dinkie. 'Here,' I said to Marina, giving her my putter, 'finish the round for me while I make sure Cook hasn't O.D.'d on cooking sherry.' Robert didn't mind. He fancied himself at clock-golf and he still hadn't noticed his girlfriend was missing.

"I caught sight of the gardener as I returned to the house—he was safe and sound, anointing the front lawn with weed-killer. But I still felt compelled to check on Dinkie in case she was making whoopee with a syringe so I went to her room—and there she was with Christian, both of them stark naked and heaving. It's hard to describe the quality of my revulsion. I'd thought I was so trendy and sophisticated but I was shocked—*shocked.* I just stood there, unable to speak. My tongue seemed glued to the bottom of my mouth.

"Then came the most shocking thing of all. Christian laughed and said: 'Come and join us!'

"He wasn't Christian any more. The dislocation was absolute. It was as if someone else had finally taken his place.

"I got my tongue unglued. I said: 'You're out of your mind'—and I never spoke a truer word, Nick, because he *was* out of his mind, he just wasn't there any more, he'd gone away, he'd been displaced by . . . but it wasn't really a person. It was a presence. It shone out of his eyes and pretended to be Christian, but it wasn't. It wasn't Christian at all.

"Then suddenly Dinkie giggled, and the scene seemed to snap sideways into another reality; it was like pressing a button on a transistor and instantly changing wavelengths. Abnormality ended, normality began and we started to behave predictably. I said: 'You bloody bitch, I never want you in my house again,' and she purred: 'What's the matter, darling? Jealous?' Funny how dialogue in real-life melodramas is far more hackneyed than any actor would tolerate on the stage . . . And the next moment the action became just as hackneyed as the dialogue. I walked right up to the bed and hit her, and when she collapsed on the pillows with her mouth wide open in astonishment I said to Christian: 'If Marina and Katie ever find out about this I'll kill you.'

"Extraordinary, wasn't it? Imagine someone like me coming out with a line like that! But oh God, I was so devastated . . . The madness, the defilement, the vilely *alien* quality of the horror . . . I ran to my room and cried out of sheer shock, but at least I cried in private. I've got this ghastly tendency to weep in public when I'm emotional, can't seem to stop myself soaking the nearest masculine shirtfront—in fact perhaps I ought to provide you with a waterproof bib before we go any further—"

"Did Christian come after you to your room?"

"Yes. Ten minutes later. I'd mopped up the tears by then. He knocked on the door and as soon as I saw him I knew he was back inside himself again, but he was in shreds. He said stammering: 'I'm sorry, Vinnie—I wouldn't have upset you for the world,' and I just whispered: 'What the hell's going on?'

"He said: 'I no longer know who I am. I've lost touch with the centre.' And he quoted Yeats: ' "Things fall apart; the centre cannot hold; Mere anarchy is loosed upon the world . . ." '

"I asked him if he was high and that was when he said he'd never got around to trying heroin. And they hadn't been smoking pot either. That bedroom was odourless.

" 'Don't worry,' he said, 'I'll work it out. But Christian Aysgarth's got to die because I can't live with him any more.'

"What do you think, Nick? What was going on? He was having some kind of breakdown, wasn't he? After he died I went straight to Albany and said to Perry: 'Was it suicide?' but he just said no, not possible because although Christian had been depressed he'd been getting better."

"Did you mention your suspicion of suicide to anyone else?"

"No, that was out of the question. Marina and Katie were upset enough by the belief that the death was accidental, and even if I'd been brutal enough to slaughter them with a suicide theory, I couldn't have told them why I suspected suicide; I couldn't have revealed that madness I'd uncovered. Even to Perry I just said that I thought Christian had been very troubled, and in fact I'm no longer sure whether 'madness' is the right word to describe what was going on. What do you call it when a personality is so dislocated that something else seems to be standing in its place?"

"Possession."

"No, I mean seriously."

"The overpowering of the ego by chaotic forces rising out of the subconscious mind." Setting down my glass I reached out and held her hand. "How did you get Dinkie to keep her mouth shut about the affair?"

"Oh, that was easy because she didn't want Marina to know. Marina's always been so good to her—in fact she's probably the only female friend Dinkie's ever had."

"When did the millionaire conveniently remove Dinkie from circulation?"

"Not long after Christian died. Of course I hoped we were rid of her for ever, but no such luck. Back she eventually came, but she's very druggy now and lives in some awful bed-sit on the outer reaches of Bloomsbury. I suppose some man must be keeping her—unless she's earning a living on the streets. Anything's possible."

"Do you have her address?"

"No, but Marina does. Katie's on heroin and Dinkie supplies her . . ." She finally started to cry.

I put an arm around her shoulders and gripped her hand harder than ever.

"We were all so alive, Nick . . . Life was such fun . . . That magical Starbridge party in the May of '63 . . ." For several seconds she was unable to speak but at last she whispered: "Say something. Anything."

"There's nothing to say. All I can do is be here and share your pain. But one day, Venetia, one day—"

"Yes?" she said, and suddenly she was smiling at me through her tears. "Come on, my Talisman! Come on, my Halley's Comet! Roll out the future and give me hope!"

"In the end," I said, "I'm going to help you beat back that Great Pollutant. Somehow. Somewhere. Someday."

"Can't it be now?" she enquired dryly. "Why do I have to wait?"

"I've no power. All I can do is pray for you."

"Doesn't sound much fun!"

"I'm not in it for the fun."

"Not in it for the fun," she said, "and not out for what he can get. What a man! But darling, if you can't rescue me just yet from my cesspit, do let's have a little fun! I hate to think of you just sharing my pain and praying—it sounds so dreadfully dreary!"

"Not half so dreary as your cesspit."

"How do you know? Even my cesspit," she said, as I suddenly realised my hand was sweating in hers, "has its interesting moments."

"Not when I'm around it doesn't." I decided I had to remove my arm from around her shoulders, but I let it slip to her waist instead. Clumsy. I tried to work out the next step I needed to take to detach myself but my brain seemed to be malfunctioning. Perhaps the debonair thing to do was to give her a brief, chaste kiss and immediately glide off the sofa to the door. I pictured a single graceful movement, all style and sophistication.

"It's extraordinary what an attractive man you've become," she said, casually removing my glasses. "How you've improved with age! You were so very plain and peculiar when I first met you."

I decided she needed another verbal biff on the nose. "Even then," I said, casting modesty aside in order to achieve the biff, "you couldn't stop watching me."

"Damn it, that's quite true, I couldn't!" she exclaimed good-humouredly, and we both started to laugh. I'm not sure what happened to that brief, chaste kiss but I certainly never made the stylish glide off the sofa.

When our mouths parted after a long, lascivious interval she said idly: "Rosalind's not relevant at the moment, is she? I mean, she's just a clerical accessory who only becomes important after ordination."

There were several replies I could have made to this falsehood but I said nothing. I was too busy giving her another kiss and telling myself it was just a further prelude to my stylish glide to the door.

"Do you like my lounger-gown?" she enquired after we had paused again for air. "It makes me long to do something erotic, exotic and eccentric—such as lying on a leopard-skin rug while fondling a diamond-studded whip and reciting 'Tyger, Tyger, burning bright.'"

"Could you discuss the imagery of William Blake's poetry while beating up a Grand Marnier soufflé with one hand tied behind your back?"

"Can't stand Grand Marnier and I'm not into bondage, but I'm more than willing to be eloquent about Blake over a hefty Rémy Martin."

We laughed and laughed. Of course I could see now what fun her cesspit was and how dreary I had been to harp on the spiritual nature of our friendship.

Then she said: "The zip-fastener of my lounger-gown is approximately six inches from your left hand, and the zip-fastener of your jeans is approximately six inches from my right. Shall we have a race and see who wins?"

I won the race with Venetia, but I lost the battle to the Great Pollutant.

Looking back I can see so clearly that the act had nothing to do with love and almost nothing to do with lust. We were using sex as an anaesthetic to escape from situations beyond our power to master, and in using sex we were abusing each other. It was a sin, as they used to say in the old days before the word lost its meaning and merely made people smirk. But although the religious word had lost its power, the reality to which it pointed was still strong as a sword designed for disembowelment. The modern word which points to that reality is alienation. That word doesn't make people smirk, not in the twentieth century. It's a word to freeze the blood and send people rushing to the nearest psychiatrist.

Sin is when you turn away from God—or, in the other language, alienation occurs when the ego, that erratic, unreliable driver of the personality, temporarily turns aside from the great quest for integration with the inner self, the self that's authentic, the self that contains the potential to be fully human, fully fulfilled and fully alive. You don't become fully human by exploiting others; you don't realise your full potential by being insensitive and uncaring. You miss the mark. You fall short of bringing to life your unique personality blueprint designed by the living God who dwells as a spark in the very core of it. The quest for integration—for self-realisation—for the start of what religious language calls eternal life—has been thwarted. Sin/alienation is psychological dis-ease which if unhealed can lead to the living hell of lost hopes and blighted lives.

But in the 1960s the curtain came down on these ancient truths explored by religion and translated into another language by psychology. In the 1960s everyone was brainwashing everyone else into thinking that we had all been set free to live happily ever after by wallowing in mindless self-indulgence. No wonder R. D. Laing believed that the mad were sane and that it was society which ought to be certified! The spirit of the age advocated a style of life which could only lead to mass psychic breakdown as people indulged their egos and became increasingly alienated from their true selves.

I suddenly realised Venetia was speaking, demanding to know my thoughts.

"I don't have any," I said, and it was true. I wasn't thinking about sin and psychic disintegration, not then. I was mentally anaesthetised.

"Are you sure? Your silence is beginning to seem distinctly creepy!"

"I'll recite some poetry. 'Tyger, Tyger, burning bright—' "

We were still rocking with laughter—and still rocking in the act of intercourse—when the door of the room opened without warning and her husband stood revealed on the threshold.

3

HE SAID at once: "I'm sorry," and walked out.

I was so paralysed with horror that there was only one part of my body that moved. No erection ever met a more sudden death.

"Bloody hell," muttered Venetia. "I thought he'd be out all morning."

"My God, if he tells Uncle Charles—Dr. Ashworth—the Bishop—"

"Oh, that's out of the question. Don't worry, we've got an arrangement: no divorce, but I do what I like and he keeps his mouth shut. Since a divorce would ruin him I've got the whip hand . . . Don't you want to finish?" she added in surprise as I replaced my glasses and began to grope on the floor for my clothes.

I treated this question with the revolted silence it deserved and eventually she turned aside with a shrug. It was only when I was dressed that I managed to say: "Forgive me. I've done you a very great wrong."

"What nonsense—it was fun! Oh darling, don't go all dreary and religious again—"

"You wanted to be helped—you said as much earlier. And I've been put into your life to help you. So what happens? I find this beaten-up body in the gutter, but do I treat it with compassion and make some attempt, no matter how inadequate, to bandage the wounds? No, I don't! I jump into the gutter and beat up the victim all over again!"

"Oh darling, do calm down! And do for God's sake stop treating me as if I were sick!"

"Only someone sick could treat that pathetic husband of yours with such cruelty."

"Oh, for the love of Christ, SHUT UP!" she shouted at once. "What do you know about my marriage, what do you know about my life, what do you know about all the hell I've been through—"

"I know you're unhappy and I know I care about you and I know I hate myself for making such a *bloody* mess of everything—"

"But you didn't. Look at me—I'm radiant!"

"Venetia—"

"No, don't let's quarrel any more," she said rapidly, "I couldn't bear it, you're too special to me—what would I do without my Talisman weaving in and out of my life while treading his mystical paths? And darling, talking of your mystical paths, promise me—*promise me*—you'll keep me informed about the Christian mystery. I'm convinced he went mad and killed himself, but what I want to know is *why* he went mad. So many of my friends are now either dead or hopelessly damaged and I feel that if only I could understand how it all happened, I wouldn't feel so . . . oh, this is a terrible time to be alive! All these years of peace—yet it's as if we've been brutalised by some invisible war." And at last she started to weep again, unhealed, unhappy, wrecked, racked and wasted.

I have no memory of saying goodbye to her. The guilt and horror produced amnesia. Stumbling west towards Queensgate I found a phone-box and somehow managed to put through a call to Marina.

4

MARINA gave me Dinkie's telephone number and tried to question me but I fended her off and hung up. Putting through the next call I found Dinkie at home.

"Hi," I said, "it's Nick Darrow."

"Who?"

"Nicky, Marina's soothsayer."

"Wow. That's wonderful, like that's wonderful, like that's wonderful."

"Can I come and see you?"

"That's over the top and out of this world and way, way out along the Milky Way."

"I'll be with you in quarter of an hour," I said, and replaced the receiver.

Dinkie lived east of Tavistock Square in a forlorn area occupied by London University students and other impoverished tenants. It was not a slum but it looked as if it could become one with the minimum of effort. The streets were dirty. Shabby people wandered around looking either bored or nuts. Stray dogs investigated dustbins overflowing with rubbish. Graffiti on a wall by a parade of shops included the slogan ALL YOU NEED IS LOVE, but the paint was flaking from the letters. I decided that now was hardly the time to dwell upon the optimism which had once characterised the decade, but as I reached the door of the tall house where Dinkie had her room, the music of 1966 drifted out of a window in the form of one of the most powerful songs those years ever produced, a record which soared far above the trite and the trivial as it expressed the timeless human yearning for a love which was "River Deep—Mountain High."

The front door swung inwards when I pushed it. I moved through a hall which needed decorating and began to climb the stairs. In one of the rooms on the second floor the record was reaching its climax, Tina Turner belting away, all the musicians lashed into a frenzy over their instruments, the A&R man throwing in everything except angels with harps, and suddenly I saw that song as a commemoration of the 1960s' dream before the nightmare began; it recalled for me all the joyous excitement of *communitas,* the group-spirit, and all the heady exaltation generated by those who had so longingly proclaimed the primacy of love.

The record ended as I reached the top of the stairs and saw the number on the last door. In the silence that followed I took a deep breath of fetid air and knocked on the panel.

The next moment I was facing a thin, middle-aged woman who looked as if she were dying of cancer.

"I'm sorry," I said, "I've got the wrong room. I'm looking for Dinkie Kauffman."

"Nicky—darling—honey—you're beautiful! Come on in!"

Of course. It was the walking corpse I had foreknown in 1963. I should have recognised her.

"Hi Dinkie," I said, somehow suppressing my horror, and forced myself to cross the threshold.

5

SHE had failed to register my lack of recognition. She was wearing a long-sleeved man's shirt which covered her bottom by about two inches, and black tights. An ornamental belt sagged around her waist. She wore no jewellery and no watch. I assumed that by this time all her valuable possessions would have been sold to pay for the habit. Her hair was unkempt. Her neck was dirty. She had slapped on some make-up in an attempt to hide the sick complexion and the effect was grotesque, thick black eyeliner over her haunted eyes, thick powder caked on her hollow cheeks, pale lipstick on her bloodless mouth.

I glanced around. The bed was unmade, the carpet unswept, the posters on the wall had faded. A smell reached me from the nearby kitchenette.

"Sit down," she said agreeably, indicating the bed. "Drink?"

"No, thanks." I took one of the two chairs by the table.

"So how are you?" she said, pouring herself a slug of bourbon. "What's new? Long time no see."

"I'm okay. How are things with you, Dinkie?"

"Just wonderful." She began to drink the bourbon neat. "I've been living in the Bahamas. My fiancé's a property millionaire with five homes and a private plane. He'll be coming back to collect me soon but meanwhile I've got to lie low because he's negotiating a real tough divorce, and if the bitch found out he was still in touch with me she'd sue the pants off him. But when I eventually get to sashaying down the aisle I'll be rich, with five homes and a private plane, and all the Coterie will come and visit me—and you'll come too, won't you, Nicky? In the old days I thought you were so cute, you were so young, as if you'd just hatched out of an egg, and so clean, your shirts were always so well-ironed, and you even had ironed handkerchiefs—Marina said: 'Look—no Kleenex!'—and now that you've grown up you're beautiful, I just love that long-limbed look and those wonderful cheekbones and those groovy glasses that signal you're so smart and serious. I really go for smart, serious men, I mean, sex isn't everything, right, there's got to be a meeting of the minds."

"Right. Dinkie—"

"What I'm saying is that a man that's just a hunk of meat is boring, right? A man's got to have a brain, right? Brains are sexy, right? So I go for clever men."

"Great. Dinkie, talking of clever men—"

"Wanna fuck?"

"What? Oh, no, thanks."

"Why not, what's wrong with you?"

"Clap." I doubted if any other excuse would satisfy her.

"Gee, that's tough! When I last had clap the doctor gave me such a big shot that I passed out and when I came to he had his hand up my—"

"I bet. Dinkie, talking of clever men, what did you think of Christian Aysgarth?"

"Who? Oh, him. I thought he was real dumb," said Dinkie with a yawn.

6

SHE altered her position, swinging her legs up onto the bed and lounging back against the pillows. "He didn't know anything," she said. "Okay, so he knew a lot about philosophy and all that crap, but he didn't know the A-to-Z of L-I-F-E. No wonder poor old Katie looked like a spaniel left out in the rain."

"Sounds as if you knew him pretty well."

"Hey man, you can say that again! But like a lot of high-class Englishmen he had no idea where it was at. Single-sex education. Cricket. Weird."

"Are you saying—"

"Listen, there he was, right—good looks, charm, brains, you name it, he had it, but he never got it all together. Katie was the only girl he'd ever been with before he got together with me."

"No kidding."

"So he said. And he'd just woken up to the fact that half his life had gone and he was still a baby in diapers. 'I want to live!' he kept saying. 'I'm dead and I want to live!' I felt sorry for him."

"How long did you and he—"

"A couple of months, maybe longer, I don't recall. But he was never much good, too old by that time and you can't teach an old dog new tricks—well, you can try, I guess I taught him a thing or two, but you hardly ever meet a man over thirty who can go on all night . . . How old are you now, Nicky?"

"Twenty-five. Was Christian upset when the affair ended?"

"It didn't end, he was crazy about me. Of course I always took care to tell him he was wonderful. You always have to tell men they're wonderful even when they're not. Fact of life." She yawned again.

"You're saying the affair was still going strong right up to the time he died?"

"Sure. Okay, I admit we couldn't meet so often at the end as we did in the beginning—when we first got together Oxford was on vacation—but after the new semester had begun he used to go sailing every weekend with Perry Palmer, so I still saw him regularly. He'd leave Oxford around noon on Friday, spend the afternoon with me and turn up at Perry's for dinner. Then the next morning they'd hit the trail early for Bosham and the boat."

"What's the story about Perry Palmer?"

"Balls cut off at birth. The knife slipped during circumcision."

"Seriously?"

"Listen, there was no story about Perry Palmer because Christian just wasn't into sex. He should have lived fifty years ago when England ruled the world and he could have raced around being a hero with a bunch of other men while the girls sat at home with their needlework. Christian was like something out of—who was that guy who scripted the movie called *The Thirty-Nine Steps?*"

"John Buchan."

"Right. Schoolboy yarns and high jinks. Like a kind of old-world James Bond. Fantasy stuff. Christian was into fantasy, and I mean *into* it, really deep. 'River Deep—Mountain High' . . ." She began to hum the song I had heard earlier, but soon broke off to yawn again. The yawns were coming faster now.

"What kind of fantasy, Dinkie?"

"He liked to disappear into France—he and Perry used to cross the Channel in that boat. 'It's like going through the looking-glass,' he said to me once. 'I leave Christian Aysgarth behind, and I'm all new, all different, I'm someone else.' And later he said: 'I've got this dream that one day I'll go through the looking-glass and never come back.' Weird, wasn't it? Pretending to be someone else . . . He even had two false passports."

I stared at her. After a long moment I managed to ask: "I'm sorry, could you just say that again?"

She said it again. "I guess Perry fixed the passports for him," she added. "Perry's a fixer at the Foreign Office." She began to scratch herself.

"Excuse me, I have to go to the bathroom and get some lotion for my heat-rash."

"Hang on, Dinkie. Are you saying you actually saw those passports?"

"Sure. We'd just had a fuck and he was asleep and I wanted a cigarette but I'd run out. So I rifled through his jacket in the hope of finding a pack, and in the inside pocket I came across the passports. His photo in both but different names. Weird . . . Excuse me, I have to go to the——"

I let her go to the bathroom to shoot up. My mind was in chaos. I was acutely aware that the evidence of a heroin addict should be regarded with scepticism and I was acutely aware that I had to prove beyond doubt that she was telling the truth, but I couldn't see how to confirm her story. Minutes passed. Dinkie eventually returned starry-eyed and suggested intercourse again. I had to remind her of my mythical case of gonorrhea.

"Dinkie, about those passports——"

"Oh honey, don't let's talk of Christian any more! He's dead, he's gone, he's way, way out on the astral plane——"

"I bet you can't remember what the false names were," I said.

"Oh yes, I can!"

Now I was sure she was lying. I thought it highly unlikely that she could remember two unfamiliar names briefly glimpsed three years before.

"I remember them because they were so wonderfully British," she said. "I sat there and smoked and looked at the passports while my high-class British lover lay out cold on the bed, and I thought: I just love England! America never worked out for me after my parents split up, but then I met this real cool British guy in New York and——"

"What were the names, Dinkie?"

"Charles Gore and Henry Scott Holland."

Then I knew beyond all doubt that she was telling the truth.

7

I WAS so stupefied that I asked the first question which entered my head. It was: "Did you ask Christian about the passports when he woke up?"

"What was there to ask? I knew it was all part of his fantasy life, and anyway I didn't want him to know I'd gone through his pockets—high-class Englishmen get real uptight about that kind of thing."

"But didn't you ever mention the passports to anyone?"

"No, because people would have wondered how I knew, and the affair with Christian was top secret, had to be, because I didn't want to hurt Marina. Marina's been a wonderful friend to me, best friend I ever had, I just love her . . . Hey, you won't tell Marina, will you? Maybe I shouldn't have told you, but there you were, so clean, so cool, so well-ironed——"

"Don't worry, Dinkie. Marina will never know." I stood up and began to head for the door.

"Hey Nicky, you'll come and visit me in the Bahamas, won't you?"

"Sure."

"And meanwhile stop by any time you like, just give me a call, you've got my number."

"Right." I hesitated with my hand on the latch. She swayed over to me but before she could attempt a kiss I gripped her shoulders, looked her straight in the eyes and said: "Kick it. Bust it. Live."

"Honey, I just don't know what you're talking about."

Silence. I went on gripping her and at last she said rapidly: "You're so cute, Nicky, so sweet to be concerned, but don't worry, I'm checking into the London Clinic next week. My fiancé's paying the bill."

I knew then there was nothing more I could do, so I left her to her drugs and her fantasies.

Another failure.

But now I could put aside the thought of failure at last because against all the odds my investigation had unfolded into a brilliant success. Driving down to the Embankment, I parked the car and gazed into the glittering waters of the Thames. I was in a state of profound excitement—fists clenched, mouth dry, heart thumping at a brisk rate—because the solution to the Christian Aysgarth mystery was finally staring me in the face.

Of course he had never drowned on that sailing trip. No wonder no body had ever been found.

I shouted to the seagulls wheeling over the water: "He's still alive!" but then I calmed down and began to plan my next move. Although Charley's theory about homosexuality had obviously been wrong, there was always the chance that someone who had chased after Christian might be able to shore up Dinkie's information and add to my conviction that there had been an escape into another life.

Finding another phone-box, I called Martin.

8

I THOUGHT it was about time you turned up again," said my half-brother, opening the door of his flat. "The water's hot. Feel free to take one of your two-hour baths."

"Never mind the bath. I want to talk to you."

"Oh, surely not! How original!"

I dumped my jacket on a fake Louis Quinze chair and plodded through the thick pile of the carpet into the living-room. The *Observer* was spread wide on the sofa. Something which could have been Ella Fitzgerald's voice was burbling softly from the stereo. On the desk was the latest montage of press cuttings, all proclaiming how wonderful Martin was.

"How's the old man?" he was saying. He was wearing casual clothes in a suede-with-everything style and looked like one of those models in a cigarette advertisement, all rugged masculinity beneath a glossy facade. His hair, now completely grey but still thick, looked as if each strand had been massaged into place. His liquid-brown eyes, inherited from his mother, the daughter of a tobacconist, had the lustrous clarity of a long-time non-drinker, and his lined face had been lightly tanned by the sun-lamp. He looked both impossibly, unbelievably handsome and subtly, indefinably vulgar. "I'm going down to see him next weekend," he was saying. "I'm worried about him."

"Who?"

"Dad." Martin had never managed to discover that our parent preferred to be called "Father." "Wakey, wakey!"

"Sorry, I was thinking of something else."

"My God, you're not high on drugs, are you?"

"Of course not!"

"Well, you certainly look as if you're in some weird state! What's going on?"

"Martin, I want to talk to you about Christian Aysgarth."

The liquid-brown eyes jelled. Naturally he had no wish to reveal his pathetic, unreciprocated passion, and a second later as his face snapped into action I knew I was to be offered a bravura performance by an actor at the top of his profession.

"Christian!" Surprise was registered, a touch of bewilderment, a hint of fascinated interest. He got it just right. Nothing was overdone. "My dear Nicholas, you do surprise me!" The projection was a hundred percent correct too, no playing to the back row of the gallery. His television experience was standing him in good stead. "Why on earth should you suddenly want to talk about Christian after all these years and why—more baffling still—should you make a special journey here to talk about him to me?"

"It's been suggested to me that you were lovers." I had decided that in order to have a profitable discussion about Christian's final months we had to acknowledge the unrequited passion as quickly and painlessly as possible.

"You amaze me," said Martin without batting an eyelid. He started to fold up the *Observer*. "Whenever I'm with you I feel like a nervous parent in the presence of his infant phenomenon; he simply can't imagine what the little love will come out with next . . . By the way, shall we have some tea? I bought some rather heavenly Lapsang Souchong at Fortnum's yesterday."

"Do you deny that you were in love with Christian?"

"Dear boy," said Martin, adopting his favourite Noel Coward manner, "regardless of how I might choose to answer that question, I consider the matter to be absolutely none of your business." And he made a superb exit into the kitchen.

9

I JOINED him as he was spooning tea-leaves into the teapot. "Sorry," I said. "Can we start again? I'm trying to help Christian's wife. She thinks he committed suicide and the guilt's driving her nuts—literally, no exaggeration; she's now in a nursing-home. Since she broke down I've been investigating Christian's death because I feel sure that if only I can prove he didn't commit suicide she'll stop feeling that she was in some way responsible for the tragedy."

"You greatly intrigue me," said Martin, setting out cups and saucers on a tray. "The noble young hero in pursuit of the Holy Grail of Truth! How attractive! But shouldn't that kind of role be left to Charlton Heston?"

"What the hell do you mean?"

"Tut-tut! Language! Don't forget your next big role is in the all-star epic 'Ordination'!"

"Now look here, Martin—"

"All I'm saying is that if you think I can't see you're heavily censoring your explanation you're more of a fool than I thought you were. You were always drawn to Christian, weren't you? A bit in love with him yourself, perhaps."

"You bastard!"

"You watch it! No one calls me names, least of all a twenty-five-year-old child who thinks he's taken out a patent on how to be a one-hundred-percent he-man. Pass me the milk from the fridge, please."

I silently retrieved the milk. Then I said: "Sorry, can we try yet again?"

"Okay, let's both work to make it third time lucky—let's put aside your distinctly curious behaviour and concentrate on me. You're quite obviously panting to discover the precise nature of my friendship with Christian, but unfortunately that's a very complex matter and I'm not sure I feel inclined to embark on an explanation to which, let us remember, you're not entitled. Let me first ask you this: who gave you the idea that Christian and I were lovers?"

"Someone saw you together at a party in the November of 1964."

"I never went to a party with Christian."

"I don't mean you went together. You went separately, but—"

"November '64? I don't remember this. Who gave the party?"

"Venetia."

"Ah, Miss Tiger-Eyes! Yes, I do remember. Okay, go on—what were

Christian and I said to be doing there? Pawing each other? Holding hands? Sighing into each other's eyes?"

"No, but—"

"I should think not! Do you really think homosexuals are incapable of behaving with good taste and discretion?"

That gave me a jolt. "You're saying Christian was a homosexual? But surely—no, wait a minute, don't answer that, let me broaden the question. Martin," I said as the electric kettle came to the boil on the counter, "can you tell me just what kind of a man you think he was?"

"I think he was the most dangerous man I've ever met and I wanted to kill him," said Martin. "Would you like a slice of angel-cake with your tea?"

IX

I

WE SAT down side by side on the sofa with the tray on the coffee-table in front of us. Ella Fitzgerald had ceased burbling on the stereo. The silence was broken only by the sound of running water as Martin poured out the tea.

"He was bisexual," said Martin. "In my opinion they're always big trouble. But let's be quite clear what I mean by 'bisexual.' I'm not talking of the man who marries young when he isn't fully mature and then slowly realises he's in the wrong sexual set-up; I'd class him as a homosexual who faced up to the truth about himself fatally late. And I'm not talking either of the people who go through a homosexual phase at school and then lead entirely heterosexual lives later on. I'm talking about individuals who in adult life go either way and are quite capable of carrying on with both sexes at the same time."

"No genuine commitment to either sex?"

"Exactly. And because these unfinished creatures are incapable of orthodox emotional involvement they're in a unique position to cause havoc. Inevitably, it seems to me, one winds up watching from the sidelines while the bisexual—who's basically only in love with himself—flits from gender to gender and treats one's own very genuine feelings as if they were symptoms of a rather embarrassing disease. 'A bad scene,' as your generation say."

"So you're implying that Christian—"

"In the beginning I got him dead wrong," said Martin, beginning to drink his tea. "I thought he was a homosexual, a late developer who had just about realised he was in the wrong sexual set-up. I discounted Perry. Perry recurs at homosexual gatherings, but no one's ever yet produced evidence that he goes to bed with anything except a good book. However, even though I discounted Perry as a lover, his presence in Christian's life seemed like evidence of Christian's latent homosexuality. I saw Christian as someone who had grown up in an emotionally repressed household in which the emphasis had been on conformity and success. So I worked out that he would have battened down the homosexuality—unconsciously, of course—in order not to jeopardise his chances of having a brilliant career and a dazzling private life."

"The theory certainly fits the facts."

"Like a glove, yes, but unfortunately for me it wasn't correct. It turned out he'd been emotionally damaged by—"

"—the death of his mother."

"That was certainly damaging, but it wasn't the whole story. After all, both you and Dad lost your mothers in adolescence, just as Christian did, but I can't seriously describe either of you as anything but heterosexual."

"But what else happened to damage Christian?"

"Dean Aysgarth's behaviour. I think that when the mother dies like that, the adolescent's relationship with the father is crucial. Dad was actually very angry with his father after his mother died, but he went on respecting him despite all their difficulties because Grandfather Darrow behaved with dignity in his bereavement and did nothing to make Dad want to reject him as a role-model. But what about Christian? Think of his father's extraordinary second marriage to that bizarre woman! And to make matters worse, Christian was convinced that the Dean became involved with her when the first wife was still alive."

"I don't believe it!"

"Well, Christian certainly did. Apparently there was a dinner-party at the bishop's palace shortly before the first Mrs. Aysgarth died. She herself didn't go but the Dean went, and—no, wait a minute, he couldn't have been the Dean in those days—"

"He was the Archdeacon. Go on. Dr. Aysgarth went to this party—"

"—and met Dido, who was then the hottest flirt in London society. The two of them wound up disappearing into the moonlit garden for half an hour of unchaperoned chat, and because of Dido's reputation everyone was shocked out of their clerical minds."

"I bet he never even held her hand!"

"Probably not, but you're missing the point. The point is that this was crazy behaviour for an archdeacon at a bishop's dinner-party in the early 1940s, and it can only be explained by saying he was so attracted to her that he threw discretion to the winds."

"How did Christian hear about it?"

"He was at Winchester with someone whose grandfather attended the dinner-party and was scandalised by the Archdeacon's behaviour. Christian did mention the old boy's name but I can't quite remember it . . . General Calthrop-something . . . was it Calthrop-Ponsonby? It was one of those names which make one simply salivate with the desire to sing 'There'll Always Be an England.' "

"So you're theorising that Christian was profoundly disillusioned with his father, even more disillusioned than was generally supposed."

"That's no theory; that's a fact. Christian said he was so appalled by the Calthrop-Ponsonby story that he couldn't even bring himself to tell Norman. The idea that his father could have looked at another woman while his perfect first wife was still alive was obviously both shattering and revolting."

"And you're saying this twofold damage to Christian—this damage from both his mother and his father—resulted in him being unable to make a genuine emotional commitment to either sex?"

"Well, of course one can never be entirely certain about anything where sex is concerned, but it seems clear to me in retrospect that the only lasting commitment he managed to make was to his brilliant intellect; he knew that wouldn't let him down. In fact looking back I suspect he regarded sex—any sex—as a last resort to ward off terminal boredom."

"When did you first realise he wasn't quite the late-developing homosexual you thought he was?"

"There was a peculiarly sordid scene when he told me he had taken to copulating with a really nasty piece of work, female, whom it suddenly occurs to me you must have met. She was a friend of Marina Markhampton's, a Miss Dinkie Kauffman, all bosom and teeth and legs set permanently apart."

"Yes, I've met her."

"Then perhaps you can begin to imagine the quality of my horror when I was informed—very casually—by Christian of his new attempt to stave off terminal boredom. 'My dear boy,' I said to him, careful not to be emotional—he *hated* emotional scenes—'if you have to bound around with girls, do you really have to pick a low-grade tart with the brains of a tick? It's so dreadfully lacking in style!' He found that amusing. He stood over there, hands in his pockets as he lounged against the door-frame, and he laughed. I'll always remember that. He'd casually disembowelled me, I was bleeding to death, and all he could do was laugh."

"Martin, I'm now quite convinced he was having some kind of breakdown. He wasn't usually such a shit."

"Oh, but I'm afraid he was," said Martin mildly. "Take off those rose-tinted spectacles of yours and face the facts: he was a shit who sent me to hell. Rather fun to be back in hell actually—I hadn't looked in on the old place for years. In fact I was so keen to celebrate my return that I rushed straight to the nearest pub and hit the vodka."

"My God!"

"Careful—remember ordination! But yes, you're right to be horrified. Fortunately as soon as I recovered consciousness I had the brains to rush to that marvellous place near Banbury and incarcerate myself until I knew it was safe to come out. Haven't touched a drop since. Happy ending . . . More tea?"

"Thanks. Martin, I do realise it's none of my business, but . . . could you possibly go into greater detail about your relationship with Christian?"

Martin thought for a long moment. His face was shadowed, his eyes dark with memory. Then unexpectedly he smiled at me.

"No," he said. "I don't really think I can. Sorry." And he returned to the kitchen to fetch the kettle.

2

AS HE topped up the teapot with hot water I said: "Okay, I accept that I can't hear the details, but I think you can still unlock the mystery surrounding the last few months of his life. It's indisputable that his behaviour during that time changed radically, and what I want to know is why it changed."

"There may be no single reason." Martin poured us both more tea. "The change could have been caused by a number of factors which happened to converge at a certain time."

"But when people have a breakdown, isn't there always a trigger? If he did get together with you," I said carefully, "perhaps the expression of homosexuality could have been the trigger—it could have turned his whole image of himself upside down—brought him face to face with a situation he couldn't master—"

"I assure you that where his sexuality was concerned he was incapable of that degree of *angst*. And I dispute your diagnosis of breakdown. His old life might have been disintegrating, but he himself wasn't disintegrating at all. He was charging along in fine fettle."

After a prolonged pause I said: "Okay, I'll buy that. What you're really saying, aren't you, is that there's not the remotest possibility of suicide."

"None. Believe me, the last person Christian would ever have killed was himself because he was the only person he really loved. However unfortunately I don't see how you can convince his wife of that without destroying her most cherished illusions."

"But all the evidence suggests he was chronically dissatisfied and un-happy—couldn't he have fallen out of love with himself?"

"He might have been chronically dissatisfied and unhappy—but with the life he was leading, not with the person he was. Let me try and sketch a parallel situation so that you can see more clearly what I'm driving at. Think of a beautiful woman who's passionately in love with her own reflection in the mirror. She has a wardrobe of clothes, all in the height of fashion, which make her appear even more beautiful. Then one day she notices her favourite outfit's looking a little tired. She tries another—and another—but they look tired too, and she suddenly realises that her outfits no longer do justice to her supreme beauty. She panics; she tries on different accessories but none of them makes any difference and finally she reaches the inescapable conclusion: she still adores herself but she's got to have a whole new wardrobe."

By this time I was sitting on the edge of my chair but all I said was: "Go on."

"My opinion," said Martin, "is that if Christian hadn't drowned in that accident, he would have ditched his old life by dropping out in the biggest possible way."

My theory was confirmed. "I don't think he did drown in that accident," I said. "I believe he's alive and well and living under another identity."

3

"TAKE a deep breath," said Martin, "and then expel it very, very slowly. Meanwhile I'll fight off any men in white coats who arrive to whisk you away to the nearest lunatic asylum."

"I'm serious, Martin!"

"That's what terrifies me. Dear boy, it's a wonderful script, but are we really due for a remake of *The Prisoner of Zenda?*"

"Look, I've heard from an eye-witness that Christian had obtained two false passports. He—"

"One false passport I can take," said Martin, "but two false passports suggest you've been talking to someone who was doped up and seeing double. Who exactly is this witness of yours?"

"Dinkie. But the story's true, Martin!"

"My dear Nicholas, it couldn't come within a million light-years of being true!"

"But that's the show-stopper," I said. "It does. She said the passports were made out in the names of Charles Gore and Henry Scott Holland."

"This is Frederick Lonsdale's territory, surely? Two characters in one of those rather brittle drawing-room comedies he wrote in the 1920s—"

"Martin, these were real people, distinguished men, but they're only famous to those who know the history of the Church of England. Charles Gore—"

"Wait a minute, I think on reflection that even I've heard of Charles Gore. Bishop of Oxford, wasn't he? One of Dad's Anglo-Catholic heroes."

"That's the one. He and Henry Scott Holland were big-time churchmen in the late nineteenth and early twentieth centuries—they were two of the contributors to a book of essays called *Lux Mundi,* a landmark in the development of Anglican thought—"

"Hardly Dinkie's literary beat!"

"Of course it isn't! Martin, it's inconceivable that she could have invented that pair of names and I find it impossible to believe she would have run across them before. So that means she really did see those two false passports, and—"

"But for God's sake, why two?"

"I don't know."

We stared at each other. Finally Martin took several gulps of tea and reached for the teapot again. "Okay," he said, "Christian had two false passports. That could certainly be construed as evidence that he was planning the big drop-out, but it's not evidence that he's alive today. He could still have died accidentally."

"Yes, but see the passports in their context," I persisted. "Some time towards the end of 1964 or possibly the beginning of 1965, Christian started to swing out of control and his behaviour became increasingly bizarre. In fact Venetia went so far as to say he behaved as if he'd been taken over by someone else—which to me suggests—"

"Dear God!" muttered Martin in a stagey aside. "He's going to talk about possession!"

"Possession's actually a very interesting subject. According to Jung—"

"No, don't get side-tracked by Jung and don't, I *implore* you, Nicholas, get bogged down in paranormal speculation. My nerves couldn't stand it."

"Okay, let's just say his behaviour became increasingly bizarre. He treated his wife outrageously, quarrelled with Marina, messed around with you and Dinkie, and bucketed through Europe on a weird trip with Perry during the course of which he played the oddest prank on his brother James."

"Colonel Blimp? What happened?"

"He and Perry took James to a transvestite bar. Then Christian told James to get him a gun and threatened to smear him with buggery allegations if he refused."

"How very baroque! Why did he want a gun?"

"He said he wanted to go into a supermarket and shoot everyone in sight."

"I know the feeling, but obviously one can't quite believe he was serious."

"The point is that he didn't need to extort a weapon from James. Perry could have got him a gun."

"I've often wondered if Perry does more in the FO than organise the canteen. However if Christian had obtained false passports—"

"The whole incident with James was like a prank played by a schoolboy who wants to shock everyone in sight—and in fact Perry did try to brush it off as just a rag. But since it was clearly an example of disturbed behaviour I asked myself what the talk of mass-slaughter indicated about Christian's subconscious mind and how much significance there was in the fact that the scene took place in a bar where people had transformed their given selves into chosen selves."

"The infant phenomenon's picking up steam!" mused Martin, addressing the teapot. "But what on earth's the little love going to come out with next?"

I ignored this. "Christian said that after he'd mown down everyone in the supermarket he'd shoot himself," I continued, "and at first I thought this was clear evidence of a desire to commit suicide, but I now believe I was wrong. Christian was talking in symbolic terms. It wasn't himself he wanted to kill; it was his way of life. And he didn't want to kill the people in the supermarket either; he just wanted to blot out everyone who inhabited his old world. Then he could move into a world that was entirely new."

"The chosen life substituted for the given life?"

"Exactly. Or in other words, I think Christian became drawn to the idea of a *psychic* suicide, the death of the *persona* which was Christian Aysgarth and the birth of someone who accurately reflected his true self."

Martin had abandoned all attempt to tease me. Now it was his turn to say: "Go on."

"My theory is that he became increasingly obsessed by the desire to disappear and he took Perry into his confidence because he couldn't have disappeared without Perry's help. He needed not only the false passports but the boat for the fake-drowning—and he probably needed money too to keep him going while he was establishing a new life. So that spring and early summer they worked out their plan, sailing regularly to France and rehearsing every step of the disappearance . . . Don't you see how it all hangs together?"

Martin absent-mindedly ate the last fragment of angel-cake on his plate and allowed a pause to develop. Then he said: "Yes, I do see. But it's nonsense."

I stared at him. "Why?"

"It's just a *Boys' Own*—style ripping yarn. It wouldn't happen in real life."

"I disagree! Thousands of people go missing every year!"

"Yes—and they do it all on their own without Perry Palmer's help! Nicholas, if I were going to disappear for good by staging an accidental death, I wouldn't confide in anyone, not even my best friend. Much too dangerous, and anyway in my opinion Perry isn't as essential as you seem to think. Why engineer a fake-drowning on a boat? Why not just leave some clothes on the nearest beach? If you had no capital of your own you'd need to raise money, I realise that, but you wouldn't have to rely on a rich friend. Over a period of months you could build up a nest-egg by unobtrusively tapping various sources—you could filch fractions of your wealthy wife's capital, for instance, or siphon a bit here and there off your current account at the bank—or possibly you could even take out a discreet little overdraft if you were friendly with your bank manager. I don't regard either Perry's boat or Perry's money as crucial here."

"What about the need for a false passport?"

"Why the need for any passport? Why go abroad? Why not vanish into somewhere like Doncaster, where no one would ever dream of looking for you, and sign on the dole as an immigrant Irish labourer? I'm not sure how much documentation you'd need, but since the Irish come here *en masse* to work, it can't be difficult to get established without English credentials."

"But can you honestly see Christian posing as an Irish labourer?"

"All right, let's take him out of Doncaster and put him in a white-collar job in Dublin. No passport needed for British subjects going to Ireland, and at least the Irish speak English. Personally I have trouble imagining Christian in a non-English-speaking environment—and not just because of his xenophobic streak. Being cut off from his mother-tongue would have cramped his genius."

"Maybe the false passports were merely to enable him to lie low on the Continent until all the fuss had died down."

"Much simpler just to pop over to Ireland. And why on earth have more than one false passport?"

"I agree that's odd, but—"

"And let me ask you another unanswerable question: what's in all this for Perry? If I had a best friend to whom I'd been devoted all my adult life, would I really be content to bend over backwards to help him disappear for good?"

"Well, I admit that's a bit of a riddle, but—"

"It's all a riddle. And tell me this: how does Christian avoid terminal boredom in a run-of-the-mill white-collar job?"

"Obviously he'd get something more stimulating later."

"How? You can't present yourself for any worthwhile interview without references and some sort of past history."

"Well—"

"Face it, Nicholas. It's not just the false passports that don't add up. It's everything else as well."

I could only say obstinately: "He's alive. I'm sure he's alive. I'm convinced of it."

"You make me extremely nervous! I have a feeling that at any moment you're going to claim you have some special psychic knowledge."

"You bet I am!" I shouted. "I know Christian's alive, I *know* it, it's *gnosis!*"

Martin carefully began to stack the china on the tray. Then having arranged the teapot and the milk-jug to form a symmetrical pattern with the pile of cups, saucers and plates, he said in his kindest voice: "May I make a suggestion? You run off and have one of your leisurely baths. After that I'll take you out to dinner at a nice little hotel nearby where the restaurant's open on Sunday. And after *that,* cleansed, watered and fed, you may with any luck revert to a state where you can think rationally."

"I can think rationally now. Martin, Christian told Venetia that he dreamed of escaping into a world where no one knew him and where there were no women. Assuming you're right about his need to remain in an English-speaking culture, where could he hope to live a secluded life and obtain interesting work without ever having to produce his Christian Aysgarth credentials?"

"Bearing in mind our father's extraordinary career, I find the answer to that question so obvious that I'm surprised you bother to ask it," said Martin. "Where else but a monastery? And the swankiest monasteries in the Church of England—just right for an élitist like Christian—are the houses of the Fordite monks. Maybe he's now running around in a black and white habit, calling himself Brother Cuthbert, or something equally quaint, and having a whale of a time with no sex, no television and first-class Anglo-Catholic stage shows every few hours in the chapel. My God, how attractive that sounds! Maybe I'll try disappearing myself. In fact next time I see Perry I'll ask him to produce a couple of fake-passports and arrange a fake-drowning just as soon as *The Rivals* has finished its run."

And having taken the tray to the kitchen, he returned to the living-room, produced a pair of spectacles and began to read the arts pages of the *Observer.*

I LAY soaking in the bath.

But although my body was inert my thoughts were sweeping along at the speed of light because I knew that in Martin's words, spoken in jest, there lay the truth which fitted all the baffling facts of Christian's last months: I had finally realised that Christian's bizarre behaviour could be explained as the run-up to a profound religious conversion.

I lay limply in the warm water while my brain charted his course with a cool, crisp logic. Christian had been brought up in a religious home by doting parents. Assuming he had had an affectionate relationship in the pre-Dido days with the father whom he resembled, I felt it was not unlikely that he would have considered following Dr. Aysgarth into the Church, and this deduction was supported by Dr. Aysgarth's conviction that Christian had had a call to the priesthood which he had later rejected.

I now reviewed the circumstances which had triggered the rejection. The first Mrs. Aysgarth had died; Christian had suffered such an emotional upheaval that he had wound up far off-course, and his father's crass involvement with Dido had ensured that Christian had never recovered his spiritual bearings. That didn't mean the call from God had ceased to exist. It merely meant that Christian had been too maimed to respond to it. Instead of responding, aiming to express the blueprint of his personality in a life which fulfilled all his God-given potential, he had turned aside, driven on by his erratic, damaged ego, and invested many years living what he had at last come to realise was an inauthentic existence, a life which divorced him from his true self. It would have been at this point that he would have become aware of the force pressing on his psyche, the force which wanted to unite him with his true self, the force which was the immanent God whose spark lay buried deep in his unconscious mind.

The unconscious mind is uncharted territory; we know it exists but most of the time we only know a fraction of what goes on there and it takes a great deal of time and effort, as all psychoanalysts know, to try to discern more than this dimly glimpsed fragment. Yet when our conscious minds are troubled we know we must try to perceive this uncharted territory more clearly—and this axiom of modern psychology isn't so innovative as most people think. The medieval mystics were well aware that the way to control the dark forces of the unconscious was to expose them to the light of knowledge; they knew as well as any modern psychoanalyst that the road to spiritual and emotional health begins with the task of knowing oneself—and knowing not just the ego but the inner self beyond.

"Swink and sweat in all that thou canst and mayest," wrote the anonymous fourteenth-century author of the spiritual classic *The Cloud of Unknowing,* "for to get thee a true knowing and feeling of thyself as thou art. And then, I trow, soon after that thou wilt get thee a true knowing and feeling of God as He is."

That writer certainly realised that the quest for God is a quest for psychic integration, a wholeness which allows the ego to be subjugated, the true self to triumph and the entire personality, conscious and unconscious, to be open to and at one with God's will and God's love. This wholeness, as I had tried to explain without success to Norman, was the unique feature of Jesus Christ. He had achieved perfect integration, something not possible in this world for human beings doomed to be imperfect; all we can do on this side of the grave is embark on that road to fulfilment and hope to travel as far as possible, but Jesus had already arrived. He was all-of-a-piece. His psyche was entirely harmonised, the ego seamlessly interwoven with his inner self. He was, as the religious language puts it, "wholly at one with the Father."

Christian's frantic words to Dinkie: "I want to live! I'm dead and I want to live!" suggested that he was by that time yearning to ditch the false ego which had created the inauthentic existence, and unite with his true self. He might still not have been aware of the renewed call from God to a religious life, but he would definitely be experiencing God as a constant pressure on the ego by the unconscious mind. (I should stress here that I'm not trying to explain God away by brandishing a scientific theory. I'm merely expressing His action in the language of psychology. Science destroys only the false ideas about religion; the true ideas it complements and explores.)

And having mentioned the false ideas about religion, I might as well add that it's strange how many people only picture God as transcendent, making Himself known by shooting off thunderbolts. God *is* transcendent, certainly, above the world and beyond it, outside time and space in a mode of being which is beyond the scope of our imaginations to conceive, but the God who makes Himself known to us is the immanent God, the God who's so close that He's at the very centre of our existence. It's strange too how much time people spend travelling round and round the circle of existence and getting nowhere. The real journey—the journey all people are required to take to achieve integration, self-realisation and fulfilment—the "eternal life" of religious language—is the journey inwards, the journey to the centre of the soul.

Viewing Christian in the light of these ancient truths, one could see him not as someone undergoing a bizarre mental breakdown but as someone enduring a profound spiritual crisis as he tried to break out of the closed circle of his inauthentic existence and embark at last on the journey to the immanent God who had designed that neglected blueprint of the man he was supposed to be. The spiritual crisis would be all the more profound for Christian because he was an atheist. Having rejected God after his mother's death, he would automatically fight God every inch of the way as soon as the spiritual crisis began to manifest itself. Or at least, the ego would fight. The true self wanted to be rescued ("I want to live!") but the ego wasn't going to relinquish absolute power without a fight, and the result, as with all violent revolutions, was very messy indeed.

God would keep right on, of course, pressing away on the psyche, but Christian's ego would keep right on too, battling away in terror against the invasive force. God isn't all sweetness and light. God can be frightening, particularly when you've decided that He doesn't exist but slowly realise there's something out there, closing in—or rather, in there, welling up. Finally Christian cracked under the pressure and the ego began to fragment in the unpleasantest manner imaginable. St. Paul's ego also suffered a messy fragmentation; while God was exerting the pressure on his psyche follow-ing the martyrdom of St. Stephen, Paul bucketed around persecuting Christians with a renewed and revolting vigour. What a relief when God finally triumphed! The famous light on the road to Damascus can be seen as a pictorial representation of a mind-blowing psychic experience in which the true self, driven on by God, finally overwhelmed that false, ferocious ego.

Eventually Christian reached a crucial point on his own road to Damas-cus and saw what he thought was the light. What he should have done at this stage was to seek spiritual counselling as he tried to solve the puzzle of how he could merge the trappings of his old life (Katie, Marina, the children, Oxford) with a new existence which was authentic. But he was a non-churchgoer who had never formed the habit of talking to a spiritual director. (If only my father hadn't fobbed him off in 1963 when Christian had realised he felt uncomfortable with his life!) In 1965, as far as Christian could work out in his confused state, his only hope was to abandon his old life completely and begin again somewhere else.

Once that decision had been reached, I reflected as I idly washed the tepid bath-water over my stomach, what could be more natural than that he should seek refuge in a monastery while he tried to come to terms with the indisputable truth that God, not the false ego, was now in the driving-seat of his personality? In addition he would by this time almost certainly be suffering a reaction from the sexual binges indulged in during the period of fragmentation. In a monastery there would be no sexual distractions and he could concentrate on the demanding journey inwards to uncover and explore more fully that true self which he had suppressed for so long.

I hooked my toe into the chain of the bath-plug and tugged. The water began to drain away. Heaving myself to my feet I drew the shower-curtain and prepared for more sensual bliss. I loved bathrooms.

It was probable, I reflected as I luxuriated under the shower, that Christian wouldn't have retired to a monastery with the idea of becoming a monk. He would merely have seen it as a sanctuary where he could sort himself out, and he would have stayed in reasonable comfort in the guest-quarters. But then he would have slowly realised that the monastic life was the life he wanted, a life free from the pressures of doting human beings and the demands of worldly success. In the monastery he could live quietly and happily, his emotional life, which had been so maimed in his previous existence, now made whole in the worship of God. Moreover, provided that he chose the right monastery, he could exercise his intellectual gifts. One of the great traditions of a Benedictine way of life was a devotion to scholarship.

I couldn't see Christian "going over to Rome." I thought it was far more likely that with his particular upbringing and his xenophobic streak he would have reverted to the Church of England, and as Martin had so correctly pointed out, the most suitable Anglican Order for him was that of the Fordite monks—the Fordite Order of St. Benedict and St. Bernard, founded in the 1840s by an old rogue called Horatio Ford, whose life provided yet another example of a mind-blowing religious conversion.

In the nineteenth century the Fordites had survived less by luck or by judgement or even by holiness than by the fact that they were rich; old Ford had made a fortune dealing in slaves. It's notoriously difficult to found an order and most attempts usually end in bankruptcy or bickering, but because of Ford's lavish endowment the monks only had to beat the bickering and keep themselves organised. This they achieved, even expanding sufficiently to found their Grantchester house in the 1890s, but then as so often happens in a well-heeled organisation, the dynamic impulse faded and the monks became dozy. This situation was cured by my father's mentor, the celebrated Cuthbert Darcy, who became Abbot-General in 1908, woke up each house, dusted down each monk and embarked on a canny public relations campaign to improve the Order's image with the Church's hierarchy. In this he was brilliantly successful, and by 1923 when my father entered the Order, the Fordites were renowned for their scholarship and their devout way of life.

They had continued to flourish until the mid-twentieth century, when, in common with all orders both Roman and Anglican, falling numbers had obliged them to contract and regroup. In addition to the Grantchester house, purchased long after Ford's death, there were three other monasteries: Ford's London townhouse, which served as the Order's headquarters; his country seat, Starwater Abbey, where I had attended the monks' public school; and Ruydale, the sheep-farm in North Yorkshire, which had been one of his property investments. But in 1963 Ruydale was closed. My father was upset by this and said the Abbot-General should instead have sold the extravagant house in London, but the Fordites were in no need of money and the Abbot-General was determined to cling to his impressive headquarters. Ruydale's insuperable difficulties had arisen because the few remaining elderly monks could no longer cope with the sheep-farm.

However, despite falling numbers the other houses appeared secure, even in the 1960s. Starwater Abbey was safe because the school was now largely run by lay-staff. London was safe because it could run on minimal man-power. And Grantchester was safe because although it was set on five acres which required a certain amount of manual labour, it had never been seriously short of postulants. This was because it appealed to two different types of would-be monk: the devotees of the simple life, who liked the idea of self-sufficiency on a smallholding, and the devotees of the intellec-tual life, who relished the Order's close association with the divinity faculty at Cambridge University two miles away.

My thoughts appeared to have wandered some way from Christian, but in fact, as I realised after my shower, the meditation on the Fordites had been productive because I now had no doubt that he was a monk at the Grantchester house. He would have avoided Starwater Abbey. Not only was it too near Starbridge, where the Aysgarths were so well-known, but the Abbot might have insisted that he teach at the school, and if Christian longed to make a break with his past he would hardly have wanted to continue teaching. The London headquarters was a possibility, but I re-membered that it had been the Grantchester house which my father had recommended to him in 1963, and I was sure that Christian would have been irresistibly attracted by that Cambridge connection.

I tried to estimate the risk he would run of being recognised by a visitor, but I concluded it was acceptable. Cambridge for him was the "Other Place," and although high-powered academics might switch from Oxford to Cambridge in the course of their careers, few Oxonians would normally venture among the ivory towers of East Anglia. There was always the risk that clerics coming to Grantchester for a retreat might be friends of his father's, but he could keep an eye on the guest-master's list of visitors and pull up his cowl if danger threatened. I myself had been a regular visitor to the Grantchester house while I was up at Cambridge, but I had come down from Laud's in the summer of 1964, a year before Christian's death, and I hadn't been back since; the Starbridge Theological College used Starwater Abbey when it sent its ordinands on retreats. My father corre-sponded with the Abbot of Grantchester, Father Wilcox, but even if the Abbot had mentioned an intellectually gifted new postulant, my father would have had no means of making an identification. Whatever name Christian was using, it wouldn't be Christian Aysgarth—and it wouldn't be Charles Gore or Henry Scott Holland either. Father Wilcox would certainly have boggled if a would-be monk had turned up with the same name as one of the *Lux Mundi* crowd.

I decided I could see Christian at Grantchester. Not literally; my powers were never visual. But I thought he would like Grantchester. I thought he would consider any risks attached to entering that particular monastery worth taking. I thought—I *knew*—he was there.

I towelled myself down. Then I dressed in clean clothes and, feigning calmness, drifted back into the living-room to rejoin Martin.

5

"*YOU* haven't asked," said Martin, "but I assume you're staying the night. Perhaps you feel you don't need to ask. However, it's generally acknowledged in civilised circles that a modest request for hospitality, preceded by the word 'please,' is required when one plans to inflict oneself on any place which isn't a hotel. Of course I'm just an old fogey, hopelessly out of touch with today's youth, but I think you'll find that even in thrillingly louche 1968, a considerable number of people still believe that 'Manners makyth man.' "

Had to humour the old bugger. "Sorry. Please may I stay the night?"

"You may. God, what a slog parenthood must be! I used to regret not having children, but now I see I've had a merciful escape."

"In that case why do you continue to play the father with me? I can't tell you how irritating I find it! I don't want you being a father—I've already got a father—"

"Yes—poor Dad! Too young to cope with me and now too old to cope with you!"

"He doesn't have to cope. We get on."

"You mean you cultivate a synthetic psychic cosiness, but that's not getting on—that's copping out!"

"Shut up!"

"Dad's very worried about you actually."

"*Shut up!*"

"You won't believe this, but I think he and I have a far more honest relationship nowadays than—"

"SHUT UP!" I stormed out in fury.

He tapped on the door of the spare-room five minutes later. "Can we take the apologies as read and have a truce? It's time for me to bear you off to dinner."

I opened the door. "Okay." I had in fact been feeling hungry for some time.

"Do you want to phone home before we leave?" said Martin neutrally.

I called the Manor. "I'm staying at Martin's flat," I said to Rowena. "Tell Father I've written him an interesting letter. How is he?"

"Well, unfortunately, Nicholas . . ."

Unfortunately his hands were bothering him so much that he could no longer hold a knife and fork.

"It's all self-induced," I said, rigid with rage and fear. "It's a psychosomatic illness brought on by this stupid, futile, utterly self-indulgent worrying about me, and quite frankly I think it's time you lot got off your bottoms and told him to stop being such a damned drag!"

"Nicholas!"

I slammed down the receiver. Martin, who had been watching me, turned away without a word.

We went out to dinner.

6

"WILL you be heading for home tomorrow?" enquired Martin casually over our sirloin steaks.

"No, I'm going to Grantchester. I want to have a chat with the Abbot and meditate for a bit."

We munched on. The steak was spongy and pink, the chips crisp, the mushrooms succulent.

"Great," I said, laying down my knife and fork at last. "Thanks."

"Glad you enjoyed it. Nicholas, why don't you admit you're going to Grantchester because you think Christian will be there?"

"Look, I've just said—"

"Yes, I heard what you said, but I've drawn my own conclusions and now I think it's time I gave you a word of . . . no, not fatherly advice. Let's call it a word of brotherly warning. Detach yourself from Christian Aysgarth."

"Martin—"

"I wasn't exaggerating earlier when I called him a dangerous man. He nearly destroyed me, and I think, if you look around, you'll find mine wasn't the only life he poisoned. I believe he's dead, but if you persist in this obsession of yours he could wind up doing you as much damage as if he were still alive—and if he *is* still alive, then all I can say is: run for cover. You could be opening up a box of horrors bigger than you ever dreamed could exist."

After a long pause I said: "Okay," and finished my Coke. "Any hope of pudding?"

Martin silently motioned the waitress for the menu.

I DREAMED about my father that night. In the dream he was about sixty-five, the age at which I could first remember him, and he was a youthful sixty-five, swift-moving, straight-backed and, to my child's eyes, huge. Those were the days before his stoop, when he was six foot three. He walked into the room where I was sleeping and turned on the light so that I woke up.

Except that I didn't wake up. But I thought I had woken up, and there he was, walking into the room and sitting down on the chair by the window. He said nothing, but suddenly I saw there was blood all over his hands and I knew he was bleeding to death like Marina's friend, poor Holly Carr, who had committed suicide by slashing her wrists. I leapt out of bed to staunch the blood, but Christian stepped in front of me, a Luger in his hand, and as I flung up my arms in a futile effort to protect myself he pointed the gun at my heart and squeezed the trigger and—

I woke up.

Except that I couldn't have woken up because I wasn't in bed. I was now dreaming I was in a black cell. There was a grey square halfway up one wall, and when I stretched out my hand towards it my fingers touched some stuff which turned out to be a curtain. A pale light flicked across the cell for a second as I exposed the window. Then I realised I stood not in an unknown cell but in Martin's living-room.

I woke up.

Except that I couldn't have woken up because I had gone to sleep in the spare-room. I could clearly remember pulling back the bedcovers, slumping down on the mattress, swinging my feet off the floor—

My feet. I had forgotten to tether my ankle. The string which I had been using was still at Charley's vicarage. I could recall rolling the string into a ball but I had no memory of packing it, and last night I had been so exhilarated by my theories about Christian that the possibility of unwanted nocturnal adventures had entirely slipped my mind.

Clutching the curtain again I dragged it aside and sank down on the moonlit sofa to struggle with the vile aftermath of somnambulism.

The shock came first, but fear followed close behind and within seconds the two of them were hammering away in tandem. My heart thumped. My fists ached as I clenched them. I was struggling with the terrible suspicion that I had killed Martin in his sleep. I knew the idea was absurd, but so overwhelmed was I by panic that I found I had to go and take a look at him.

He was alive, breathing peacefully. Weak with relief, I tiptoed out of the room but was then bludgeoned by the dread that I might have gone outside and killed a stranger in the street. I looked at the soles of my feet. They were clean. I hadn't left the flat. It seemed I had merely walked from the spare-room to the living-room, and all I now had to do was calm myself down.

I began to recite the mantra and when I stopped twenty minutes later I knew I had once more succeeded in squeezing my consciousness back behind the orthodox boundaries. Moving to the kitchen, I searched the cupboards until I found a ball of string. Then I returned to the spare-room and tethered myself to the bed.

But I was unable to sleep again.

8

MAKING an early start, I drove north out of London up the A1. Rush-hour traffic chugged slowly in the other direction but I sped along in my Mini-Cooper until I reached the road to Biggleswade, the point where I could head cross-country to Cambridge. I began my drive through rural Bedfordshire. Huge fields undulated around compact, workmanlike little villages. A succession of church towers pierced the horizon.

After crossing the county border into Cambridgeshire I eventually reached the summit of the hill beyond Orwell where the spires of the University could be seen in the distance, and as I drove down onto the plain I pictured Cambridge itself, that city of the mind, with its bookshops and bells and bicycles, its smooth lawns and hidden gardens and its somnolent river flowing through the meadows of the Backs. It was in Cambridge that I had first met Marina and begun my journey towards Christian. How neat it would be if I could end my quest where it had begun, but no, I wasn't destined to enact that famous line from the "Four Quartets"; I was heading for Grantchester, the village which a lesser poet than Eliot had immortal- ised in drivel about the church clock standing at ten to three and was there honey still for tea.

The Grantchester monks kept bees and since the 1920s had traded brazenly on the Rupert Brooke connection. My father had redesigned the packaging of the honey long ago in 1937 after Father Darcy had yanked him out of Ruydale, his home for fourteen years, and dumped him at Grantchester to be the abbot. The community had gone soft and someone from another house had been required to toughen it up. "There was even a cream-cake in the larder!" my father used to reminisce, scandalised. "Father Darcy said . . ."

What a bore my father was about that old thug, but old people had to talk about the past, it was necessary for them, their psyches required to be stroked by memory in that way. Yet it was curious which sections of the past my father selected for the stroking. He never reminisced about his marriages and only occasionally did he mention his childhood with his parents. What he talked about was his great monastic soap-opera which had run from 1923 until 1940.

I knew that soap-opera inside out. I knew not only all about Father Darcy but about Francis Ingram, the debonair aristocrat who had succeeded him as Abbot-General; I knew about Aidan Lucas, my father's abbot at Ruydale, and about Cyril Watson, who had been abbot of Starwater; I knew too about the minor characters such as Wilfred and Ambrose and Bernard and Barnabas and . . . The list went on and on. I even knew the entire life-story of the original Whitby, the house-cat at Ruydale. This vast accumulated knowledge was why I always found it so strange, almost uncanny, to visit the Grantchester house where my father had spent three years as a Fordite abbot. I wasn't just visiting a monastery. I was stepping onto one of the sets of my father's epic soap-opera.

The house had been built in the late nineteenth century and was one of those solid, unspectacular country mansions which the Victorians special- ised in producing once their architects had recovered from the national love affair with medieval fantasy. On one side of the house was the extension, designed by my father in 1938, where the guests stayed; he had wanted to encourage visitors but at the same time guarantee the monks greater privacy. This wing was connected to the main house by a long, low building which contained not only the linking passage but the confes- sionals, small rooms where guests could discuss spiritual matters with the priest-monks.

The gravelled drive wound gracefully up to the front door of the house, flowed on to the front door of the guest-wing and then looped around to rejoin itself so that its final shape resembled a curvy letter P. Around this elegant design were neat lawns bordered by beech-trees. A fence on the perimeter preserved the monks from prying eyes, but the gates stood open. Having parked my car by the guest-wing, I rang the bell, turned the handle and walked in.

Across the hall was a kitchen. Lunch—which the monks called dinner— was brought over from the main house every day, but a light evening meal was produced in the guest-wing after the monks had supped off bread and cheese in their refectory. Guests also used the kitchen to make themselves tea when they fancied it. On the left of the kitchen was the guest-master's office, where he attended to the running of his miniature hotel, and on the right was the dining-room, where all the visitors ate sitting around a long table. Beyond the dining-room was the common-room, painted the deadest of dead whites but furnished with colourfully upholstered armchairs and well-stocked bookcases.

As I entered the hall the guest-master bobbed out to meet me and I saw he was a stranger. He was drying a plate with a scarlet tea-towel which might have been specially designed as a striking accessory for his black and white habit.

"Good morning!" he said with that peculiarly relentless cheerfulness which is so often found among practitioners of the cenobitic life. "I'm Daniel, the guest-master. How may I help you?"

My father would have hated this modern chumminess. In his day only the monks themselves had called one another by their Christian names, and outsiders had used surnames preceded by the title "Father," if the monk was a priest, or "Brother," if the monk was a layman. Although the Fordites had made no distinction in dress between the two groups, there had been no problem of classification for visitors because in the old days the priests were the ones who were gentlemen and one always knew a gentleman as soon as he opened his mouth. Nowadays when social boundaries were hazier the Fordites still refused to make a distinction in dress but had encouraged the use of Christian names both to reflect the informality of the *zeitgeist* and to simplify monastic protocol.

"Hi Daniel," I said, shaking the hand he offered me. "What happened to Christopher?" That was the guest-master I remembered from my last visit in 1964.

"He's Bursar now, Mr.—?"

"Darrow—Nicholas Darrow. Son of Jonathan Darrow, your abbot from 1937 to 1940," I said shamelessly, knowing I had to pull out all the stops to gain an instant audience with Father Wilcox. (Abbots, to my father's relief, were still addressed formally by outsiders.)

"Aha!" said Daniel, rising to the bait and becoming very chummy indeed. "Welcome to Grantchester, Nicholas!"

"Thanks. Any chance of seeing Father Wilcox for five minutes? My father asked me to say hullo to him."

Daniel, oozing good will, said he would see what he could do.

I wandered into the common-room to wait and found a limp middle-aged cleric reading Thomas Merton's *Thoughts in Solitude*. I liked Merton, an emotional monk but tough and modern. It occurred to me that the Fordites could do with a few Merton clones. That Daniel was much too precious.

The limp middle-aged cleric said "Good morning" in an alto-tenor, and I realised he was precious too. I found myself longing for a replay of 1937 when my father, then in his fifties, had swept through the front door to tone everyone down and toughen everyone up.

I was still reflecting on this dramatic incident in my father's monastic soap-opera when Daniel pattered back to announce his success in securing me an audience with the Abbot. Leaving the common-room we crossed the hall, walked down the interlinking passage and entered the hall of the main house.

The Abbot was waiting to meet me, and as soon as I saw him again I forgot the spectre of decadence now haunting the Church because I knew I was in the presence of a man who had no time for the thought that we were all dissolute and effete and fit only for the nearest drain. Here was someone who accepted us as we were, warts and all, and looked upon us with faith and hope and love because he knew we were made, no matter how imperfectly, in the image of God. Here was a real disciple of Christ, someone who made me want to put up with the Church for the sake of Christianity.

He was a friendly old buffer, with mild eyes and a stout frame—quite different from my father, but that didn't matter. All that mattered was that he exuded the right aura of intelligent compassion, the aura of a devout man who was a conscientious, balanced leader.

"How nice to see you again, Nicholas!" he said, shaking my hand and ushering me into the parlour where he received visitors. "Is your father well? I haven't heard from him lately."

"Yes, he's fine, said he'd write soon." The room was amazing, a museum-piece unchanged since the 1890s when the Fordites had acquired the house from the bankrupt merchant who had built it. The most riveting feature was the high, wide marble fireplace, which bore a sculpted frieze of naked nymphs doing gymnastics with animals. Or at least I supposed that was what they were doing. My father had said it was a most unsuitable frieze for a monastery but Father Darcy had ruled that allowances had to be made for great art. Naughty old thug. Of course it wasn't great art at all, but I suspected he had been unable to resist the chance to have a dig at my father's uncertain artistic taste.

Recalling my attention from the raunchy frieze, I said politely: "Thank you for seeing me so quickly, Father. I promise I won't keep you long."

"But there's no need to rush along at top speed for my sake! Sit down, relax and tell me all your news—the big day's coming up very soon now, isn't it?"

"Yes, but I didn't come to talk to you about my ordination. I wanted to ask you about a man who made a retreat here in the last quarter of 1963. He was sent by my father and his name was Christian Aysgarth."

"I certainly remember that unusual name," said Father Wilcox as we sat down facing each other in the high-backed chairs which flanked the fireplace. "He was the brilliant young don who drowned in that sailing accident, wasn't he? As soon as I read the report in the paper I wondered if he was related to Dean Aysgarth of Starbridge and later I heard he was the eldest son. A terrible tragedy . . . But you're mistaken about the retreat.

He never came here, and in fact I don't even remember receiving the letter of referral from your father."

"I don't think he wrote one. He just pointed Christian in your direction," I said, busy savouring the fact that Father Wilcox had never met anyone called Christian Aysgarth. The report he had read of the accident would have been the one produced by *The Times,* the only newspaper allowed to cross the monastic threshold, but *The Times* had printed no photograph. If Christian had arrived at Grantchester to embark on a new life he would have been unrecognised.

"Father, have you anyone here at the moment who's six foot tall, dark, good-looking, slim, fortyish, with an educated accent and a trick of either drawling his words or else speaking unusually fast with a very slight, barely noticeable stutter?"

"No," said the Abbot bemused, but added as an afterthought: "Are you talking about a monk or a guest?"

"Well, I thought he might be a monk by now, but—"

"You'll have to ask Daniel about the visitors, but I can assure you we have no professed monks, no novices and no postulants here who answer that description. May I ask who this man is?"

"He's connected with Christian Aysgarth, and I'm trying to trace him. Father, has anyone ever applied to you for admittance to the Order and said his name was either Charles Gore or Henry Scott Holland?"

Father Wilcox was astounded but responded good-humouredly: "No, we don't go in for ghosts here, Nicholas!"

I laughed. Then I suddenly realised I had no idea what to say next, but fortunately Father Wilcox was eager to steer the conversation into other channels.

"Now do tell me all about your father!" he exclaimed warmly. "He'll be eighty-eight in May, won't he? Amazing! I can so clearly remember when I was a novice back in 1937 . . ."

Back we went into the past again. Out came the monastic soap-opera for another rerun, but this was different, this was the story filmed from another angle, and this time the hero was not Father Darcy but Father Darrow.

". . . and I always felt sorry that I only knew Father Darcy at the end of his life when he was so crusty and cantankerous—dear me, how we used to shake in our shoes before his annual visitation! 'You're saying the words you want me to hear,' he'd declare when he interviewed us, 'but I hear the words you can't bring yourself to say!' How terrifying that was, especially for the novices! But your father had quite a different approach; he *never* ruled by terror. What a leader he was, so wise, so compassionate, so understanding, so spiritual . . ."

I switched off and began to plan my cross-examination of Daniel.

". . . but quite difficult for you, I should imagine," Father Wilcox concluded suddenly.

I realised I had to tune in again. "Difficult for me?"

"Having such a very outstanding man as a father," said the Abbot kindly. "A hard act to follow, perhaps, but I'm sure you'll do equally well in the Church in your own way."

I murmured some polite banality, dredged up some neutral news about my father for him and made a tactful escape.

Returning to the guest-wing I found Daniel typing with two fingers in his office. The typewriter looked like a prop from a pre-war film-set. "Excuse me," I said, "but is there any guest here who . . ." I described Christian but again drew a blank. Daniel said with a sigh of regret that none of the current guests could be classified as tall, dark and handsome. "Will you be staying to dinner, Nicholas?" he added. "Today it's roast lamb with bread-and-butter pudding to follow."

I hesitated, confused by the apparent failure of my psychic *gnosis* and uncertain what I should do next. Feeling that I needed to be somewhere quiet in order to think, I glanced at my watch to see how much time remained before the midday meal. The hands pointed to eleven-twenty.

"Thanks," I said to Daniel. "Yes, I'd like to stay. Meanwhile can I go and sit in the garden?"

"Of course you can, but keep an eye open for the sections that are out of bounds. They're all marked, but visitors sometimes get absent-minded and overlook the signs."

This was a tactful order not to stray from the area set aside for guests. Assuring him that I already knew exactly where not to go, I left his office and stepped out once more into the drive.

There was a wooden seat under one of the beech-trees in the front garden, but I knew I would be disturbed there by the noise of passing traffic, so I began to pad around the side of the guest-wing. A monk was weeding a flowerbed nearby, and as he heard the crunch of my footsteps on the path he turned to smile at me. He was about fifty, thick-set, bald—definitely not Christian, but of course I now knew Christian was not at Grantchester.

I reached the section of the back garden which was reserved for guests. The section was divided in two: directly behind the guest-wing lay the lawn, and beyond the lawn was the herb-garden. The latter formed a small square with a sun-dial in the centre and a bench at one side, but I thought the smells might prove distracting so I sat down instead on the seat which stood at one end of the lawn. Yet another beech-tree rose behind me to provide shelter from the unseasonably hot sun.

I now have to describe exactly what I saw as I sat on that seat. This is difficult; not having been trained as either an artist or a policeman I seldom notice a view in detail, but this is where I must make a big effort to achieve total recall in order to set what became a very bizarre scene.

There I was, as I have just stated, sitting under the beech-tree which overshadowed one end of the visitors' lawn. Let me first summarise the general view which met my eyes: on my left was the guest-wing, the interlinking passage and, in the distance, the main house; straight ahead of me on the other side of the lawn was the wall of the kitchen-garden; to my right was the herb-garden, bounded by the perimeter hedge which marked off the visitors' precinct from the monks' smallholding, and behind me this tall perimeter hedge continued towards the front of the house. In other words, I was sitting in an area bounded on two sides by a tall, thick hedge and on the other two sides by bricks and mortar.

There were three exits from this area. One: the path I had just traversed, the path which led around the side of the guest-wing. Two: the gap in the perimeter hedge at the back of the herb-garden, the gap which provided an entrance into the smallholding. And three: the archway in the wall straight ahead of me, the wall of the kitchen-garden. Beside the archway and beside the gap in the perimeter hedge were notices telling guests that the kitchen-garden and the smallholding were out of bounds.

So much for the general topography. Now for the details.

The wall ahead of me—the wall of the kitchen-garden—ran from the back of the main house on my left to the tall perimeter hedge on my right. Through the archway a small section of the vegetable beds was visible to me, and at the right of the archway my attention was quickly drawn to a magnificent peach-tree which had long ago been trained to grow against the wall in such a way that its main branches formed four lines parallel to the ground. The wall was high, about eight feet, and it surrounded the kitchen-garden on three sides; the main house itself stood on the fourth side.

At the point where the kitchen-garden wall met the perimeter hedge a shed had been constructed to house the lawn-mower and various gardening implements. Another hedge had been planted to screen this eyesore from visitors, but the hedge was not yet tall enough to hide the shed's corrugated iron roof. I remember looking at it and wondering why the monks had been content to build something so ugly in their quiet, serene, restful visitors' garden.

It was a perfect April day, the sky cloudless, the sun hot. It must have been around seventy degrees. I'd left my leather jacket in the car and I was wearing a short-sleeved shirt with my jeans, but I felt comfortable and although my thoughts were scampering around I was physically relaxed. I sat there for some minutes while my brain flickered away inconsequentially, but at last I decided I should get down to some serious thinking.

I glanced at my watch again. The time was now twenty-eight minutes past eleven.

I looked up from my wrist, and at that moment a monk appeared at the other end of the lawn. He emerged from behind the small hedge, the one which was inadequately screening the shed, and began to walk along the path beside the kitchen-garden wall. At once I deduced he had been in the shed for some minutes sorting out or perhaps cleaning tools, but the only implement he now carried was a rake. As he walked from right to left across my field of vision I saw him in profile but his features were shadowed because he was wearing his cowl drawn forward. Then as he passed the magnificent peach-tree he turned his head and looked straight at me across the long expanse of lawn which separated us.

It was Christian.

9

HE NEVER stopped. He never even paused. He just looked at me and turned his head away again. A moment later he had disappeared through the archway into the kitchen-garden.

How long did I take to react? Five seconds? Ten? All I know is that there was a brief interval during which all movement was blocked by my blank mind. Then a burst of energy blasted me to my feet. I shouted: "CHRISTIAN!" and pounded across the lawn to the archway.

Gasping for breath I erupted into the kitchen-garden.

No one was there.

I stared at the vegetable beds in disbelief. Automatically I rubbed my eyes but when I looked again at the garden it was unchanged. I was definitely awake and everything I was seeing was real. There was no confusion in my mind about that. But I had apparently witnessed the impossible: a human being vanishing into thin air.

Then I realised that although the back door of the main house was some distance away across the kitchen-garden, it was nearer to the archway than my bench under the tree. Mystery solved. Christian had reached the back door while I'd still been pounding across the lawn.

I plunged through the archway into forbidden territory. Racing down the path, I shot across a paved yard and burst through the back door of the house.

The monk peeling potatoes at the scullery sink nearly passed out; the peeler flew from his hand as he reeled against the wall. But he wasn't Christian. He was short, red-haired, under thirty. Ignoring him I blazed on through the scullery into the main kitchen, and again I shouted "CHRISTIAN!" at the top of my voice.

The four monks engaged in the task of preparing the midday meal had already been transfixed by my noisy entrance. The one by the larder was about five foot nine, middle-aged, grey-haired; the one by the dresser was around six foot, fat and bald; the two by the table were wrinkled old men.

"All right, where is he?" I demanded, striding into the room. "Where's that monk who just came in?"

They continued to stare at me. No one spoke.

"I know he's here!" I shouted, enraged by their silence. "Don't try and deny it!" I was about to start searching the nearby cupboards when I realised that there was no reason why Christian should hide in the kitchen. All he had to do to avoid me was to retire to his cell. Swinging back to confront the monks again, I said furiously: "What's he calling himself? That monk who just came in—tall, dark, fortyish—what name's he using now?"

One of the monks finally took charge. The grey-haired man who had been standing by the open door of the larder turned to the fat bald monk by the dresser and said quietly in an educated voice: "Thomas, fetch Father Abbot." Then he closed the larder door and added to me with immaculate courtesy: "I'm sorry, sir, but I'm afraid there's some mistake. No one came in here just now from the garden, and we've no monk in this house who fits that description."

"You're lying." I wiped the sweat from my forehead. "This is a conspiracy," I said. "You're all in it together, you're all ganging up to deceive me, you're all—" I ran out of breath. When I wiped my forehead again I realised my hand was trembling.

Nobody said anything. They merely looked at me with appalled fascination, as if I were quite insane.

Then, of course, I realised that I was.

It was as if something had silently removed cool, rational Nicholas Darrow and filled the resulting physical shell with someone else.

I tried to say: "Jesus is Lord," but I couldn't. Naturally I couldn't. Possessed people never can.

Pressing back against the nearest wall, the physical remnant of Nicholas Darrow sank down, covering his face with his hands, and curled himself into a foetal position.

Then he began to shudder from head to toe.

PART TWO

THE JOURNEY
TO THE
CENTRE

"*Perhaps the only way to avoid attaching ourselves to some false centre, whether a cause, a person or some aspect of our selves, is to discover and submit to the authority of our true centre, the place where God makes his presence and purpose for us known. To be attached to a false centre inevitably leads to division within the personality . . .*"

CHRISTOPHER BRYANT
Member of the Society of St. John the Evangelist,
1935–1985
THE RIVER WITHIN

"*It may be that stories of demonic possession are explicable rather as stories of psychological disorder.*"

MICHAEL RAMSEY
Archbishop of Canterbury, 1961–1974
CANTERBURY ESSAYS AND ADDRESSES

X

"In other words human life is under threat from destructive forces or evil. It was one of Jung's complaints about Christian theologians that they did not take evil seriously enough."

CHRISTOPHER BRYANT
Member of the Society of St. John the Evangelist,
1935–1985
JUNG AND THE CHRISTIAN WAY

I

A THOUGHT crawled from a crevice. The thought was: no one must know I'm possessed.

A reason crept after the thought. The sentence was extended to become: no one must know I'm possessed, because if I'm possessed I can't be ordained.

Then a welcome deduction arrived: I really do want to be ordained.

And finally, mercifully, the revelation was received. It was: if I still want to be ordained I can't be possessed because a person infested by the Devil would never want to serve God.

Streaming back into my body, I found myself still hunched in a foetal position and shuddering from head to toe.

A hand suddenly touched my shoulder. Father Wilcox said: "It's all right, Nicholas. I'm here now."

I tried unsuccessfully to speak. It seemed I was still in shock despite the fact that I was now capable of rational thought. My glasses had steamed up. I managed to remove them from my nose but could do no more. I sat clutching them tightly.

Meanwhile the Abbot was saying: "Don't worry, we'll sort everything out, I'm sure there's a rational explanation. Now, if you'd like to get up I think you'll find you'll be more comfortable sitting on a chair . . . Peter, fetch Mr. Darrow a glass of water, please, and then go to the infirmary for brandy . . ."

More rational thoughts occurred to me. They were: Christian's alive. Therefore his spirit couldn't have manifested itself to me in the garden and it certainly couldn't now be infesting me in a demonic form. Therefore it's time I stopped behaving like a shell-shock case.

I sat up.

"That's right, Nicholas, that's it, that's better . . . Yes, give your glasses a good polish so that you can see this is just an ordinary old-fashioned kitchen, very humdrum, no horrors . . . Now, have a drink of water—light a cigarette if you like—do you smoke?—no?—and just tell me how you came to be here. I know you would never have entered any enclosed area without the best possible reason."

By the time he had finished this speech I was sitting at the kitchen table with my glasses back on my nose and a tumbler of water in my hand. I opened my mouth. Words came out. I was recovering.

"I was in the back garden," I said. "I was sitting on the seat by the beech-tree and I saw this monk walking along by the kitchen-garden wall." I managed to look Father Wilcox straight in the eyes before stating: "It was Christian Aysgarth."

Father Wilcox said immediately: "Matthew, find Paul and say I want the grounds searched at once—tell him to use the novices. Thomas, I want you to go round the house and make a note of where everyone was five minutes ago—but don't bother about the novices because they'll have been together in the scriptorium. When you've done that, go to the guest-wing and find out from Daniel where all the guests were. Timothy"—he turned to address the young sandy-haired monk who had been peeling potatoes—"find Andrew and ask him to count the spare habits in the linen-chest. I also want him to go to the laundry-room and count all the habits that are being washed. I want to know if one's missing. Now"—he turned back to me—"Nicholas, I suggest we go to the parlour—ah, here's Peter with the brandy."

As the monks rapidly dispersed we left the kitchen, I clutching the glass of water while Peter followed, like a butler, with the brandy bottle and a clean glass on a tray. Surreal. Yet paradoxically I felt the world had returned to normal, and having allowed myself to be amused by Peter I began to feel embarrassed by the memory of my collapse.

In the parlour the naked nymphs were still frolicking with the animals in the marble frieze. I swallowed some brandy. Then I was finally able to say to Father Wilcox: "I'm very sorry I crashed through enclosed areas."

"That's all right, Nicholas. I'm sure if I'd seen a dead man I'd have chased him to London and back in order to satisfy my curiosity."

"I'm convinced he's alive. I came here today because I thought he was one of your monks."

"So that man you described earlier—"

"—was Christian. What baffles me is how he managed to vanish in the kitchen-garden. I'm sure the monks never saw him—their astonishment was obviously genuine—but if he didn't escape into the house, where did he go?"

"Let's take one problem at a time. Nicholas, I give you my word that he's not a monk at this house."

"But I saw him! I mean, there he was, dressed as a Fordite monk—"

"As I see it, there are two explanations," said Father Wilcox briskly. "The first one is that you saw a monk who lives here. It's true we don't have anyone who exactly fits the description you gave me earlier, but we do have some monks who are slim and around six foot tall."

"You're saying I made a mistaken identification, but I assure you—"

"The second explanation is that we have an intruder, probably one of the undergraduates livening up his vacation by gatecrashing our house as a 'dare.' That happened once in the past, although the young man didn't manage to get hold of a habit. He wore a white dressing-gown with a black shawl and looked like a pantomime dame."

"This habit was completely orthodox. He even had the regulation brass crucifix hanging from his belt—I saw it flash in the sun."

"Then it must have been one of the monks. Don't worry, we'll track him down."

"But Father"—I decided it was no use trying to convince him I had seen Christian—"how did he manage to vanish into thin air?"

"Well, obviously he didn't and there's a rational explanation which we'll uncover shortly. Ah, there's the bell for the noon office. I must leave you for a short while, but please do continue to rest here—would you like me to send someone to keep you company?"

"No, I'm all right now," I said, and indeed thanks to the brandy I was feeling very well, well enough to attempt to recall every detail of the scene in the garden. I began to wonder if Christian could have hidden among the vegetable beds, but it was the wrong time of year to try to disappear in a kitchen-garden and I could remember no cover dense enough to conceal a man dressed in non-camouflage black and white. Could he have scaled the eight-foot wall? Possibly, but not quickly, not in a monk's habit. The sheer oddness of the disappearance began to bother me more than ever, and I was still staring uneasily at my empty glass when Father Wilcox returned to the room.

"I'm afraid the mystery's still unsolved," he said. "No intruder's been found, and no one was seen escaping. Assuming the man somehow eluded you in the kitchen-garden and doubled back through the archway—"

"He couldn't have done."

"I agree it does seem improbable, but since he didn't enter the house, how else could he have escaped? However, even if he did succeed in eluding you there, I don't see how he escaped unobserved from the back lawn. Hugh was weeding at the side of the guest-wing and swears no one came along the path. Two monks mending the chicken-run fence swear no one came into the enclosed area of the grounds from the herb-garden. And Daniel is quite convinced that either he or a visitor who was in the common-room would have seen and heard anyone who tried to scramble through one of the windows of the guest-wing."

"Was one of the habits missing?"

"No, they've all been accounted for. So have the monks. So have the visitors. I'm now convinced that the man you saw was an intruder, but the big question is how on earth did he escape?"

I took a deep breath, gripped the arms of my chair and said: "I saw this monk. I know I saw him. He was real, as real as you are now."

"Yes, I accept that," said Father Wilcox without hesitation. "Obviously you wouldn't have charged into enclosed areas unless you were convinced of the reality of what you'd seen, but nevertheless the situation as it stands is disturbing and what troubles me is that it might be given a bizarre interpretation once the story begins to circulate within the Community."

"What do you mean?"

"Well, first of all you claim to have seen a man who's officially dead— but luckily at the moment I'm the only one who knows that. Much more serious is this apparent disappearance into thin air. You'll notice I use the word 'apparent'; I still believe that a rational explanation for the disappearance will present itself, but a disappearance into thin air isn't normal, Nicholas. It's paranormal, and once the monks start to regard the incident in that light we're in trouble. Even the most disciplined house can quickly become infested by gossip which leads to hysteria; it's the Devil wriggling in through the breakdown of order, of course, and causing havoc. In fact very often the paranormal event which triggers the crisis is demonic, although I can't think why it should be in this case."

I suddenly realised I was no longer feeling well. The effect of the brandy had worn off, my Dutch courage had ebbed and the fear was streaming back across my psyche.

"There was nothing particularly wrong with Christian Aysgarth, was there?" said Father Wilcox. "I assume that in addition to his brilliant career he had a happy marriage, a good relationship with his family and so on? He wasn't dangerous or destructive in any way to those who knew him?"

I opened my mouth but found I was dumb again. My hands ached as I continued to grip the chair.

"I'm not going to ask you why you're so sure he's still alive," said Father Wilcox, too busy pursuing his train of thought to notice my reaction. "No doubt you have good reasons, but if you're wrong and he's dead, the likelihood of this being a paranormal experience certainly increases. Yet what kind of a paranormal experience can this possibly be? If you've seen his ghost, why should you see it here and why should it be dressed as a Fordite monk? It makes no sense . . . Nicholas, I'll tell you what I'd like to do: I'd like to call in a man who's an expert at solving this kind of problem. He's perfectly respectable—a priest, of course—and by coincidence he's from your diocese. In fact maybe you even know him: Father Lewis Hall."

I looked blank. But I wasn't merely registering the unfamiliarity of the name. I was now so frightened that all expression had been wiped from my face.

"Of course the monks might say the incident was consonant with possession," mused Father Wilcox, still absorbed in his reflections. "They might think you were seeing your possessor in the form of a hallucination, and although it's obvious to me you're not possessed, the monks in the kitchen will remember how you curled yourself into that rather sinister foetal position when you were so unnerved, and once they start to speculate about what was going on . . ."

I tried to tell myself I knew Christian was alive, but to my horror I found I was no longer sure. I then tried to tell myself again that a man who wanted to be ordained couldn't be possessed, but instead I realised that the Devil might want me to be ordained so that he could use me more effectively.

". . . so you do see, don't you," Father Wilcox was concluding, "why I want to summon an expert straight away to—my dear Nicholas, you're white as a sheet! Lie down on the sofa and I'll fetch the infirmarian!"

"I don't want the infirmarian," I said. "I want the expert," and at once Father Wilcox left the room to make the call.

2

AT THAT point I tried to recite the mantra but I found this was impossible; my powers of concentration had been shredded. I could only wish futilely that I were stroking Whitby's fur in my father's cottage far away.

"Father!" I shouted in my head, but he was so old, so sick, and I sensed he had fallen into such an exhausted sleep that for once he was psychically deaf to my fear. I was alone and helpless, as alone and helpless as I was going to be once he was dead, and suddenly I found the tears had sprung to my eyes. But I couldn't even summon the strength to despise myself for such weakness. I was too disabled, too terrified, too utterly laid waste by forces far beyond my control.

I tried to nerve myself to say: "Jesus is Lord." If I succeeded, I would survive because no demon, as my father always said, could withstand the power of Christ, and if I could invoke Christ's lordship I could invoke his power. Or in other words, I would survive because no fragmented mind could resist the drive to integration generated by the most potent symbol of wholeness of all time, provided that the symbol was allowed to reverberate in the psyche with sufficient faith.

To stimulate the necessary faith I turned back to religious symbolism and pictured the demons reeling backwards, keeling over and biting the dust once they were confronted by their exorcist, but I remained silent, too terrified to attempt the invocation of Christ's lordship for fear I would fail and prove myself possessed. At that moment it seemed my faith was insufficient to heal me; my fear of madness remained greater than my belief that I could be healed by an invocation.

Father Wilcox returned to the room. Fortunately by that time I had wiped my eyes and repolished my glasses.

"Here's a bit of luck," he was saying. "Lewis is less than twenty miles from here at Ely. I've left a message with the Bishop's secretary and asked Lewis to ring me as soon as he gets back to the palace. I expect he's on one of his hush-hush missions." And he added lightly in explanation: "He describes himself as a 'trouble-shooter'—such a delightful example of American slang, I've always thought!—but perhaps 'consultant' would be a more appropriate word for an English priest. At least three bishops now rely on him to solve any little diocesan problem that's not quite conventional."

"Ah," I said. I could think of no useful comment but at least by making an intelligent noise I could stop Father Wilcox from doubting my sanity and summoning a doctor. I noticed he himself was looking much more relaxed, and the next moment he was suggesting kindly that I should return to the guest-wing for the midday meal. "Daniel can allocate you a bedroom if you don't want to face the other guests . . ." I found it hard to absorb what he was saying, but I knew my best policy was to be docile so I followed him to the guest-wing. Daniel was found. I was led to a small, austere bedroom which faced the back garden, scene of . . . whatever it was. As soon as Daniel had departed I drew the curtains, unhooked the crucifix from its nail over the bed and sat down on the chair by the table.

Eventually Daniel returned. "Here's your roast lamb," he said, trying not to give me a fascinated look as he set down the tray. God only knew what word had reached him from the main kitchen along with the roast lamb. "I've put the mint sauce in a separate dish in case you didn't fancy it . . . Would you like me to sit with you for a while? Father Abbot did suggest—"

"No, thanks."

Daniel departed with reluctance. I went on gripping the crucifix while the roast lamb grew cold on the plate. There was no question of eating.

Since I was too close to madness to say "Jesus is Lord" I needed to hold the crucifix with both hands to repel the demons of doubt and terror which the Devil had summoned to destroy me.

Some time passed. Dimly I became aware that I couldn't face another conversation with Daniel and that I had to escape before he returned to collect the tray. I crept downstairs with my crucifix. The scrape of cutlery against china indicated that the guests were still busy in the nearby dining-room, and I calculated that I could bolt for the front door without being seen.

I bolted. Clasping the crucifix to my chest with one hand, I drew back the latch with the other and slipped out. In the drive I took a huge gulp of air. Then I scuttled over to my car and fell inside. The interior was hot, so I drove the necessary few yards into the shade. I had to drive using only one hand. That was because I had to keep holding the crucifix.

Switching off the engine, I settled down to wait in the knowledge that there was nothing else I could possibly do. I began to feel as immobilised as the paralysed man in the New Testament story, the man whose friends had lowered him through the roof on his pallet into Jesus' presence.

To pass the time I began to picture the ecclesiastical trouble-shooter, Father Hall. I saw him driving briskly around the Fens near Ely in a modest black Ford which needed a wash. His cassock would be dusty too after his trouble-shooting, but despite his travel-worn appearance he would exude sufficient respectability to impress three bishops who needed someone to sort out those awkward little problems which refused to fit into a conventional diocesan filing cabinet. His scanty hair would be short and neat, his rimless glasses shining, his lined face immaculately shaved. He would almost certainly be retired, no longer engaged in a formal ministry but glad to have part-time work which would supplement his pension. Rounding out my portrait I gave him an ancient mother, a celibate life, an impoverished middle-class background, a devotion to church music and an interest in something slightly nutty, such as UFOs or the mating of butterflies.

I suddenly realised Father Wilcox was crossing the drive towards me. "I've just heard from Lewis," he said as he approached the open window at my side. "He should be here by four. Why don't you come and sit in the parlour again, Nicholas?"

"No, thanks, I'm fine."

He hesitated, eyeing the crucifix. It must have been obvious to him that I was disturbed, but he was an intelligent man and he made no attempt to argue with me. Instead he said: "Very well, but please call on me at once if you need help. You're sensible enough to do that, aren't you, if the need arises?"

I told him I was. He went away. Probably he ordered someone to watch over me from one of the windows, but whoever he appointed was so discreet that I saw nothing. More time passed. I tried to imagine leaving the sanctuary of my car but I couldn't. I couldn't imagine ever relinquishing the crucifix either, but I told myself I would worry about all minor problems later. My present sole task in life was to stop myself disintegrating completely before Father Hall arrived to produce the rational explanation which would deliver me from insanity. But supposing there was no rational explanation to produce?

I shuddered.

Time dragged by. A few visitors turned up, delivery vans, a couple of Morris Minors, a priest on a bicycle. Nobody stayed long. The garden shimmered somnolently in the spring sunshine.

And then at one minute past four there was, as we used to say in the 1960s, a "happening." A Volkswagen roared through the gates, a Volkswagen Beetle, very cool, very trendy, a white Beetle it was, pristine and glistening, a Beetle with a pink and orange psychedelic flower painted on the driver's door.

My eyes widened. Naturally I assumed the car belonged to some groovy drop-out who was pausing at the house to sample the vibes. I went on waiting for my elderly consultant in his dusty black Ford.

The Volkswagen screeched to a halt. As the engine died a man leapt out. I was some yards away so I was unable to form a detailed impression of him, but I saw he was stocky and dark, probably in his forties, a man of medium height. He wore a black shirt with his black trousers, and when a speck of metal on his chest flashed in the sunlight I realised he was wearing a small pectoral cross.

It suddenly occurred to me that this could be Father Hall.

He grabbed a black hold-all from the back seat, slammed the door shut and ran up the steps of the main house. The front door opened and closed. I waited, assuming that he would be talking for some time to Father Wilcox in the parlour, but within five minutes I saw him again. He was moving swiftly past the windows of the interlinking passage, and seconds later he emerged from the front door of the guest-wing. He was now empty-handed. I deduced he had dumped his black bag in Daniel's office.

He wasted no time glancing in my direction but disappeared around the side of the building to the back lawn. Another five minutes elapsed. I pictured him prowling around by the peach-tree as he placed the Abbot's story in its setting.

Then he reappeared. He walked right up to me, planted himself by the open window of my car and said: "It's okay. You're going to be all right. Come indoors and we'll have some tea while I tell you what I plan to do."

I was reminded of the New Testament again. Just as the paralysed man had picked up his bed and walked, so I now opened the door of my car and got out.

Around me in the psychic world the demons bit the dust.
For the time being, at least, I was saved.

3

"I'M LEWIS HALL," he said over his shoulder as he led the way towards the
front door of the guest-wing. "You'd better call me Lewis—I don't believe
in standing on ceremony in a crisis. Are you Nicholas or Nick?"

"Well, the older generation usually call me Nicholas, but—"

"Fine. I'm nearly forty-seven and I've never aspired to be Peter Pan. I'll
call you Nicholas." He flung open the front door. "Tea, Daniel, please!"
he called, and added as Daniel came at the double: "We'll take it upstairs
in my room—shout when it's ready and I'll run down to collect it."

"Oh, there's no need for that, Father, I'll—"

"Did you find a second chair for the table?"

"Yes, Father, I put it in your room."

"Excellent. Oh and by the way, I'd deeply enjoy a sandwich. Marmite
would do." He began to ascend the stairs. "Come along, Nicholas."

Clutching my crucifix I hurried along in his wake.

He had been assigned the room next to mine. "Now," he said as we
reached the door, "why don't you go and hang up that crucifix—it's from
your room, isn't it? Standard fitting, Fordite guest-room—very nice, but
if you continue to lug it around you're going to get some strange looks.
I'll lend you this"—he whipped off his little pectoral cross—"to wear
instead. Much more practical."

"Oh thanks, I—"

"I'll just unpack my bag and change my shirt—it was so hot in the car
that I've been sweating like a pig all the way from Ely. Give me five
minutes, would you?"

"Yes, of course." I retired dazed to my room, hung up the crucifix and
after only a brief pause drew back the curtains. It occurred to me that I
could now go to the lavatory. I had been suppressing the need for some
time because I had been unable to leave the sanctuary of my car.

When I returned down the corridor Daniel was arriving with tea and
sandwiches. "I thought you too might like a bite to eat, Nicholas," he said
in his most solicitous voice, "since you didn't eat your roast lamb."

The door of the nearby room flew open. Lewis said firmly: "Thank you,
Daniel, that looks wonderful," and whipped the tray out of his hands.
"Come in, Nicholas."

Daniel pattered away, and as I entered the room Lewis dumped the tray
on the table by the window. It was clear that he had been washing
vigorously at the corner basin, for water was scattered over the linoleum

and the towel lay askew on the rack. He was now wearing a green sports-shirt, open at the neck, and had replaced his small pectoral cross with something much larger on a thick chain. I could see part of the chain, but the shirt concealed all but the outline of the object at the end of it.

Suddenly my voice said: "That's not just another cross you're wearing. That's a crucifix."

"Yes, it's a nice one," said Lewis agreeably, pouring out the tea. "I'm fond of it." And passing me my cup he added: "Help yourself to milk and sugar."

I slumped down on the nearest chair. Then I managed to say: "I've been very slow on the uptake. Father Wilcox mentioned the words 'trouble-shooter' and 'consultant,' but they're just euphemisms, aren't they? You're an exorcist."

"Yes, I do the occasional exorcism," said Lewis vaguely, rather in the manner of a housewife confessing that she sometimes felt obliged to add bleach to her wash, "but my ministry's primarily concerned with healing, not deliverance. Have a Marmite sandwich."

I took a sandwich, and when he remained silent in order to eat at high speed I had the chance to observe him in detail.

He wore his dark straight hair on the long side at the back, but it had been trimmed with care and was now neatly parted and brushed. However, his most fashionable feature was not this longish hair but the thick side-burns which reached down to the level of his ear-lobes. He had an aquiline nose and a thin-lipped mouth which, unlike Dr. Aysgarth's, conveyed an impression not of brutality but of resolute common sense; I decided this was because Aysgarth's mouth turned down at the corners while Lewis's mouth was dead straight. I thought he was probably overweight in propor-tion to his height, but because his build was broad the excess pounds were not immediately noticeable. His dark eyes, set deep in shadowed sockets, were the only part of his appearance which could have been described as sinister, but as he sat munching the sandwich their expression was tranquil and benign.

"That's better," he said when his plate was empty. He poured himself some more tea. "Now let me tell you how I intend to proceed. We're going to talk in three sessions and basically what you'll be doing is briefing me. In the first session I want you to tell me how you became involved with Christian Aysgarth and how you were led step by step towards that moment this morning when you saw him in the garden. In the second session I want you to describe exactly what you saw, and we'll try to clarify your description as far as possible. And in the third session I want you to tell me a little about yourself—no two-volume biography is required, but an extended thumbnail sketch would help me to see the situation in the round."

"Do you think—"

"I don't think anything at the moment. I'm only operating on Father Wilcox's summary of this morning's events—which is why it's so important that I spend time talking to you in detail. The three sessions will take the rest of the day. Then tomorrow morning we'll stage a reconstruction."

I digested this information for a moment in silence before asking: "And after that?"

"After that I believe I'll have some sort of idea what's going on. I doubt that I'll be able to shout 'Eureka!' and instantly produce the correct solution, but I think I'll have established certain possibilities so that I'll know the next step to take."

I said astonished: "Are there so many possibilities?"

"At least half a dozen, yes, but they're not all equally likely. By the way, perhaps this is the moment when I should state unequivocally that I believe you could have seen Christian Aysgarth and that I'm more than willing to consider any theory you care to put forward."

Then I knew I was no longer alone.

4

"EAT up your sandwich," said Lewis. "I don't want you to faint for lack of food—it would be so time-consuming. Now, where shall we hold our first session? Shall we stay here? Or should we take advantage of the fine weather by sitting in the front garden?"

He was watching me intently, and at once I knew that for some reason my response to these innocuous questions was crucial. "You decide," I said confused, "but if we go into the garden I'd like to sit in the shade because a hot sun doesn't suit me."

"Was that why you were sitting in your car when I arrived?"

"No, I only went there to escape from Daniel."

Lewis stopped watching me intently and relaxed in his chair. "Daniel must find it hard to keep a rule of silence!" he commented. "How clever of Father Abbot to make him guest-master and give him plenty of opportunity for authorised chat!" And before I could reply he added: "Let's make a move."

I followed him downstairs, and when he opened the front door I saw that the bench in the garden ahead of us was already standing in the shade. We began to cross the lawn.

"We can go to the back garden if you like," I said, anxious to prove to myself as well as to him that I was no longer too panic-stricken to look at the scene of the incident, but I was relieved when he shook his head.

"There are two visitors out there at present," he said. "I saw them from the bedroom window." And as we moved on across the lawn he said unexpectedly: "Let me tell you a little about myself. I think it would be unfair if I milked you for information and yet offered no information in return."

I recognised this manoeuvre. My father had told me he always adopted it when the person he was counselling was disturbed enough to be distrustful of all strangers. It was a form of stroking the psyche by befriending; the aim was to reassure by presenting oneself as a person with a background which could be grasped and understood; it was a method of making the unfamiliar non-threatening. "In fact one gives little away," my father had explained, "but the important thing is to adopt a friendly tone and offer one's few facts as a gesture of good will." My father had acquired this somewhat Machiavellian technique from his abbot at Ruydale, Aidan Lucas, during the monastic years.

"I was brought up in the country—in Sussex, to be precise," Lewis was saying as we sat down on the bench and I prepared to judge his skill as a befriender. "My father died when I was two but my uncle took me over when my mother went to live with him and his wife, so I had a standard family upbringing. In 1939 I was supposed to go up to Oxford but I thought it was more important to fight Hitler instead. The result was that when I was demobbed in 1945 I was too old to find Oxford anything but unbearably juvenile so I went straight to theological college.

"After I was ordained I worked in the Chichester diocese and was eventually appointed to one of those plush parishes inland from Worthing. I lasted there five years. Then I became chaplain of a large mental hospital in the diocese of Radbury.

"However in 1965 it seemed clear to me that I was being called back into some kind of parish situation in order to use the skills I'd developed in my hospital work, so I decided to approach the Bishop of Starbridge for help—not merely because I didn't think much of the new Bishop of Radbury, but because I'd heard through the Fordite grapevine that Ashworth was sympathetic to the ministry of healing, particularly when it involved counselling people who had suffered breakdowns, and I thought he might be able to use me somewhere in his diocese. I'd never met him; I knew he wasn't an Anglo-Catholic, as I was, but he was a traditionalist with Catholic leanings and I had a hunch we'd get on.

"He set me up in my present ministry. I'm attached to an Anglo-Catholic city parish—St. Paul's, which is in the part of Starbridge known as Langley Bottom—and although I do assist Desmond Wilton, the vicar, I also work independently, running a small healing centre in the crypt."

I had long since forgotten I was supposed to be judging his technique. I had realised in amazement that this was one of the priests whom the Principal of Starbridge Theological College had dismissed as Anglo-Catholic cranks and whose services my father had asked me not to attend. But I now knew exactly why my father had tried to keep me out of Langley Bottom. He had wanted to steer me away from that ministry of healing which, inevitably, he would have heard about from Uncle Charles.

I could only exclaim feebly: "I never knew there was a healing centre in Starbridge!" but Lewis was unsurprised. "I don't advertise," he said, "and I don't go in for big, flashy services of healing. I see people by appointment and everything is done *sotto voce* within the context of a parish church where the emphasis is on the daily mass . . . You know Starbridge well?"

"Very well indeed! Didn't Father Wilcox tell you about me?"

"I'm afraid I didn't give him much chance—I was too anxious to get my teeth into a Marmite sandwich. He just gave me the bare facts of the case and told me you were an ordinand called Nicholas Darrow."

"Well, I'm at Starbridge Theological College, and—"

"No wonder you've never heard of my ministry! Your Principal thinks I'm a dangerous maverick, and even if he didn't he's such a snob that he'd take good care to steer his lily-white ordinands away from a working-class parish like St. Paul's. What's your opinion of that College?"

"Awful."

"I'm not surprised. I hear the ordinands emerge spouting Eusebius but unable to counsel the average bereaved widow . . . Do you smoke?" he added as an afterthought as he pulled a packet of cigarettes from his pocket.

"No." I opened my mouth to tell him that my father had been Principal during the College's golden era in the 1940s, but before I could speak Lewis was observing: "I'm an incorrigible smoker, but I do give up cigarettes in Lent. For forty-eight hours." And he smiled at me before adding casually: "To conclude my self-portrait I should tell you that I married during the war and that my wife and daughter now live in London. My divorce, of course, provided me with the impetus to chuck up conventional parish work, but as I was the so-called 'innocent party' there was no problem about continuing in the Church. There'd be a problem if I wanted to remarry, but I don't consider that remarriage is an option for a divorced priest." He paused to exhale a cloud of smoke. "Okay, so much for me. Now let's turn back to you. Session One: your involvement with Christian Aysgarth. When did you first meet him?"

"1963. Did you by chance ever—"

"No, we never met. I seem to remember that he was still around when I came to Starbridge in 1965, but I was never in with the Cathedral Close set. How did you yourself meet him?"

"I *was* in with the Cathedral Close set. My father is Bishop Ashworth's spiritual director."

Lewis stared at me. "Your father's a priest?"

"Yes."

"*Your father's a priest called Darrow?* Jonathan Darrow? The Darrow who was abbot here before the war?"

"Yes."

"Great balls of fire!" said Lewis astounded, and scattered ash all over his trousers as he dropped his cigarette.

5

I WAS not unaccustomed to this reaction. My life had been regularly punctuated by the gasps of churchmen who had discovered I was the son of Jonathan Darrow. Sometimes I enjoyed basking in my father's fame and sometimes I didn't, but on this occasion I merely felt relieved. Aware of my dependence on Lewis I was anxious to enhance his interest in me.

Automatically I asked: "You've met him?"

"No." Lewis retrieved his cigarette. "He left the Order in 1940, didn't he? But I never visited the Fordites here at Grantchester until I was an ordinand after the war—and by the time I reached the Starbridge diocese years later he was living as a recluse. How amazing to think he's still alive! How old is he now?"

"Nearly eighty-eight. Fancy you remembering when he left the Order!"

"Oh, it was a sensation at the time. In fact the events of 1940 rocked all four houses: Cuthbert Darcy dying, your father leaving—what a challenge for the new Abbot-General!"

Picking up this last reference, I said fascinated: "You knew Francis Ingram?"

"Yes, I knew Francis."

"And did you know Aidan Lucas? He was Abbot of Ruydale when my father was Master of Novices there."

"Yes, I knew Aidan."

"And Cyril—Cyril Watson?" I was enthralled that someone else outside the Order should be so familiar with the major characters in my father's long-running cenobitic soap-opera.

"Yes, I knew Cyril," said Lewis. "He was the Abbot of Starwater during my schooldays there."

"I was at Starwater Abbey too! Did you know—"

"Probably. Shall we get back to Christian?"

But a mesmerising thought had occurred to me. "Did you ever meet Father Darcy?"

"Yes, I did."

I was deeply impressed. "You knew everyone!"

"But not Christian. Now, you said you were a member of the Cathedral

Close set, but nevertheless he must have been considerably older than you. How did your paths manage not merely to cross but to interweave?"

With reluctance I abandoned the subject of Lewis's distinguished acquaintances among the Fordite monks and began to describe the innocent "orgy" which Marina had given at her grandmother's house in the May of 1963.

6

HE WAS a superb listener. He soaked up my story with the efficiency of blotting-paper absorbing ink, grasped instantly who was who, picked up every nuance of my narrative and punctuated the briefing with summaries which were remarkable for their accuracy. I held nothing back except my three disastrous sexual lapses, the complex torment I was currently experiencing with my father, and the interminable abrasiveness of my relationship with Martin. I thought it was important not to clutter up the narrative with irrelevancies.

When I had finished my story Lewis made no immediate comment on it but said he was interested in my psychic gift, and in response to his mild, friendly questions I described my powers in detail.

". . . but I've never had a vision," I concluded. I thought it wise at this point to use my firmest voice to stop him jumping to conclusions about Christian's appearance in the garden. Now that my panic had subsided I found I was less inclined to believe my sighting had been paranormal; in fact the more I replayed the memory the more convinced I became that I had seen Christian in the flesh. "My father has visions occasionally," I said, "but I'm not nearly so gifted as he is."

"Why do you say that?"

"Well . . ." I was so taken aback that I found it hard to explain this obvious fact of life. "He's exceptional and I'm not. He's so distinguished, so wise, so devout, so—"

"Yes, I dare say he is, now that he's nearly eighty-eight, but what was he like when he was your age?"

"Oh, I'm sure he was always far more gifted than I am. His visions—"

"What's the big deal about having a vision?" said Lewis. "If your appalling bout of foreknowledge at Marina's party had been translated into visual terms would you have known any more than you actually did? Does a radio play automatically become more exalted when someone adapts it for television?"

I stared, amazed by this cavalier approach. My father and Aelred Peters had always referred to the subject of visions with so much awe and reverence that it had never occurred to me that my failure to have a vision could be anything but a psychic deficiency.

"All the best spiritual guides say that psychic manifestations are a distraction to those following the spiritual way," said Lewis. "If you don't have visions, consider yourself lucky."

I suddenly realised I longed to egg him on into further displays of iconoclasm. "But at least one of my father's visions was very special!" I protested. "It was the vision calling him to leave the Order. His superior ruled that it was a direct communication from God."

"Fine. If God chose to communicate in that way with your father, so be it. But God has many less spectacular ways of communicating with his creation, and they're just as valid as any vision."

"So what you're saying is . . . well, what you seem to be saying is . . . I mean, are you saying that just because I don't have visions—"

"—you're not necessarily less gifted than your father. Okay, let's pause there so that I can summarise your description of yourself as a psychic: you regularly experience moments of 'knowing,' but most of the time these could simply be the result of a well-developed intuition working in conjunction with a sharp intelligence. However, far less frequently you experience powerful moments of either 'knowing' or 'foreknowing,' and these can't be written off as anything but the operation of a psychic gift. Would you agree that was a fair summary of your powers?"

"Well, I think you're downgrading my regular moments of 'knowing' just a little—"

"You don't like your clever guesses being written off in that way?"

"They're not just clever guesses! The true psychic *gnosis* is independent of—"

"*Gnosis!* What an evocative word! But don't let's get side-tracked, because I'm keen to build up your psychic portrait in even greater detail. Have you ever suffered from uncontrolled outbursts of kinetic energy and generated the phenomenon that's known as poltergeist activity?"

"That happened in my teens after my mother died."

"And what about the deliberate use of such energy—have you ever stopped a watch, for instance, just by looking at it?"

I said evasively: "My father always forbade me to do psychic parlour-tricks."

"Oh yes, yes, yes!" said Lewis, very benign and good-natured. "But knowing teenagers, I'm sure you were tempted to go your own way whenever your father wasn't breathing down your neck."

"Well, as a matter of fact . . ." Reassured by the absence of criticism I threw caution to the winds. "Yes, I did give the trick a try—several times—but I never actually succeeded in stopping a watch. I just used to make the girls think I did."

"You mean you hypnotised them."

"Well . . ."

"Good at it, were you?"

Again I was lured on by the benign tone and the absence of criticism. Adopting my most modest voice I said: "As it happens, hypnotism's my forte. In fact to be quite honest—"

"You're a knock-out."

"Yep. I can put a girl under just like *that.*" I snapped my fingers. "Men take a little longer, but girls are instant. When I was up at Cambridge—" But instinct now told me it was time to apply the brakes. Cutting short my reminiscences I said carefully: "When I was young and insecure I relied on parlour-tricks to make people notice me, but I'm older and more self-confident now."

"And wiser too, I hope," said Lewis pleasantly. "Okay, let's just sum up again: you have exceptional hypnotic skills and there's been at least one occasion in your life when you've been the centre of paranormal activity— although the poltergeist phenomenon is not uncommon, as I'm sure you know, in households where an adolescent is under stress, so perhaps we shouldn't make too much of that particular experience. Have you been involved in any poltergeist bouts since then?"

"Yes. I mean, no. Well, maybe." I suddenly found myself wondering what he was trying to prove. "I was doing some voluntary work in a mental hospital," I said warily, "and some plates got smashed in the kitchen at odd hours, but I'm pretty sure now that one of the inmates was responsible."

"Were you still a teenager?"

"No, I was twenty-three. I did voluntary work for two years when I came down from Cambridge."

"Stressful, was it?"

"Well . . ."

"Challenging?"

"Challenging, yes. Sure. Challenging."

"Anything challenging going on in your personal life right now?"

I said coldly: "You're trying to prove I hallucinated this entire incident as the result of stress."

"I'd be very stupid to try to prove that particular possibility before I knew exactly what you'd seen—it would be putting the cart before the horse."

"Then why all the questions about—"

"Just adding the finishing touches to your psychic profile. It's important, you see, that I know exactly what kind of psychic I'm dealing with; I don't want to make the mistake of writing you off as a nut-case, particularly when you seem to be commendably rational and intelligent. Now let's just try and wrap the profile up as quickly as possible. Have you ever suffered from sleep-walking?"

Immediately I said: "No," but the next moment I was so confused by this lie that I wanted to retract it. "What's that question got to do with me being a psychic?" I demanded instead when I found retraction was impossible. "Anyone can sleep-walk!"

"That's quite true," agreed Lewis, "but I sometimes wonder if psychics aren't peculiarly inclined to somnambulism. Their pathway between the conscious and the unconscious mind is better developed—more flexible, one might say—than the pathway of ordinary people, and when a psychic's under stress that pathway can bend in odd directions."

"I'm not under stress."

"In fact sometimes," reflected Lewis, gazing across the lawn, "the pathway can become almost fluid, blurring the lines which separate sleeping and waking. Have you ever had difficulty knowing when you were asleep and when you were awake?"

"Never."

"You've no sleep problems at all at the moment?"

"None."

"Good. That, as far as I'm concerned, completes your psychic profile, and I have only one more question to ask before we complete this session: was Christian a psychic?"

Although startled, I was in no doubt about the correct reply. "No," I said, "he wasn't. Why?"

"I was wondering if that could have been one of the reasons why he interested you so deeply, but obviously I was mistaken. Are you always able to recognise other psychics?"

"Yes, always. *You're* a psychic," I said as I looked straight into his eyes. "Your psyche's supple but very strong, like a top-quality rope."

He smiled before glancing at his watch. "We seem to have missed Vespers," he said, "but perhaps later we can make it to Compline. Shall we take a break for supper?"

We began to drift back across the lawn towards the guest-wing.

7

THERE were four other guests in the dining-room. While we ate macaroni and cheese, Daniel read aloud a passage from William Law's *A Serious Call to a Devout and Holy Life.* Conversation among guests at meal-times was not forbidden but it was discouraged.

I ate some of the macaroni but refused the stewed apples which followed. In contrast Lewis ate every scrap on his plate much too quickly and even asked for more. I found myself wondering if his unusual ministry required an equally unusual intake of calories.

Once the meal had finished we adjourned to his room and he drew the black blind over the window.

"Okay," he said as we sat down opposite each other at the table. "Session Two: the appearance. There you were, sitting in the back garden. And then—"

I began to describe what had happened.

8

AFTERWARDS Lewis lit a cigarette and said: "Before Christian appeared, did you notice a change in the light?"

"No—but I know what you're thinking," I said at once. "My father experiences certain alterations in reality immediately before he has a vision, and colours become very bright, just as they do in an LSD trip. I suppose God's creating such a pressure on the psyche that certain chemicals are released in the brain."

"Have you ever taken LSD?"

"Certainly not! I've taken no drug except alcohol—which I don't particularly like. Believe me," I said strongly, "my psyche's quite active enough as it is. The last thing it needs is to be jacked up with chemicals."

Lewis merely said: "I'm interested in the flexible way you use the word 'psyche.'"

"I've picked that up from my father. He uses it to describe the special force in each personality which varies from individual to individual and is as unique as a fingerprint. The psyche's related to the ego and the conscious mind, but essentially it's rooted in the inner self and so has access to the unconscious."

"The soul in action?"

"Something like that. All language is really so inadequate—"

"You favour Jungian terms, I notice."

"I suppose you disapprove."

"Why should I? Jung talks a language it would pay Christians to master. Have you ever heard of an Anglican priest and monk called Christopher Bryant? He's one of the Cowley Fathers, and he's interested in the possibility of a Jungian-Christian synthesis."

"My father's met him, I think. He's a spiritual director, isn't he? But I didn't know he was an admirer of Jung."

"Is Jung ever mentioned at the Theological College?"

"Nothing interesting's ever mentioned at the Theological College."

"I'm surprised your father sent you there! Isn't he appalled by its inadequacies?"

"Oh, he doesn't know about them." I realised that this sounded odd so

I added quickly: "He's so old, you see, and at his age any shock or anxiety could be fatal. So I always go to great lengths to ensure he's never upset."

"Really," said Lewis. He used the word as only an Englishman can use it. The syllables were so impregnated with courteous neutrality that it was impossible to know what he was thinking. "But Nicholas, just explain to me: why *did* you go to that College? I can understand your father being sentimental about the place where he was once the Principal, but that was a long time ago now and it's not even Anglo-Catholic any more."

"I needed to be near my father. Because he's so old it's not good for him to be separated from me for too long."

"Ah."

"If we're apart he tends to worry about me, you see, and of course I mustn't let him get upset."

"Quite so. How did he manage when you were away at school?"

"I was never farther away than Starwater, and anyway he was younger then. And it was all right when I was up at Cambridge because the University terms were so short. But then I began my two years' voluntary work by going to Africa, and that was a mistake. Africa," I said, examining my thumbnail, "didn't work out."

"Where did you work when you came back to England?"

"Starmouth. Then Starbridge."

"Moving steadily closer to home?"

"Well, it was safer."

"Safer?"

"Yes, it made me feel more secure," I said, "to know that I could get home quickly if anything went wrong. I mean, if he fell ill. Once people get over eighty, any illness can be fatal."

"True. Bit of a worry for you, having this elderly parent."

"Oh, but he's always anxious never to be a burden and he's always encouraged me to lead my own life! He's been a model parent in that respect."

"Ah," said Lewis, "so in fact he's not the one who feels you have to be around. You're the one who likes to stay close."

"Well, I've got to look after him, haven't I? It's my moral duty, and so long as I'm there to make sure he's never upset there's no reason why he shouldn't live to be a hundred."

"You're saying it's very important to keep him alive."

"Well, of course it's important! What kind of a son do you think I am?"

"Devoted. All right, let's end this digression about your father and return to the subject of Christian's appearance. I'd asked if the light had changed beforehand, but I wasn't in fact expecting you to say that you'd experienced the enhancement of colour which can sometimes precede a vision. I was thinking along much more prosaic lines, and what I had in mind was a very slight shift in the quality of the light—as if a cloud, for instance, had passed over the sun."

"Oh, I see." I thought for a moment. "But there were no clouds," I said. "It was a perfect morning."

"So there was no change in the light at all?"

"None."

"Was there any slight change in sound? Did you notice, for instance, that the birds had ceased to sing?"

"I didn't notice any birdsong either before or during the appearance— although I suppose it must have been going on," I said confused, "because birds always sing in gardens."

"So there was no change in sound. Was there a slight change in temperature? Just before the appearance, did you feel either hotter or colder?"

I thought hard but could only reply in the negative.

"Were you aware of any new smell at that moment—possibly a strong smell such as burning rubber?"

"Burning rubber!" I stared at him. "That's a symptom of schizophrenia!" I tried not to panic. "What are you getting at? What do you mean? What are you trying to—"

"You've been studying the mind, haven't you? Reading Jung, investigating the symptoms of mental illness—"

"When you have a mind like mine you want to work out just what the hell's going on!"

"Yes, that's very natural. Have you ever suffered from epilepsy?"

"No. Do you think I'm crazy?"

"I see no sign of mental illness."

"Do you think I'm having a nervous breakdown?"

"I see no sign that you're having a breakdown."

"Do you think I'm possessed?"

"I see no sign of possession."

"Then what on earth's happening to me?"

"That's what we're trying to find out. Do I take it that you weren't aware of any unusual smell at the time of the appearance?"

"No smell," I said, soothed by his tranquil, confident statements. "No change in light, noise or temperature."

"So you're saying that this was all one reality; the humdrum experience of sitting on a garden bench flowed without break, change or interruption of any kind into the bizarre experience of seeing Christian dressed up as a monk."

"That's correct. It was all one and all real."

"There's one point that puzzles me: why do you think Christian wore his cowl up?"

"Outdoor work. The cowl gives protection from the sun in summer, the wind in winter and the rain all the year round."

"But it wasn't excessively hot today, was it? About seventy, I'd say— very pleasant, unless one's incarcerated in a small car as I was this afternoon."

"Some people can't take much sun," I said. "My own skin, for example, is so fair that I always have to be careful in hot weather."

"But was Christian fair-skinned?"

That gave me a jolt. "He had brown hair and eyes," I said at last, "but he wasn't all that dark. I admit he wasn't as fair-skinned as I am but he wasn't swarthy either."

Lewis paused before saying: "There's a peach-tree by that kitchen-garden wall and the branches grow roughly parallel with the ground. As Christian walked along, can you remember where the top of his head was in relation to the nearest branch?"

This defeated me. "No, I can't. I was barely aware of the peach-tree while I was watching him."

"But you're sure this was a man about six foot tall."

"Positive."

"How tall are you yourself, Nicholas?"

"Six foot."

"That could be useful tomorrow when we do the reconstruction . . . Is that why you're so certain of Christian's height? You were aware during your meetings that you and he quite literally saw eye to eye?"

"Yes, I remember looking at him in a mirror once and seeing we were the same. In height, I mean."

Lewis was silent.

Immediately I became nervous again. "Have I said something peculiar? Was it the mirror? Schizophrenics can get obsessed with mirrors—they look at their reflections but fail to recognise themselves—"

"Has that ever happened to you?"

"No, but—"

"Then don't worry about it. Why worry about something which will probably never happen? Waste of energy. All right," said Lewis as the bell in the chapel began to toll for Compline, "I've only one more question to ask before we adjourn: why do you think Christian was carrying a rake as he headed for the kitchen-garden? I'm no gardener, but judging from my quick reconnaissance earlier I think a spade would be more appropriate than a rake at this time of year."

"Not necessarily. You're getting hung up on the image of a gardener raking the autumn leaves, but in fact—"

"Talking of images, let's suppose for a moment that the rake was a symbol. How would you interpret that if you were a psychoanalyst?"

I said outraged: "Are you trying to imply this incident was just a dream?"

"No. You're reacting as if symbols only exist in dreams, but that's not true; think of the historical life and death of Jesus where a unique number of powerful symbols met and merged. We actually deal all the time with symbols because the truths to which they point are beyond adequate expression in language."

I knew this was true but I still felt he was downgrading the reality of Christian's appearance. Obtusely I said: "I don't see how you can say much about a mere rake."

"No?" said Lewis. "Well, Freud would have thought it was a substitute for a penis, of course, and theorised that it represented the drive to sex. Adler, on the other hand, would have said it was substituting for a gun and represented the drive to power. And Jung . . . now what would Jung have made of that rake? Slightly cruciform, isn't it, except that the top of the cross is missing."

I was hooked. "Jung would have seen both the man and the implement as an archetype," I said immediately. "The Christian form of the archetype is the shepherd with the crook. It represents the saviour, the redeemer, the one the little sheep has to have around if it wants to avoid getting eaten up by the big bad wolf."

"Poor little sheep," said Lewis. "It just can't survive without that shepherd, can it? And what happens when the shepherd dies and isn't around any more to keep the big bad wolf at bay?"

There was a profound silence.

I realised at once that I could protect myself by pretending that I only understood the conversation at its most facile level, but for a moment I was too stunned to speak. So subtle had Lewis been in extracting the symbolic description of my central problem that we were now in a situation where I knew that he knew and he knew that I knew that he knew, but we didn't have to talk about it until I felt ready to do so. Consumed with admiration for his technique yet enraged that I had been so effortlessly read, understood and packaged for future counselling, I found I could only offer him the cold comment: "Sheep are very stupid animals. Humans are quite different."

"Quite different," agreed Lewis, "but nevertheless Jesus always spoke as if no sheep was so stupid that it ceased to matter, and no sheep was so lost that it couldn't be found and brought home." He stood up and added over his shoulder as he moved to the door: "You'll want to come with me to Compline, of course."

I was unable to decide whether this was an order or a suggestion, but by that time I was too mesmerised to do anything but follow him downstairs.

In silence we headed for the chapel.

"*I WOULDN'T* mind some tea and biscuits," said Lewis after the service. "I'm feeling a trifle peckish."

Daniel, who was on his way to bed, revealed the existence of flapjacks baked specially for the guests. The Fordites never stayed up late. The night office had been abolished at the beginning of the 1960s—my father had at once declared that the monks were being fatally pampered—but the first service now began earlier and lasted longer; Matins had been merged with Prime.

"I'll make the tea, Daniel," said Lewis. "Off you go."

Daniel flapped away. As the other guests too headed for bed they murmured "Good night" to us and Lewis, waiting for the kettle to boil, gave a succession of robust responses. He was already halfway through a flapjack.

"We'll take the tea to one of the confessionals," he said. "If we talk in my room we're bound to keep someone awake. But how do you feel about tackling Session Three? If you're tired it would be better to postpone it till tomorrow."

"I'm all right." I was unsure how true this statement was but I was certain I wanted to complete the interviews so that we could focus on discovering what had happened in the garden.

When the tea had been made, we withdrew from the kitchen to the passage which linked the guest-wing with the main house.

"Cosy, isn't it?" remarked Lewis as we entered the first little room on our right. "I like the Grantchester confessionals. Less baroque than London, less austere than Ruydale—alas, poor Ruydale!—and less fussy than Starwater."

I said suddenly: "Were you ever a Fordite monk?"

"No, but I became very involved with the Order when I was a mixed-up psychic teenager at Starwater Abbey. The monks and their Anglo-Catholicism represented the stable religious framework which I came to realise I had to have."

"I see," I said. "So that particular little lost sheep needed a whole gang of shepherds to bring it back into the fold."

We looked at each other and then, much to my surprise, we both laughed. I had had no intention of laughing. I had made the comment out of a desire to hit back at him for his brilliant extraction of a truth I had had no wish to reveal, yet now I found my animosity had dissolved. Perhaps that was because he was genuinely amused by my remark and his humour was infectious; or perhaps his skill at befriending was finally bearing fruit; or perhaps the psychic affinity between us was strong enough to override any clash of our personalities. I didn't know. I couldn't decide. I was even unsure how well I liked him. I sensed he could be difficult, possibly hot-tempered, certainly domineering, not a priest who would ever find it easy to fit into conventional ecclesiastical structures—and not a priest who fitted the conventional image of the patient, self-effacing listener, the model to which modern counsellors were supposed to aspire. Yet in his unorthodoxy, in the sheer originality of the style which displayed his gifts as a priest, I felt at ease. The conventional men of the Church had all failed me. But this man understood. What did it matter how likable or dislikable he was? All that mattered was that I trusted him and that he wanted to help me survive.

"Oh, I know all about being a little lost sheep!" he was saying amused. "But most of us have to endure a woolly phase when we're young . . . Am I forgiven now for using the symbolic rake as a scalpel?"

I merely said: "It's good to meet a priest who talks the language of psychology as well as the language of religion."

"If one believes in the unity of knowledge, then all languages point to one truth."

By this time we were sitting down. Although the room was so small, it contained a table and two chairs in addition to the prie-dieu in front of the little altar; it had long been a Fordite custom that a formal confession at the prie-dieu should be preceded by an informal talk at the table.

"Right," said Lewis, producing his cigarettes and reminding me that we were to examine my life-story, not the state of my soul. "Session Three: your self-portrait. Begin: 'I was born on . . .' and continue from there."

I thought: this'll be the easy session, the one where I'm wholly in control from start to finish.

But I was wrong.

1 0

"*I WAS* born on the twenty-fourth of December, 1942," I began, "at my mother's family home, the Manor House at Starrington Magna. My father . . . well, you know all about my father. My mother—"

"No," said Lewis. "I don't know all about your father. Tell me about him."

"Well, he's a fabulous priest, a famous spiritual director, a former abbot of Grantchester—"

"Yes, I certainly know all that. But what was he like as a husband and father?"

"Fantastic. He's never put a foot wrong."

"How very remarkable. So he coped well, did he, with your development as a psychic?"

"Brilliantly. I learnt from the start that he could always keep the Dark at bay."

Of course Lewis never asked what I meant by "the Dark." He already knew. So enrapt was I by the sheer luxury of this easy communication that I failed to hear his next question and had to ask him to repeat it.

"I said: when did he start to train you to do without him? Psychics need careful training if they're to avoid getting into messes in later life."

"Well, of course my father recognised that. He started to train me before I went away to school at Starwater. I hadn't been away from home before. I'd been a day-boy at the Cathedral Choir School."

"What form did his training take?"

"Before my first term at Starwater he tried to get me into a religious routine. I already went to mass every Sunday, but I'd never bothered about attending church during the week and he'd never pressed it. He'd just encouraged me to say my prayers daily."

"But if you were at the Choir School, surely you were attending at least one service almost every day?"

"I wasn't one of the choir, and apart from Sundays the choir only sing Evensong anyway. Even if I'd been a chorister I'd still have been a long way from a daily attendance at mass."

"I see. Go on."

"Well, when my father started to train me he said: 'No demon can withstand the power of Christ'—that was his big slogan—and he told me that the best way to develop an awareness of Christ, an awareness strong enough to keep the demons at bay, was to adopt a more frequent pattern of worship and recollection. He said one of the reasons why he wanted me to go to Starwater was that the monks provided a good daily service for the boys and I'd have every opportunity to build up my spiritual strength."

"And what did you, aged twelve or thirteen, think of all this religion being rammed down your throat?"

I blinked at this coarse description but said without hesitation: "I thought it all made sense. But somehow when I got to Starwater . . . well, you know what public schools are like. My first priority was to survive community life without going crazy. Fortunately there wasn't much bullying because the monks took a firm line on that, but I soon found out it didn't do to be 'churchy,' even in a school like Starwater, because the tough boys would think you were soft. So I wound up just paying lip-service to the religious routine."

"Did you tell your father that?"

"Oh no, I couldn't bear to disillusion him! He'd gone on a scholarship to a minor public school which was Low Church Evangelical, and he was so happy to think I was getting the kind of religious education he'd never had."

"But didn't your father—this almost superhuman psychic—intuit that you had problems?"

"He realised I was having a little trouble settling down, but he thought that was normal—as I suppose it was. But it never occurred to him that I wasn't tuning in properly to the religious life because he couldn't imagine Starwater being a failure in that respect."

"But surely as time went on—"

"Oh, I'm sure he would have intuited the truth eventually, but then the catastrophe happened: my mother died." I described how the death had affected my father. "He couldn't cope with anything," I said. "All he could do, when I generated the poltergeist activity at school, was arrange for me to be counselled by someone else. He did make a new effort to train me once he was better, but somehow it didn't work out and soon he said he was too emotionally involved to carry out the training successfully. But the parent-child relationship often fails to work as a teacher-pupil relationship, doesn't it? That's not unusual. There were boys at school whose fathers nearly had strokes as the result of trying to teach their sons to drive."

"I certainly had to abandon the attempt to teach my daughter. So who did train you in the end?"

"I just continued with my counsellor at Starwater, Aelred Peters . . . Do you know Aelred?"

"Yes, a nice old boy, quite bright but rather a limited psychic range. He'd do well in a prayer-group for the sick, I've always thought, but in my opinion dealing with the psychic aftermath of a catastrophe would be well beyond his powers."

I said defensively: "He did stop the poltergeist activity."

"No doubt he did—I can imagine him praying hard for you and teaching you some appropriate meditation techniques. But did he shore up your spiritual life? And did he make any real attempt to come to grips with what was going on in your mind?"

"Well, he was very knowledgeable about paranormal phenomena—"

"So are a lot of people who believe in anything from devil-worship to UFOs, but unfortunately a knowledge of the paranormal doesn't guarantee the ability to give good spiritual direction. It would seem, wouldn't it, that throughout the crucial years of your adolescence your father was disabled and the substitute he appointed was inadequate . . . Or am I being much too unfair to your father?"

"You're not just being unfair—you're being bloody unjust!"

"Just take a moment to revise that last sentence, please."

" 'You're being very unjust.' " I was now furious but anxious to control myself in order to vindicate my father with conviction. "My father cared very much what happened to me," I said. "He often gave me good advice. It wasn't his fault if I was too stupid to take it."

"Advice on what?"

"Well . . . psychic parlour-tricks, for instance."

"What did he say?"

"I told you earlier. He said: 'Don't do them.' "

"I suppose I just couldn't believe he actually said that."

"What do you mean?"

"You have to be much more subtle when you're trying to deflect a young man from risky behaviour! Nicholas, your father may be a brilliant spiritual director, brimming over with gifted advice on prayer, but he seems to have had only the sketchiest idea of how to deal with his adolescent son. Of course if one tells a teenager anxious to establish his own identity: 'Don't do this!' he immediately longs to rush out and do it."

"I wasn't eager to establish my own identity."

There was a slight pause before Lewis said: "You weren't?"

"No, I wanted to be just like him. But because I'm so inferior to him, so much less gifted, I can't always live up to his high standards."

"I thought we agreed earlier that just because you don't have visions you shouldn't automatically assume you're less gifted than he is? But never mind, let that pass—and let me assure you that I do believe your father's always tried his best to be a good parent. Now I want to go back for a moment to your birth in 1942. What was your father doing in those days?"

"He'd started to work at the Theological College—but only as a lecturer. He didn't become the Principal till later."

"And what did he do between 1940, when he left the Order, and 1942, when he began to work at the College?"

"Got married. Worked temporarily as a parish priest, but that didn't pan out."

"Why not?"

"He made a mess of a ministry of healing. But he was soon blazing around being dynamic again. He was fantastic, he really was—well over sixty by that time but with so much energy, so much charisma—"

"How did the marriage fare while all this was going on?"

"Oh, everything was fantastic. They were really happy. My mother had her work too—she ran her family estate. She was great, lots of personality, strong but sensitive—one of those vital, competent brunettes who can have a career and a family and a social life, all with one hand tied behind her back while reading Shakespeare. She was twenty-eight years his junior but it didn't matter, never bothered them, it was all just—"

"Fantastic. Yes, I see. Did they have any other children?"

"No. Well, there was Gerald. He was their first son, but he died at birth. For some reason they always made a great fuss about him, can't think why, it was pointless."

"What sort of fuss?"

"Oh, they used to lay flowers on his grave and remember his birthday every year as if he'd been a real person. I thought it was all very stupid, sentimental behaviour. I doubt if he'd have added up to much if he'd lived."

"Why do you say that?"

"Because *I* was the special one, not Gerald. My father saw me in a vision well over a year before I was born. He told me that after my mother died. The vision made it clear to him that I was to be exactly the son he wanted, a replica of himself. So Gerald would inevitably have been inferior to me and a disappointment to him. Like Martin."

"Who's Martin?"

"That's my father's son by his first marriage, the marriage he blundered into when he was too young to know better, but fortunately his wife died when Martin was seven and Ruth was eight. Ruth's dead now. She had two children, but Colin's farming in New Zealand and Janet's married to an American so they're not around."

"What does Martin do?"

"Act. Martin Darrow. Stage, TV and all that crap."

"Good heavens, yes—a most distinguished actor!"

"Yes, but he's a big disappointment to Father. He's queer."

"Homosexual? Or just odd?"

"Both. And he's a reformed alcoholic."

"Reformed! But how admirable! It's not every alcoholic who can reform with such spectacular success!"

"Yes, but he doesn't really count. *I'm* the one who counts because I was specially designed by God to make Father happy after his vicissitudes."

"That's your father's interpretation of the vision, of course. But what's your interpretation, Nicholas?"

"Mine?" I stared at him. "I don't have one. I mean, Father's interpretation is my interpretation. We think exactly alike. We *are* exactly alike, except that I'm not so gifted as he is, but I'll put that right by living his life for him all over again."

"Is that what he wants you to do?"

"Yes. Well, he does say: 'I don't want you to be my replica,' but that's not what he really thinks—that's just what he knows he's supposed to say. But I *know* he wants me to be a replica, I just know, it's *gnosis*. How can I be 'me' anyway? There *is* no 'me.' I'm him—not literally, of course, but sometimes I think it's exactly as if we're Siamese twins joined at the psyche, and—" I stopped.

There was a long pause.

Lewis, who had taken such a strong hand in the conversation earlier, was now utterly silent.

At last my voice said: "I'm getting mixed up, everything's coming out wrong, I'm saying things I've never said to anyone before because you've got under my guard, but you're not getting under my guard any more, I'm shutting you out before you start thinking I'm nuts. The truth's simply this: I love my father and he loves me; I loved my mother and I know very well she loved me too; we were a happy family and everything was perfect and if you try to tell me it wasn't perfect, I'll—"

"Indeed I shan't try to tell you it wasn't perfect. You're the one, I think, who's secretly longing to tell someone how imperfect it all was."

And as I stared at him in horror he said neutrally: "These parents of yours who spent their time rushing around being fantastic—how much did you actually see of them?" Then he added: "How much did they see of each other?" And finally he said, no longer speaking neutrally but in the gentlest possible voice: "What really lay at the bottom of your father's terrible grief when she died?"

Then I knew I no longer wanted to shut him out.

I I

IT WAS so hard to find the right words.

"It was okay," I said. "I was all right. I had Nanny. I was always loved and looked after. But it's true my parents were very busy. The problem, my mother used to say when she was explaining why my father wasn't around, was that there were only twenty-four hours in a day. I saw more of her than I did of him. I minded her dying when she did. I'd have liked to know her better. I couldn't talk about her to my father once she was dead, of course. He got too upset.

"The worst part of her death was the effect it had on him. I know I've already told you he was ploughed under, but that was an understatement. I just can't describe . . . no, wait a minute, maybe I can. Maybe you'll understand what I mean if I say his psyche was one long scream. I used to hear it at school. It used to get to me at night. I'd wake up—or rather, not wake up—and—"

I broke off. Couldn't admit to somnambulism. Not now, not after telling the lie about it. I waited, staring down at the surface of the table as I tried to decide where to go next.

Opposite me Lewis never said a word.

At last I said: "My father felt so guilty. That was the problem; his grief was so muddied with guilt. I said to him: 'But she understood. She knew there were only twenty-four hours in a day.' That nearly killed him. He said: 'I neglected her and I've neglected you too.' I thought he might commit suicide because his guilt was so unbearable. He swore he wouldn't, but then I thought he might go into a decline anyway and die of natural causes.

"I don't know what happened with the marriage. They did love each other, I know they did, but something wasn't right. My mother used to get so upset sometimes. She was looking forward to his retirement, but he wouldn't stop working and when he retired he became busier than ever . . . Why did he keep working so fanatically? Of course he was so famous, so sought after, so successful . . . but it wasn't right. Okay, the Church needed him, but we needed him too. 'Why do I always have to come second to the bloody Church?' I heard my mother yell at him once. But he did love her. It was just that he . . . well, what was it?

"Sometimes I think that although he himself became convinced that he'd been called from the Order to run that College in those chaotic, demanding years after the war, it wasn't the kind of work he enjoyed best. He was good at administration, good at leadership, good at teaching—he'd proved all that as a monk—but what he really loved was being a spiritual director, not just giving straightforward advice on prayer but helping people overcome the problems that were cutting them off from God. Father Darcy had always approved and welcomed his development as a spiritual director, but even so my father had had to put other work first: teaching the novices at Ruydale, running the community at Grantchester . . . And then finally, when he was seventy, he found himself in a situation where he didn't have to put other work first; he found he could devote himself entirely to spiritual direction, and his delight was so great that my mother and I got lost in the clouds of euphoria . . . Or at least that's how it seems to me sometimes, but I do now wonder if that was just one aspect of what was really going on.

"Sometimes I think the age-gap might have begun to bother him. When he was seventy, my mother was forty-two, and perhaps he felt he had to go on being dynamic for her sake in order to keep old age at bay. My father wasn't very good at becoming old. He adjusted to it in the end—no choice—but he didn't like it. It offended his pride. My father knows holy men should display humility, but he's not actually very good at being humble himself . . . In fact there are a number of things he's not very good at, but because he's so charismatic people tend not to notice his shortcomings. Well, you wouldn't notice them unless you actually had to live with him. But if you do live with him you realise eventually—and I suppose this is the rock-bottom truth—that family life isn't quite his scene.

"He's not very clever at being married, you see. It's not that he dislikes family life. He just doesn't understand it. I think he had a rather peculiar life as a child, with his parents not communicating and no one ever saying much to one another, with the result that the three of them wound up living separate lives under one roof. He seemed to regard my mother and me as rewards sent to him by God to compensate him for having to leave the monastery, but I've wondered in retrospect if he was ever sure what to do with us.

"He missed the Order a lot. Still does. He'd never admit it to me, of course, but the happiest days of his life were spent as a monk. The Order was really the kind of family he preferred, I can see that now. Lots of brothers, giving emotional support. No women and children making emotional demands. My father's so gifted at dealing with other people's problems, but he has to operate from a very clear, emotionally uncluttered base. That's why a life without women and children suited him so well."

I sighed as I reflected on my father's peculiarities, but then concluded: "I couldn't be a monk, but that's all right because he knows no one can be a monk without the strongest possible call, and if I don't have the call, that's God's decision and there's nothing to be done about it. So all I have to do now is be a priest and marry a nice girl—which reminds me, I forgot to tell you about Rosalind, my fiancée. She's the grand-daughter of old friends of my mother's. My father's very pleased."

Lewis at last spoke. Having allowed himself to look politely interested in the existence of Rosalind he said: "How's your father's psyche at the moment?"

"Screaming. I have to keep tuning him out. But he can't help himself, he's so old and he can't control his powers as he used to."

"Why's his psyche screaming?"

"Worried about me. Can't think why. I'm fine." I glanced restlessly around the room. "Well, I know I have one or two minor problems," I said, "but I'm coping, I'm functioning, I can manage."

Silence fell again.

"Well," I said, rising at last from my chair, "that's it, that's my autobiographical thumbnail sketch—although we seem to have spent a lot of time on digressions which are hardly relevant to 1968. Have you any more questions? Because if you haven't—"

"I've no more questions," said Lewis, "but I'd like very much to do some more listening. Can you tell me a little more about your brother Martin?"

I sank slowly back in my chair.

I 2

TRUCULENTLY I said: "What do you want me to say?"

"Oh, anything'll do. I'm very easily pleased."

"Balls! I know exactly what you want me to confess!"

"You do?"

"Yes, you want me to say I'm jealous of him, but I'm not. You're thinking I'm bound to be jealous of him because he's so good-looking and successful whereas I'm just an obscure misfit of an ordinand, but you'd be wrong because I'm not jealous of him at all. Why should I be jealous of an elderly queer?"

"No idea. But I'm intrigued by how deeply you dislike him."

"I know what you're thinking!" I cried. "You're thinking—following Jung—that we project onto others what we hate and fear in ourselves. You're thinking I hate Martin because I'm a repressed homosexual!"

"What a deduction!" said Lewis admiringly. "What ruthless self-analysis! But I think it's more likely that you're being abusive about Martin not because you're a text-book homophobe but because it gives you relief from some very deep-seated rage. After all, Christian's homosexuality doesn't seem to have bothered you."

"Well, of course that never happened."

"No?"

"No, that was just Martin hamming it up—converting his unconsummated yearnings into a grand passion. Don't forget, he never actually admitted to me that he'd gone to bed with Christian."

"But didn't he nonetheless give the unmistakable impression—"

"I tell you, that was just Martin hamming it up. Christian was one hundred percent heterosexual. Had to be."

"Why did he have to be?"

"Well, he just was, that's all, I knew he was, it was *gnosis* . . . What's all this about me having a deep-seated rage?"

"Maybe I've got it wrong. How would you yourself describe this powerful emotion which surfaces in your conversation whenever Martin's name is mentioned?"

"Dislike."

"All right," said Lewis. "I accept that. For all I know he may be thoroughly dislikable. But what about poor little Gerald? I thought I detected the same deep-seated rage there, but he never lived long enough to be either pleasant or unpleasant."

"I didn't dislike Gerald. I just disliked the Gerald cult."

"The Gerald cult provided a focus for your anger, but why were you so angry in the first place?"

"I didn't see much of my parents when I was a child and I resented them paying attention to a dead baby when they could have been paying attention to me. It was the same with Martin. He was always muscling in and grabbing my father's attention."

"Yes, but that was when you were a child. We can certainly allow you a little commonplace jealousy of your siblings when you were in the nursery, but surely now that you're twenty-five—"

"Don't adults ever get jealous?"

"Of course. But the interesting question here is: what do you now have to be jealous about? After all, you discovered in adolescence that you were the special one, the son your father saw in his vision. Why aren't you now saying indulgently: 'Poor little Gerald—what a pity I never knew him!' And more baffling still, why aren't you saying: 'Funny old Martin, what a character, I'm really rather fond of the old boy!' As I see it, you can afford to be generous. You're alive—unlike Gerald. And you're the apple of your father's eye—unlike Martin. So what's the problem?"

"It must be the aftermath of the childhood jealousy."

"Must it? Then answer me this: you dislike that Community too, don't you—the Community which runs your home. In Session One when you mentioned the set-up at Starrington Manor you spoke of the members with a contempt which again seems to mask some very profound rage. Yet why should that be? Your father surely can't prefer their company to yours!"

"Why can't I be allowed a little simple dislike? Why are you so busy ferreting for a complex explanation?"

"Because your dislike strikes me as being violent enough to be irrational, and yet I believe you're essentially a rational man. I had a case once," said Lewis, lighting another cigarette, "in which an apparently rational young man was quite irrational about his twin brother who had died at birth. He came to me saying that his brother was resentful that he hadn't been allowed a crack at life, so resentful that he had decided to infest the living twin."

I forgot to be truculent. Instantly I said with interest: "How did you interpret that old-fashioned picture-language?"

"The old-fashioned picture-language, as you call it, was a perfectly valid way of describing his feeling of being mentally oppressed by unpleasant emotions which he connected with his dead brother, but there was more going on than he was initially prepared to admit. It turned out that he had a difficult private life with a very demanding mother—in fact it was so difficult that he felt envious of his dead brother for being lucky enough to escape it. The envy festered and gave rise to complex feelings of guilt and anger—guilt that he should resent his innocent little brother, and anger that he couldn't control the resentment. This seething mass of emotions eventually tied him into such a knot that he began to feel haunted by them, and in the heart of the seething mass, as he well knew, was the memory of his brother. That was why he became convinced he was infested by his brother's spirit."

"How did you heal him?"

"By listening, by prayer, by counselling. Working with a psychotherapist, I took the patient through the relationship with the mother, which was at the bottom of the mess, and eventually got him to the point where he could try to forgive her, forgive his brother and forgive himself—the point where, in other words, he could start a new life unburdened by the pressures which had been distorting his personality. Then I turned back to the religious language: we prayed that the spirit of his dead brother would depart and find peace at last with God. After that the patient still needed regular psychotherapy to assist him in the new relationship he was forging with his mother, but the demons of hatred and jealousy had been exorcised."

I savoured this satisfying conclusion. Then before I could stop myself I was saying: "I've always wanted to be a priest in the ministry of healing, but I can't be because my father says it wouldn't work. It didn't work for him so it couldn't possibly work for me."

Another silence began. I knew what Lewis was thinking—I knew what I was thinking—but such thoughts were so difficult, so dangerous, that it seemed impossible to articulate them. I traced a cross with my finger on the table, and concentrating hard on that invisible drawing I began to answer the question that Lewis had not asked.

"I can't go against my father's wishes," I said. "He mustn't be upset. He's so old, so fragile, that in order to keep him alive I've got to do exactly what he wants. And he's got to be kept alive because if he dies . . ."

My voice trailed away. I started to trace the four points of the cross again. Reality is quaternal, Jung had written. Reality is fourfold.

"Life could be a little awkward for me without my father," I said at last. "That's why I have to do everything I can to keep him alive. But recently no matter what I do it doesn't seem to be enough, and I can't understand it. He's just getting sicker and sicker, and sometimes I feel so angry, *so angry,* because here I am, making all these sacrifices for his sake, yet he just refuses to get well." Dimly I realised I was sounding petulant and selfish. Hastily I tried to backtrack. "Don't get me wrong," I said. "I'm glad to make sacrifices for his sake. I mean, that's what I'm here for, isn't it? To sacrifice my own needs so that I can live his life for him all over again."

"No," said Lewis flatly.

XI

"Jung was very conscious of the mysteriousness of the human personality and the difficulty of penetrating the outward appearance and discovering the real individual."

CHRISTOPHER BRYANT
Member of the Society of St. John the Evangelist,
1935–1985
JUNG AND THE CHRISTIAN WAY

I

"*I KNOW* what you're thinking," I said at once. "You're thinking I'm badly mixed up, but I assure you that I've spent a long time examining my situation and submitting it to rational analysis."

"In that case I'd be most grateful if you could share your conclusions with me."

"Sure. My logic runs like this: one, like everyone else I've got to seek my true self in order to achieve integration—by which I mean that my task is to realise as far as possible in this life the unique blueprint designed for me by God, because to be at one with God's will is to be happy and fulfilled. Two, God intends me to be a replica of my father. Three, that must mean my personality blueprint is in all important respects identical to my father's. Four, that in turn must mean I can only achieve integration—happiness, fulfilment, wholeness—by striving to become my father's replica."

"Very sound," said Lewis. "Well done. But aren't you forgetting something?"

"What's that?"

"The whole point about a unique personality blueprint is that it's unique, and as far as I know cloning exists only in the pages of science fiction. Did your mother play no part in your genetic make-up or was her womb merely leased by God so that He could have fun and games overriding the law of biology?"

"Well, of course if you want to make a joke of it—"

"I assure you I'm taking what you say very seriously indeed. What a strain your life must be at present! This acute anxiety about your father's life-span, the non-relationship with your brother which makes it impossible to turn to him for help, the inevitable emotional demands of a fiancée—and to cap it all, ordination looming on the horizon! No wonder you seized the chance to escape from all those pressures by investigating Christian."

I ignored this speech. "Despite all your smart talk of cloning and womb-leasing," I said, "you can't knock down the fact that my father saw me in a God-given vision well over a year before I was born and knew at once that I was going to be a replica."

"That tells me a great deal about your father," said Lewis, "but I'm not sure it tells me anything about God. The problem with visions, Nicholas, no matter how God-given they are, is that they have to be interpreted by fallible human beings."

"But my father's so wise, so gifted, so holy—"

"He may well be all those things, but that doesn't mean he's incapable of making mistakes. How interesting it must have been for you to see how Christian coped with—or failed to cope with—his own very successful clerical father! In fact I can quite see now why Christian intrigued you so much. Here's a man with a curiously similar background to your own: the distinguished clerical father who adored him, the mother who died in his teens, the paternal expectation that he would go into the Church, make an excellent marriage—"

"Talking of marriage," I said, "I still haven't told you much about Rosalind, have I?"

"The phrase 'nice girl' speaks volumes—and implies we must add sexual abstinence to your list of difficulties. How are you coping with that?"

"Fine." I was already on my feet and heading for the door. "Well, if you'll excuse me, I think I'll—"

"If you can bear to hang on a moment longer," said Lewis, "perhaps we can make a plan for tomorrow morning. I assume you'll be coming to mass?"

"Well, I hadn't got as far as thinking about it, but—"

"It's extremely important," said Lewis, turning on the full power of his personality, "that you should be in good spiritual health when you're dealing with a situation which is potentially demonic. When did you last attend mass?"

"Friday. With my father in our chapel."

"And when did you last make your confession?"

"A formal confession? To a priest?"

"Well, since you claim to be an Anglo-Catholic—"

"Yes, of course, let me think. It must have been—oh, not long ago. Quite recently, in fact. At College before the end of term."

"I'm sure a lot of water's flowed under the bridge since then. Why don't we return to this confessional at seven tomorrow morning? Then you can make your confession to me before we attend mass."

"Okay."

"If you'd prefer," said Lewis pleasantly, "I can arrange for one of the monks to hear you."

I nearly fell into the trap but scooped myself back just in time. If I refused to confess to him he'd think I had something to hide. "Oh no!" I said. "I'm quite happy for you to hear me! Why not?"

He smiled, his eyes very dark in their shadowed sockets, and followed me from the room.

2

HALFWAY up the stairs I succumbed to a bout of profound uneasiness and came to a halt. "What can you be thinking?" I said nervously. "All those questions . . . and all my answers . . . Have you secretly concluded that I'm crazy?"

"I can come to no worthwhile conclusion until we've staged the reconstruction, but so far one of the most interesting aspects of this case is your apparent sanity."

I slumped against the wall for a moment before resuming my journey up the stairs.

On the landing Lewis said: "If you have trouble sleeping or if for any reason you feel uneasy during the night, do please wake me up so that we can talk things over. Oh, and wear your cross. Don't leave it on the bedside table."

"Okay."

Five minutes later I was tethering my ankle to the bedpost and preparing for a quick dive into oblivion.

3

I AWOKE slowly, drifting back through the levels of consciousness until I became aware that the room was bright with moonlight. That startled me because I knew I had pulled down the blind earlier, but suddenly I realised that it had been the flutter of the rising blind which had woken me. Someone had drawn it up. I was no longer alone in the room.

A monk was standing motionless by the bed.

I gasped but when he said: "It's all right—it's only me," I knew it was Christian.

He was wearing his cowl up again so that his face was in shadow, but I recognised his trick of speaking fast with a barely perceptible stutter. I whispered: "So Father Wilcox was lying!" but he only answered: "Sorry I couldn't stop in the garden. Come back to the shed now and we can talk."

I scrambled out of bed and the string tugged at my ankle. "Wait!" I said urgently to Christian, and he paused by the door as I untied the knot. The texture of the string was rough against my fingers and the linoleum was cool against my bare feet. "Should I get dressed?" I asked as I became aware of the chill in the air, but he answered: "Just put your jacket on over your pyjamas," and when I obeyed him he added: "You can take off that cross you're wearing because my crucifix will do for us both."

I saw him touch the little brass crucifix which hung from his belt. I was unable to see the shape clearly but the brass was gleaming in the pale light.

As I put my cross on the bedside table I said: "Lewis lent me that— Father Lewis Hall from St. Paul's in Langley Bottom. Father Wilcox called him in so that they could say I was a hallucinating psychic who hadn't really seen you at all."

"There's no Lewis Hall at St. Paul's."

I was transfixed: "Then who the hell is he?"

"He's one of the London monks, and his real name is Darcy."

"Darcy?"

"Shhh. Come outside and I'll explain everything."

We left the room. It was very dark in the passage but Christian had no trouble seeing his way and I followed close on his heels. In the hall he said unexpectedly: "You must be the one who unlocks the door—monks are forbidden to unlock doors at night," so I stepped forward to draw back the bolt. "Leave it on the latch," he said as the door swung wide. "We don't want to lock ourselves out."

I pressed down the button, drew the door noiselessly back into the frame and followed him along the path which led to the back garden.

The lawn was shining in the moonlight. The branches of the beech-tree, black against the pale sky, were soughing softly in the faint breeze and I was aware of the scent floating towards me from the herb-garden. The dew on the grass was so cold that I gasped.

"How stupid!" I muttered. "I've forgotten my shoes."

"Never mind, it'll be dry in the shed."

We reached the peach-tree and followed the path alongside the kitchen-garden wall towards the hedge that screened the shed from the lawn. The area behind the hedge lay in deep shadow, and again Christian took the lead, moving past me through the blackness to open the shed's door. "I put a candle in here earlier," I heard him say. "Wait till I've struck the match."

I waited on the threshold. When light flared a second later I stepped forward but Christian remained with his back to me. Having lit the candle on the shelf in front of him he picked up the three-pronged gardening fork nearby and raised it aloft as if it were a sword.

I said sharply: "What are you doing?"

He laughed. Then he spun to face me, flung back his cowl and I saw he was the Devil.

In terror I shouted: "Father, save me!" but even as I spoke I knew I was beyond saving. I'd slipped too far over the rim of the psychic world and now I was to be savagely destroyed.

"You're mine now," said the Devil. "All mine," and as he laughed harder than ever I saw that his crucifix was hanging upside down.

The candle burst into flames. The raised fork glittered in the light. Every prong was now a spear, and in the intense heat the alien lines of the Devil's face blurred into a mess of red eyes and bleached bones and black blood. Blind with terror I turned to run but I was too slow and the next moment the spears had struck me in the back. I sank to my knees, my breath coming in great tearing gasps, the tears streaming down my face, my voice shouting: "My God, my God, why hast thou forsaken me?"—and then as I crawled dying from the shed into the moonlight I saw Lewis standing motionless in front of me, his crucifix held high in his hand.

4

"LEWIS, Lewis, Lewis—"

"Yes, you're all right, you're safe—"

"No, I'm dying—Christian's killed me, he turned into the Devil and he killed me—"

"That was the dream. This is the reality, and I'm saying to you that you're *going to wake up*—look at me, Nicholas, *look at me,* I'm telling you IN THE NAME OF JESUS CHRIST—"

I suddenly became aware that this last hallucination of a dying man was taking a new direction. I had been lying gasping on the ground, shuddering from head to toe, but now I dreamed that Lewis was yanking me into a sitting position and ramming his crucifix against my chest.

"Feel the metal," he was saying urgently. "Feel the image of Christ on the cross. It's all real, isn't it? It's not a dream. You know it's not a dream, you know you're alive because you're waking up, Nicholas, *waking up*—"

"No, I've been through this before. I think I'm waking up but in fact it's an illusion because I'm still asleep. So I wake and I wake and I wake, but I don't wake and now I'll never wake because I'm—"

I stopped. I had suddenly realised that the crucifix was still warm from its contact with his living flesh. But perhaps the fire in the shed was heating everything nearby. I glanced in panic over my shoulder at the fires of hell—

But I saw only darkness.

The door of the shed was open but there was no fire within. Farther down the path the peach-tree was basking in the moonlight. An owl hooted. The branches of the other trees were still soughing faintly in the night breeze.

"Oh my God," I said. I reached up and touched Lewis's face. It was warm, heated by real blood which was circulating in a real body. "Oh my God." I dropped his crucifix and covered my face with my hands.

Lewis retrieved the crucifix instantly, slipped the chain over my head and tucked the crucifix itself into the open neck of my pyjamas. All he said was: "Are you awake or asleep?"

"Awake."

"Are you alive or dead?"

"Alive."

"Was Christian a reality or a dream?"

"A dream."

"Good. Now lie flat on your back and take some slow, deep breaths . . . That's it . . . Yes, hold the crucifix if you like . . . And keep breathing deeply—"

"Jesus is Lord."

"That's right, make it clear you're not possessed . . . And now relax your muscles, beginning with your toes and working upwards . . ."

I said "Jesus is Lord" again to reassure myself that the first time was no fluke. The crucifix seemed glued to my sweating palm.

When the shuddering finally stopped and I was once more able to stand I said: "I was possessed earlier. But you delivered me."

"No," said Lewis firmly. "You were merely having a nightmare and I was there to help you recover from the shock when you woke up. Rule number one when dealing with the paranormal: always look first for the normal explanation because nine times out of ten the normal explanation will be the correct one."

"But Lewis—"

"You weren't possessed, Nicholas. If you'd been possessed you'd have tried to kill me. The dream was caused not by the Devil but by the most profound stress, so what we now have to do is not exorcise you but explore what your unconscious mind was spelling out to you during that nightmare."

I said tentatively: "A rational analysis?" and began to feel better.

Lewis smiled but merely said: "You need to be wrapped in blankets and dosed with sweet tea to counter the shock. We'll go to the kitchen."

WHEN the kettle came to the boil I was at last able to say: "What exactly happened?" Wrapped in the eiderdown from my bedroom, I was sitting at the kitchen table. Lewis, fully dressed, was standing by the counter and spooning tea-leaves out of the caddy.

"I had a hunch you'd sleep-walk," he said. "I know you'd denied suffering from somnambulism but I thought you'd almost confessed to sleep-walking after your mother died, and since you were once again in a stressful situation—"

"I don't know why I lied to you."

"No? I'd imagine it was easier to blot out the memory than to confront it. After all, somnambulism's an unnerving activity, isn't it? Not to be consciously in control of one's actions—to wake in a place where you're not supposed to be—to have no idea what you might have been doing along the way—"

"I thought I'd killed Martin the other night. Of course now I can look back and laugh at the idea, but at the time I was terrified."

"Of course. Somnambulism's no joke—which is why I was on my guard tonight."

"So when I started out—"

"I'd left the door of my room open and I heard the creak of your bed as soon as you began to get up. I took a look and there you were, undoing the string around your ankle, putting on your jacket and taking off your cross. The removal of the cross intrigued me. It suggested that you were gearing yourself up not to beat back the Dark but to examine it in a confrontation which required you to be spiritually vulnerable."

"How did you know I was asleep?"

"You remained unaware of me. And you were exuding that mechanical air common among sleep-walkers, the air of someone moving in accordance with a pre-set programme. I knew at once you weren't awake."

"So what happened next?"

"I followed you downstairs where you unbolted the door and left it on the latch. Interesting, isn't it, how sleep-walkers can take trouble over little details; you should have been too far under to worry about locking yourself out of the house, but not a bit of it—you were determined not to suffer any inconvenience." He made the tea before adding: "Off we both went into the garden, I keeping a respectful distance behind you, like the Duke of Edinburgh accompanying the Queen. When you reached the shed you went inside and stood in the middle of the floor for about twenty seconds while I watched from the threshold. I did dutifully hold up my crucifix in case there were any demonic forces around, but I saw no abnormal manifestations and you, in fact, were behaving in a very typical manner for a sleep-walker. Sleep-walking always looks so sinister but most of the time there's nothing particularly interesting going on.

"Then just as I was thinking it would be more fun to watch a robot the action began. You yelled: 'Father, save me!' and I realised you were having a big nightmare, but usually it's best not to wake a somnambulist. So I drew back and prayed you'd somehow find your way out of the drama without waking, but the next moment you're staggering out of the shed, falling flat on your face and shouting: 'My God, my God, why has thou forsaken me?' At that point I knew I had to intervene . . . Here, have some tea. I apologise for the sugar, but think of it as medicine."

The tea tasted disgusting. For a while the silence was broken only by the sound of Lewis reopening the tin of flapjacks, but at last when my cup was almost empty I began to describe my dream to him.

"Did Christian explain why he didn't stop to talk to you yesterday?" said Lewis as I recalled the dialogue in my bedroom.

"No. He gave the impression that he shouldn't have been communicating with me and that he was breaking a rule by seeking me out."

"It's certainly a rule that the dead don't normally communicate with the living."

"But it never occurred to me that he was dead! My reaction as soon as I saw him was: so I was right—he's alive."

"Maybe your subconscious mind was cleverly juggling with both possibilities. Was it he who told you to take off your cross?"

"Yes, he said his crucifix would do for both of us."

"That suggests that you felt you had to align yourself with him in order to gain some new insight. Did you argue with him?"

"No, but for some reason I mentioned that my cross belonged to you. Then Christian said—" I stopped.

"Yes?"

"Well, I know this sounds crazy, but—" I broke off again.

"I shall have a stroke in a minute," said Lewis.

I laughed, finally seeing the absurdity of my embarrassment, and said: "He told me there was no Lewis Hall at St. Paul's."

"So you secretly doubt my reality! Quite right too. Always treat an exorcist with grave suspicion! However"—he pulled out his wallet and produced his driving licence—"let me instantly offer proof of my identity."

"Good heavens, Lewis, of course I don't seriously think you're a fraud!" I protested. But I did take a quick look at the licence.

"Did Christian deign to inform you who I was or was I just written off as an anonymous con-man?"

"He said you were one of the London monks and that your real name was Darcy."

Lewis dropped his half-eaten flapjack. Crumbs from the edges spun across the kitchen table towards me. "But how extraordinary!" he exclaimed. "Why should your subconscious mind have been playing with that idea?"

"Oh, that's no mystery—my father's been wishing for years that I could meet a modern version of his mentor, and obviously I must have been thinking that you fitted the bill."

"I realise you intend that remark as a compliment," said Lewis dryly, "but I think we should get right away from this notion of yours that human clones are either possible or desirable. Would it really be beneficial for you if we staged a rerun of the Darcy-Darrow drama? I'd heard they had a tough, abrasive relationship whenever they weren't seeing psychic eye to psychic eye."

I said sharply: "Who told you that? It's not the kind of thing anyone outside the Order would know."

"Oh, but think how indiscreet those old monks can be after a couple of glasses of claret!"

"Even so—"

"No, let's waste no more time discussing the monastic weakness for gossip. There was Christian, you said, telling you that my real name was Darcy . . ."

I continued to recall my dream while Lewis gathered up the fragments of his flapjack and ate them. Finally I was able to conclude: "Now that I've reviewed the dream I think I can analyse what it all means."

"This is what impresses me," said Lewis at once. "Your dedication to rational analysis means that you're always trying to grasp reality and beat back illusion. You may not always succeed, but at least you keep trying. I regard this as strong evidence of your basic stability."

This remark completed the restoration of my self-confidence. Sweet tea, the fading of shock, the re-emergence of common sense—all had contributed to my recovery, but the major contribution had come from Lewis as he subtly smoothed my mind back into shape.

Embarking on my interpretation of the dream, I said: "The first thing I have to admit is that I hadn't faced up to the whole truth about Christian. I'd refused to accept the facts I didn't like, and the purpose of this nightmare was to force me to face the dark side of his personality."

"Why do you think you'd been so reluctant to face this?"

"I wanted him to be just like me. So I rejected all the evidence—such as the bisexuality—which indicated he wasn't. You'd already grasped that I needed him to be just like me—you signalled as much at the end of our third session—but I couldn't discuss it with you then because I couldn't tolerate the implications. I chose to change the subject and bury the memory of what you'd said, but once I was asleep the memory began to rise up through my unconscious mind until it produced the dream symbolising the dark side of Christian, the side I didn't want to know."

After a pause Lewis said: "Perhaps I shouldn't have tried to force the pace, but I wanted to find out how far you were aware of the identity-game you were playing with him."

"I was both conscious and unconscious. I always knew he seemed to have a special message for me, but I couldn't work out what it was or how his life could connect with mine. All I knew in the end was that I had to sort out the mystery of his final months, and when I found out he was alive, the meaning of my quest at last became obvious. But I couldn't talk about it, even to you, because I recognised it was bizarre."

"Let's see if your explanation matches my deductions."

I hesitated in order to choose my words with care but at last I said: "I was in a muddle about many things. Then one day I looked across at Christian and saw someone who had apparently mastered similar problems. I thought he could show me the way out of my muddle."

"So the more like him you were, the more chance there'd be that he could offer you salvation."

"That's it. He had to be an alter ego because if he wasn't, his situation would differ, his solutions would be inapplicable and his life would hold no message for me. And if there was no message for me—" I broke off before saying: "No, I still can't face that. If there are no solutions after all, what do I do? I was absolutely relying on Christian to provide me with the answers, and when I realized he was alive—oh, how excited I was! The idea of rebirth, of slipping out of a suffocating life and moving sideways into another identity . . . I thought: if he can do it, I can do it too, and amidst all my despair I began to hope. My fundamental problem," I said, finally summing up the crisis, "is that I hate being me and I want to be someone else."

"No," said Lewis. "Your fundamental problem is that you hate being someone else and you want to be you."

6

AS THE silence lengthened I stared down at the coarse-grained wood of the table in front of me. The kitchen, brightly lit, seemed to be without shadows. I felt like a fugitive with no place to hide.

At last I said: "I can't be me, can't separate myself from my father, it's too late."

"Your first task," said Lewis, "is to separate yourself from Christian, not just because you've been using him to avoid facing up to your central problem, but because his message for you is demonic. If he's alive, he did a terrible thing by abandoning his family and disappearing into the blue. That's not self-realisation, the subjugation of the ego and the emergence of the true self in a fully integrated personality; that's selfishness in its most lethal form, the ego running rampant and trampling underfoot God's design for the true self. You can't build an integrated life on the sufferings of others; your new house will rest only on the shifting sands of guilt. And if Christian's dead, all one can say is that he died while pursuing a self-destructive course which indicates a mind falling apart under pressure. Whichever way you look at his life, Nicholas, there's no message for you there. You can only say to yourself: Christian lost and went under, but I'm going to win and survive."

"But I can't survive once I'm separated from my father! I'm just a shadow of him and once he dies the Dark will blot me out!"

"Of course no shadow can exist without the presence of light. That's why you have to give birth to your true self, the self that won't be a shadow, the self substantial enough to exist whether your father's present or not. Don't you see, Nicholas? It's the replica, not your true self, that can't withstand the Dark! It's impossible to create a living truth out of a lie."

"But if I ditch the replica my father will get so upset that he'll die and then I'll be crucified by guilt and then the Devil will take me over and then—"

"Never mind the Devil for the moment. Let's give him a well-earned rest. And never mind your father for the moment either. We'll deal with him later. Let's take this situation one step at a time—and the first step, as I see it, is to detach you from Christian by solving the mystery surrounding his death. Then you'll be free to set him aside and confront your real problem."

I found these rational statements calming. Making a big effort I tried to analyse the current state of my attachment to Christian. "Could one say," I began tentatively, "that Christian has to be exorcised from my psyche? Could one say that the shadow side of him has been converted into an evil force which by infesting me has almost driven me mad?"

"Well, if you really want to sound like an actor in a Victorian melodrama, I'm not going to stop you," said Lewis, "but since we're trying to give the old-fashioned language a rest, why don't we just say you've been experiencing an obsession which we now have to terminate by uncovering the truth and allowing you to make a satisfactory adjustment to reality at last?"

"But if you, an exorcist, had to describe what was going on in religious language—"

"Let me hold my fire until after the reconstruction. There are certainly demonic elements in this case, but so far I'm not convinced that the Devil's directly involved . . . One of the dangers of being an exorcist," remarked Lewis, moving to the sink to rinse out the teapot, "is that one tends to see the Devil everywhere—just as Senator McCarthy and his anti-communist fanatics saw reds under every bed."

I dried our cups and saucers as he washed up. Eventually I managed to say in a nonchalant voice: "I'm a little worried about attempting to sleep again. It bothers me that I untied the string when I was unconscious."

"It would bother me too, but I've got a hunch tonight's episode represents the end of your current bout of somnambulism. Now that your conscious mind has acknowledged the shadow side of Christian, there's no longer any need for your unconscious mind to put you through such unpleasant hoops."

"Even so——"

"Even so, I'll keep my door open and if necessary I'll play the Duke of Edinburgh again to make sure you come to no harm."

As we went upstairs I suddenly realised I was exhausted, and in my room I paused only to give him back his crucifix and slip his cross around my neck. Then once I was alone I tethered my ankle, fell into bed and sank instantly into unconsciousness.

7

WHEN he woke me at six-thirty I was so deeply asleep that he had to wake me again five minutes later. I dragged myself out of bed. Shaving was obviously a task to be postponed. Standing by the basin I stared blearily at the taps and remembered the horrors of the night.

"Time for the confessional," said Lewis, appearing for the third time. "Are you ready?"

I wasn't. He had to wait while I finished buttoning my shirt. Meanwhile I was reflecting that the very last thing I felt like doing was confessing—or rather, not confessing. Staggering after him downstairs, I tried to summon my wits and think intelligently.

He himself seemed unaffected by the broken night. He was wearing his green sports-shirt again with his black suit, but despite the absence of a cassock he contrived to exude an aura appropriate for a priest. He was shaved, washed, brushed and neat. In contrast I felt less like an ordinand than like a hung-over hippie.

Entering the confessional where we had talked before, we sat down again at the table for the informal discussion which would precede the formal confession at the prie-dieu.

"Okay, how's the batting going under stress?" said Lewis, selecting a casual opener to put me at ease. "Any particular fallen wicket you'd like to examine?"

"Anger," I said promptly. "I've got to be more tolerant of the Community—I was very struck when you mentioned yesterday how hostile my attitude towards them was. And I've got to stop being angry with Martin too—I quite see I must work at improving that relationship."

"Any idea why you should feel so angry with these people?"

"It's all bound up with pride. I feel superior to Martin because he's queer and superior to the Community because they're cranks. But could I be subconsciously compensating myself for a poor self-image? It's just possible that I'm looking down on these people because I have a psychological compulsion to boost my ego."

"What an intriguing theory! But how does it link up with your anger?"

"Well, my pride means I classify these people as fools, and I don't suffer fools gladly—or in other words, I get angry when I think people are stupid. What I have to do in future is fight this pride by reminding myself that I can often be stupid too. The way to be less angry," I said, very meek, very earnest, "is to adopt an attitude of greater humility."

"I see. Go on."

"Well, that's my main fallen wicket, and I do realise it's a very unattractive one. Now let me see. Gluttony: no. Avarice: no—except that I rather coveted your VW! I like that groovy flower on the door."

"My daughter's handiwork. Tell me, how far do you blame your current stressful situation for this anger of yours?"

"Oh, the stress only aggravates a situation which already exists. I don't want to make excuses for myself," I said, pitching the remorse just right and hitting the humility spot-on. "I just want to lay the sin before God and pray for the grace to do better in future."

"Uh-huh. Anything else that's particularly bothering you?"

"No, only sex—I suppose I ought to give that a mention, but there's nothing special going on there, just the usual impure thoughts—oh, and masturbation, but of course that'll all sort itself out when I'm married. Meanwhile I'm very sorry about the lapses and I'll try hard to keep myself on the rails while I'm waiting for the wedding."

"Splendid," said Lewis.

"Well," I said, "that's about it, I suppose. Anger, pride, a little dash of lust—and a few very minor incidents which I can list at the prie-dieu—"

"That won't be necessary," said Lewis, shedding his casual manner so suddenly that I jumped. "If you think I'm going to let you offer such a load of rubbish to God, you've made a very big mistake. Why don't you leave the room, come back and begin all over again?"

I stared at him. I did open my mouth to reply but found I could only slide my tongue around my lips in the classic manifestation of guilt. When I finally managed to speak I could only utter the feeble lie: "But I've told you everything!"

"No," said Lewis, grinding the lie into dust. "You said the words you wanted me to hear, but I heard the words you couldn't bring yourself to say."

I freaked out.

8

"WHO are you?" I whispered. "What is this? What the hell's going on?"

"My dear Nicholas!" exclaimed Lewis with pardonable astonishment. "What on earth are you talking about?"

I floundered in the search for words but eventually managed to say: "This is the past being replayed. You're Father Darcy and I'm my father."

Lewis stared at me. Then he ran his fingers through his hair and said in his firmest, kindest voice: "No, I'm Lewis Hall, you're Nicholas Darrow and reincarnation is quite definitely not on the psychic menu today."

"But you used Father Darcy's exact words—the words he used to unsatisfactory penitents!"

"So what? He never took out a patent on them!"

"But if you were never a monk, how could you have known one of his favourite phrases?"

"Good heavens, you don't imagine he confined his *mots justes* to the monks, do you? Remember, I was educated at Starwater Abbey in the 1930s when Darcy was in his third decade as Abbot-General, and that particular saying of his was notorious. We all knew about it."

I took off my glasses and rubbed my eyes as if I were erasing a hallucinatory view. Then I said: "Sorry. You must be thinking I'm ripe for a strait-jacket after all." And replacing my glasses I added as crisply as possible: "Where were we?"

"You'd just realised you had to revise your neat little shopping-list of sins."

"Ah yes." I tried to concentrate on forming a new list but found my curiosity was overpowering me. "How did you know the list was no good?" I demanded. "Was it sheer psychic *gnosis*?"

"Nicholas, I'm a Christian priest. I leave *gnosis* to the Gnostics."

"Then how did you know I was holding out on you? I was so convincing!"

"*Convincing?* But it was quite obvious you were lying to the back teeth! For instance, although I found it easy to believe that you weren't sleeping with that 'nice girl,' your fiancée, there were a number of reasons why I thought you might be having trouble with sex. One: it's 1968 and unfortunately some of today's ordinands, particularly cool, hip young ordinands in jeans, delude themselves into thinking that a little discreet sex is acceptable behaviour. Two: your unflinching exposition of the theory that you could be a repressed homosexual suggested to me that you were in fact secure in your heterosexuality and that your security almost certainly arose from regular experience. Three: your roll-call of glamorous ladyfriends implied that women find you attractive and that the opportunities for you to misbehave, particularly recently, would have been considerable. And four: despite your sinister boast that you can hypnotise women instantly—a skill which must have enhanced your confidence with them—you seem strikingly reticent about the opposite sex. I don't think for one moment that you've formed the habit of seducing a different woman every week by abusing your hypnotic powers, but this modest silence on the subject of girls certainly contrasts with the need of so many young men to talk big to boost their self-esteem."

"Say no more," I said. "Obviously this is the most catastrophic confession I've ever—"

"My suspicions increased," pursued Lewis, "when I remembered you were under stress yet obviously not interested in relieving the tension by an overindulgence in food and drink. Moreover, when I raised the subject of sex last night you nearly fell over yourself trying to bolt from the room—and when you yourself raised the subject this morning, you behaved very shiftily indeed, wriggling in your chair and assuming a bashful air which was so patently false that I could only consider it a mercy you've never been tempted to follow your brother onto the stage. By this time it's quite clear you're not being honest about your sex-life, just as it's equally clear to me that you're not being honest about this anger that's consuming you, but I think you may genuinely not understand yet why you're so angry. What I'm sure you do understand is—but no, it's not for me to say out loud what you've been doing. That's your task, as I believe you'll agree."

I finally faced the fact that this was the one man I could never manipulate, and at last, knowing there was no alternative, I embarked on an honest confession.

9

"*EVERY* time it happened," I said after I had told him about the episodes with Katie, Marina and Venetia, "I said to myself: well, that's it—I can't possibly be a priest now, it's clear I'm unsuited, the call's false. And I felt relieved. Yet at the same time I felt horrified because I knew very well I did still want to be a priest. Ever since I first heard about Jesus the healer

I knew not only that I wanted to be a priest but exactly what kind of a priest I wanted to be."

"I remember you saying you felt drawn to the ministry of healing."

"Then you'll remember I also said my father was dead against it. He doesn't want me to work on the fringes of orthodoxy."

"So long as the ministry's conducted in the right manner by a priest with a genuine call, it ought to fall well within orthodox boundaries," said Lewis firmly, but added in a more neutral voice: "Maybe because your father failed in this particular ministry he now has a subconscious urge to run it down."

I felt driven to say: "To be fair to my father, I think he honestly believes that it's too dangerous for a psychic to work in an area where there's such a risk of demonic infiltration."

"And I'm afraid that objection merely suggests to me that he's fallen into the parental trap of being overprotective. There's no reason why a psychic shouldn't take on a high-risk ministry so long as he operates within a strong, traditional religious framework which will keep him in order."

"The framework of the Catholic tradition?"

"I'm sure it could also be Protestant. But the Catholic tradition is the one that's worked for me, and given your background it's probably the one that'll work for you."

"And within this framework you feel safe from demonic infiltration?"

"As safe as I'm ever going to feel. It's all a question of spiritual health; if you devote the necessary time and energy to a keep-fit programme which has been tried and tested for many hundreds of years, you're less likely to fall sick when you move into areas of infection."

I was unable to resist saying: "What I can't understand is why my father, who's so very orthodox and Catholic, came to grief when he tried his ministry of healing. What do you suppose went wrong?"

"Not knowing your father I can only speculate, but it's possible he took up the ministry for the wrong reasons. Or maybe he took it up for the right reasons but found he was temperamentally unsuited to it. But no matter why he failed, he's wrong to think you'd be automatically doomed to fail too."

"He'll never believe he's wrong. He believes—"

"He believes you should be one sort of priest but you believe you should be quite another—and what you were saying a moment ago, I think, was that your frustration is now so great that you're tempted to chuck up your whole call; you were saying that the sex with these girls was part of a subconscious attempt to convince yourself you had no option but to reject ordination."

"But at the same time I was also trying to play the healer with them, trying to convince myself I really was cut out to be the kind of priest I wanted to be—"

"So in fact what you were doing was rejecting your father's vision of your call while simultaneously affirming your own."

"But even that's not a complete picture of what was going on," I said in despair, "because my pride was mixed up in the mess too—I wanted to appear strong and powerful because I knew I was really so weak, so utterly dependent on my father—"

"A fact which you no doubt resented—"

"—because it underlined to me that I couldn't be free of him, couldn't be my true self, and that made me feel very angry, but I can't be angry with him, can't be my true self, because if I do he'll get upset—and once he gets upset he could die—and once he dies the Dark will wipe me out—"

"Wait." Lewis paused in his task of playing midwife to the truth and sought to calm me down. When I was silent he said mildly: "That Gnostic shorthand of yours makes it sound as if you're describing something uniquely sinister, but before you die of fright let me at least make some attempt to cut your nightmare down to size. Isn't this situation really rather commonplace?"

"*Commonplace!*"

"I believe the nightmare you're describing is simply this: people who spend their lives trying to be something they're not become very unhappy. When people are unhappy they try to blot out their unhappiness in various ways—taking to drink is the most obvious example, but of course there are others. This self-destructive behaviour saps the will to change and so leads into a downward spiral which results ultimately in despair, a spiritual death; this spiritual death, as we know from suicide figures and the prevalence of diseases such as cirrhosis, is all too often linked to physical death." He paused before concluding: "Wouldn't you say that was a fair longhand translation of your shorthand sentence: 'The Dark will wipe me out'? And wouldn't you agree that far from being a unique nightmare it happens all the time everywhere?"

I knew the answer to both questions was "yes," but all I managed to say was: "Is that supposed to make me feel better?"

"No, it's supposed to strip away the melodrama so that we can see exactly what's going on; then we'll be better equipped to deal with it. Now let's take the translation a step further. You know that only your father's sustaining love and prayers are preventing you from being drawn into that downward spiral; that's why you're so convinced you can't do without him. A stranger might think that once your father's dead you would at last have the freedom to be yourself, but you know this isn't true; you know your father has such a hold over you that you'll feel crucified by guilt if you try to be anything other than his replica—and we all know what happens to people crucified by guilt: it's the main gateway into the downward spiral. In short, you've wound up in a very tight corner, and although you love your father you're also very angry with him for leading you into it. Now take a look at Martin again. Can you finally begin to see why you're angry with him too?"

My voice said: "I'm jealous. I'm jealous because he *has* realised his true self, he's done it, he's got a happy successful life independent of our father, and he's not in this terrible mess I'm in. And neither's Gerald—lucky little sod, I hate him too for leaving me all alone to carry this crushing burden, sometimes I hate everyone, I even hate the members of that pathetic Community because they're the lucky ones, they're living authentic lives, the lives they feel God's calling them to lead, whereas I . . . I'm cut off from what I should be, I'm being twisted into the wrong shape, and although I have this longing to heal I can't heal myself, I just keep getting sicker and sicker, I'm trapped in a blind alley with no way out, and all I can think is: the Dark will wipe me out. I'm going to die."

I could say no more. I could only sit in my chair and stare at my clenched fists on the table in front of me.

There was a long silence.

Then Lewis's hands covered my fists and Lewis's psyche wrapped itself around mine in an infusion of hope and Lewis's voice, very calm and matter-of-fact, said simply:

"You're going to live."

10

"BUT how? I just don't see—"

"No, you're too frightened and confused to see the way out. That's why we have to concentrate now on taking one step at a time; it makes life less complex and intimidating. So let's refocus on your confession because our current step, in case you've forgotten, involves putting you back in good spiritual health." He released my hands, and suddenly I became aware that my fingers were behaving as if they had received a muscle-relaxing drug. My clenched fists had uncurled. My hands were limp. A warmth was spreading from my forearms to my shoulders. In admiration I exclaimed: "That's the classic healer's touch! How did you do it?" and Lewis said laughing: "You and your passion for rational analysis!"

"But seriously, Lewis—"

"Seriously I think we should wrap up your confession. Are there any more girls in your life at present?"

I sighed and began to talk about Tracy.

11

TALKING of Tracy led inevitably to a description of my past life with the Doreens and Debbies on the one hand and the Lavinias and Celias on the other. ". . . and I know it was wrong," I concluded, "but compared with so much that goes on today, it wasn't really all that bad. I mean, I don't think the girls minded being screwed—in fact I'm sure they didn't—and I always tried to be very kind when I traded them in."

"Traded them in? You're saying you thought of them in the same way as a second-hand car?"

"No, of course not! I was just speaking colloquially. The point I was trying to make is that whenever I broke off an affair I did it as decently as possible, gave the girl a nice present, told her I still thought she was great—"

"This is decency?"

"Well, what would you call it?"

"Expensive insincerity. Tell me," said Lewis, "have you ever been traded in?"

After a fractional pause I said: "No."

Lewis said nothing. I found myself shifting uneasily in my chair.

"All right," I said truculently at last. *"All right!* Haven't I already admitted I was in the wrong? But at least I was responsible enough to ensure the girls weren't seriously hurt!"

"How do you know they weren't seriously hurt?"

"How do I know?"

"Yes, how do you know? After the trade-in did you look them up to see how they were getting on?"

"But nobody does that once a love affair's over!"

"Maybe they should. It might prove to be quite an eye-opener."

"But I'm sure the girls were all right! I mean, none of them got pregnant!"

"You think an unwanted pregnancy is the only damage you can inflict on a woman?"

"No. But I'm still sure I didn't harm them."

"You're saying they cared nothing for you?"

"No. Yes. I mean, no, I'm not saying that. They did care, of course, but—"

"You're saying that people who care aren't vulnerable when they're abandoned?"

"No, I'm not saying that either! Okay, I take your point, maybe they did shed a tear or two afterwards, but I'm sure there was no real harm done—"

"How can you be sure of that when you never checked on them?"

"Well . . . they weren't the type to be harmed, were they?"

"I see," said Lewis. "You cause considerable distress by bedding three upper-class women and you're overcome with shame and remorse. But you can bed a bunch of working-class women and go merrily on your way without a second thought."

"But the circumstances were quite different! Working-class girls do it all the time, to them it's just like having a cup of tea—"

"You're saying they're a subhuman species incapable of feeling pain and humiliation?"

"Of course I'm not saying that!"

"Then exactly what are you saying?"

"Well, I'm saying . . . well, I . . . well—"

"You're saying that although you rejected these girls who cared for you—traded them in as if they were inanimate objects—denied them their basic humanity—it was all good clean fun?"

After a long pause I said: "Okay, I was snobbish, selfish and insensitive." "Is that all?"

I stared at him. "Isn't that enough?"

"Don't you think you were also a little forgetful? The gospel of Christ, I seem to remember, teaches that each one of us has worth in the eyes of God and that therefore each one of us should be treated with love and respect. It's common practice, of course, for non-believers to treat working-class girls like lumps of meat, but surely an ordinand who feels called to a ministry of healing—"

"Okay," I said rapidly, now feeling very hot and very uncomfortable, "I was un-Christian. Okay. But you see, it didn't occur to me—I mean, I just didn't think—"

"No," said Lewis, "you just didn't think. But try thinking now. People's psyches are so frail, so vulnerable, that it can never be right to be an invading force, no matter how harmless the invasion may seem at the time. That's because an invading force contains the seeds of the demonic; in fact any ego bent on self-gratification contains the seeds of the demonic, and that's why we live all the time in such danger that no one—not even a working-class woman—perhaps least of all a working-class woman— survives emotionally unscarred."

After a silence I managed to say: "I never want to be a demonic force. I never want to side with the Dark. I want to heal people, not destroy them."

"And how may you best do that?"

"By striving for integration. By trying to lead a disciplined life within the strong religious framework I need to survive. By worship. By prayer. By grace."

There was another silence. Then again Lewis reached across the table, and again he covered my hands with his.

12

HE HAD only just pronounced the words of absolution after my formal confession at the prie-dieu when the bell started to toll for mass. I felt exhausted. Despite my relief that I now stood right with God after my days of alienation, I barely heard the service or registered the powerful symbolism. I supposed I was experiencing a reaction after being spiritually turned inside out, washed, scrubbed and hung up to dry. I received the sacrament like a zombie. Afterwards I wanted to shut myself in my room but I knew Lewis would object if I skipped breakfast so I drank tea and ate bread.

As we left the dining-room he said: "I don't want to stage the reconstruction until the sun's at the same angle as it was yesterday at the time of the appearance. Why don't you take the chance to catch up on your sleep?" Then I knew he had sensed my longing to be alone. Returning to my room I fell on my bed and buried myself under the eiderdown.

When Lewis called for me later I was sitting at the table and pretending to read a psalm. The eiderdown had smothered all tears at birth but sleep had proved impossible.

"How are you feeling?" he said.

"Terrible. I'm so worried about my father." To my horror I felt the need to burrow under the eiderdown again. Slamming shut the Book of Common Prayer I said in despair: "I'm so afraid he's about to die. And when a Siamese twin dies, the other twin knows he's got to die too."

"But they separate Siamese twins nowadays," said Lewis. As I wiped the mist from my glasses I was aware of him parking himself on the edge of the table; there was no second chair in my room. "It's very natural that you should be so worried about him," he said, "particularly now that you're finally turning to face the problem he represents, but why don't we try to ease your anxiety by offering him psychic support? We'll take a moment to enfold him in prayer."

"I don't seem to be any good at praying at the moment."

"We'll keep it simple. What we have to do is visualise our minds stroking his. What was the name of that cat you mentioned in Session One? 'My father lives in one large room with a cat,' you said when you described how you went to see him after the séance—"

"Oh, that's Whitby."

"*Whitby?*" repeated Lewis as if doubting he had heard correctly.

"As in the Synod of Whitby."

"Ah yes, of course." Lewis paused to regain his concentration before saying: "All right, now visualise your father's psyche as Whitby's fur. You're stroking it with slow, smooth, soothing movements of your fingers. Whitby's been feeling bedraggled but the stroking relaxes him. He's pleased. He starts to purr."

We fell silent. The image was faint at first but gradually it became strong enough for me to start stroking, praying wordlessly to God for my father's healing. At last I realised I was strong enough to enfold my father's psyche because Lewis's psyche was enfolding mine.

Letting my hands fall from my face I said: "We're better now."

Lewis crossed himself and rose to his feet. "It's time for the reconstruction."

With enormous relief my mind slipped away from my father and began to focus once more on Christian.

I 3

WE WERE to take it in turns to play the monk.

Lewis had borrowed a spare habit, complete with the regulation brass crucifix, and had even obtained a pair of monastic boots. The habit was tailored to fit a man of medium height ("Too short for you," he said, "but at least I won't be tripping over the hem") and the boots had been selected to fit my feet. ("I've got lavatory paper to stuff in the toes when it's my turn to play the monk," said Lewis, who had thought of everything.)

In the back garden I struggled into the habit and found the extreme unfamiliarity distracting. "Just be thankful you don't have to put on the underwear," said Lewis when I complained. "I'm told it hasn't been updated since the founding of the Order." He adjusted the crucifix hanging from my belt and stepped back to take a critical look at me.

"That's good enough," he said. "Now let's review the plan: you go to the shed, you collect the rake—yes, it somehow got itself back in the shed after the appearance—and when you're ready to start you bang the door to let me know you're on your way. Then you emerge from behind the hedge that screens the shed, and you walk down the path to the archway. Try to get right not only Christian's pace but the exact spot where he turned his head to look at you. After that you go through the archway, and as soon as you pass out of my sight you begin to count the seconds. We want to know how much time the monk had to disappear into thin air before you showed up in the kitchen-garden—oh, and talking of counting the seconds, how much time should I allow to elapse before I rush after you? I assume you were too shocked to rocket off the bench straight away."

"Yes, I was. But I can't quite remember—"

"I'll count to five. Now, as soon as I shout 'Christian!' you start to run. Run all the way to the back door—I've got Father Abbot's permission to enter the kitchen-garden, of course—but when you reach the back door, don't go in. Just wait outside and continue to count the seconds until I show up in the archway . . . Okay, pull up your cowl and let's get going."

I dragged the black cloth forward over my head to shadow my face and moved quickly away across the lawn, but despite the protection afforded by the cowl I was aware of the heat of the sun as it once more shone from a cloudless sky; the habit seemed intolerably heavy and cumbersome.

When I reached the shed I found that Lewis had left the rake outside, propped against the wall. For a moment I hesitated, mesmerised by the notion that Christian himself might reappear, but I felt no awareness of him and finally I accepted that he was absent. Three times I recited the Jesus prayer to steady my nerves. Then having banged the door as a signal to Lewis, I began to walk, rake in hand, down the path towards the archway.

14

I HAD already spent much time trying to recall the exact spot where Christian had turned his head, and I had finally decided that the movement had been made just after he had passed the trunk of the peach-tree. Conscious that the cowl was shadowing much of my face, I began to walk past the outstretched branches to the right of the trunk, and a second later the crucial moment came: I turned to stare at Lewis and by the time I glanced aside I found myself within two paces of the archway.

Moving into the kitchen-garden I began to count the seconds.

Lewis's voice called: "Christian!" but he seemed far away, perhaps because the wall now rose between us to muffle the sound of his voice.

Instantly I began to run, haring down the path past the vegetable beds. The habit was horrible, flapping and flopping around my legs like some dead creature out of a science fiction film. I remember wondering how women could bear to wear skirts.

Breathing hard I reached the back door, swung round to face the garden and continued to count the seconds.

"Bingo!" shouted Lewis, appearing in the middle of the archway.

I hurried back to join him. "Sixteen seconds," I reported as he lounged panting against the wall. "I was out of your sight for sixteen seconds, and

I could easily have disappeared through the back door before you arrived on the scene."

"But we know Christian didn't do that. And now look at the windows. Unlike the windows of the guest-wing, the ground-floor windows here are all raised well off the ground because of the basement. If he ran across to the house and climbed through an open window in full monastic gear in under sixteen seconds he must have had the speed and agility of a cat-burglar."

"And as for scaling the eight-foot kitchen-garden wall—"

"No, he'd need wings for that. And in fact we're talking about a time of less than sixteen seconds because you almost certainly ran across that lawn faster than I did."

"So that proves it—he vanished into thin air!"

"No, all we've proved is that he didn't escape into the house or over the wall. By the way, I assume those glasses give you normal distance vision; how well could you see me as I sat on the bench?"

"Very well."

"If you hadn't known I was going to be there, would you still have recognised me instantly?"

"Well, I suppose I might have hesitated for a couple of seconds out of sheer surprise, but—"

"Exactly. You'd have hesitated. Do we know for a fact that Christian had normal sight?"

"I certainly never saw him wear glasses. Are you implying—"

"It's odd that he didn't even falter. Never mind, let's keep going with the reconstruction before the sun moves far enough to change the angle of the shadow from the cowl."

We swapped roles, Lewis pulling on the habit, the boots, the belt and the crucifix. I was startled how greatly the uniform altered him; his individuality was diminished by the trappings of the corporate Fordite identity.

"It's an odd phenomenon, isn't it?" agreed Lewis when I remarked on the change. "It reminds me of the effect created by Middle Eastern women who wear the chador." He picked up the rake before adding: "Let's run through the plan again. I'll bang the door of the shed to let you know I'm starting out. When I appear I'm bound to look different from Christian because I'm the wrong build, but don't let that distract you. Note very carefully where the top of my head comes in relation to the outstretched branches of the peach-tree—use the branches on the right as markers—and note also how clearly you can see my face when I turn to look at you. And once you rush through the archway in pursuit of me, don't stop. Got that? *Don't stop.* Keep right on running till you reach the back door."

"Okay, but why—"

"I'll answer all questions afterwards." He set off towards the shed.

I sank down on the bench and waited, fidgeting with the little borrowed cross around my neck, but in the end I became so tense that my fingers stiffened into stillness.

The door of the shed banged. Seconds later Lewis, looking bulky in the habit, appeared with the rake from behind the hedge and walked along the path by the wall. As he reached the peach-tree my memory was jolted and I almost failed to notice, when he turned his head to look at me, that his face was in shadow. He looked away again, walking on without faltering, and seconds later he had disappeared through the archway into the kitchen garden.

Having allowed time for my original stupefaction, I leapt to my feet. "CHRISTIAN!" I shouted, replaying the scene to perfection, and once more I began to pound across the lawn.

I reached the wall, I cannoned through the arch, I erupted into the kitchen garden.

But it was empty.

Lewis had vanished into thin air.

XII

"Those who have investigated the evidence of extra-sensory perception—telepathy, clairvoyance and the phenomena which attend spiritualistic seances—have built up massive support for the conviction that everywhere mind flows into mind, that individuals are not wholly separate from each other but are unconsciously linked together. Like islands of an archipelago, joined together underneath the sea that separates them, we are knit together by invisible and unconscious ties."

CHRISTOPHER BRYANT
Member of the Society of St. John the Evangelist,
1935–1985
THE RIVER WITHIN

I

AT ONCE I remembered the instruction to keep running so I stumbled on down the path, but I tried hard to see where he was hiding. Even if he had been sheltering behind the row of stakes which supported peas in summer he would still have been visible in that black and white habit, and nowhere else offered any hope of concealment. Reaching the back door I immediately swung around, unable to accept the reality of that empty garden, but no one was there.

"LEWIS!" I bawled, and immediately, hearing the note of panic in my voice, he reappeared.

But he was on the other side of the archway.

I tore back to him. "How in heaven's name did you do that?" I demanded between gasps. "How in heaven's name did you do it?"

"As the RAF used to say in my young day," said Lewis satisfied, "it was a piece of cake." He stepped back into the kitchen-garden and led me along the wall to a point where it embraced a slim pillar, built to provide support. Placing his back to the wall he lined himself up with the pillar and flattened his body against the bricks. "The niche isn't deep," he said, "but when you bounded through the archway I was sufficiently hidden to ensure you never saw me out of the corner of your eye. Provided you didn't look back I was invisible, and you weren't going to look back immediately because you were going to be much too busy trying to work out if I was hidden among the vegetables. As soon as you were well past me I nipped out and doubled back through the archway." He patted the pillar and added: "I noticed the niche when I made a reconnaissance of the garden on my arrival yesterday."

"I can't think how I missed it!"

"You haven't had an army training. One develops an eye for cover out in the field." He turned aside. "Let me shed this habit before I pass out. One of the biggest arguments against being a monk is that one has to wear such impossible clothes."

I hurried after him. "But Lewis, this is a sensational discovery! It proves I really could have seen a flesh-and-blood person!"

"Yes, but it doesn't prove that you did."

"At least it gives me some sort of defence against a charge of hallucination!"

"You don't need the defence because I've no intention of bringing the charge. Where did the top of my head come in relation to the peach-tree?"

I turned to look at the wall. "The second branch from the top was the crucial one," I said, pointing to our markers, the branches on the right-hand side of the trunk. "Your head came just below it—and as soon as I saw that, Lewis, I remembered that the top of Christian's head came above the branch, but that makes sense, doesn't it, because you're shorter than he is."

"You're sure about that position?"

"Positive. What happens next?" I demanded as he began to strip off the habit.

Lewis smiled at me. Then he said: "Let's go down to the pub and have a drink."

2

WE DROVE in his glistening white Beetle to a pub called The Laughing Fish which overlooked the river half a mile beyond the village. A curvy-mouthed trout was painted on the signboard. In the garden I chose a secluded table shaded by an umbrella while Lewis bought two pints of bitter.

When we were both seated with our tankards he said: "Okay, let's do a complete run-through of all the solutions, normal and paranormal, and see where we get to. We'll start, as one always should in such cases, with the most obvious explanations before we let rip with the fantastic." And he paused to drink deeply from his tankard.

"The most obvious explanation," he said, pulling out his packet of cigarettes, "is that you're mad. However, I've already made soothing noises to you on the subject of your sanity, and I'll now explain exactly why this obvious explanation isn't, in my opinion, the correct one." He lit a cigarette before continuing: "If you were suffering from a specific mental illness and were sick enough to be hallucinating, I think your behaviour would be abnormal in other respects. Even if you weren't hearing voices and believing Russian agents were trying to kill you, you'd have betrayed to me by now in your general behaviour that you weren't quite tuned in to the rational world—or alternatively, could only tune in erratically. But what's so striking about you, as I've already remarked, is that not only do you appear completely tuned in but you're even capable of analysing your situation. Of course it's clear you have your problems and your hang-ups, but that's normal. I've yet to meet the man who has no problems or hang-ups of any kind.

"It also occurs to me that if you'd suffered a hallucination triggered by mental illness, the hallucination itself would probably have been far more bizarre than it was. After all, what happened? All you saw was a monk in the garden of a monastery. You didn't see six topless dancers or Genghis Khan.

"So we discard the possibility that you're suffering from a specific mental illness, but can you be suffering from what is euphemistically known as a nervous breakdown? Now, nervous breakdowns come in various shapes and forms, usually as the result of prolonged stress, but I see no sign that you've actually broken down. You're still functioning, still going out and about, talking to people, having a drink with me now at the pub. People who have broken down to the point where a hallucination becomes a possibility can't function as normally as that. The typical sufferer from a nervous breakdown prefers to stay in bed all day with the blinds drawn—or if he gets up he's fearful of going outside. Remember how I asked you yesterday if you minded conducting Session One in the garden? But that didn't bother you in the least. No agoraphobia there.

"So we discard the possibility that you're hallucinating as the result of a nervous breakdown, but on the other hand this is where we have to acknowledge that you're quite clearly suffering from stress. I don't believe sheer stress alone could have caused a hallucination so long as you were still functioning normally, but I do think that stress is almost certainly a factor in this case. You'll remember me implying yesterday that psychics can get up to odd tricks when they're under stress. I was referring then to somnambulism—which you rightly pointed out isn't confined to psychics—but I could well have been referring to the fact that a psychic under stress is more receptive to paranormal phenomena. His psychic faculty is rubbed raw; the protection provided by the rational faculties is weakened and he's more exposed to both malign and benign forces. You've never, you say, had a visual psychic experience. But that doesn't mean you're incapable of having one.

"But we'll get to the paranormal later. Let's refocus on the normal explanations and consider the possibility that you experienced something which I'll call 'a waking dream,' a phenomenon closely related to somnambulism and triggered, like somnambulism, by stress. In this form of abnormal day-time sleep you'd think yourself awake and be convinced that what you were seeing was actually happening but in fact you wouldn't be fully conscious and what you saw would be a dream.

"At first glance this seems a promising explanation, particularly when we know you're currently prone to somnambulism, but I don't think the theory can be right. It's true that directly after the somnambulism last night you were unable to distinguish between reality and the dream, but that muddle only lasted seconds and was entirely consonant with the fact that you'd received a severe shock. If Christian's appearance had been a waking dream I think that afterwards you would have recognised it for what it was; you'd have been able to look back and see the kink in reality which occurred not only when the dream ended but when it began. Yet you're absolutely certain that the episode formed part of one uninterrupted reality. If I believe you—and I can't think why I shouldn't as you're so obviously *compos mentis*—then this experience of yours can't have been a waking dream.

"Another hypothesis is that you might have unconsciously hypnotised yourself into believing you saw Christian. People under stress can do this—it's part of a syndrome known as 'conversion,' and at first sight this theory too looks promising, particularly when we remember how clever you are at hypnosis. But I just don't believe that someone like you, who's still functioning, still tuned in full-time to reality, would suffer a full-blown hysteric experience like that. The hysteric temperament is just as common among males as among females, as the medical records of the world wars prove, but with your analytical mind and your notable mental toughness, you'd be most unlikely to experience a hysteric episode unless you were already suffering from a complete nervous breakdown. I'll back up that opinion by saying that if this was unconscious self-hypnosis, triggered by your urge to communicate with Christian, I believe you'd have done just that: communicated with him. One of the most interesting aspects of this appearance is that Christian did no more than appear.

"All right, so much for the theories arising from the possibility that this experience was the result of disturbed mental activity. Let's turn to the next most obvious possibility: that this was, as you put it, a flesh-and-blood person whom you saw.

"Now, there are two possibilities here: one, you saw Christian Aysgarth. And two, you saw someone physically like him and made a mistaken identification."

At once I said: "I'm one hundred percent certain I saw Christian."

"I know you are, but that analytical mind of yours must surely realise we have to consider every possibility in order to reach the right conclusion. Try not to feel threatened. I'm very willing to believe you saw Christian, but it's my job to test the theory thoroughly."

I drank some beer and forced myself to say: "Go on."

"The reconstruction underlined the fact that whoever the monk was, his face was in shadow and even when he turned to look at the bench, the shadow was only partly reduced. When you were the monk I recognised you without difficulty but one must remember that (a) my distance vision is exceptionally good and (b) I knew it was you. You wear glasses which give you normal sight, but your distance vision may still not be as good as mine; I don't know. What I do know is that if I'd had no idea beforehand whom I was about to see, I doubt if I'd have been quite so sure, even with exceptional distance vision, that my identification was correct. When I prepared to play the monk you remarked how a habit changes a man's appearance by muting his individuality, and I don't see how one can avoid saying that the habit heightens the risk of making a mistaken identification.

"But if this man wasn't Christian, who was he? We know it couldn't have been one of the monks or visitors because everyone was accounted for. It could certainly have been an undergraduate frolicking around as the result of a bet, but if we accept that idea we soon run into difficulties. How did he get hold of the habit? The surplus ones are in the enclosed section of the house, and none of them was missing from the linen-room. Monday's laundry day here; all the habits in this house, apart from the surplus ones, were either in the wash or being worn by the monks. You can't order a Fordite habit from an ecclesiastical shop like Wippell's; they don't supply them. Could you have it specially made? Or could you make it yourself? Yes, but why go to all that trouble and expense? The whole theory bristles with improbabilities which only multiply when one pursues it further.

"For instance, supposing he eluded you, as I did, in the kitchen-garden, why did he bother to replace the rake in the shed? Surely his main preoccupation would be to escape without delay. And when he did deign to escape, how did he do it? We know that the monks working in the garden would have seen anyone who took either the herb-garden exit or the path around the side of the guest-wing, and we have the evidence of Daniel and the visitor in the common-room that no one broke into the guest-wing through a window. He could have flown over the perimeter hedge, but we don't seriously think he grew wings. The mystery of how he vanished from the visitors' lawn is, as it turns out, far more intractable than the mystery of how he vanished from the kitchen-garden.

"Now let's put aside the idea that the monk was an unknown impostor and return to your conviction that the monk was Christian. We must accept Father Abbot's word that Christian is not and has never been a member of this community, so that means he too has to be an impostor, facing all the difficulties I've just listed—and confronting us with the additional complication of a complete absence of motive. If it was Christian you saw, what on earth was he doing here dressed as a monk? And again, how did he get hold of the habit and how did he escape from the visitors' lawn?"

I said obstinately: "There must be an explanation."

"If there is, I'd very much like to hear it. In my opinion the theory that you saw a flesh-and-blood person just doesn't work out."

After a pause I said: "So where does that leave us?"

"At the point where we turn to the paranormal. Let's once again start with the obvious explanation and work through to the fantastic: the most obvious explanation, of course, is that you've seen a ghost, but unfortunately we must discard that possibility straight away."

"We must?"

"Father Wilcox confirmed to me that there's no ghost at the Grantchester house."

"Would he necessarily know about it?"

"Yes, it would have been recorded. Paranormal occurrences have to be taken very seriously in an enclosed community because they can cause such trouble."

"But couldn't the ghost have been making his first appearance?"

"I did ask Father Wilcox if anyone had died here recently in unfortunate circumstances, but he said no, and in fact you wouldn't normally expect to find a ghost in a modern monastery because the monks tend to die in a state of grace. It was different in the pre-Reformation monasteries, many of which were run-down and corrupt."

"So what's the next possibility?"

"A much more promising theory: you may have experienced a slip in time. In other words, you could have seen either the past or the future or the present—but not the present that was happening here at Grantchester; you'd be looking sideways in time and seeing a monk somewhere else. The American scientists investigating paranormal phenomena call that process 'remote viewing.'"

This excited me. "Christian could be a monk at the London house or at Starwater Abbey! I could have looked across and—"

"You could have done, yes, but did you? I've never heard of a 'remote viewing' case where a present event occurring somewhere else was extracted from its setting and instantly replayed in the viewer's own environment. I'm not saying it couldn't happen—the human mind is capable of the most amazing psychic feats—but it would be extremely unlikely. If you'd seen Christian against the backdrop of the London garden or the Starwater grounds, I'd find it much easier to accept the 'remote viewing' theory—but don't be downcast by my scepticism, because the best of the time-slip theory is still to come."

"If I saw the past—"

"If you saw the past, you couldn't have seen Christian because we know he's never been a monk in this community. The other possibility is that you saw a past monk and made a wrong identification. That wouldn't be the same as seeing a ghost, of course. When you see a ghost, you and the ghost are in the present. When you experience a time-slip backwards, you and the person you see are in the past. The theory that you wrongly identified a past monk is actually quite attractive, but the trouble is—"

"Supposing I saw the future?"

"Ah!" said Lewis, willing to be diverted. "This is the time-slip theory in its most compelling form because it's the theory that chimes most harmoniously with your belief about what happened to Christian. One could argue: yes, he did choose to disappear, and yes, Perry did take him to France, and yes, he's still there, but he *will* eventually be at Grantchester, for all the reasons you've already deduced. Father Wilcox pointed out to me that he would never accept as a postulant a man who had abandoned his wife and children, but if Christian were to build a new identity in France for, say, five years, he'd reach the stage where he could produce the right references and none of the referees would know of his marriage. Of course it would be a gross deception to attempt to enter the Order in that way, but although it would be immoral it wouldn't be impossible."

I set down my tankard with a thump. "So that's it—that's the answer! Mystery solved!"

"Unfortunately," said Lewis with regret, "there's a fly in the ointment. I was about to say so just now when I was commenting on the possibility that you could have wrongly identified a past monk. The theory of the time-slip, attractive though it is, seems to be fatally flawed—and for the same reason which led us to reject the idea that you'd had a waking dream: when you looked back on the experience afterwards you remained quite convinced there'd been no break in reality."

"But does there always have to be a break?"

"There has to be a point when the time-slip begins and reality alters. Usually this is easy to pin-point—people appear dressed as Cavaliers and Roundheads, for instance, or trees which should be bare are suddenly seen in full leaf. However in your case the monk is a timeless figure and you noticed no change in the garden, so we're forced to search for more subtle markers—a slight change in light or temperature, sound or smell. Yet there was no change of any kind, was there?"

"Maybe I'm overlooking something." I started to search my memory but broke off to ask: "Have you ever had this experience?"

"Yes."

"Could you describe what happened? I feel I need some yardstick of comparison."

Lewis nodded to show he understood. Then he said casually, as if the incident he was about to describe were in no way abnormal: "Well, it was like this . . ."

3

"*I WAS* visiting a National Trust stately home for a chamber music concert," said Lewis. "The concert was held in the main hall, but the Trust had opened up all the ground floor rooms so that in the interval the members of the audience were able to wander around for a free look.

"The rooms had been restored in the style of the late eighteenth century, and when I reached the hall at the back of the house I found a room where the Trust had apparently excelled itself in its efforts to produce an authentic atmosphere. I was drawn to the threshold of this room because I noticed that the lighting was dimmer there than it was everywhere else, and the next moment I saw that a small sitting-room had been so faithfully recreated that there were even lighted candles in the candlesticks. A nice touch was provided by an open sewing-basket on the table alongside some unfinished embroidery. For a moment I just stood there, fascinated by this extreme authenticity, but then I realised the room had a bad aura, very heavy, very stifling, full of sorrow. Turning aside I found my companion had joined me and I said: 'Let's go back.' "

Lewis paused to stub out his cigarette. "I was unaware of the time-slip when it was happening," he said. "The truth only dawned on me after the concert when my companion commented on the beauty of the house and I said: 'Yes, I liked everything except that unpleasant little room with the lighted candles.' At that point she turned to me in astonishment and said: 'What lighted candles?' "

"So the time-slip began—"

"It began when I noticed the change in the light and it ended when I turned aside from the threshold. Once I'd realised what had happened the markers seemed very obvious."

"Did your companion see the sewing-basket and the embroidery?"

"No, they were back in the past along with the candles." Lewis paused to drink before concluding: "The interesting question is why the experience happened to me. There seems always to be a link, I find, between the viewer and the viewed, and in this case I theorised that someone had spent hours in that room mourning a broken romance and that I'd been sufficiently receptive to pick up those grief-laden emanations. I was under stress; the friendship with my concert-companion was to break up later that night; I could well have been in a similar state to the person who impregnated that room with sorrow."

At once I said: "If there's always a connection between the viewer and the viewed, then it must have been Christian I saw because there's no reason why I should have seen a stranger. And I must have seen him as the result of a time-slip into the future because there's no other explanation. I admit the lack of markers is a puzzle, but maybe I didn't notice them because I was so astounded by Christian's appearance."

"The markers should have preceded the appearance. But let's put the time-slip theory aside for the moment and consider the most fantastic theory of all. Have you ever heard of bilocation?"

"Wait a minute. Yes, I do remember reading somewhere—"

"The phenomenon of being in two places at once. It's exceedingly rare but it's well-documented because the most famous practitioner of bilocation in this century was a highly revered Roman Catholic priest called—"

"Padre Pio."

"That's right. He was a man who regularly experienced all manner of paranormal phenomena, including the stigmata, and these experiences made him so famous that people flocked to see him from all over Europe. He lived an enclosed life in Foggia but nevertheless he used to turn up in the homes of people who required healing. When these people eventually journeyed to see him in Foggia—which, of course, he had never left—he not only recognised them but was able to remember the exact nature of their illnesses. When asked how he achieved this truly extraordinary phenomenon of being in two places at once, he said he did it by the 'prolongation of his personality.' "

"I don't believe it."

"Neither do I, but since there's evidence that it happened several times maybe we'd be wise to try."

"But it's incredible!"

"I agree, but when you failed to disclose any markers which would have indicated a time-slip, I began to toy with the possibility of bilocation. Working on the theory that Christian was a monk at either London or Starwater, I thought he might have been psychically aware that you were trying to find him and responded by a 'prolongation of his personality.' As a monk he couldn't leave his monastery without permission, but with a huge psychic effort perhaps he could still turn up at Grantchester and exhibit himself to show you that you were on the right track in believing he was still alive."

I boggled at him. "But do you really think that's possible?"

"No," said Lewis with the sigh of the *bon vivant* who accepts that the best bottle on the wine-list is beyond his price-range. "It's an enthralling theory but it won't do—not because it's fantastic but because it doesn't quite fit the facts. You're certain, you told me yesterday, that Christian wasn't psychic, and this phenomenon couldn't possibly be achieved without the use of extraordinary psychic power."

I was unable to resist asking: "How do you think Padre Pio did it?"

"I don't know. I've never encountered a case of bilocation. The real issue, I'd guess, would be: is this merely a psychic encounter between the viewer and the viewed, or is it an encounter which is capable of being witnessed by uninvolved spectators? The Padre Pio stories I've read didn't make that clear." He finished his beer. "Well, that's the end of my survey of possibilities. Drink up and let's have another round."

"But Lewis, you've just wound up destroying every possibility!"

He laughed. "It's plain I've gone wrong somewhere but without more information we've no way of progressing further."

"But what on earth do we do next?"

"After so much uncertainty I'm delighted to tell you that's obvious," said Lewis, picking up our empty tankards and rising to his feet. "We establish beyond doubt whether Christian's alive or dead."

"But how can we possibly do that?"

"That's also obvious, because there's one person who knows for sure."

"You mean—"

"We call on Perry Palmer," said Lewis, departing with our tankards for the bar.

4

"IF CHRISTIAN'S dead," said Lewis when he returned to the table, "we destroy the theory that you saw him as the result of a time-slip. We already know you couldn't have seen him in the past; he was never a monk here. And if he's dead you couldn't have seen him either in the present, by means of 'remote viewing,' or in the future. As a spin-off we also prove, if proof were needed, that you couldn't have seen him in the present as the result of a bilocation phenomenon."

"I'm beginning to be convinced again that I saw him in the flesh. If only I could think why he should have been dressed as a monk in that garden—"

"If we establish he's dead we destroy the possibility that you saw him in the flesh."

"If we establish he's dead we destroy the possibility of everything! But no, wait a minute—there's one possibility you haven't mentioned at all. What about the Devil? You seem to have tossed him aside in a very cavalier fashion for an exorcist! What makes you think the appearance wasn't the Devil manifesting himself?"

"Lack of evidence that it was. As I said last night, it's clear there are demonic elements in this case—for example, think of all the pain and misery you uncovered in your investigation—but so far I've seen nothing which indicates the Devil himself is actually involved. Or in other words, there's plenty of evidence of suffering but none of a force which could be categorised as militantly evil, and if the appearance was generated by some form of evil psychic activity I'd be very much surprised."

At once I fastened on the two crucial words. "You said *so far* you've seen nothing which indicates the Devil's present. Does that mean—"

"Oh, we could still run across him in connection with Christian. But I've a hunch we'll be able to write the Devil out of this mystery entirely once we've talked to Palmer and heard the final word about Christian's death."

"But what makes you think that Perry Palmer, the human clam, will now open up on that particular subject?"

"I think you'll find he'll be much more forthcoming if you confront him not with the run-of-the-mill suicide theory but with the mind-bending idea that Christian's still alive. If we play the scene right he'll be much too shocked to remember how to act the clam."

But I remained sceptical. "He'll just deny everything and we'll be no further on."

"Not necessarily," persisted Lewis. "Think positive—for all you know he may be longing to spill the beans. Perry is actually the most enigmatic figure in this story, far more enigmatic than Christian, who seems to have been sliding into a fairly conventional nervous breakdown after making the discovery—rather late in the day—that worldly success isn't a passport to heaven. If Perry did help Christian to disappear, I'd like to know why. What's in it for him?"

"That was the question Martin asked."

"And why in fact should Christian have needed Perry's help at all? The false passports weren't essential. He could have gone to Ireland."

"Martin said that too."

"How did you answer him?"

"I couldn't."

"Without doubt we need to talk to Mr. Palmer," said Lewis, glancing at his watch, "but unfortunately we can't do it today because I've got to be at my vicarage for a parish meeting this evening. What I propose is that you should come back with me to Starbridge. Tomorrow morning I have a bunch of appointments to keep, but in the afternoon we can go up to town and ambush Perry when he returns home from work."

"I could stay overnight with the Fordites in London—"

"I think not," said Lewis. "It would be best if we kept together at present."

I suffered a pang of uneasiness. "You're secretly thinking I need a keeper," I accused, trying to speak lightly, but without hesitation he answered: "Not a keeper. You're neither mad nor under age. But while your present level of stress persists you need an adviser who's instantly accessible."

Shying away from this reference to my central problem I found myself saying abruptly: "You're sure Christian's dead, aren't you? I mean, you don't just suspect—you *know*. It's *gnosis*."

"Psychics don't *know* anything in that specialised sense," said Lewis dryly. "They merely believe. A surprising proportion of their beliefs may turn out to be true, but that doesn't alter the fact that many of their beliefs turn out to be either false or just plain nuts. If I were you I'd use the verb 'believe' to describe your clever hunches and save the verb 'know' for facts that are indisputably true."

We drank our beer in silence for a moment but finally I was unable to resist saying: "I saw Jung on TV once. He was asked if he believed in God, and he answered: 'I don't need to believe. I KNOW.' "

Lewis smiled, and I wondered if he was thinking that Jung was a Gnostic, hardly an adequate model for a young Christian priest. Having gulped some more beer, I found I had the nerve to say strongly: "When I was growing up I hated the fact that if I said: 'I KNOW God exists,' people thought I was crazy. So I stopped saying: 'I KNOW.' But then I saw that old man, that sage, that scientist, and when he said: 'I KNOW'— on TV! To millions!—I thought: that's cool. And I wanted to stand up and cheer."

"Of course you did. And Jung's declaration was hardly original; the great mystics have all, in their different ways, said: 'I KNOW.' But I think the Church is right to warn that ordinary mortals such as you and I should be very careful when we're claiming to have special knowledge, particularly the special knowledge which arises from psychic powers."

"Oh, I'm sick of the Church being careful! If the Church said 'WE KNOW' more often and laid more stress on its great mystical tradition, its witness today wouldn't be so damned feeble. Where's the Church in the 1960s? What's it doing? Either hailing radical books which say it's impossible to know anything about anything or else fawning over pop stars in an effort to be trendy!"

"Isn't that a little harsh?" said Lewis mildly. "The Devil never has it all his own way! I seem to remember that last year at Keele there was a very positive and exciting conference—"

"I can't connect with the Evangelicals."

"At least they're not writing books saying it's impossible to know anything about anything!"

"Maybe not, but they've no time for mysticism or the Catholic tradition."

"And how much time do you have for non-mystics and the Protestant tradition?"

"Well—"

"And don't forget everything changes, Nicholas, even the Evangelicals. You may find in the future that—"

"I can't cope with the future, it's gruesome enough trying to cope with the present, and as I see it we're all currently having a mass psychic breakdown, we're all demoralised, and no one's more demoralised than those old buffers in purple who are supposed to be leading the Church. Okay, I agree the Archbishop of Canterbury's a great man, so holy, but we don't need holiness right now, we need—"

"We always need holiness," said Lewis.

"—we need a whole army of mystics saying 'I KNOW' and translating the eternal truths into a modern language which everyone can understand. We don't need the liberals with their pathetically narrow view of reality, we don't need the Evangelicals bawling away in outdated thought-forms like a bunch of religious fascists—"

"—and we certainly don't need Gnostics claiming to belong to a spiritual élite. But I'll tell you this, Nicholas: so long as the Church can still attract ordinands of your originality perhaps it's not in quite such a demoralised mess as you think."

"The Church doesn't attract me," I said violently. "I was brought up to think it was so wonderful, but the glorious glittering days are over and all that's left is this effete institutional disaster. I feel I've been swindled and let down."

I had never before admitted such disillusionment and I thought Lewis might be shocked, but he only answered: "When the ecclesiastical structures are weak there's always a resurgence of mysticism, which eventually breathes new life into the Church—and that means the spirit of the coming religious age may well be right up your street."

Even in my beer-inspired belligerence I found this a soothing thought. Tentatively I said: "I'd like to believe that. I so much want things to get better." And on an impulse I added: "I suppose I must love the Church all the time I'm hating it because it's never occurred to me not to stay loyal. After all, when the chips are down it matters, doesn't it, who stands up for you, and here we all are, there's darkness at noon, and it's my job to stand up and be counted."

Lewis said: "Maybe the Church needed this experience of darkness at noon. Maybe when I was growing up before the war it was just a little too glorious and very much too glittering. Maybe the purpose of this current pulverising lesson in humility is to remind us all that the Kingdom of Christ is not of this world and that God has no office in the corridors of power." Pushing aside his half-finished drink he stood up and added: "Time to move on."

It was only when we reached his car that I remembered the suspicion I had voiced earlier. "You never answered my question," I said to him.

"Which one was that?"

"You think Christian's dead, don't you?"

"I believe it's the most likely explanation," said Lewis, "but as an exorcist I'd be the first to say unlikely things do happen. Think of Padre Pio."

I thought of Padre Pio. That was much easier than thinking of likely explanations.

We drove back to the Fordites' house for lunch.

5

AFTER the meal Lewis advised me to rest before we embarked on our journey, and I realised I was being told to rid myself of any post-alcohol doziness before I put myself behind the wheel of my Mini-Cooper. By that time my fiery pugnacity had ebbed and I was more than willing to subside on my bed. To my surprise I slept soundly for twenty minutes. Then I packed my bag and left the guest-wing with Lewis soon after two.

"How did you leave matters with Father Wilcox?" I asked him in curiosity as we crossed the drive to our cars. "Did he want you to exorcise the garden?"

"I told him it was unnecessary and explained that in my opinion the Devil wasn't involved. I also said I thought the garden was a mere backdrop to the incident and that the community wasn't involved in any way."

"Oh, I see. Or do I? Wait a minute, are you saying—"

"The appearance—whatever it was—is attached to you," said Lewis, "and if you now leave Grantchester there'll be no recurrence here."

"But does that mean I might witness a second appearance somewhere else?"

"Without knowing exactly what the appearance was, I can't answer that question. And talking of leaving Grantchester, let's get going or we won't reach Starbridge in time to dine at a civilised hour."

Lewis always had to think ahead to the next meal.

We drove in convoy cross-country to the A1 and then headed southwest, avoiding London by a route which I had discovered during my years at Cambridge. Eventually, after joining the A303, we turned off to Starbridge. (Those were the days before the motorway.) I had been driving in silence, but during that last stretch of the journey I turned on the radio which had been installed to stop me becoming somnolent on long journeys, and as the thump of a popular beat instantly grazed my eardrums I saw the Cathedral ahead of me in the gap between the hills.

John Lennon started to sing: " 'Give me money! That's what I want!' " and the Cathedral vanished as the road looped back behind the hill. I'd evidently struck a request programme where current hits weren't guaranteed to spin. When had Lennon recorded "Money"? Long, long ago when the Beatles still had short hair. Perhaps it had been the year of Marina's Starbridge orgy: 1963. But I didn't want to think about Marina.

I turned up the volume. Lennon screamed on, and suddenly at the next twist of the road the Cathedral appeared again, a little nearer, a little larger. Thump, thump, thump, went the beat. Bang went the Cathedral, wiped out again. But of course it hadn't been wiped out. Lennon's voice would die, the record would end, but the Cathedral would come back—again—and again—and again—

The turntable stopped, the DJ whooped and chortled, Mick Jagger began to croak "It's All Over Now." What year was this? Couldn't remember. Maybe it was 1964, the year I went to Africa, but I didn't want to remember 1964. Thump, thump, thump, banged the Rolling Stones, insisting that it was All Over Now, and yes, some things *were* all over, but not the Cathedral, back it came again, huge on its mound now, bursting from the floor of the valley, brilliant in the red glow of the dying sun. But the voices were dying alongside the sun, dying away in a calculated fade-out, and the DJ began to whoop again as the Cathedral disappeared for the last time behind the hill. I pressed down the accelerator, the car roared towards the final curve of the road and suddenly, as the great view of the valley opened up in front of me, the DJ fell silent, the Cathedral towered above us all and I heard the opening bars of that 1960s song of songs, "River Deep—Mountain High."

I drove down into the valley, but now I no longer saw the Cathedral. With my psychic eye I saw the Holy Spirit moving ceaselessly across those dark twentieth-century waters, and I knew God had not after all turned His face away from the Church in which I had grown up, from my friends with whom I still felt so connected, from the joyous, exciting, dynamic decade which the Devil had soured and ruined. The Devil might have done his worst, but the Holy Spirit would pour back over the ravaged landscape to restore and renew it, to heal the brokenness, to raise up those who suffered, to redeem death with life, and meanwhile God was there in the middle of all the mess, suffering with Katie, enduring with Marina, hurting with Venetia, screaming with Dinkie, grieving with Martin, in torment with me and a million others, right there He was, right in the midst of His creation, His spark buried deep in every one of us, and He was *here* too, just as Starbridge Cathedral was here, not standing aloof in a timeless silence, but right in the heart of that valley in the centre of that city, the Dream in our midst, the Truth in our time—and in all time—and at that moment my time *was* all time as the cross on the spire of the Cathedral stood silhouetted against the blood-red clouds and on the radio Tina Turner shouted out in ecstatic celebration of that indestructible love which proved eternally river-deep and mountain-high.

I suddenly realised that I was passing the sign which said WELCOME TO STARBRIDGE.

I glanced in the mirror to check that Lewis was still tailing me in his Volkswagen, and when I glimpsed the reflection of his face I saw him not as the off-beat priest who had become so familiar so quickly, but as the mysterious healer, brought into my life by the most mysterious force of all, to renew and raise up all that was damaged, to realign and reintegrate all that was dislocated, so that I could move forward at last on my journey to the centre and embark on the river within.

Turning aside from the Cathedral I began to head north beside the railway tracks into the drab city parish of Langley Bottom.

6

THE PART of Starbridge known as Langley Bottom consisted of a network of mean streets around the railway station. On the outer rim of the area the new Starbridge by-pass, a concrete ribbon on stilts, bore a steady stream of traffic around the city. I could hear the faint drone of engines in the distance after I had parked my car in the vicarage forecourt and emerged to stretch my legs after the long drive.

The vicarage was a large Victorian house pregnant with shabby self-importance, a déclassé relation of Charley's highly buffed home at Fairlight Green. Nearby stood the church, also Victorian, also pretentious, a building designed by an architect determined to bring Gothic art to the slums. It had a certain sooty grandeur, but I knew the diocesan office would be impervious to its minimal charm; both church and vicarage would be ill-suited to modern needs and unpleasantly expensive to maintain.

"A smooth journey, wasn't it?" remarked Lewis, removing his bag from the Volkswagen. "That was an excellent route of yours."

He led the way across the forecourt to the front door. Inside I found a gloomy hall redeemed by a wide, handsome staircase which needed polishing. I wondered if the vicar, Desmond Wilton, had a wife, but any woman working on her own would have been fighting a losing battle against dirt in a house designed to be run by several servants.

As Lewis moved to the hall table to pick up some messages which had been left for him, I noticed on one wall a board similar to the boards kept in the halls of pre-war blocks of London flats to indicate whether the residents were at home. On the left-hand side of the board someone had painted the names DESMOND and, underneath, LEWIS. Opposite the names were two columns, headed IN and OUT, and in the columns were two black rectangles which could be moved from one column to the other. Both rectangles were now in the OUT column.

"Desmond's probably over at the church," said Lewis, stuffing the messages unread into his pocket and moving his rectangle from OUT to IN. "We'll go straight up to my flat." And as he reached the stairs he added: "Desmond has the ground floor, I have the second floor, and the first floor is the buffer-state where we can put up guests if the need arises. Since Desmond and I both like solitude we decided right from the beginning that to make a success of sharing the house we had to live wholly apart."

At the top of the stairs was a landing even gloomier than the hall below.

"Are you officially the curate?" I said as we began to ascend a second, more modest staircase.

"No, there's no money for a curacy."

"You mean your salary's included in the diocesan grant for the healing centre?"

"No, I don't take a salary. I have a private income," said Lewis, and in that one sentence spoken so casually I glimpsed the past that he had concealed from me.

I thought: that home in Sussex was very large, very rich, there was a county background like my mother's but much smarter, and the uncle and aunt who had taken him in were well-meaning but didn't understand him, preferred their own children, secretly resented the fact that Lewis had been palmed off on them, because of course the mother had palmed him off, she was very sophisticated, very sexy, blazing away in the Roaring Twenties, lots of lovers, and Lewis had minded that, resented the scandal, become, as he had put it, a mixed-up psychic schoolboy until he had been rescued and sorted out by the monks at Starwater Abbey . . .

I suddenly realised that Lewis was speaking again. Recalling my attention with an effort, I realised we were approaching the front door of his flat.

"I'm afraid there's nothing much in the refrigerator," I heard him say, "but I do have some interesting tins, and—"

He was dramatically interrupted. The door flew open. A woman's voice demanded in fury: *"Where have you been?"* and Lewis came gasping to a halt.

"Good heavens—Rachel!" he exclaimed faintly. "But you're not supposed to be here till Thursday!"

"No, Tuesday, you great big duffer, *Tuesday!*"

"But I wrote it down in my desk-diary—"

"Yes—in the wrong place! I suppose you just saw the capital letter *T* and guessed the rest—it's sheer vanity, bragging about your distance vision and never admitting you can see nothing less than twelve inches from your nose! And if you try and tell me again you'd temporarily mislaid your reading-glasses, I'll—"

She stopped. She had finally seen me. And I had long since seen her. I found myself gazing at the steamiest of steamy brunettes, a girl probably no more than twenty years old. She had curvy hips, an eye-catching waist cinched in with the aid of a silver-studded belt, and long legs which were tantalisingly encased in navy-blue slacks patterned with white flowers. Above the slacks she wore a high-necked, hot-pink top, skin-tight, which erotically emphasised all it concealed. Curtains of long straight black hair framed her face and brushed idly against the erotic outlines. She had dark eyes, full lips and a squarish, resolute, almost pugnacious jaw which I instantly admired for its originality. It both contrasted with and enhanced the femininity of that moist, passionate, kiss-me-quick mouth. I wanted to grab her with both hands and hit the nearest horizontal space.

"Ah yes," Lewis was saying, still uncharacteristically flustered, "let me introduce you. This is Nicholas Darrow, who's been doing some work with me before his ordination. Nicholas, this is my daughter Rachel."

"Hi," I said.

"Hi," said the girl.

We each spoke very quietly, very politely. I didn't dare offer her my hand for fear of what might happen if she touched it. I almost fancied I could hear my jeans creaking at the zip.

"I do apologise," Lewis was saying to her as he moved across the threshold. "If I'd realised you were coming I'd have bought some food and raided the wine merchant, but—"

"Relax," said the girl, turning away from me to follow him into the living-room. "I haven't been sitting on my bottom all day. Once Desmond told me you wouldn't be back till this evening—oh, by the way, that parish meeting tonight's been cancelled—I trawled the supermarket, whipped up a large pot of spaghetti Bolognese, slapped together a fruit trifle, cleaned the flat, ran all the towels through the washing-machine— that dish-cloth was *filthy*—defrosted the fridge and scraped the goo off the floor of the oven. All I've got to do now is toss the salad and warm the garlic bread. Would you like to open the Chianti Classico?"

"My dear Rachel," said Lewis, "what on earth have I done to deserve you?"

"I often wonder." She allowed herself to be kissed and patted. Then she said to me: "Well, don't just loaf there in the doorway! Come on in and have a drink!"

I glided greedily forward into the room.

"*I MADE* a note of your phone calls," said Rachel to her father, "and Desmond's left some messages in the hall. All sorts of women are gasping to see you, including someone called Miss Peabody who phoned three times."

"That's the Bishop's secretary," said Lewis, drawing the cork from the wine bottle. "I'll deal with her before my appointments tomorrow morning."

"Should I myself make an appointment to see you? Or would you only write it down in the wrong place again?"

"I'll leave you alone with him after dinner," I said hastily. "In fact I can leave you alone with him now."

"Certainly not!" said Rachel severely. "Stay just where you are!"

I smiled. She smiled. It was only after three smiling seconds that I realised Lewis was not amused. He was gripping the Chianti bottle as if longing to wring its neck.

"Well, go on, Daddy!" said Rachel brightly. "Pour out the wine!" And to me she added: "Have a seat!"

"Thanks." I settled myself at one end of the two-seater sofa and left plenty of space for her to join me.

Lewis, wearing his most inscrutable expression, poured out the wine.

"We don't want to eat just yet, do we?" Rachel was saying as she retrieved a clean ash-tray from the kitchen.

"Yes, we do," said Lewis. "I'm feeling extremely peckish."

"Oh, that's all right, I bought those lovely cheese nibbles for you, the ones you like so much . . ."

Lewis, outflanked, was marooned in an armchair with his cheese nibbles and the clean ash-tray while Rachel joined me on the sofa. Casually I managed to conceal the front of my jeans behind a small cushion which I began to stroke as if it were a cat. Perhaps I felt that I needed to do something to justify its presence. The Chianti tasted so pleasant that I almost forgot it was alcohol. The little sitting-room, lined with books, began to assume a rosy glow.

"Which university are you at?"

"How did you know I was at university?"

"It's your aura, your ambience, your *je ne sais quoi*."

"What rubbish! Daddy probably told you—or perhaps you realized I'd be unlikely to have time off at the moment unless I was a student. You'll be saying next you can tell from my *je ne sais quoi* what subjects I'm reading!"

"I see you studying languages—French certainly—and perhaps a little German or Italian as well—"

"But that's extraordinary! How did you know? I'm reading French with a German subsidiary!"

"Ah, but I knew at once you were a linguistic sort of person, sensitive to language, musical—"

"You're *amazing!* How could you possibly have known that I like music?"

"He saw the sleeve of your Berlioz record," said Lewis crisply. "It's lying over there on the table alongside your copy of Balzac (in French) and your headscarf. Realising that I would be unlikely either to wear a headscarf or to read a book with a French title, he made the simple deduction that both the book and the record were yours and then he pretended he was being psychic. Could we have dinner now, please?"

"Crosspatch!" said Rachel annoyed. "The Berlioz record is actually a present for you—I thought you might be ready for a break from all that chamber music you've been so keen on lately. Excuse me, Nicholas, I must just put the garlic bread in the oven."

"Can I help?" I said, rising smartly from the sofa.

"Nicholas," said Lewis before Rachel could reply, "I'm sure you'd like a wash and brush-up after your journey. The bathroom's at the end of the passage and you'll find a towel in the airing-cupboard."

"I bet you'd like a wash and brush-up even more than Nicholas does," said Rachel to him. "You know how you always love to throw water everywhere and change your shirt after a long car journey. Would you like to lay the table, Nicholas, while you're waiting for Daddy to finish with the bathroom?"

"Oh, I'll lay anything," I said before I realised what I was saying. "I mean—that's to say—what I meant was—"

"Super!" said Rachel. "Run along, Daddy, and leave Nicholas and me to do our own thing."

I took one look at Lewis's face and headed instantly for the bathroom.

Having used the lavatory, washed my hands and combed my hair I returned to the living-room to find Lewis was still sitting grumpily in his armchair and a startling amount of wine had disappeared.

"Do you fancy tossing the salad, Nicholas?" called Rachel from the kitchen nearby, and scurrying past my host I reached the sanctuary of the draining-board, where a large bowl of interesting green vegetation waited to be mixed with tomatoes, radishes and a jug of Italian dressing. A magnificent aroma had already reached me from one of the saucepans on the stove.

"Sorry I was so long," I said to Rachel, "but I did need to spruce myself up."

"It's heavenly to meet someone who doesn't smell. Do you spruce often?"

"More wine, Nicholas?" said Lewis, appearing in the doorway to keep an eye on us.

"Great," I said warily. "Thanks."

"Do go to the lavatory, Daddy," said Rachel. "I'm sure you must be bursting. Why are you so reluctant to leave Nicholas alone with me?"

Lewis was so livid at this direct question, which not only made him look like a neurotic parent but was impossible for him to answer truthfully, that he spilled the wine he was pouring into my glass.

Urgently I said to him: "It's okay—I understand," and muttering something inaudible he retired wrathfully to the lavatory.

"Sulky old bear!" said his daughter, giving the simmering pasta a stir. "It's just as well he and I don't normally live under the same roof because if we did I'd never get anything that resembled a social life. Hung up on sex, of course."

"You are?"

"No, he is! It's all this Anglo-Catholic business. He ought to remarry but he never does."

"He did mention a girlfriend and a concert—"

"That was his lady-violinist. I quite liked her, but she drifted away, just as they all do, when she realised nothing was going to come of it. I often feel it would be easier both for him and the women if he was a Roman Catholic priest because then there'd be no question of marriage and everyone would know exactly where they stood right from the start, but he'll never go over to Rome, he loves his Church of England too much, loves the scope it gives him to be eccentric."

"He certainly has an unusual ministry."

"Unusual! Well, I suppose that's one way of putting it," said Rachel, but as she spoke I knew she had no real idea what his ministry involved. "I just think it's tragic he's not a bishop bounding around being glamorous in purple."

"I suppose the divorce—"

"Oh, he'd lost all interest in a big ecclesiastical career before the divorce! Mummy simply couldn't understand it—that's why she traded him in and went off with someone else. She was really looking forward to living in a palace, and when she realised there was no chance of it ever happening—"

"I somehow can't quite see Lewis as a bishop."

"That's because you've only seen him with hippieish sideburns and off-the-peg clothes, but in the old days he was really stylish. Believe me, he could have been a bishop, he could have been anything—if he hadn't married, he could even have been the Abbot-General of those ghastly Fordite monks—he had all the necessary money and all the right connections, but look what's happened! He's an unpaid curate in a slum-parish attended by a horde of lame dogs!"

"And just as big a success," I said, "as any bishop in a palace."

"How terribly Christian of you to say so, but let's face it, Daddy's choice of ecclesiastical career wasn't quite normal and Mummy and I are both dead normal, always have been, we like all the normal things of life like amusing dinner-parties and interesting people and smart cars (that *pathetic* little Volkswagen Daddy drives! Honestly! If he's got to have a German car why doesn't he buy a Mercedes?) and—where was I?"

"Interesting people, smart cars—"

"Oh yes, and winter holidays and shopping at Harrods and champagne at the Ritz—"

"All this is normal?"

"All right, I admit it's a creative interpretation of normality, but—"

"I always admire creativity!"

"And now I suppose you're thinking I'm just another godless debutante, but actually I'm rather keen on religion; I just don't see why one has to be churchy and boring about it, that's all. Poor Mummy's not religious any more, she says she's had religion, absolutely *had* it, after coming second to God and the Church for years as a clerical wife, but I think it's all rather marvellous, I love the pageantry, and it's so nice to think of God being around somewhere, the old man with the long white beard playing peek-a-boo in the clouds—"

"A magnificently normal heresy!"

"Well, of course I don't *literally* believe that—"

"Of course not. That's normal too. And what's the next normal thing you're going to do once you're through with university?"

"Have an extraordinary career. That'll be thoroughly normal for girls in the 1970s. I'm going to train as a buyer for a top London store and then work my way up until I'm jetting all over Europe doing fantastic deals. Eventually, I suppose, I'll take a few weeks off to get married and have a baby, but not until I'm at least thirty and well established in the power structure . . . Why are you looking at me as if I'm pulling your leg?"

"But I'm not! I'm just so mesmerised by all this dynamic normality!"

"Well, is this 1968 or isn't it? And have we read Betty Friedan or haven't we?"

"Betty who?"

"Gosh, you ordinands had better wise up fast—how do you think you're going to deal adequately with women in the 1970s? But hey, wait a minute—why am I letting my hair down in this outrageous style when I've only just met you? Maybe you've spiked the Chianti, but no—I know what's happened: Daddy made me so cross by behaving as. if I were a Victorian heroine and you were a sex-maniac that I've cast discretion to the winds out of sheer rage! Quick, before he pads back from the lavatory, do tell: how on earth did you get mixed up with him?"

"We met through the Fordite monks at Grantchester," I said as Lewis returned to the living-room, "and I've come back with him to discuss a case."

"Oh God, are you a Fordite fan too? I'm sorry I was so rude about them a moment ago, but all-male institutions always strike me as being so dreadfully abnormal . . . Oh hullo, Daddy! Dinner's almost ready."

"Splendid!" said Lewis, having cunningly decided to change his tactics and produce his best behaviour. "Well, this is really a great treat! Thank you very much, my dear, for all the time and trouble you've taken today to produce such a wonderful surprise!"

Rachel, greatly mollified, gave him a radiant smile.

I thought they were probably quite fond of each other.

8

THE sauce had just the right texture, the pasta was *al dente,* the salad was crisp, the trifle was delectably enhanced by sherry. Abandoning any lingering ascetic inclinations I ate like a horse and drank like a fish—not a large fish, perhaps, but certainly a small one with a thirst. The normal conversation bounded along through all the normal subjects, providing a lavish antidote to my recent travels through abnormal landscapes. We talked about where my home was, where I had been educated, where Rachel's home was (Cadogan Square) and where she had been educated (St. Paul's Girls' School before her arrival at King's College, London). We then talked about how London had gone downhill since the tourist industry had exploited Carnaby Street, how the Beatles had gone downhill since their early days, how America had gone downhill since the escalation of the war in Viet Nam, and how even though Hollywood had gone downhill French films were still worth seeing . . . We began to survey the French cultural front, past and present, and having ruminated over Truffaut and Proust we returned to the subject of Berlioz. Within minutes Rachel and I had discovered a mutual interest in Beethoven.

"Beethoven's for one's twenties," said Lewis, "Mozart's for one's thirties and after forty it's really Bach or nothing."

"What happens after fifty?" said Rachel. "Is there anything except the 'Dead March' in *Saul?*"

"Perhaps after fifty one reverts to Beethoven and begins all over again," I said. "In one's end is one's beginning. Life's a circle. The wheel of fortune. Boethius." By this time another bottle of Chianti had been opened.

"Bo who?" enquired Princess Normality.

"Boethius. He was a philosopher who—"

"Oh, I can't bear philosophy! What a waste of time to sit on one's bottom thinking when one could be dancing around having fun! Philosophy's abnormal."

"Eat your hearts out, Plato and Aristotle!"

"No wonder the Greeks had such a low opinion of women," said Lewis.

"I think philosophy's futile too," I said, ignoring him, "because the greatest truths are beyond the power of words to express."

"That sounds a bit peculiar," said Her Royal Highness. "If there are no words, why not just invent a few more?"

"Well, all words are symbols, and—"

"Rubbish! Where's the symbolism in 'the cat sat on the mat'?"

"My daughter, the logical positivist," said Lewis.

"That sounds very rude, Daddy. Watch it. And you're sounding increasingly peculiar, Nicholas. I do hope you're not secretly abnormal."

"Come to Starrington Manor with me tomorrow and I'll show you exactly how normal I can be!"

Lewis slammed down his glass. "Is Rosalind interested in philosophy, Nicholas?"

"Who? Oh, Rosalind—"

"What did she read at university?"

"Rosalind didn't go to university," I said, suddenly realising I was being blitzed. "She went to Winkfield to learn *cordon bleu* cookery and flower-arranging."

"Who's Rosalind?" demanded Rachel.

"My ex-fiancée," I said, outmanoeuvring Lewis. "I'm just about to break off my engagement."

"Oh dear," said Rachel, "I'm so sorry, but I'm sure it's the right decision. I can't quite see you wedded to a flower arrangement."

"I'll show you to your room, Nicholas," said Lewis, rising to his feet. "No doubt you'd like to unpack and have an early night."

I realised this was an order but I was unable to resist saying to Rachel: "Can I help with the washing up?"

"How extremely kind of you," said Lewis, "but since you're our guest I insist that you now relax."

Rachel pulled a face behind his back.

With regret I allowed myself to be dragooned from the room.

"*NOW* just you listen to me," said Lewis, having led me to a sparsely furnished bedroom on the first floor. "This won't do. You've got to focus entirely on your current crisis in order to survive it, and if you now take time out to frolic around, you could be endangering your entire recovery."

"Lewis, with all due respect, don't you think you're slightly—just very slightly—overreacting?"

"No."

"But Lewis—"

"No, don't whine 'but Lewis' at me! This ego-building flirtation is nothing but a dangerous exercise in escapism, and you'll solve nothing, I assure you, by tap-dancing into a dream-world where you play Fred Astaire to Rachel's Ginger Rogers!"

"You're talking exactly like a celibate priest who's hung up on sex!"

"Well, at least I'm not talking like a perpetual virgin who has no idea what sex is all about! Look, let me try and put this in the simplest possible language—like the language in those easy-reader books designed for primary school children. You're in danger, Nicholas. You have a big bad dangerous enemy who's trying to destroy you. But luckily you also have a friend who wants to save you. The friend's taken you into his house, bolted all the doors against your enemy and said to you: 'So long as you do as I say, you'll be safe.' Meanwhile your enemy's outside, roaming around the house in the dark and gnashing his teeth because he can't get at you. Now, what do you do? Do you follow your friend's advice and stay safe? Or do you fling wide the front door and cry to your enemy: 'Oh, do come in!' "

"You're surely not suggesting that the Devil's trying to get at me through Rachel!"

"Okay, let's scrap the easy-reader approach and try again. While you're under acute stress, Nicholas, you've got to avoid all behaviour which could exacerbate your mental and emotional fragility and lead you into the kind of mess I'm sure you'd prefer not to imagine. If you were a heavy drinker I'd tell you to stay off the booze in order to avoid disaster, and you'd know exactly what I was talking about. But your problem isn't booze, is it? So I have to say to you instead: steer clear of the girls. At this particular stage of your crisis it's a question not just of morality but of self-preservation."

"I see your line of argument," I said tactfully, trying to calm him down. Unfortunately I was then unable to resist adding: "But are you sure you're not getting steamed up just because you're Rachel's father?"

"Well, of course I'm getting steamed up because I'm Rachel's father! I'm steamed up because I'm her father and I'm steamed up because you're in my care, and how I haven't exploded like an abused pressure-cooker long since I've no idea. What do you think I am, some sort of spiritual robot? Now pin back your ears, unscramble your brains and get this: put Rachel aside for the time being because if you persist in chasing her now I could no longer counsel you. I'd be far too emotionally involved."

My little rebellion collapsed and died. Subsiding on the bare mattress I said: "Okay, you can stop beating me up. I get the message, but I really liked her, Lewis! It wasn't just mindless escapism!"

"No, it was just a mindless sexual attraction. But what could be more natural for a young man who thinks being hung up on sex constitutes certifiable behaviour?"

"Look, I'm sorry I said—"

"Forget it. Celibate priests get used to cheap gibes."

"Of course I know you're not really hung up on sex—"

"What if I am? And why shouldn't God use the hang-up to make me the kind of priest He wants me to be? It's one of the big fallacies of the ministry of healing," said Lewis as I boggled at him, "that everyone should aspire to be perfectly 'whole.' Quite apart from the fact that perfection isn't obtainable in this world, God can work through one's afflictions to transform them into a powerful source for the good—provided that one works with Him to use them in the best possible way." He turned aside. "I'll get you a sleeping-bag."

I went on sitting motionless on the edge of the bed, but by the time he returned I was able to say: "I've been very rude and very ignorant. I'm sorry." And without giving him time to reply I added: "I'm worried in case I sleep-walk."

"I'm ninety-nine percent sure that won't happen, but by all means let's allow for the additional one percent. Before I go to bed I'll rig up a device which will make a crash on my landing if you open your door. If you want to pee during the night, use the pot under the bed." He dumped the sleeping-bag on the mattress and a pillow-case on the pillow.

I felt reassured. Tentatively I said: "And tomorrow?"

"You'll want to start the day in church, of course. Desmond and I say Matins at seven-thirty and celebrate mass at eight before we breakfast together to discuss parish matters. After breakfast I'll leave you with Desmond while I keep my morning appointments, and after lunch I'll spend some time with Rachel. Be ready to leave for London with me at three-thirty."

"Should I phone Perry to warn him we're coming?"

"Good heavens, no! Never give a clam time to close up!"

"But supposing he's out?"

"Let's take the risk. And talking of phone calls, I expect you want to ring home before you go to bed. There's an extension downstairs in the hall."

I stood up with reluctance. "I'm almost afraid to phone in case he's worse."

"What exactly are these physical troubles of his?"

"Oh, all the usual psychosomatic ailments—and the latest fiasco is eczema on his hands. Why he won't see a doctor and get the right cortisone ointment I just don't know, but sometimes I think he wants to be ill."

"Why?"

"Because he knows at heart I'm a poor replica and so he feels there's no point in staying alive any longer. He only survived my mother's death because he thought he was going to see the replica living his life all over again for him."

There was a lengthy pause. Lewis remained motionless, staring at the boarded floor, but at last he looked at me and said: "If I were him I'd want to live. I'd be too worried about what might happen to you if I died."

"But if he's reached the end of his tether—"

"One doesn't reach one's late eighties unless one has a very long tether. Ring home and find out how he is. You may be pleasantly surprised."

We went downstairs together and I phoned the Manor. Agnes said my father was a little better. He had been very pleased with my letter and hoped to hear from me again soon. ". . . and if you're now in Starbridge, Nicholas, I really don't see why you can't come home and—"

"I'll ring again tomorrow." Replacing the receiver I said to Lewis: "You were right. He's better. Do you suppose—"

"Keep praying," said Lewis. "Keep stroking his psyche. Remember Whitby's fur."

I nodded but was unable to comment.

We returned upstairs.

I O

AFTER I had prayed for my father I lay awake for some time planning how I could trade in Rosalind while causing the smallest possible distress to all concerned. The problem was acute because I was very fond of her. I found her restful. Since I had known her from birth, she had the familiarity of a nursery teddy-bear which was retained after childhood for sentimental reasons; the reasons might be sentimental but the affection they reflected was genuine enough. Rosalind was the only person apart from my father with whom I could be silent without feeling embarrassed. The truth is one doesn't need to talk to one's favourite bear; one just holds its paw and feels comforted by the way it so effortlessly symbolises loyalty and devotion. Teddy-bears also have the great virtue of being predictable. Their joints can only move in certain directions; their glass eyes have an unchanging glare. Being so conscious of unpredictable forces, I loved the predictable, the reliable, the secure.

But that was all very dull, I could see that now, just as I could see that I had only proposed to Rosalind because I had felt unable to maintain my sexual double life a moment longer—and because Rosalind had been there, just as she always was, and the desire to play safe had been so overpowering. But now I realised I needed someone more stimulating. I still wanted someone normal—God preserve me from marrying a psychic and acquiring yet another set of peculiar problems!—but I wanted someone who made normality hum with excitement, I wanted to put my teddy-bear away in the toy-cupboard, I wanted to move out of the cosy nursery at last into a bright brash adult world.

I pictured myself saying to Rosalind: "We can still be friends, can't we?" and I could picture Rosalind replying good-naturedly: "Silly old Nicky, of course we can!" And I heard myself say: "We can still listen to Beethoven, can't we, and go for walks in the woods and toast crumpets for tea in winter and laugh at *The Avengers* on TV and be silent together while you arrange your flowers in those beautiful patterns? Because I wouldn't really be trading you in, would I, if I married someone else— you're woven into my life so seamlessly that I couldn't begin to cut you out." And in my imagination I heard Rosalind answer: "Darling Nicky, don't worry—whatever you do I'll love you and stand by you for ever . . ."

I toyed with this fantasy for some time but finally, realising it was a fantasy, I blotted out the thought of Rosalind in order to focus on Rachel. I began to visualise the smart London parish she would require. So long as I had Rachel I was sure I could adapt to any environment, and how relieved my father would be if I wound up working in the mainstream! In fact I could see plainly now that my father had been right and that I had to avoid the ministry of healing. I didn't want my wife thinking I was an incomprehensible failure who had wasted his opportunities for a conventional ecclesiastical career.

I slept, and dreamed I was killing Christian because he had tried to take Rachel away from me.

But despite this frenzied mental activity I neither got out of bed nor untied the string that tethered my ankle. It was as if the thought of Rachel had acted as a charm to keep all abnormality at bay.

I I

THE following morning I attended Matins and mass at St. Paul's. Any Roman Catholic would have felt quite at home there. So would any pre-war Anglican ritualist who got his kicks out of flouting the rubric. At first I felt gloomy, more convinced than ever that Anglo-Catholicism needed to be yanked out of this esoteric rut (could anything have been more old-fashioned in the 1960s than the florid touches which had given the Protestants such apoplexy in an era which was as dead as a doornail?), but after five minutes I began to feel comforted by the familiar patterns. Here was another of my old nursery teddy-bears symbolising security and predictability in a world of chaos. The liturgy suddenly seemed as soothing to me as a mantra.

Only a handful of creased old women joined us as we said Matins, but a surprising number of people turned up for mass. On a weekday this was unusual. It forced me to acknowledge that the old-fashioned ritualism might not be as irrelevant as I'd supposed, and it made me look more closely at the two priests in charge. Father Wilton, bald, rosy-cheeked and asexual, had a mild, tranquil air; I found it easy to imagine him being very kind, very humble and very good—an easy victim for the parish harpies, but at least no one could accuse him of not being a devout Christian. Lewis, in contrast, looked like a prize-fighter who had wound up in the wrong ring. It was the first time I had seen him in a cassock, and instantly I remembered my father confessing to me once that he had always felt more comfortable as a priest when he wore a monk's habit, because a black cassock, even when muted by a surplice, tended to stimulate quite the wrong response among the ladies.

Breakfast at the vicarage turned out to be a substantial meal; I might have guessed that Lewis would need to be well-fuelled. The daily house-keeper produced eggs, bacon, sausages, fried bread, toast and an enormous pot of tea. Father Wilton had toast with marmalade. I had toast with eggs. Lewis had toast with everything. Conversation centered on parish affairs, although Father Wilton took care to include me in a couple of digressions. When he asked no questions about my presence at the vicarage I realised that Lewis had briefed him earlier.

After breakfast Father Wilton said gently: "Would you like to settle down in my study with a good book, Nicholas?" and I realised he was to be not merely my host but my baby-sitter. We passed most of the morning in his study, he writing letters, answering the phone and occasionally with-drawing to the morning-room to deal with callers, I rereading Anthony Hope's *The Prisoner of Zenda* in a battered edition which was a relic of Father Wilton's remote boyhood. Time passed while Rudolf Rassendyll, having escaped into another identity, encountered the ravishing Princess Flavia.

At eleven o'clock my own princess surfaced, flashing long lissom legs beneath a mauve mini-skirt, and flew off in her father's Volkswagen for another raid on the supermarket. With reluctance I returned to Ruritania.

Lunch consisted of sandwiches with Father Wilton who said kindly: "Shall we eat in silence this time? I always feel that after a working breakfast with Lewis I need a quiet lunch." Lewis himself, returning home late from his work, looked in on us briefly but retired upstairs to have lunch with Rachel.

After the meal my baby-sitter suggested I might enjoy a little sunshine in the garden, but bearing in mind what had happened on the last occasion when I had tried to enjoy a little sunshine in a garden, I turned down this suggestion and began to read *Rupert of Hentzau,* the sequel to *The Prisoner of Zenda.* It all ended in tears, of course. You can't escape into another identity. Poor old Rudolf. But it was a good try.

Lewis collected me just as I was skimming the final pages. "Ready, Nicholas?"

I thanked Father Wilton for his hospitality and set off on the journey to London.

I 2

IT WAS well after six when we left the car on Albemarle Street; we had stopped for coffee during the journey. Lewis, wanting to signal to Perry that all admissions would be held in confidence, was wearing a dark suit with a black stock and clerical collar. I was wearing my black trousers, taken reluctantly from my wardrobe the previous Sunday, and a black jacket which had been lent to me by Father Wilton. This unusual ascent into conventional clothes was the result of Lewis's insistence that we would dine at a Jermyn Street restaurant after calling on Perry. I still had my white shirt open at the neck but Lewis had brought his old school tie for me to wear later.

We had already agreed that I was to open the interrogation in order to give Perry time to adjust to Lewis's presence. We were operating on the assumption that Perry would be reticent but not hostile.

"This is essentially a good-natured clam," I said as we moved into the forecourt of Albany. "I think you'll like him. He's very pleasant and civilised."

The uniformed doorman stepped forward to meet us but waved us on when Lewis said we had come to see Mr. Palmer. We entered the Rope Walk.

It was now six-thirty, the hour when Perry was most likely to be pausing to relax after work before leaving for an evening engagement. But I was still worried that he might be either working late at the office or out drinking at a cocktail party, and my anxiety increased when no one answered the doorbell.

Lewis rang the bell a second time but again there was no reply.

"Third time lucky," he commented phlegmatically as I groaned in an agony of suspense, but before he could press the bell again the door began to open.

The next moment Perry stood revealed on the threshold but I hardly recognised him.

He looked as if he were terminally ill.

XIII

I

I TOOK a step backwards. Uncertainly I murmured: "Perry?" but found I had no idea what to say next. I was aware that Lewis was motionless beside me.

"Nick," whispered Perry. He passed a hand over his forehead. "Good God, how extraordinary, I've been thinking of you. Christ, how odd everything's become, how crazy, how . . . Well, never mind, come in, excuse me looking beaten up but I seem to have hit a rough patch, nothing's quite . . . But come in, always nice to see you, come in and have a drink."

"Thanks," said my voice. "We won't stay long, but if you could spare us a few minutes—" I broke off. Having stepped into the hall I found that the atmosphere was horrific, psychically searing, conjuring up images of decay and clotted blood, and I could see clearly now that Perry looked like a rotting corpse, his smooth face gaunt, his skin grey, his eyes sunk deep in his skull. As he closed the front door I noticed his hand was shaking. Again he had to wipe the sweat from his forehead.

"Sorry, Nick," he said, "sorry, everything's rather a wreck, not my usual self, but nothing to worry about, tomorrow I'm going to start eating again and then I'll be fine. Who's your friend?"

As I groped for the conventional response Lewis introduced himself and held out his hand. "Wait a minute," said Perry, looking at it, and at last I realised how drunk he was. "Wait a minute. A clergyman. Do I know you? Are you connected with the Aysgarths?"

"No, but I'm from Starbridge."

"Any relation to that Hall who was at Winchester in the early forties?"

"No."

"Ah." Perry took Lewis's hand but dropped it as if the effort of behaving normally had exhausted him. "Well, never mind, I'm used to clergymen because of the Aysgarths, so come in, come in . . . Whisky?"

"Very nice," said Lewis. "Thanks."

The atmosphere in the high-ceilinged, old-fashioned drawing-room was equally appalling, lifeless as concrete but permeated by a rancid, fetid miasma which I found revolting. But there was no odour in the room other than cigarette smoke. This stench was one no nose could ever smell.

"I don't have any Rose's lime juice, Nick—"

"That's okay, Perry. Whisky will do." I never drank whisky. But then I had never before experienced such psychic pollution. I hardly knew what I said.

"I'm so sorry," said Lewis, suddenly exuding great charm, "but could I possibly have some ice?"

During the Chianti-swilling dinner with Rachel he had deplored the American habit of drinking whisky on the rocks. I began to wonder if we were all mad.

"Of course," said Perry. "No problem, as the Yanks say, no problem. I'll just go to the kitchen to get it—sit down, sit down, sorry it's all such a mess, I'm not very organised at present, couldn't get to work, all so odd but just a temporary malaise, must be, that's the only logical explanation and I'm a deeply logical man, wholly rational, devoted to positive logical-ism—I mean logical positivism—Christ, I've got to get myself together, excuse me."

He blundered out into the hall and we heard his footsteps stumbling down the stairs to the basement. The atmosphere lightened. I sank down stupefied on the sofa.

"Okay," said Lewis in a low voice. "Change of plan. Leave this entirely to me."

"Lewis, the *atmosphere*—"

"There could be a number of reasons for that. Keep calm and don't jump to conclusions." As he spoke he was moving through the communicating door into the dining-room, and the next moment he had paused by the table. When I followed him I saw his eyes were closed.

"Lewis, what is it? What's happening? Why are you—"

"Shhh." He returned to the drawing-room. Meanwhile Perry had begun his return journey with the ice-tray, and as we heard his footsteps on the stairs Lewis said in a low voice: "Concentrate on looking relaxed."

By the time Perry re-entered the room I was sprawled on the sofa with one leg crossed over the other, and Lewis, sedate in his clerical suit, was standing with his hands in his pockets before the unlit gas fire.

"I'm sorry to descend on you without warning, Mr. Palmer," he said, "but it suddenly occurred to me that you might be able to help us."

"Fine, but call me Perry, won't you, why not, same generation if I'm not mistaken, I'm forty-one, you look about forty-five, same generation. Suppose we ought to be calling each other 'Palmer' and 'Hall,' but that tradition's dying out, isn't it, and now it's all Christian names—oh God, Christian, Christian, Christian—Nick, ever since you came here last Friday . . . Yes, that's when I date it from, that's when it all started, it's all so bloody odd and Norman Aysgarth always said *you* were so bloody odd— did you put some sort of spell on me when you came? No, don't answer that, of course you didn't, I don't believe in magic, I'm rational. Here you are, Hall—what did you say your first name was?"

"Lewis. Thanks, Perry. Has this phenomenon been getting steadily worse?"

"Yes, couldn't eat, only drink, extraordinary, but I'm sure I'll get better soon. Well, cheers, everyone." He raised a tumbler of neat whisky and drank deeply. "That's better," he said, coming up for air. "That's much better. Now I can think. Well, Nick, well, Lewis, how can I help you?"

"As you know, Nicholas has been troubled about Christian," said Lewis fluently, "and he decided to talk to me about the matter because he knew he could trust a priest to hold everything he said in the strictest confidence."

"Marvellous. Not a churchgoer myself, but . . . marvellous. Always admired first-class clergymen—old Aysgarth—a great man. Go on."

"Nicholas no longer thinks Christian committed suicide."

"Oh, good. Wizard. God, how that word 'wizard' takes me back! Do you remember, Lewis, when everyone used to exclaim 'wizard prang'? Before Nick's time, of course. There was 'topping' and there was 'ripping' and there was 'wizard'—and now there's 'fab.' Amazing thing, slang. And the Americans! My God! I met a Pan Am steward last week who . . . Wait a minute, I'm wandering—sorry, got to concentrate. Nick no longer thinks Christian committed suicide, you said."

"No. That's because he saw Christian last Monday."

There was a crash of smashing glass as Perry dropped his tumbler in the fireplace.

"*ONE* of us is crazy," said Perry, "and contrary to all the evidence I don't think it's me. Or maybe it *is* me, maybe I'm imagining you both, maybe this whole scene is a grand prelude to a long holiday in a lunatic asylum." Ignoring the broken glass he sank down in the nearest chair.

"You think Nicholas is mistaken?" said Lewis with interest as the room began to reek of whisky. He spoke as if the subject under discussion was an unusual weather forecast.

"*Mistaken!* Well, of course he's mistaken!" Turning to me he added unevenly: "Nick, Christian's dead. Okay, I admit I didn't see him die, but if he'd survived that fall overboard I'd have found him, I swear I would . . . Lewis, could you please pour me some brandy from that decanter on the right?"

Lewis moved to the sideboard.

"I must have been mistaken," I said quickly, "although at the time—" I stopped. Behind Perry's chair Lewis was holding up a hand warning me to say no more.

"There was no inquest, was there," he said, handing Perry the drink. "I can only remember reading about the accident directly after it happened."

"That's right. No body, no inquest. The coroner must 'have his carcase,' as the saying goes." Perry was making a mighty effort to regain his composure.

"And you're quite sure you'd have found him if he'd survived? I was wondering if he could have been picked up by another boat."

"No, that's impossible—there was no one near us at the time. Even the bloody tanker was probably two miles away."

"What tanker?"

"The one I think must have caused the freak wave. I can't prove it because I never saw the brute and so there were no details I could give the coastguard, but some of those foreign supertankers charge up and down the Channel so fast that they create monstrous wakes. They're a well-known hazard."

"But surely you'd have seen a supertanker?"

"Not if it was two miles away. We wouldn't have heard it either at that distance."

"You're saying the visibility was poor?"

"It wasn't too bad. But there was a haze. Certainly we couldn't see as far as two miles."

"I take it you're an experienced sailor?"

"Yes, I'd kept that boat at Bosham for years. A wonderful boat it was, my pride and joy, a thirty-one-foot sloop built by Camper and Nicholson . . . Do you know anything about boats?"

"Nothing at all," said Lewis with an apparently genuine regret.

"Okay, I'll skip the nostalgic details. They're all past history now anyway. After the accident I sold the boat and never went near Bosham again."

"So despite this first-class boat and all your years of experience—"

"Oh, they counted for nothing in the end. That was the cruel part about the accident: it was so utterly undeserved. It was a warm June morning and the sea was like a millpond—too much like a millpond, I remember thinking at the time—and it was still early; Christian and I used to leave London at five on those Saturdays, unless we were going as far as France. Then we'd try to get down to Bosham on Friday night, but that wasn't always possible as Christian could be delayed in leaving Oxford."

"So you didn't plan to go to France on the day of the accident?"

"No, we were just heading east along the coast."

"And what were you actually doing when the wave struck?"

"Nothing much. We were waiting for some wind, and in fact I was thinking of starting the engine. Christian was in the bow with his field-glasses. He was studying the coast, which was just about visible, and I was at the tiller keeping an eye on the buoyage. Then while we were both looking in the wrong direction this bloody wave slunk up and slammed into us. It must have been at least fifteen feet high and it was a miracle we didn't capsize. Everything was flung around and wrecked in the galley. I was flung around and pretty well wrecked myself, and as for Christian . . . well, he must have lost consciousness, as I did, and drowned soon after hitting the water."

"Weren't you wearing life-jackets?"

"Good God, no! They're for women and children . . . Nick, where the hell did you see this person you thought was Christian?"

"Near Cambridge," said Lewis.

"Cambridge! But he'd never go there—he could barely admit the place existed!"

"Nicholas thought he might have wanted to begin a new life under another identity."

"Balls!" said Perry, knocking back the brandy.

"In that case," said Lewis, very courteous, "what was the purpose of his false passports?"

"Oh my God!" cried Perry. "Charles Gore and Henry Scott Holland!" And slamming down his glass he buried his face in his hands.

"SORRY," he said, letting his hands fall seconds later. "I was just overcome with exasperation. That idiotic hang-up of Christian's has caused me nothing but trouble . . . Damn it, I'm out of cigarettes, and Nick, I know, doesn't smoke. Lewis, do you by any chance—"

Lewis gave him a cigarette. "When you say 'idiotic hang-up,' what exactly—"

"Well, he was nuts, you see—kept saying he was alienated from the ground of his being, out of touch with his true self—he said the Christian Aysgarth identity was a prison and he had to escape from it. But he wasn't suicidal, Nick," said Perry, turning to me, "and although he talked of going on a journey, it wasn't a physical, geographical journey he had in mind. He called it the journey to the centre. He said he wanted to paddle upstream in his canoe towards the source of his own private river—the river of the self—but he kept being swept downstream and smashed against the rocks. The whole concept was allegorical, even religious. I think once he even mentioned God."

"Fancy!" said Lewis, somehow contriving to sound both deeply surprised and mildly gratified. "But why are you so certain that he didn't want to act out this allegorical journey by disappearing into the blue?"

"Oh, I think he did flirt with the idea, but my point is he would never have done it. Oxford was his life-blood—he loved being a don, loved luxuriating in the academic spotlight. I know his career was going through a bland patch, but if he'd lived he'd have sorted that out."

"But just supposing," said Lewis, "he had indeed been planning to drop out. Would you necessarily have known about it?"

"I'm quite certain he'd have confided in me. I was one hundred percent in his confidence."

"That's what Nicholas thought. And that's why he was tempted to reason that having obtained the false passports you could have taken Christian to France in your boat and faked the effect of a freak wave to support your story of an accident at sea."

"But that makes no sense at all!" cried Perry. "Christian was my best friend—I'd have fought tooth and nail to stop him vanishing into the blue!"

I could keep quiet no longer. "Then why the false passports?" I demanded, and although Lewis winced at such an aggressive approach Perry answered willingly enough: "I told you—he was nuts. But I was providing him with therapy."

"*IN ORDER* to grasp what was happening," said Perry to Lewis, "you've got to understand my relationship with Christian. Otherwise nothing will make sense. God, my mouth's so dry I can hardly speak! I'd better have some soda-water."

"I'll get it for you," said Lewis instantly, heading for the siphon on the sideboard.

"Thanks. Sorry, I seem to be treating you as a butler . . . But I think the two of you must have shocked me into a recovery because I'm beginning to feel better." He drank deeply from the glass of soda-water before saying to Lewis: "I had a rotten childhood, parents in India, shipped off early to school in England, boarded out in the holidays—but everything changed when I went to Winchester and met Christian. That wasn't just because he proved to be such a good friend; it was also because his family more or less adopted me, and I finally began to realise that life could be fun.

"Now how do I describe Christian to Lewis in a single sentence, Nick? I can only say: he was so gifted that he often seemed arrogant, but the arrogance was only superficial and beneath it he was a good person, very decent—very 'white,' as we used to say in the old days. Funny how all that schoolboy slang keeps coming back to me.

"You're probably thinking by now, Lewis, that you're listening to someone talking about the big romance of his life, but you'd be wrong. Of course nowadays, when everyone's continually leaping into bed with everyone else, it's hard to remember that there used to be a less frenetic era—in fact it's probably impossible for someone as young as Nick to understand that relationships don't always have to be about sex, that sex isn't the be-all and end-all of existence, that it's even possible to do without bloody sex altogether, but maybe you, Lewis, as a member of my generation—"

"I'm not merely a member of your generation; I'm a priest who considers himself called to celibacy. It's really all a question of how you want to organise your energy, isn't it? If you pour enough energy into your work, you're not going to feel so driven to romp around in your leisure hours."

"Exactly! Well, if you believe that, you won't be overcome by scepticism if I say that Christian's energy before he married all went into his work. And so did mine. It still does. Never mind why." He paused but when Lewis made no attempt to cross-question him he exclaimed impatiently: "Damn it, why am I pussy-footing around when you're both men of God who know the Boss will strike you dead if you break a confidence! If you really want to know," said Perry, allowing us no time to comment on this sinister vision of God, "I was seriously assaulted when I was seven. That was one of the reasons why I was so relieved to form an alliance with Christian at Winchester. Some boys never get bullied or brutalised; they're too golden, too successful, too popular.

"But the friendship didn't just consist of my cowering in a golden boy's shadow. I became of great importance to Christian. Always he was the subject of attention from both sexes, but although when he was young this was gratifying to his ego he soon got very bored with people worshipping him passionately, and my virtue in Christian's eyes was that I was invariably, indestructibly non-sexual. So you can see, can't you, how we suited each other? I was the person he could always relax with; he was the person I could always trust never to involve me in sex. But let me make one thing quite clear: he was heterosexual. And so was I. I like women, although for some years now I've tended to run with a homosexual crowd because I discovered that relationships with women inevitably ended awkwardly when I backed down. Homosexuals are capable of behaving awkwardly too, of course, but if you reject a homosexual he's much more likely than a woman to say: *'C'est la vie!'* and pass on to the next possibility . . . Sorry, Lewis, you probably think I'm digressing, but unless I make the sex-angle absolutely clear you could jump to all manner of wrong conclusions."

"I'm more than grateful to you for putting me in the picture."

"Well, now I've set up the picture, let me turn on the spotlight. Christian began to unravel towards the end of 1964, but it wasn't an overnight phenomenon; the trouble had actually been brewing for a long time. He'd become dissatisfied with his marriage. That was obvious by 1963, but in my opinion the dissatisfaction began after Helen was born in 1961. (That's his second daughter, Lewis.) Katie had had a tiresome sort of pregnancy and Christian said to me: 'Why can't she be more like my mother? My mother never whined and moaned like this.' That was when it dawned on him, I think, that he'd wound up with the wrong wife."

"Why do you think he chose Katie in the first place?"

"Oh, he idolised his dead mother and wanted a wife who was just like her. I know how Freudian that sounds, but it needn't be a recipe for disaster, need it? It seems to me that a lot of men marry women who remind them of their mothers yet manage to live happily ever after."

"That's certainly true."

"However, unfortunately Katie's resemblance to the first Mrs. Aysgarth was only skin-deep. Christian's mother was one of those middle-class women who appear delicate but are actually much tougher than they look; when her husband was Archdeacon of Starbridge, she ran that vicarage at St. Martin's and looked after her five children with the minimum of hired help. But Katie the aristocrat not only looked delicate; she *was* delicate, the exotic flower perpetually wilting in the conservatory. And worst of all she mooned over Christian like the heroine of the dreariest kind of romantic novel, and the one thing Christian couldn't stand was being doted on with unceasing passion. He found it oppressive and exhausting. He was fond of Katie, of course—loved her certainly in the beginning—but he should have married someone like Venetia (does Lewis know who I mean, Nick?), a woman who's neither conventionally beautiful nor conventionally feminine but who nevertheless has tremendous brains and style. Venetia's just as much an aristocrat as Katie, but she doesn't cling, she doesn't dote and she could have kept Christian constantly amused.

"Marina helped the marriage to some extent—she too had the style and brains to keep him amused—but since Christian wasn't suffering from a conventional form of the seven-year itch, the amount of help she could offer was limited. In fact what happened was that although the marital trouble was temporarily eased, his dissatisfaction spread to other areas of his life and he became noticeably depressed—although the word 'depressed' nowadays is so overworked that you may misunderstand me when I use it. Christian's depression was what medieval men would have identified as the sin of sloth. The word was—oh God, I've forgotten, how typical, brain failing—"

"Accidie," said Lewis.

"That's it. A sort of listless world-weariness which becomes debilitating. He went on functioning, but it was a tremendous effort and in the end he was barely able to go through the motions of his day-to-day existence. His last book was poor. He couldn't be bothered to offer hospitality to his undergraduates. He couldn't be bothered to take his family for a holiday. He couldn't be bothered to do anything much. He was just marking time, it seemed, waiting for someone to put the spice back into his life . . . And eventually someone did." Perry stopped. "Wait a moment," he said. "I've just realised this is tricky. I'm not sure how to go on."

"It's okay, Perry," I said. "I've talked to Martin."

"You have? But how extraordinary—I never thought you and Martin were that close! Well, in that case—my God, I must have a splash of brandy in this soda-water—no, don't get up, Lewis, I'll do it, I've got to stop treating you as the butler. Well, in that case," repeated Perry, darkening the soda-water, "I can speak freely. What on earth did you think of the story, Nick, when Martin talked to you?"

"Martin was in fact very cagey," said Lewis before I could reply. "Nicholas realised there'd been an emotional involvement but was left uncertain how far, if at all, it had been satisfied."

"Well, in the beginning nothing happened," said Perry. "They met in the summer of 1963—not long after Marina's classic Starbridge orgy,

Nick—when Martin was appearing at the Starbridge Playhouse in the pre–West End run of *Present Laughter* and the Aysgarths threw a party for the cast at the Deanery. Christian and Katie had come down from Oxford for the weekend and I'd come down from London. I sensed that Martin was deeply attracted, but Christian was behaving with his usual detachment and I felt sure Martin would soon realise he was wasting his time. Martin wouldn't have been put off by the fact that Christian was married, of course—married men often have a busy time on the homosexual circuit—but since Christian never encouraged Martin by even the flicker of an eyelash it seemed doomed to remain a one-sided love affair. In addition I knew from my theatrical friends that Martin had for some reason taken to living like a monk—someone even said he'd started going to church—so in those circumstances I thought he'd make every effort to overcome the attraction.

"After that first encounter they met a few times at various social gatherings and still nothing happened, but then at the end of 1964 they met at a cocktail party of Venetia's. This time I wasn't present; there was a flap on at the office and I had to work late. Christian said nothing to me afterwards, but obviously Martin had decided to chuck up the ascetic life and obviously Christian had given the required flicker of an eyelash because the next thing I knew my homosexual pals were all gossiping about Martin and Christian.

"I didn't believe it. I just didn't believe it. My first instinct was to find Christian, shake him till his teeth rattled and shout: 'Have you gone out of your mind?' but then I calmed down and realised I had to be ultra-cool. After all, that was the secret of my relationship with Christian: no messy emotional scenes.

"So I got a grip on myself and tried to work out why Christian was behaving in a way that I knew was wholly out of character—and the more I thought about it the more convinced I became that Christian really had blown his mind and that the preceding months of 'accidie' had been the necessary psychological prelude to this complete freak-out. That sounds as if I'm saying a man has to be mad to have a homosexual affair, but of course I don't mean that at all. What I'm saying is that I don't think a man who was as heterosexual as Christian was would have had a homosexual affair unless he was under abnormal stress—like the men in prisons, for example, who in the absence of women feel driven to turn to their own sex."

"He'd never had a homosexual affair before?"

"Never. If he had I'd have known about it."

"A case of repression, perhaps."

"No, he just had no interest. He wasn't even interested in verbal queer-bashing. His indifference was monumental."

"No wonder you were shocked by the affair!"

"Yes, but when I finally concluded he was in deep psychological trouble I was able to put on my best neutral manner and seek him out. He was wary at first but when he saw I had no intention of criticising him he was overpoweringly relieved. I remember thinking: miracle number one: I've saved our friendship. Now for miracle number two: saving Christian.

"But obviously it was going to be tough. 'I'm in another world!' he said as he tried to explain what was going on. 'I've escaped from Christian Aysgarth! Whenever I'm with Martin I'm someone completely new!' And *that,* you see, was what fundamentally attracted him. Not Martin. Not the homosexual expression of love. But the escape into another identity, the psychological release obtained from behaving as if he were someone else. And as soon as this truth dawned on me I knew the romance was doomed."

"How did it all end?"

"Messily. Christian ditched poor Martin in the nastiest possible way, cutting him dead at a straight party, referring to him as a bloody queer, doing everything, in fact, except spitting in his face. It was wrong, rotten, revolting, and I was very angry, but I knew I still had to keep calm, just as I knew that this monster walking around being bloody awful wasn't the Christian I knew any more. It was as if his old personality had terminal cancer—as if it were being eaten away by a malign growth which was taking him over—but no, that sounds much too fanciful and I don't deal in fantasy. I'm a rational man.

"Meanwhile, parallel to the Martin fiasco, there was another sexual horror-story going on. You won't believe this, Nick, but—"

"Dinkie."

"My God, you know everything, don't you? Talk about Sherlock Holmes! Yes, he took up with bloody Dinkie, who even then was nearly always stoned on some drug or other, and he ran the two affairs in tandem like one of those ghastly bisexual bores who treat their acquaintances as a sort of smorgasbord. Well, of course yet again it was quite incredible that Christian should behave in such a way, but when I found out about Dinkie at least I knew I had to act; I could no longer go on sitting on the sidelines and playing it cool while my friend disintegrated before my eyes. So after he'd told me about Dinkie—still bragging that he'd escaped from Christian Aysgarth—I said to him: 'If you really want to sample new identities maybe I can offer you more interesting possibilities than either Martin or Dinkie.' And I volunteered to get him a false passport so that he could rocket around Europe doing all the things Christian Aysgarth would never do.

" 'Wonderful!' he said. 'I can see the end of the dark tunnel at last—*Ecce lux!*' Then he laughed and exclaimed: *'Lux Mundi!'*—which he told me was the title of a famous book of nineteenth-century essays on theology. He said he'd use the names of all the contributors in turn, starting with Charles Gore, who I gather was the ring-leader of the gang.

"Well, by that time it was clear he was mad as a hatter, but I reasoned that the first step towards a cure was for me to take control of the madness and manoeuvre it into less self-destructive channels. Bucketing around Europe pretending to be someone called Charles Gore struck me as being the hell of a lot better than bucketing around bedrooms with Martin and bloody Dinkie."

"I certainly see the logic," said Lewis. "But how successful were you in achieving a cure?"

"Well, I did get him away from Martin, although it was hardly my fault that Christian chose to disembowel him as a farewell gesture. And eventually I did get him away from Dinkie, so at least I achieved my aim of channelling the madness out of the bedroom. I started my campaign by luring him away on a holiday to the Continent, where we whizzed around behaving like a couple of undergraduates—we even played a crazy rag on his brother James in Germany, but that was a mistake because Christian couldn't be Charles Gore with James and afterwards he just felt rather a fool. God knows what James thought. Meanwhile everyone was criticising Christian for leaving Katie on her own when she was eight months pregnant, but I couldn't help that. The emergency was too acute to wait, and Christian had to have this therapy in order to avoid a complete breakdown."

"So apart from the incident with James, the holiday was a success?"

"I thought so. It enabled Christian to let off a lot of steam—and as we all know, a volcano's far less dangerous after an eruption. But then, damn it, he wanted to do it all over again! No more being Charles Gore—he'd 'done' Charles Gore and now he had to be Henry Scott Holland.

"However, we soon ran into problems. I did get the Scott Holland passport, but I was carpeted by my boss, who wanted to know what the hell was going on; someone had tipped him off that I was on a false passport kick, and although I do have access to a number of peculiar departments, I'm not normally in the business of providing false identities. I told him the passports were all part of an entertainment being planned for an old Wykehamist reunion, and luckily my boss, who's an old Etonian, was very willing to believe that old Wykehamists were capable of a really esoteric degree of inanity. So I crawled out of that tight corner and swore blind that both passports had been destroyed, but I knew I couldn't go to that particular well for water again so Christian's plan to work his way through the *Lux Mundi* theologians came to an end. But at least he did still have those two passports and at least every weekend I could take him sailing and enable him to escape into another identity. Even if we didn't go to

France he always kept the passports with him to make him feel liberated
. . . Nick, how in God's name did you find out about them?"

"Dinkie said she searched his pockets once when he was asleep."

"But he'd given up Dinkie by the time I got him the Scott Holland
passport! In fact I made that a condition of the deal: I'd only get the
passport, I said, if he'd . . . Bloody hell, he double-crossed me! He kept
on with her!"

"In retrospect," said Lewis as Perry blundered back to the brandy
decanter to refill his glass, "what do you yourself see as the source of this
compulsion to be someone else?"

"Well, to be honest I didn't believe all that allegorical rubbish he was
spouting about the journey to the centre to find the source of the river
within. That was just his intellectual way of dressing up a basic problem
in high-flown language in order to make it bearable. I thought at the
time—and I still think—that this split identity arose because he was a
decent man who knew he was going to have to behave like a bastard."

"You mean—"

"I think he was subconsciously winding himself up to ditch the wife
who loved him." Perry slumped down in the chair again with his glass.
"It was like this," he said. "Christian, the real Christian, was such a good,
moral, decent man that he couldn't consciously face up to what he had to
do to get his life back on course. So his escape into other identities where
he played the bastard was in a bizarre way an acting-out of what he had
to do in his real life but which simultaneously he couldn't bring himself
to do at all. That was the conflict that was driving him crazy, and at the
time he died he still hadn't come close to resolving it."

Lewis merely said: "You're sure that ditching Katie would have been
the answer to his problems?"

"Positive. With the marriage out of the way he would have had the
strength to reorganise his career—maybe he would have gone back to the
classics. His first degree was in Greats, Lewis, and the classical languages
were his favourite subjects at Winchester. If he could have lived in the
classical world during his working hours and afterwards returned not just
to the twentieth century but to the right wife . . . But he didn't. He died.
End of story . . . Or is it?" Drinking his brandy he relapsed into silence.

"It was the end of the story until Nicholas Darrow started to bob around
saying Christian was alive."

"But that's what's so bloody odd! When Nick turned up last Friday,
he wasn't saying Christian was still alive—he was just dredging up the old
suicide theory. So why, ever since Nick's visit, have I felt . . ." He stopped
again.

"Haunted," I said.

Lewis looked as if he wanted to throw me out of the window.

"Don't be ridiculous!" said Perry at once. "I'm a rational man. I don't see ghosts."

"No, of course you don't," said Lewis briskly. "Why should you? The real issue is this, isn't it: what did Nicholas do last Friday that had such a profoundly unpleasant effect?"

"Exactly. Well done, Lewis. But I don't know the answer. What is it?"

"Well now, I wonder," said Lewis, offering him another cigarette.

5

I'M SURE there's a rational explanation," he added, "but before I offer a theory I need some more facts. Can you describe more precisely what's been happening since Nicholas visited you?"

"I seem to be unable to do anything except sit around and drink."

"Have you been out?"

"Once. I bought some cigarettes, but in Piccadilly I thought I saw him—I mean *him*—Christian. All right, I know that's ridiculous, but I haven't been able to face going out again."

"Did you have any doubt about the identification?"

"Well, of course I did! The pavements were crowded, the look-alike was some way off and Christian's at the bottom of the Channel, so I knew at once I was mistaken. But nevertheless . . ."

"It seemed very real."

"Yes. So when you said just now that Nick had seen him too, I nearly had a stroke. For God's sake, why are we both seeing Christian like this and what happened last Friday to turn us into hallucinating lunatics?"

"I doubt if either of you were hallucinating in the medical sense of the word," said Lewis mildly, "and I doubt too if Nicholas's sighting arose solely from his visit here last Friday. But if I may venture a tentative theory about the trouble that's overtaken you yourself since then, I would suggest you seem to be exhibiting some excruciating symptoms of bereavement. A lot of people hit the bottle and become paralysed with inertia when the full shock of bereavement begins to bite. And the sighting in Piccadilly, which you recognise wasn't real, can also be explained in this way because the bereaved often do make mental projections involving the deceased; the most common example is for them to be acutely aware of the dead person's presence in the family home."

"My God!" said Perry, much struck by this diagnosis and regarding Lewis with a genuine, though wary, respect. "Well, that's certainly cut all my irrational terrors down to size! But I suppose that as a clergyman you're well accustomed to bereavement symptoms."

"Deal with them all the time."

"Wonderful. So what you're saying is that last Friday—no, hang on, I'm still not with you. What exactly happened last Friday when Nick came here?"

"I think he must somehow have resurrected all the horror and grief you experienced when Christian died. He cross-questioned you, didn't he, about Christian?"

"Very persistently. Much more persistently than anyone else who's ever trotted here to serve up the suicide theory."

"We were in the kitchen, weren't we, Perry," I said. "I remember you getting up in the middle of the meal and taking a bottle of wine from the fridge. I could see you were rattled."

"What often happens after a traumatic accident," said Lewis, "is that the sufferer represses the memory, perhaps for some considerable time, but eventually it breaks back into his conscious mind and demands to be constantly replayed. Tell me, what happened after the sighting in Piccadilly? Did you become more acutely aware of your memories of him here at Albany?"

"I hate to admit it but yes, I even started to feel he was actually present in the set—although of course I knew that was quite irrational—and when the feeling persisted I began to wonder if I was going mad. In fact I reached the point where I only felt sane when I was drunk, and now every time I stop being drunk I feel as if he's cleared a spot in my brain and moved in—it's as if he's taken possession, like an occupying army, and . . . No, I'm sorry, I'm talking rubbish, I know I'm talking rubbish, and Lewis, that's exactly what's so extraordinary: I can listen to myself saying all these crazy things but I know quite well they're crazy—so that must mean I'm sane, mustn't it? If I was completely mad I wouldn't know I was talking rubbish."

"Let me reassure you again by saying that these bereavement symptoms of yours are very common and the likelihood is that you're still far from certifiable. Have there been any other visual projections in addition to the incident in Piccadilly?"

"No, but . . . well, you won't believe this—"

"Aural projections, perhaps?"

"Right. Last night I heard—or thought I heard—his footsteps in the kitchen. Frightful. Of course there was no one there. I had a slug of brandy and thought: come on, Perry, you're rational, be rational. But I couldn't sleep again."

"Has there been any unusual smell? Any change in the light or temperature?"

"No smell. No change in the light. But . . . now, this sounds preposterous, but there was a cold spot. I noticed it as soon as I passed by."

"Is it still there?"

"Don't know. I've kept away ever since."

"Whereabouts is it?"

But Perry, finishing his brandy, remained silent.

"I've encountered the cold-spot phenomenon before," said Lewis. "In fact I'm not infrequently called in to remove it. There are various things a priest can do to alleviate an unpleasant atmosphere, and if you like I'd be very willing to deal with this problem for you."

There was a long pause. Then Perry said, staring into his empty glass: "I'm not a believer."

"That wouldn't necessarily matter, although of course it would be helpful if you were. So long as you believe that *I* believe and that I'm opening up a channel of power that can wipe out this form of pollution, then my prayers should be sufficient for us both."

"No, I . . . No, I'm sorry, I know you mean well, but—"

"Would it help if I gave a demonstration of my experience in this field? Let me walk around both floors of the flat. If I can tell you where the cold spot is, perhaps you'll be more willing to believe I have access to a power that can rid you of it."

"No, no, we're getting into very superstitious waters here and I can't have that, I'm rational. Sorry, Lewis—no offence meant, but—"

"None taken. But can I at least give you my card so that you can contact me if you change your mind?"

"Well . . ."

"Or you might simply wish to talk. I'd always be very willing to listen."

"To be honest I don't usually go in for chats with clergymen—except old Aysgarth, marvellous man, never put his foot in it by mentioning God—but since you seem a very decent sort of chap, respectable, properly dressed, not the sort of nutty-fringe clergyman who runs around in mufti with a guitar . . ." He took the card.

"Nicholas," said Lewis, "we must be going."

I followed him from the room in silence, but as Perry paused at the head of the stairs, such a wave of psychic pollution washed past him from the kitchen that I could no longer contain myself. "Perry," I said urgently, "change your mind and trust Lewis! The atmosphere in this place is enough to drive anyone round the bend!"

Perry looked startled but Lewis said swiftly to him: "Thanks for the drink. I hope things improve soon, but if they don't, please do get in touch."

"For heaven's sake!" I exclaimed, exasperated beyond endurance by this inexplicable reticence. "Why can't we all call a spade a spade? Perry, Christian's spirit's trying to possess you. Lewis is an exorcist who knows all about dealing with demonic infestations. He—"

"I do apologise!" said Lewis ruefully to Perry. "I'm afraid the child's been reading too many horror comics. Come along, Nicholas—time to find an antidote to all that whisky you've been putting away."

I was outraged, but not so outraged that I failed to notice Perry's response. He was looking at us both as if a black pit of irrationality had opened up at his feet, and as soon as I saw this reaction the *gnosis* hit me between the eyes. The trigger was the image of the black pit. Instantly the word "coal" flashed on the screen of my psyche.

"The coal-cellar!" I shouted at once. "That's where the trouble is! Lewis must exorcise the coal-cellar!"

Perry was now looking not only horrified by the irrationality but incredulous, as if he felt that no normal person could have uttered such an opinion.

"Lewis has no intention of exorcising anything except his very considerable hunger," said Lewis, still effortlessly conveying the impression that he was in charge of a precocious child who was determined to embarrass him by showing off. "I'm off to Jermyn Street for a good dinner. Goodbye, Perry—good luck." And he placed his hand firmly on my shoulder in order to propel me outside.

We left the flat. Lewis closed the front door behind us with a tug of the door-knocker and shoved his way past me into the Rope Walk.

"Lewis—"

"BE QUIET!" He paused only to glare at me in fury before striding ahead again.

Much shocked by this violent reaction I hurried after him, but as we entered Piccadilly my shock faded and I too gave way to fury. I was livid that I had been treated like a child, livid that my helpful advice had been brushed aside and livid that poor Perry had been so feebly abandoned. In fact I felt ready to lose my temper with Lewis, but since he had lost his temper first I felt I had been in some subtle way outmanoeuvred, and as I became increasingly aware of his rage I found I was too nervous to do more than scuttle along in his wake.

We ploughed across Piccadilly, plunged downhill past the side-entrance of Fortnum's and pulled up at last on the brink of Jermyn Street. By this time I was experiencing such a disturbed reaction from all the chaotic abnormality at Albany that when Lewis paused as if to remember the exact location of the restaurant, I tugged the sleeve of his jacket and muttered an apology; I felt an urgent need for him to resume his normal manner without delay.

He swung to face me. Then he sighed and to my relief I realised he was no longer angry. In a resigned voice he said: "Someone will really have to do something about you, and I have the terrible feeling that the someone's going to have to be me. You've got to be trained. You're a menace."

"But what did I do wrong? I was only trying to help, and you see, I knew, I absolutely *knew*—"

"You knew blank-blank nothing," said Lewis, not hostile but clearly welcoming the chance to sound robust. "However, that's no surprise. People under thirty hardly ever do know anything, even though they're usually pig-headed enough to think they know everything there is to know."

"Excuse me, Lewis, I don't want to upset you all over again, but don't you think you're being just a little unfair to the younger generation?"

"You wait. I haven't started yet. Come along, I'm feeling extremely peckish."

We hurried down Jermyn Street. Outside the door of one of those quiet, dimly lit, dark-panelled establishments where the menu prices are not intended to be read by the timid, Lewis produced the school tie he had brought for me and said: "Put that on. And put it on quickly."

But the design at once made me hesitate. Automatically I said: "This isn't a Starwater tie."

"No, it's a relic of my ill-fated days at Charterhouse. My Fordite mentor said later that it would be a useful exercise in humility if I kept the tie and looked at it once a year to remind myself of my expulsion . . . Now, why are you gaping at me like a goldfish? I told you I was a mixed-up psychic teenager!"

"But if you were expelled from Charterhouse, how on earth did you manage to get into Starwater Abbey?"

"Nicholas," said Lewis, "I'm quite extraordinarily hungry after witnessing your psychic pirouetting at Albany, and my patience could by no remote stretch of the imagination be described as infinite. If you think I'm going to loiter on the pavement of Jermyn Street while you cross-question me about a part of my youth which I'd prefer to forget, I assure you you've made a very big mistake."

I apologised hastily, knotted the tie and hurried after him into the restaurant.

6

NOW just you listen to me," said Lewis once we were established in a secluded booth and a waiter had produced a bottle of claret. "You may be a grown man but as a psychic you're a baby. You're gifted, you show promise, but you're a baby. Psychically you know nothing, and the main reason why you know nothing is that your so-called *gnosis* isn't special knowledge at all—it's just a heaving mass of belief, intuition and wild, woolly guesswork."

"But Lewis—"

"No, you still don't understand. The concept is too advanced for your infant mind. Let's try again. Of course I'm not denying that you have genuine psychic experiences. Nor am I denying that very occasionally the meaning of the experience is so obvious that even you can understand it; your bout of foreknowledge at Marina's party would fall into that category. But every psychic should have hanging over his bed a sign which says: I CAN BE WRONG. Now, just reflect on that sentence for a moment. Say to yourself quietly, calmly, intelligently: 'I CAN BE WRONG.'"

"But I'm not wrong most of the time, and—"

"Ye gods and little fishes," said Lewis, finishing his first roll and grabbing another from the bread-basket. "At this rate I shall wind up as demented as poor Perry." He took a large gulp of claret.

Nervous in case he lost his temper again, I said hastily: "Okay, I know nothing. I can be wrong."

"That's better. Now apply those two vital facts to the concluding moments of our visit to Albany, the moments before you went clean over the top with your weird and wonderful talk of a coal-cellar. You were trying to force Perry to accept my help, weren't you? But that was a bad mistake. Never force paranormal help on anyone, because the resulting backlash is usually so great that all possibility of such help is destroyed."

"But surely in order to save Perry—"

"The trouble with the young is that they always want instant results. I *was* saving Perry. I think he'd have come round to the idea of receiving help from a priest, but now, of course, thanks to you bawling out debased and inflammatory words such as 'demonic' and 'exorcist'—words which I took immense care never to use—"

"Okay, I blew it. I'm sorry. But surely in order to save Perry you've got to exorcise that flat before it drives him completely round the bend?"

"No, the flat's not of the first importance here."

I stared at him. "But the atmosphere! As soon as we crossed the threshold—"

"Yes, but that had nothing to do with the flat."

"Nothing to do with the flat? But I know it did!"

"No, Nicholas, you don't *know.* You believe."

"But—" I broke off in great confusion but finally said: "In that case I understand nothing here."

"Well done," said Lewis. "You're growing up."

"But surely—"

"An exorcism of the flat would be helpful, certainly; I'm not denying that. It would have the therapeutic effect of showing Perry that I was on his side, helping to fight the force that's threatening him, and there's nothing wrong whatsoever in offering that kind of support to someone who's in extreme distress. Oh, and I could eliminate the cold spot, of course, but that's a minor detail because the cold spot isn't the source of the trouble. It's a symptom of trouble—perhaps very bad trouble—but it's not the source. The real evil isn't centred on the flat."

"You mean—"

"It's centred on Perry," said Lewis.

7

AT THAT point our first course arrived and while it was being served I drank some wine to calm me down. Lewis was already poised for action with his soup-spoon.

"When you encounter a bad atmosphere like that," he said as soon as we were alone again, "your first task is *not* to jump to conclusions but to form a rational opinion about where the atmosphere's coming from. You said you noticed the atmosphere as soon as you crossed the threshold; so did I, but who was across the threshold? Perry. And now cast your memory back to that moment when I deliberately got rid of him by asking for ice. Did you notice—"

"The atmosphere lightened."

"So you did notice. Well done. If I can only train you not to jump to conclusions, not to think your psychic powers make you infallible and not to crash around like a runaway bulldozer at the wrong moment, you may one day cease to be a menace and even, if you're very lucky, become a useful member of society."

I ignored this. "Why did you go into the dining-room in Perry's absence and listen with closed eyes?"

"I wasn't listening. I was sampling the atmosphere. The closed eyes were an aid to concentration, and the purpose of sampling the atmosphere of another room was to check that the pollution wasn't emanating from the flat."

I took a deep breath. "Is Perry possessed?"

"I don't know. That's the next thing you must learn, by the way: the humility to say not only 'I can be wrong' but 'I don't know.' "

"But if he's producing an atmosphere like that, something must be horribly wrong!"

"That's indisputable, but psychic impressions such as the one we both received tonight are usually capable of more than one interpretation and you can't rely on your much-vaunted *gnosis* to tell you which is correct. Try to understand, Nicholas: what makes a first-class psychic isn't the psychic experience itself; any fool can have one of those. The first-class psychic is the one who can interpret the experience correctly, and a correct interpretation requires reason, intelligence, maturity and training."

I finally accepted my psychic infancy. After a moment spent thoughtfully stirring the soup in my bowl I said in my politest voice: "Please could you explain why you're unsure whether or not he's possessed?"

"The evidence was contradictory and therefore inconclusive." Lewis, eating much too fast as usual, paused to shovel away some sliced onions. Then he said: "But let's be sure you can define 'possession.' We can distinguish it from mental illness because the sufferer is sane; he feels he's periodically being invaded by a malign force, but this isn't a delusion stemming from paranoia. However, the condition's extremely rare and the resemblance to some forms of mental illness makes it difficult to diagnose."

"But you've had experience, surely," I persisted, "in making the diagnosis."

"Yes, but don't run away with the notion that the classical exorcism of people is a normal part of my ministry. The exorcism of places—yes, that's usually straightforward and I'm often called out to deal with ghosts and cold spots (which are just two different aspects of one problem). And modern exorcism—the casting out of psychological suffering by prayer and counselling—yes, that too forms a significant strand in my ministry. But the classical exorcism of a possessed person requires extensive preparation and an army of helpers—in fact I'd never attempt such a thing unless I had a psychiatrist, a psychotherapist and possibly a social worker in attendance along with at least three strong men, all of whom, ideally, should be priests. In other words, it's quite definitely not the sort of challenge one encounters regularly and wraps up in half an hour."

"Are you implying it's most unlikely that Perry's been afflicted by something so rare?"

"It's certainly unlikely, but that doesn't mean it hasn't happened. What I'm really implying is that one should approach the possibility of possession with extreme caution, and the first point to note in this particular case is that I saw no physical sign that Perry was, in the classical sense, possessed. There are certain movements of the body which indicate possession—and sometimes you can even see the possessor in the eyes when the possessed is temporarily overpowered—but none of those symptoms was on display this evening. On the other hand, he did present the famous mental symptom of possession: he was convinced he was sane but being periodically invaded by a hostile force."

"Couldn't this be the onset of possession," I suggested, "with the physical symptoms occurring when we weren't there?"

"It could. But it could also be the onset of paranoid schizophrenia or, more prosaically, a nervous breakdown."

"I don't think we should have left him," I said. "I think we should have stayed."

"And done what? Held his hand? Let me repeat, Nicholas: you can't force your help on people. That's because the healer's a mere channel for the Holy Spirit and the power won't flow effectively if there's a faulty connection between the channel and the mind of the sufferer. There's got to be faith and trust between the healer and those who require healing, and because faith and trust can't be extorted on demand, the healer's first task is to try to create the conditions in which they can exist."

I digested this lesson as I ate my soup. Then I said: "I think—that's to say, I tentatively believe—though I could be wrong"—Lewis laughed— "that Perry is possessed by Christian's spirit."

"Fine. But now tell me the objections to that theory."

I stirred my soup thoughtfully again but was finally forced to say: "Okay, I give up. You tell me."

"Well, for a start, why should Christian possess Perry so unpleasantly? It seems an odd way to treat a loyal and devoted friend. And why should Christian's spirit be so malign?"

"Those last six months of his life—"

"Yes, I agree they were a disaster, but if he was on the verge of a nervous breakdown he could be classified as sick, so perhaps he should still be viewed with compassion. One can say with confidence, I think, that he was muddled, miserable and occasionally downright monstrous (one thinks of your brother) but was he actually evil? I'm inclined to think not. But of course . . . I could be wrong."

"But if Perry's sure it's Christian who's taking him over—and in a way that creates such revolting psychic pollution—surely that implies Christian's an evil force?"

"Not necessarily. The boot could be entirely on the other foot."

I boggled at him. "What do you mean?"

"Christian's memory could be activating an evil force in Perry."

I continued to boggle. "So you're saying the Devil's already planted a demon in Perry? Or are you saying it's the Devil himself who's now taking Perry over? Or are you saying—"

"Stop!" said Lewis good-humouredly, polishing off the remains of his soup and setting down his spoon. Food was making him more benign. "Rein in the old-fashioned picture-language before you're tempted to sell your ideas to Hollywood, and let's see if we can get a clearer picture of the truth by adopting the primary school easy-reader approach. Now, using the simplest possible language, how would you describe Perry as he appeared to us tonight?"

"Drunk, disturbed and frightened."

"Correct. Very well, we know this behaviour is linked with Christian's death but we don't know why. How do we know there's a link?"

"Because the behaviour began after I visited him and resurrected the subject—"

"Correct again."

"—and because the paranormal incidents he's experienced since have all involved Christian."

"I wouldn't call any of them paranormal except the cold spot, and we don't actually know that's connected with Christian at all."

"But the sighting—the footsteps in the kitchen—"

"Both those incidents are unremarkable if you remember he was unbalanced by bereavement and stoned by drink."

"Yes, but—"

"Let's just set the paranormal aside for the moment and keep this very simple. The most obvious explanation of Perry's collapse is that he's suffering from an excruciating form of survivor's guilt and that he can't forgive himself for living while his friend died; he suppressed this guilt at the time of the accident when he was in a state of shock, but now it's surfaced in a form which is additionally virulent because it's been untreated for so long."

"But what about the cold spot?" I persisted, impressed by the psychological explanation but reluctant to have all my paranormal phenomena treated as irrelevant.

"The cold spot may or may not be real. Let's focus for the moment on what we know to be real: Perry's collapse. Now if my theory's right, the solution to the problem is not to submit him to a classical exorcism but to refer him to a first-class psychiatrist."

"But couldn't you counsel him yourself?"

"Yes, but as a non-believer he'd probably be more comfortable with a medical man. Ideally, of course, the psychiatrist and I would work together, but I don't think Perry would want that."

Our soup-bowls were collected, our wine glasses refilled; someone brought us more rolls. When our privacy had been restored I said: "So what you're saying is he's having a nervous breakdown."

"That's the most likely explanation," said Lewis, "but it needn't be the correct one. Your theory that Perry's possessed by Christian's spirit still remains a possibility, but we'd have to prove that at the end of his life Christian wasn't just behaving badly as the result of stress but was deliberately choosing to act in a manner which could be classified as evil. As I've already indicated, that seems unlikely to me, but nevertheless I can imagine a possible script. Supposing, for example, Christian tried to kill Perry but Perry killed him in self-defence."

"But why would Christian want to kill Perry?" I said amazed.

"Oh, I can imagine a possible script for that too—in fact I can imagine numerous scripts, but wild speculation unsupported by a shred of evidence is merely a waste of time and energy . . . And talking of wild speculation, what's all this about a coal-cellar?"

I described Perry's celebrated museum-piece.

"And how exactly did you make the connection between the cold spot and the coal-cellar?"

"Oh, I was just jumping from hunch to hunch. Of course I'm sure now I got everything wrong."

"I hate to undermine this newfound humility of yours," said Lewis, "but there's always the chance you got everything right. Can you outline your journey as you jumped from hunch to hunch?"

Carefully I reviewed my memory. "We decided to leave," I said, recalling the events one by one. "We went out into the hall. In the hall a wave of psychic pollution seemed to surge up the stairs from the kitchen—although now I realise that was a false impression; the pollution must have been emanating from Perry who was by that time standing at the head of the stairs. However, even though the impression was false it nailed the word 'kitchen' to the front of my mind, and this automatically linked up with information that Perry had given us earlier: he said the sound of Christian's footsteps had come *from the kitchen.* At that point I was associating the kitchen with both psychic pollution and paranormal phenomena, so it was hardly surprising that I jumped to the conclusion it was also the location of the cold spot."

"But what made you zero in on the coal-cellar?"

"Oh, that was mere *gnosis,* or what I now recognise as a wild, woolly guess based on a mindless word-association. After I'd unmasked you as an exorcist and bawled out all the stuff about possession, I noticed Perry was looking at me as if a black pit had opened up at his feet. The word 'black' then instantly conjured up the word 'coal'—which in turn produced the memory of the coal-cellar. But of course it was all a false hunch."

"But was it?" said Lewis. "That's the question."

I stared at him but he was looking around restlessly as if hoping to see the waiters approaching with the main course. "I too was suspicious of the kitchen," he said, turning back to me when his hope was disappointed. "My immediate reaction was to wonder why the sound of the footsteps had come from there and not from anywhere else. Then almost simultaneously I remembered that the kitchen was where your interview with Perry last Friday had taken place—"

"So it was!"

"—and I asked myself if Perry had been disturbed not just by the persistent questions but by the fact that they were being asked in a room which had some sinister significance for him. Then Perry mentioned the cold spot. Now, there was certainly no cold spot in either the drawing-room, the dining-room or the hall, which were the three rooms I visited tonight. It could have been in the bedroom, the bathroom or the lavatory, but Perry clearly stated that after his encounter with the cold spot he had kept well away from it. This seemed to rule out the possibility that a small room was involved, and I thought that in an old-fashioned place like Albany a basement kitchen would be not only large but would include an area by the tradesmen's entrance which could be avoided for some time. So I decided this was the most likely location of the cold spot, and if the coal-cellar's in that area then maybe your wild, woolly guess isn't so wild and woolly after all."

I was sufficiently encouraged to say: "I did think at the time that I'd hit a nerve."

"Why?"

"It was the way he looked at me when I said the coal-cellar should be exorcised. Didn't you notice?"

"I was too busy trying to will you to shut up. How did he look at you?"

"As if he'd just seen a bear-cub transform itself into a six-foot grizzly. People often look like that when a psychic hunch hits the mark, so naturally I did wonder if—"

"Nicholas, you're on no account to go back to that flat unaccompanied, and if Perry invites you there I want to know about the invitation straight away."

I stared at him again. "But why?"

"I think he might try and kill you," said Lewis as our main course finally arrived.

8

I COULD hardly contain myself until the waiters had departed but as soon as we were alone again I said incredulously: "Lewis, you can't seriously think that dear old Perry—"

"Despite his drunken state 'dear old Perry' struck me as being a tough, resourceful customer who'd survived a considerable amount of adversity. Try this script: Perry kills Christian in the kitchen and buries the body beneath the floor of the coal-cellar. Three years later you bounce along asking such searching questions that the horrific guilt, which Perry's been suppressing in order to live close to his friend's corpse, starts to rise to the surface of his mind. He gets himself in such a state that even he, the dedicated rationalist, becomes aware of the cold spot, an area of abnormally dense psychic pollution caused by the projection of an evil memory so intense that it can even be sensed by an uninvolved third party. Then just when Perry reaches the point where he feels haunted by Christian's ghost, back you bounce and declare that the coal-cellar should be exorcised. Don't you think that in those circumstances Perry would feel tempted to liquidate you?"

"But Lewis, why would Perry kill Christian?"

"Oh, lovers often kill each other. Happens every day."

"But they weren't lovers."

"So Perry says."

"But Lewis, even supposing they were lovers, we know for a fact that Christian died on that boat!"

"But we don't," said Lewis. "That whole story rests on Perry's uncorroborated evidence. Let's now expand the script: Christian arrives at Perry's set on that Friday for another sailing weekend; Perry kills him that evening and the big question immediately becomes: what can he do with the body? Obviously he can't carry it through the front door of Albany and dump it outside the Royal Academy. There's the time-honoured solution of the trunk and the railway left-luggage office, but a taxi-driver is going to remember a man who leaves a posh address like Albany with a trunk so heavy that two men are required to carry it. However, fortunately Perry has his coal-cellar, the perfect makeshift grave. No megawatt cables there and no concrete foundations—not in an old-fashioned coal-cellar where the flooring would be primitive—and he realises that given sufficient time he could haul out the coal, haul up the floor and conceal the corpse. No need to carry out a massive excavation. All that's required is a depth which will seal up the smell of decay.

"But his first task isn't to embark on this lengthy burial. It's to create the fictional story of Christian's death, and leaving the body temporarily concealed in the coal-cellar he heads for Bosham as planned. I'd guess he left even earlier than five to ensure that no one saw him either when he left Albany—using the back entrance, of course—or when he arrived at Bosham. Obviously it was vital that no one should notice he was on his own.

"He sails around for a time and creates below deck the disorder which can be blamed on the freak wave. Finally he returns with the story of a disaster and everyone believes him. Why shouldn't they? He's an experienced sailor who's no doubt heard all about freak waves, and he knows exactly what to say.

"On returning to Albany he begins the long, laborious task of burying the corpse where it may well never be discovered. Full marks to Mr. Palmer! A highly successful murder. The only thing he fails to foresee is the lethal effect of his fermenting guilt."

I laid down my knife and fork. I leaned back in my chair. And I said: "You're crazy."

WE DISCUSSED the theory for the remainder of dinner and during the entire journey back to Starbridge. We shared the task of driving, but during my stint Lewis had to remind me more than once to keep my eyes on the road.

"I freely admit I could be wrong," he said when we were still at the restaurant, "but once one accepts that your hunch about the coal-cellar hit the mark the theory evolves with no obvious flaws. If it didn't hit the mark—if Perry's expression of horror and incredulity merely arose from the fact that he couldn't stand you holding forth like a fairground charlatan—then my theory bites the dust."

"But if your theory's right," I said later, "he must have been lying extensively during our interview with him, and I found him plausible throughout." We were both in the car by that time and Lewis was driving. I think we were somewhere near Basingstoke.

"Detecting false notes in a confession is an art which I wouldn't expect you to have mastered."

"But which notes struck you as false?"

"The ones relating to his sexuality."

I was very surprised. "You didn't believe him when he said he'd been assaulted when he was seven?"

"Oh, that rang true enough; one would expect a mental castration of some kind in order to account for the remarkable consistency of his reputation for being a sexual abstainer. But just because he chooses, for whatever reasons, to abstain, one shouldn't automatically assume he's uninterested in sex—and neither should one assume he's incapable of doing anything except living up to his reputation. If he has the standard physical equipment and all the right hormones, some form of sex could still occasionally appeal to him."

"But there's no evidence for that!"

"There's certainly circumstantial evidence. I regard it as suspicious that he runs with this homosexual crowd. I accept that he has to be very careful because of his work, but maybe he's just that: very careful. As I've already said, he struck me as being a tough, resourceful survivor, just the kind of man who could get away with leading a sexual double life."

"But he clearly stated how much he liked women!"

"Well, he would, wouldn't he? But I didn't find his assertion of heterosexuality convincing. You don't tune in to the homosexual circuit just because women become emotional when you turn them down."

"So are you saying that he and Christian—"

"I can certainly accept that Perry's extreme devotion to Christian had no physical expression while Christian was leading a wholly heterosexual life. But if Perry's not wholly asexual, what would his reaction be when this adored friend embarked on a love affair with your brother? We know he was shocked and incredulous. But don't you think that once he'd calmed down he'd be anxious for a piece of the action?"

"No," I said. "The whole structure of the relationship was built around the understanding that there would never be any sex between them."

"That's what Perry wanted us to think," said Lewis, "but is it true? Surely the real structure of the relationship was built around an unspoken understanding that Christian could do what he liked with women—even marry—but never betray Perry with another man."

"But what grounds have you for saying that?"

"It was all there between the lines of his narrative. He was disgusted by the Dinkie affair because Dinkie the drug-addict wasn't worthy of Christian. He disapproved of Katie but it seems he was still able to treat her courteously. He found it easy to tolerate—even like—Marina and Venetia, who weren't sexually involved with Christian but who both cared deeply for him. Yet what he just couldn't stand was the affair with Martin, and once Christian had rewritten the sexual rules why shouldn't Perry have started to wonder if the rules of their relationship could be rewritten as well?"

"So you think that the continental holiday—and all the sailing week-ends—"

"It's impossible to say for sure what was going on, but it's certainly a fact that Perry was the one Christian was seeing regularly at the end of his life."

I took some time to consider my thoughts but finally I commented: "If we believe Perry's story that the continental holiday, the sailing trips and the false passports were all part of a scheme to save Christian from breakdown, then sex needn't have featured on the agenda at all."

"That's quite true," Lewis agreed, "and I do believe that Perry's prime concern was to save Christian by providing what he thought was appropriate therapy. But Perry's ideas on how to save his friend were so misconceived that he might well have reached the conclusion that the therapy should include sex."

"Were they so misconceived? I can certainly see the logic behind Perry's ideas—"

"So can I, but it was faulty. You don't heal someone's personality disorder by providing him with false passports and sailing trips; Christian needed intensive counselling, not John Buchan–style escapades. And I'm afraid Perry's theory that all would have been sunshine and roses after a divorce strikes me as being psychologically naive. A man like Christian, brought up in that religious, conventional, middle-class home, would almost certainly have been unable to abandon a loving wife and three young children without suffering the most catastrophic guilt which would have destroyed his career and ploughed him right under."

"But if he was being ploughed under anyway—"

"A divorce would have buried him six feet deep. Don't think I'm automatically hostile to the notion of divorce; after all, I'm a divorced man myself. But I don't believe it would have been the answer for Christian. What he needed to do was to find out who he was and be helped to love and accept who he was. Then he would have been better equipped to love and accept those who were closest to him."

After we had stopped the car to change places and give Lewis a break from the driving, I said: "I still don't believe Christian and Perry were ever lovers, and I still don't believe—sorry, Lewis!—that Christian's buried beneath Perry's coal-cellar. A far more likely possibility, it seems to me, is that they quarrelled badly on that Friday night but survived to go sailing together as planned. I don't see a quarrel as unlikely. After all, Christian was being intolerable to just about everyone; why shouldn't he have started being intolerable to poor old Perry? So my theory is that they came to blows by the coal-cellar—perhaps Perry was trying to walk out of the back door in disgust and Christian lost his temper and clobbered him. However, then Christian patched up the quarrel because he wanted to go sailing and escape into another identity as usual. After the accident Perry's consumed by survivor's guilt, just as you theorised earlier, and the cold spot is the physical projection of Perry's current grief—the grief that he actually came to blows there with his friend on the night before the disaster at sea. Perry's expression when I started bawling about the coal-cellar can then be explained by saying he was appalled to be reminded of that painful quarrel and stupefied that I should apparently know about it."

Lewis said: "You could be right. But so could I. We just don't know."

Later—I was still driving and the car had begun to wind through the hills near Starbridge—I said: "So what do we do now?"

"Nothing. There's nothing we can do."

"But Lewis—"

"Perry has my card and I hope that eventually he'll phone me. If he does, I'll have the chance to help him."

"But supposing you're right and Christian's buried in the coal-cellar? Surely we should do something!"

"What do you suggest? Do you really propose to turn up at Scotland Yard and say: 'Excuse me, I've no proof and I'm not likely to get any, but by a series of psychic insights I've deduced that a Dr. Christian Aysgarth, believed drowned in 1965, was in fact buried in a coal-cellar at Albany after being murdered by his best friend'?"

"So the whole expedition was a complete failure!" I said violently. "We haven't helped Perry and we're left picking over theories we can't prove!"

"Oh no," said Lewis as the car turned the final corner and we saw the floodlit Cathedral in the valley below. "The evening was a great success. You've finally been weaned from your conviction that Christian's still alive."

I stared at the Cathedral. I remember being surprised that it was still floodlit. The lighting was turned off at eleven.

"That's true, isn't it?" Lewis was saying. "You now accept that Christian's dead."

After a pause I said: "Yes, I do. Perry wouldn't be coming apart at the seams in that particular way if Christian were still alive."

"And I think you'd agree now, wouldn't you, that Christian has no message for you."

I knew only one answer was possible. "None. He never found the way to the centre. He was just bucketing down a dead-end street." I sighed before adding: "I suppose all that's left for me to do now is to thank you for straightening me out and ask you to close the case."

"On the contrary," said Lewis, "this is where the case splits wide open at last. If Christian's dead, you couldn't have seen him at Grantchester in the present or future—and we already know that you couldn't have seen him in the past. So just who was it, in fact, that you saw in the garden on Monday?"

All the lights around the Cathedral went out and the valley was plunged into darkness.

PART THREE

SELF-REALISATION
ETERNAL LIFE

"But the eternal life which is a major theme of St. John's gospel is not simply unending life, but an enhanced quality of life, a fuller, richer, freer life which begins in this world though it is consummated in the next. The psychologist can shed a flood of meaning on the 'this world' meaning of eternal life. One of the ways the psychotherapist understands the goal of life is as the attainment of self-realisation. He works on the assumption that each person has an inborn need so far as possible to realise his capacities to the full."

CHRISTOPHER BRYANT
Member of the Society of St. John the Evangelist,
1935–1985
THE RIVER WITHIN

"The goal of the gospel of Christ is the restoration of the right relation [of man's to his maker] . . . This right relation is itself 'eternal life': it is here and now, but here and now cannot exhaust or define it."

MICHAEL RAMSEY
Archbishop of Canterbury, 1961–1974
CANTERBURY PILGRIM

XIV

I

"*I'LL* take over the driving again," said Lewis as I pulled out of a skid to the accompaniment of screaming tires.

"No, I'm okay."

"But I'm not. I'm sweating blood. Pull over, please."

We changed places. As Lewis drove off again I said: "Sorry. Stupid reaction. Of course the figure in the garden is easily explained by saying it was the result of unconscious self-hypnosis."

"You think so?"

"Isn't it obvious? I so strongly wanted to believe Christian was a monk at Grantchester that I couldn't accept Father Wilcox's denial and willed myself to create the figure in the Fordite habit. It was a hallucination caused not by mental illness but by stress."

"I agree that your extreme stress, your desire to see Christian and your conviction that he'd become a monk at Grantchester are all of great significance," said Lewis. "I believe they enabled you to make a wrong identification so positive that even now you're very reluctant to abandon it. But as I've already explained, I don't believe the appearance was due to self-hypnosis."

"Believe what you like," I said. "The man I saw was Christian—but we know now I couldn't have seen him. Therefore I was hallucinating."

"I quite understand that it may be easier for you at this point to believe that," said Lewis, "but I now strongly suspect you were seeing not a hallucinatory image (something which didn't exist on any level of reality) but a psychic event which was taking place on a level of reality not normally accessible to the conscious mind. And the man you saw wasn't Christian."

"You can't prove that!"

"Well, as a matter of fact," said Lewis, "I can. The man you saw was taller."

It was fortunate that I was no longer driving. I would have crashed the car. When I could speak I whispered: "How the hell do you know?"

"The peach-tree. At a distance the crucial branch appears to be just a thin line but it's actually three or four inches thick. The top of my head came below the branch. The top of your head matched the branch exactly. And the top of the monk's head was above the branch altogether. You and Christian were the same height. That means it couldn't have been Christian you saw."

There was a long silence while I watched the beams of the headlights rake the road ahead as the car continued its journey downhill into the valley. Finally I said: "I don't want to talk about it."

"Okay."

"The man was Christian and I was hallucinating. You made a mistake when you used the peach-tree to measure my height. Case closed."

"Okay."

Having reached the valley we began to travel through the dark meadows. As we approached the housing estate by the cemetery I said: "Now that the case is closed I'm going to spend tomorrow enjoying myself. Will you behave like a Freudian casebook if I ask Rachel out?"

"I think you'll find that even Freudian theory allows a man to feel annoyed if he sees his daughter being exploited."

"But I'm not exploiting her! I realise you think my interest in her is pure escapism, but maybe this is one of those occasions when you should say to yourself: I CAN BE WRONG."

Lewis made a noise which sounded like "Arrrgh!" and halted the car much too abruptly at a red light.

"Naturally I'd like to proceed with your approval," I said, "but if you continue to be so unnecessarily obstructive—"

"Don't threaten me," said Lewis. "I don't want to get tough when you're in such extreme psychological distress, but it would be quite wrong if I let you get away with behaviour that shouldn't be tolerated."

"I'm not in extreme psychological distress!"

"Okay," said Lewis.

The light turned green. We drove on and within five minutes we had reached the forecourt of the vicarage. The silence which fell as Lewis switched off the engine instantly became uncomfortable.

"My God!" I burst out. "From the way you carry on, anyone would think I intended to rape her!"

"Don't use God's name in that way, please."

"I wish I'd never made that confession to you. If I hadn't admitted all that sex—"

"—I'd still have deduced what was going on. Your confession's quite irrelevant in this context, Nicholas. You confessed your sins, I gave you absolution and from a spiritual point of view the matter's closed. What concerns me now is the thought of you embarking on a close relationship, sexual or otherwise, while this case is still open."

"THE CASE IS CLOSED!"

"Okay." He switched off the lights and we both got out. "But before you set out on an expedition with Rachel," he said, "could you take me to Starrington Manor? I think it's time I met your father."

"He doesn't see strangers."

We stood facing each other. The light from the porch slanted across his face and made his eyes seem more sunken and shadowed than ever. His expression was unreadable.

"If you chose," he said, "you could introduce me."

"But I don't choose. You'd make him upset."

"You think so? But my aim would be to help him. For instance, I might well be able to heal his hands by easing his anxiety."

"There's nothing wrong with his hands that a tube of cortisone ointment can't cure, and I quite definitely don't want you to meet him. If you did, you'd wind up telling him that I can't be a replica any more, and then he'd die."

"But my purpose would be to bring not death but new life. For both of you."

"You couldn't do that unless you separated us, but you can't separate Siamese twins joined at the psyche, it's too dangerous. My father's so old, so fragile, and he'd never survive."

"Maybe he'd be prepared to take the risk."

"But I wouldn't. I'd rather trust in God. He set this situation up. It's His will that I should be a replica."

"Is it, Nicholas? Is it really? This suppression of your true self in order to be someone else, this turning away from the centre of your God-given personality, this rejection of integration and self-realisation? Can this really be the will of the God who sent his son into the world to show us not just how to exist but how to fulfil every ounce of our human potential?"

I was aware of the Light trying to enfold me but I remained in darkness.

The demon of fear had tied me in such a knot that I was dumb before my exorcist, and in my disabled state I was unable to open up my psyche to that channel of the Spirit. The element of faith was missing. I just couldn't believe I would survive without my father. I just couldn't believe I had any choice but to keep him alive as long as possible by doing everything I could to make him happy. And I just couldn't believe I could make him happy except by being his replica and living his life for him all over again.

Turning my back on Lewis I walked up to the front door and stood silently, waiting to be let in.

2

I WENT straight upstairs to the first floor, used the lavatory and shut myself in my room. Half an hour later Lewis tapped on my door and said: "I'm setting up the alarm which will warn me if you sleep-walk," but I lay motionless on my bed in the dark and said nothing.

The hours passed. All prayer was impossible, even the wordless prayer which took place when I flipped the switch in my head. I did try and flip the switch but it had jammed. Something large and heavy was stifling the mechanism and crushing my psyche. I began to feel increasingly frightened.

I dozed for two hours and woke at six. By the time Lewis disconnected the alarm I was sitting on the edge of the bed and staring at the floor.

"I don't want to go to mass," I said when he looked in on me. I didn't want to go anywhere. I wanted to lie in bed all day with the blinds drawn.

"That's all right," said Lewis, "but why don't you at least listen while Desmond and I say Matins? Following the routine of the Office can rest and refocus your mind."

I wanted to say no but the word which came out was: "Okay." I was aware of Lewis's psyche wrapping itself around mine in order to draw me out of my apathy, and in reflection of this invisible rescue I abandoned the bed to get dressed.

I attended Matins. And in the end I stayed on for mass. During the services I had become even more aware of the power of Lewis's psyche as it pulled me smoothly along in his wake.

Again I found myself breakfasting with him and Father Wilton in the ground-floor dining-room. I ate a corner of burnt bread and passed the meal in silence, but I was not allowed to sink back into apathy. In the hall after the meal Lewis said to me: "I hope you're still planning to take the day off and relax. I now think that's an excellent idea, and I'm sorry I was so negative about it last night."

"Ah," I said—not very brightly, but at least I was speaking again after my long silence.

"In fact," said Lewis, "I think you should take two or three days off now that the case is closed. Why don't you stay on here at the vicarage until Rachel goes back to London?"

"Ah!" I said, becoming much brighter.

"I've got some calls to make this morning, but I'm sure Rachel would be very happy to keep you company. Of course," said Lewis pleasantly, "I don't have to lecture you, do I, about how you should behave with her."

"I'll be Sir Galahad reincarnated!" I said, now very bright indeed.

"Then just make sure you keep your eyes fixed on the Holy Grail. Why don't you shave and smarten yourself up and come up to my flat for coffee? Rachel should have surfaced by this time."

I ran buoyantly up the stairs to my room.

3

WHEN I entered Lewis's flat I found Rachel lounging on the sofa with a mug of coffee and a copy of the *Guardian*. Lewis himself, seated at his desk, was in the middle of a telephone call. When he waved his arm towards the kitchen I saw the coffee-jug on the counter.

"Hi!" said Rachel, mindful of the phone conversation and speaking in a low voice. She was wearing a shiny white dressing-gown over scarlet pyjamas. No slippers. Her naked feet were exquisitely narrow. I was aware of a vague urge to fondle her toes. Odd. I'd never before thought of myself as a foot fetishist. I wondered what it meant, and at once longed to look up foot fetishism in the medical dictionary.

"Hi!" I said, noting the return of my passion for rational analysis and realising that I was very, very much better. Having helped myself to coffee I sat down beside her on the sofa, but conversation was still restricted by the phone call. Lewis was talking to someone called Annette who I soon deduced was a social worker; they were discussing the case of an old-age pensioner who was trying to starve herself to death.

"Want some of the *Guardian?*" whispered Rachel.

"No, thanks. Doing anything this morning?"

"Just planning tonight's five-star menu. Daddy's graciously informed me that he intends to be in."

"So do I. I've been invited to stay till you leave."

"Good God, what's the old bear playing at?"

"I think he's realised he's been behaving like a Freudian casebook and he's making an effort to shape up."

At that point Lewis replaced the receiver. "I've got to call straight away on this old lady in Jubilee Walk," he said, rising to his feet. "Nicholas,

I suggest you take your coffee downstairs to Desmond's domain and then Rachel can join you there when she's dressed."

"Sure," I said, leaping smartly to my feet to show him how keen I was to play Sir Galahad. Obviously I couldn't be left alone with a bunch of naked toes.

"Shall I wear my chastity-belt?" said Rachel to her father. "Or will a whalebone corset be sufficient?"

"You can wear anything so long as it's not your birthday suit. I shall be coming back here after I've made this call, and when I return—"

"—you'll find us behaving immaculately downstairs," I said. "We'll be like two characters from *Barchester Towers*."

"Oh yes?" said Lewis, very bland. "I seem to remember that in *Barchester Towers* there was a very fast young adventuress and a very shady young clergyman."

We indignantly denied any resemblance to Madeline Neroni and Mr. Slope. There was much laughter. We were all getting on wonderfully well.

"I shall say no more, Nicholas," said Lewis as we parted downstairs in the hall, "but remember the Holy Grail."

He left. I wandered into the dining-room and sat down at the table to finish my coffee. Five minutes later the housekeeper departed to do Father Wilton's shopping and barely had the front door closed when the telephone began to ring. I went out into the hall. On the board both rectangles were in the OUT column. I was just eyeing the extension and wondering if I should pick up the receiver when the ringing stopped, and seconds later Rachel called from the top landing: "Nicholas, it's for you!"

"I'll take it down here!" I shouted back. Naturally I assumed I was about to be bombarded by one of the Community with more advice to return home without delay, and having grabbed the receiver I said very curtly into the mouthpiece: "Hullo?"

"Hullo, Nick," said Perry Palmer.

4

FOR a second my brain went blank. Then it began to tick over smoothly with increasing speed. "Perry!" I said. "How are you?"

"Better. You and Lewis evidently galvanised me into something that resembles sanity."

"I'm afraid Lewis is out at the moment, but if you want to leave a message—"

"No, it was you I wanted to talk to. I rang Starrington Manor and someone there gave me this number—which I now see is the number on Lewis's card. Look, can we meet? I didn't tell you the whole truth last night, not in front of a stranger—although don't misunderstand, I liked Lewis, nice chap, no limp wrists, sensible sort of fellow, but after all I didn't know him from Adam, did I, and as a general rule it's better not to spill every bean in the bag to someone who's just materialised on one's doorstep, as it were, in a puff of smoke."

"I understand." I was trying to keep my voice casual. "Do you want me to come back to Albany?"

"My dear chap, I wouldn't dream of asking you to trek all the way to London just because I'd expressed a wish to see you! Now that I'm no longer climbing the walls I think a trip to the country would do me good, but I'm rather thrown by the news that you're not at Starrington Manor. Is there any chance you could meet me there?"

"Yes, of course. Come to the house and—"

"Well, as a matter of fact I don't think I'm quite strong enough to face that religious gang your father sponsors, so I was wondering if we could meet in the grounds. Venetia told me once that there's a nice little chapel tucked away in a wood, and it occurred to me that it would be the ideal place for us to meet and talk. How would I find my way there from the main gates?"

"Forget the main gates. When you leave the village, follow the wall of the grounds for about a mile and you'll come to a door which opens directly onto the path leading to the chapel."

"Will the door be unlocked or will I have to wait for you to come and let me in?"

"It's always unlocked during the day because it's the quickest way of getting to my father's cottage."

"Oh God, I'd forgotten your father—"

"No, it's all right, we won't disturb him because he won't see us. He's in bed, temporarily a little under the weather. What time shall we meet?"

"Noon?"

"Fine. I'll be there," I said, and hung up.

"Anything wrong?" said Rachel, who had sped down the stairs to join me. "You look as if you're about to pass out."

All I said was: "Do you want to help me trap a murderer?"

5

WHEN Rachel demanded an explanation I summoned my creative powers and gave her a version of the truth so bowdlerised that it was almost unrecognisable. Omitting all mention of the séance, I said that Katie had suspected her husband had committed suicide; I had made some enquiries for her and had mistakenly thought I'd seen Christian at Grantchester, where I had happened to meet Lewis; acting on his advice I had approached Perry, who had made a fatal slip during the interview and revealed that a murder might have taken place, but Lewis had said that without proof we could take the case no further.

"But why are you so convinced that Perry now wants to liquidate you?"

"Why else would he come all the way from London to meet me at a secluded spot? Quick, get dressed and we'll go to Starrington."

Rachel, who had only got as far as applying her make-up, disappeared upstairs again but returned ten minutes later in a new pair of flowered slacks and a burnt-orange sweater. "I've left Daddy a note," she said. "I always have to do that or he thinks I've been abducted and there's a big scene."

"Funny old Lewis . . ."

Can I make excuses for myself? No, I can't. I was young but old enough to know better. I was spiritually sick but still capable of understanding that I was moving deep into fantasy as I fled from a reality too complex to master. I was also, I think, childishly determined to prove to Lewis that I wasn't quite the psychic baby he thought I was. I was aware of saying to myself: I know I can fix Perry, I *know,* it's *gnosis.* But as I felt the confidence surge through me I knew that what I wanted most of all was not to confound Lewis but to prove beyond dispute to Rachel that I was a tough, courageous hero.

Horrific. As Lewis had already said, I was a menace. And as I myself had already proved, I was a disaster-carrier wreaking havoc wherever I went, an untrained psychic at the mercy of his pride and his random impulses. It's strange how the media strive to package the paranormal as something which could be described as entertainment. The efforts resemble an attempt to convert a man-eating tiger into a domestic pet, an outsize cat whose only hobby is playing with a ball of wool.

"Poor Katie will get better now, won't she?" said Rachel as we drove to Starrington in my Mini-Cooper.

"Of course. Once she knows about the murder she can no longer blame herself for Christian's death," I said, and as I spoke I thought of the séance when Christian's spirit had erupted, hooking onto Katie's guilt and igniting it in that searing psychic explosion. Tormented Christian, "unhousel'd and unanel'd," not at peace with God despite all the prayers which had been said for him, but surviving in the guilt and grief and pain of the living, his memory moving incessantly through the inaccessible levels of so many unconscious minds to create the ghost which had haunted the bereaved.

"What are you thinking about?" said Rachel. "You're being fabulously strong and silent."

But of course I couldn't tell her about the séance. She would have thought it abnormal, as indeed it was. "I was thinking about you," I said, "and how normal you are." And then I clearly saw that my father had never married a Rosalind, someone whom he had known all his life and who perhaps knew him a little too well. He had married the strangers who had enchanted him with their normality, first the tobacconist's daughter, then the country lady, neither of them with a paranormal thought in their heads.

"I wish you could have met my mother," I heard myself say to Rachel, and the next moment I was busy imagining my mother drawing me apart from my father, stepping into the space she had created between us and saying briskly: "Now, Nicholas, no more talk of Siamese twins joined at the psyche. It's not only medically impossible, it's morbid. And Jon, no more nonsense about a replica—you're being very naughty." And I could see her kissing the top of his head as he sat at the dining-room table and she left the room on her way to work. At once in my head I cried: come back, *come back!* But the door had closed and she was lost beyond recall.

Rachel had been speaking but I had to ask her to repeat what she had said.

"I was asking if your mother was pretty."

"No, but she was attractive. She was tall and curvy, with marvellous legs."

"Super! My mother's beautiful, which is such a handicap because it means she has to devote almost all her free time to making sure she stays that way. Thank God I've been educated and have other things to think about—although of course, not being beautiful, I don't have poor Mummy's problems."

"I think you're the sexiest girl I've ever met."

"Sexier than the flower-arrangement? Who was this flower-arrangement anyway?"

"Just someone I'd known all my life."

"Sort of comfy and familiar, like an old boot?"

"Sort of. But if your mother's so beautiful, why has she never re-married?"

"She tries too hard. I used to think it was because she was still secretly in love with Daddy. My God, the hours I spent as a child praying for him to forgive her! Of course I got it all wrong. She was the one who couldn't forgive him for paying more attention to God than to her."

"Why didn't she marry that man who triggered the divorce?"

"Oh, he ditched her before she could lure him to the altar. Daddy then offered to have her back, but she wouldn't go and I don't think he really wanted her back anyway."

"How old were you when all this was going on?"

"Six. I don't remember much about it. I stayed with Granny most of the time."

"And how do your parents get on nowadays?"

"Oh, they never meet, they're so sensible. If they meet they have a row. Daddy never complains to me about her, but she's always going on about him, I get so tired of it. 'I can't stand that temper of his,' she says, but she always takes care to rub him up the wrong way. 'I can't stand all that psychic business,' she says, but why shouldn't he make the study of the paranormal his hobby? 'All he ever wanted from me was sex and regular meals,' she says, but all men want sex and regular meals, they're abnormal if they don't, and anyway, what else did she have to offer him? She never took any interest in his work. Sometimes I think all she ever wanted from him was sex and success. Poor Mummy, I know she's only bitchy because she's unhappy, but she shouldn't be so beastly about Daddy—who's really rather wonderful whenever he's not being bossy and pig-headed and old-fashioned and driving me round the bend." Then as I swung the car into the drive of my home she exclaimed: "Oh, what a *beautiful* house!" And I could hear her thinking: poor old flower-arrangement, poor old boot, missing out on all this, of course she wasn't sexy enough, bored him to tears, no idea how to play her cards, poor thing, very sad.

I was hoping we could avoid the Community but Rowena was lurking in the hall and I knew straight away that she disapproved of Rachel's skin-tight, burnt-orange sweater. I mumbled the necessary introductions and whisked Rachel upstairs. I could tell Rowena's disapproval then doubled, so acting on the principle that one might as well be hanged for a sheep as for a lamb I removed my glasses, grabbed Rachel as soon as we entered my sitting-room and allowed myself the luxury of a hot smooch. However, this was a bad idea as I soon began to lose sight of the Holy Grail, so after ten incinerating seconds I tore myself away with the comment: "Too bad we didn't come here just to romp in the hay."

"A major tragedy! But the funny thing is I can't quite work out why you're so more-ish. Those glasses make you look like an owl."

" 'The Owl and the Pussy-Cat went to sea in a beautiful pea-green boat...' " Replacing my glasses on my nose, I extracted the portable tape-recorder from my old toy-cupboard and inserted the batteries I had bought that morning in Starbridge. By the time I tested the new tape seconds later we were reciting Edward Lear's poem in unison.

" '... O lovely Pussy! O Pussy, my love, What a beautiful Pussy you are!' " our voices proclaimed fervently as I played back the tape.

"Okay," I said, pressing the rewind button and glancing at my watch. By this time it was eleven o'clock. "This is what we do: we go to the chapel; we set up this little toy underneath the altar which, as you'll see, is a rectangular table covered on all sides by a heavy embroidered cloth; then you'll sit under the table with the toy and turn it on when the conversation begins—we'll have the microphone at the edge of the cloth but it'll be invisible except at floor-level. My job will be to get Perry close to the altar for the big dénouement."

"Supposing he takes a peep under the cloth?"

"Why should he?"

"James Bond always checks to see if a room's bugged!"

"Perry's not James Bond—he's just a paper-shuffler at the FO, and he's long since written me off as a mere kid. He'll underestimate me."

"But what do I do if he tries to kill you?"

"Nothing. I'd knock him out. No old man over forty could hope to win a fight with a fit man of twenty-five."

"But if he's coming down here to kill you, wouldn't he have a gun?"

"No, much too dangerous—it could be traced to him. He might have a blunt instrument tucked into his waistband," I conceded, "but I'll be on the watch for that, and anyway he won't try to kill me immediately because he'll want to find out exactly what I know. My way of ultimately controlling the situation, of course, is to say that Lewis knows everything and that if I disappear he'll go straight to the police. Then I'm sure Perry will crack and confess everything—if he hasn't confessed everything already."

"*You're* the one who's James Bond!" exclaimed Rachel enthralled. "This is a James Bond book come to life!"

"Just what I was thinking! Okay, Pussy Galore, let's transfer to the chapel for the big climax . . ."

Insane. Criminally insane. Off we went, two overgrown children bouncing along to toss their lighted matches into the keg of dynamite, and never, *never once,* did it occur to me to say those saving words: I CAN BE WRONG.

6

WE REACHED the dell where the chapel stood glowing in the sunshine. Rachel voiced all the right words of admiration, and as she spoke I noticed with relief that the blinds on the windows of my father's cottage were drawn; I knew how important it was that he should be out of the way while I completed my James Bond mission.

I passed Rachel the tape-recorder and the microphone. "You go into the chapel and have a look around," I said. "I just want to run down the track to the boundary wall to make sure the door's unlocked. Since my father's unwell the Community may have left the door locked to make sure no one disturbs him."

"I thought he never saw visitors?"

"There are just a handful of people, like the Bishop, who are authorised to drop in at any time." Leaving her I jogged down the track to the wall, but the door opened as soon as I turned the handle. Without bothering to glance out into the main road I pushed the door shut again and jogged back to the chapel. The nearest entrance, when one approached from this direction, was at the back of the building where a door led into the vestry. Walking in I called out: "It's only me!" and moved out of the vestry into the chancel.

Those were the last carefree words I spoke that morning.

A second later I had stopped dead.

Rachel was standing white with terror by the altar, and facing her was Perry with a small black gun in his hand.

7

IT WAS strange how the chapel looked exactly as usual, clean and well-ordered despite my father's numerous Anglo-Catholic ornaments; the altar-cloth was carefully draped, with every fold in place, and the plain oak cross stood in polished splendour between the ornate silver candlesticks.

It was strange too how my mind fastened on an irrelevant fact as I stood paralysed by horror and fear. As I looked at Perry's gun I could think only of my father making that beautiful cross in a monastery long before I'd been born.

"Oh hullo, Nick," Perry was saying casually. "Sorry to commit the social sin of arriving early but I wanted to case the joint—and check for bugs, of course." He looked pityingly at the little tape-recorder, now abandoned on the altar-table.

I had by this time grasped that I could no longer keep reality at bay with thoughts about my father's cross, and I knew that whatever happened I had to keep Perry talking. I managed to say: "How could you possibly have got down from London so quickly?" and I found it all too easy to sound not only incredulous but appalled.

"I made one of my early starts. When I phoned you I was already in Starbridge." He beckoned me forward with his free hand but he appeared to be both unrushed and untroubled. "I hardly need add that as soon as you left last night I started to plan what to do."

Rachel, who had been standing transfixed by the table, gave a convulsive shudder, but I couldn't allow myself to be diverted by her. I knew I had to focus the whole weight of my psyche on Perry and try to hypnotise him into an error, but my psyche was in tatters, shattered and shredded by shock, and my powers, those "glamorous" powers which had got me into so much trouble in the past, had now deserted me so that I was defenceless.

"I think I should tell you straight away," I said as panic engulfed me, "that Lewis knows I'm meeting you here."

"I'd be very surprised if he did," said Perry mildly. "If he knew about the meeting he'd be here too—or alternatively, bearing in mind that he's older and wiser than you are, he'd have made damned sure you never kept the appointment."

"But he does know exactly what happened to Christian, and—"

"Lewis can have no proof. There'll only be the statements you've made to him, and that sort of hearsay evidence is inadmissible in a court of law."

"But if you kill me, Lewis will make sure the police suspect you—and once they find out you own a gun, they'll—"

"The gun's unregistered. I picked it up in Berlin. And who's to know you've been murdered? Plenty of scope for unmarked graves around this corner of the world."

"But if I disappear into the blue—"

"Kids disappear into the blue all the time these days, and everyone's always known you were a bit odd. If you disappear they'll just think that you and this quite extraordinarily attractive girl have dropped out and run off to California to smoke pot or found a new religion or, quite possibly, both. But why are we talking of murder? It seems a trifle wild and uncivilised."

"Well, since you're standing there with a gun—"

"Oh, that just seemed a sensible precaution to take, since I'm an elderly forty-one and you're an active twenty-five, but I assure you I don't make a habit of shooting people and it's possible that you don't in fact have any hard evidence that would inconvenience me. But I've got to be sure. Who or what put you onto the coal-cellar?"

"It was a psychic hunch."

"Oh, come on, Nick! You don't really expect me to believe that, do you?"

"But it really was a psychic hunch! You made me suspicious when you talked about the cold spot in the kitchen!"

"I never said the cold spot was in the kitchen."

"Oh God, no, that's right, you didn't—"

"Look, forget the psychic nonsense and tell me the truth. It was Dinkie who made you suspicious of the coal-cellar, wasn't it?"

By this time I couldn't think straight at all. "But why would Dinkie believe you'd buried Christian in the coal-cellar?"

"So you do know Christian's there! Thanks for confirming my worst suspicions!"

With horror I realised I had made a catastrophic error and that he now had no alternative but to kill me. Then a second later I realised that he had already been convinced I knew the truth and had planned to kill me from the start; his hint a moment ago that he might let me live had been no more than a manoeuvre to soften me up and gain the essential information more quickly. But what was the essential information? It seemed he thought Dinkie had provided me with some kind of hard evidence. Obviously he wanted to know whether he had to kill her too.

"Sorry, Perry, I'm sort of confused and I can't quite see where to begin. If you could give me a helping hand to start me off—"

"Okay, I suppose I must make allowances for shock. Christian, as I learnt for the first time last night, had double-crossed me with Dinkie. If he was carrying on with her right up to the time he died, he could have told her he was planning to reject me as ruthlessly as he'd rejected Martin. And if she'd told you that—"

"I'd see you had a motive for murder."

"Well done—that peculiar brain of yours is finally starting to unscramble itself!"

"And if I'd realised Christian had been planning to ditch you, I'd wonder if in fact the two of you ever got as far as Bosham that weekend—"

"Excellent! Keep going!"

"—and then I'd suspect that Christian ditched you soon after his arrival at Albany, with the result that you killed him at the flat."

"And of course once I'd killed him at Albany—"

"—you had the problem of getting rid of the body—"

"—and since I've never fancied being a surgeon I soon abandoned the idea of cutting the body into small pieces on the kitchen table. After that it was only a matter of time before I worked out that the one place where I could bury the body was the coal-cellar . . . But Nick, tell me this: if Dinkie knew Christian had no intention of going to Bosham with me that weekend, why on earth didn't she say so after I'd staged the drowning? Was it because she couldn't bear the thought of Marina knowing about her affair with him?"

"Oh no!" I said, saving Dinkie's life. "You've misread Dinkie's role altogether—you're forgetting how dumb she is. When she heard Christian had drowned she just assumed he'd changed his mind and decided to keep the sailing weekends going for a while after all. And on that last day of his life he didn't actually say he was going to ditch you. He just said he was getting fed up with the sailing, but of course as soon as I heard that I put two and two together and realised—"

"So he did see her on that final day!"

"Yes, but she knows nothing—there's no 'hard evidence' at all—"

"He saw her on that final day."

"Yes, but it doesn't matter, can't you see? And Perry, it was Lewis who worked out about the coal-cellar. If you kill me you'll still have to deal with him—"

But Perry was now moving beyond rational argument. "He swore to me he'd given her up—Christ, what a swine he was, how could he have turned into such a—"

I abandoned rational argument. Instinctively I knew I had to damp down that soaring emotional temperature. "He treated you very badly," I said, attempting to calm him with a lavish display of sympathy. "I can quite see how you must have hated him."

"Hated him?" said Perry blankly.

"Well, if you were lovers and he ditched you—"

"We were never lovers. But I loved him. I loved him right up to the end."

"Then why did you kill him?"

Perry said vaguely: "They shoot mad dogs, don't they?" Then he said: "It wasn't Christian I killed. Christian had gone away and this—this *creature* had taken his place. 'Kill me, Perry!' it said. 'Kill me so that I can escape into you—the ultimate identity switch!' Well, of course, I knew then he was incurably mad and that my therapy had been worse than useless, so I killed him. I grabbed the poker from the fire-irons by the kitchen range, and as he turned his back on me I . . . well, it was the only thing to do. He couldn't have gone on, could he? He'd become such a monster, destroying everyone who cared, that it was really a kindness to kill him. In fact looking back," said Perry, now speaking quickly, far more quickly than he normally spoke, "I regard the killing not as murder but as euthanasia." And as he stumbled very slightly over the T-H in that final word he smiled at me and I saw Christian shining behind his eyes.

"Just a minute, Perry," I said. "I think I'm beginning to understand this—"

"I'm afraid it doesn't matter whether you understand it or not, old chap, because now I'm going to have to kill you too—which is rather a shame because I always thought we got on so well, but there we are, terrible things happen in life, and if one wants to survive, one can't afford to be sentimental."

"But Perry, can you just tell me—"

"No, old chap, sorry, but it's only in books that the hero keeps the villain talking while he waits for the police to arrive on the final page."

"Okay," I said, and in my head my voice was shouting: FATHER, FATHER, SAVE ME! as I finally faced annihilation by the Dark. "Okay, I accept that you can't tell me any more, but you'll allow me a moment to pray, won't you, Perry, I know you're an atheist but after all you're a civilised man and you surely wouldn't want to be so uncivilised as to deprive a believer of the chance to put himself right with God before he dies. Just one moment, Perry—it'll only take a moment—just let me take off my cross so that I can hold it in my hand—"

I had a fleeting glimpse of Rachel, shivering from head to toe, eyes black with terror, but I couldn't allow myself to look at her for more than a second because I was risking everything on this one last desperate manoeuvre. We were now standing in a triangle based on the altar-table. Rachel was at one end, I was at the other and Perry was facing us with his back to the pews.

I took off the small cross which Lewis had lent me at Grantchester. I thrust the cross high in the air. And I drew breath to yell with all my strength: "IN THE NAME OF JESUS CHRIST—"

But then I froze.

I had seen the figure at the back of the chapel.

He had slipped in soundlessly through the main door, a tall man dressed formally in a clerical suit with a black stock—a very tall man he was, six foot three, taller than I was, taller than Christian, taller than that crucial branch on the peach-tree—*so tall* he was, that priest who had once been a monk at Grantchester long ago before I was born, and that priest, that monk, was of course my father—yes, *my father* had now appeared in response to my shout for help, but he was not the father who lived in 1968. The father before me now was the father who lived in my earliest memories, straight-backed, swift-moving, radiating authority, the father who had been Principal of the Theological College long ago in the 1940s.

"Father!" I shouted in panic, because he was so real—*so real he was*—that even though I could see he was not in my time I still feared he could die if Perry fired at him. "Father, get back—get out—he's got a gun!"

Perry knew at once that I could never have faked such terror. He swung round to face the intruder, and the moment he turned his back on us Rachel lunged forward, grabbed the wooden cross from the altar and slammed it with all her strength into Perry's skull.

8

I WAS blasted onto a different level of reality.

The demonic spirit screamed.

The cross shuddered in my hand.

"IN THE NAME OF JESUS CHRIST—" I recognised my voice but I was severed from it. My psyche had been dislocated, jolted from my body as the forces of darkness were battered by the forces of light.

"IN THE NAME OF JESUS CHRIST, CHRISTIAN AYSGARTH, DEPART AND REST WITH GOD—"

I knew I had to stop that demon-infested spirit moving sideways out of Perry into someone else, but I was so weak, so shattered, so disorientated that I hardly had the strength to draw breath.

"IN THE NAME OF JESUS CHRIST—"

And then it happened. The Light exploded, pouring down upon us, and I saw the Dark disintegrate. Black blood gushed from the corpse. The demon died. And Christian's spirit was finally set free.

"DEPART AND REST WITH GOD!" I shouted again with my last ounce of strength, and he was going, he was escaping at last, he was streaming forth on his journey towards all the freedom which had eluded him in life, and only the demon remained rotting in his place.

Then I found that the chapel was now a charnel-house, awash with blood and gore.

My psychic eye closed.

The stench of sulphur cut off the oxygen supply to my brain.

I lost consciousness.

9

WHEN I opened my eyes again—my physical eyes—I was back in my body and my face was inches from the embroidered altar-cloth at the point where it touched the floor. Somewhere near me a woman was sobbing. The sobs were punctuated with words distorted by shock and terror. They were: "I killed him, I killed him, I killed him . . ."

I failed to recognise the voice. I failed even to remember who she was. "The police . . . I'll have to go on trial and everything'll be ruined, my whole life, everything," she was weeping, and then enlightenment arrived because it was Lewis who answered tersely: "Over my dead body."

Memory assaulted me. I levered myself into a sitting position and looked at Perry, who was lying in a heap on the marble floor before the altar. The back of his head was bashed in and his brains had burst out. The wooden cross lay nearby in a bog of blood. Beyond the chapel's open door the birds were singing.

I looked around for my father but he was no longer there. Instead I saw Lewis and Rachel. They were halfway down the central aisle as if each had rushed to meet the other as soon as Lewis had entered the building. Rachel appeared to be glued to his chest as she shuddered and sobbed. He was clasping her tightly. As I hauled myself to my feet he glanced up the aisle and ordered: "Get her some water." His face was very pale.

I suddenly realised my little cross was lying at my feet. Retrieving it I put it back around my neck and stumbled to the vestry. My body felt as if it had been injected from top to toe with that drug dentists use to neutralise pain.

I was just filling the chalice—the only drinking vessel on the premises—when Lewis walked in. He strode over to me, removed the chalice from my hands and set it down in the sink with a thud. Then he grabbed my shoulders, spun me to face him and said in a voice which shook with rage: "You ignorant, arrogant, idiot of a boy, how *dare* you put my daughter in such danger, HOW DARE YOU!" And he hit me on the cheek with the open palm of his hand.

I reeled back against the wall but he only closed in again. "I tell you," he said, renewing his grip on my shoulders and punctuating his phrases by giving me a series of violent shakes, "I tell you specifically—in words of one syllable—that Palmer might want to kill you. I explain—in great detail—why he could be dangerous. And *still*— STILL—you prance along into his trap because you're so damned juvenile that you think you're a comic-strip hero who's discovered the secret of immortality! You ought to be flogged into a bloody heap!" And he slapped me again before giving me such a blow on the jaw that I lost my balance and crashed against the cupboard where the vestments were kept.

I hit the floor. Lewis picked up the chalice and walked out, but a second later he had walked back, the chalice still in his hands. "I'm sorry," he said. "That was unforgivable behaviour for a priest. I'm sorry." But then the rage roared through him again and he shouted: "No, damn it, I'm not sorry! Some people have to be beaten up before they can get it into their thick skulls that humility saves and arrogance kills!" And once more he stalked out, without looking back.

I lay on the floor. Then I managed to sit on the floor. I did try to get up but something seemed to have happened to my legs. Eventually I crawled on all fours to the sink and by gripping the rim I managed to lever myself to my feet. I stood there, breathing hard. Seconds later I was sick. I sluiced the mess away. Then I found my legs were working again so I crept back into the chancel.

Lewis and Rachel were now sitting in a pew halfway down the nave, and Rachel was sipping water from the chalice. Her tears had stopped but her eyes were swollen. Her make-up had streaked. She looked ill.

Lewis said curtly to me: "I've bolted the main door. Where's the key which locks the door of the vestry?"

"It should be in the lock."

"Turn it and come back here."

I did as I was told. Afterwards he motioned me to the pew in front of him and I sat down, turning to face them both. Rachel never looked at me. She was still taking little sips from the chalice. Lewis's right arm tightly encircled her body.

"You'd better read this," he said, passing me a folded sheet of paper from his pocket. "It'll stop you wasting energy wondering how I came to be here."

Unfolding the paper I read: "Dear Daddy, Nicholas and I are off to Starrington to meet the arch-villain Perry Palmer, who's just phoned to suggest a rendez-vous in the Manor's chapel! Don't worry, Nicholas has worked out there's nothing he can do to us. We're going to tape his confession. Back this afternoon sometime. Love, R."

The paper slipped from my fingers but I made no attempt to retrieve it. I was feeling very sick again.

"Now," said Lewis, "I need to know exactly what happened. Nicholas, I'll hear your story first."

I talked disjointedly for a while. The words only flowed rapidly when I recalled the horror at the end.

". . . and suddenly Perry spoke as Christian used to speak—he spoke in Christian's voice at that same quick pace with the very slight stutter—he tripped on the T-H of 'euthanasia'—and when I looked at him I saw Christian shining behind his eyes and I knew he was possessed, I knew the Devil had annexed Christian's soul at the end of his life and planted a demon in it, and this demonic spirit was now infesting Perry in revenge for the murder, and the demonic spirit wanted to destroy Rachel and me. So I took off my cross and held it high to exorcise the demon, but at that moment I saw my father had entered the chapel, my father as he'd been in the 1940s— which meant he wasn't dressed as a monk this time but as an ordinary priest—and I shouted: 'Get out! Get back!' because he was so real, you see, so real, and it was all one reality, there was no break, I wasn't in the past and seeing the past, he and I were both in the present, even though he was only in the present as his past self, and I thought he was in danger of being killed with us. Then when I shouted, Perry—who was Christian—the demonic Christian—spun round to face my father and Rachel grabbed the cross and swung it, though it's amazing that she had the strength because it's very heavy, but of course fear does give one abnormal strength—and she swung the cross and the moment he fell I knew I had to exorcise him before the demon could slip sideways into someone else, so I invoked the name of Jesus and commanded Christian's spirit to rest with God, and suddenly the demon died, it split wide open and all the black blood spewed out, and as Christian went to God at last I was overpowered by the stench of sulphur from the dead demon, and I passed out."

I stopped speaking. Several seconds passed. Then slowly, very slowly, I looked past Lewis's inscrutable face and saw Rachel's revolted expression. She whispered to her father: "He's gone mad."

"I'll sort him out later. Now darling, tell me if you can—but only if you want to—how it all seemed to you during those last moments."

But Rachel had no trouble speaking her mind. She said to him strongly: "It's rubbish to talk about possession. The only thing that changed was that Perry became dreadfully upset."

"Did you hear the change in his speech?"

"It's true he did begin to talk more quickly, and maybe he stammered slightly over 'euthanasia,' I can't remember, but there was certainly nothing weird shining in his eyes! They were just tears. He was grieving, that's all, and when he said he regarded Christian's death as euthanasia I thought he was going to break down. It was obvious he'd loved Christian very much—well, he was confessing to a *crime passionnel,* wasn't he? And that was tragic, of course it was, but there was nothing bizarre about it, and to suggest that Christian's soul had been annexed by the Devil and im-planted with a demon which had taken over Perry—well, I mean, it's so fantastic that no one rational—no one *normal*—could possibly believe it. That sort of thing doesn't happen in real life, and if you think it does, Nicholas, you should have your head examined. In fact maybe you should have your head examined right now because of course there was no man dressed in a clerical suit at the other end of the chapel, no demon splitting wide open, no black blood pouring out and quite definitely no reek of sulphur. All that happened was that I—I—I—"

"It's all right, my darling, there's no need to speak of that now. What did Nicholas do after you'd done what had to be done?"

"Bloody nothing! He didn't lift a finger to help me, he just bawled out some religious rigmarole and passed out. Wonderful! A real hero on a white horse! Thanks a lot, James Bond!" She started to sob again.

Lewis calmed her down. Then he said: "I'm not having my daughter standing trial for manslaughter just because a young man she barely knows used her to act out a fantasy. I'm going to detach you both from this disaster. I'm not going to let—" But he decided not to utter the name of his old adversary. "I'm not going to let the wrong side win," he said instead, and as he spoke I saw him not just as an exorcist vowing to outwit the Devil, but as the maverick priest willing to travel beyond the law in order to serve God as he thought fit.

"Now listen to me, both of you," I heard him say. "This is what we're going to do . . ."

10

"WE'RE going to remove the body," said Lewis, "and leave it in his car, which is hidden away under the trees opposite that door in the wall. Once the body's removed from the grounds of the Manor there'll be no direct connection with any of us."

I found myself saying: "How did you know the quick way to the chapel?"

"Luckily for you the village pub happens to be one of my favourite watering-holes, and the landlord told me long ago about the famous little chapel at Starrington Manor." He paused before adding: "My own car's parked near Perry's—or at least I assume that car under the trees belongs to Perry; we'll find out for sure when we try his key in the lock. But it doesn't matter if any witness reports later that the two cars were parked within yards of each other, because I can always say I'd never seen Perry's car before and therefore there was no way I could know it was his."

My brain was beginning to function normally again. "You want the police to assume he picked up a hitch-hiker who turned violent?"

"It's as good an explanation as any other."

"In that case, should we take his wallet to make it look like robbery?"

"No, we take nothing. If we take something, then we have the difficulty of getting rid of it. Let's keep this very simple and then there'll be less chance of anything going wrong—let's leave it to the police to work out why he was carrying an unregistered gun and driving in the Starrington area. As far as we're concerned we know nothing. You never spoke to him on the phone this morning, none of us saw him today, we had no idea he was planning to come down here."

"But what are we all doing at the Manor?"

"You'd invited Rachel to see your home and eventually you brought her here to show her the chapel. In response to another invitation of yours, I then presented myself to be introduced to your father. We'd arranged to meet at the chapel, so I left my car by the door in the wall. However, Father Darrow's turned out to be unwell so I'm not able to see him after all—or maybe I am; let's wait and see what happens, because what we've got to do now is to stick to the truth as closely as possible. Then there'll be less chance of making a mistake when we talk to the police."

"Did we meet Perry at Albany last night?"

"Certainly we did, as that porter on duty will remember. I'd decided to treat myself to a dinner in London and I invited you to join me. We asked Rachel to come too, of course, but she had a headache and preferred to stay at home—which suited us well, as we had spiritual matters to discuss over dinner. Arriving in Mayfair at cocktail time you suddenly remembered your friend Perry and we decided to drop in at Albany on the chance that he'd be at home. I was interested to meet him because I thought he might have been related to the Palmer who was at Starwater Abbey with me in the thirties."

"But why should you and I be such friends?"

"We're not. But when we met at Grantchester you realised I could be the spiritual director you were looking for, and I invited you to the vicarage so that we could further our acquaintance. Now," said Lewis, rising to his feet, "we'd better start clearing up the mess. Rachel darling, I want you to sit outside on the steps of the porch so that you can warn us if anyone approaches. Nicholas, is any member of the Community likely to turn up?"

I glanced at my watch. "No, it's almost lunch-time. They'll be up at the house."

"As your father's ill, mightn't someone come down to prepare him a meal?"

"Not in the middle of the day—although I suppose they might just want to check on him to see if—"

"Which way would they come?"

"For a quick visit they'd drive around to the door in the wall."

"Run down and lock it. And take Perry's keys so that you can make sure that car under the trees is his, but keep your wits about you and don't leave your fingerprints all over the place."

I somehow managed to extract Perry's keys from the pocket of his jacket without vomiting all over his brains. I have no memory of my journey to the door in the wall. Across the road outside I saw the black Bentley. One of the keys opened the driver's door, which I opened and shoved shut with my hand masked by a handkerchief. Seconds later I was locking the door in the wall.

When I reached the chapel I found that Rachel had retired outside and Lewis was using his vest to mop up the blood on the floor. He had found the bucket which was kept in the cupboard below the vestry's sink.

"We don't want to risk treading in this mess when we move the body," he said, "so I thought I should do at least a partial clean-up, but I'll finish off more thoroughly later. Are you wearing a vest?"

"Yes."

"Take it off and we'll wrap the head in it. We don't want blood dripping everywhere . . . Did the key open the car?"

"Yes." I began to unbutton my shirt.

The head was appallingly mutilated, and when Lewis wrapped it without flinching I realised he had dealt with dead bodies in the war. To my humiliation I began to feel nauseated again.

"We'll burn all our clothes later in the vicarage furnace," Lewis was saying. "The police forensic scientists are so clever that we can't take any risks." By that time he had secured the head. "All right, are you ready to move him?"

I had to say that I was.

"If you're going to be sick, do it now, in the vestry sink. We don't want you making a mess in the wrong place."

I went to the vestry sink but nothing came up. Everything had been vomited earlier.

"Okay, take his legs," said Lewis on my return, "and concentrate on keeping in step with me. Then we'll move more efficiently."

We set off, leaving the chapel through the vestry door, and somehow maintaining a steady pace down the track. The journey to the wall seemed endless. I was again abnormally conscious of the birds singing among the sunlit trees.

"Now for the tricky bit," said Lewis as we reached the door. "Put your end down and take a look outside to see what's going on."

I took a look. No one was there. The Bentley stood waiting for us on the other side of the road.

"We'd hear a car coming," said Lewis, "but let's hope no one bowls around the bend on a bike. Okay, now when I give the word we head for the car *at the same pace.* Got that? If we try to hurry, the odds are we'll get in a muddle."

A new phase of horror began. We got across the road but on the verge I stumbled and dropped one of the legs. As the body tilted the gun fell out of the jacket. Lewis muttered a string of obscenities.

"Sorry, Lewis, I—"

"Don't start apologising, just—"

I scooped up the gun, shoved it back in the pocket and retrieved the fallen leg.

"Oh God, my fingerprints—"

"I'll deal with them. Just get going, Nicholas, *get going—*"

We blundered on and seconds later reached the far side of the car. "At least we've now got some cover," said Lewis, and he had barely finished speaking when a van passed by. We ducked out of sight. As we straightened our backs I said: "Where are we putting him?"

"In the boot. Our mythical homicidal hitch-hiker would be anxious that the body should remain undiscovered for as long as possible."

"Isn't that what we want too?"

"Certainly. The more we obscure the exact time of death the more we distance ourselves from it." As he spoke he was unlocking the boot and raising the lid. We both looked around. The road was empty. There was no noise of approaching traffic. Once more we stooped over the corpse.

At that stage I would have succumbed to the dangerous impulse to hurry, but Lewis took his time. After the body had been stowed in the boot, he removed the gun from Perry's jacket, wiped off my fingerprints and re-marked the gun with Perry's prints before locking it in the glove compartment.

I said suddenly: "Why not wipe off Perry's prints to make it look as if the gun belonged to the hitch-hiker? It would destroy any theory that

Perry was a murderer on the loose and required killing in self-defence."

"I'm sure we should stick to the decision I made earlier to keep every-thing simple. The more we mess around the more likely we are to make a fatal mistake."

"Yes, but—"

"If the gun belonged to the hitch-hiker, why didn't he shoot Perry instead of bludgeoning him? And why should he leave the gun to be found by the police?"

I was silenced.

"I'm uneasy about that gun too," admitted Lewis after a pause, "but if Perry's job at the Foreign Office really was as hush-hush as everyone was so keen to believe, maybe the Special Branch will stop the police from asking too many awkward questions. Certainly no one will want any scandal. In fact it may be in everyone's best interests to cover up the murder." Handing me the vest which he had removed from the battered head he added: "Hold that for a moment."

I watched in silence as he wiped clean the surfaces he had touched. He even wiped the steering wheel and the hand-brake, neither of which he had touched at all.

"It's what the hitch-hiker would have done," he said when I questioned him. "I'll run through the story with you, but let's wait till we're safely back in the grounds." He locked the driver's door, locked the boot and shoved the keys up the exhaust pipe before taking one last look around. Then back we ran across the road to the wall. The relief, as I slammed and locked the door behind us, was so great that my legs felt unsteady again.

"Right—this is the script," said Lewis as we both slumped against the wall to recover, "and let's hope it seems moderately obvious to the police. Last night when we visited Albany we both thought Perry was tired and needed a break. When we left, I gave him my card and told him to look me up if ever he was in the Starbridge area visiting you, but at no time did Perry say he would take a break the very next day; certainly if you'd known he was to be visiting the Manor, you would have expected him to drive up to the front door just like any other visitor; as far as you were aware he had no knowledge of the door in the wall and there was no reason why he should have parked there. The presence of the Bentley under the trees is a complete mystery to you.

"With any luck the police will think: cheered by his visitors Perry feels much better the next morning and on an impulse heads into the country—to the Starbridge area which he knows so well from his visits to the Aysgarths. Acting on a further carefree impulse he decides to drop in at the Manor unannounced, but while he's still some miles from Starrington he picks up a hitch-hiker. Away they drive, but shortly afterwards the hitch-hiker's homicidal instincts get the better of him and he pulls out the blunt instrument which will be the murder weapon. He forces Perry to stop the car and get out. Then—"

"Why didn't Perry produce his gun?"

"No opportunity. The gun's locked up in the glove compartment."

"Oh, of course . . . Sorry, go on."

"Another theory would be that this was a sexual episode and Perry left the car voluntarily. Anyway, the result's the same: Perry's bludgeoned to death. The killer then stows the body in the boot—"

"Why not just leave the body where it was?"

"If he removes the body from the scene of the crime he removes it from any clues lying around on the ground—footprints, for example."

"Okay. So with the body in the boot he drives off—"

"—and decides to ditch the car at Starrington, a village with a mainline railway station ideal for a quick getaway. By one of those amazing coincidences which happen more often in life than in fiction, he dumps the car by the wall of the Starrington Manor estate; he figures that a Bentley will be less conspicuous tucked under the trees on the outskirts of the village than sitting in the station car park. Being mad but not mentally defective, he then takes care to wipe all his prints from the interior of the car before he and the Bentley part company."

"I'm almost beginning to believe in this hitch-hiker."

"So much the better." Moving forward again, he took the bloodstained vest from my hands and hid it under the nearest bush. Then he said: "After I've finished cleaning up with the other vest I'll come back here and put both vests in my car. They'll have to be wrapped up but fortunately I've got a rug in the back which can be burnt along with everything else."

We headed up the track. Rachel, who had been waiting for us at the side of the chapel, disappeared from sight again as she resumed her position on the front steps.

It was Lewis who completed the task of cleaning up. He said that no one who hadn't been in the services knew how to clean properly. All I had to do was to run back and forth to the vestry sink in order to change the water in the bucket. I had to do this several times.

The last thing he cleaned was the wooden cross.

"Put that back on the altar," he said, giving it to me, "and then double-check the altar-cloth to make sure there's no speck of blood on it. After that you can try and work out if there's anything we've forgotten."

"Where are you going?"

"To disinfect the bucket and put both vests in my car."

He disappeared. I checked the altar-cloth and looked around. As he re-entered the building I was stooping to retrieve Rachel's note from the floor.

"I'll burn that," he said as soon as he saw the folded paper, and reached for his cigarette lighter. Having flushed the ashes down the sink, he himself checked the chapel to make sure nothing had been overlooked, and it was only when he declared himself satisfied that I finally managed to say to him: "I'm very sorry for what I did. I know I deserved to be beaten up like that."

Lewis never hesitated. He said: "No," and sinking down on the nearest pew he began to fumble for a cigarette.

"No?" I said, so startled that I forgot my shame and stared at him.

"No. You didn't deserve to be beaten up and I'm the one who should be apologising. Of course the person I really wanted to beat up was myself."

I went on staring at him. "I don't understand."

"I was so involved with your problems that I was prepared to do anything to keep you under my supervision until the case was closed. I was even prepared to put my daughter at risk; I knew you were in an unstable state and I should never have left you alone with her." And when his cigarette was at last alight he managed to add: "Healing's a dangerous ministry. You only need to make one slip—one little ego-trip such as the one I made this morning when I put my longing to achieve a cure above my daughter's welfare—and then the Devil's on the loose. There's no room for pride and arrogance in the ministry of healing, Nicholas. You need humility, more humility and still more humility—and even then there's never enough humility for all you have to do."

I could only say: "I've learnt my lesson. I'll never forget."

"Neither of us will forget." He paused to inhale from his cigarette. Then he said: "I want to take Rachel up to the house now. When we talk to the police we'll say we took her back so that she could listen to your records while we talked to your father; she wasn't included in the invitation to meet your father, of course, because he sees so few visitors and certainly never meets more than one new person at a time."

"And why are we really taking Rachel back to the house?"

"We've got more work to do here—the exorcism—but now that the mess has been cleared up and the immediate danger has passed I'd rather she got right away from the chapel and waited for me in a comfortable place within calling distance of other people . . . Is there brandy at the house?"

"Yes."

"I think we could all do with some."

We went outside. Rachel stood up, hesitated, then hurtled into Lewis's arms again. Stroking her hair he said: "It's going to be all right. You never saw him, and now that you and I have finished our sightseeing tour of the chapel, I'm taking you back to the house so that you can relax with Nicholas's record collection while I meet Father Darrow as planned."

All she said was: "I don't want to listen to Nicholas's records."

"Then you can just wait quietly for us."

"I can lend you a book, if you like," I said, speaking directly to her for the first time since the catastrophe, but she just said: "No, thanks," and turned away.

We set off up the path which led out of the dell. None of us spoke. Beyond the edge of the woods the back lawn stretched to the house, but I made a detour around it because I had no wish for the members of the Community to see us from the windows of the dining-room and interrupt their lunch in order to meet Lewis. I felt unable to cope with the Community at that moment.

"I'll meet them later," said Lewis as I explained my reason for the detour. "But let's get Rachel settled first."

"Why do you need to meet them at all?"

"It would be useful to have people who could confirm that we brought Rachel back to the house. Any corroboration of our story would be helpful at this stage."

But in the end we didn't need the Community to bear witness to our return. Because of the detour we wound up in the drive at the front of the house, and just as we were crossing the gravel sweep towards the front door, a white Ford turned through the main gates.

"Who's that?" said Lewis sharply to me.

"No idea." I was just as alarmed as he was, and we all halted to stare at the approaching car.

Suddenly Rachel said: "It's Charley."

"Charley who?" I said, but even as I spoke I was recognising the driver. It was Charley Ashworth.

"Okay," said Lewis to us quickly. "I'll do the talking."

But he never got the chance. The car halted and out bounced Charley, bursting with energy. "I was just making a flying visit to Starbridge in order to see Dad during Holy Week," he announced, "and I suddenly thought: Nick Darrow! What a splendid opportunity for a lightning pastoral call! So here I am, cantering up your drive on my white horse, and lo and behold, what do I find? Rachel—wonderful to see you! And Father Hall—terrific! What a splendid surprise to bump into you both here—Raye, why didn't you tell me you were a friend of Nick's?"

"I'm not," said Rachel. "We barely know each other." She gave a muffled sob.

"Hey!" exclaimed Charley, instantly concerned. "Are you all right? I must say, you look a bit—"

"Spring's a bad time for allergies," said Lewis. "All that pollen."

"What a nuisance. Never mind, Raye, you still look gorgeous—I love those psychedelic trousers!"

Rachel suddenly said in a high voice: "Oh Charley, it's so wonderful to see you!" and the next moment she was stumbling into his arms which, I saw with shock, were only too ready to receive her.

Realising he had to abandon all talk of pollen, Lewis said: "Life's rather tricky for Rachel at the moment. Various unexpected problems," and Charley cried: "Poor little thing!" as if outraged by the malevolence of a fate which could saddle Rachel with even the smallest difficulty. "Never mind," he added swiftly to her, "let me carry you off instantly for a good stiff drink and a delicious lunch—you don't mind, do you, Nick, if I bear Rachel away on my white horse? Or—wait a minute, are the Halls arriving or leaving? I assumed that as you were all grouped around Nick's car he was about to give you a lift to the station, but perhaps—"

"Thank you very much, Charley," said Rachel. "Daddy's not ready to leave yet but I am. Goodbye, Daddy. Don't worry. I'll be all right now."

"Leave her entirely to me," said Charley masterfully to Lewis. "I'll look after her. Nick—sorry my lightning pastoral visit turned out to be no more than a quick flash, but of course one must always rescue a maiden in distress whenever she's thrust across one's path! I'll be in touch later. Come along, Raye." And having eased her into the passenger seat, he bounded back behind the wheel and drove off.

Rachel didn't look back.

She didn't even look back once.

I'd been traded in.

I I

I FELT as if an entire universe, blazing with light, had folded itself up and vanished down a black hole. I forgot Perry and the horror of the morning, shut it right out. I even forgot Lewis, motionless by my side. The present had been obliterated by that lost future. Sinking down on the step by the front door, I covered my face with my hands.

I found myself trying to take refuge in incredulity. I thought of Charley-the-Prig, that pathetic creature who had never made it with the girls, but that image, as I well knew from my visit to his vicarage, belonged to another era and now Charley-the-Prig had been succeeded by Charley-the-Superpriest. I remembered that band of attractive girls all eager to help him with his parish work, and suddenly as I remembered him radiating happiness in his vicarage I saw that *I* was the pathetic creature, not Charley; *I,* Nicholas Darrow, that ignorant twenty-five-year-old child who had thought he was making it with the girls but who had never once got beyond first base. No wonder I had stalked around flaunting my shoddy, shady, shabby "glamorous powers"! I had been disguising from myself just how immature and inadequate I really was.

I let my hands fall from my face and found that Lewis was sitting beside me on the step. All the bright colours of the garden looked incongruous. I felt I should be seeing a landscape of ice and ashes.

All I said in the end was: "How long's that been going on?"

"Not long. They met soon after I came to the diocese in 1965 when the Bishop very kindly invited us both to dinner, but Charley was shy with girls then and of course Rachel was very young. However last Christmas they met again, and since then they've been seeing something of each other. Charley's parish is less than an hour by train from London."

No wonder Charley had been able to describe the girl of his dreams to me so graphically. I should have realised the portrait had been more than a mere fantasy.

"I rather like him," Lewis was saying idly. "He's a little volatile, perhaps, but he's certainly got all those gregarious, outgoing qualities which Rachel admires so much. I'm sure he'll do very well in the Church."

After a moment I managed to say: "He's okay." Then I said: "Not quite my sort, but he's okay." And finally, ashamed by this lack of graciousness to a lifelong acquaintance who had always been kind to me, I succeeded in saying: "He's a good man, much better than I am, and he'll never see black blood gushing from a dead demon."

"No," said Lewis, "she'll feel quite safe there."

We sat and thought of Rachel feeling safe. Then Lewis said casually: "What would Rosalind say if you told her about the demon?"

"Nothing. But she'd hold my hand."

Lewis allowed several seconds to elapse before commenting in a neutral voice: "My wife hated and feared my psychic gift. I could never share it with her." He stood up. "Let's have that brandy I suggested earlier."

Having retrieved the brandy bottle from its home beneath the kitchen sink, I led Lewis upstairs to my sitting-room where he poured out two hefty measures. We had met no one. The members of the Community were still at lunch.

The thought of lunch prompted me to say worried to Lewis: "You must want something to eat."

"No, food can wait," said Lewis, acting out of character, and suddenly I sensed how keyed up he was, as if he stood on the brink of some very great occasion.

I said: "You want to meet my father."

"Yes."

"And it's not just because of me and my problems, is it? You want to see him because you've heard so much about him and because he was the only one of all those senior Fordite monks whom you never met back in the 1930s."

"Never mind what I want. The most important thing now is what you want, but do you know yet what it is? You could still be feeling too shocked and confused by the catastrophe to know your own mind."

But at once I said: "This morning's demonic mess nearly destroyed me. The next demonic mess *will* destroy me. I can't go on being this fake-person who's powerless before the Dark. I've got to—" I hesitated but then remembered a phrase he himself had used. "—I've got to give birth to myself by achieving a psychic separation from my father, but I still don't see how it can ever be done."

"Does a surgeon explain every single detail of an operating procedure to the patient beforehand?"

"No, but—"

"The big question isn't: how can it be done? But: do you have faith that you and your father can be healed?"

Only one answer was now possible. I thought of Lewis not only saving me from breakdown at Grantchester but saving me from ruin that morning in the chapel, and I knew then he could save me from annihilation when my father finally died.

"I won't be the one who heals you, of course," said Lewis, watching me. "I'll just be the channel."

But I believed now that he could be the channel. I believed now that he was being offered to me as a channel. I believed now that I was being called to life, the richest possible life, the life that would be uniquely my own.

I drank the remainder of my brandy. Then I set down my glass, stood up and said: "I'll take you to my father."

12

AS WE retraced our steps to the dell I said: "I'm worried in case my father doesn't trust you as I do and rejects the possibility of healing."

"Oh, I think you'll find he'll trust me," said Lewis.

"But you're so much younger than he is and he might not approve of you wearing casual clothes. He's very old-fashioned and thinks priests should always be in uniform unless they're on holiday."

"I think you'll find he won't even notice my clothes," said Lewis.

But I continued to worry. "Supposing he simply refuses to discuss me with a stranger?"

"What makes you think he isn't longing to talk about you with some-one who understands?"

"Yes, but he doesn't know you understand, and—" I stopped. We had reached the point on the path where we could look down on the chapel, and suddenly I found I could go no farther. The memories which I had wiped from my mind in order to dwell on my lost future with Rachel and my possible future with my father now surged back in a tidal wave of horror, and when I looked at the chapel I saw sacrilege instead of holiness and obscenity instead of beauty. Filth oozed from every clean pure architectural line.

I said: "He's killed my chapel." Then I wept. I wasn't even crying decently, privately, under an eiderdown, but I was so stricken that I no longer cared. Sinking to the ground I tucked myself close to the nearest tree-trunk and whispered: "Sorry, Lewis, sorry, got to stop, can't go on."

"It's the delayed shock." He knelt beside me. "But listen, Nicholas. I shall heal your chapel, and you'll be with me when I do it. We'll open wide the doors and we'll cast out the Dark and then every stone will be bathed in light again."

Some time passed. Lewis sat down cross-legged on the ground and lit a cigarette. Eventually I was able to say: "I'd like to base my ministry at the chapel one day. But how am I to hang on to this estate? Rising prices . . . taxation . . . the burden of a big house . . . the truth is it would be nothing but a millstone round my neck. Perhaps God polluted the chapel to signal that I'm to let go of it."

"It was the Devil who polluted the chapel, Nicholas, not God, and ours is a gospel of hope, not a creed of despair. Dream the impossible! Why shouldn't you? And stand by your chapel! Why not? I promise you we'll heave out the demon's carcase and mop up his black blood as efficiently as we wiped out all the evidence of Perry's murder."

A longing for rational analysis flickered in my mind and I realised I was getting better. Having wiped my eyes with my cuff I said tentatively: "About that demon . . ." But I was unsure how to go on.

"Yes, I was waiting for you to want to work that one out."

"And my father's appearance . . . Don't tell me I didn't see him, because I know very well that I did. He was present. He was there."

"Of course he was. So was the demon. And so, luxuriating in all the murder and mayhem, was the Devil. Or whatever you choose to call it in 1968."

"But according to Rachel—"

"You and Rachel told different stories," said Lewis, "but in fact you each told the truth. You each described a different facet of one underlying reality."

"You mean I saw with my psychic eye and Rachel saw with her physical eyes?"

"Exactly. Your extreme stress once more gave you access to a level of reality not normally accessible to the conscious mind, and that means what you saw was much harder to describe. It was easy for Rachel; she only had to use everyday language, but you were driven to use an archaic and largely discredited vocabulary to describe events which can't accurately be represented in words at all." He paused to let me digest this before adding: "Rachel was right, I think, to label Christian's murder a *crime passionnel.* It's interesting that she was able to pick out Perry's grief—the grief which, combined with guilt, had driven him mad. You only saw the madness itself—which you identified as possession. You see how the two of you picked out different aspects of the truth? He *was* grieving and he *was* mad. It's not a question of 'either/or.' It's a question of 'and.'"

"But if Perry and Christian were never lovers, how could it have been a *crime passionnel?* Or do you think Perry was lying when he said—"

"Why should he lie at that stage? And why should you think a *crime passionnel* can only arise from a consummated passion? In fact if they were never actually lovers then the murder becomes much easier to understand."

"Does it?"

"Well, consider the background for a moment. I suspect that the heavy emotional side-effects of the affair with Martin made Christian feel bisexuality was not a way of life he wanted to pursue and reinforced his conviction that the last thing he ever wanted from Perry was sex. Meanwhile Perry was thinking just the opposite: he was thinking that the Martin affair would lead Christian to rewrite the rules of their friendship. Since Christian was no fool and since no one knew Perry better than he did, I'm sure he realised what was going on in Perry's mind, just as I'm equally sure his instinct was then to back away—but he couldn't back away because he needed Perry for those escapist weekends. So as the weeks passed a very tense situation built up and eventually reached dangerous proportions."

"So you think that on that last Friday evening at Albany—"

"—there was an emotional explosion. My guess is that Perry's patience snapped and he declared his feelings, but of course Christian, when he finally had his back to the wall, was quite determined to turn him down."

Making an effort to recall the horrific dialogue in the chapel, I said: "Perry did talk of a rejection."

"So you said earlier when you were telling me what happened. He thought, didn't he, that Christian had told Dinkie he was planning to reject Perry just as he'd rejected Martin."

"And once Perry had been rejected—"

"Murder was on the cards. If I read Perry correctly, it was the huge frustration in addition to the agony of rejection which finally drove him right out of his mind. Someone as self-controlled as he was wouldn't go over the edge unless he was experiencing provocation on a grand scale."

"What surprises me," I said, "is that Christian did reject Perry as brutally as he'd rejected Martin. You'd think that as they were such old friends Christian would have tried to let him down lightly."

"Maybe he did. Remember, we've only heard Perry's side of the story. Christian may well have tried to reject him as kindly as possible, but unfortunately by that time there was no kind way of handing out the rejection."

"But if Christian was mad, why should he have bothered to be kind?"

"We don't actually know he was mad."

"But what about Christian saying at the end: 'Kill me so that I can escape into you—the ultimate identity switch!' Surely that was the demon talking—and surely that implies Christian was raving?"

"Well, yes," said Lewis. "Possibly. But if you make a big effort to imagine this scene in a way that allows Christian to act in character, don't you think it's more likely that he was trying to laugh the whole thing off as a joke? There's Perry saying: 'I'm going to kill you,' but naturally Christian doesn't believe him. Dear old Perry, his friend for over twenty years! At the same time he can see Perry's in a most embarrassing emotional state and needs to be calmed down, so instinctively Christian resorts to humour to defuse the situation. 'Kill me so I can escape into you!' he jokes. 'The ultimate identity switch!' But unfortunately by that time Perry's lost his sense of humour and interprets the joke as the mockery of a lunatic."

This explanation struck me as being impressively plausible but I felt more confused than ever by the issue of Christian's sanity. "Even if you write off that final raving as an exercise in misguided wit," I said, "do you really believe Christian could still have been sane?"

"Certainly—although I agree he was profoundly disturbed. I also concede he was probably on the road to a complete mental collapse, but it seems clear that this particular journey was uncompleted when he died. After all, he was still functioning, still going out and about, still bedding Dinkie and enjoying his sailing."

"So when Perry described Christian as a mad dog—"

"Oh, that was all projection, of course. It was actually Perry who broke down, Perry who ceased to function normally, Perry who swung so far out of control that he committed murder. What Perry was doing in his confession this morning was projecting his own madness onto his victim."

"So he was the one who was possessed by the Devil—or by a demon implanted by the Devil. But if Christian was sane, a victim, and not an evil man infested by a demonic spirit . . ." I stopped, unable to articulate the problem.

"You're confused because if Christian was a sane victim you couldn't have seen his demonic spirit shining behind Perry's eyes—and yet you know that you did. But let's give the old-fashioned picture-language another rest and try a more flexible approach to this very complex truth.

We can still say that Perry was possessed," said Lewis, "but we'll now say he was possessed by his grief, his guilt, his shame and his horror that he had killed the friend he loved. And we can still say that Perry was possessed by Christian's demon—except that we might now follow Jung and call it the shadow side of Christian. This dark side—the demonic aspect—was in fact embedded at the centre of all those destructive emotions, with the result that when the emotions took over Perry's mind, the dark side of Christian was there at the heart of the take-over, shining in Perry's eyes and echoing in Perry's speech."

"So Christian could have been a sane victim and yet still have had his dark side—"

"—just as we all do, yes. Again, it's not a question of 'either/or' but a question of 'and.' "

"So when I saw Christian shining behind Perry's eyes and heard Christian in Perry's speech, I wasn't hallucinating?"

"Certainly not. What you were doing was giving yourself a psychic interpretation of reality. The shining eyes and the stutter were real events; Rachel's our witness for the eyes, and I'm quite prepared to believe you heard the stutter. But then what happened was that your psychic eye saw much further than your physical eyes and interpreted these events as sinister markers which indicated the climax of the scene was at hand. By seeing the shadow side of Christian—the demonic presence—you knew Perry's madness was about to erupt again and this advance warning gave you the inspiration to produce your last defence: exorcism."

"But it wasn't much of an exorcism, was it?" I said with regret. "I should have named the demons in order to cast them out—the demon of guilt, the demon of shame, the demon of grief, and so on. I shouldn't just have named Christian and ordered him to rest in peace with God."

"My dear Nicholas, you were hardly in a position to conduct a leisurely classical exorcism! You needed one name which encapsulated the whole demonic force which was occupying Perry's dying mind and you found it. What happened then, as you ordered Christian to be at peace with God, was that the dark side was destroyed and the bright side went home. In my opinion that was a highly successful exorcism—in fact a triumph."

I was amazed. "Are you sure?"

Lewis smiled and said: "The acid test is whether it had a saving effect on you, and obviously it did: you're not now walking around convinced you're possessed by either Christian or Perry."

"Oh, I see. Or do I? Hang on, wait a minute, are you saying—" I hesitated.

Lewis smiled again. "It was real," he said. "It happened. It worked. You called on the greatest exorcist of all time and aligned yourself with his power. On one level of reality Rachel was given the chance to strike the physical blow, and on another level of reality you were given the chance to strike the spiritual blow. Rachel saw Perry die and you saw the demon split apart in a shower of black blood, but what you both saw with your different eyes was the Dark receding before the Light."

"Rachel will never believe I saw what I saw."

"No, but try to forgive her. Remember that her blindness is God's gift to her, just as your sight is God's gift to you." He stubbed out his cigarette and carefully buried the butt. "How are you feeling now?"

"Better." As I stood up I said: "I'm glad I can think of Christian not as a crazy bastard but as a tormented man searching for truth. But I'm sorry he died before he could begin his journey to the centre, sorry he spent his life going round and round on the edge of the circle."

"I'm afraid his case is far from uncommon. So many people fail to realise that the greatest journey one can ever take is the journey to the very centre of one's being."

We fell silent, but in the centre of my own being the immanent God, who had designed the blueprint of my true self and who longed for me to become the man he had created me to be, began to exert a strong, ardent pressure on my psyche.

Without another word I stepped forward along the path which led to my father.

I 3

"YOU go in first to prepare him," said Lewis as we reached the cottage. "I'll wait here."

I knocked on the door and opened it a few inches. "Father?"

"Nicholas!" He sounded faint with relief.

Leaving the door ajar I went in. He was fully dressed, a fact which surprised me, and lying on his bed. Several pillows propped him up high enough to make reading comfortable but the book he had selected was lying face down at his side. I recognised his favourite copy of *The Cloud of Unknowing*.

I took his bandaged hands in mine and sat down on the edge of the bed, but before I could ask him how he was he said in a trembling voice: "You've been in such danger."

"Yes, but that's over now."

He closed his eyes for a moment as if he was too relieved to speak. At last he said: "I'm so tired. Keeping you safe takes so much energy, and what will happen when I'm no longer here to look after you?"

"That's what I've come to talk to you about. Father, it's going to be all right. I've finally found the priest who can help me. He—"

"Wait." My father was staring across the room at the open door, and as I glanced over my shoulder I saw that Lewis's shadow had fallen across the threshold.

My father whispered to me: "Who is it? Who's there?"

"It's this priest. I think Uncle Charles may have mentioned him to you. He runs a healing centre at St. Paul's in Starbridge, but you mustn't let that prejudice you against him."

Lewis, hearing his cue, gently opened the door wider and stepped into the room.

My father gazed at him. Lewis paused. Then suddenly my father's whole expression changed. Utter relief mingled with awe-struck excitement as he sat bolt upright on his bed, but all he said in wonder was:

"So you finally came."

XV

I

LEWIS appeared riveted to the floor. I had never before seen him at a loss for words, and to my amazement I realised he was shy. But then my father was so distinguished, and Lewis was, after all, forty years his junior.

"I've been waiting for you," said my father to him. "You've been close now for some time, I think."

"I've just told you, Father," I said. (How one has to repeat oneself to the old!) "He works in Starbridge." And to Lewis I added in explanation of my father's mysterious statement: "He's been praying for years that I'd find a priest who could help me."

But my father wasn't listening. "We'll sit at the table," he said to Lewis. "Nicholas, help me get up."

"Please," said Lewis, finally finding his tongue and moving forward awkwardly, "there's no need." But my father waved these words aside. "Important guests must be received in style!" he said smiling. He was getting younger by the second. I barely had to help him walk to the table.

"Let me introduce you both," I said. "Father, this is Lewis Hall. Lewis—"

"Get the folding chair out of the cupboard, Nicholas," said my father, ignoring the introduction, "and shut the door. There's a draught."

Old people can be very autocratic sometimes. With resignation I closed the door, produced the folding chair and took it to the table, where my father and Lewis were already sitting opposite each other. Since my father normally only received one visitor at a time the folding chair was seldom used.

I sat down. Whitby appeared fleetingly around my ankles but was unable to resist the lure of my father's lap.

"You remember the cat, of course," said my father to Lewis.

My blood ran cold. My father did occasionally get confused about the past, but such confusion had always fallen a long way short of senility. I wondered if his extreme exhaustion had affected his brain, and the thought was unbearable. If Lewis should find himself confronted not by the heroic figure of Fordite legend but by a senile old man . . . I sat rigid with dread on my chair.

But Lewis seemed untroubled. Reaching into his memory of our recent conversations he said easily to my father: "That's Whitby, isn't it?" and the next moment my father was beaming from ear to ear.

"So you even remember the name!" he said delighted. "I wasn't sure whether you would. But of course this isn't the original Whitby, the house-cat up at Ruydale. We're not in that time now . . . Forgive me, that sounds a trifle odd, I know it does, but for me past and present seem so fluid that occasionally I have trouble remembering which time I'm in. But you're here, aren't you, Father, you're in the present, and you've come to look after Nicholas at last."

By this time I was in agony. "Father," I said, so embarrassed I could hardly speak, "I'm afraid you're a little confused. This is *Lewis Hall*. He—"

"It's all right, Nicholas," said Lewis suddenly. "I understand." And to my father he added: "The walls of time are very thin sometimes, aren't they?"

"As paper," said my father, setting Whitby down on the floor. "That's why I was so sure that one day you'd tear them apart. Father, I'm so worried about Nicholas—I can't tell you how worried I've been about him—"

"I know." Reaching across the table, he turned my father's bandaged hands upwards and laid his fingers across the damaged palms.

There was a long, long silence.

Eventually my father whispered: "You understand, don't you?" and Lewis said: "Of course."

My father sighed, closing his eyes briefly in relief, and I felt the tension begin to seep out of him.

"I told you about the eczema, didn't I?" I felt compelled to say to Lewis. "If you can now convince him to see a doctor and get the right ointment—"

"Oh, do be quiet, Nicholas!" said my father irritably. "It's got nothing to do with eczema."

I stared at him. "But you always said—"

"Well, I had to say something, didn't I? I had to explain the need for bandages." He turned back to Lewis. "Do you need to see the wounds?"

"No, the bandages are no barrier to the healing."

"What wounds?" I demanded, my scalp prickling with fright. I could remember reading about self-mutilation during one of my bouts of psychiatric research.

"It's all right, Nicholas," said Lewis again, and added to my father: "Do you regard the wounds as a gift from God?"

"No," said my father without hesitation. "It was a mere reflection by my body of what was going on in my mind."

"The reflection of very powerful psychic activity?"

"I knew you'd understand," said my father, and as he spoke I saw his hands were now fully relaxed as they lay limply beneath Lewis's fingers. "I knew you would."

"Tell me how it happened."

My father said very willingly, as if he could hardly wait to confide in someone who would display neither revulsion nor incredulity nor—worst of all—hysterical wonder: "I knew that only Our Lord could keep Nicholas safe. I knew that only by holding Nicholas and Our Lord constantly together in my mind could I ensure my son's survival. For hours and hours I'd pray by focusing my entire psyche on the crucifix as I begged Our Lord to protect Nicholas . . . and of course it was a very great strain on my body as my mind reverberated day and night with images of the crucifixion. I was hardly surprised in the end when the blood started to well up in the palms of my hands and burst through the skin. The wounds don't bleed all the time, I hasten to add, but the marks of the nails go right through the palms—I can hold up my hands and see the light through the membranes . . . Father, say something to that boy, say something before he passes out—"

"Your father's been suffering from a rare but well-documented phenomenon, Nicholas," said Lewis crisply. "In some past cases the stigmata have been regarded as a gift from God and indicative of great holiness: St. Francis is the most famous example. But your father's being very honest and saying that in his case the manifestation was caused not by God but by his own psyche, straining to accomplish such a difficult form of prayer."

"It's wonderful how well you understand!" said my father simply, and as he relaxed still further he added: "What a healer you are, Father! I see you haven't lost your touch."

"My touch at present is just easing the symptoms, as I'm sure you realise. The real cure will only take place when you no longer have to endure this crippling anxiety about Nicholas."

"But you'll cure that, won't you, Father? You know that despite all our difficulties I always had absolute faith in you when it came to healing. Do you remember—"

"Father," I said in a loud voice, "perhaps we should take a break now and resume this conversation later when you're better. Perhaps you should lie down and rest again. Perhaps—"

"Take no notice of him," said my father to Lewis. "He's still such a child that he doesn't understand anything and no matter how hard I try to explain he doesn't listen because he thinks he knows everything already. Oh, what a relief it is to open my heart at last to someone who'll understand the situation in all its many dimensions—and particularly the psychic dimension, which is so baffling and so apparently intractable. None of my remaining friends—and I'm thinking in particular of Charles Ashworth, who's so very kind to me—none of them can grasp the scope of this problem and help me to solve it."

"It's been very hard for both you and Nicholas."

"Poor Nicholas," said my father, "he's such a good boy at heart, and if he's gone wrong, it's all my fault. I've tried to bring him up properly, but I'm so old and God never designed me to be a parent and I've made such a mess of everything."

"Oh, stop talking such rubbish!" I exclaimed horrified, and swung round on Lewis. "I can't have this," I announced. "He's getting upset. The conversation must end at once."

"Oh, I think not, Nicholas," said Lewis. "I think this is where the conversation really begins."

2

"WHAT'S wrong with speaking the truth?" said my father truculently to me. "Why aren't I allowed to say I've made an awful hash of bringing you up, almost as bad as the hash I made of bringing up Martin and Ruth?"

"Because it's not true! You're perfect, the best father in the world, and I absolutely forbid you to get upset like this!" I turned on Lewis again. "He's not to be upset," I said fiercely. "It's very bad for him, very dangerous. *I refuse to let him be upset.*"

"But Nicholas," said Lewis, "can't you see? It's the lie that's upsetting him, the lie that he's perfect, the lie that he's satisfied with the way things are, the lie that he's well and happy because you've chosen to be his replica—"

"REPLICA!" cried my father. "Oh, don't mention that word to me! I hate the very sound of it!"

Instantly I dredged up my most soothing voice. "I know you do, Father, I know you do. Don't take any notice of him, don't let yourself be upset—"

"*Be* upset!" said Lewis to my father. "Be very, very upset! Go on— you've got the right, you've earned it after suffering in silence for so long!"

"Shut up!" I shouted in panic to Lewis. "He doesn't talk about anything upsetting, he never does, never—"

"Then now's your chance!" said Lewis to my father. "Talk about what's upsetting you—shout it from the rooftops! Yell out that truth that'll set you free!"

"You see?" said my father to me. "He understands."

"But Father—"

"I want to talk, Nicholas."

"No, you can't—you mustn't—"

"But I shall. In fact if I can't talk now about how upset and unhappy I am," said my father, somehow managing to inject a shred of humour into such a desperate situation, "I swear I shall burst a blood vessel and die in a fit of pique."

I was finally rendered speechless with horror.

3

"*I SEE* Nicholas has told you all about this replica business," said my father confidentially to Lewis. "How appalled you must have been! What a monster of pride and selfishness you must have thought me, demanding that my son should be a mere replica of myself! But Father, the situation's far more complex than you might imagine, and in fact it's so complex that I hardly know now where to begin in my attempt to describe it. I suppose I must start with my wife's death when Nicholas was fourteen. After she died I felt my life was so diminished, so damaged, that I hardly knew how to go on. Of course now I can see I was merely suffering from an acute form of bereavement, but at the time I was in darkness and Nicholas was my only ray of light. It was then that I began to dwell again on a vision which I had had well over a year before he was born: I'd seen him in the garden of the Manor when he was three or four years old. There he was, looking just as I'd looked at that age, and when I saw him I thought God was promising me a replica to compensate me for . . . well, I'd had a tough time since leaving the Order and at that moment I felt very estranged from both my children, and . . . dear me, how spiritually immature this sounds, but I thought I could do with a little present from God to cheer me up. But Francis Ingram, who was by then my confessor, always said the vision was a delusion and I came to accept he was right.

"But in 1946 that vision was actually replayed in reality, and I started to wonder about it all over again. 'All this proves,' said Francis, 'is that your excessively peculiar brain occasionally glimpses the future. It doesn't prove the vision came from God.' And of course I saw he was right. We also discussed (not for the first time) how very wrong it was for fathers to expect their sons to be replicas. 'Never tell Nicholas about this vision,' said Francis. 'It might give him all manner of false ideas about who he's supposed to be.' You'd be surprised, I think, Father, by how able Francis proved as my spiritual director—that worldly scepticism combined with the shrewd common sense certainly stripped down my psychic illusions and kept me on the rails . . . If only Francis had lived a little longer! But he died before Anne, back in the fifties.

"Well, I made up my mind never to tell Nicholas about the vision, but one day when I was so unbalanced by my bereavement—one day when Nicholas was being such a comfort to me—one day when I was quite overpowered by the need to cheer myself up—"

"You told him."

"Yes. Of course I shouldn't have done it—I knew I shouldn't have done it—but I saw him there, just like me, and I remembered my vision, and I thought: how I'd love to share it with him! And the next moment I was thinking: how wonderful it would be if he could live my life for me all over again but without making my mistakes! Guilt played a large part in my bereavement, I'm afraid, and I see now I had a great psychological need to redeem my errors by rewriting my life, reshaping it, editing out all the pain and mess and unhappiness, and offering the revised product to God with the message: 'I got so much wrong the first time, but at least, thanks to you giving me a replica, I'll get everything right now.' Absurd, wasn't it? Absurd and disgraceful. All I can say in my defence is that I was very sick then, very depressed. Anyway, I told Nicholas about the vision and I couldn't help getting excited when I spoke about it, and of course as soon as he saw that the idea of a replica cheered me up and gave me a much-needed interest in life—"

"—he realised what he had to do. When did you eventually come to your senses?"

"About a year after Anne died. By that time I'd organised the Community to take care of the house and grounds, and my cottage here had been built. I hardly need add that as soon as I was on my own in absolute silence with no distractions I was able to realign my mind with God and see clearly just how far I'd gone astray."

"And then I'm sure you tried to put things right."

"Yes, but by then it was too late! I said very firmly to Nicholas on several occasions: 'I don't want you to be my replica. I want you to be your true self,' but he didn't believe me. 'Yes, yes!' he would say. 'Don't worry about it—don't get upset!'—and he went right on trying to be my replica. But I tried so hard to communicate the truth to him, Father! I explained all about the personality and the concept of the self—how clever it was of Carl Gustav Jung to put those ancient religious truths into modern scientific language!—and finally I said: 'God's given you a unique blueprint which you have to uncover and fulfill.' But all he said was: 'Yes, but don't worry, it's identical to yours, so I'll be following in your footsteps and living your life for you all over again.' He was deaf to all reason, Father, utterly irrational! 'Nicholas,' I said, 'you can't be identical to me. It's biologically impossible.' And do you know what he said? He said: 'The vision was God's assurance that He intended to override the laws of biology. No need for you to get worried or upset, no need at all.' And then, Father, *then*—oh, I hardly know how to find the words to make such a terrible confession, but—"

"You began to believe him."

"Yes. Well . . . no. I mean, half of me knew I mustn't believe him, but the other half . . . oh, what shameful ambivalence! I must have started sending out confused signals to him again, but I was in such a muddle, Father, that I couldn't work out where the truth lay. In fact I'm still in a muddle. Is it possible, do you think, that Nicholas has more spiritual insight on this point than I do and that he really is my replica after all?"

"I think it's more likely that Nicholas's behaviour stems not from spiritual insight but from psychological difficulties. But there's one thing I do know for sure: in 1942, when he was born, it was scientifically impossible to produce a clone of a human being. In fact I believe it's still impossible. So that means we must relegate all ideas about replicas to the pages of science fiction."

"But if the vision was a sign from God that He intended to override the laws of biology—"

"Why on earth should He? What's so special about you that you have to be exactly reproduced?"

"Lewis!" I shouted in fury, but my father was much too interested in these questions to pay me any attention.

"You're absolutely right," he said to Lewis. "There's no reason why I have to be exactly reproduced, and only sheer pride and arrogance could have made me entertain the idea in the first place. But nevertheless, if God sent the vision—"

"I thought you agreed with Francis that He didn't? With all due respect, I think you've allowed yourself to become so mesmerised by this vision of yours that you've been seduced into building psychic castles in the air."

"You believe Francis's view of the vision was right?"

"To be honest, I have to say that I do. All the vision proves is that you're capable of an extraordinary degree of clairvoyance—and let me go further than Francis could when he was discussing the vision with you all those years ago; let me say that in my opinion it's now patently obvious that the vision couldn't have come from God."

I said sharply: "You can't be sure of that!" but even as I spoke my father was saying: "Go on."

"The gifts of the Spirit," said Lewis, repeating the famous Christian maxim, "can be recognised by their fruits, but isn't it obvious that the fruits of this vision have been disastrous? The vision wrapped you in the sentimental delusion that a replica of yourself was possible, pampered your ego by encouraging you to believe you were special enough for God to override the laws of science on your behalf, and finally laid the foundations for a lot of trouble between you and Nicholas. I'd forget that vision, if I were you. Take it firmly between your thumb and forefinger and drop it in the nearest psychic wastepaper-basket. Then your mind will at last be sufficiently uncluttered to see Nicholas as he truly is."

"I can't tell you how utterly I disapprove of that advice!" I said outraged. "My father needs this vision, it's one of his favourites, he loves it, it's cheered him up so often, given him strength and hope when he's upset—and *I won't have my father deprived of a source of strength and hope when he's upset!*"

"You see?" said my father to Lewis. "You see how he's quite beyond rational argument when I'm under discussion?"

"You continue to believe your vision was from God, Father!" I said strongly, overriding this comment. "Don't let yourself be upset by any talk of psychic wastepaper-baskets!"

"I want to be upset!" bawled my father. Back he turned again to Lewis. "Father, what do I do?" he said in despair. "How can I stop him clinging to this notion—which I now see is utterly false—that the vision was from God and that he has to be my replica?"

"Try talking to him of his mother," said Lewis.

4

MY FATHER'S eyes filled instantly with tears.

"Right—the conversation's now closed," I said, rising to my feet. "It's too much for him, he's too old, he can't cope."

"*You're* the one who can't cope!" cried my father. "You cut me off whenever I try to speak of her!"

"That's because you get so upset."

"No, *you're* the one who gets so upset, Nicholas!"

"I only get upset because you get upset. After she died you said: 'It hurts even to mention her name.'"

"Yes, but—"

"I had to stop you getting upset."

"If you mention that word 'upset' one more time," said my father in a frenzy, "I swear I'll grab that vase of daffodils on the mantelshelf and smash it against the wall!"

"Well done!" said Lewis admiringly. "Excellent! That's a tremendous step forward!"

"Shut up!" I yelled.

"What I just can't understand," said my father, much encouraged, to Lewis, "is why he's got this malignant *idée fixe* that I must never be upset."

Immediately Lewis turned to me. "Are you ready, Nicholas? Now it's your turn to shout the truth from the rooftops, your turn to—"

"I can't."

"Why not?" demanded my father.

"He thinks you'll get too U-P-S-E-T," said Lewis, "and what'll happen, Nicholas, if your father gets too U-P-S-E-T?"

"He'll die."

"Nonsense," said my father. "Why should I?"

"You nearly did after Mum died. You wanted to. If you'd got any more upset you would have done."

"But I gave you my word I'd never take my own life!"

"Yes, but you were so upset you could have died without meaning to. You were terrible when you were upset. Terrible."

"You were frightened when he got upset, weren't you, Nicholas?" said Lewis. "He frightened you very, very much, didn't he?"

"No, no," said my father aghast, "that can't be right—"

"Of course it's not right," I said. "It wasn't your fault." And then before I could stop myself I said: "It was hers."

"*Hers?* Your mother's? But—"

My voice said: "She wrecked everything, dying like that. She wrecked our home, she wrecked our family life, she changed you into a recluse. And once you wanted to be a recluse you rejected me."

"*Rejected you?* Oh but Nicholas, that's not true! You know it's not true!"

"OH YES IT IS!" I yelled. By this time I was almost gasping with emotion, but I managed to say: "You rejected me, you went off on your own, you withdrew here to this cottage and abandoned me with that bloody Community—"

"But Nicholas, I was so bereaved, so upset—"

"Yes," I shouted, "YOU WERE UPSET! And if there was one lesson I learnt from that terrible time it was that I had to make sure you were never, never upset again!"

"But I got better—I did get better—"

"I made you get better," I said. "I willed it. I couldn't have let you die. Mum's death destroyed my home, but your death would have destroyed *me,* I knew that, I knew it as surely as I saw you being eaten away by the Dark. But I rolled the Dark back, I gave you hope again, I gave you something to look forward to, I made you believe your most cherished dream could come true—"

"Dear God!" whispered my father, and covered his face with his hands.

"It was no good being *me* any more," I said. *"Me* just reminded you of *her,* and that made you upset. We had to cut her right out. No more *her.* And no more *me.* Just you and the replica. Just you and the dream that was going to keep you alive. And it did keep you alive, didn't it? The replica won. So long as I was the replica we could live happily ever after—although, of course, I always had to take great care never to let you get upset."

My father let his shaking hands fall. "Father, help us," he begged Lewis. "Tell him—explain—make everything come right—"

"But you can do that," said Lewis. "No need for me to interfere. Just tell him about his mother."

"I don't want her name mentioned," I said. "I blame her entirely for this mess."

"Blame me," said my father, "but don't blame Anne. She was so proud of you, Nicholas—she loved you so much—"

"I can't blame you because you'll get upset."

"Help us!" my father begged Lewis again. "Please—we're locked up in this terrible prison and we've got to have someone to rescue us—"

"Nicholas is going to rescue you both," said Lewis. "He's going to proclaim the password which will open the prison gates."

"What password?" said my father, but he knew.

"There's no password," I said, but there was.

Silence fell.

"She needs to come back, you see," said Lewis, addressing my father but talking principally, as I well knew, to me. "When she died everything went out of alignment. It wasn't your fault. Her death devastated you to such an extent that you became temporarily disabled, unable to focus on your son. His solution was to heal you by evicting her from that space which she occupied between the two of you, but of course he was very young and he didn't know how to heal properly. What we have to do now is to clear that space, the psychic space she occupied during her lifetime, and welcome back her memory into it."

"But if Nicholas insists on blaming her for everything, how can he ever welcome her back?"

"But do you really insist on blaming her, Nicholas, for the fact that your father found his bereavement so disabling?"

I said uncertainly: "Someone's got to be to blame." But I knew no one was, not even the God who was still creating his world, still suffering with his creation, still working ceaselessly to redeem the darkness with light. And as the thought of Christ flickered through my mind—that symbol of light triumphing over darkness, of life over death, of hope over despair—I said vaguely: "It seemed important to blame someone," and I realised I was no longer using the present tense but the past. "I didn't know how else to live with my anger," I said. "I was so angry that my world had been smashed up and I had to be a replica."

"It was a moment of great darkness," said Lewis, "and it lasted a long time. But now the darkness is under such pressure that one word—the password—will ensure its end."

I nodded. Then I said to him: "The word's 'forgive,' isn't it?"

And as I spoke I saw the prison gates swing wide.

5

LEWIS said briskly to my father: "Bring her back," and at once my father said: "Oh Nicholas, how well Anne would have understood your difficulties! She spent a great deal of her youth trying to please her father and become a young woman who had little relation to her true self, and how unhappy that made her! But in the end she uncovered the person God had created her to be and she was able to live out her own truth, just as I hope you'll now live out yours. Once she's rejoined us she'll always be there to remind you that you must be your true self, and every time you feel I want you to be my replica, you'll find it easy to picture her saying: 'Nonsense, Nicholas! Take no notice of him—he's being very silly!' You remember, of course, how sensible and down-to-earth she was, how magnificently rational. Rational analysis was very much her forte."

"Nicholas takes after her in that respect, I think," said Lewis.

"Yes, that's why I feel Nicholas's gifts are really very exceptional, even more so than mine. He has my psychic gift combined with a scientific detachment and curiosity—a most unusual and striking combination. In fact I never wanted him to give up science at school in order to specialise in the arts, but since he was determined to be my replica—"

"We must accept the past, I think, and make the most of it. Perhaps God was merely ensuring that Nicholas would become a special kind of priest."

"Anne was interested in scientific matters," pursued my father, so keen on his reminiscences now that he merely nodded in response to this comment. "Of course circumstances demanded that she took an interest in the science of agriculture, but there's no doubt she did have a flair for it; she always seemed to know exactly what to do at the Home Farm. But her interests were very varied. She shared my fondness for Shakespeare . . . Nicholas rebelled against us when he was twelve and said he found all poetry boring, but after Anne died he studied Shakespeare hard in order to please me. Oh, how Anne would have been angered by that replica! She loved Nicholas just as he was, and he was so precious to her—her only surviving son . . . How sad it was that she never had another child, but she'd had two babies in two years and she thought she should make time for me instead . . . But I didn't make time for her." My father's eyes filled with tears again.

"But you can make time now, can't you?" said Lewis. "That's something you can still do for her. You can talk about her to Nicholas, tell him when he reminds you of her, share your memories so that she becomes someone cherished again, not just the symbol of an unbearable tragedy. And if you do all those things then I think eventually you'll find you'll be able to look back and wonder in amazement how you could have imagined Nicholas to be anyone other than the unique person you and your wife created."

"I'm already wondering in amazement," said my father, "but I must tell you that great difficulties still remain. First of all, Nicholas will find it well-nigh impossible to let go of me so that Anne can fill the space between us. It's because the desire to be my replica has turned him into a sort of psychic parasite—poor Nicholas, how bizarre that sounds, but I can think of no other way of expressing it!—and he needs to have his psyche constantly fortified by mine."

"Nicholas sees you both as Siamese twins joined at the psyche. But it's the replica's psyche which needs constantly fortifying, isn't it? So once he begins to live the life God's called him to lead, he'll develop the capacity to be independent at last."

"Yes, but now we come to the second huge difficulty, Father. You know how hard it is to discern God's will, and I'm quite sure that once Nicholas feels free to go his own way he'll jump to all the wrong conclusions about what God's calling him to do."

"You think so?"

"I'm sure of it. You see, what he really wants to do—when he's not trying to be my replica—is to be a priest in the ministry of healing. It's the most unfortunate obsession and I regard it as potentially disastrous. I myself had a catastrophic experience of the ministry of healing, and I'm firmly convinced—"

" 'I,' " said Lewis. " 'I, I, I!' But we're not talking about you now! We're talking about Nicholas, that unique person who's not your replica!"

My father looked much taken aback. "I realise that," he said in a polite voice which only narrowly failed to mask his annoyance. "But the point is this: I failed in the ministry of healing because I was temperamentally unsuited for it, and since Nicholas is temperamentally exactly like me—"

"In no respect is he exactly like you. Take that word 'replica,' please, and add it without any more delay to all the other rubbish in the psychic wastepaper-basket."

"But—"

"Of course Nicholas appears to be temperamentally like you—he's been slaving away to create that effect for years! But I think that talent of his for rational analysis can be trained and used to foster the spirit of humility which all healers require; he'll master the art of seeing himself and his work without the false illusions generated by pride."

"In my opinion," said my father, perfectly polite still but now very cold and grand, "you're mistaken. Of course I see the point you're trying to make and I realise you mean well, but I myself remain quite convinced that Nicholas is not called to the ministry of healing. He must work in the ecclesiastical mainstream."

Lewis leapt to his feet.

My father and I were so startled we nearly fell off our chairs. Certainly we both gasped. My father even clutched the edge of the table to steady himself.

"JONATHAN DARROW!" thundered Lewis, piling on the histrionics. "I can hardly believe my ears! Nearly eighty-eight years old and still blazing arrogance in all directions—*how disgraceful!* When was the last time you looked in the glass and said to yourself: 'I CAN BE WRONG'?"

My father, already pale, became ashen.

I thought in panic: he's going to die of rage—

But he didn't.

He lived. He laughed. And he looked utterly enthralled.

6

"HOW this reminds me of the old days!" he said delighted to Lewis. "Never shall I forget how forcefully you used to harangue me on my need for humility! Very well, Father. You mustn't think that I've reached the age of eighty-seven and learnt nothing from my past battles to overcome my

greatest weakness. I accept that I could be wrong, jumping to an arrogant conclusion about Nicholas's future ministry, and I realise that I must be humble enough to seek your guidance."

"And I must be humble enough to admit I'm not sure what Nicholas is being called to do," said Lewis, sitting down again. "Discerning the will of God is never easy, but I'll say this: if Nicholas works hard to become a devout priest and a well-trained psychic, then I believe the way will unfold before him and all our doubts about his future will be dissolved."

My father nodded and said: "Yes, I can agree with that." And turning to me he added: "Very well, Nicholas, I shall keep an open mind on the subject. At least I can feel confident that you'll thrive spiritually now that all my prayers have been answered and you've met Father Darcy at last."

I cringed. "Father," I said, speaking loudly and clearly, "this is *Lewis Hall,* not Cuthbert Darcy. He's a priest at St. Paul's—you remember St. Paul's, that big Victorian church in Langley Bottom—"

"I recognised you at once, of course," said my father to Lewis. "Psychically you're unmistakable. Most psyches are blunt and cumbersome, but yours is so supple, so flexible, and driven all the time by that tremendous power. You were the greatest exorcist I ever met, the most formidable priest I ever knew . . . How interesting it is to meet you at this stage of your life! What age are you at the moment?"

"Nearly forty-seven."

"Ah yes, I never knew you then. You were in your early sixties by the time we met, but Aidan always used to say how delightful you were when you were younger. He knew you before the war—the First War, I mean. How long ago those days seem now that we're in—no, don't tell me!— now that we're in 1968. Strange how easily the past and present interweave nowadays, but time's all an illusion, I know that now. Reality is beyond time. Reality is spiritual."

I looked at Lewis to try to signal some sort of apology for this senile behaviour, but he was unaware of me. He was too busy curling his supple psyche around my father in order to bear him forward into the future along that river where the present mingled so effortlessly with the past.

"Reality is spiritual," he was saying, repeating my father's words, "and often we have to use symbols, don't we, in order to express that reality when it's beyond the power of mere words to describe. We've talked of creating a space so that your wife can come back to you both and realign that relationship which has become so crippled. But to create that space the two of you must begin to move apart psychically—and because we're talking of things our physical eyes can't see, we have to find some way of enacting this event so that it becomes real to us; we have to find some way of showing on a material plane how the parting of your joined psyches will create the space which will allow your wife to come back and play her vital part in the realignment; we have to deal now entirely in symbols because we've reached the point where no words can express what has to happen."

He paused. Then he said to my father: "Do I have your consent?"

"For the operation? Yes, of course. It's vital that Nicholas should be separated from me so that he can set out at last on his own special journey."

"And you believe that it's possible?"

"I believe," said my father, "that by the grace of God all things are possible."

"And you, Nicholas—what do you want most at this moment?"

I said: "I want to live."

Lewis stood up and indicated without words that I should sit down in his chair opposite my father. When I was seated he pulled my folding chair aside and stood beside the table. My father was now on his left and I was on his right.

There was a long silence while Lewis rested his fingertips on the table, closed his eyes and bent his head in prayer. Then he crossed himself and said without looking up: "In the name of Jesus Christ . . ."

The operation had begun.

7

POWER began to stream from his psyche. It wrapped us up, propped us up, supported us. It was like a blood transfusion, a triple brandy and a steel corset all rolled into one. I remember feeling high, as if I'd had more to drink than normal. I wonder now if he had somehow managed to release in us a supply of the morphine-like substance which the brain is capable of producing naturally.

"In the name of Jesus Christ Our Lord . . ." The words, though referring to a real person, were simultaneously reverberating with symbolism, the multi-symbolic image of the Eternal Christ. Light began to flicker across my psyche in kaleidoscopic patterns. I wondered if my father, with his visual gift, was seeing bright colours. "In the name of the healing power of the Holy Spirit . . ." I tried to focus on the words of the prayer but I kept losing my grip on it. It was as if the rational side of my mind was slowly being submerged beneath a deeper level of consciousness. ". . . we pray that we may be aligned with Thy will. Our Father, Which art in heaven . . ." I thought: is he hypnotising us? But I didn't think he was. We weren't being put under. We were being in some extraordinary way raised up, offered to God, as it were, on a platter. ". . . *Thy will be done* . . ." I thought: I must concentrate, must take all this in, must analyse exactly what he's doing . . .

Then I realised I was no longer capable of analysis.

"... FOR thine is the kingdom, *the power and the glory* . . ."

The prayer was like a blow-torch, each word sending catherine wheels of sparks in all directions.

". . . for ever and ever . . ."

I was thinking of the Book of Revelation. All those symbols. Apocalyptic. "I saw a new heaven and a new earth . . ."

"Amen," said Lewis in such a brisk voice that I opened my eyes with a start.

I tried to say "Amen" too but nothing happened, and a second later I realised my father also was silent. It was as if we were conscious but paralysed.

"You can both hear me, can't you?" said Lewis in his most matter-of-fact voice. "Now whatever you do, don't start hypnotising yourselves into believing you're hypnotised. We want to keep hypnosis right out of this. The effects of hypnotism wear off. We're looking for a permanent cure involving grace and will, not a temporary relief generated by mind-control. Say something to me, would you, Nicholas, just to prove you haven't hypnotised yourself into being a zombie."

The power of speech was instantly restored to me. "I was thinking of that quote from 'Revelation': 'I saw a new heaven and a new earth.' "

"Fine. What were you thinking, Jonathan?"

"I was thinking: 'Strait is the gate and narrow is the way which leadeth unto life and few there be that find it.' "

"Good. Both of you ultra-receptive but both of you *compos mentis*. We're getting on. Now lean forward and grip each other's forearms."

Instantly we obeyed him, and as I noted the lack of hesitation I suddenly saw what it meant. All our minds were now operating in unison. It wasn't a case of hypnotism, where Lewis's mind would have been in control of ours. All three minds were now flowing into and out of one another without impediment.

"Not much room there," reflected Lewis, for the table was not large and our arms covered most of the surface. He paused, the surgeon contemplating the body on the operating table, and then to my surprise moved to the fireplace. On the mantelshelf stood the vase of daffodils which my father had earlier threatened to smash against the wall. As I watched, Lewis selected the largest, yellowest daffodil, brought it back to the table and laid it with care across our joined forearms.

"Now," he said, "take a moment to reflect how confined you are by your present position, how handicapped you are by those joined forearms which deter all spontaneous movement. Think what your lives would be like in the physical world if you were permanently welded together like that. Imagine what a narrow world it would be, how distorted and fragmentary and frustrating."

The silence began.

He allowed it to last a full five minutes, and throughout that time he was not controlling our psyches but supporting them with that unceasing, phenomenal power. It gave us the strength to concentrate, to focus on the horror of a crippled, diminished existence, and by the end of the fifth minute I could hardly wait to tear myself free.

But Lewis said: "Keep holding each other; maintain that position but allow your fingers to relax. I want you to reflect for a moment on three texts, all from St. John's Gospel." And when we had slackened our grip he added: "The first is from chapter eight. Jesus says: 'I am the light of the world: he that followeth me shall not walk in darkness, but shall have the light of life.' "

He paused again, and in that silence I heard the sentence resonate as the footsteps of mysticism and Gnosticism echoed and re-echoed in that classic Christian corridor. Then I saw Truth as a multi-sided diamond with the themes of heresy and orthodoxy all glittering facets of a single reality, and beyond the facets I glimpsed that mysterious Christ of St. John's Gospel, not the Jesus of history but the Christ of Eternity who in turn pointed beyond himself to the Truth no human mind could wholly grasp. And I thought: there is no truth but Truth, but that sounded so paradoxical, so odd, just as words always do when they're labouring at the outer limits of human understanding, and meanwhile Lewis was speaking again; Lewis was saying:

". . . and the second text is from chapter ten. Jesus says: 'I am come that they might have life, and that they may have it more abundantly.' "

I felt my father tremble.

Or perhaps I was the one who was trembling. The author of that Gospel seemed so close, speaking my language, striving to express the inexpressible, reaching deep into the well of mysticism to grasp the symbols which illuminated eternity. And I thought: he's present, he's here—although of course that was impossible, but now we were moving along the boundary of the possible and the impossible, and Lewis was talking again; Lewis was saying, raising his hands at last to touch us:

". . . and the third text is from chapter eleven. It's the text which so many people nowadays associate with funerals, but that's such an irony as it's the greatest call to life that's ever been uttered. Jesus says—" He broke off, then began again. It was as if he were shifting into a higher gear, and simultaneously, as the timbre of his voice changed, I felt his power lifting us to the very top of his psychic range.

"—Jesus says: 'I am the resurrection, and the life: he that believeth in me, *though he were dead,* YET SHALL HE LIVE—"

The Force erupted in our midst.

9

THERE was no sound, but the air was rent from top to bottom as that boundary wall between the possible and the impossible was finally blasted to pieces. I saw Lewis, the channel, shudder under the impact of the explosion, but a second later as his right hand pushed down on my head, a brilliant light blinded my eyes, and I saw my mother—

* * *

—and there she was, sitting in the nursery rocking-chair and reading me a bedtime story about my hero, Jesus the healer. She was quoting: " 'Suffer the little children—' " but I was interrupting impatiently: "No, not that bit, read the story where he raises the little girl from the dead!" and my mother laughed.

I was in 1949—how did I know it was 1949?—I've no idea, but it didn't matter because my mother in 1949 was now side by side with my hero the healer in the first century—but both were present with me in 1968. And as this truth shot through my consciousness I realised that the walls of time were buckling beneath the mighty power of the Spirit—

* * *

—and then suddenly the walls collapsed completely so that we were all eternally present in the mind of God, the child raising his tin soldiers from the dead, my mother laughing in the nursery, my father striding through the front door after a day at the Theological College—and with us was not only the Jesus of history but the Christ of Eternity, holding us together in a moment of triumph over death and victory over darkness. 1949—1968—it didn't matter, it was all one, because the power of Christ was beyond time, no other power could withstand him, and now the darkness generated by my mother's absence was being rolled back and back and back—back until it was utterly extinguished—by that light which was the light of the world—

* * *

"—Light of the World. In the name of Jesus Christ—"

I heard the voice of the exorcist in 1968, the exorcist who was delivering us from the Dark, and when I opened my eyes the first thing I saw was the daffodil shivering on our forearms.

"In the name of Jesus Christ—"

Some sort of arrow-prayer followed—a brief sentence—something about going forth separately—new life—in harmony with the indwelling spirit . . . But I could barely hear the words because I was so mesmerised by the daffodil. I found I couldn't stop looking at it, couldn't stop, couldn't stop—

Lewis suddenly removed his hand from my head. I almost passed out as the power was withdrawn, but I couldn't pass out because I had to keep looking at the—

". . . Amen," I heard Lewis say in a voice barely above a whisper. Then slowly, very slowly, he drew my left arm from my father's right, and slowly, very slowly, he drew my right arm from my father's left. Exhausted we slumped back in our chairs, but between us in the open space created on the uncovered table, the daffodil glowed, brilliantly present, in the spring sunshine which streamed through the window.

I O

LEWIS drew the folding chair back to the table and sat down.

Then nobody spoke and nobody moved for a long time.

I just sat listening to the silence. I could not remember when I had last heard such a silence, but at last I realised why it was so silent. My father's psyche had stopped screaming. The torment was no more.

I took a quick journey around my new self and patted the ragged edges into place. Birth's an untidy business. My new self felt very vulnerable. I enfolded it instinctively with my psyche and waited.

In the end it was my father who spoke first. He began to recite the General Thanksgiving, and I closed my eyes in prayer but when I opened them afterwards I saw him with heightened clarity. He looked very old, very frail, very tired, but his eyes were luminous, as if still reflecting the light which had flowed through Lewis. I had barely been aware of my father during the healing, but Lewis's left hand had been placed on his head, just as Lewis's right hand had been placed on mine.

I looked at our healer. He was grey with exhaustion, limp as a corpse, his eyes closed.

"Nicholas," said my father, "fetch the brandy from the medicine cupboard."

"No, not brandy," said Lewis, opening his eyes. "It has no effect immediately afterwards. Tea's best. With sugar in it."

I made the tea while they sat in silence. In the kitchen I found Whitby hiding behind the door. Odd how sensitive animals are to atmosphere; they always know when something peculiar's going on.

When I returned with the tray my father said, picking up the daffodil: "I shall press this and frame it and hang it on the wall, and every time you come here, Nicholas, it'll be a sign that I want you to be yourself, just as Anne would have wished." My father had no pictures on the walls, only a crucifix over the bed.

I nodded. Then suddenly I felt so weak I couldn't even pour out the tea. But my father was able to do it. I could see he was stronger now.

We drank the tea. Lewis's face lost its greyish tinge and he made a series of normal minor movements, rubbing his nose, scratching the back of his head, shaking his watch to get it going again. I said: "Does it often stop when you heal? And why exactly does it stop? Is it to do with an alteration in the magnetic field?" but Lewis merely said: "You and your passion for rational analysis!" and I knew it was the wrong time to cross-question him.

Meanwhile my father was fingering the bandage on his right hand and saying: "I felt no pain when I picked up that heavy teapot. Perhaps my hands are already cured."

"I'd be very surprised if they were," said Lewis dryly, at last sounding like his normal self. "I don't go in for miracles."

"But they'll get better quickly now, won't they?"

"Yes—provided you take care to eat properly and get plenty of rest. I'm sure you've been very debilitated for a long time."

My father said simply: "I can hardly remember what it's like not to feel ill with exhaustion. It required such an enormous effort to keep Nicholas safe—and in fact after that journey to Grantchester—" He stopped.

I drew in my breath sharply, but before I could speak Lewis said in his most sympathetic voice: "It must have taken every ounce of strength you had."

My father was stunned. "You know?" he said as if he could hardly believe his ears. "You know about my journey to Grantchester?"

"I know about it in the sense that I've grasped what happened, but I confess I'm still in the dark about how you managed to do it. I've never before encountered a case of bilocation."

"Oh, as a case of bilocation it was all rather a failure," said my father with a deep sigh. "Obviously I'm too old now to make a success of it. I found I couldn't travel as I am, you see. Insufficient strength. So I had to travel as I used to be—which made a mess of everything."

"You mean you made a conscious effort to travel in that form?"

"No, it just happened that way. The problem was that I needed all my energy to break down the spatial barrier, and when I got to the temporal barrier there was no energy left so I couldn't, as it were, bring myself up to date . . . But Father, tell me: how did you know about this journey?"

"Nicholas saw you at Grantchester."

"But how extraordinary!" My father was suddenly tense with excitement. "I saw him, but I didn't think he saw me. He just sat there on that bench and . . ." His voice trailed away as he became absorbed in re-examining the experience.

I said: "Tell us how it happened," and my father, collecting his thoughts, answered willingly: "It all began when Martin phoned on . . . was it Monday? I was beside myself with anxiety," he added, turning to Lewis, "because I knew Nicholas wasn't confiding in me and I could feel such evil engulfing him. Then Martin telephoned the house and left a message to say Nicholas had gone to Grantchester and I wasn't to worry because he'd be safe with the monks. Martin's so kind to me. Down he comes here regularly to listen while I talk about my worries—what an old bore I must so often seem to him! But he's so good and he never complains.

"As soon as I got Martin's message telling me not to worry I began to worry myself to death. I thought: he wouldn't be sending that special message unless he felt Nicholas was behaving so oddly that I needed extra reassurance. And in my agony I said to myself: if only I could be there! If only I could rush at once to Grantchester to protect Nicholas from the evil that's engulfing him! But it seemed I could do no more to save him than align myself once more with Our Lord in that very difficult and demanding form of prayer.

"But as I prayed I was conscious of my longing growing. I longed and I longed and I longed to be at Grantchester, and in my mind I could see the house so clearly just as it was in those days when I'd been the Abbot. Then suddenly, Nicholas, I knew—I *knew*—you were in the visitors' garden, and at once I thought: if I could be the Abbot again before the war I could be in the garden, doing my stint of outdoor work—we all had to help in the garden in those days—and instinctively I thought not of the spring but of the autumn, when I'd so often raked up the leaves. I always found that particular task so satisfying, tidying up the garden and making it neat, and soon the scene was so vividly imprinted on my mind that I could almost smell the smoke from the bonfire.

"The next moment, before I could stop myself, I was taking my crucifix down from the wall, and holding the cross in both hands I said aloud: 'I *will* be there, I *will*, I WILL!' And I called on God to bestow his grace upon me and give me the strength I needed for the journey.

"Then the colours of the objects around me began to change and I moved out of my body to the corner of the ceiling up there and I looked down on my body, just as I always do prior to a vision, but within seconds the darkness, moving from left to right, blotted out the room and I covered my eyes with my hands.

"When I opened my eyes again I was at Grantchester, but it took me a moment to work out where I was because I was in the tool-shed and I had expected to be on the visitors' lawn; I suppose I had been thinking so hard of getting the rake in order to tidy up the leaves. However, once I'd got my bearings I found the rake and went out. Then I got another shock because there was a hedge in front of the shed, a new hedge—what a surprise! As I stood staring at it I realised how strong the sun was, so automatically I pulled up my cowl—and the moment I drew it forward I began to get very confused about what time I was in. The new hedge and the warm sunshine certainly suggested I was in the spring of 1968, but as I stood with the rake in my hand I had the terrible feeling I was revisiting a hot autumn day thirty years earlier; I had a picture of two times juxtaposed but not touching, a picture of myself watching another time through a wall of glass which I knew I could never break. It was then that I glanced down at my hand, and when I saw the Abbot's ring on my finger I knew my worst suspicions had been confirmed.

"But I told myself stubbornly: it won't matter. I'm here, and when I see Nicholas I shall come up to date.

"I didn't put the rake back in the shed. I was too confused. I just walked on with it down the path towards the peach-tree—doing *very* well that peach-tree was, so much more substantial than I remembered—and then as I glanced across the lawn . . .

"The strange thing was, Nicholas, that as soon as I saw you I knew beyond any shadow of doubt that communication was impossible. I couldn't bring myself up to date after all, so you remained *now,* in 1968, while I remained *then,* in the late 1930s. I saw the spring around you, the green leaves on the beech-tree, the flowers blooming along the border, but it was no spring I could ever enter as I was.

"I was so stunned, so absorbed in this conundrum, that I moved like an automaton. I didn't stop, I just walked into the kitchen garden—I think I had some last desperate hope that once I passed through the archway I might find myself in my eighties again, restored to 1968, and indeed that did happen but not in the way I wanted. My journey was terminated, not extended. Once I was in the kitchen garden the darkness returned, moving from right to left to cut off my vision, and when I next opened my eyes I was lying on my bed in this room and feeling so exhausted that I thought I might die.

"How Padre Pio achieved his psychic journeys I've no idea but obviously he was considerably younger and very much more gifted than I am. How depressed I felt afterwards! I didn't believe you'd seen me, Nicholas. Certainly I hadn't been able to help you in any way. All I'd done was project the image of my past self through space, and I couldn't be more surprised now to learn that I was in fact visible to you. But was the projection something which could have been witnessed by people other than you? Or was it only an image transmitted between two abnormally gifted psyches which were also abnormally linked together?"

I said firmly: "I saw you with all my eyes—the two physical ones and the psychic one. They were all working together." Then I became aware of Lewis looking at me quizzically so I added: "But I could be wrong." And finally I concluded: "I don't know."

"All that matters," said Lewis to my father, "is that you were there in some form or other, just as you were present in the chapel this morning."

At once my father said: "I was terrified. I could feel Nicholas's psyche screaming, begging me to save him, and I knew he was in the chapel, but I was so weak that I realised it would take me several minutes to get there if I tried to walk. So I grabbed the crucifix again and begged God for His help, and the moment I opened my eyes after the prayer I was at the chapel; the translation was immediate. I was standing outside the main door—but once again I was in the wrong time. I was at least twenty years younger, I knew that, because nothing ached, although I could see the age-spots on my hand when I raised it to open the door.

"Inside I saw Nicholas beside the altar with two people—or was it three? I couldn't look at the other people properly. I was so terrified that I just shouted Nicholas's name at the top of my voice—but of course he was in 1968 and couldn't hear. So then I shouted: 'Lord Jesus Christ, Son of God, SAVE HIM!' and the next moment I saw the flash of metal in Nicholas's hand as he held a little cross aloft. He was invoking the power of Our Lord, just as I'd done, and as soon as I'd realised that, every muscle in my body relaxed—it was like a sign that he was going to be all right. I had to wipe away tears of relief, and when I opened my eyes again I was lying slumped on my bed at the cottage."

"That time you did help me," I said. "You saved my life."

"He can hear about that later," said Lewis, standing up. "At present nothing's more important than that he should rest."

"No, wait!" said my father, clutching his sleeve. "I know Nicholas is out of danger now and I know you'll train him how to keep himself safe in future, but Father, I must just take a moment to beg you to be patient with him. As I've already said, he's a good boy at heart, but he's *very wilful,* so wilful at times that you may well be tempted to hit him as you once hit me—and that reminds me of a question I've always wanted to ask you: did you regret your behaviour afterwards? I understood, of course, why you acted as you did. You weren't just giving vent to a sadistic impulse; you genuinely felt I had to learn the hard way that humility saves and arrogance kills. But of course, your violence was very unbecoming conduct for a priest, wasn't it?"

I could bear the senility no longer. By that time I was emotionally exhausted and my patience finally snapped. "Father," I yelled, "this is *not* Father Darcy! This is—"

But then I found I was no longer so sure who he was.

THE years of the twentieth century cascaded at random around me like the cards of a loosely shuffled pack. I looked at the door of the room and was no longer sure it opened onto the grounds of Starrington Manor. I looked at my father and for a split second saw him as a man in his forties. I couldn't quite bring myself to look at . . . whoever it was, but out of the corner of my eye I thought I saw the flash of rubies in the Abbot-General's pectoral cross.

I rubbed my eyes with my hands.

"Oh, do stop treating me as if I were senile, Nicholas!" my father was saying crossly. "Of course I know he's Lewis Hall, but I'm not confined to 1968 as you are and I don't see why I shouldn't roam around the century psychically if I please! What we're really talking about here is the saving power of the Holy Spirit which flowed through the channel of Cuthbert Darcy, whom I met in 1923, and which is now flowing through the channel of Lewis Hall, whom we've both met in 1968. The channels are as one in their dedication to God—which means that in the light of the Holy Spirit those psyches can be seen as identical. The Holy Spirit is, as you well know, timeless, and insofar as those identical channels convey the power of that Spirit, they too are beyond time. 1923—1968—it doesn't matter. Jesus Christ is the same yesterday, today and for ever, and our selves—our *real* selves—can never be the prisoners of either time or space."

He stooped to pick up Whitby, who had finally dared to venture from the kitchen. Then he commanded: "Nicholas, help me to stand!" and after I had eased him to his feet, he tucked the cat in the crook of his left arm before holding out his right hand to Lewis.

"Goodbye, Father," he said. "I'm sure you're a very busy man, but I hope you'll find time to come back here soon. Between four and five is a good hour to visit me, and you'll find the door in the wall will be unlocked." He glanced down at the cat again and smiled. "Fancy you remembering Whitby's name!" he said enchanted. "Dear old Whitby, what a character he was! By the way, talking of Whitby, I think I've finally managed to forgive you for—but no; we won't talk of the past any more now. Poor Nicholas finds it embarrassing."

Lewis laughed, shook hands with him and said: "God bless you, Father. I'll come back soon, I promise."

"Why aren't you calling me Jonathan? You called me Jonathan during the healing—well, of course you did, you always called me Jonathan, everyone in the Order had to call me Jonathan, you insisted on that even though I hated the name and wanted to change it! Do you remember how

I asked if I could choose John as my monastic name and you refused point-blank because you didn't want to pamper me?"

"How very cantankerous!"

"No, you weren't cantankerous in those days, just tough. You only became cantankerous later when the arthritis gave you so much pain in your hip." He opened the front door and stood aside to let us pass. "Nicholas, come back later, after Evensong."

"Okay."

No race is more hopeless than the English in emotional moments. We looked at each other, tried an awkward, untidy hug—Whitby yowled in fury as he was shoved against my father's chest—and parted in relief with our upper lips impeccably stiff. All I said was a gloomy: "I suppose you'll still go on worrying about me to some extent."

"I shall always worry a little," said my father. "That's natural for a parent. But the crucified days are over. And that's as it should be. God bless you both," he concluded serenely, and stood there smiling, healed at last, with his tabby-cat purring in his arms.

I 2

"LEWIS —"

"I know what's coming."

"We don't really believe in reincarnation, do we?"

"Certainly not!"

"So you're not really Father Darcy, are you?"

"Don't be absurd!"

"Then how do you explain yourself?"

Having paused by the chapel to light a cigarette, Lewis now blew smoke at the sky and made an indeterminate growling noise in his throat.

"Lewis?"

"Nicholas, I've been having an unusually active day and I've now reached the stage where I'm too weak to be cross-questioned. I need a stack of sandwiches and another pot of tea immediately. Keep your mouth shut and provide them."

We staggered on towards the house.

I 3

"I THINK I'm ready for an infusion of alcohol," said Lewis as we stepped into the hall. "Can you produce that bottle of brandy again along with the tea and sandwiches?"

I raided the kitchen and eventually retired upstairs with a large tray loaded with food and drink. Lewis was waiting for me in my sitting-room. He was lying flat out on the sofa but the sight of the tray revived him.

I somehow managed to contain my curiosity until the last sandwich had been consumed. Then I said: "Can I start asking questions again?"

"Yes, but I don't guarantee to answer them. What time's Evensong?"

"Six-thirty."

"Good. That allows us a little time to rest before we embark on the exorcism of the chapel. We don't want to wind up being carried away from here on stretchers."

But I was barely listening. Having taken a deep breath I announced: "Lewis, I've been analysing the mystery you present, and I'm now more convinced than ever that there really is something very odd going on."

"That sounds more like psychic *gnosis* than rational analysis, and I assure you there's nothing odd going on at all. Do you remember me saying to you once: 'When dealing with the paranormal, always consider the normal explanation first because nine times out of ten the normal explanation will be the correct one'?"

"This could be the tenth time. Okay, put your cards on the table. What's your connection with Cuthbert Darcy?"

"Oh, I'm a clone. He grew me in a test-tube at the Fordite HQ."

"Lewis!"

"Well, since you seem to have reached the stage where only a fantastic explanation will satisfy you—"

"Don't try and tell me there's no connection between the two of you," I interrupted, "because I shan't believe it. I know we can write off my father's peculiar behaviour towards you as senility, but there are other mysteries which can't be so easily dismissed. For instance, you never actually said when you met Darcy, and I assumed the first meeting came when you were a pupil at Starwater and he made his annual visitation; but how did you get into Starwater after your expulsion from Charterhouse? A school like Starwater Abbey doesn't take rejects unless someone in authority pulls some very strong strings."

I paused but when Lewis remained silent I added: "Then there's the second mystery: how did you come to know so many of the top men in the Order—and know them so well that you picked up information which normally someone outside the Order would never hear? You knew exactly what kind of relationship my father had with Darcy, and that certainly wasn't public knowledge."

Again I paused but still Lewis remained silent. "And finally there's the third mystery," I pursued. "I've got a hunch you knew about Whitby—the original Whitby, the house-cat up at Ruydale. When I first told you what my father's present cat was called, you reacted with something which could be described as a double-take, but it's unlikely you ever saw the original Whitby during a visit to Ruydale because he died in 1930, when you were still a child. So that means you must have heard about him on the Fordite grapevine, but the gossip about Whitby—the Whitby affair—was so scandalous that the likelihood of an outsider hearing about it would have been almost non-existent. The poor cat got mixed up in a bout of witch-craft hysteria, and . . . But I don't have to tell you, do I? You already know, but *how* do you know? I know because I have a special connection with the Order: I'm Jon Darrow's son. But you—"

"Quite," said Lewis. "Very closely reasoned. But don't, I beg you, now start speculating that Darcy tiptoed out of his monastery in 1920, ravished my mother in the nearest moonlit rose-garden and sent a silver spoon to my christening in 1921. Leave that kind of fiction to Sir Walter Scott."

"Truth is stranger than fiction—"

"Not this truth."

"I just can't understand why you're so reluctant to speak of him!"

"My dear Nicholas," said Lewis, rising to his feet, "isn't it patently obvious by this time that I'm hopelessly and hellishly hung up on the subject of that monstrous old monastic maverick?" And leaving me open-mouthed on the sofa he retired abruptly to the lavatory.

I 4

"IRONIC, isn't it?" said Lewis on his return. "Think of all I've done today! I've rescued my daughter, disposed of a corpse, healed a couple of ailing Darrows—but that's all easy, no problem, I sail through the morning on a tide of brandy and sweet tea. Yet the moment you start questioning me about Cuthbert Darcy I start to fall apart at the seams."

"I'm sorry, I didn't mean to make you upset—"

"Oh, don't start waving that word U-P-S-E-T in my face or I swear I really will start to climb the walls! Darcy spotted my potential, Nicholas, when I was just an adolescent mess, and unlike anyone else I'd ever met he decided he was called to do something about it. You're right in thinking I knew him before my Starwater days, but he wasn't interested in children. He wasn't much interested in adolescents either, but after I was expelled from Charterhouse and my uncle refused to have me in his house and my mother ran off to Paris with her latest lover, the old boy thought he'd take a look at me, and what he saw so horrified him that he decided to keep me at the Fordite HQ while he straightened me out. I was treated rather like a destructive puppy who required strict house-training; Francis Ingram was even assigned to take me for daily walks in the park . . . But Darcy succeeded in saving me, Nicholas, and I suspect that the training he gave me was the main reason why I seemed so familiar to your father; I was reflecting all the Darcy techniques, even the flamboyant and unorthodox ones which I'm sure other priests prefer not to use."

"But why are you so hung up about him?"

"Because I owe him everything and I'm haunted by the thought that I've let him down."

"I don't understand."

"He told me I should be a monk. He said I'd never make a success of marriage. He said I'd never be able to endure a conventional ministry. He insisted I wasn't cut out for a big ecclesiastical career. He warned me that unless I served God in a monastery I'd wind up perpetually on the brink of scandal. Nasty old brute, I thought after his death, when I was at the sex-mad, know-it-all age of nineteen, I'll prove him wrong even if it's the last thing I ever do—and of course all I managed to do was prove him right. Oh, the horror of it! The horror of realising I was unsuited to marriage, the horror of being a priest with a wife bent on divorce, the horror of telling that conventional parish, where I'd been so miserable, that my marriage vows had gone up the spout, the horror of being cut dead by the ecclesiastical establishment which had once fawned on me, the horror of trying to lead a celibate life before I received the call which made celibacy possible—and worst of all, the horror of remembering how proud of me the old monster had been and what high hopes he had held for my future . . .

"It was a nightmare. I was beside myself, couldn't stop thinking about him, he began to haunt me day and night. 'Cast him out!' I begged my spiritual director. 'Cast him out!' All guilt, of course, but no other demon has a better record for driving people nuts. I only broke free from the nightmare and hauled myself back from that particular hell when I embarked on my ministry of healing. No more constant preoccupation with myself; just constant preoccupation with others. Excellent. A God-given Christian solution. He would have approved."

"But surely then you were at peace with him at last?"

"Depends what you mean by peace. I stopped sitting around thinking of him and feeling guilty; I just sat around thinking of him. And now I don't even sit around, I just think. I think: what would he do in this situation, what would he do in that, would he think I wasn't acting with sufficient humility, would he tell me to make my confession more often, would he . . . The questions go on and on. I still discuss him endlessly with my spiritual director—but I must discuss him no more with you. Just remember, Nicholas, that we all have our hang-ups, and that the archetypal figure of the wounded healer is by no means confined to the pages of myth."

Cautiously, anxious to show sympathy but acutely aware I might say the wrong thing out of sheer inexperience, I commented: "My father told me once that all successful healers have to have been wounded at some time or other, because only through suffering can they develop the breadth of understanding required for healing others." Then on an impulse I added: "But Lewis, in view of all you've said, how traumatic it must have been when my father started treating you as if you were Darcy! How did you keep so calm?"

"Oh, but I *was* him then, of course," said Lewis vaguely. "He'd taken me over." Glancing at his watch he rose to his feet and added: "We must go."

But I remained transfixed on the sofa. "Wait a minute," I said. "Wait a minute. Are you saying . . . no, you can't be . . . or are you? Lewis, are you trying to tell me—"

"Time for your next lesson," said Lewis. "Now, this'll be really big news to you. In fact you may even find it highly disturbing."

"What's that?"

"Not all mysteries can be solved by rational analysis. Let's go and exorcise the chapel."

I 5

HE MOVED with precision, just as a priest should when conducting an important ritual. Words can be tossed off rapidly, but symbols need time to reverberate in the mind.

First he filled a bowl with water from the tap in the vestry and placed the bowl on the altar, where he blessed the water and allowed a minute of silence. The psychic atmosphere in the chapel still recalled images of sewage and offal, and as I prayed during the silence it was hard not to despair.

But once Lewis began to work I soon noticed the improvement. Using the water he made the sign of the cross on the doors and the pews, and I became increasingly aware of the image of a powerful solvent, fracturing the putrefaction so that it could be easily washed away. Lewis moved to the altar. Having anointed the wooden cross, he finally traced a large cross on the floor where the body had fallen and we knelt there to pray in words; he asked that Perry's soul as well as Christian's might rest in peace with God, and he called on the Holy Spirit to cleanse the chapel by pouring its healing power through the channels marked out by the water.

The images of sewage and offal, already faint, faded away altogether; the atmosphere was now no longer reminiscent of the slaughter-house but of the operating theatre, scrubbed down with disinfectant. I waited, still kneeling, still praying but knowing no polluted corner could survive.

At last Lewis rose from his knees, took the wooden cross and raised it high above the altar as he rededicated the chapel to Christ. The sentences were short, his voice firm. After he had set down the cross he allowed another silence for prayer but at last he said: "Now we celebrate mass," and as an afterthought he added: "I always celebrate mass if a ghost has actually been seen."

"But was a ghost seen?"

"You saw Christian in Perry and sensed his presence. And don't you remember your father saying he thought there might have been three people with you at the altar?"

I shuddered, but long before Lewis had reached the end of the service the image of the operating theatre had disappeared and I knew my chapel had been restored to me. Opening my eyes I found that the late afternoon light was slanting through the west window, and that I could now smell the furniture polish and incense which mingled with the mustiness resulting from innumerable damp winters. This was the chapel's special smell. I looked around. The brass tablet which commemorated a Barton-Woods who had died in the Boer War was gleaming. So were the silver candlesticks on the altar. The embroidery glowed on the altar-cloth. The chapel's special emanations, special beauty and special holiness were once more unmistakably present, and I knew that on a psychic level everything was shining.

I sat down in the front pew, and when Lewis joined me I said: "What really goes on during the exorcism of a place? Does the exorcist set tormented souls at rest and cast out the pollution they leave behind? Or does he set free the living by willing away the shadows the dead leave on their subconscious minds?"

"It's not a question of 'either/or.' "

"But you said the acid test of the exorcism I performed this morning was the psychological effect it had on me. That rather implies, surely, that exorcism's really just a method of triggering a healing in the living."

"I certainly didn't mean to imply that and I certainly don't believe exorcism's 'really just' anything; the moment you try to simplify it you cut back on your ability to understand a very complex phenomenon."

"So you really do believe that exorcism affects both the living and the dead?"

"Yes, but of course we can't directly see the effect on the dead. That's something which can only be psychically intuited, but what we do see, often very clearly, is the effect of the exorcism on the living who have been reflecting the dead person's torment. The phenomenon's similar to that psychic connection I mentioned earlier between the viewer and the viewed in paranormal puzzles."

I remained silent, considering what he had said, but eventually I accepted that it hardly mattered how the exorcism had worked. All that mattered was that I knew my chapel had been cleansed and healed. Then I thought again of Lewis saying: "It's not a question of 'either/or,' " and it seemed to me I was being given another glimpse of the multi-faceted diamond which was truth.

"Truth is certainly more complicated than a lot of people think it is," said Lewis when I had put my thoughts into words, "but I think if I were to use the metaphor of the diamond I'd make it clear that some facets glitter more brightly than others."

"You mean some truths are more truthful than others?"

"Well, aren't they? Isn't orthodox Christianity, for example, closer to the spirit of the Eternal Christ than Christian Gnosticism, which leans so heavily on the idea of a spiritual élite? Orthodox Christianity may not be the last word in truth—God is always the last word, not the Church—but maybe it's the last word in facets. For the time being."

"Uncle Charles behaves as if the Church is the last word in everything," I said, "and I don't think he'd approve of those words 'for the time being' at all. He always talks of the 'absolute truths,' and insists they never change."

"Your Uncle Charles always strikes me as being a great deal more subtle than his public reputation, and I suspect his talk of 'absolute truths' is merely his private shorthand for those facets which he regards as essential for a Christian life."

"Like chastity and continence." I shuddered again before saying rapidly: "If he knew the whole truth about what I've been doing during the past week, he'd refuse to ordain me."

"I agree it's best Ashworth never knows about your recent activities," said Lewis, "but I say that for the purely pragmatic reason that Perry's death has made all disclosures relating to the Christian Aysgarth affair very dangerous; I'm not saying it because I think Ashworth would refuse to ordain you."

"But put yourself in his position, Lewis! Would you ordain me if you were a bishop?"

"Of course," said Lewis surprised. "You'll be a much better priest now than you would have been if all this hadn't happened. You'll be a real priest, not a replica-priest, a man experienced in horror and suffering, not a mere boy who's spent his life wrapped in cotton wool."

"So you're saying that out of all that tragedy and death—"

"—will come life and truth. *Your* life, Nicholas, and *your* truth. And in your life and in your truth, Christian's tragedy will be redeemed."

THAT dialogue would end my reminiscences neatly, but life is far untidier than a smoothly rounded memoir. The police saw no reason to disbelieve our professed ignorance on the subject of Perry's death even though the Community produced the information that Perry had phoned the Manor on the crucial morning and asked for me. (This was something we'd forgotten amidst all the horror.) Remembering that Rachel and I had been alone in the house when Perry had phoned the vicarage, I at once said that I had never heard from him; I then suggested that having been obliged to abandon the idea of an impromptu visit to the Manor he had decided not to interrupt my visit to friends by calling at the vicarage; possibly too he had had no wish to waste his day in the country by spending time in Starbridge's nearest approach to a city slum, Langley Bottom.

The police said yes, that all made sense, and went away to think again.

So far so good. But just as we thought all the fuss was dying down the police horrified us by arresting a vagrant for the crime. Fortunately they had to release him almost at once for lack of evidence, but there was a moment when we thought we might have to confess in order to save an innocent man. However, that crisis passed and eventually Perry's death became a mere unsolved murder in the police files.

The next agonising time came when Perry's flat passed to a new occupant. Would he or wouldn't he modernise the kitchen, and what would be discovered when the coal was finally removed? Eventually I heard from Marina that a friend of a friend of her brother's had moved in and had been permitted by the authorities to embark on a modest programme of refurbishment. "My dear, the sacrilege!" wailed Marina. "He's cleared out the coal and turned the historic masterpiece into a wine-cellar!" This information made me feel very queasy, but no police descended on Albany and no corpse was found. It was essential that Christian's body remain undiscovered because it would have linked me too closely with Perry. Everyone knew I had been asking questions about Christian's death. If the police turned up evidence that Perry had murdered him, they could easily have theorised that I had found out too much and that Perry had driven to Starrington to silence me. Then indeed I would have had a hard time convincing the police that Perry had abandoned his hope of seeing me when he had visited the Starbridge area that morning. They might never have proved a theory that he had been killed in self-defence, but the scandal attached to "helping the police with their enquiries" could well have finished me.

I went to Perry's funeral, just to keep up appearances, and found to my relief that there was no religious service at the crematorium. It made the ordeal easier to survive because without the need to concentrate on prayers I could just switch off and think of something else.

Katie was not among the mourners as she was still at Banbury, but the next day I wrote to her to say I had become convinced that Christian had not committed suicide. "He wanted to go on a journey," I wrote, "and the last thing he would have welcomed at that stage of his life was death." Then after considerable thought I wrote: "Sorry I can't explain further and reveal my sources, but I give you my word that the above sentence is true." It was hard to know how to end the letter but finally I put: "Sorry, Katie, sorry for everything, NICK."

I expected and received no reply but at least I felt I had made some attempt to excise the dread of suicide from her mind. Marina told me the attempt had been successful and demanded to know more details, but I said I was bound by the rules of the confessional. "I suppose he was planning a second continental jaunt with Perry," she said, hoping I would at least either nod or shake my head, but I made no more disclosures and eventually she went away.

Soon afterwards Katie became well enough to leave the nursing-home and resume her life in Oxford, but she never remarried.

Rachel married, of course, and she certainly didn't wait till she was thirty, as she had sworn she would. She waited only till she had graduated from university and recovered from her traumatic experience in the chapel. But Rachel was resilient; those extroverted types seem better equipped to withstand trauma than people who are prone to introspection. I assume she told Charley everything eventually, although he never mentioned the matter either to me or to Lewis. Being Charley, a good man but with an increasingly ambitious and sophisticated streak, he probably thought it was much wiser simply to pray for us.

The wedding took place after various stormy scenes involving Mrs. Hall, who was livid that Rachel was marrying a priest and determined to proclaim that it would all end in tears. At one stage Lewis was so furious that he even accused her of being jealous of Rachel's success in finding a good man who loved her, and Mrs. Hall tried to assault him with a gin bottle. However Charley eventually ironed out his warring in-laws. He told me once with a radiant smile that he just loved a good pastoral challenge.

He and Rachel now have four children who are all wonderfully clever, wonderfully good-looking and wonderfully charming (or so Grandfather Lewis always insists on telling me after an extra glass of whisky). Occasionally nowadays I bump into Charley (swarming rapidly up the ecclesiastical ladder of preferment) and ask politely how his family's getting on, but everything's always unbelievably wonderful. In fact sometimes I wish the children would wind up drug-addicts and/or pregnant out of wedlock, but that's hardly a very Christian thought so I always do my best to suppress it. Once in a while I think of Rachel tossing off Grand Marnier soufflés, raising four perfect children, running a huge ecclesiastical home, being the ideal clerical wife and working on her doctoral thesis—all with one hand tied behind her back—but the thought's too exhausting to sustain for long. She would have worn me out in no time, I can see that now. Lewis always realised that, always knew he had merely witnessed a sexual attraction between two people who were radically dissimilar, but I still sigh occasionally when I think of her. She's such a very outstanding steamy brunette, and one doesn't meet even run-of-the-mill steamy brunettes every day.

"Better to sigh for her than live with her," said Lewis dryly once, and he was right. So when I'm sighing I thank God she's living with Charley, the best possible husband for her—though he's not quite my sort, but I fear that's my problem, not his.

His brother Michael married Marina, as planned, and for some time they had a most peculiar marriage, very 1960s, but now it's lapsed into a conventional success. Venetia said Marina always became a devoted friend of any mistress of Michael's who lasted longer than six months, but Venetia was drunk at the time she made that statement, so she was probably exaggerating. Venetia's husband died not long after she and I sipped champagne together, but like Katie she never remarried.

Now, in 1988, Marina and Michael are about to celebrate their twentieth wedding anniversary and I've just received a card inviting me to the inevitable orgy. Marina's scrawled on the bottom: "This is the successful marriage that no one, *not even my Soothsayer,* predicted!" I'm tempted to send her a card saying: "I CAN BE WRONG."

How ironic it is that I should find Michael so much more congenial than Charley! You'd think I'd have more in common with a Christian zealot than with an agnostic who's mixed up about religion, but perhaps I empathise with Michael's tormented streak which drove him to escape into wild behaviour when he was young. And Michael's the one who reminds me of Uncle Charles. Those two certainly had problems back in the 1960s, although by the time Uncle Charles died Michael was mature enough to get on well with him. Sometimes I think Uncle Charles used to look at Michael's dissolute behaviour and see the shadow side of himself that he repressed. But perhaps I'm being too Jungian. All I can really state with certainty, as the result of various heart-to-heart talks with Michael over the years, is that Uncle Charles had a very curious family in some ways, but that, as they say, is another story.

That other curious family, the Aysgarths, bucketed along in their usual wild style. Cynthia recovered from her breakdown but Norman never beat the drink. He's dead now. He died in . . . Can't remember. But it was after his father. Dr. Aysgarth died in 1975; he had a good innings, tough, sentimental old brute. Dido's still around, talking continuously. Nymphomaniac Elizabeth became Dipsomaniac Elizabeth, following in the family tradition. Sandy eventually got married, although I'm not sure he knew what to do with his wife afterwards. James is still soldiering on in darkest Surrey. Little Pip passed up the Church and went to work for the classical division of a big record company; I'm glad he stuck to his music in the end. But Christian's sister Primrose was the real success of that family. She's a big wheel now in the Movement for the Ordination of Women. Uncle Charles could never stand her, but he could never really stand any of the Aysgarths and he was too much one of the old school to approve of women's ordination. He outlived his old enemy Dr. Aysgarth. I used to see Uncle Charles regularly in his final years, but my abiding memory of him is not of the tranquil retired priest, but of the courageous bishop who proclaimed his "absolute truths" in the 1960s when relativity and relevance were the idols of that Devil's decade.

I'll always remember Uncle Charles proclaiming his absolute truths. Nothing rocked him, and the only time I ever saw him disconcerted in public was at Charley's wedding. Charley declared at the end of his speech: "And now I want to pay a very special tribute to my father, the best father any man could wish for . . ." And when I looked at Uncle Charles I saw he was overcome, quite speechless, and the tears were shining in his eyes.

It's strange how weepy men get when they grow older. But in my ministry I see men of all ages weep.

I was ordained as planned in 1968 and somehow survived two years of conventional parish work as a deacon and curate. Lewis was a great support to me and kept me going whenever I became frantic. I worked near Starbridge, partly to be close to him but also to be close to my father, now enjoying a new lease of life. Eventually I embarked on a chaplaincy at Starbridge General Hospital and life became simultaneously easier (because I enjoyed the work) and harder (because the work was very demanding).

On June the twelfth, 1972, the fifteenth anniversary of my mother's death, my father died in his sleep.

I took over Whitby but he pined and died soon afterwards.

I lived.

I can say no more about my father's death. I give thanks for his life and remember him by striving to be the man God created me to be. That's what he would have wanted. That's what I do.

Desmond Wilton retired a year later and I was given the chance to be vicar of St. Paul's but Lewis and I concluded that I would get too involved in the healing centre, with the result that the parish would suffer. So I continued my chaplaincy at the hospital, but in the early 1980s after a similar chaplaincy in London, I applied to be the rector of one of the Guild churches, St. Benet's-by-the-Wall. The Guild churches of the City of London open their doors from Monday to Friday for all those who work in the area, but the doors are closed on weekends when the City becomes deserted. Each church has different affiliations, different specialities. I made St. Benet's a centre of healing.

There's a big rectory attached to it, but Rosalind decided straight away that the City was an unsuitable place for children, so she lives in one of those fake farmhouses in Surrey and I go down at weekends. This suits me rather well. I don't have either the time or the energy for family life during the week. Lewis (now very cantankerous) doesn't approve and says it's not a marriage, it's a liaison. But Rosalind and I understand each other. I don't have to explain myself to her or make excuses; she just accepts me as I am, peculiarities and all, and makes the best of me. At least I haven't made the mistake my father made twice—marrying a fascinating stranger—but I know now I'm very different from my father in some ways. And of course Rosalind's not an old boot. She's a pair of extremely elegant, handmade shoes, the kind that never give a moment's discomfort.

We have two sons whom I can't connect with at all. They say they want to be accountants, drive Porsches and make loads of money. Rosalind says they'll grow out of it. I wouldn't know. Meanwhile Charley's two sons are already talking of being priests, but then Charley's sons would be. Lewis says I should stop being a weekend father and order Rosalind to London. I don't know what century he thinks he's living in. Nobody orders women about these days. Anyway the boys are away at school most of the year now. I do go down to Starwater regularly to see them but whenever I turn up they whine that the Abbey's boring and that they want to go to Rugby. Rosalind says they'll grow out of that. I wouldn't know. Meanwhile Charley's two sons are doing brilliantly at Westminster, both of them happy as larks. Sometimes I wish I had a . . . no, not a replica, God forbid that I should ever hanker for a replica, but a daughter who shared my interests would be very far from unwelcome. However, Rosalind says she can't face a third pregnancy. Lewis says that's rubbish and I should take no notice. Quite what he means by that, I don't know. Obviously he's not sanctioning rape. I think he just wants to express solidarity with me. Meanwhile Charley's two daughters are preparing to embark on their schooling at Cheltenham. But then Charley's daughters would be.

Lewis has been with me for five years now. He turned up on my doorstep one evening in 1983 and asked if he could stay the night. It turned out he'd got in a mess with some woman and the new Bishop of Starbridge had given him the sack. Poor Lewis. He was drinking too much, eating too much, saying that his career as a priest was finished and that the Devil had finally won.

I said: "The Devil never finally wins," and devoted myself to the necessary rehabilitation. The key to a new life was the licence to work as a priest in the diocese of London. Lewis said I would never be able to obtain the licence for him, but I went to the Abbot-General of the Fordite monks and together we won over the Bishop. Once Lewis had the prospect of working again, pouring out his exceptional gifts as a priest, he soon succeeded in embarking on a new life. He cut back on the drink, put himself on a diet (this was hell for us both) and emerged streamlined and bursting with energy three months later. How I ever managed without him at the Healing Centre I have no idea. He not only assists me in ways too numerous to mention, but he holds the fort whenever I'm called out to deal with paranormal phenomena. The paranormal's a growth industry at the moment; I'm a consultant to several dioceses now.

Lewis started out by living in the curate's flat at the top of the house, but lately he's moved down to a large room on the ground floor and I've had the cloakroom converted into a bathroom for him. He says he doesn't need much space now, but the truth is that an arthritic hip has made climbing the stairs too painful. He'll have to have the hip replaced, but he keeps putting off the operation; he says that hospitals are where you pick up an infection and come out in a box. He really is getting very cantankerous—quite as cantankerous, I'm sure, as his Great-uncle Cuthbert—and Rosalind occasionally asks me how I stand it, but I like having an old man to look after. It reminds me of my youth.

Strange how Lewis looked after me and now I've wound up looking after him. I suppose it *is* a father-son relationship in that respect, but at present I feel he's more like a brother—and I was always accustomed to a brother who was much older than I was. Martin's death left a void in my life; we got on far better once I was no longer jealous of his success in living the life God had called him to lead. After he died I organised a lavish memorial service for him at St. Paul's Covent Garden—the actors' church—and all the show-business celebrities said to me afterwards how much Martin would have enjoyed it. That was a long time ago but I often think of him. He was a good brother to me, better than I deserved.

Sometimes when I try to work out my current domestic situation, I wonder if the time has come for me to return home and begin a ministry centered on the chapel, but I always wind up deciding that I'm not ready yet; I feel such a move must wait until I begin to leave middle age behind. The Community broke up after my father died, but the Abbot of Starwater approached me for a lease and the monks at present use the house for the retreats which they conduct for clergy and laymen. The Fordites are on the increase again; the tide has turned. Their temporary acquisition of Starrington Manor represented a small but significant expansion after their massive retrenchment in the 1960s.

The tide has turned in the Church too with the Evangelicals on the march at last, the Liberals in retreat and the Anglo-Catholics beginning to realise they should change their outdated image and promote a new dawn for Anglican Catholicism. And mysticism is everywhere, pouring into the ecclesiastical structures which were so weakened in the 1960s, and acting as the cement which binds together all the bricks in a wall. Books on prayer and spirituality sell in thousands now, and at times I'm tempted to think all the world is trying to go on retreat. Or if people aren't trying to go on retreat they're speaking in tongues and joining the charismatic movement. Lewis takes a dim view of this mass outbreak of glossolalia and says it's enough to make any decent exorcist's hair stand on end, but I just say to him: "Remember the empty pews of the 1960s?" and he shuts up. At least he approves of the burgeoning popularity of retreats and the monks' current work at my home.

"The Fordites' lease is coming up for renewal soon," I said last week to Rosalind. "Are you by any chance secretly wishing I'd reclaim the Manor so that we could begin a new life in Starrington?"

"Starrington's heaven, of course," said Rosalind, "but I do realise you've got lots of work still to do at St. Benet's, and since I'm quite happy in Surrey . . ."

I wonder what she gets up to down there.

Nothing, probably.

But I wonder sometimes.

"Rosalind should come up to the rectory more often," growls Lewis. "She should make more effort to share your life here."

Quite. But Rosalind knows I'm so busy during the week that in the evenings all I want is silence and solitude. The ministry of healing's exhausting. I never accept social invitations when I'm in London. Venetia's just asked me to dine with her, but I shan't go.

"I'm very suspicious of this woman," says Lewis, growling away again. "I don't think you should counsel nymphomaniacs, Nicholas. It's all a very bad idea."

But finally after all these years I've got the chance to deliver Venetia from a way of life she despises, and I'm not going to let her languish any longer in her spiritual prison. I'm going to help her beat back that Great Pollutant at last, and no one, not even Lewis, is going to stand in my way.

"I thought I'd never get past that crusty old curate you keep!" Venetia said crossly on the phone when she rang about her proposed visit to St. Benet's for counselling.

"He's not my curate. He's my colleague at the Healing Centre."

"Well, chain him up somewhere—I can't bear misogynists . . ."

After the phone call had ended I said to Lewis: "That's the only woman

I've ever met who can instantly recognise a quotation from Wittgenstein."

Lewis looked at me as if I'd just signed my own death warrant.

But I'll be all right. I'm going to heal someone who's sick, and by the healing I shall transcend and transmute the past . . . But didn't I once think along those lines when I tried to heal Katie? Perhaps I'm being too arrogant. I pray daily for the grace to approach my work with humility but I don't pretend to be perfect and I know that it only takes one crack in the psyche, one lapse into weakness, for the Devil to wriggle his way in and cause havoc. No matter how strong the Light is, the Dark is always battling away to blot it out.

What am I going to do about Rosalind and that awful fake farmhouse in Surrey where I spend such comfortable weekends? What am I going to do about those two strangers, my sons? Should I go on at St. Benet's or should I try to draw my family together by returning home to the Manor? And last, but by no means least, can I really afford, at this stage of my life, to refurbish the soul of a magnificently original woman with whom I was once very much too intimate after an unwise dose of champagne?

I know I must lay all these questions before God and pray.

And now once more I see with my psychic eye the Holy Spirit moving across the dark waters of the earth in a ceaseless outpouring of light and life. The power of the Spirit never fails; that's what Uncle Charles would have called an absolute truth, a truth no pollutant can ever destroy. And as I see far beyond time and space to the mystery that veils the Godhead, I can feel at the very centre of my being the spark which connects me to that ultimate mystery, the mystery which no man will ever unfold on this side of the grave. All one can do in this life is to embark on that journey to the centre, where the immanent God dwells, and fight to continue that journey no matter how many obstacles are thrust in one's path. I know that in order to serve the mysterious transcendent God to the best of my ability I must continually work to align myself with the immanent God, the God within; I must continually strive to realise the blueprint of my personality and become the man God created me to be.

I must lay my problems before God, pray that His will be done, pray that my will be united with his, pray that I may move forward with faith and hope and love upstream on the river I'm called to navigate. And now another absolute truth seems to be pressing so hard on my psyche that I seem to see it written in letters of fire: serve God, love God, trust God, and the door will open into eternal life. Or in the other language: don't violate your true self by worshipping only what your ego demands, don't override the call of your true self in order to respond to the summons of false gods, don't sink into disintegration by turning your back on the one road which can guarantee you the happiness of fulfilment. Our task is to be whole, not fragmented, to be fully human, not mere naked apes, to reach upwards towards the Light, not to dive headlong into the Dark, and always God is there, calling us to integration, to self-realisation, to eternal life, by pressing on our psyches to lure us on towards Him. We may have to struggle on our inner journey through the labyrinth of the unconscious mind, but the guiding light is always there ahead of us at the source of the river within.

The telephone rang, interrupting my meditation.

Perhaps it was Rosalind, phoning to announce that she was running off with another man or that the boys had staged a break-out from Starwater. Or perhaps one of the people I was counselling was ringing to threaten suicide. Or perhaps the Archdeacon was calling to say I ought to take a firmer line against militant Christian homosexuals. Or perhaps the militant Christian homosexuals were calling to say I had to give the Archdeacon hell. Or perhaps the Anglo-Catholic die-hards were calling to tell me my attitude towards women's ordination was unacceptable. Or perhaps the Movement for the Ordination of Women was calling to demand that I should sack Lewis. Or perhaps—

Unable to stand the suspense a moment longer I picked up the receiver. "Father Darrow."

"Darling, it's Venetia again. Forgive me for pestering you like one of those ghastly neurotic women who go wild at the sight of a cassock, but I've been thinking so much about the extraordinary way you've now recurred in my life—and of course the extraordinary way you've so often recurred in the past—"

"Something tells me we should avoid certain excursions down Memory Lane, Venetia."

"Darling, that's exactly why I'm ringing you up! It occurred to me that you might be a little nervous in case I was planning to drown you in nostalgia, and I just wanted to reassure you that you have absolutely nothing to worry about. I want to turn over a new leaf, not romp around a compost heap of shady memories, but darling, are you really so sure I can heave my new leaf over? I mean, I'm such a raddled old wreck of a society woman! Do you truly believe I can resurrect myself from the dead and begin a new life at last?"

I thought of Lewis quoting St. John's Gospel long ago in my father's cottage: " '. . . he that believeth in me, *though he were dead,* YET SHALL HE LIVE—' "

It was the call to self-realisation, to the integrated life designed by a Creator who was bent on triumphing over death, and as I remembered those famous words, I thought how my own life had been so radically transformed.

"I don't just believe you can rise from the dead, Venetia," I said, speaking not as a Gnostic soothsayer but as a Christian priest proclaiming the eternal Christian message. "I KNOW."

"Darling!" she cried, much moved. "I adore you!" And she blew a kiss into the phone before replacing the receiver.

I fingered my pectoral cross and wondered what on earth the future would bring.

Author's Note

MYSTICAL PATHS is the fifth in a series of novels about the Church of England in the twentieth century. Each book is designed to be read independently of the others, but the more books are read, the wider will be the view of the multi-sided reality which is being presented.

The first novel, *Glittering Images,* was set in 1937. *Glamorous Powers,* narrated by Jon Darrow, opened in 1940, *Ultimate Prizes* was narrated by Neville Aysgarth after the war, and *Scandalous Risks* viewed the Church in 1963 through the eyes of Venetia Flaxton. The sixth and final novel, *Absolute Truths,* will take place in 1965, three years before the main events described by Nicholas Darrow in *Mystical Paths,* and Charles Ashworth, the narrator who opened the series, will narrate the novel which brings the series to a close.

THE ecclesiastical era of Nicholas Darrow's youth was dominated by ARTHUR MICHAEL RICHARD RAMSEY, who was born in 1904. While still in his thirties he became the Van Mildert Professor of Divinity at the University of Durham and a Canon of Durham Cathedral. Two years later he married. A short period as Regius Professor of Divinity at Cambridge preceded his appointment as Bishop of Durham at the age of forty-seven, and his ascent to the top of the Church's hierarchy continued to be rapid: by 1956 he was Archbishop of York, and in 1961 he became the one hundredth Archbishop of Canterbury.

Ramsey combined a first-class intellect with a striking appearance and a considerable degree of eccentricity and originality in his speech, manner and dress; a member of the Catholic wing of the Church, he was the first Archbishop of Canterbury to adopt the uniform of a purple cassock instead of the traditional frock-coat and gaiters. The combination of eccentricity and a deep personal holiness made him seem a remote figure to some in the turbulent days of the 1960s, but others appreciated his traditionalism at a time when all traditions were coming under attack. Hostile at first to the outbreak of radical theology, he later adopted a more flexible approach, recognising that the widespread questioning of both Christianity and the Church needed careful answering, not instant condemnation.

"It may be the will of God that our church should have its heart broken," Ramsey said before his enthronement at Canterbury, and this proved a prophetic statement. During the secular triumphalism of the 1960s, the Church suffered a loss of confidence and a numerical decline, but Ramsey provided the spiritual leadership needed to sustain it during the dark days of demoralisation and lead it towards more fruitful times.

Having retired from Canterbury in 1974, he died in 1988 in the midst of an era very changed from the one over which he had presided twenty years before.

THE thought of Jon and Nicholas Darrow reflects the work of CHRISTOPHER BRYANT, who was born in 1905 and ordained not long after he had graduated, like Michael Ramsey, from Cambridge University. In 1935 he became a professed member of the Society of St. John the Evangelist, known as the Cowley Fathers, which is the oldest religious community for men in the Church of England. For almost all of the next twenty-five years he was based at the Society's house in Oxford; he became first novice guardian, then assistant superior, and it was here that he began to make a special study of psychology.

In 1955 he was put in charge of St. Edward's House, the Society's London home, and he became increasingly famous as a spiritual director. As he approached seventy his writing career began: he embarked on committing to paper the insights into religious belief which he had obtained from studying Jung's psychology. The book failed to find a publisher, but another religious community came to the rescue and published it under their own imprint as *Depth Psychology and Religious Belief.* His other books, however, found favour with a well-known religious publisher and all his work came to have a wide readership. *The River Within, The Heart in Pilgrimage* and *Jung and the Christian Way* were published before his death. *Journey to the Centre* was published posthumously. He died in 1985.

A NOTE ON THE TYPE

THE text of this book was set in Bembo, a facsimile of a typeface cut by one of the most celebrated goldsmiths of his time, Francesco Griffo, for Aldus Manutius, the Venetian printer, in 1495. The face was named for Pietro Bembo, the author of the small treatise entitled De Aetna in which it first appeared. Through the research of Stanley Morison, it is now acknowledged that all old-face type designs up to the time of William Caslon can be traced to the Bembo cut.

THE present-day version of Bembo was introduced by the Monotype Corporation, London, in 1929. Sturdy, well balanced, and finely proportioned, Bembo is a face of rare beauty and great legibility in all of its sizes.

COMPOSED by ComCom, a division of
The Haddon Craftsmen, Inc.,
Allentown, Pennsylvania
Printed and bound by R. R. Donnelley & Sons,
Harrisonburg, Virginia
Book and ornament designed by Margaret Wagner